STAR WARS

THE RISE OF SKYWALKER

STAR WARS

THE RISE OF SKYWALKER

A Random House SCREEN COMIX™ Book

Random House
New York

For Lucasfilm

Senior Editor: Robert Simpson

Creative Director: Michael Siglain

Art Director: Troy Alders

Project Manager, Digital & Video Assets: LeAndre Thomas

Lucasfilm Art Department: Phil Szostak

Lucasfilm Story Group: Pablo Hidalgo, Matt Martin, and Emily Shkoukani

ISBN 978-0-7364-4147-6

rhcbooks.com

Printed in the United States of America

10 9 8 7 6 5 4 3 2 1

A long time ago in a galaxy far, far away....

The dead speak! The galaxy has heard a mysterious broadcast, a threat of REVENGE in the sinister voice of the late EMPEROR PALPATINE.

GENERAL LEIA ORGANA dispatches secret agents to gather intelligence, while REY, the last hope of the Jedi, trains for battle against the diabolical FIRST ORDER.

Meanwhile, Supreme Leader KYLO REN rages in search of the phantom Emperor, determined to destroy any threat to his power....

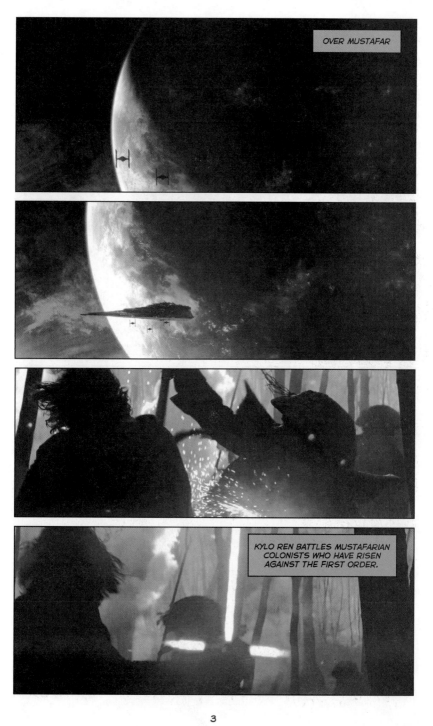

OVER MUSTAFAR

KYLO REN BATTLES MUSTAFARIAN COLONISTS WHO HAVE RISEN AGAINST THE FIRST ORDER.

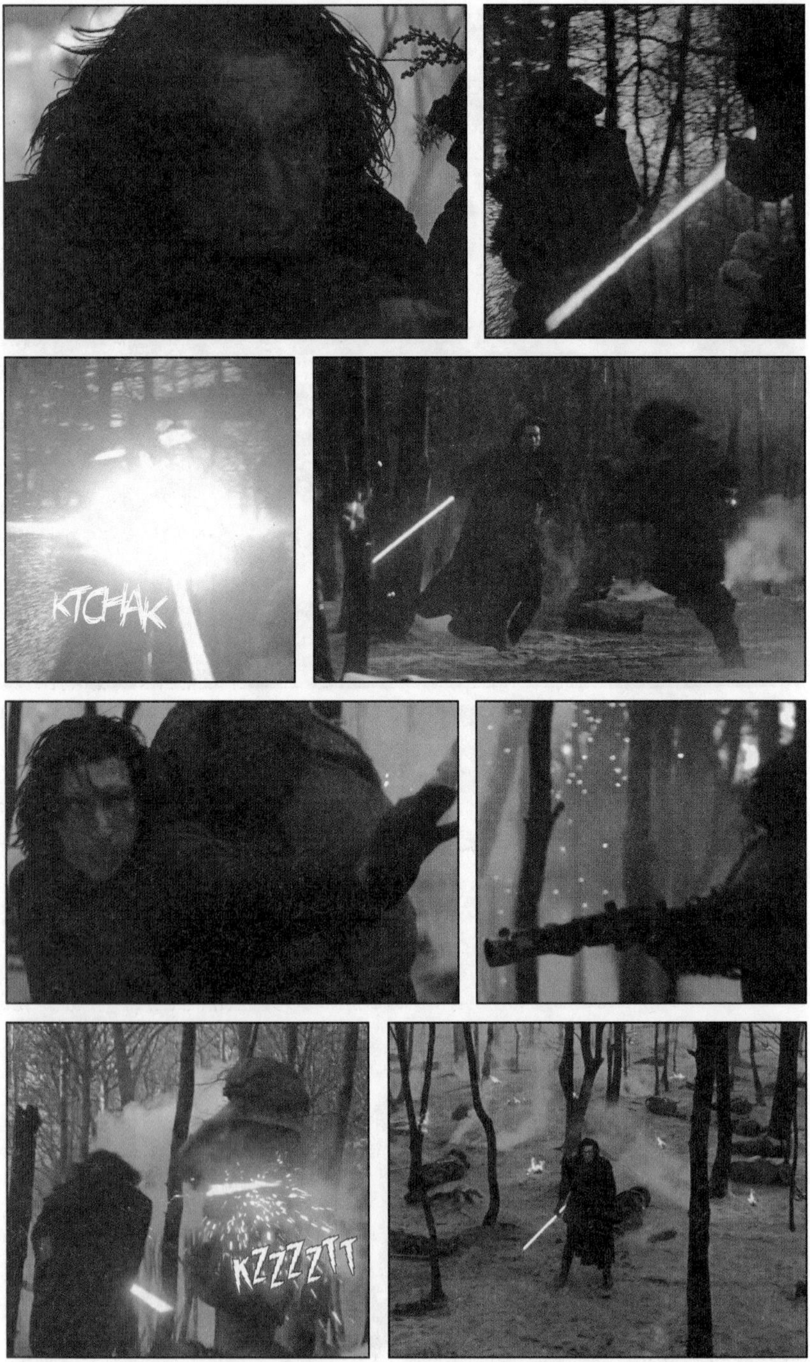
KTCHAK
KZZZZTT

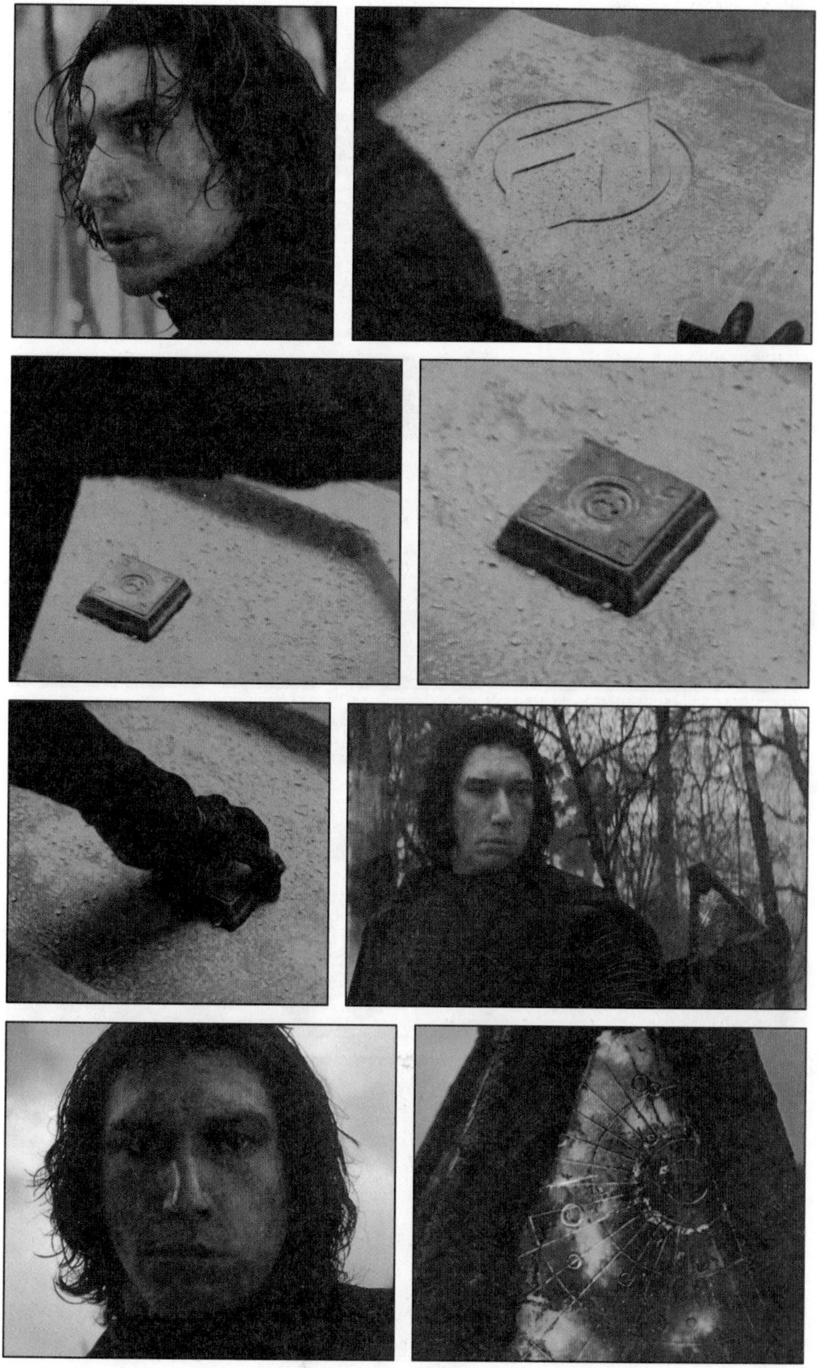

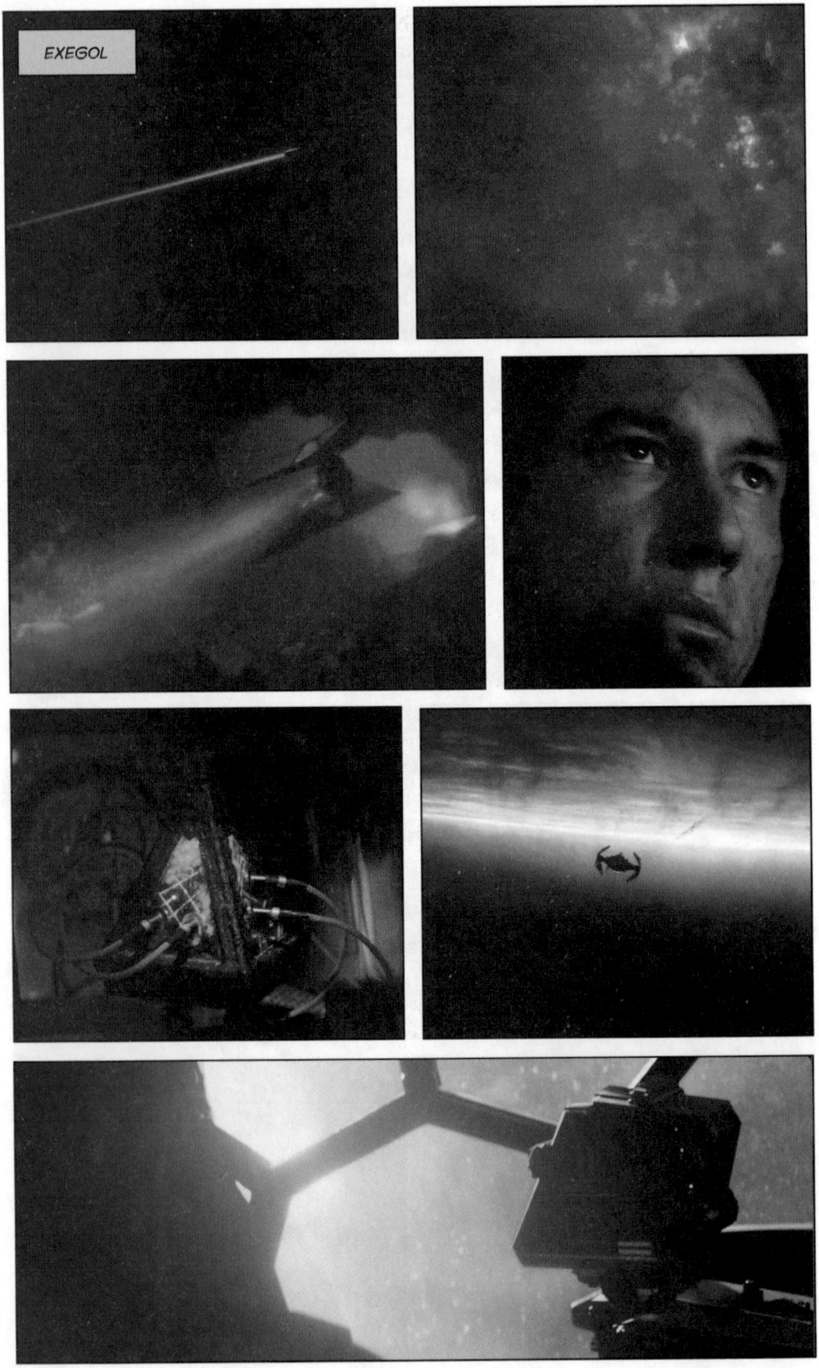
EXEGOL

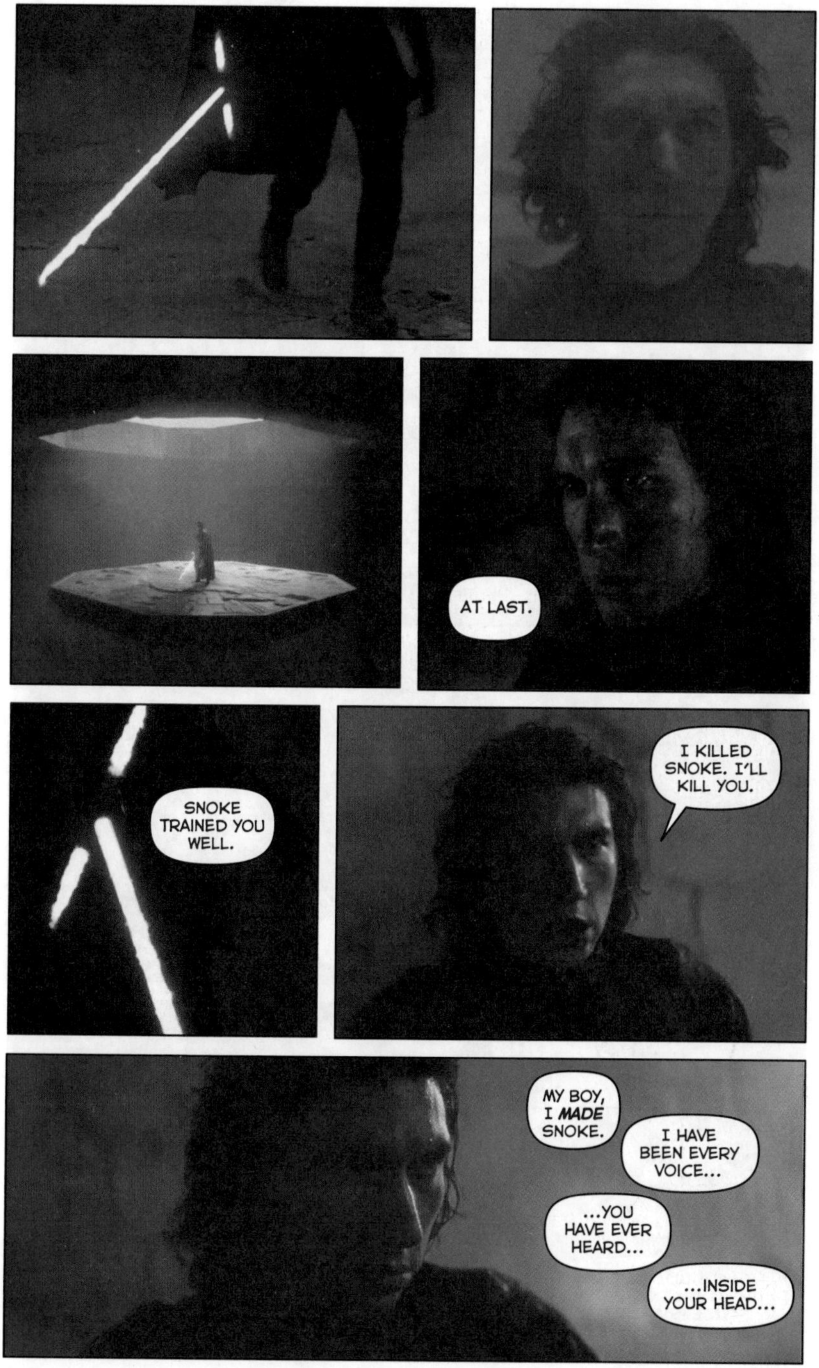
AT LAST.
SNOKE TRAINED YOU WELL.
I KILLED SNOKE. I'LL KILL YOU.
MY BOY, I *MADE* SNOKE.
I HAVE BEEN EVERY VOICE...
...YOU HAVE EVER HEARD...
...INSIDE YOUR HEAD...

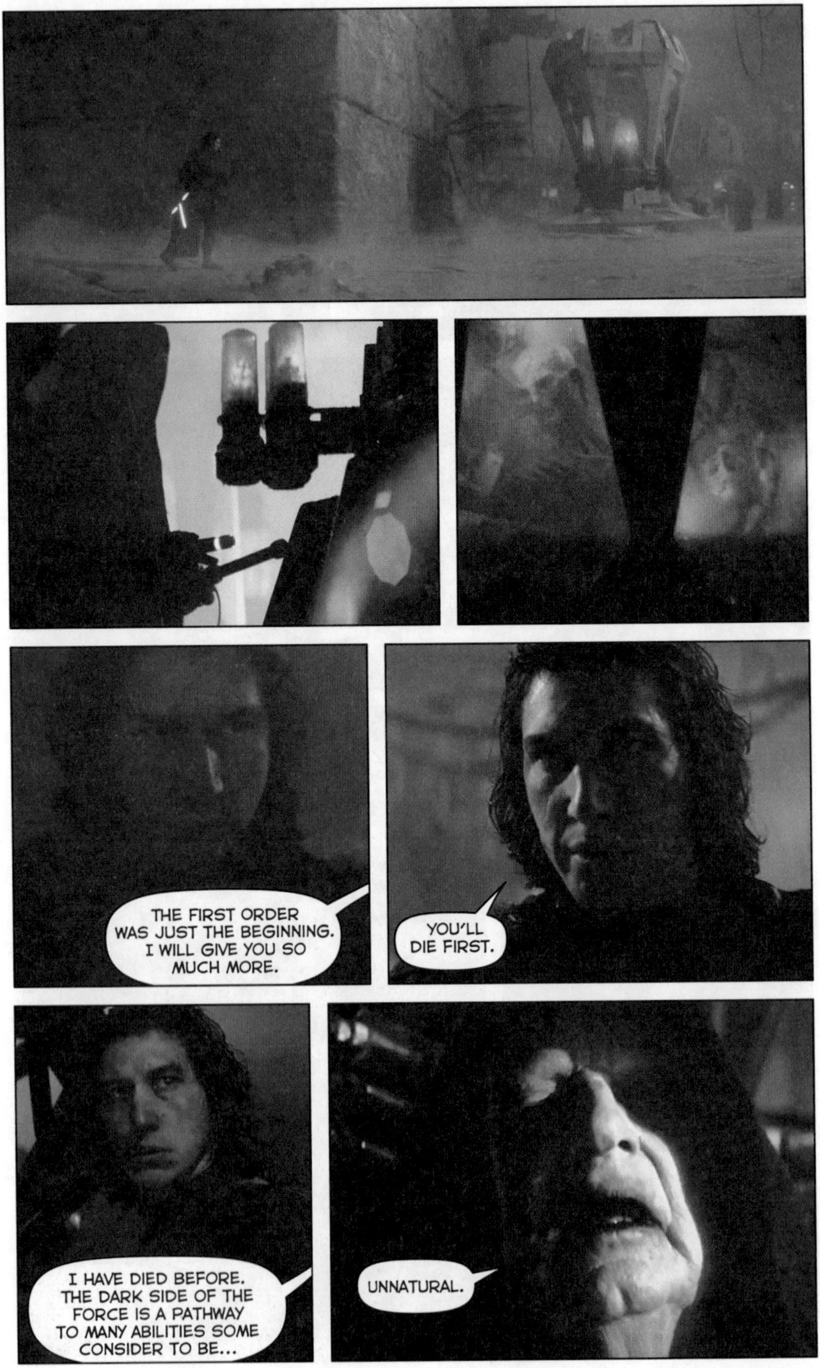
THE FIRST ORDER WAS JUST THE BEGINNING. I WILL GIVE YOU SO MUCH MORE.
YOU'LL DIE FIRST.
I HAVE DIED BEFORE. THE DARK SIDE OF THE FORCE IS A PATHWAY TO MANY ABILITIES SOME CONSIDER TO BE...
UNNATURAL.

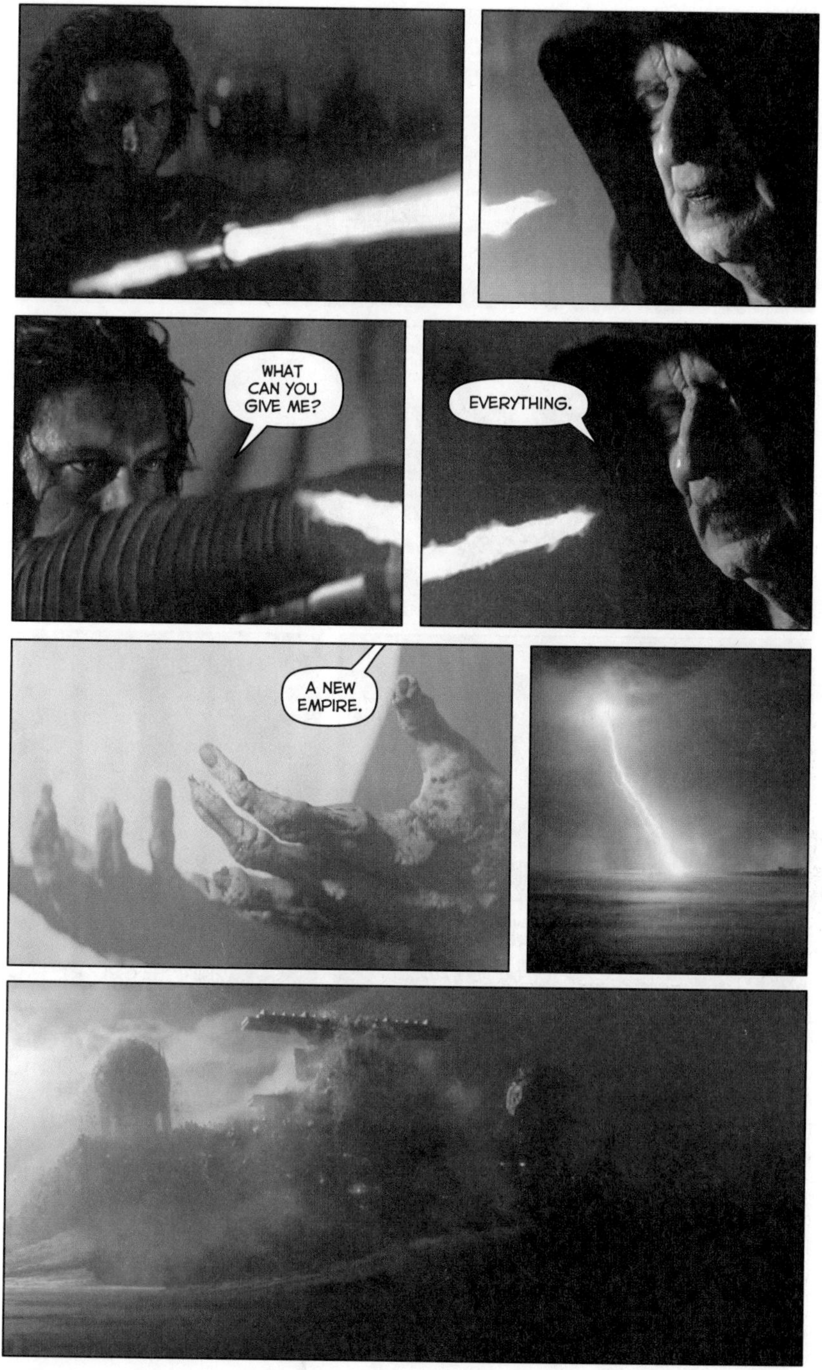
WHAT CAN YOU GIVE ME?
EVERYTHING.
A NEW EMPIRE.

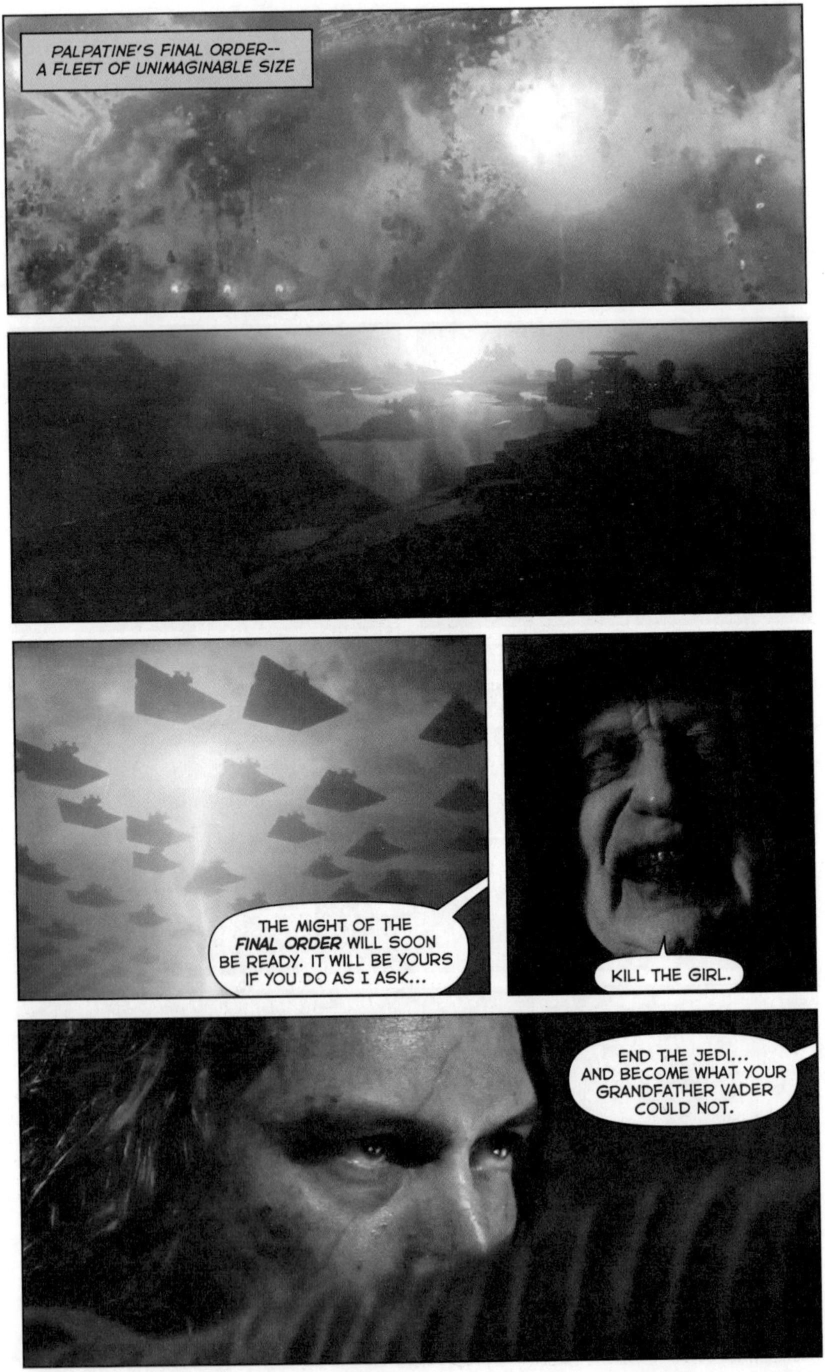
PALPATINE'S FINAL ORDER--
A FLEET OF UNIMAGINABLE SIZE
THE MIGHT OF THE ***FINAL ORDER*** WILL SOON BE READY. IT WILL BE YOURS IF YOU DO AS I ASK...
KILL THE GIRL.
END THE JEDI... AND BECOME WHAT YOUR GRANDFATHER VADER COULD NOT.

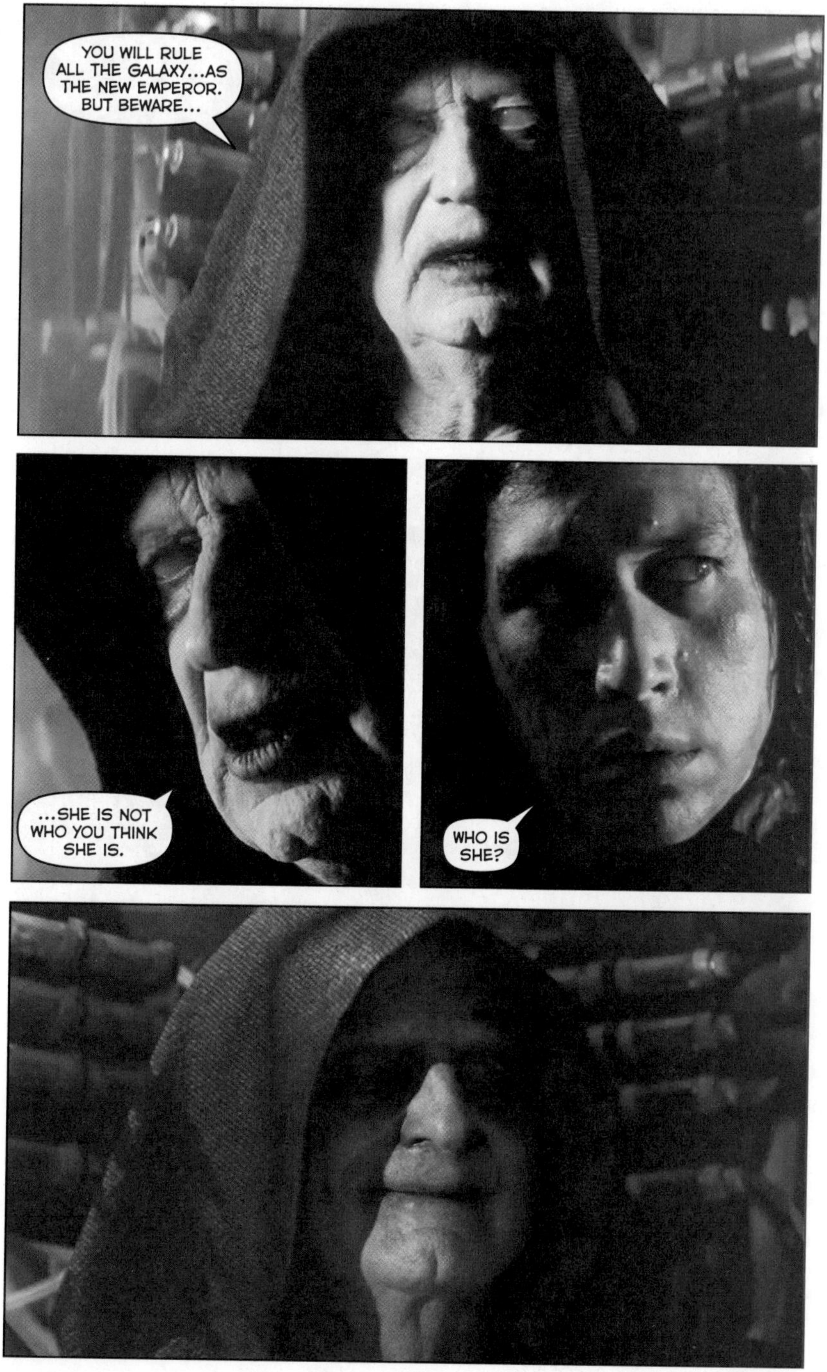
YOU WILL RULE ALL THE GALAXY...AS THE NEW EMPEROR. BUT BEWARE...
...SHE IS NOT WHO YOU THINK SHE IS.
WHO IS SHE?

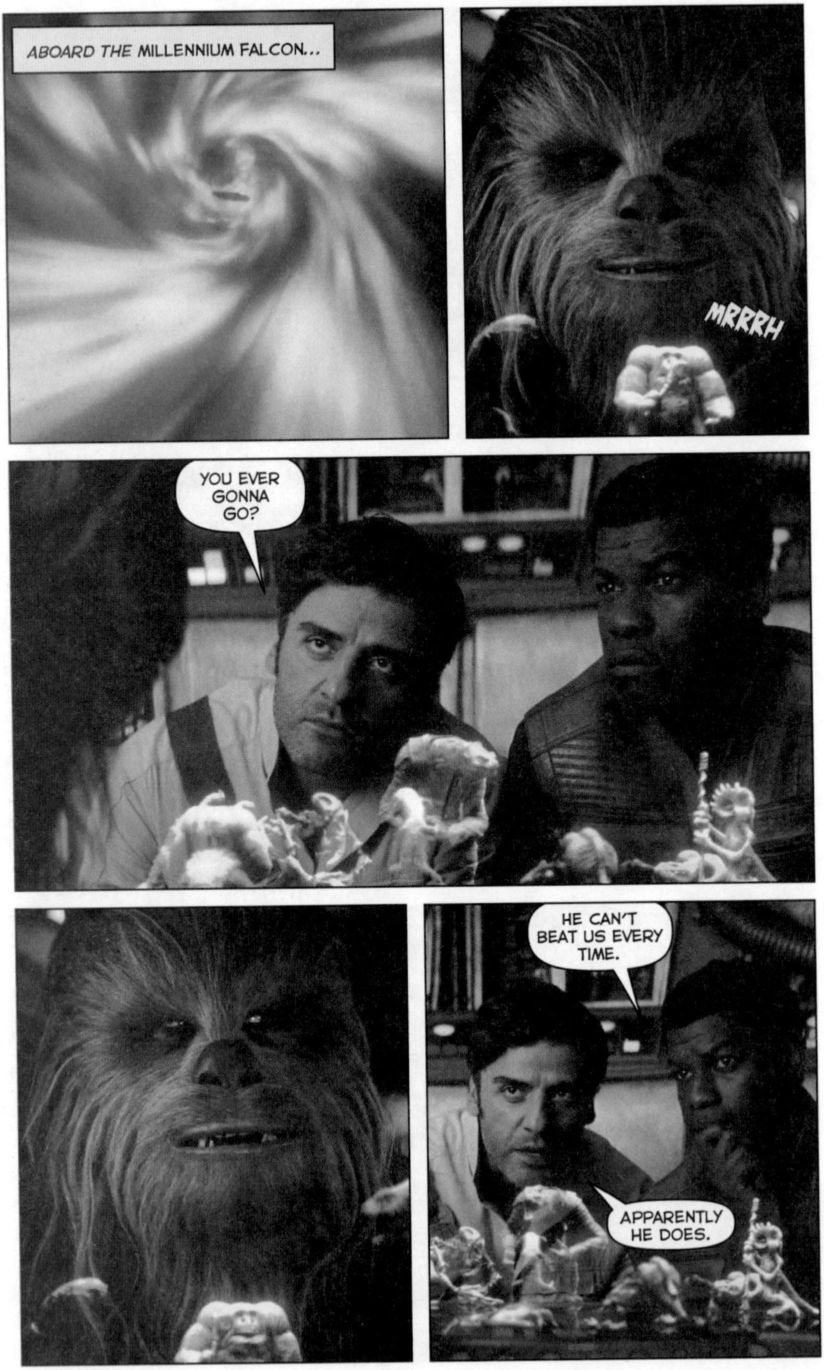
ABOARD THE MILLENNIUM FALCON...
MRRRH
YOU EVER GONNA GO?
HE CAN'T BEAT US EVERY TIME.
APPARENTLY HE DOES.

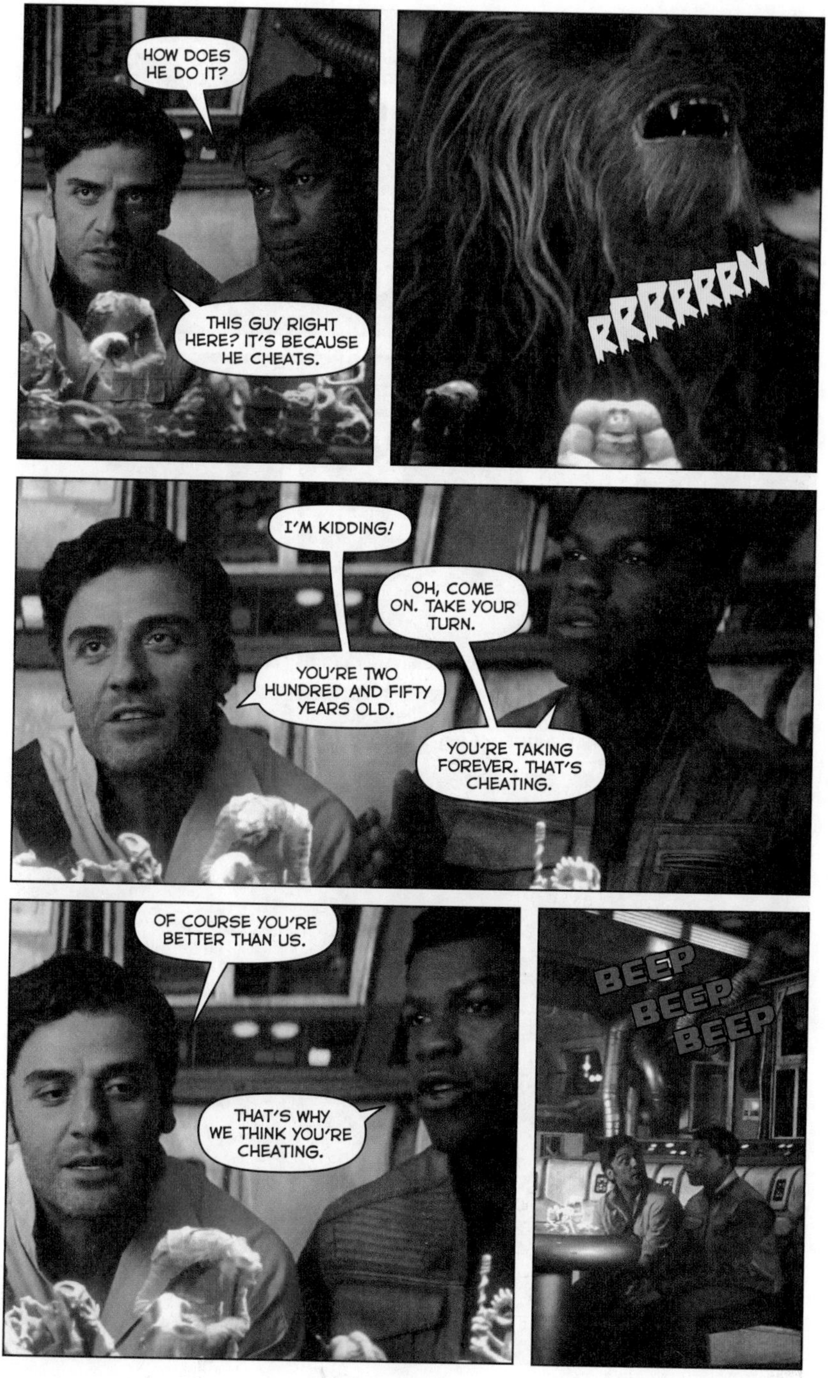
HOW DOES HE DO IT?
THIS GUY RIGHT HERE? IT'S BECAUSE HE CHEATS.
RRRRRRN
I'M KIDDING!
YOU'RE TWO HUNDRED AND FIFTY YEARS OLD.
OH, COME ON. TAKE YOUR TURN.
YOU'RE TAKING FOREVER. THAT'S CHEATING.
OF COURSE YOU'RE BETTER THAN US.
THAT'S WHY WE THINK YOU'RE CHEATING.
BEEP
BEEP
BEEP

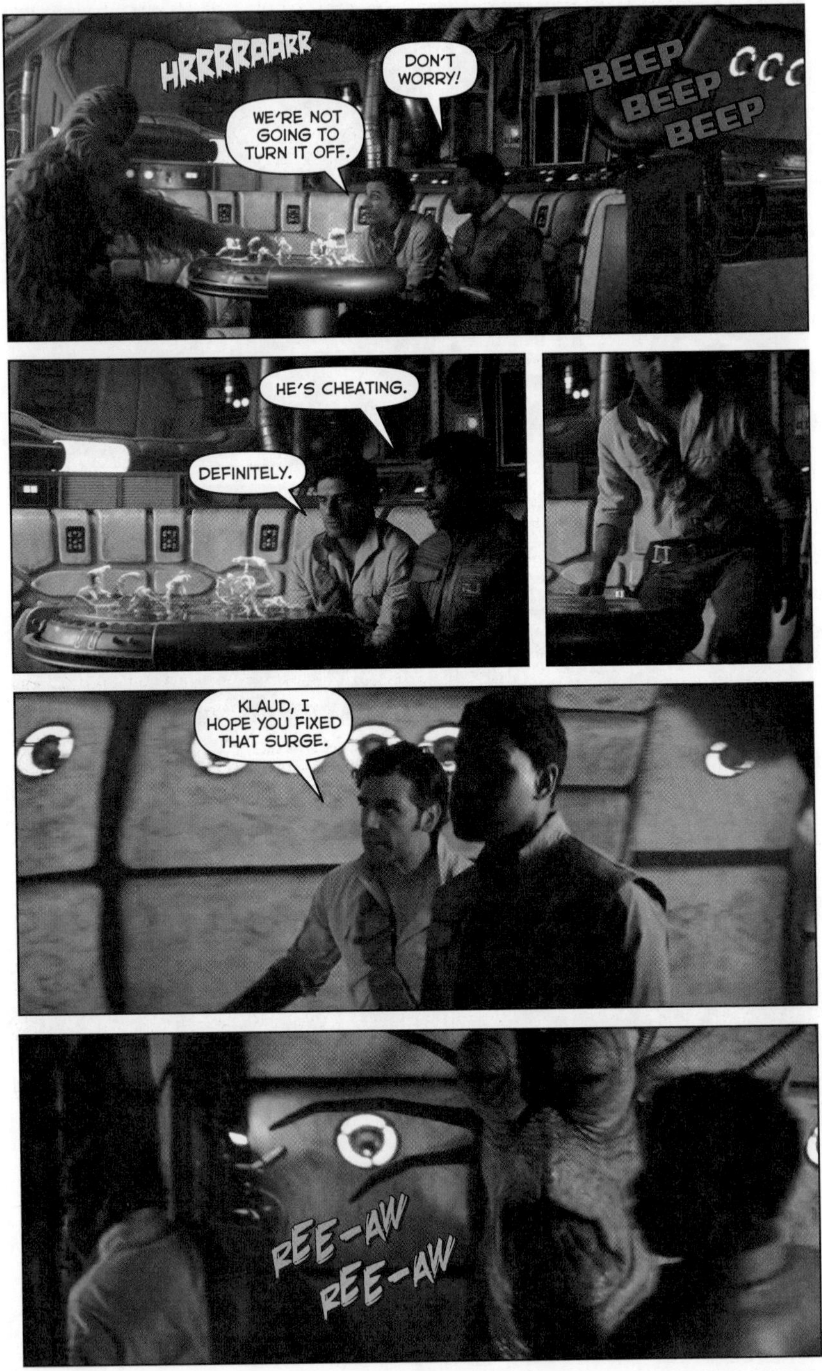
HRRRRAARR
DON'T WORRY!
WE'RE NOT GOING TO TURN IT OFF.
BEEP BEEP BEEP
HE'S CHEATING.
DEFINITELY.
KLAUD, I HOPE YOU FIXED THAT SURGE.
REE-AW REE-AW

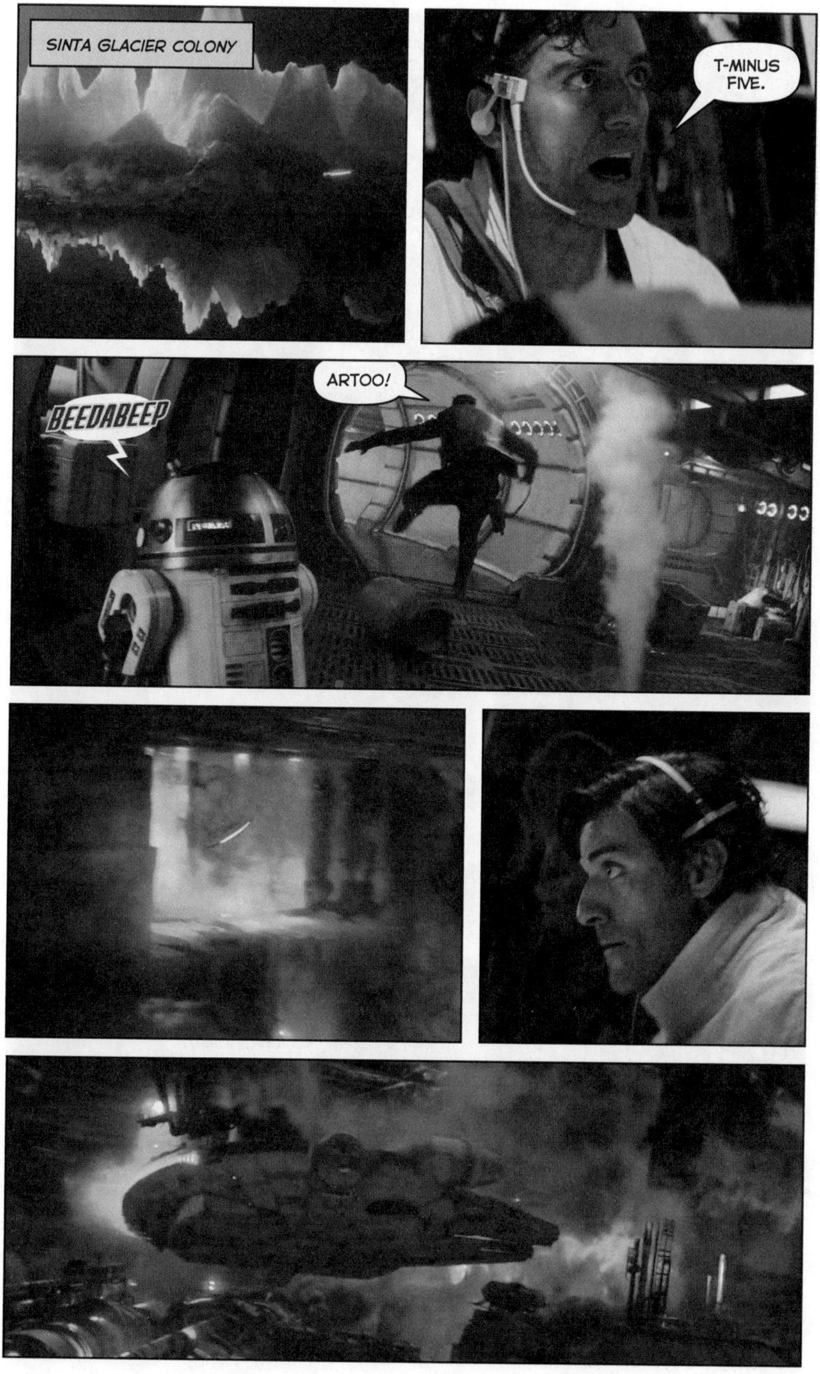
SINTA GLACIER COLONY
T-MINUS FIVE.
BEEDABEEP
ARTOO!

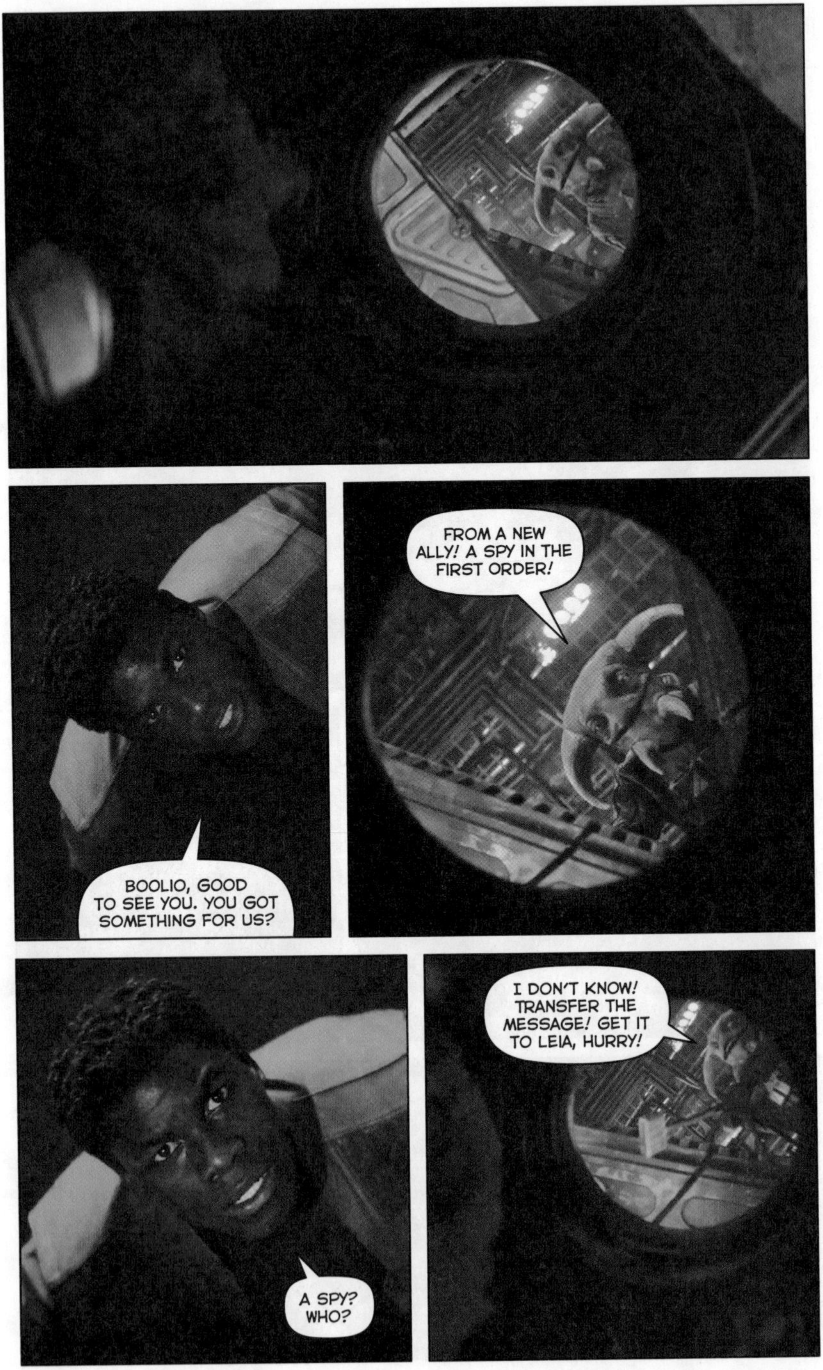
BOOLIO, GOOD TO SEE YOU. YOU GOT SOMETHING FOR US?
FROM A NEW ALLY! A SPY IN THE FIRST ORDER!
A SPY? WHO?
I DON'T KNOW! TRANSFER THE MESSAGE! GET IT TO LEIA, HURRY!

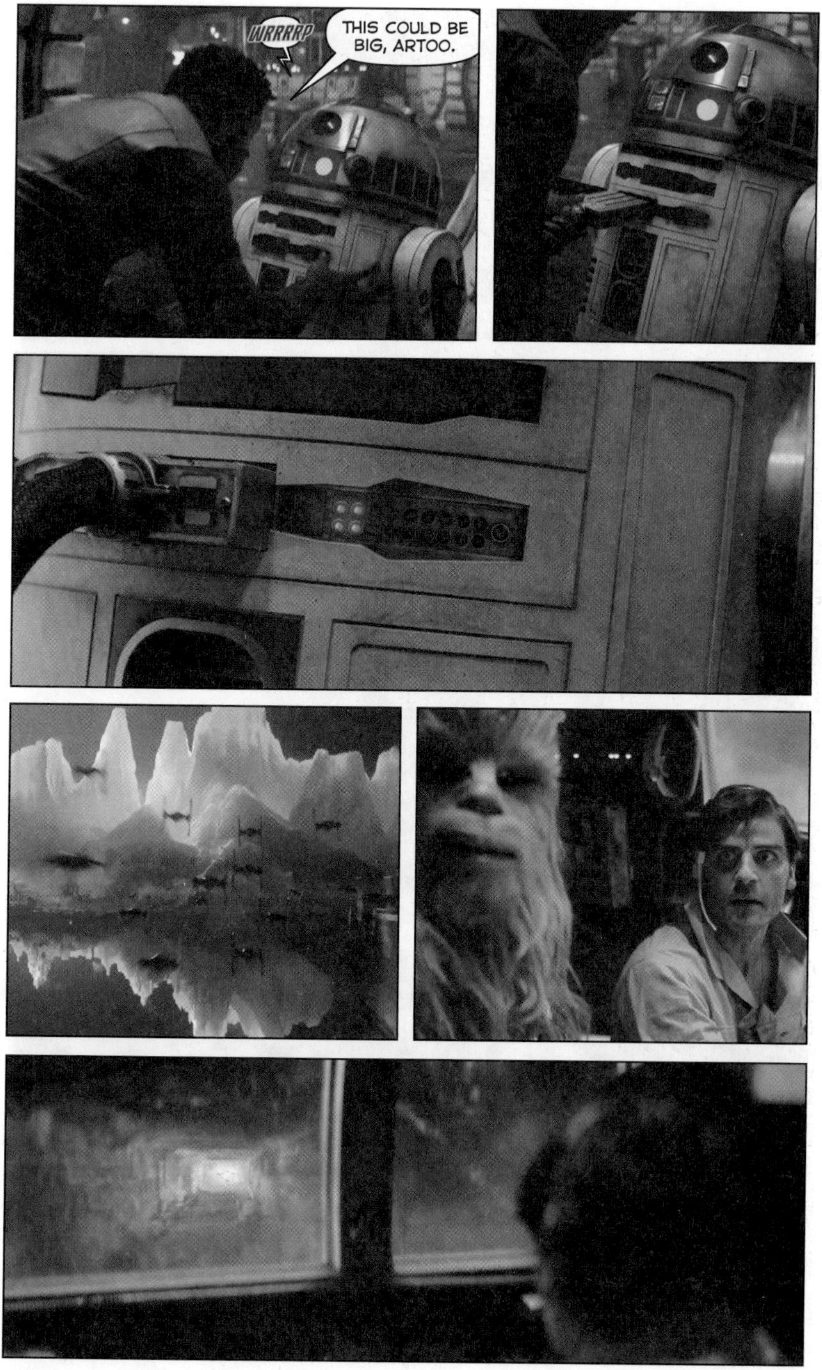
WRRRRP
THIS COULD BE BIG, ARTOO.

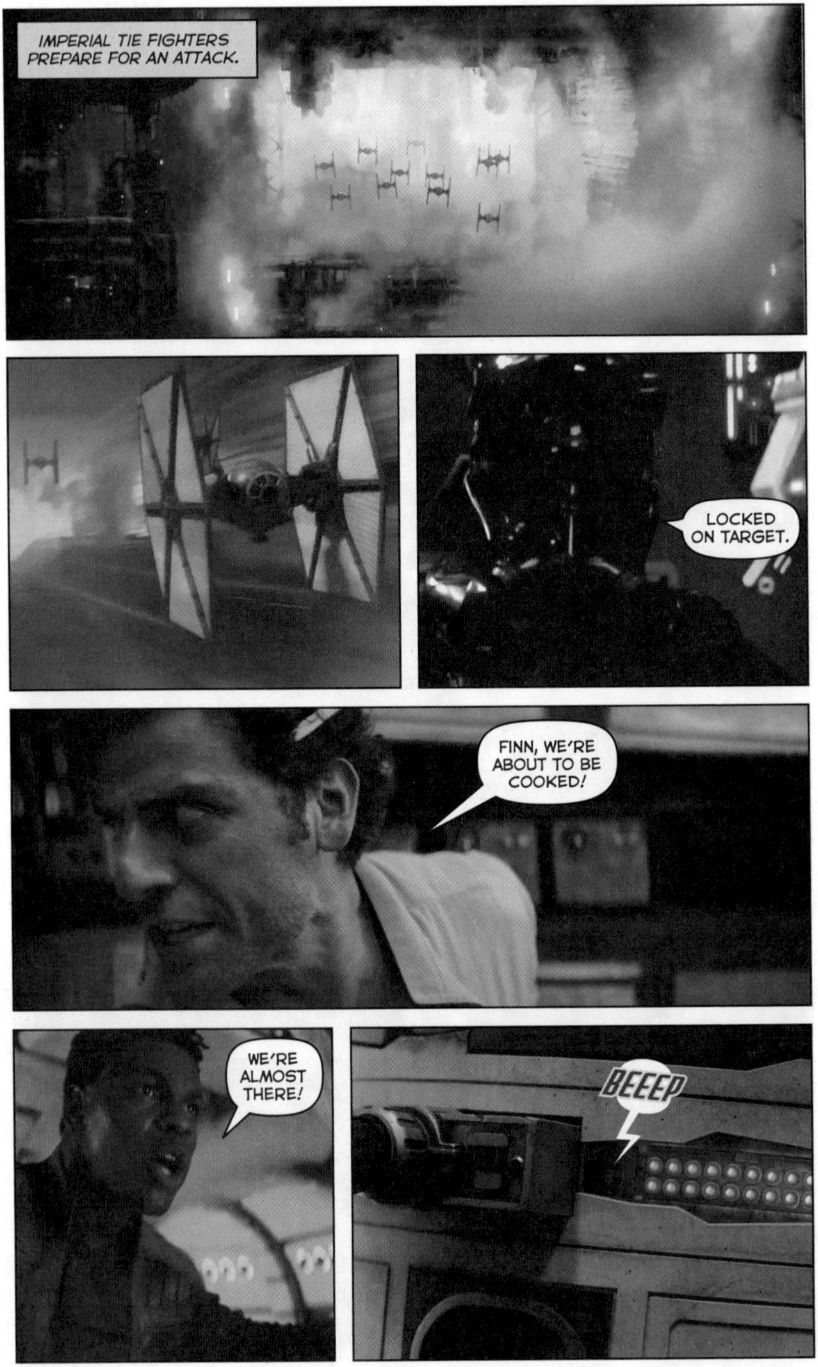
IMPERIAL TIE FIGHTERS PREPARE FOR AN ATTACK.
LOCKED ON TARGET.
FINN, WE'RE ABOUT TO BE COOKED!
WE'RE ALMOST THERE!
BEEEP

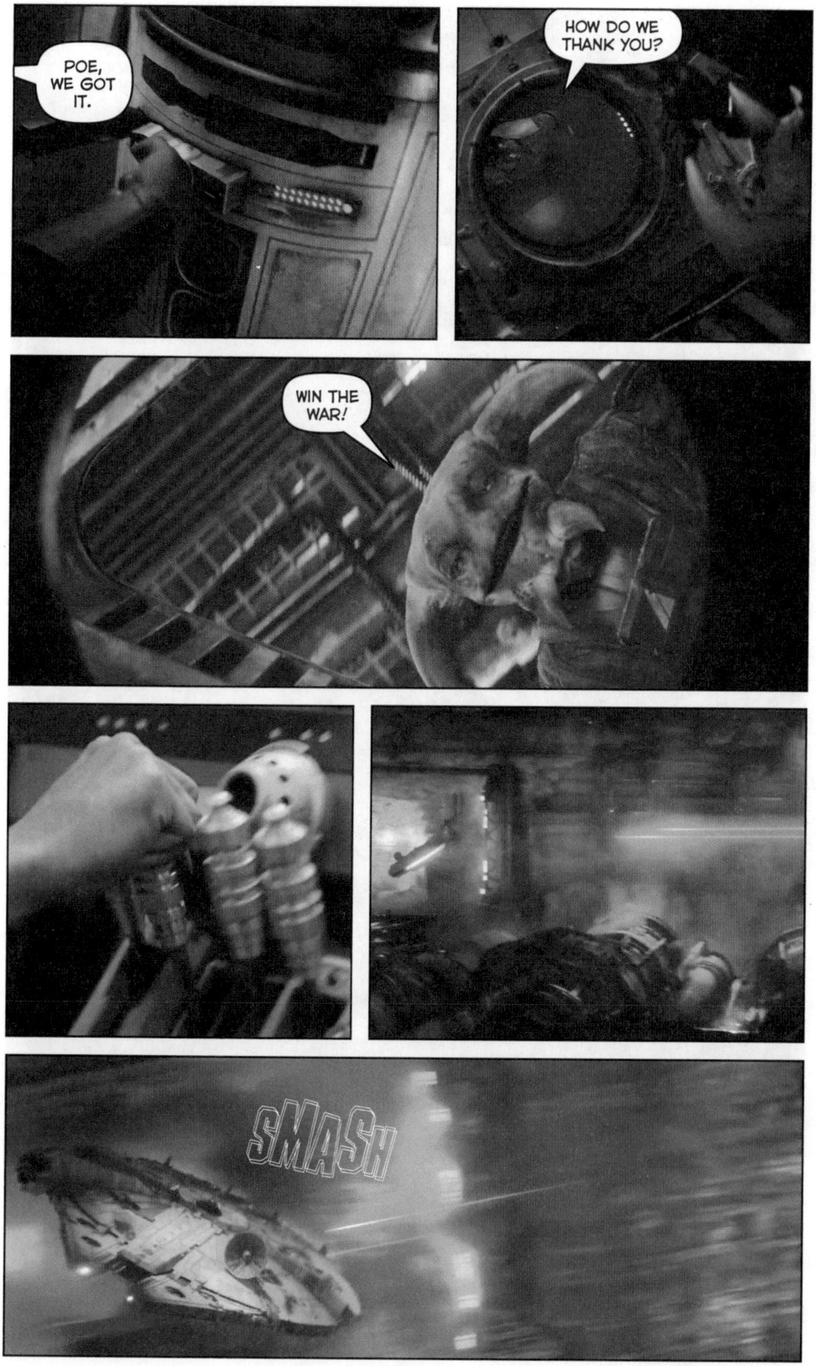
POE, WE GOT IT.
HOW DO WE THANK YOU?
WIN THE WAR!
SMASH

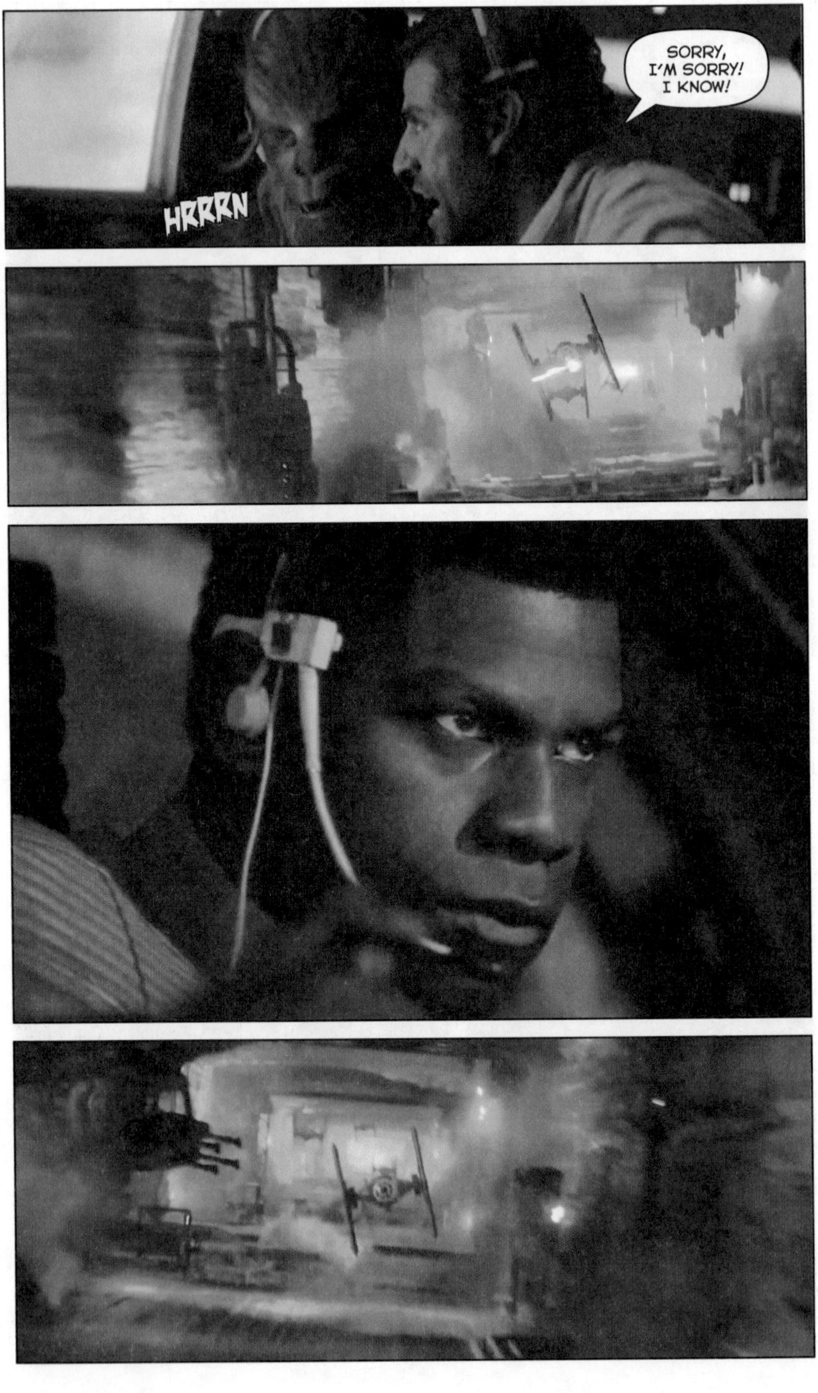
SORRY, I'M SORRY! I KNOW!
HRRRN

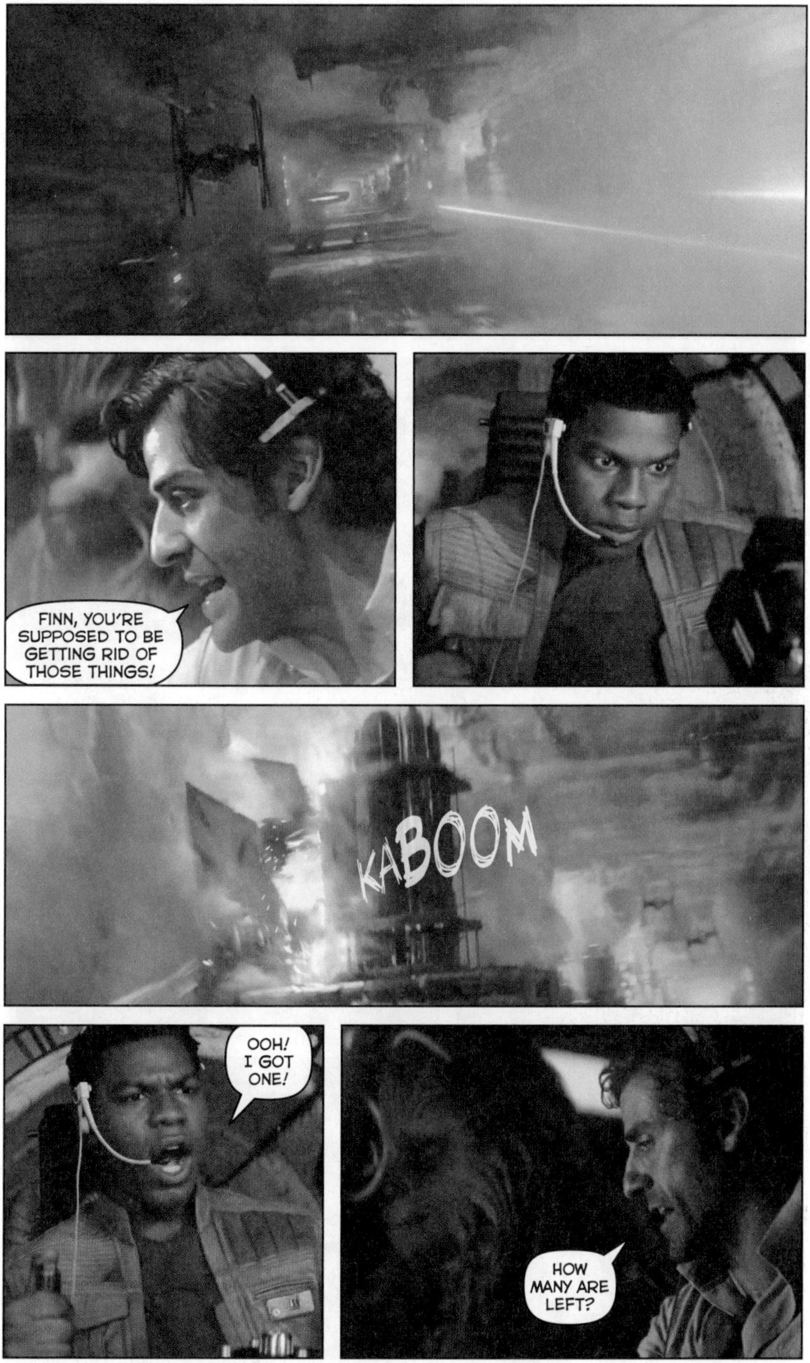
FINN, YOU'RE SUPPOSED TO BE GETTING RID OF THOSE THINGS!
KABOOM
OOH! I GOT ONE!
HOW MANY ARE LEFT?

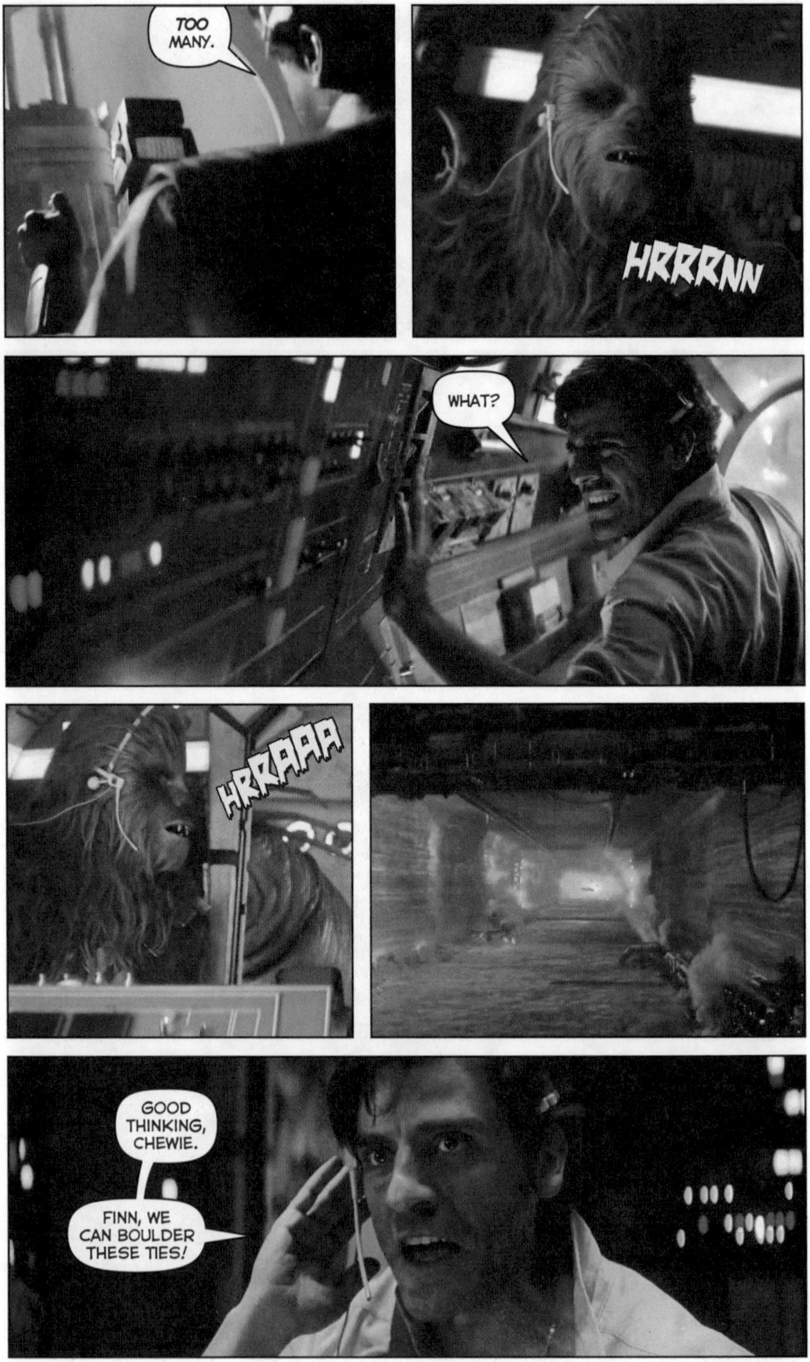
TOO MANY.
HRRRNN
WHAT?
HRRAAA
GOOD THINKING, CHEWIE.
FINN, WE CAN BOULDER THESE TIES!

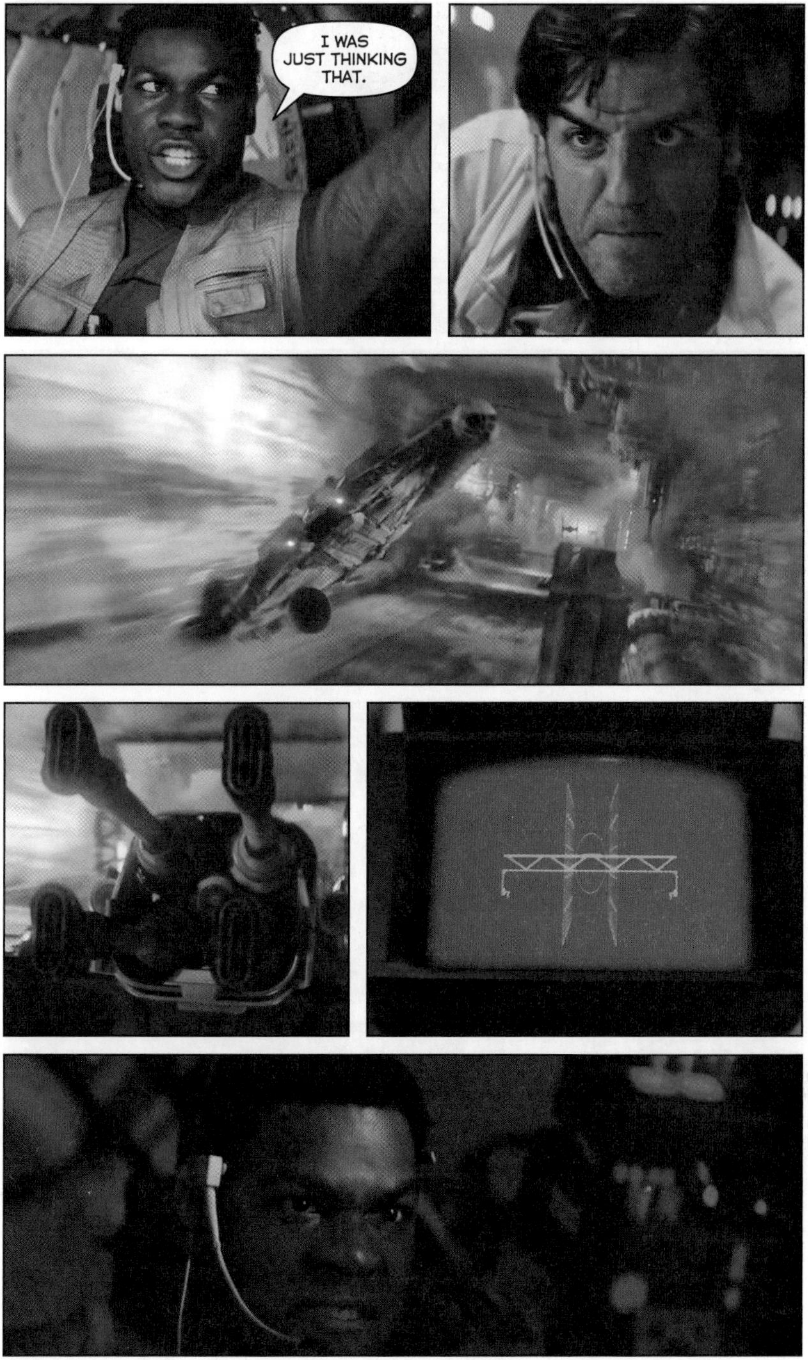
I WAS
JUST THINKING
THAT.

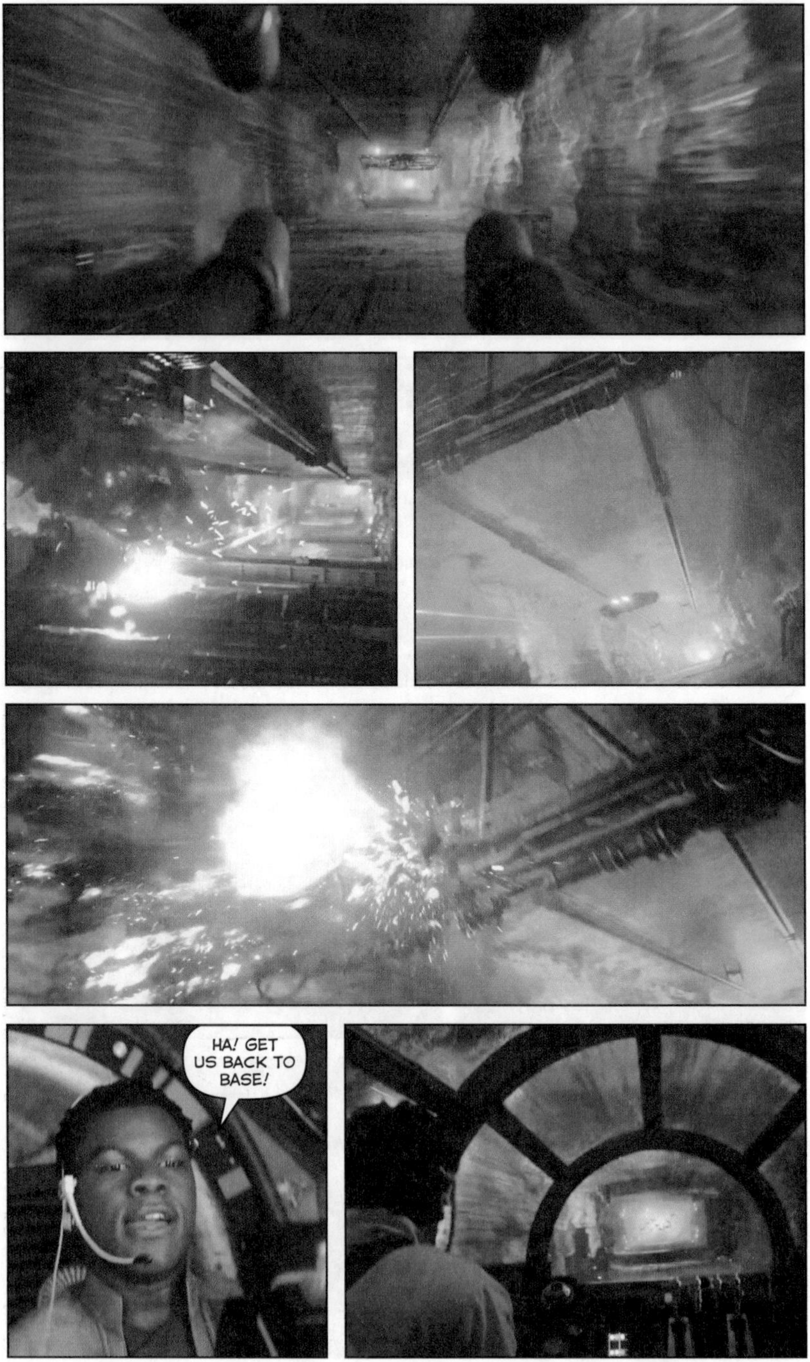
HA! GET
US BACK TO
BASE!

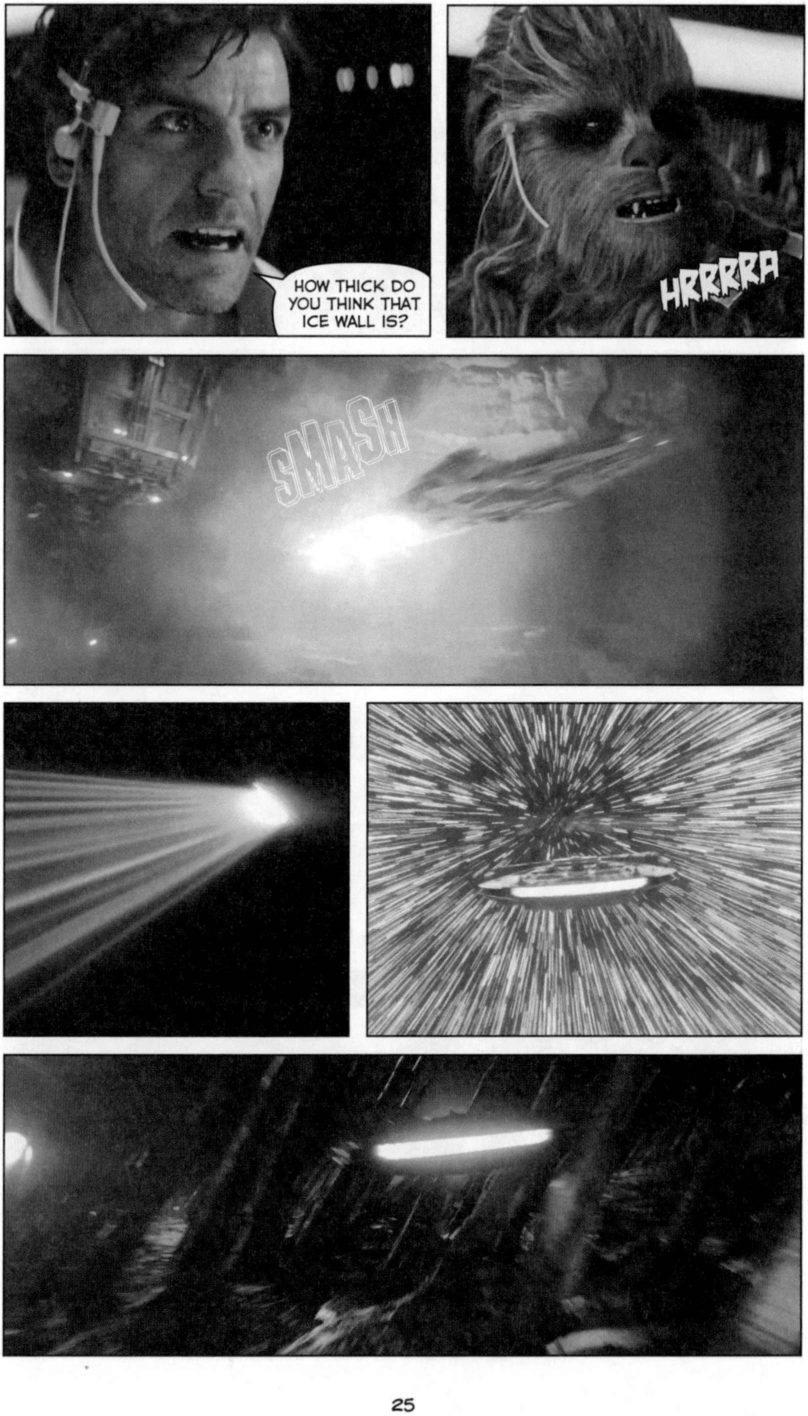
HOW THICK DO YOU THINK THAT ICE WALL IS?
HRRRRA
SMASH

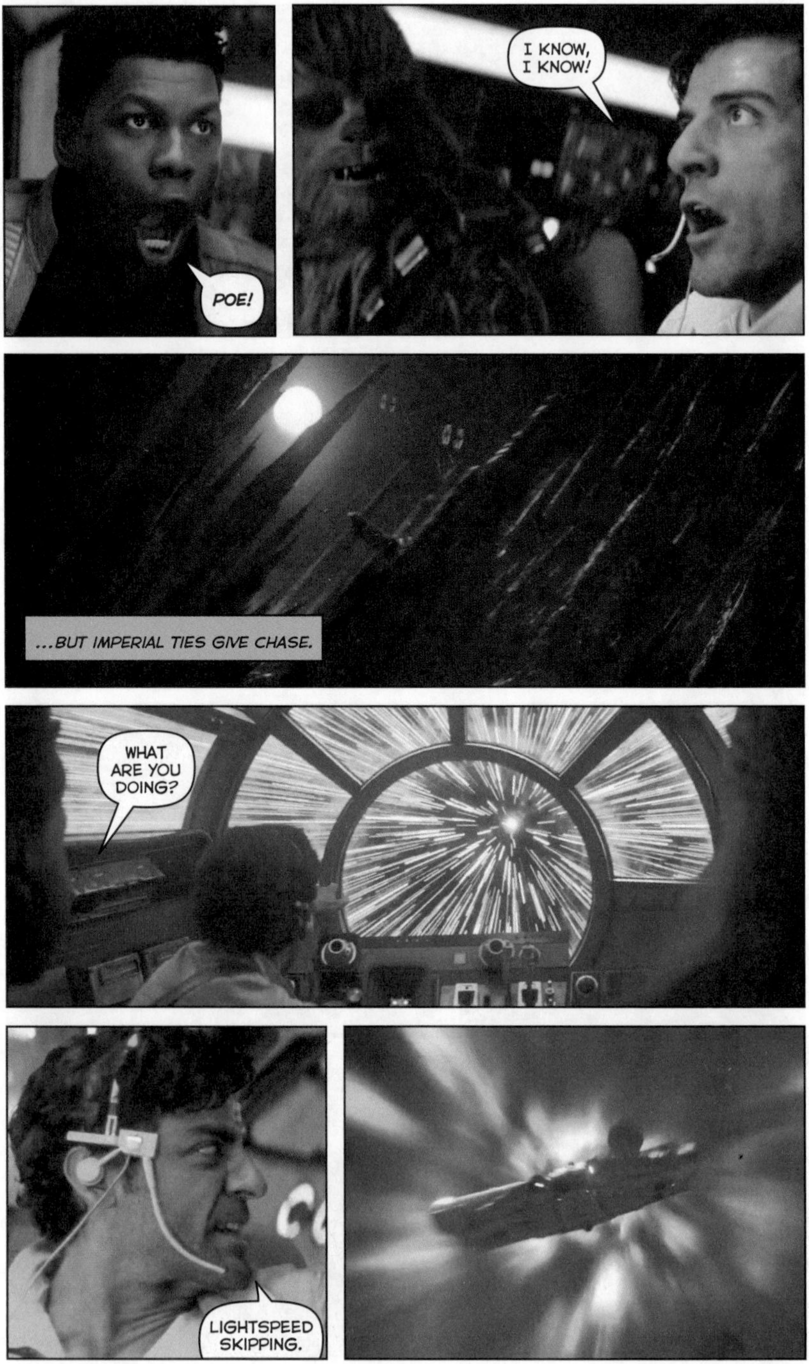
POE!
I KNOW, I KNOW!
...BUT IMPERIAL TIES GIVE CHASE.
WHAT ARE YOU DOING?
LIGHTSPEED SKIPPING.

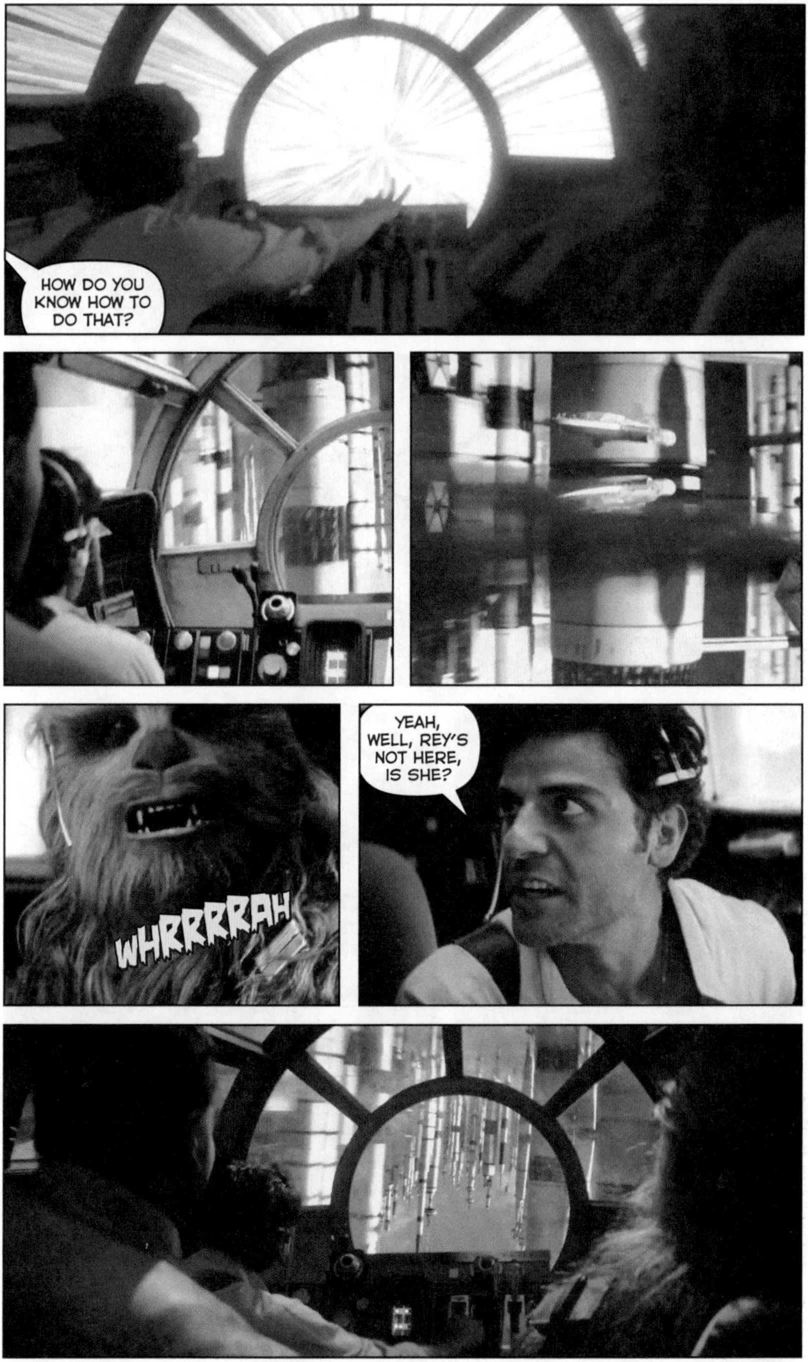
HOW DO YOU KNOW HOW TO DO THAT?
WHRRRRAH
YEAH, WELL, REY'S NOT HERE, IS SHE?

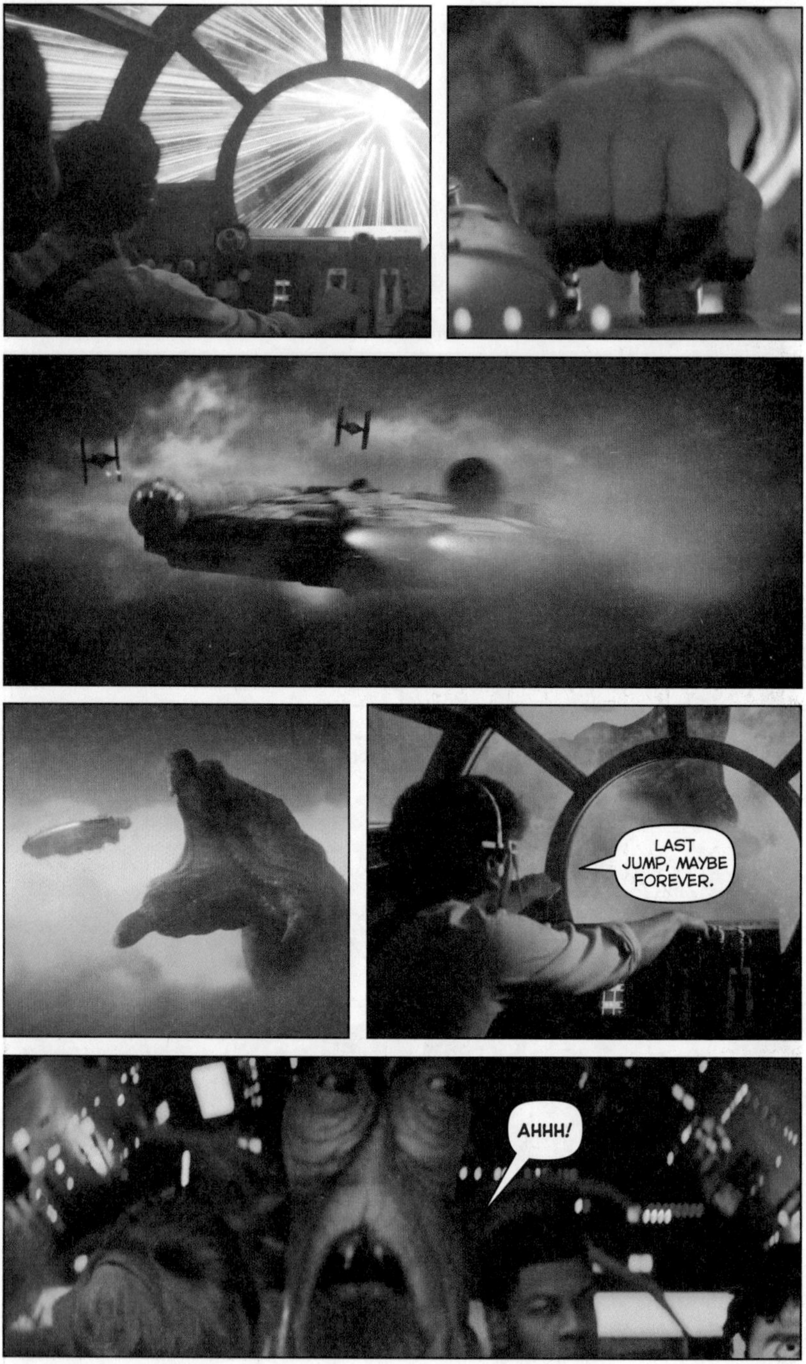
LAST JUMP, MAYBE FOREVER.
AHHH!

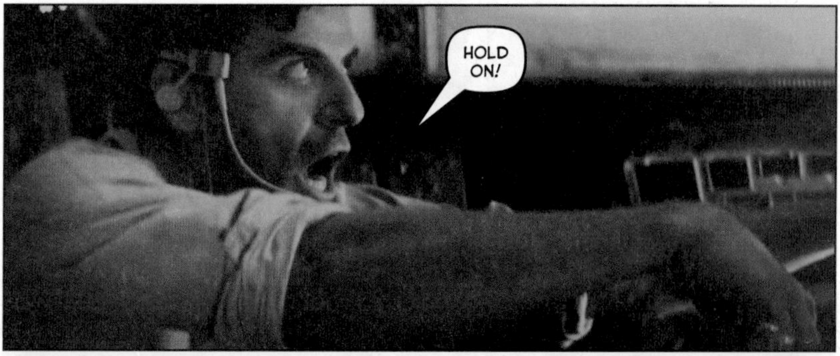
HOLD ON!

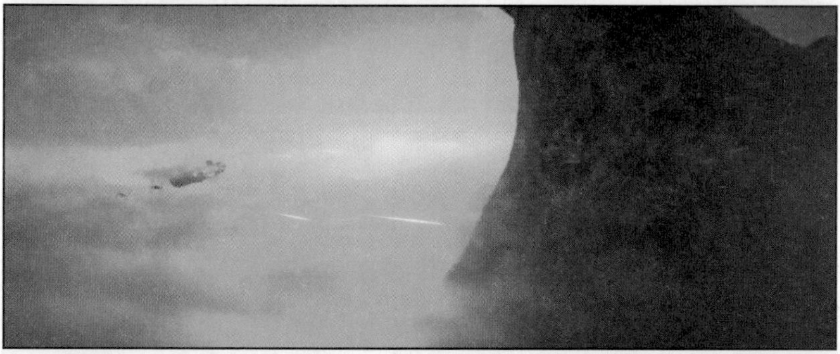

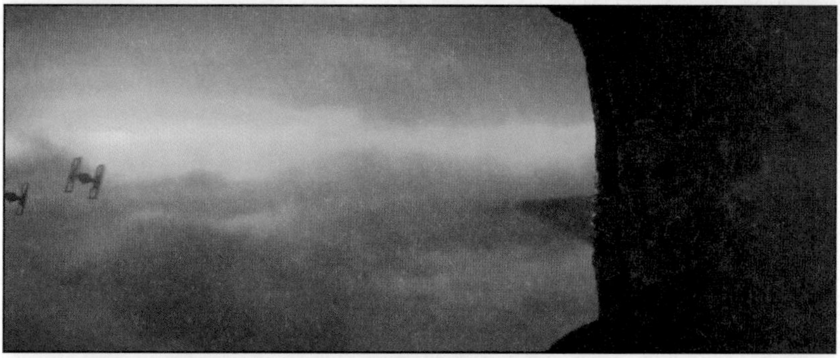

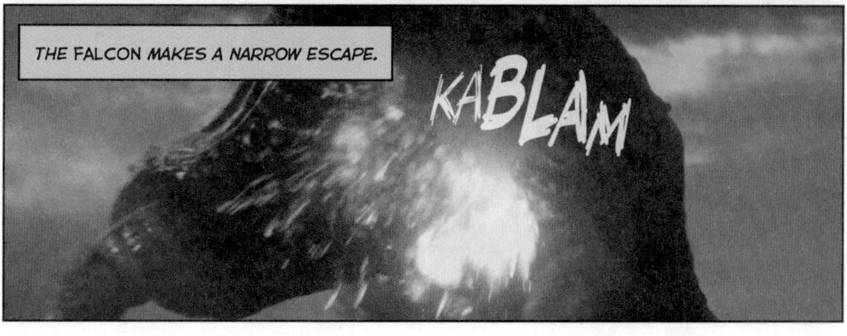
THE FALCON MAKES A NARROW ESCAPE.
KABLAM

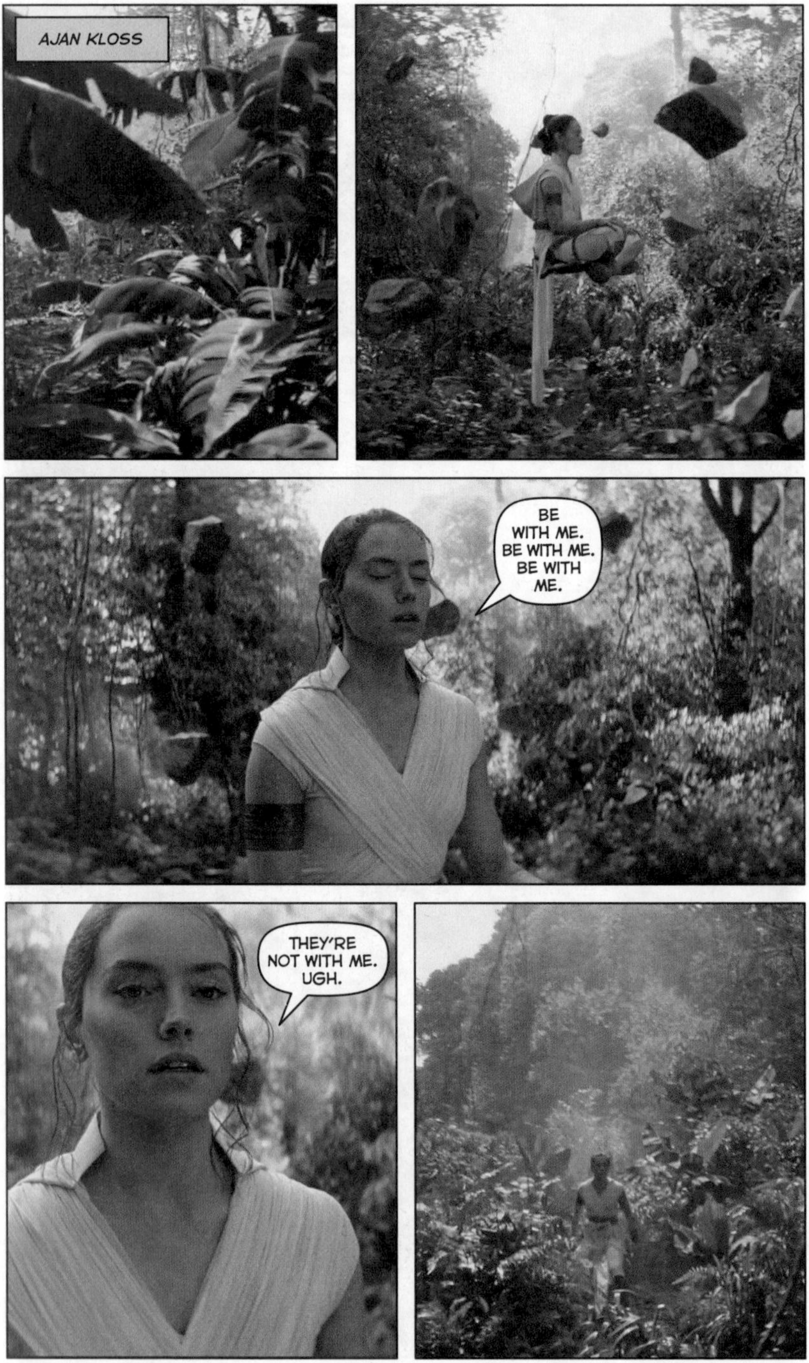
AJAN KLOSS
BE WITH ME. BE WITH ME. BE WITH ME.
THEY'RE NOT WITH ME. UGH.

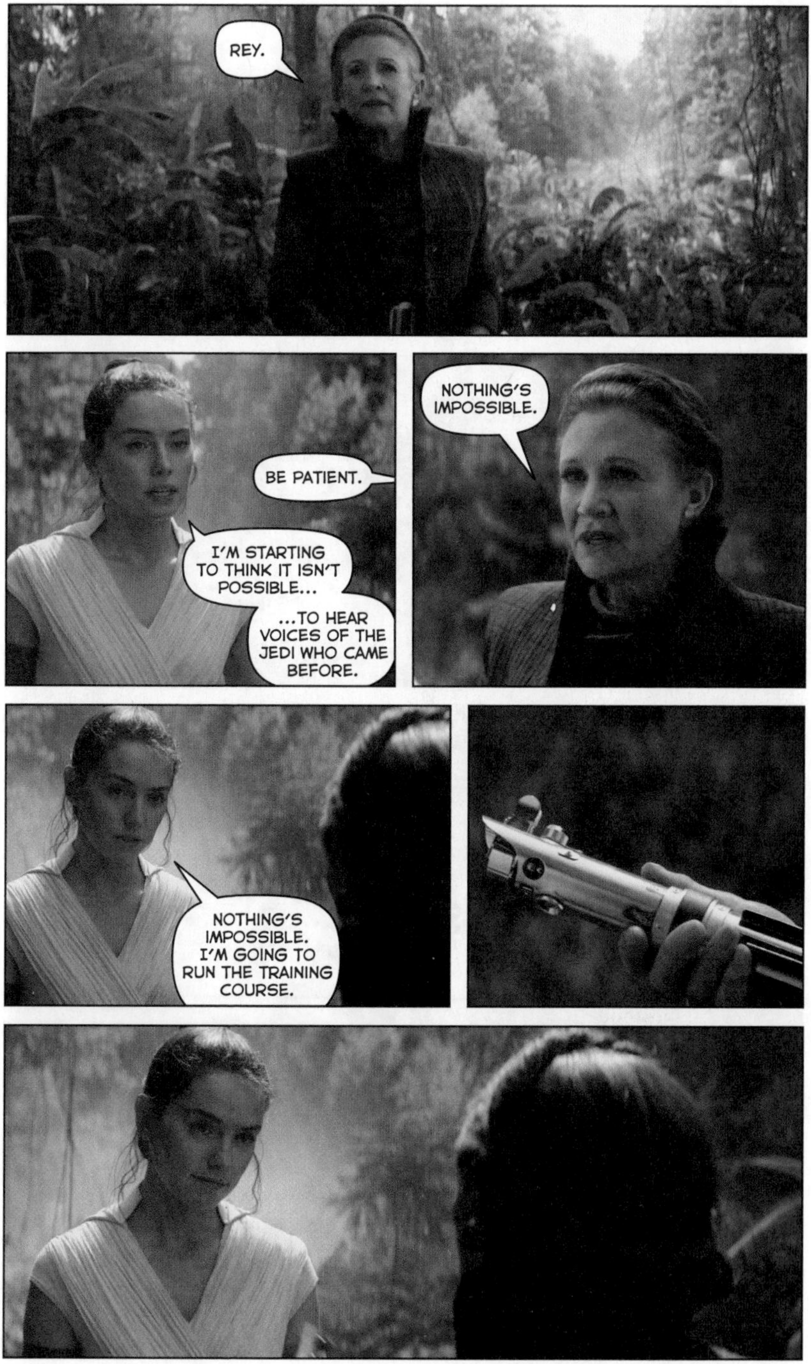
REY.
I'M STARTING TO THINK IT ISN'T POSSIBLE...
...TO HEAR VOICES OF THE JEDI WHO CAME BEFORE.
BE PATIENT.
NOTHING'S IMPOSSIBLE.
NOTHING'S IMPOSSIBLE. I'M GOING TO RUN THE TRAINING COURSE.

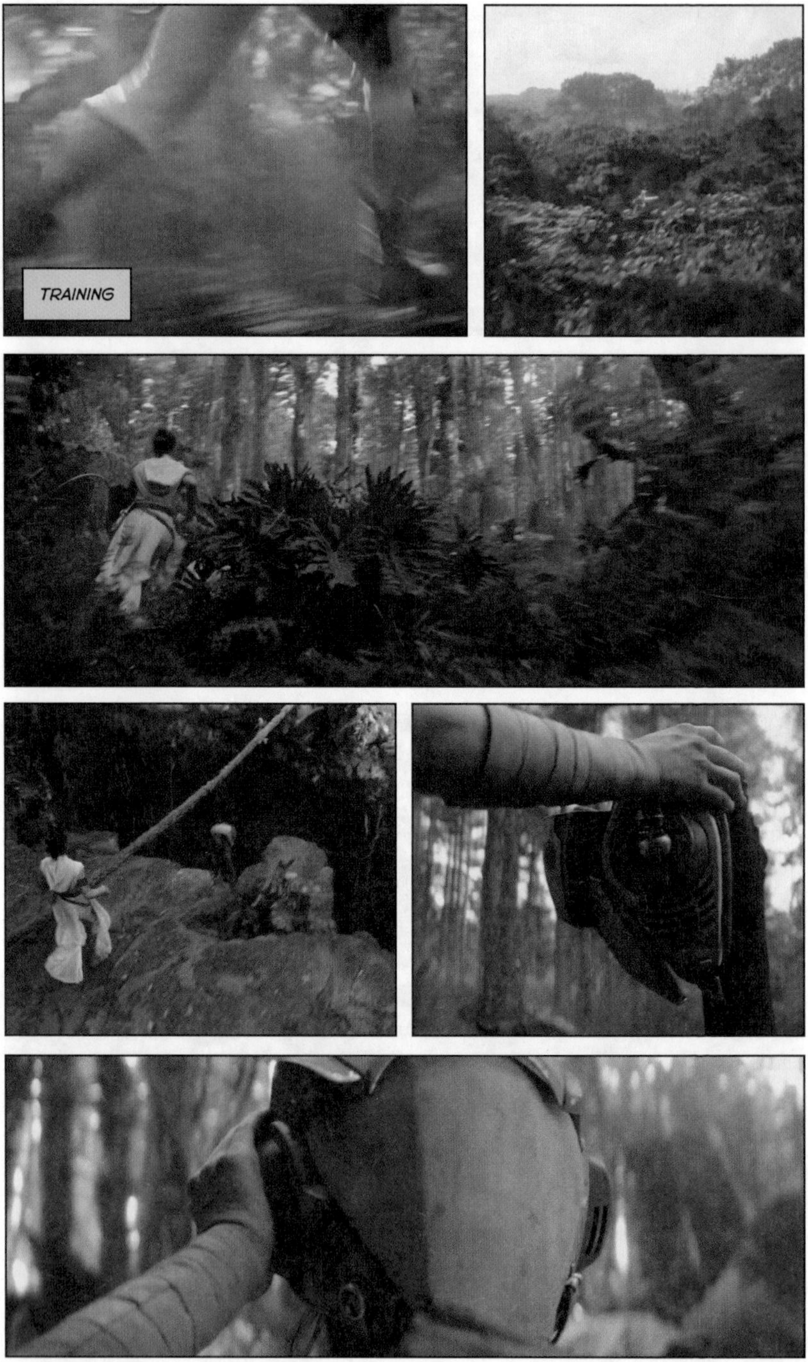
TRAINING

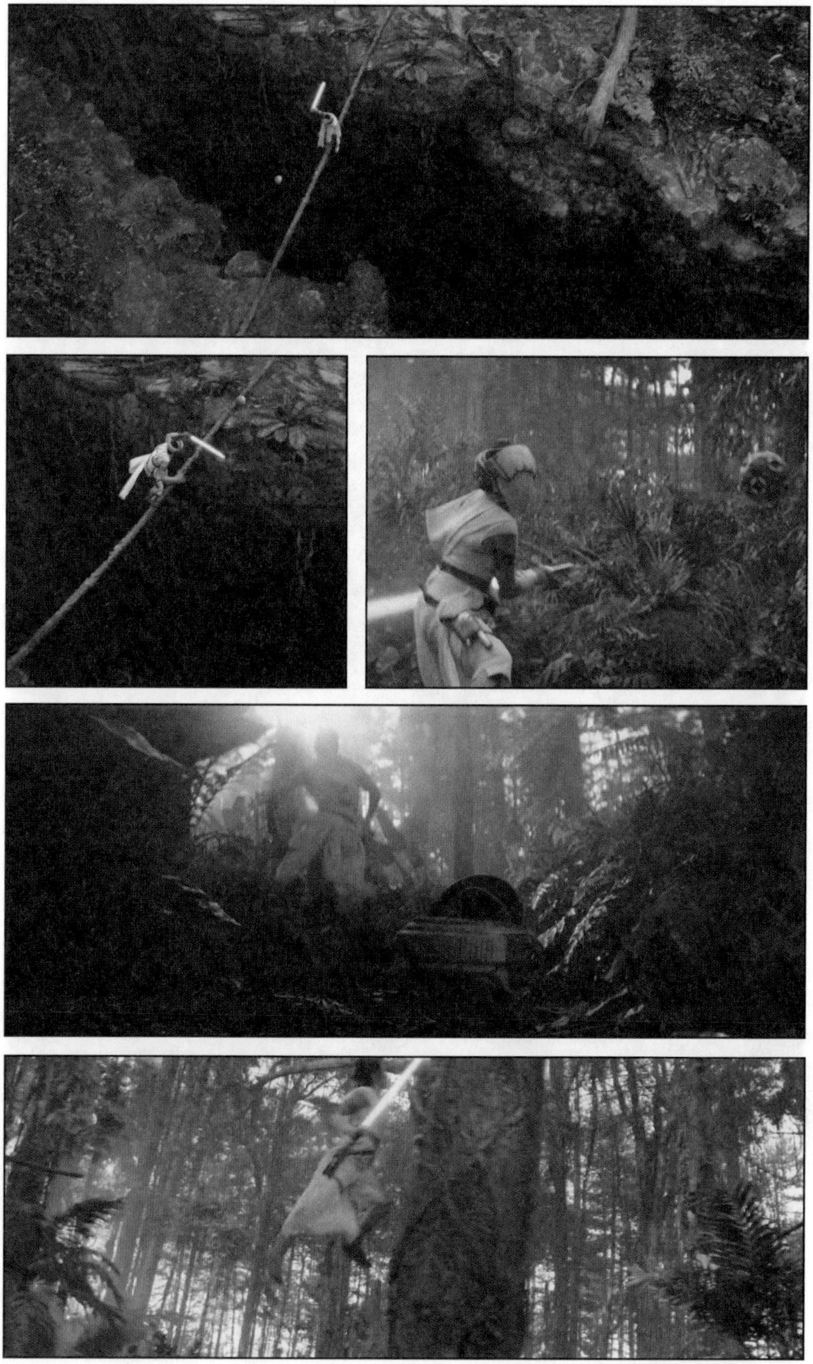

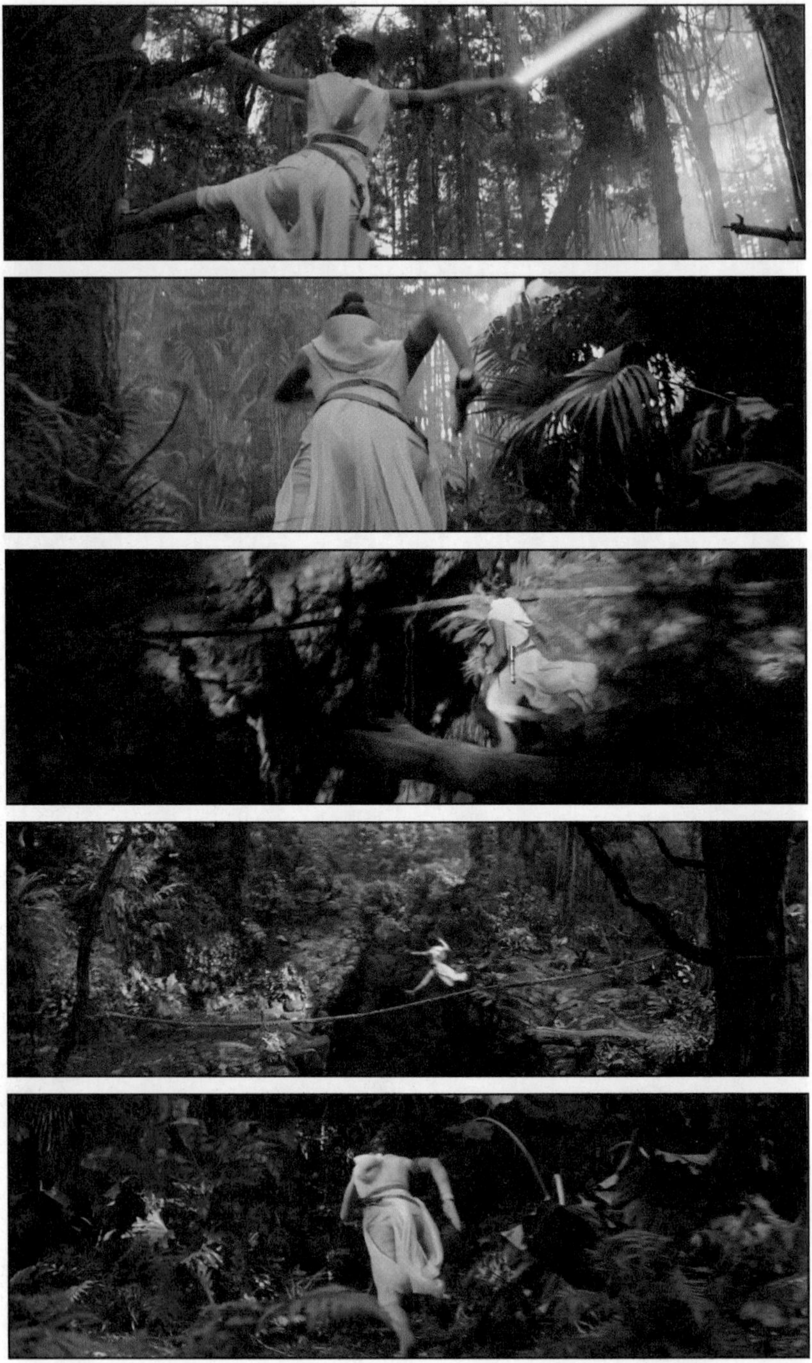

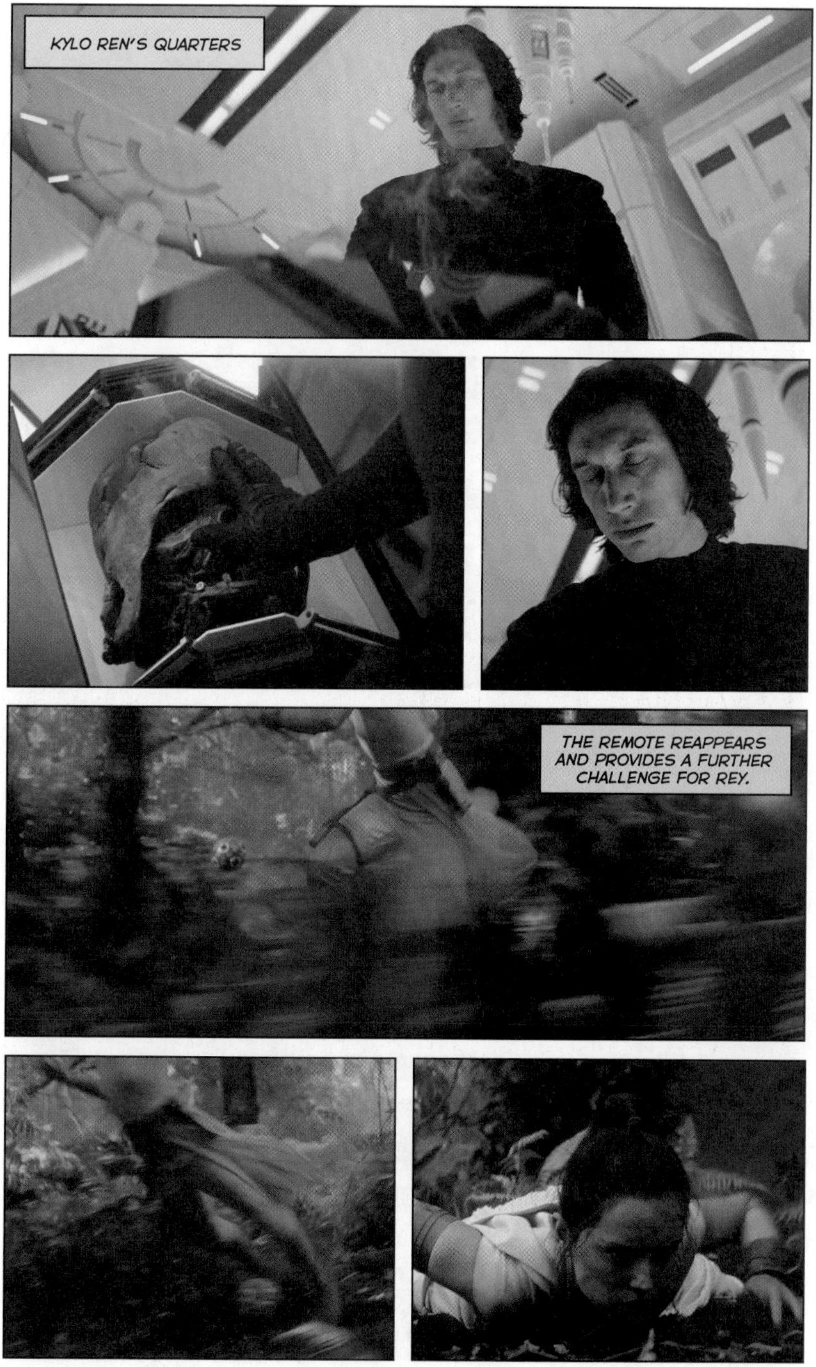
KYLO REN'S QUARTERS
THE REMOTE REAPPEARS AND PROVIDES A FURTHER CHALLENGE FOR REY.

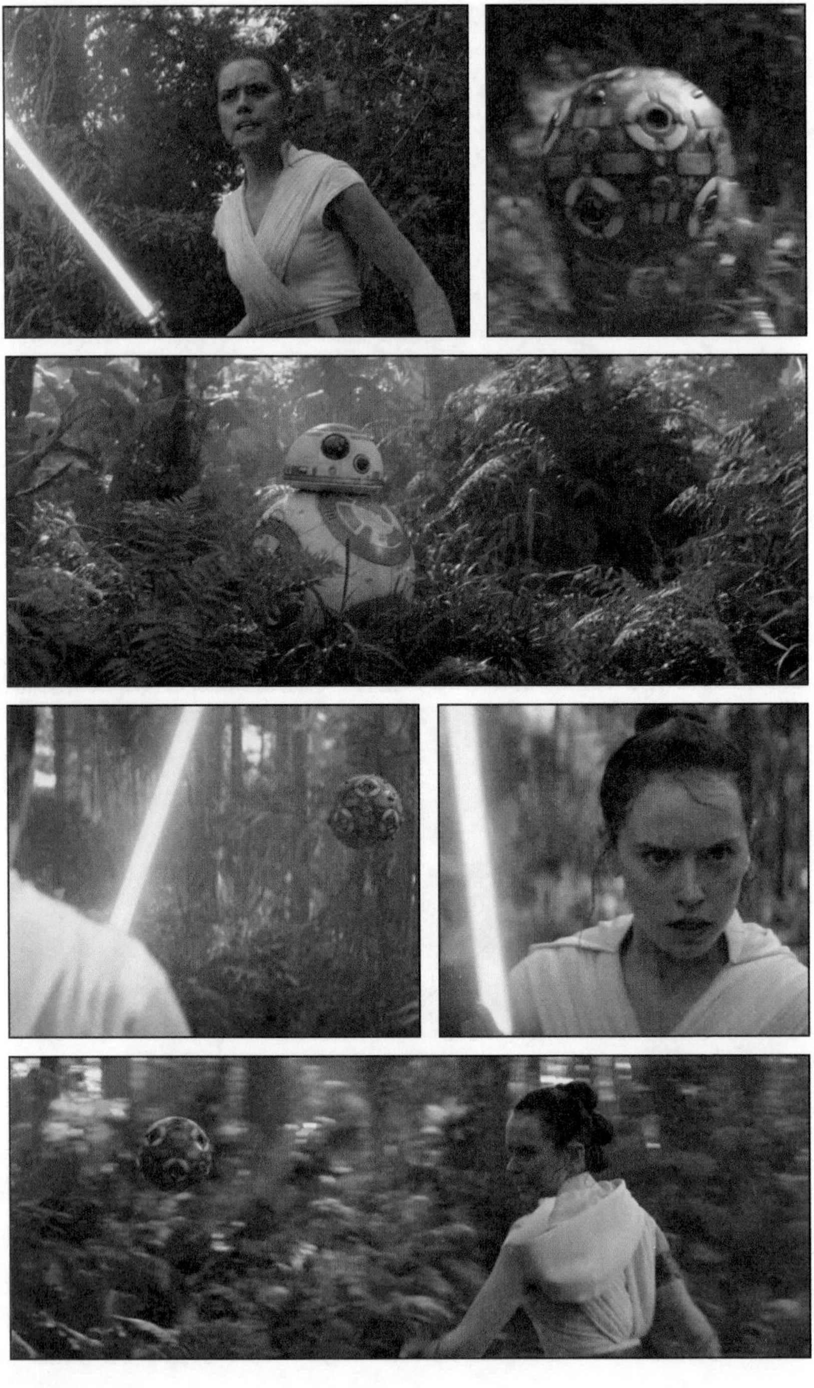

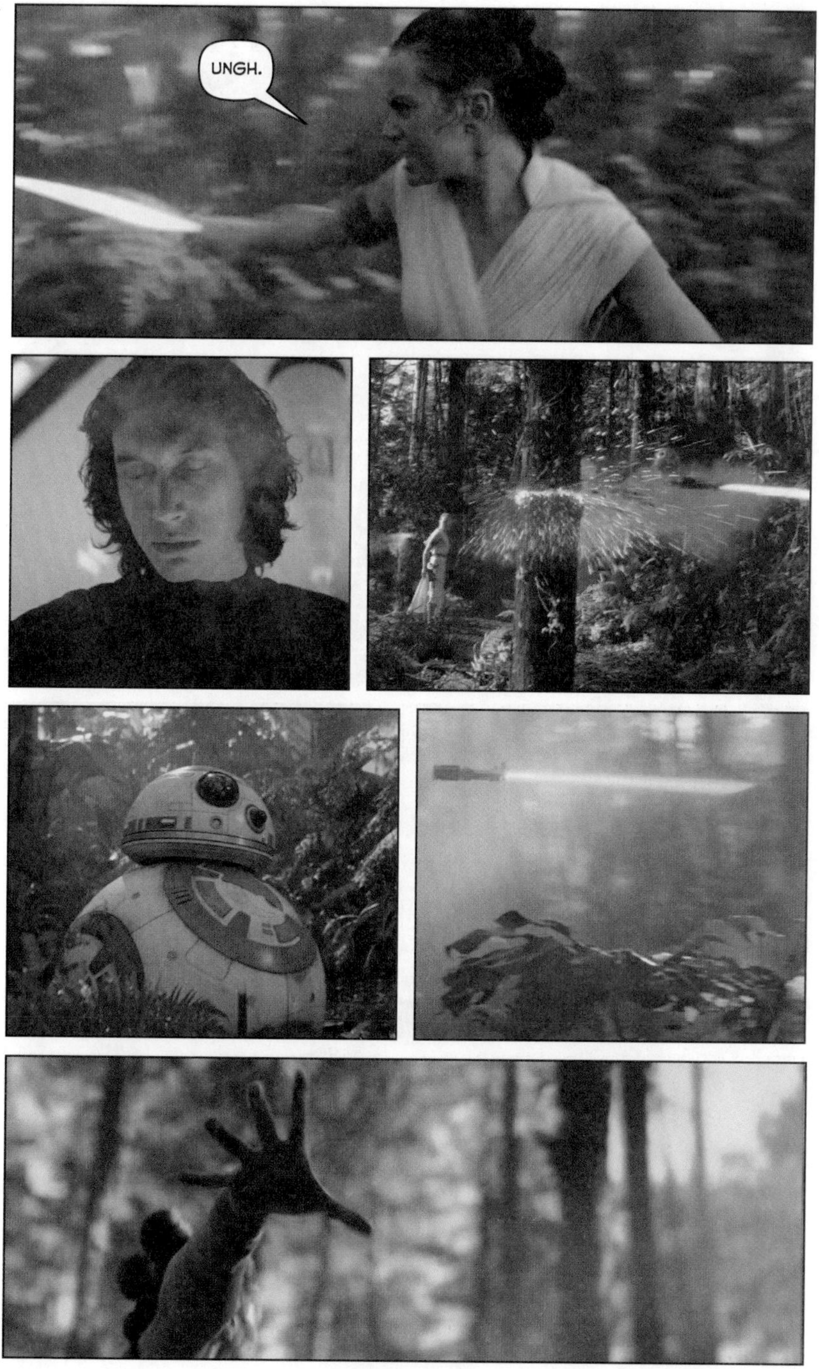
UNGH.

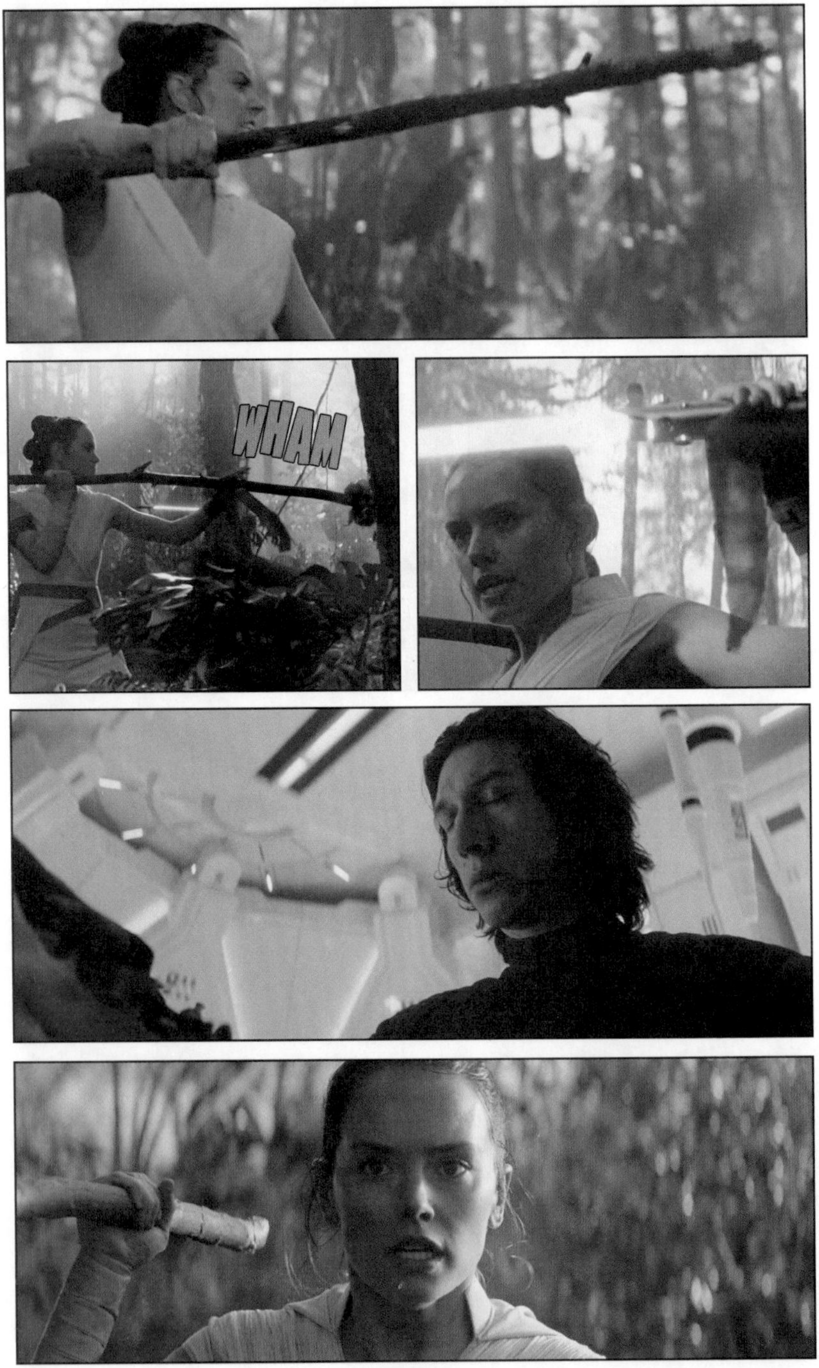
WHAM

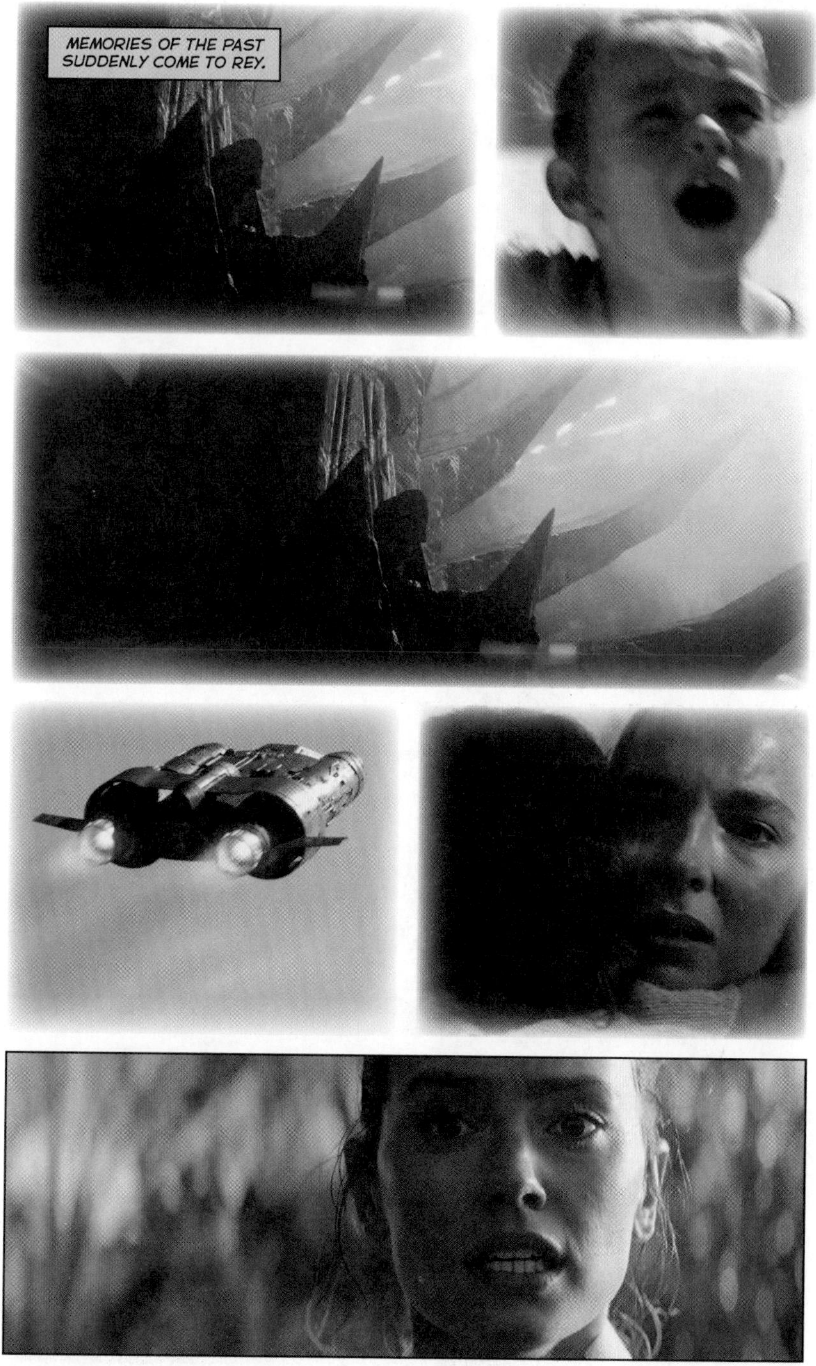
MEMORIES OF THE PAST SUDDENLY COME TO REY.

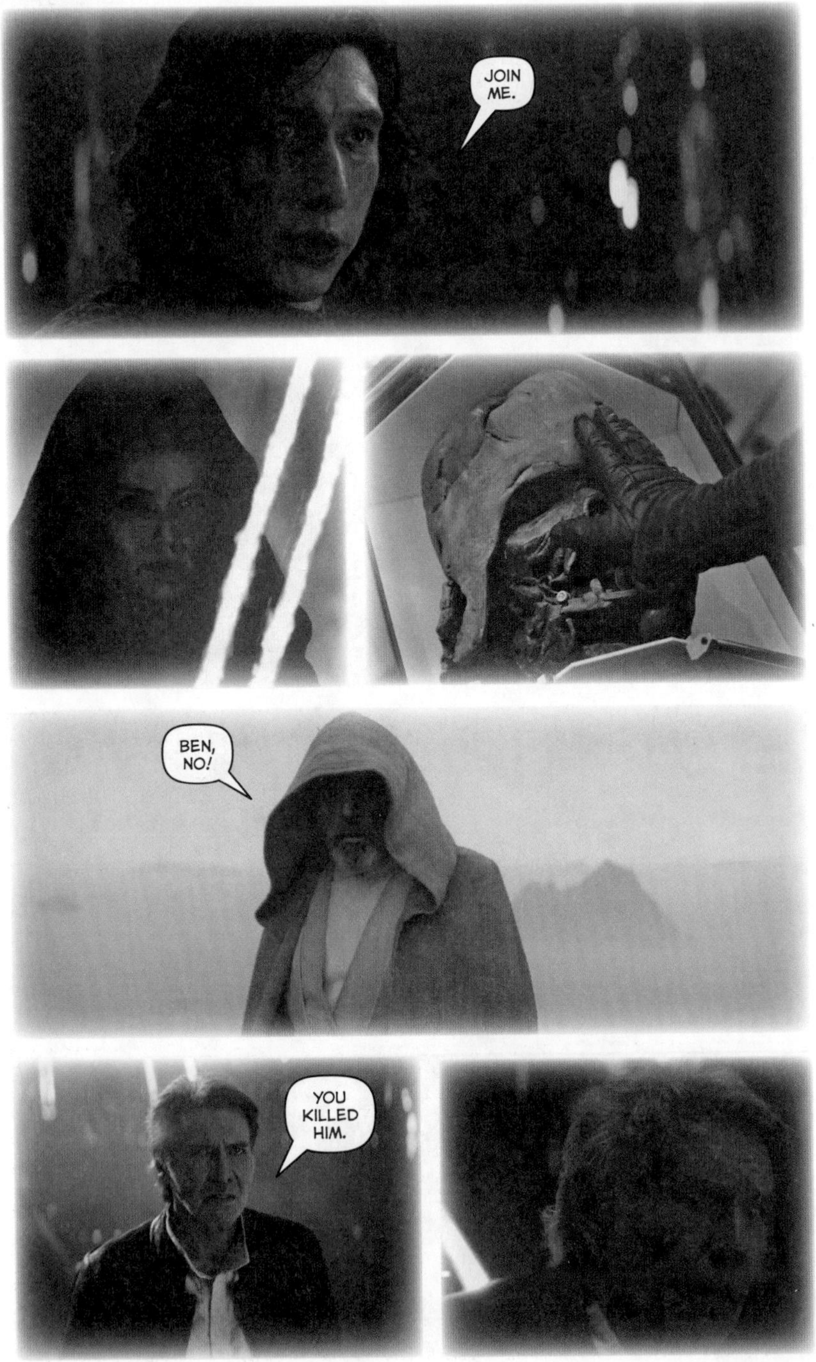
JOIN ME.
BEN, NO!
YOU KILLED HIM.

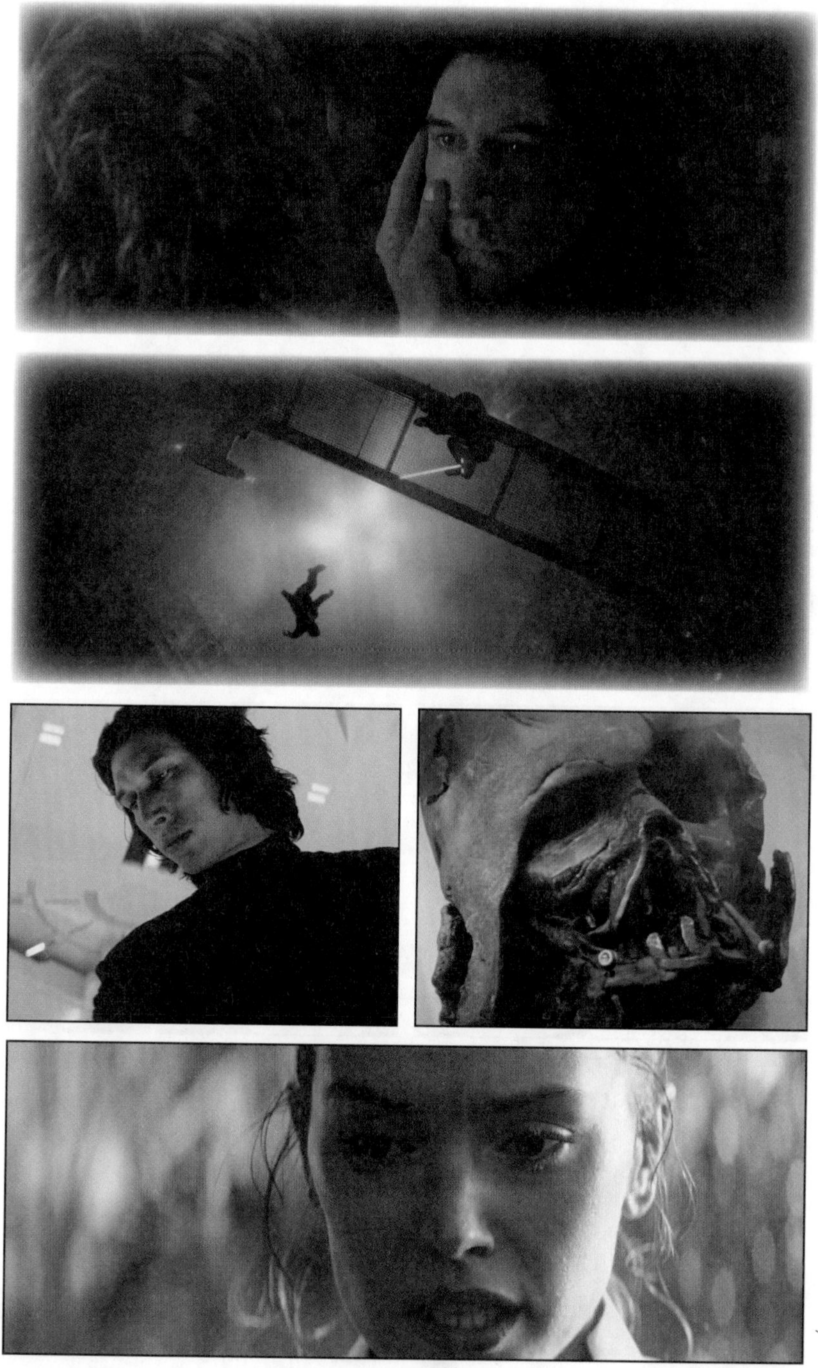

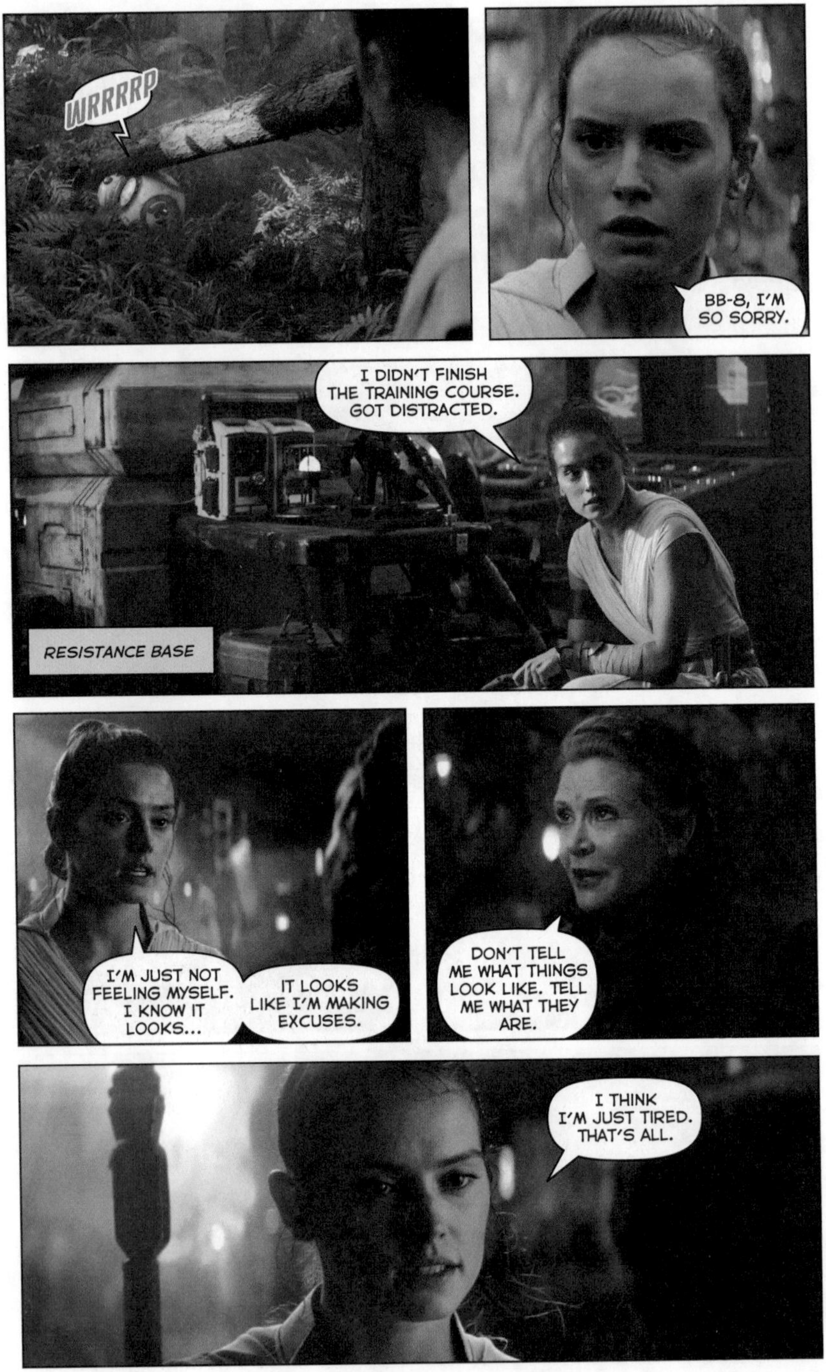
WRRRRP
BB-8, I'M SO SORRY.
I DIDN'T FINISH THE TRAINING COURSE. GOT DISTRACTED.
RESISTANCE BASE
I'M JUST NOT FEELING MYSELF. I KNOW IT LOOKS...
IT LOOKS LIKE I'M MAKING EXCUSES.
DON'T TELL ME WHAT THINGS LOOK LIKE. TELL ME WHAT THEY ARE.
I THINK I'M JUST TIRED. THAT'S ALL.

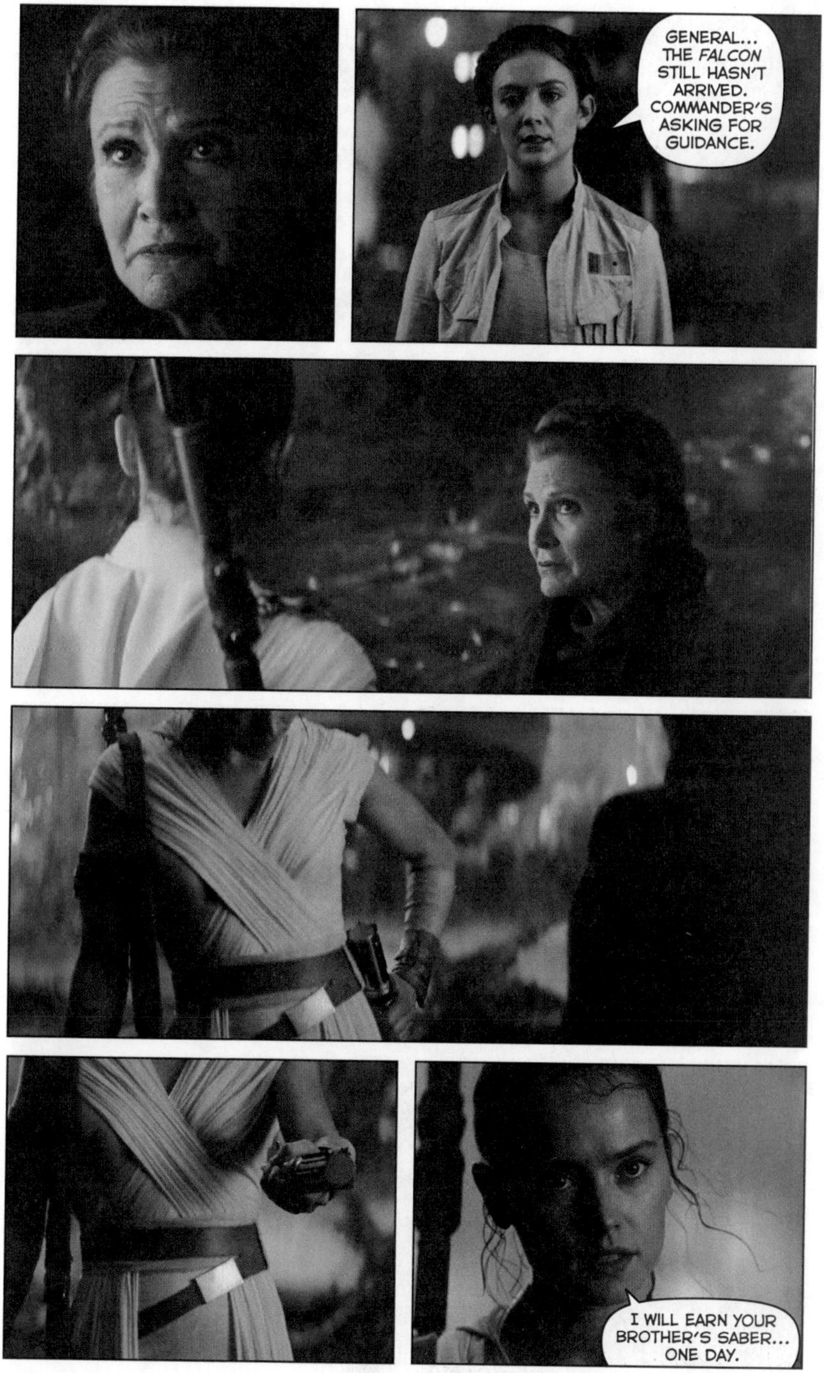
GENERAL... THE FALCON STILL HASN'T ARRIVED. COMMANDER'S ASKING FOR GUIDANCE.
I WILL EARN YOUR BROTHER'S SABER... ONE DAY.

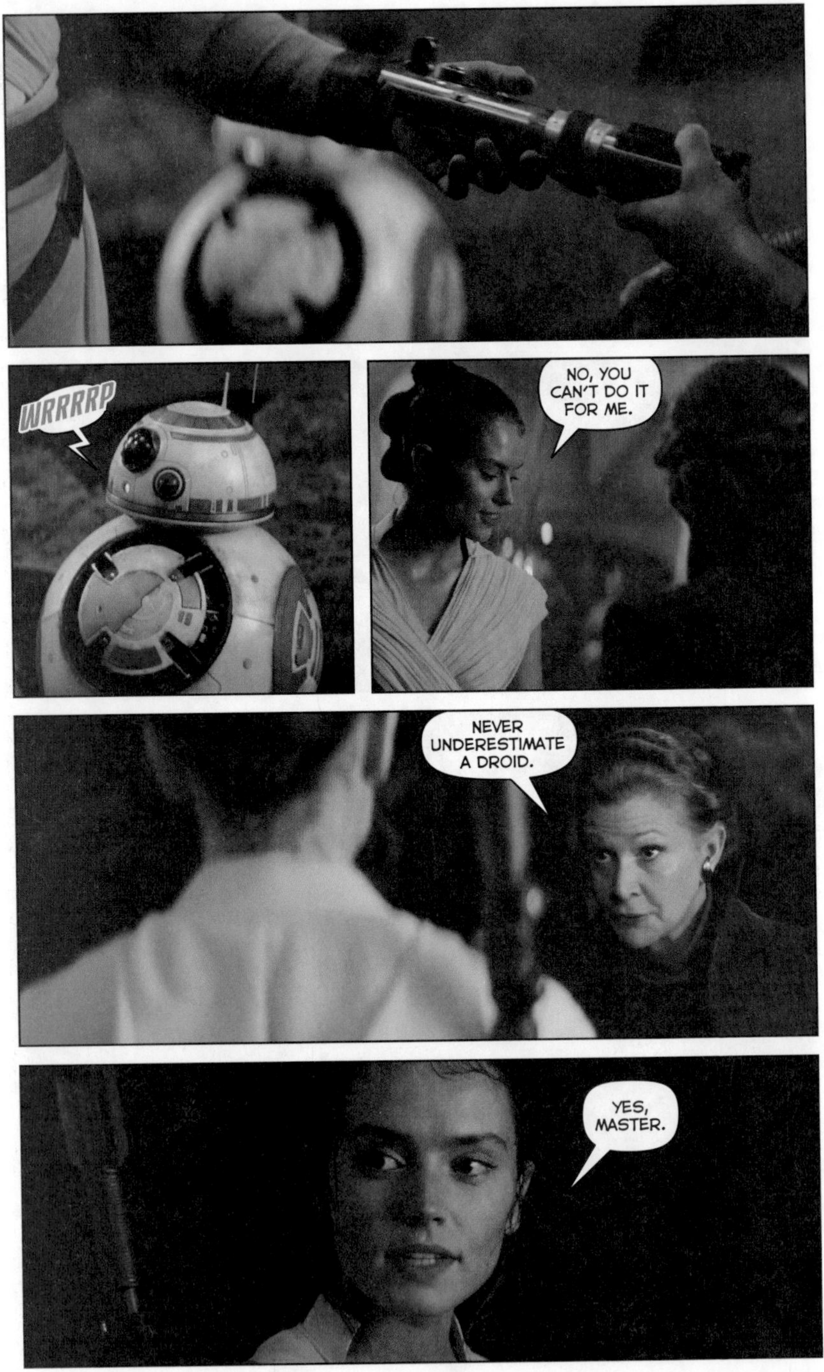
WRRRRP
NO, YOU CAN'T DO IT FOR ME.
NEVER UNDERESTIMATE A DROID.
YES, MASTER.

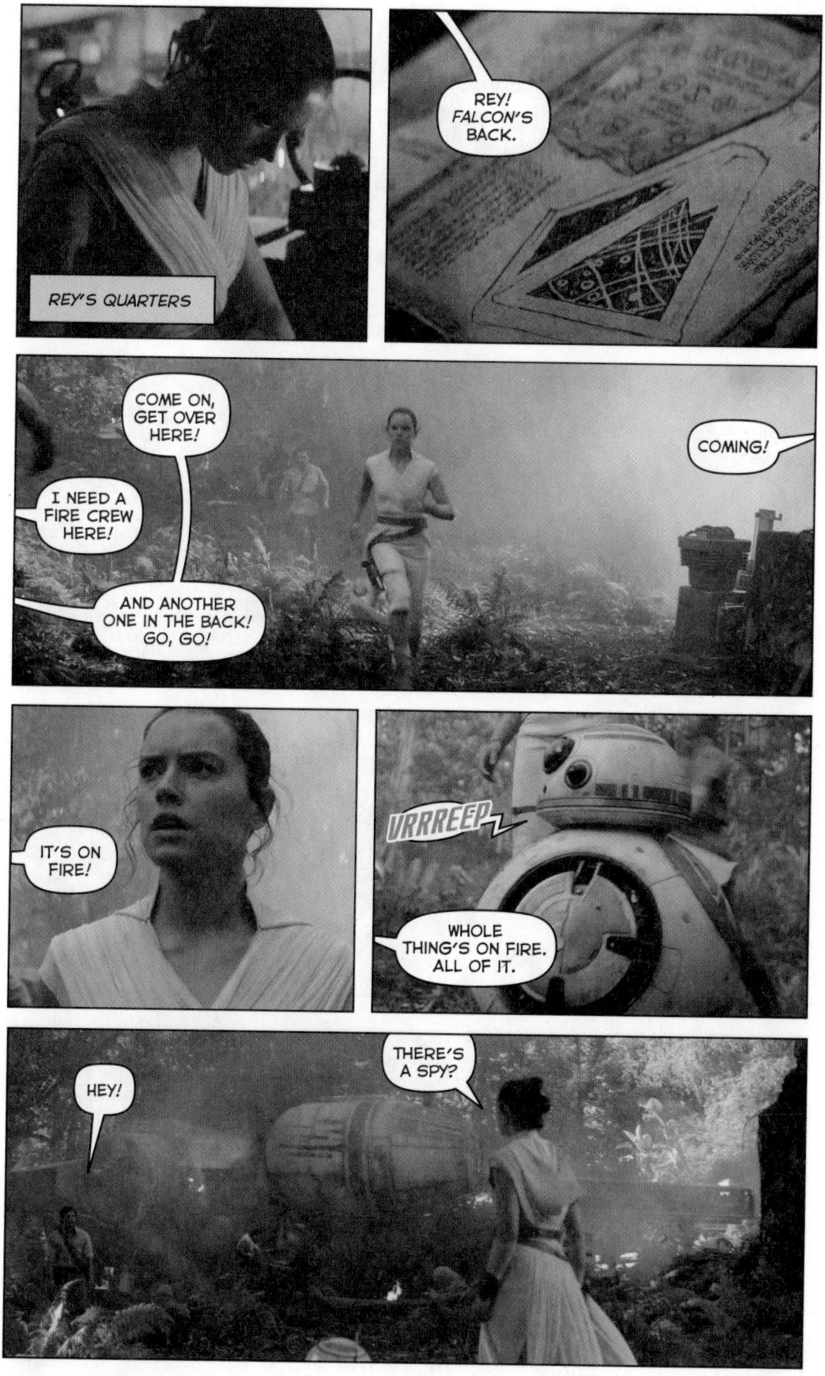
REY'S QUARTERS
REY! FALCON'S BACK.
COME ON, GET OVER HERE!
I NEED A FIRE CREW HERE!
AND ANOTHER ONE IN THE BACK! GO, GO!
COMING!
IT'S ON FIRE!
URRREEP
WHOLE THING'S ON FIRE. ALL OF IT.
HEY!
THERE'S A SPY?

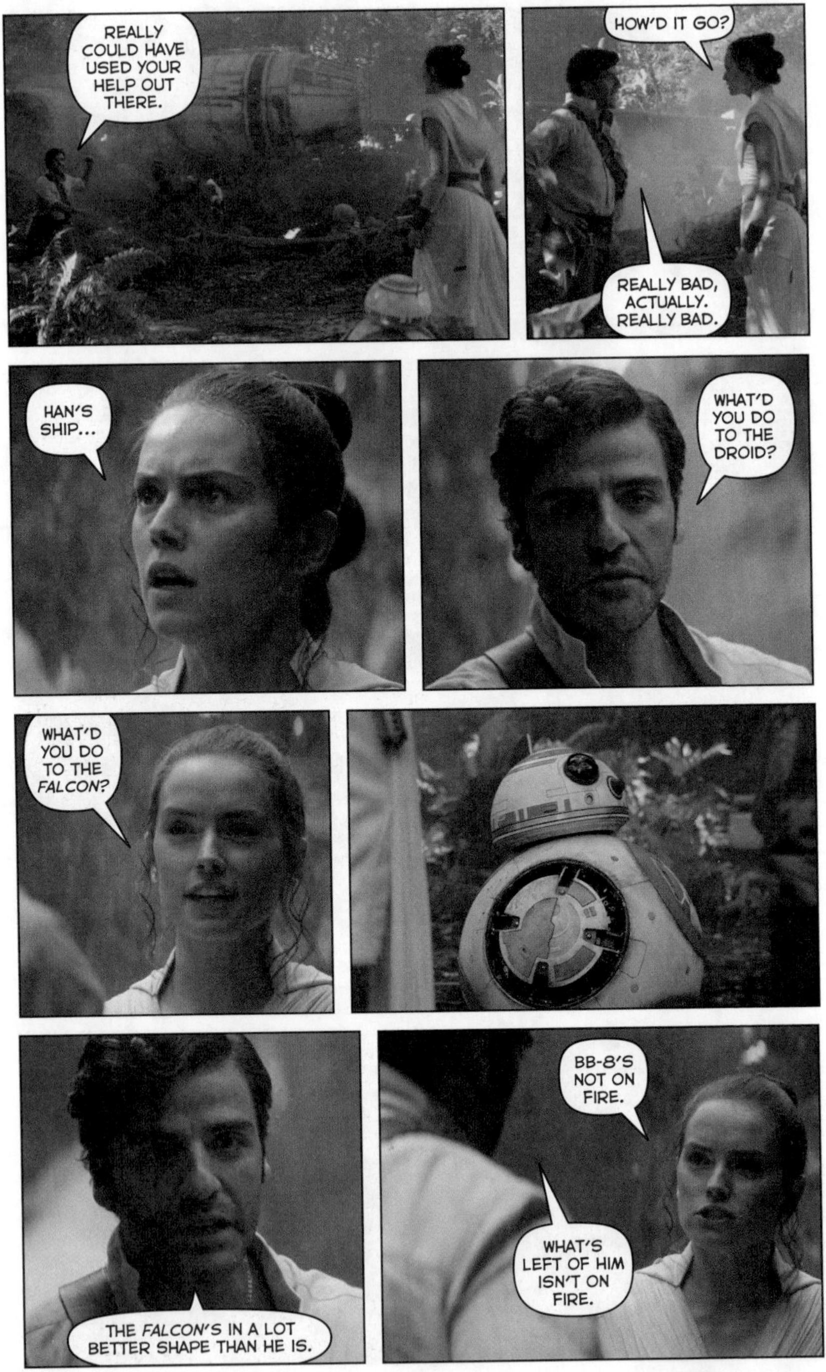
REALLY COULD HAVE USED YOUR HELP OUT THERE.
HOW'D IT GO?
REALLY BAD, ACTUALLY. REALLY BAD.
HAN'S SHIP...
WHAT'D YOU DO TO THE DROID?
WHAT'D YOU DO TO THE *FALCON*?
THE *FALCON'S* IN A LOT BETTER SHAPE THAN HE IS.
BB-8'S NOT ON FIRE.
WHAT'S LEFT OF HIM ISN'T ON FIRE.

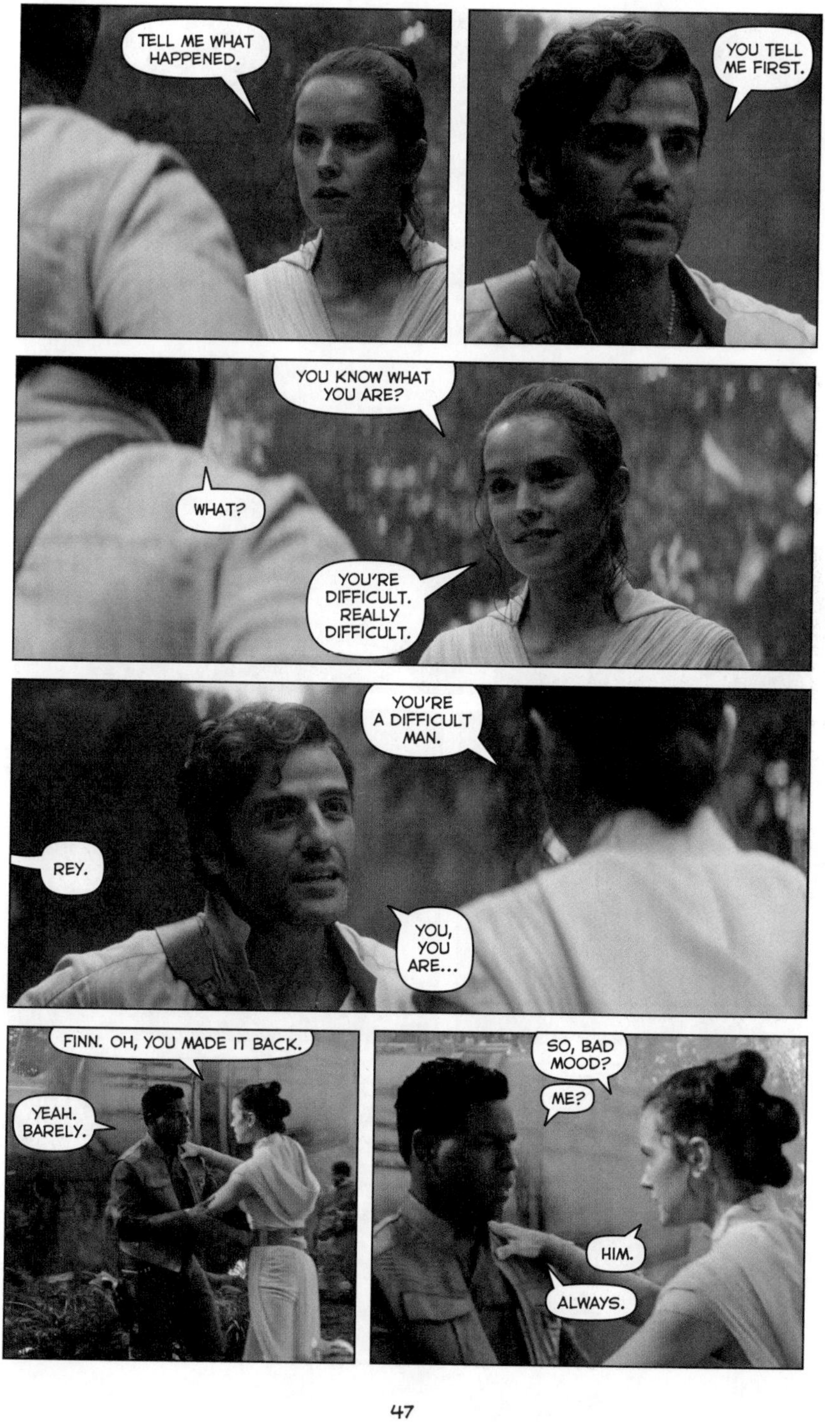
TELL ME WHAT HAPPENED.
YOU TELL ME FIRST.
YOU KNOW WHAT YOU ARE?
WHAT?
YOU'RE DIFFICULT. REALLY DIFFICULT.
YOU'RE A DIFFICULT MAN.
REY.
YOU, YOU ARE...
FINN. OH, YOU MADE IT BACK.
YEAH. BARELY.
SO, BAD MOOD?
ME?
HIM.
ALWAYS.

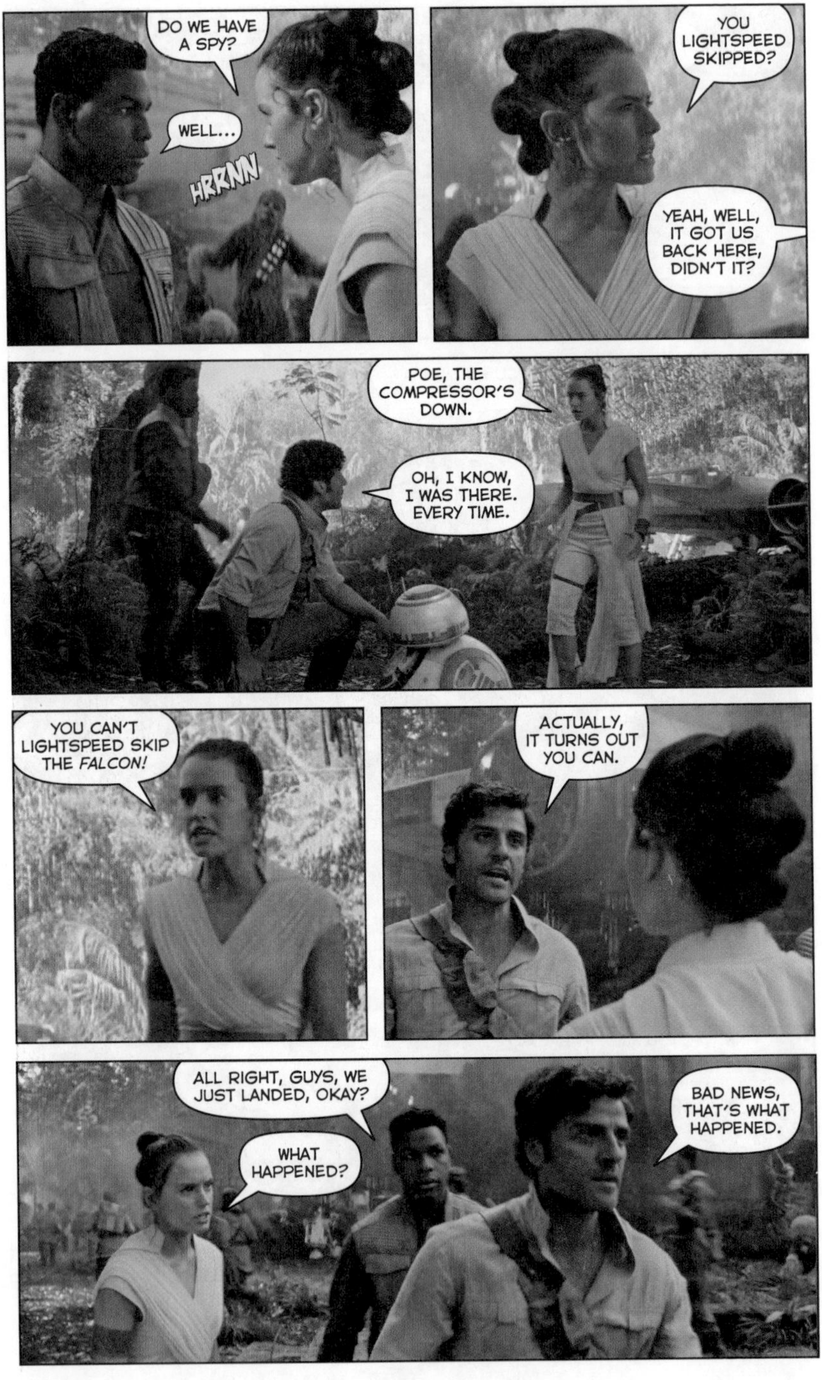
DO WE HAVE A SPY?
WELL...
HRRNN
YOU LIGHTSPEED SKIPPED?
YEAH, WELL, IT GOT US BACK HERE, DIDN'T IT?
POE, THE COMPRESSOR'S DOWN.
OH, I KNOW, I WAS THERE. EVERY TIME.
YOU CAN'T LIGHTSPEED SKIP THE *FALCON!*
ACTUALLY, IT TURNS OUT YOU CAN.
WHAT HAPPENED?
ALL RIGHT, GUYS, WE JUST LANDED, OKAY?
BAD NEWS, THAT'S WHAT HAPPENED.

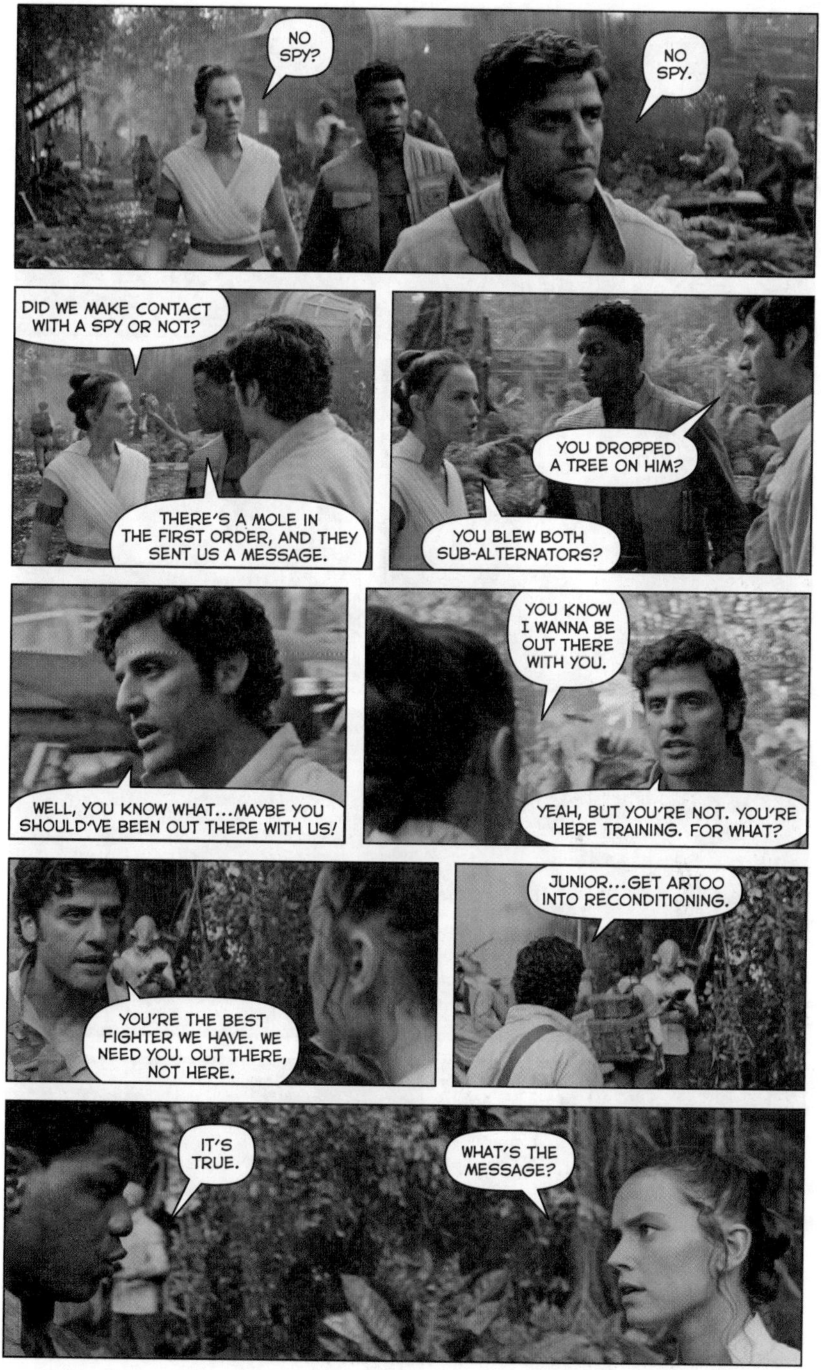
NO SPY?
NO SPY.
DID WE MAKE CONTACT WITH A SPY OR NOT?
THERE'S A MOLE IN THE FIRST ORDER, AND THEY SENT US A MESSAGE.
YOU DROPPED A TREE ON HIM?
YOU BLEW BOTH SUB-ALTERNATORS?
WELL, YOU KNOW WHAT...MAYBE YOU SHOULD'VE BEEN OUT THERE WITH US!
YOU KNOW I WANNA BE OUT THERE WITH YOU.
YEAH, BUT YOU'RE NOT. YOU'RE HERE TRAINING. FOR WHAT?
YOU'RE THE BEST FIGHTER WE HAVE. WE NEED YOU. OUT THERE, NOT HERE.
JUNIOR...GET ARTOO INTO RECONDITIONING.
IT'S TRUE.
WHAT'S THE MESSAGE?

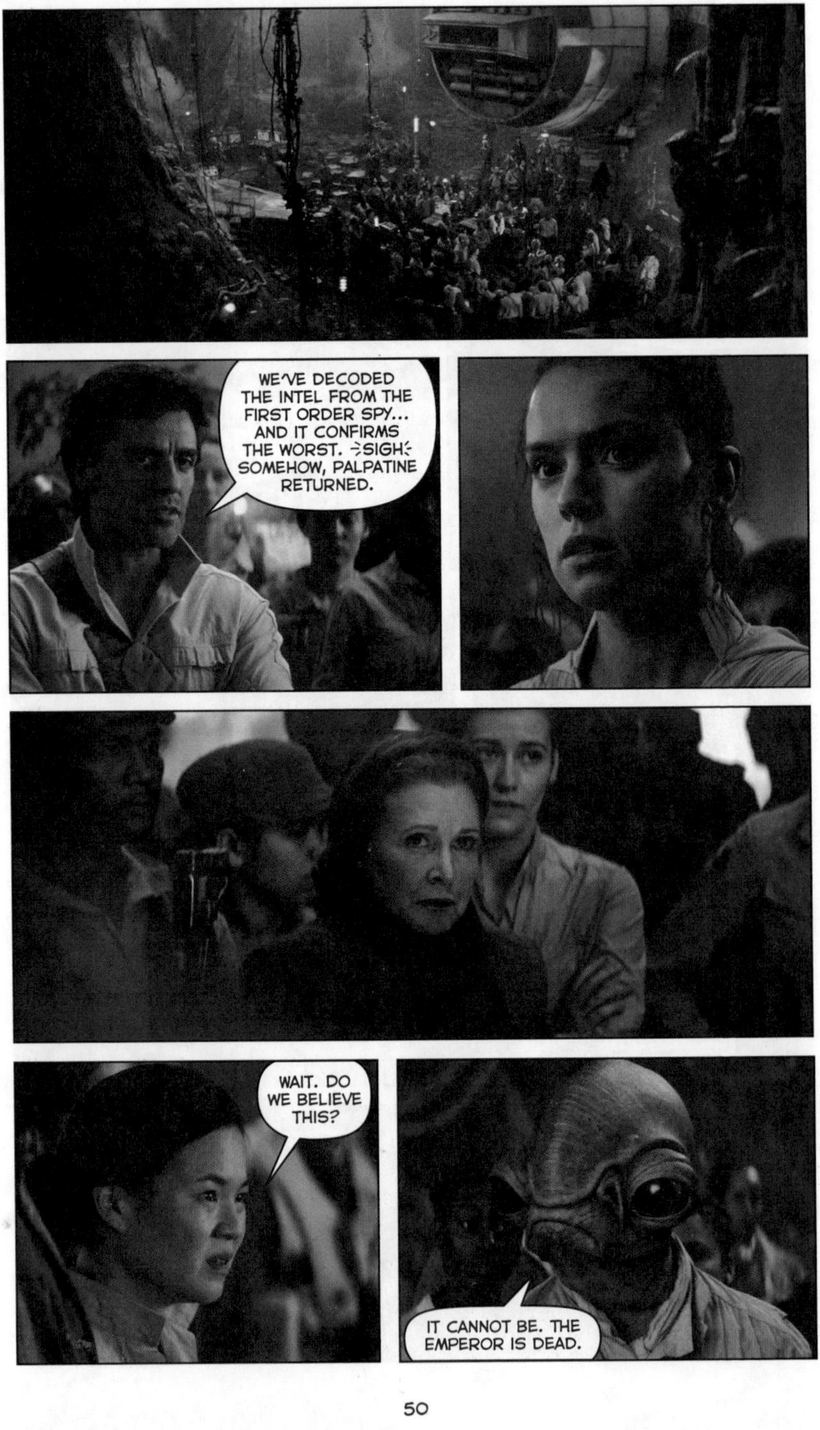
WE'VE DECODED THE INTEL FROM THE FIRST ORDER SPY... AND IT CONFIRMS THE WORST. SIGH SOMEHOW, PALPATINE RETURNED.
WAIT. DO WE BELIEVE THIS?
IT CANNOT BE. THE EMPEROR IS DEAD.

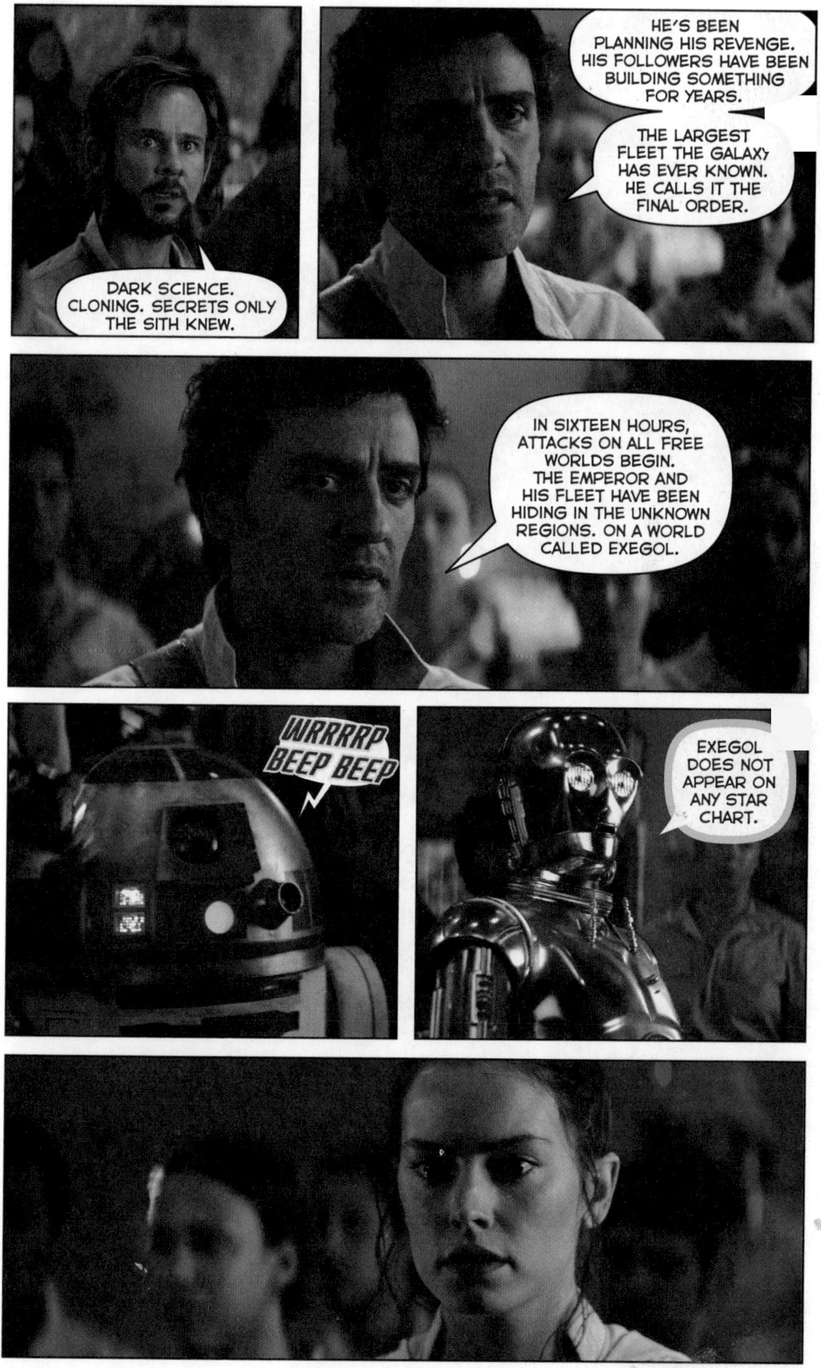
DARK SCIENCE. CLONING. SECRETS ONLY THE SITH KNEW.
HE'S BEEN PLANNING HIS REVENGE. HIS FOLLOWERS HAVE BEEN BUILDING SOMETHING FOR YEARS.
THE LARGEST FLEET THE GALAXY HAS EVER KNOWN. HE CALLS IT THE FINAL ORDER.
IN SIXTEEN HOURS, ATTACKS ON ALL FREE WORLDS BEGIN. THE EMPEROR AND HIS FLEET HAVE BEEN HIDING IN THE UNKNOWN REGIONS. ON A WORLD CALLED EXEGOL.
WRRRRP BEEP BEEP
EXEGOL DOES NOT APPEAR ON ANY STAR CHART.

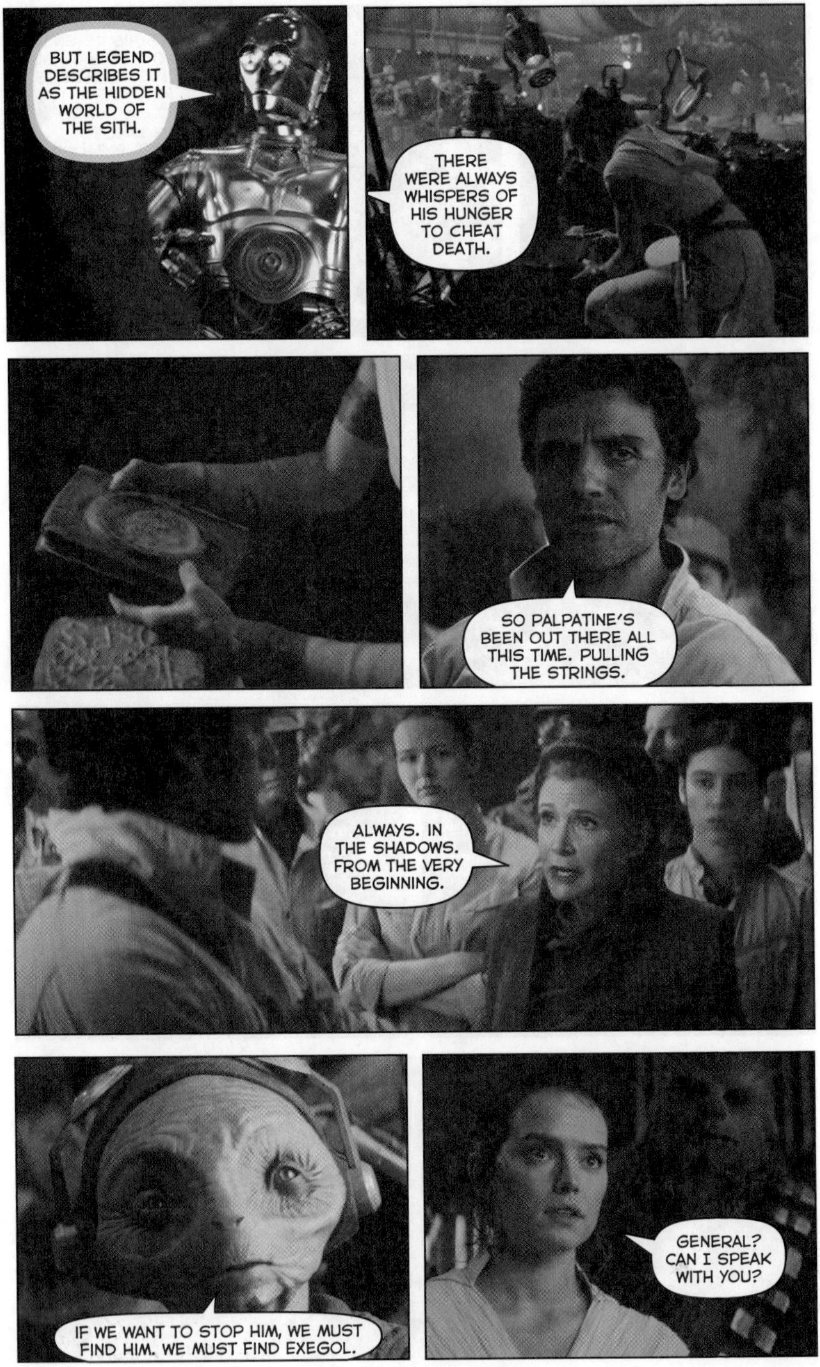
BUT LEGEND DESCRIBES IT AS THE HIDDEN WORLD OF THE SITH.
THERE WERE ALWAYS WHISPERS OF HIS HUNGER TO CHEAT DEATH.
SO PALPATINE'S BEEN OUT THERE ALL THIS TIME. PULLING THE STRINGS.
ALWAYS. IN THE SHADOWS. FROM THE VERY BEGINNING.
IF WE WANT TO STOP HIM, WE MUST FIND HIM. WE MUST FIND EXEGOL.
GENERAL? CAN I SPEAK WITH YOU?

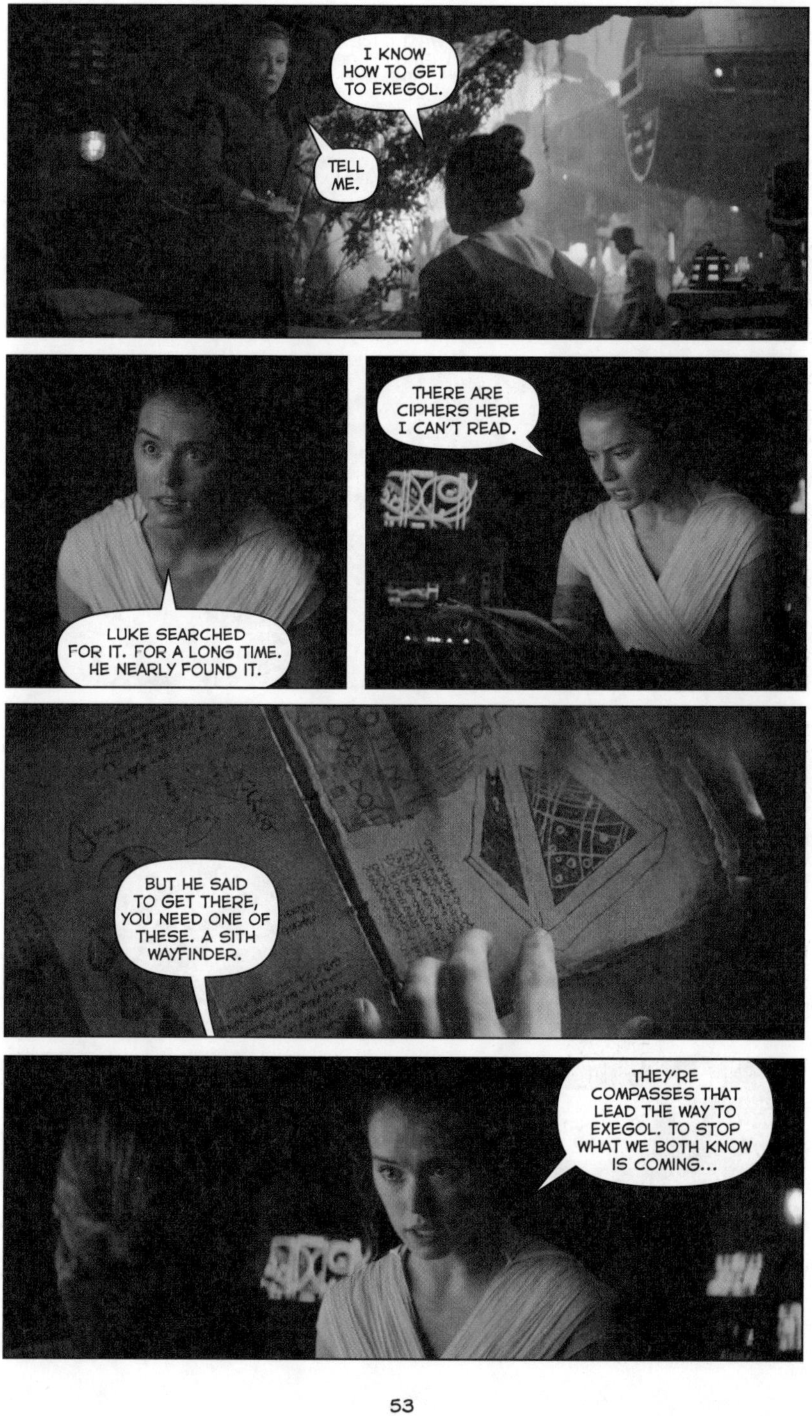
I KNOW HOW TO GET TO EXEGOL.
TELL ME.
LUKE SEARCHED FOR IT. FOR A LONG TIME. HE NEARLY FOUND IT.
THERE ARE CIPHERS HERE I CAN'T READ.
BUT HE SAID TO GET THERE, YOU NEED ONE OF THESE. A SITH WAYFINDER.
THEY'RE COMPASSES THAT LEAD THE WAY TO EXEGOL. TO STOP WHAT WE BOTH KNOW IS COMING...

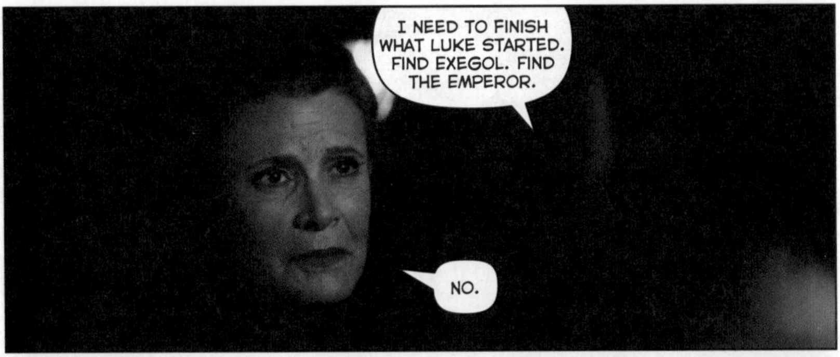
I NEED TO FINISH WHAT LUKE STARTED. FIND EXEGOL. FIND THE EMPEROR.
NO.

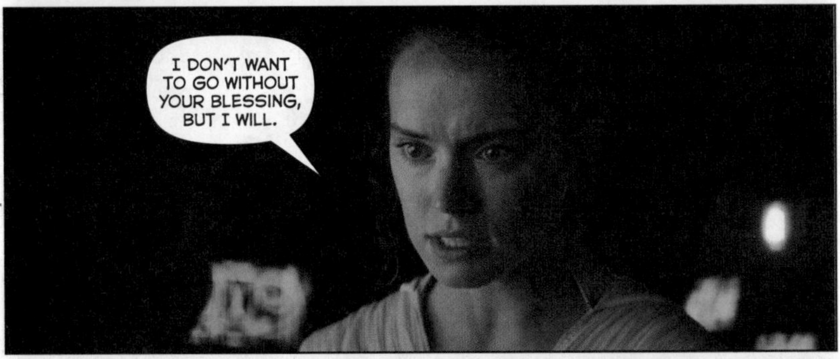
I DON'T WANT TO GO WITHOUT YOUR BLESSING, BUT I WILL.

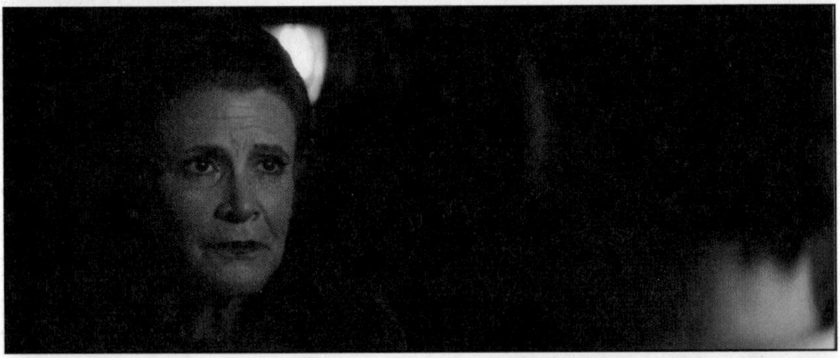

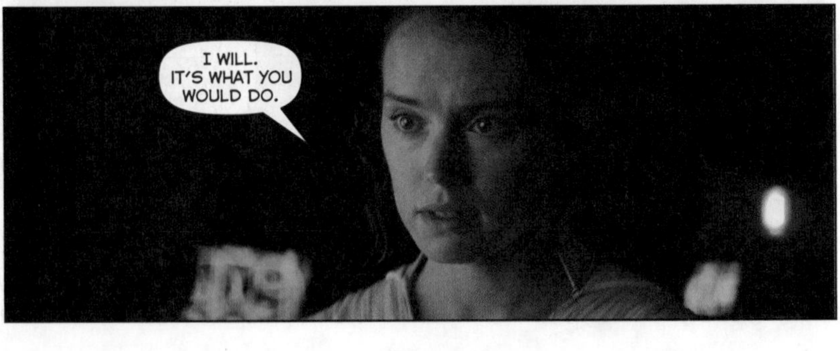
I WILL. IT'S WHAT YOU WOULD DO.

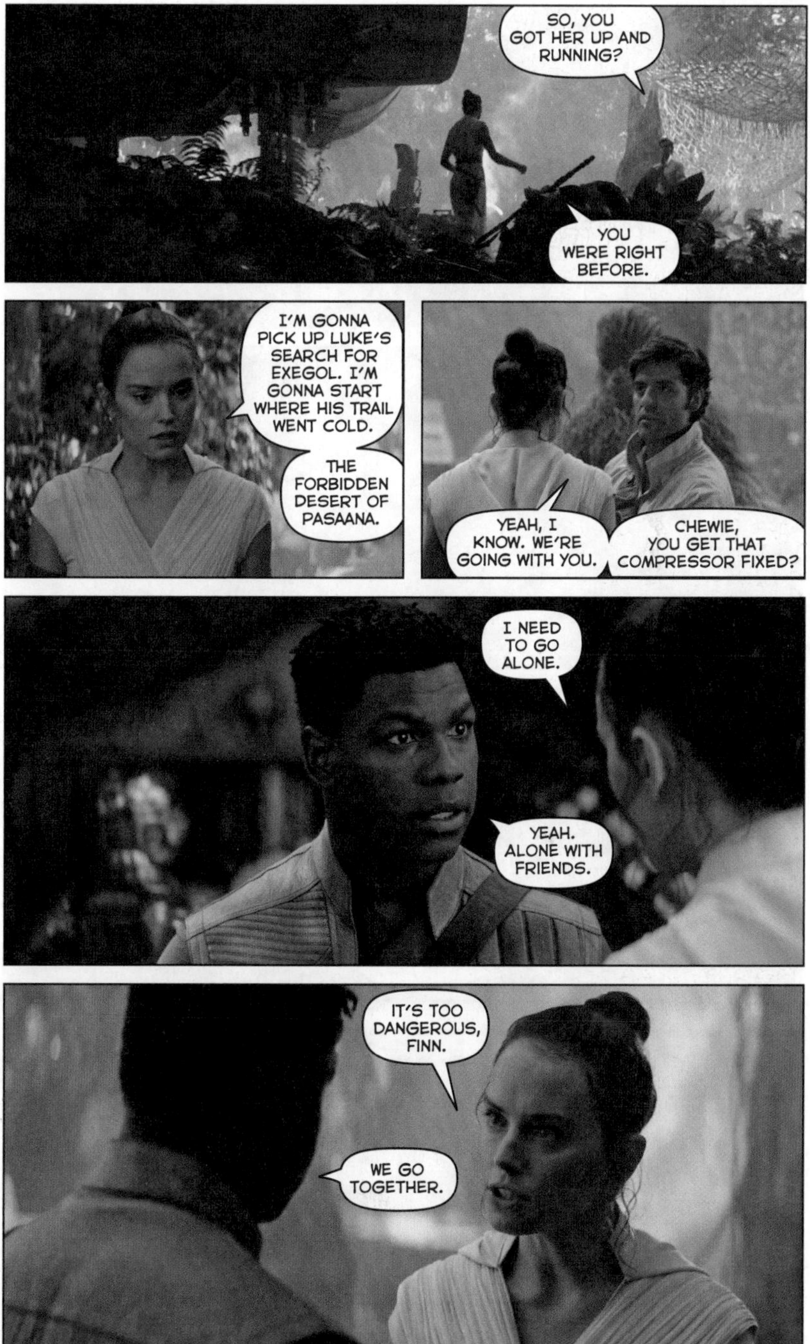
SO, YOU GOT HER UP AND RUNNING?
YOU WERE RIGHT BEFORE.
I'M GONNA PICK UP LUKE'S SEARCH FOR EXEGOL. I'M GONNA START WHERE HIS TRAIL WENT COLD.
THE FORBIDDEN DESERT OF PASAANA.
YEAH, I KNOW. WE'RE GOING WITH YOU.
CHEWIE, YOU GET THAT COMPRESSOR FIXED?
I NEED TO GO ALONE.
YEAH. ALONE WITH FRIENDS.
IT'S TOO DANGEROUS, FINN.
WE GO TOGETHER.

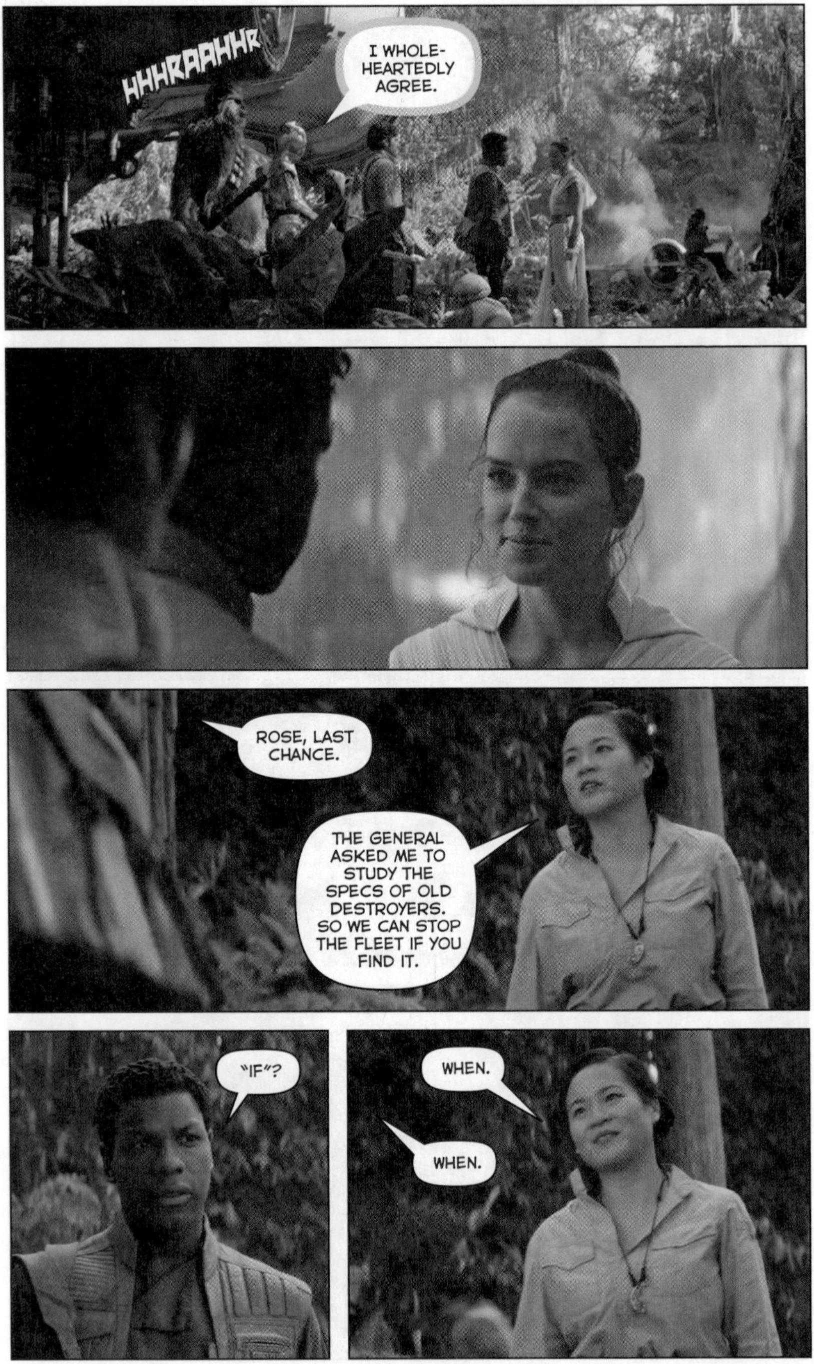
HHHRAAHHR
I WHOLE-HEARTEDLY AGREE.
ROSE, LAST CHANCE.
THE GENERAL ASKED ME TO STUDY THE SPECS OF OLD DESTROYERS. SO WE CAN STOP THE FLEET IF YOU FIND IT.
"IF"?
WHEN.
WHEN.

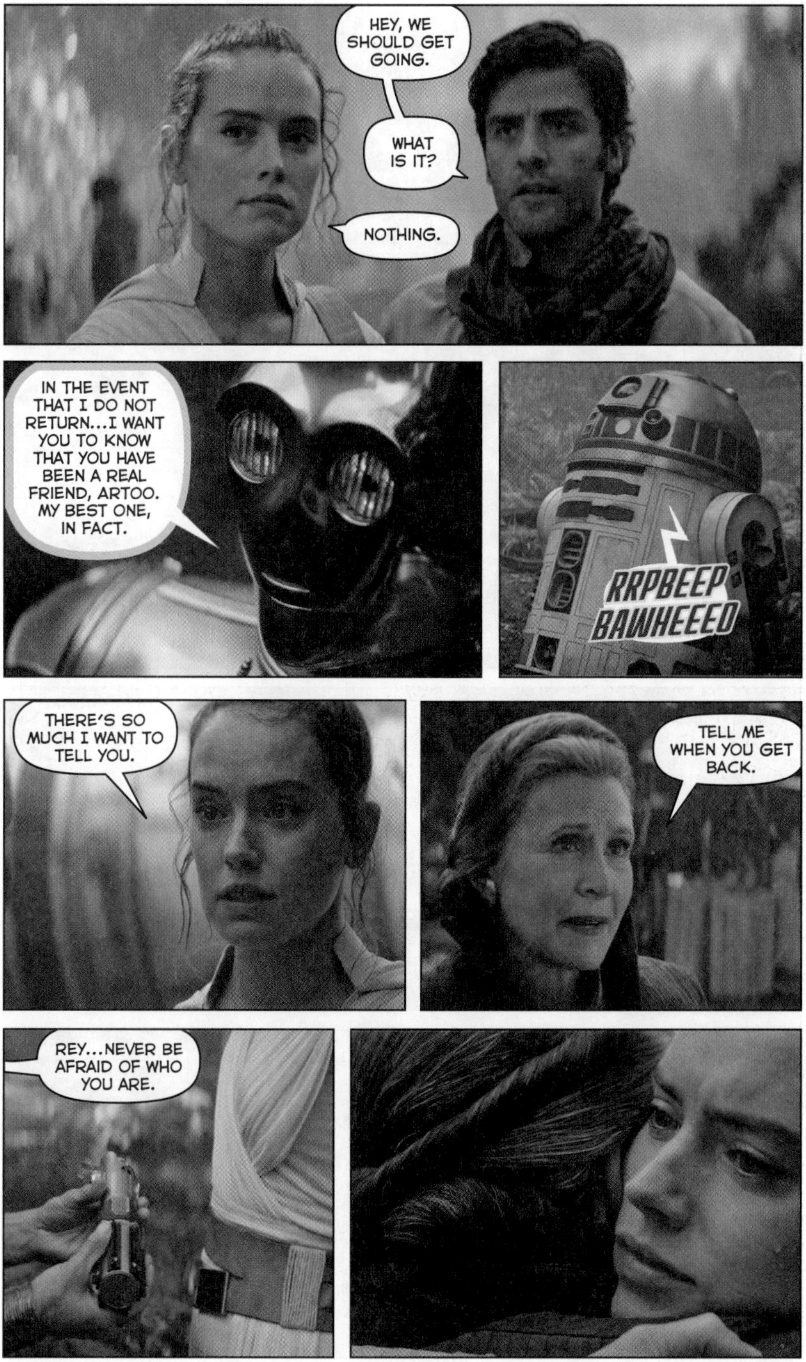
HEY, WE SHOULD GET GOING.
WHAT IS IT?
NOTHING.
IN THE EVENT THAT I DO NOT RETURN...I WANT YOU TO KNOW THAT YOU HAVE BEEN A REAL FRIEND, ARTOO. MY BEST ONE, IN FACT.
RRPBEEP BAWHEEED
THERE'S SO MUCH I WANT TO TELL YOU.
TELL ME WHEN YOU GET BACK.
REY...NEVER BE AFRAID OF WHO YOU ARE.

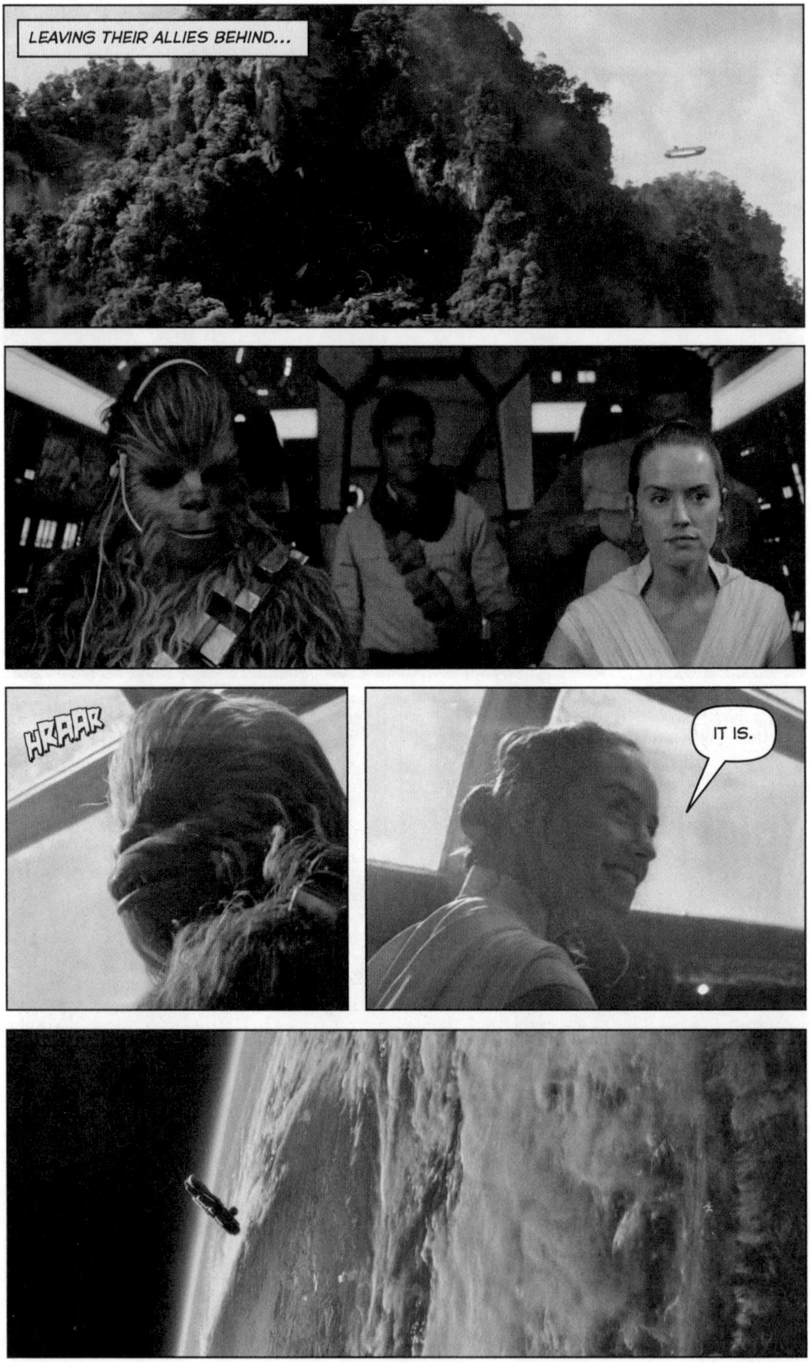
LEAVING THEIR ALLIES BEHIND...
HRAAR
IT IS.

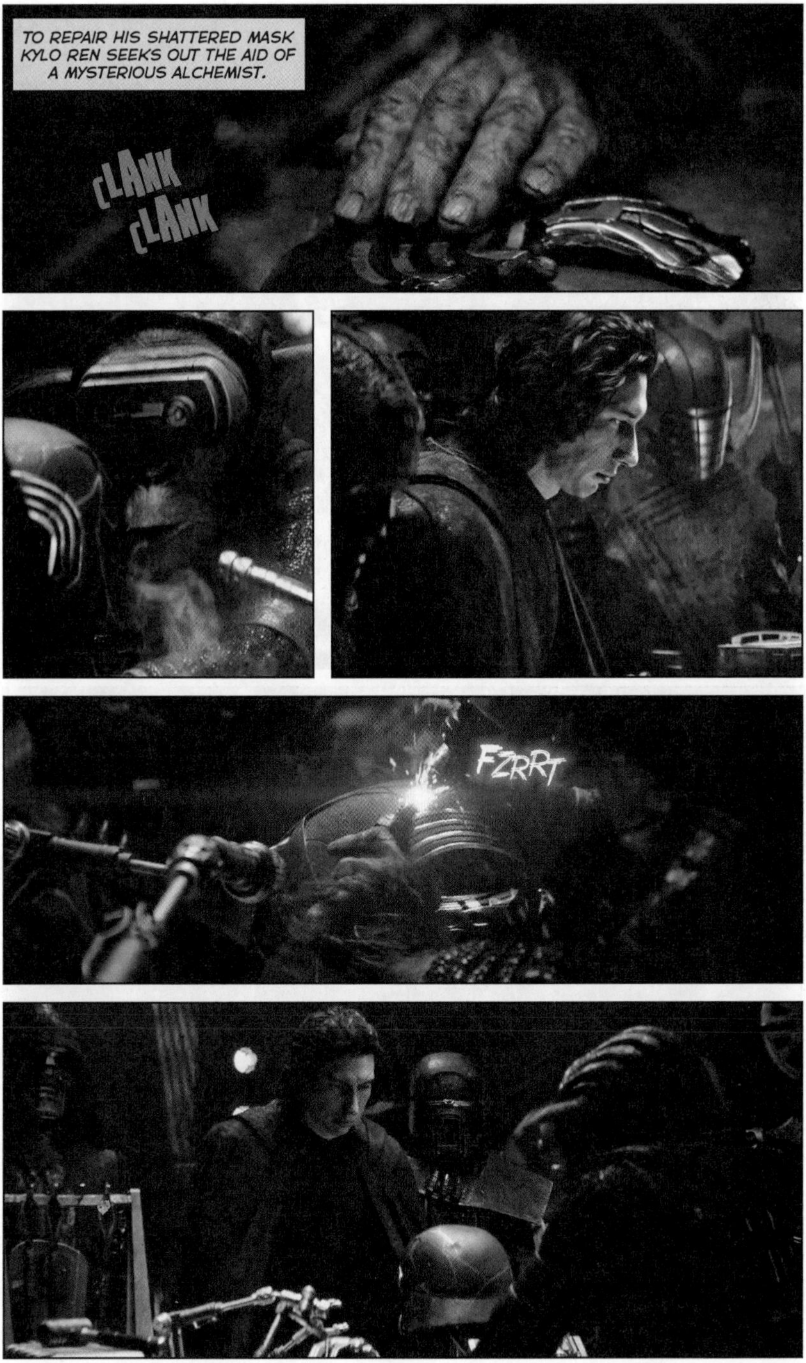
TO REPAIR HIS SHATTERED MASK KYLO REN SEEKS OUT THE AID OF A MYSTERIOUS ALCHEMIST.
CLANK CLANK
FZRRT

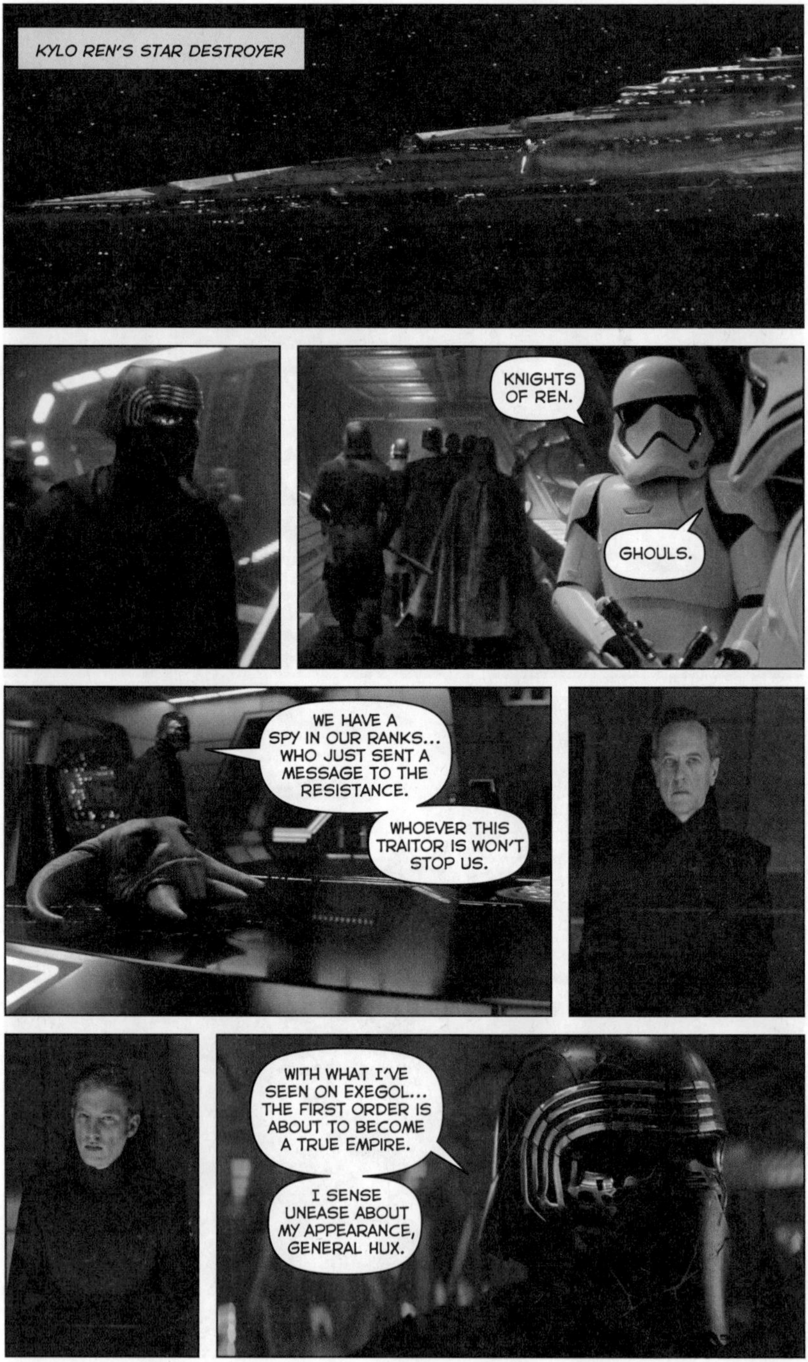
KYLO REN'S STAR DESTROYER
KNIGHTS OF REN.
GHOULS.
WE HAVE A SPY IN OUR RANKS... WHO JUST SENT A MESSAGE TO THE RESISTANCE.
WHOEVER THIS TRAITOR IS WON'T STOP US.
WITH WHAT I'VE SEEN ON EXEGOL... THE FIRST ORDER IS ABOUT TO BECOME A TRUE EMPIRE.
I SENSE UNEASE ABOUT MY APPEARANCE, GENERAL HUX.

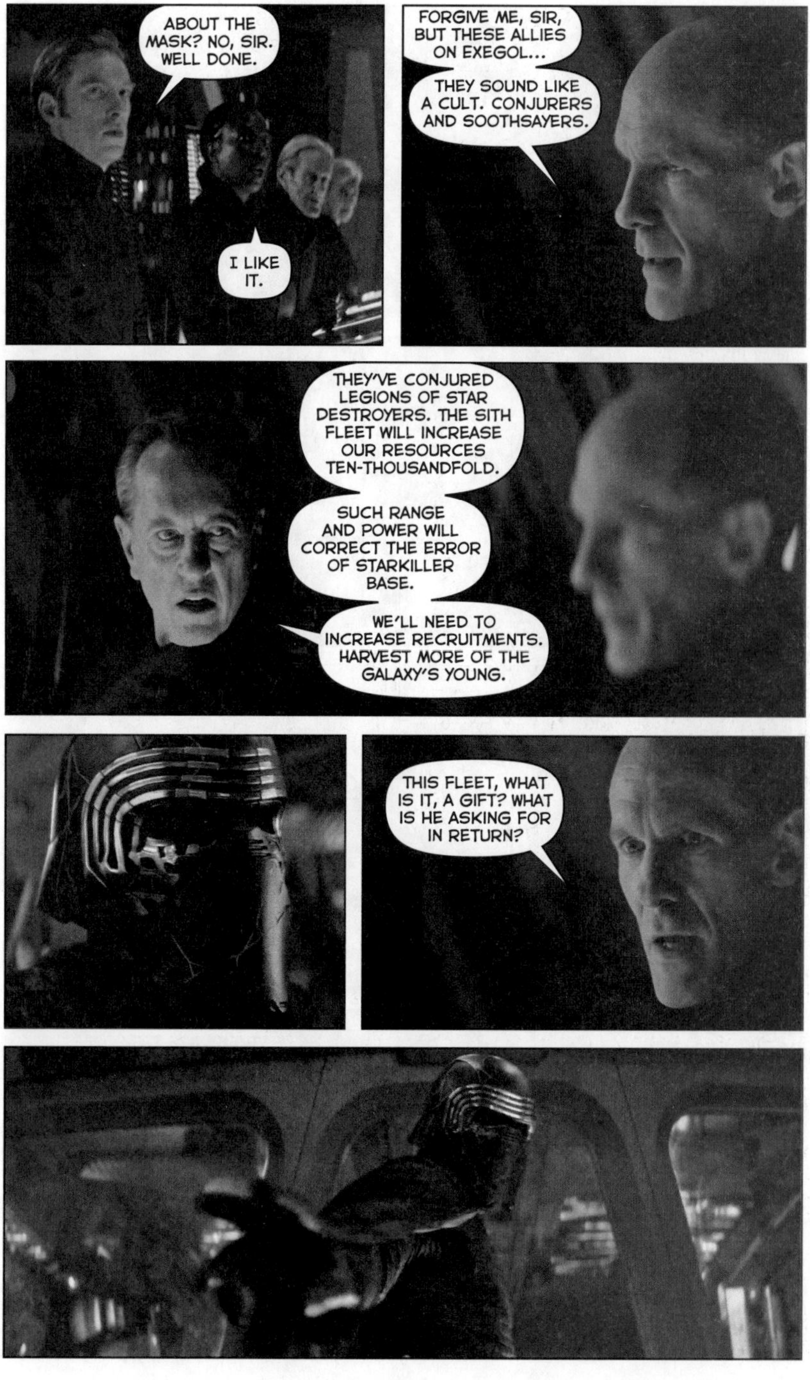
ABOUT THE MASK? NO, SIR. WELL DONE.
I LIKE IT.
FORGIVE ME, SIR, BUT THESE ALLIES ON EXEGOL...
THEY SOUND LIKE A CULT. CONJURERS AND SOOTHSAYERS.
THEY'VE CONJURED LEGIONS OF STAR DESTROYERS. THE SITH FLEET WILL INCREASE OUR RESOURCES TEN-THOUSANDFOLD.
SUCH RANGE AND POWER WILL CORRECT THE ERROR OF STARKILLER BASE.
WE'LL NEED TO INCREASE RECRUITMENTS. HARVEST MORE OF THE GALAXY'S YOUNG.
THIS FLEET, WHAT IS IT, A GIFT? WHAT IS HE ASKING FOR IN RETURN?

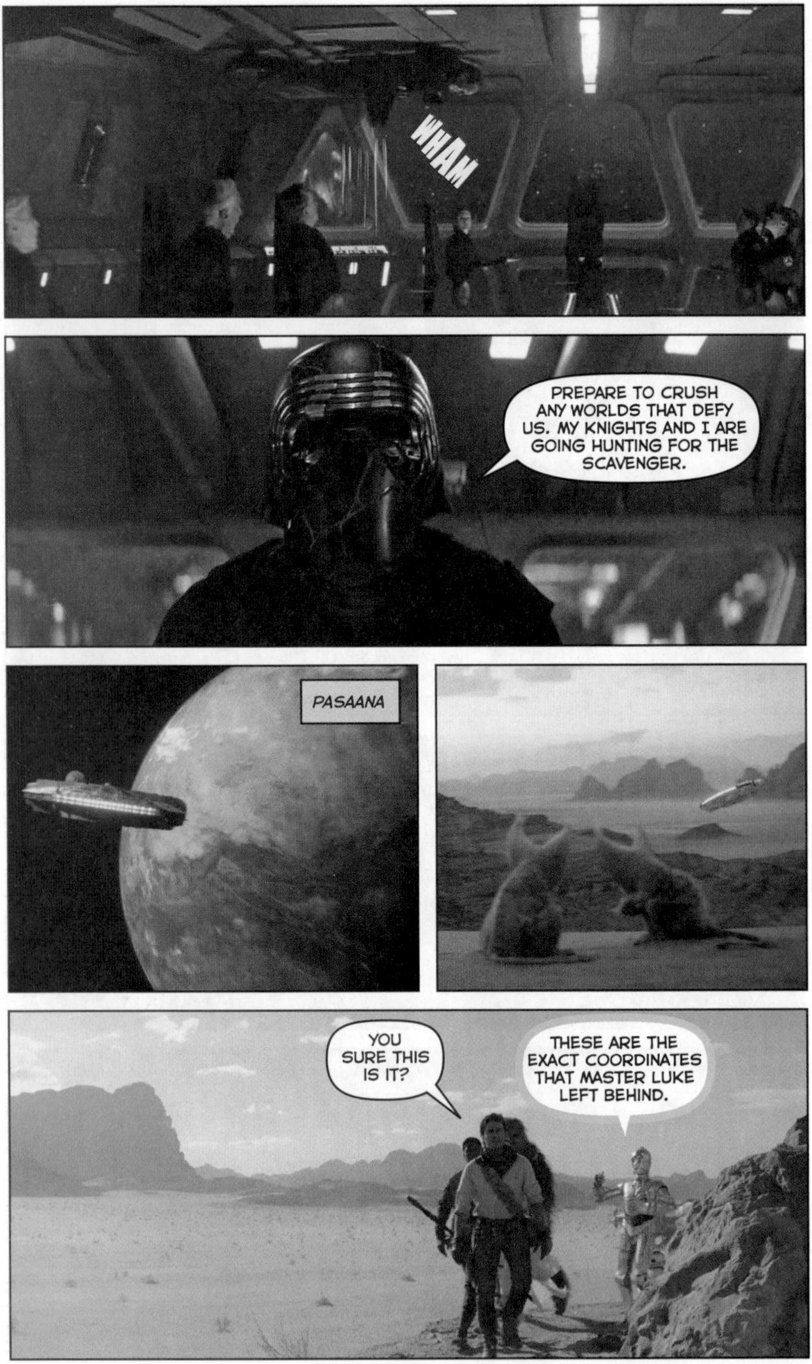
WHAM
PREPARE TO CRUSH ANY WORLDS THAT DEFY US. MY KNIGHTS AND I ARE GOING HUNTING FOR THE SCAVENGER.
PASAANA
YOU SURE THIS IS IT?
THESE ARE THE EXACT COORDINATES THAT MASTER LUKE LEFT BEHIND.

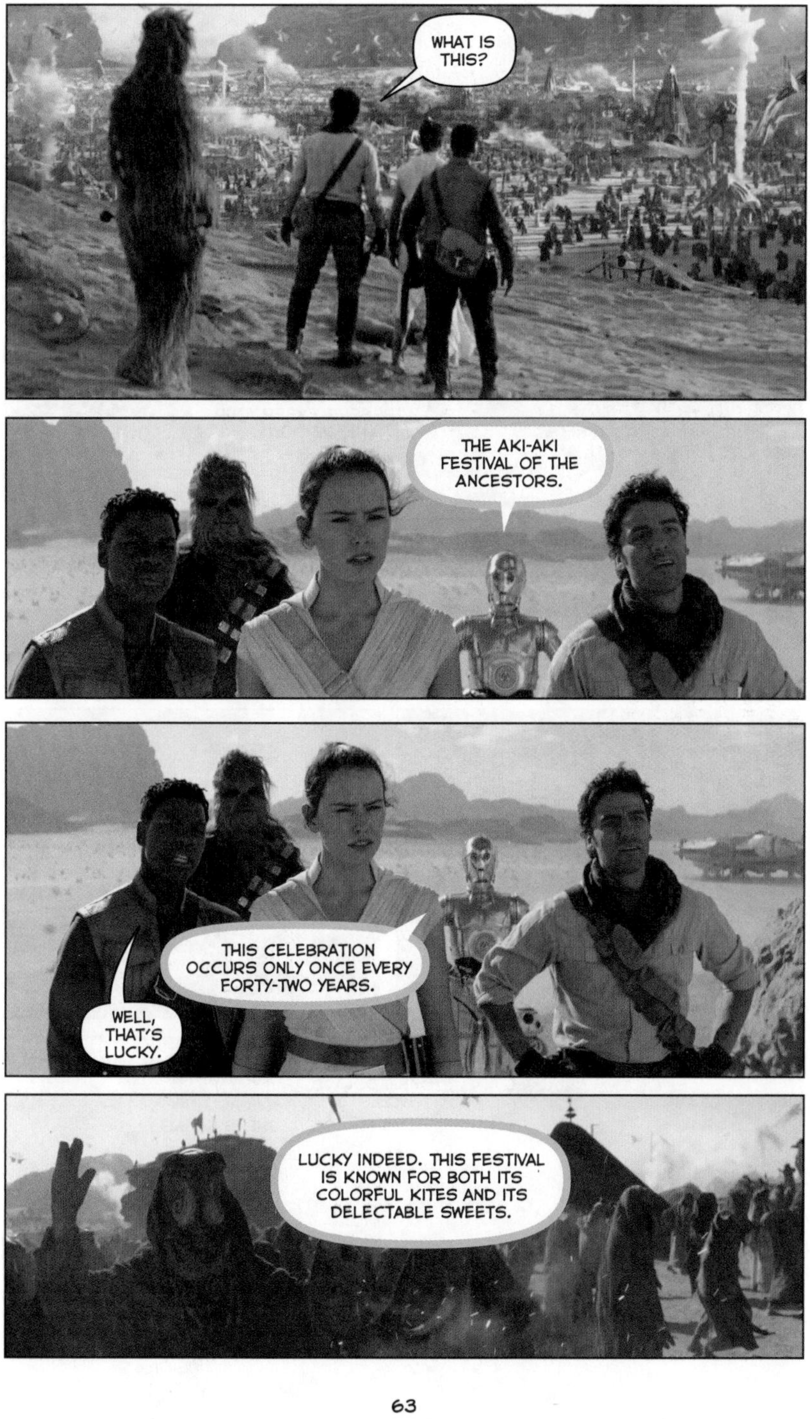
WHAT IS THIS?
THE AKI-AKI FESTIVAL OF THE ANCESTORS.
THIS CELEBRATION OCCURS ONLY ONCE EVERY FORTY-TWO YEARS.
WELL, THAT'S LUCKY.
LUCKY INDEED. THIS FESTIVAL IS KNOWN FOR BOTH ITS COLORFUL KITES AND ITS DELECTABLE SWEETS.

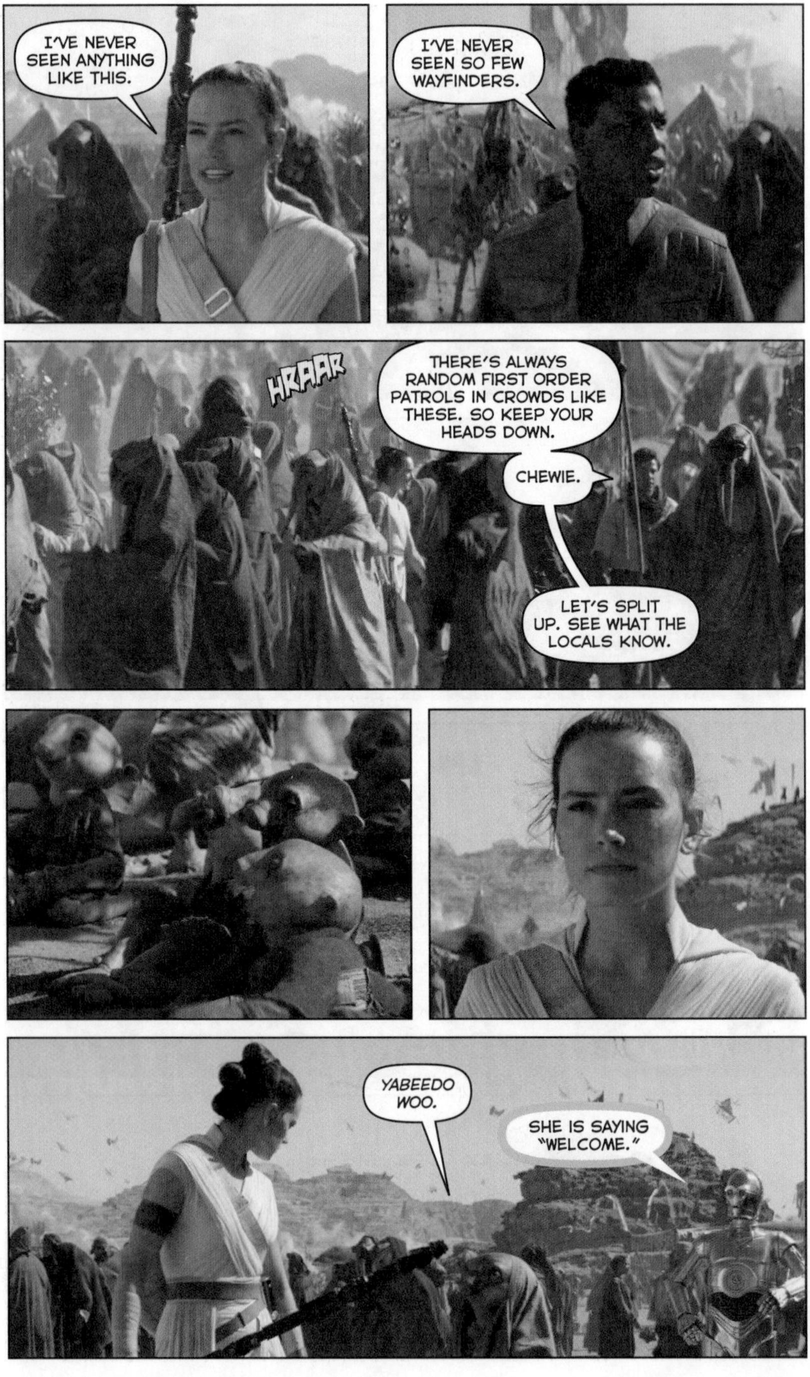
I'VE NEVER SEEN ANYTHING LIKE THIS.
I'VE NEVER SEEN SO FEW WAYFINDERS.
HRAAR
THERE'S ALWAYS RANDOM FIRST ORDER PATROLS IN CROWDS LIKE THESE. SO KEEP YOUR HEADS DOWN.
CHEWIE.
LET'S SPLIT UP. SEE WHAT THE LOCALS KNOW.
YABEEDO WOO.
SHE IS SAYING "WELCOME."

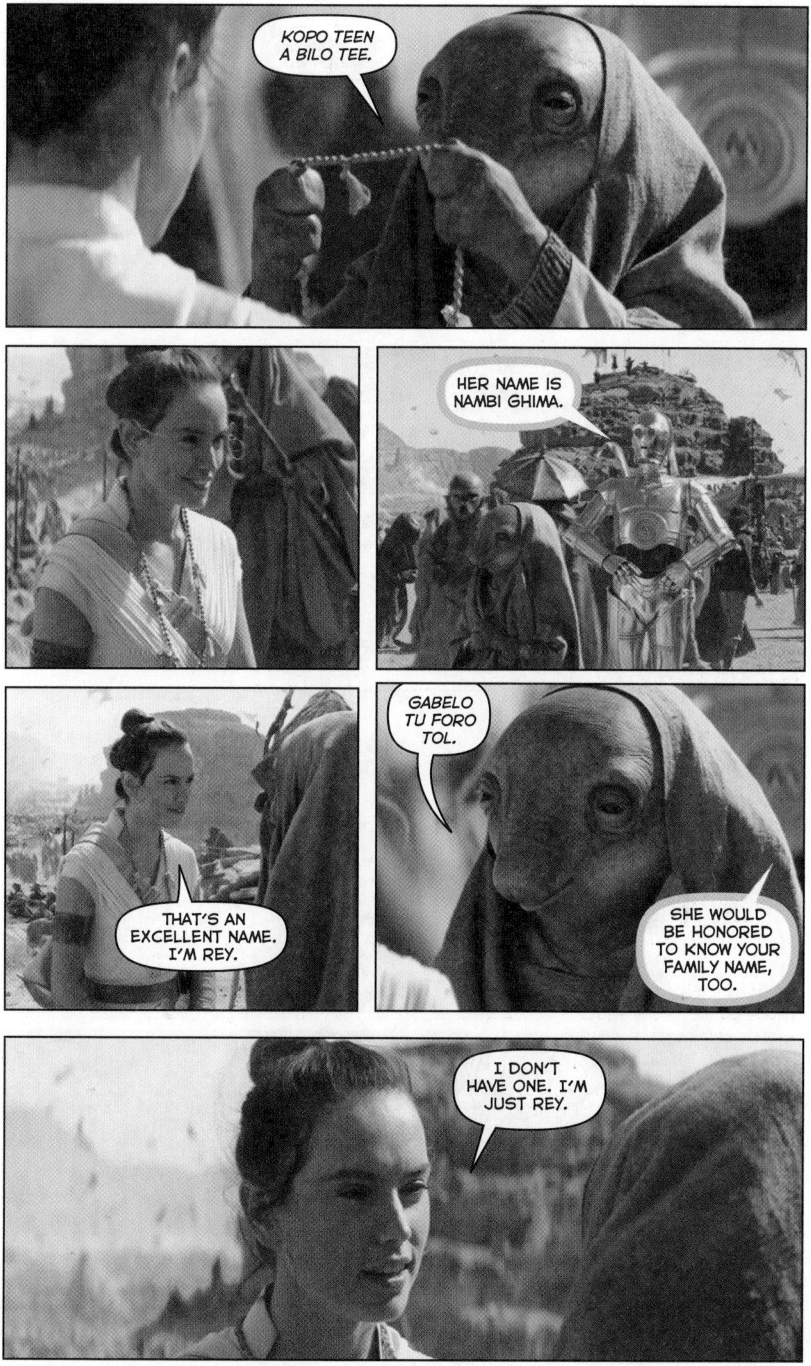
KOPO TEEN A BILO TEE.
HER NAME IS NAMBI GHIMA.
THAT'S AN EXCELLENT NAME. I'M REY.
GABELO TU FORO TOL.
SHE WOULD BE HONORED TO KNOW YOUR FAMILY NAME, TOO.
I DON'T HAVE ONE. I'M JUST REY.

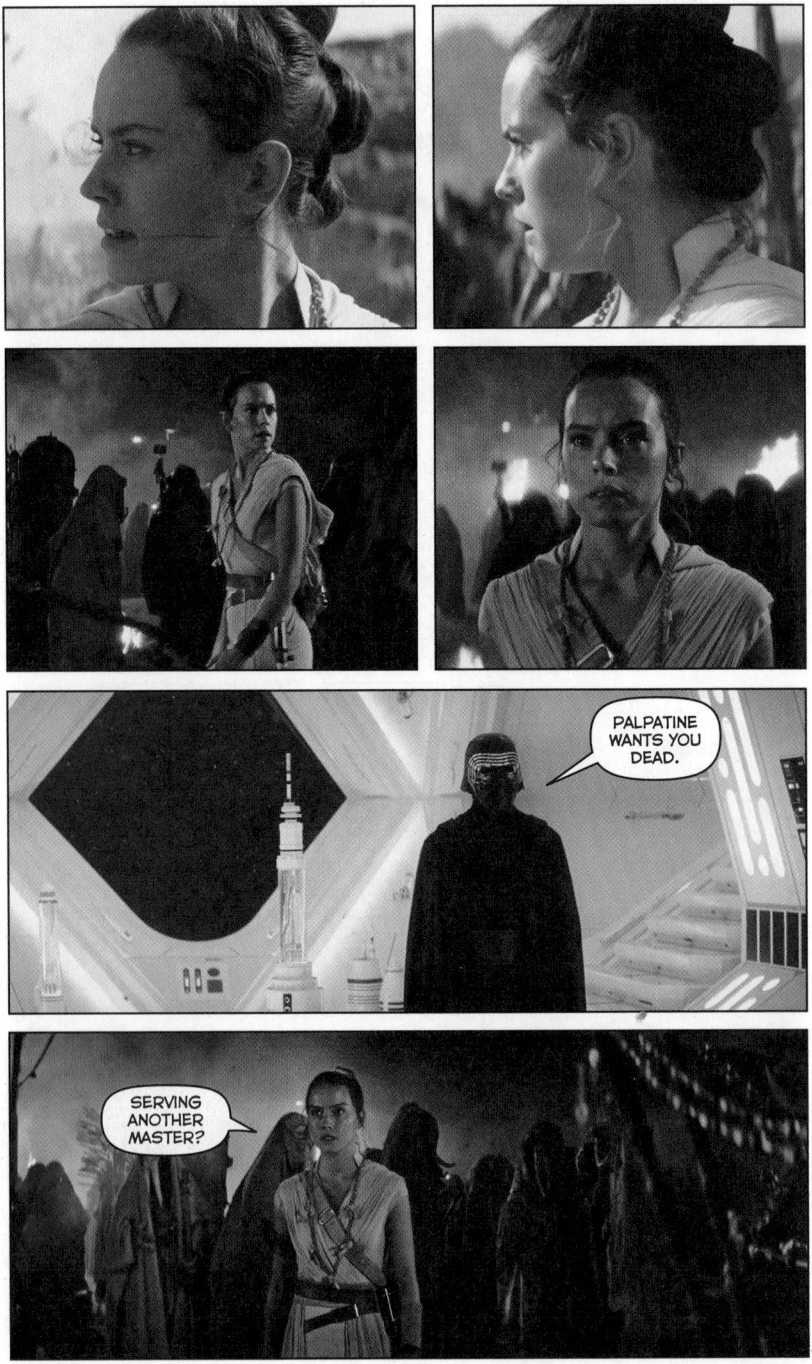
PALPATINE WANTS YOU DEAD.
SERVING ANOTHER MASTER?

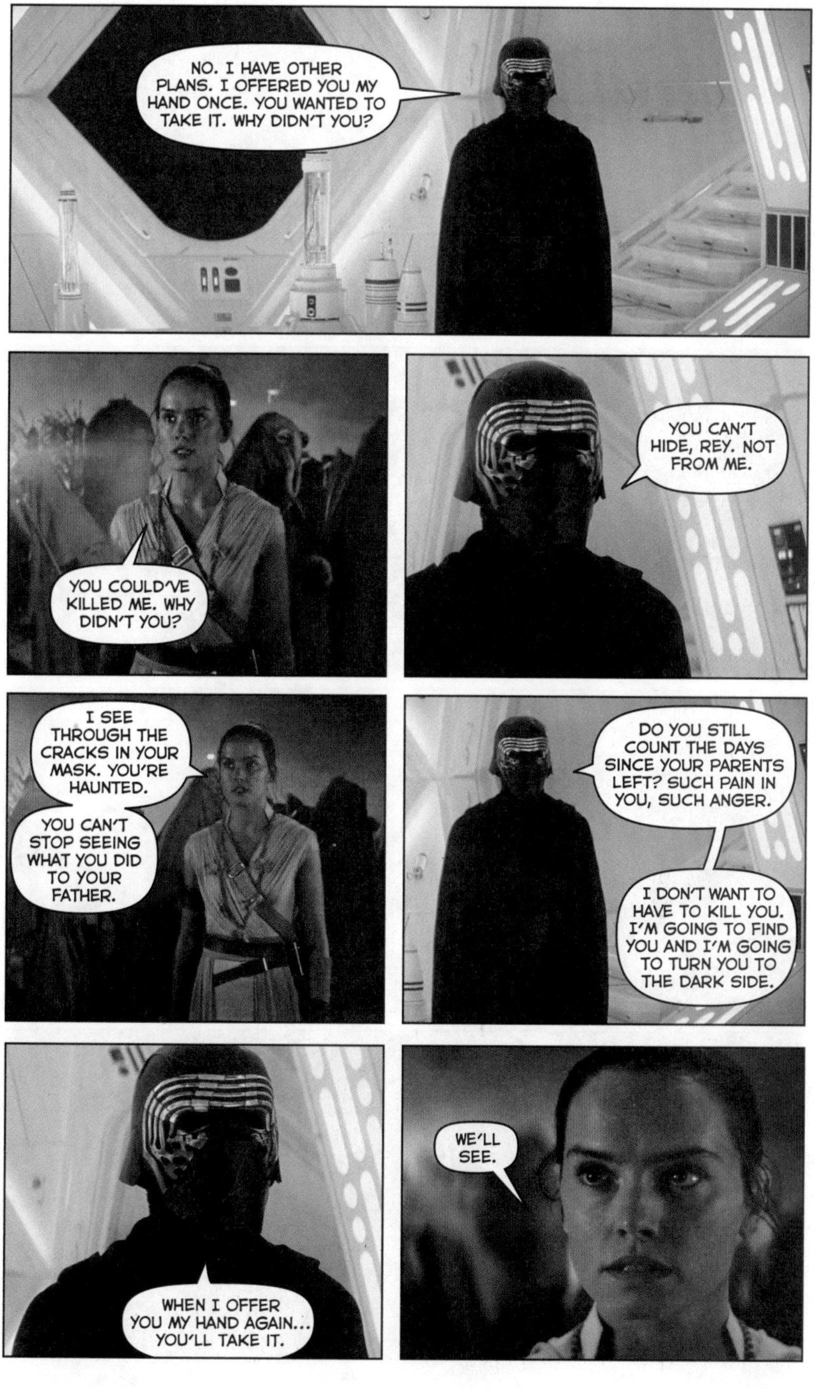
NO. I HAVE OTHER PLANS. I OFFERED YOU MY HAND ONCE. YOU WANTED TO TAKE IT. WHY DIDN'T YOU?
YOU COULD'VE KILLED ME. WHY DIDN'T YOU?
YOU CAN'T HIDE, REY. NOT FROM ME.
I SEE THROUGH THE CRACKS IN YOUR MASK. YOU'RE HAUNTED.
YOU CAN'T STOP SEEING WHAT YOU DID TO YOUR FATHER.
DO YOU STILL COUNT THE DAYS SINCE YOUR PARENTS LEFT? SUCH PAIN IN YOU, SUCH ANGER.
I DON'T WANT TO HAVE TO KILL YOU. I'M GOING TO FIND YOU AND I'M GOING TO TURN YOU TO THE DARK SIDE.
WHEN I OFFER YOU MY HAND AGAIN... YOU'LL TAKE IT.
WE'LL SEE.

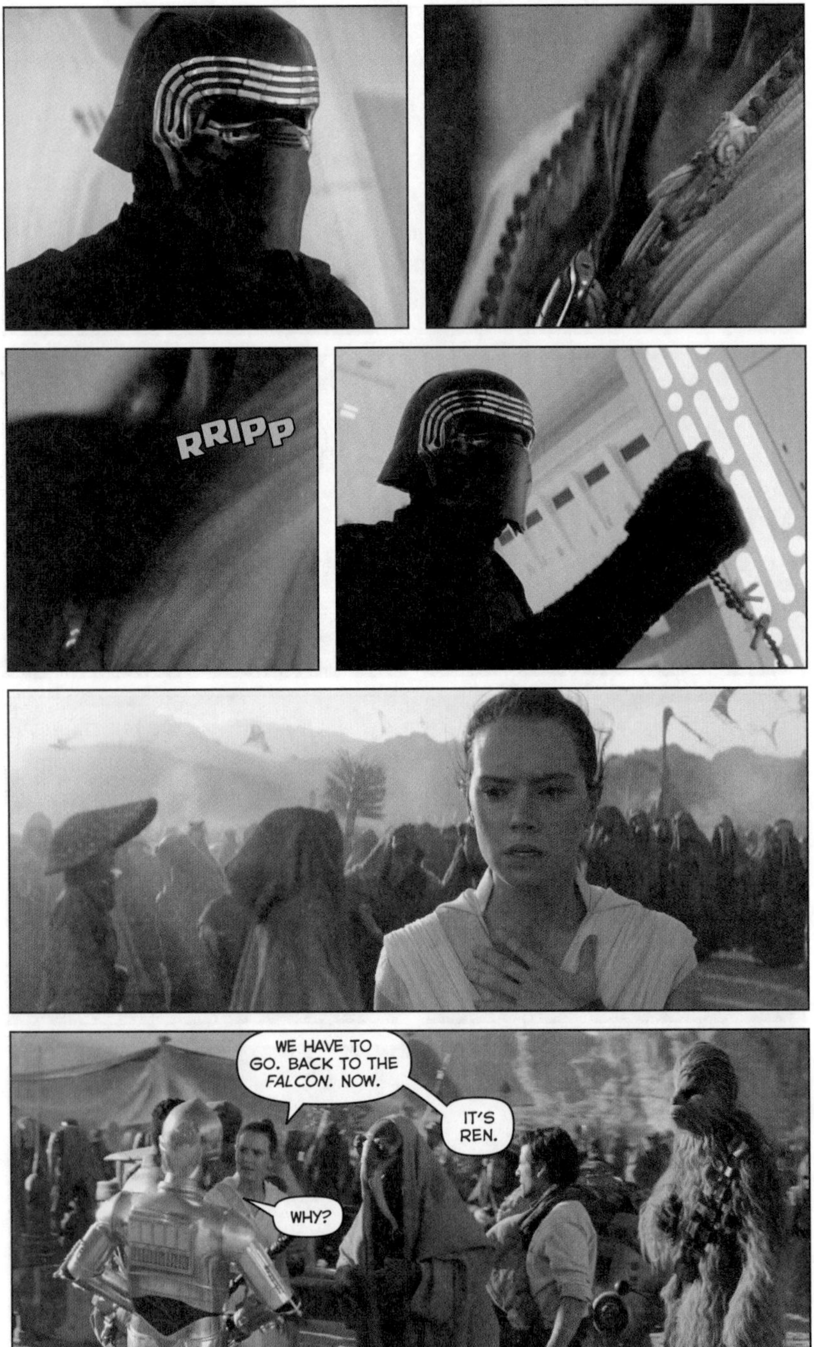

RRIPP
WE HAVE TO GO. BACK TO THE *FALCON*. NOW.
IT'S REN.
WHY?

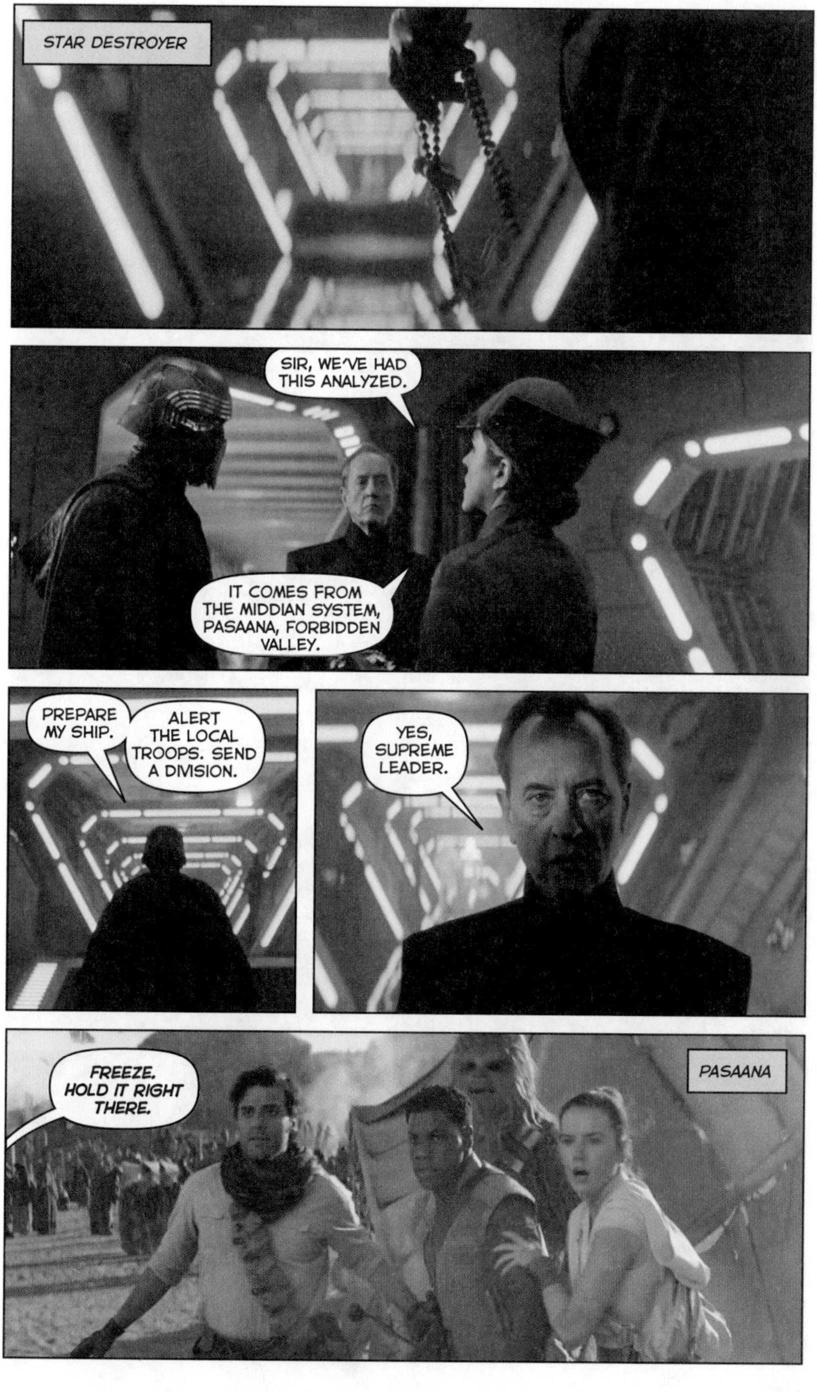
STAR DESTROYER
SIR, WE'VE HAD THIS ANALYZED.
IT COMES FROM THE MIDDIAN SYSTEM, PASAANA, FORBIDDEN VALLEY.
PREPARE MY SHIP.
ALERT THE LOCAL TROOPS. SEND A DIVISION.
YES, SUPREME LEADER.
PASAANA
FREEZE. HOLD IT RIGHT THERE.

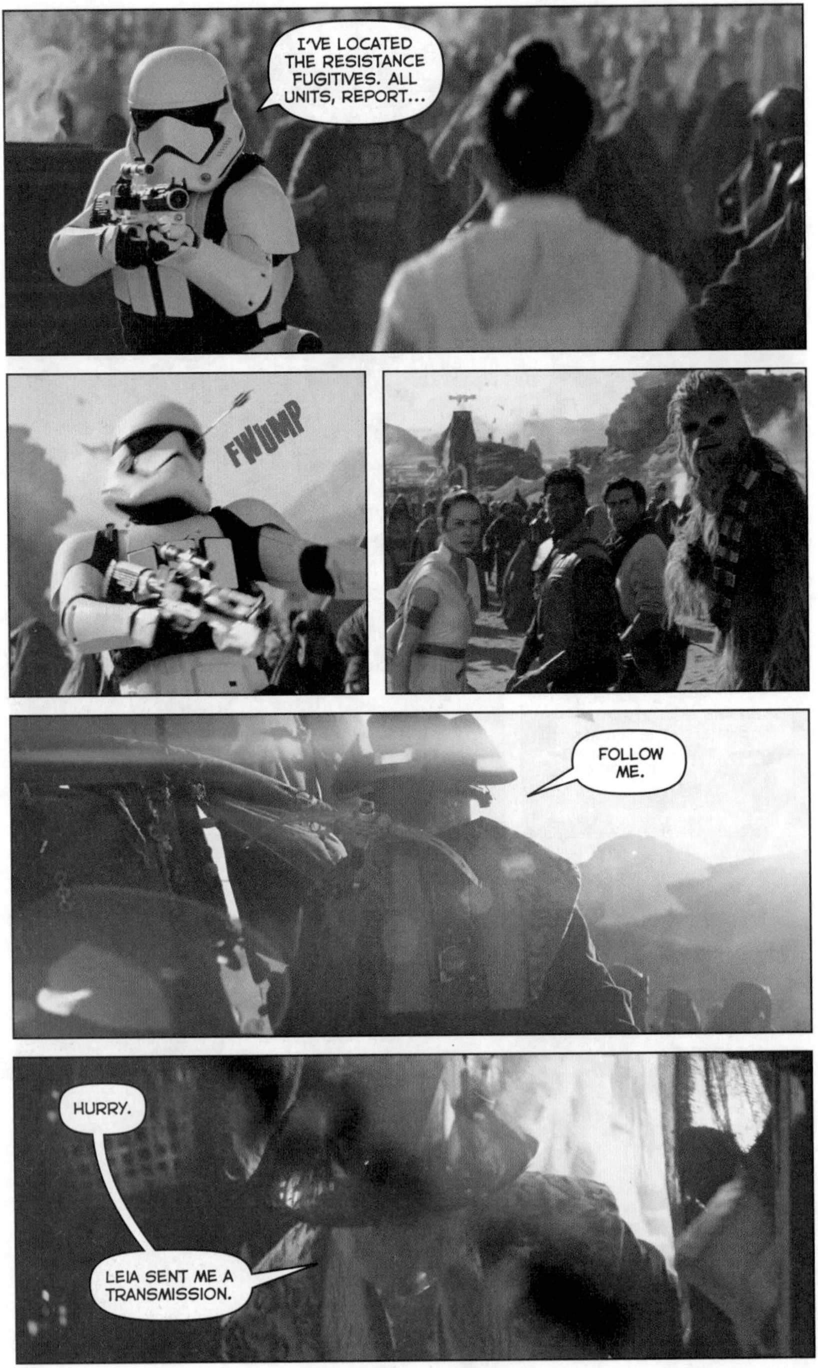
I'VE LOCATED THE RESISTANCE FUGITIVES. ALL UNITS, REPORT...
FWUMP
FOLLOW ME.
HURRY.
LEIA SENT ME A TRANSMISSION.

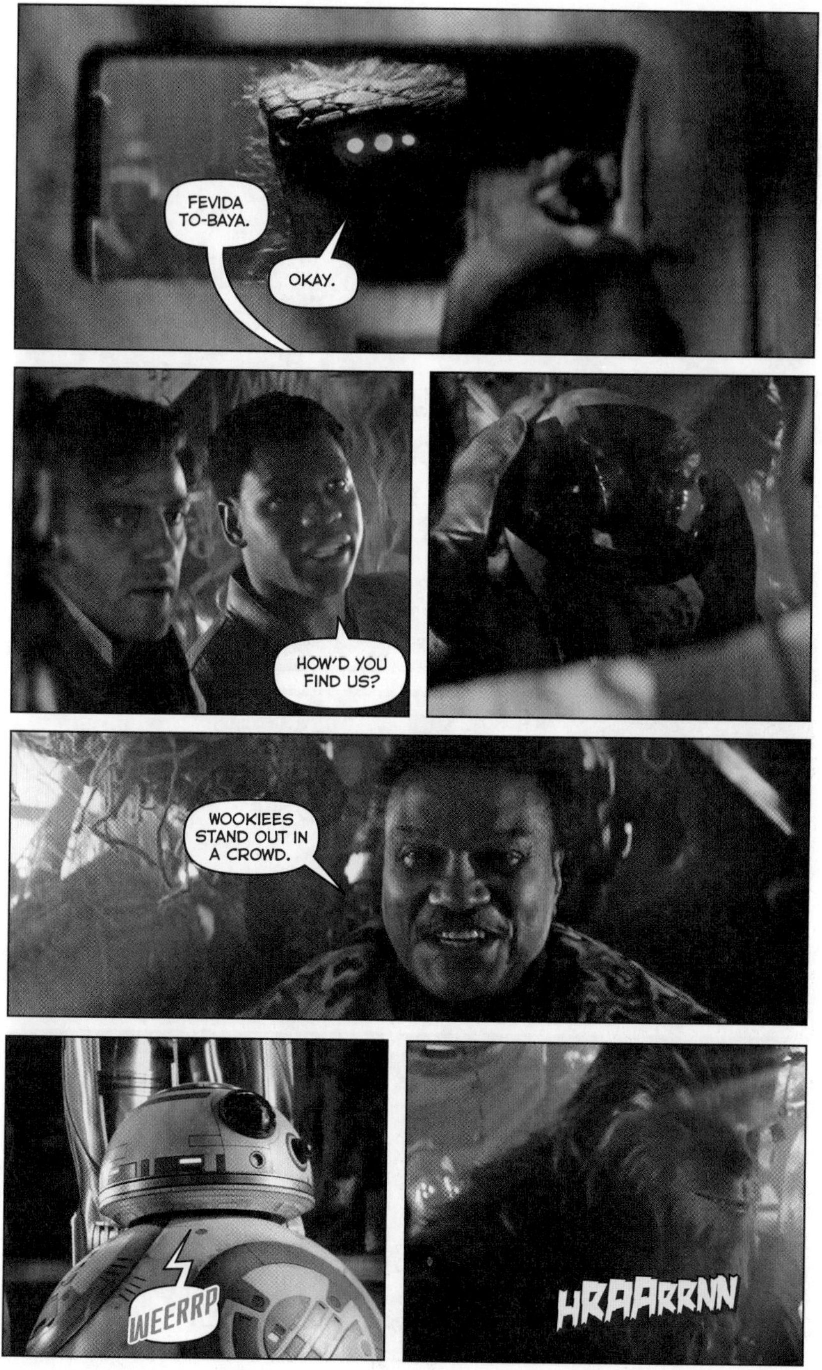
FEVIDA TO-BAYA.
OKAY.
HOW'D YOU FIND US?
WOOKIEES STAND OUT IN A CROWD.
WEERRP
HRAARRNN

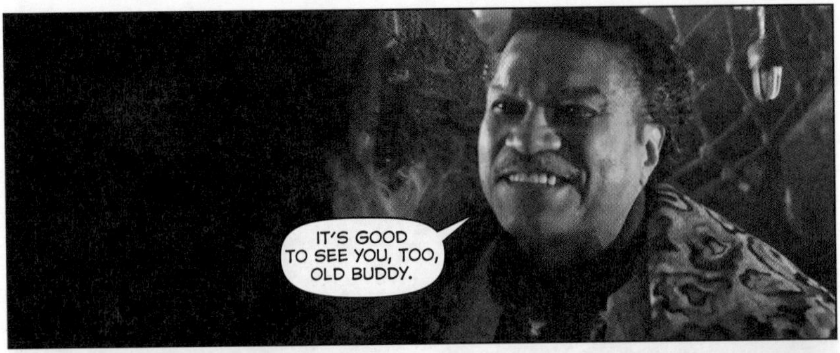
IT'S GOOD TO SEE YOU, TOO, OLD BUDDY.

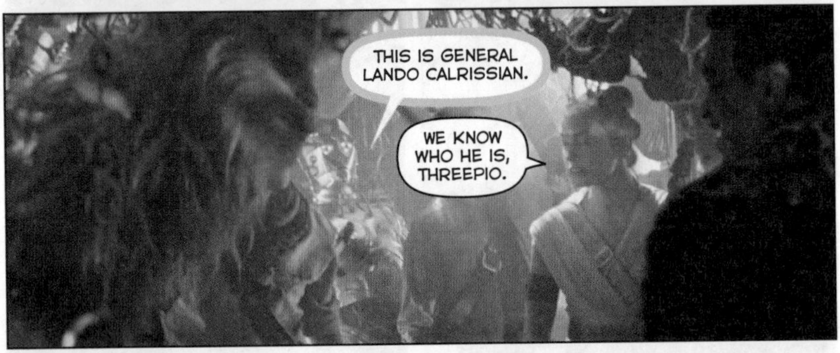
THIS IS GENERAL LANDO CALRISSIAN.
WE KNOW WHO HE IS, THREEPIO.

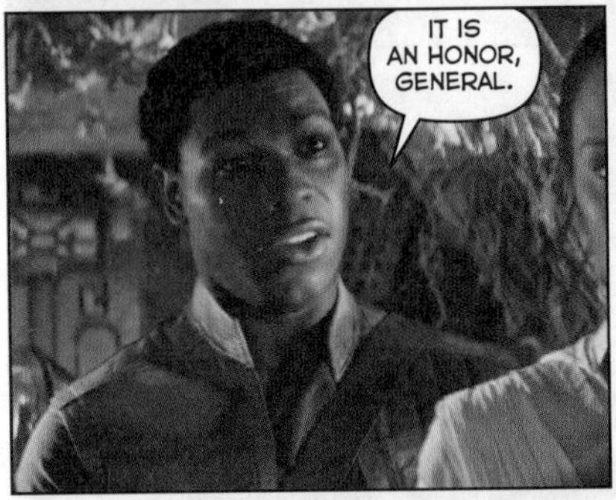
IT IS AN HONOR, GENERAL.

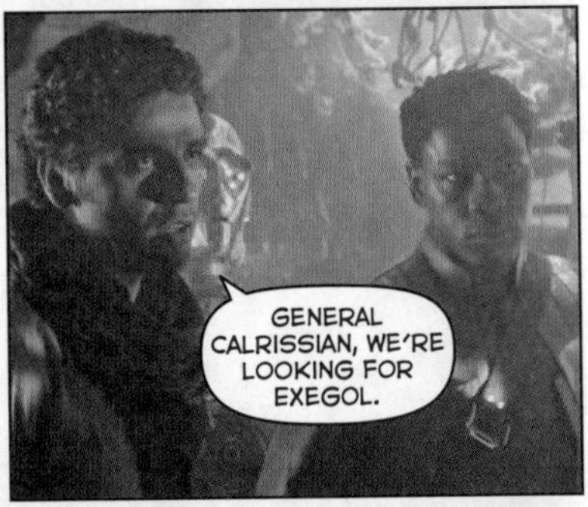
GENERAL CALRISSIAN, WE'RE LOOKING FOR EXEGOL.

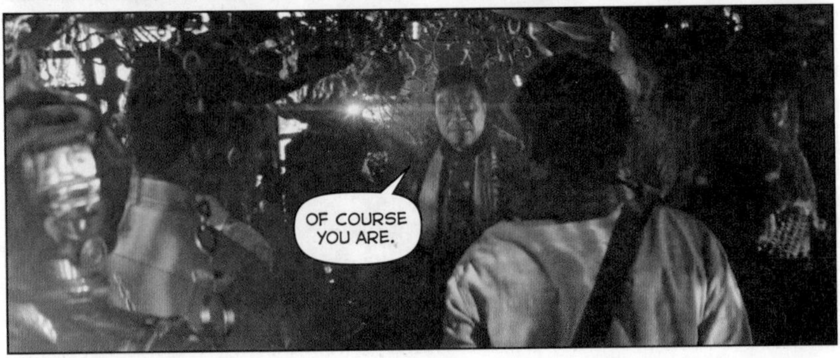
OF COURSE YOU ARE.

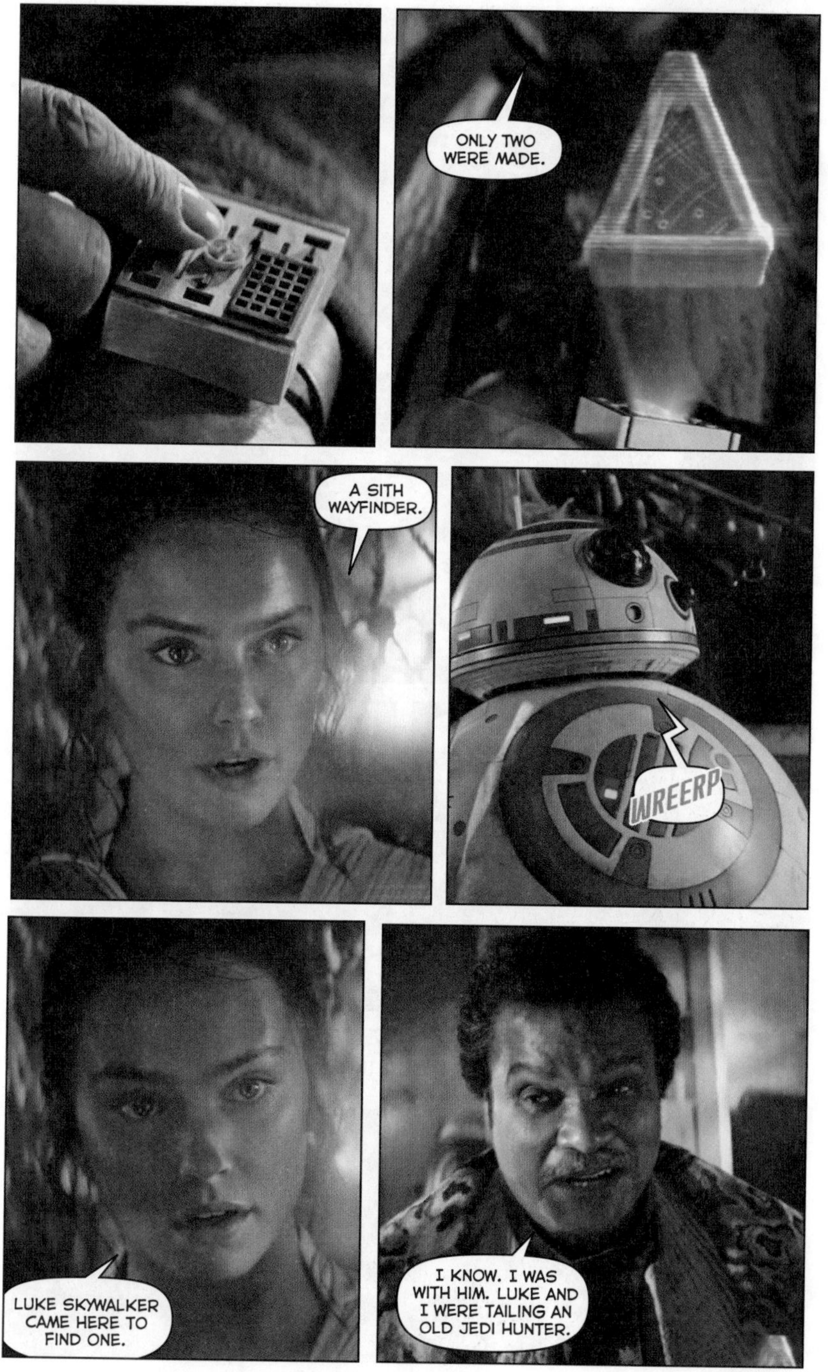
ONLY TWO WERE MADE.
A SITH WAYFINDER.
WREERP
LUKE SKYWALKER CAME HERE TO FIND ONE.
I KNOW. I WAS WITH HIM. LUKE AND I WERE TAILING AN OLD JEDI HUNTER.

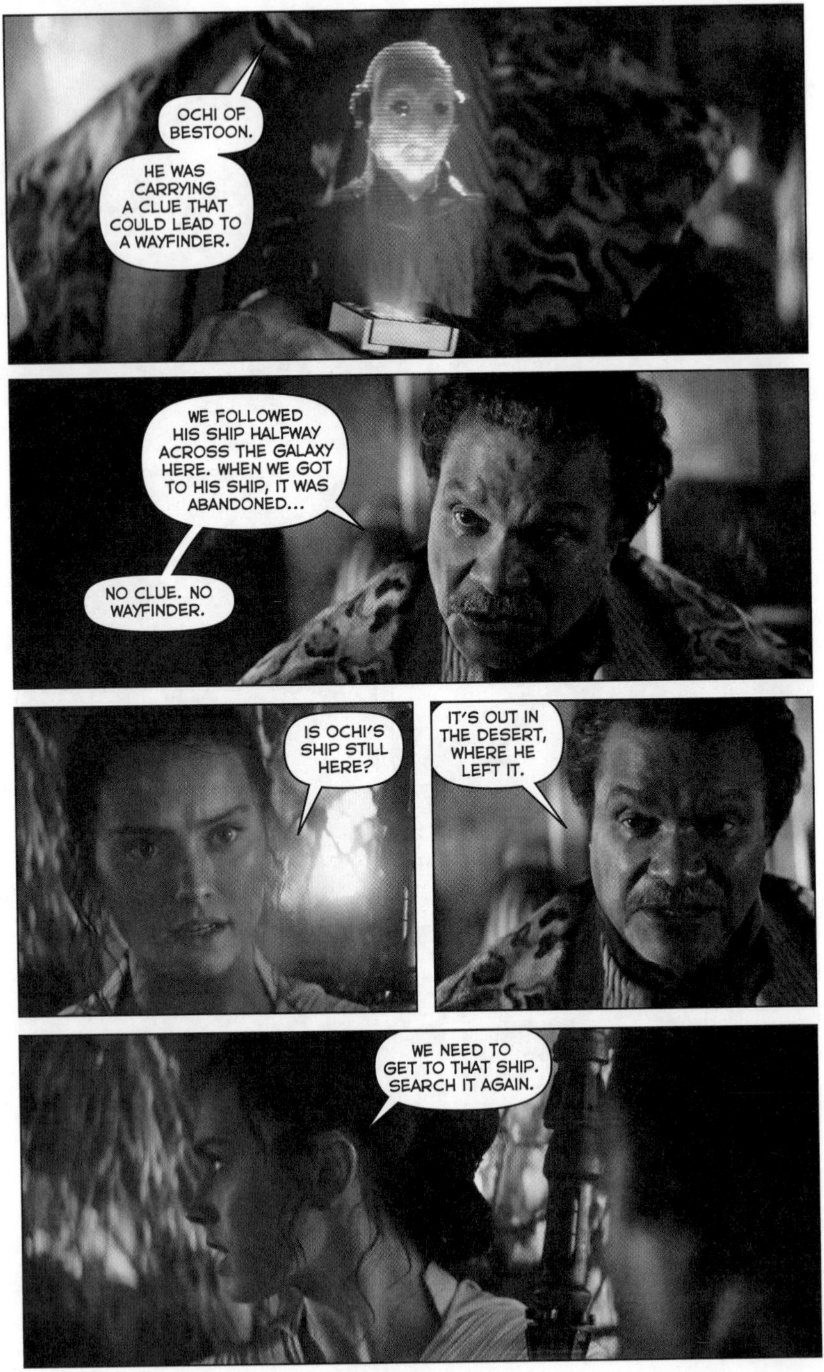
OCHI OF BESTOON.
HE WAS CARRYING A CLUE THAT COULD LEAD TO A WAYFINDER.
WE FOLLOWED HIS SHIP HALFWAY ACROSS THE GALAXY HERE. WHEN WE GOT TO HIS SHIP, IT WAS ABANDONED...
NO CLUE. NO WAYFINDER.
IS OCHI'S SHIP STILL HERE?
IT'S OUT IN THE DESERT, WHERE HE LEFT IT.
WE NEED TO GET TO THAT SHIP. SEARCH IT AGAIN.

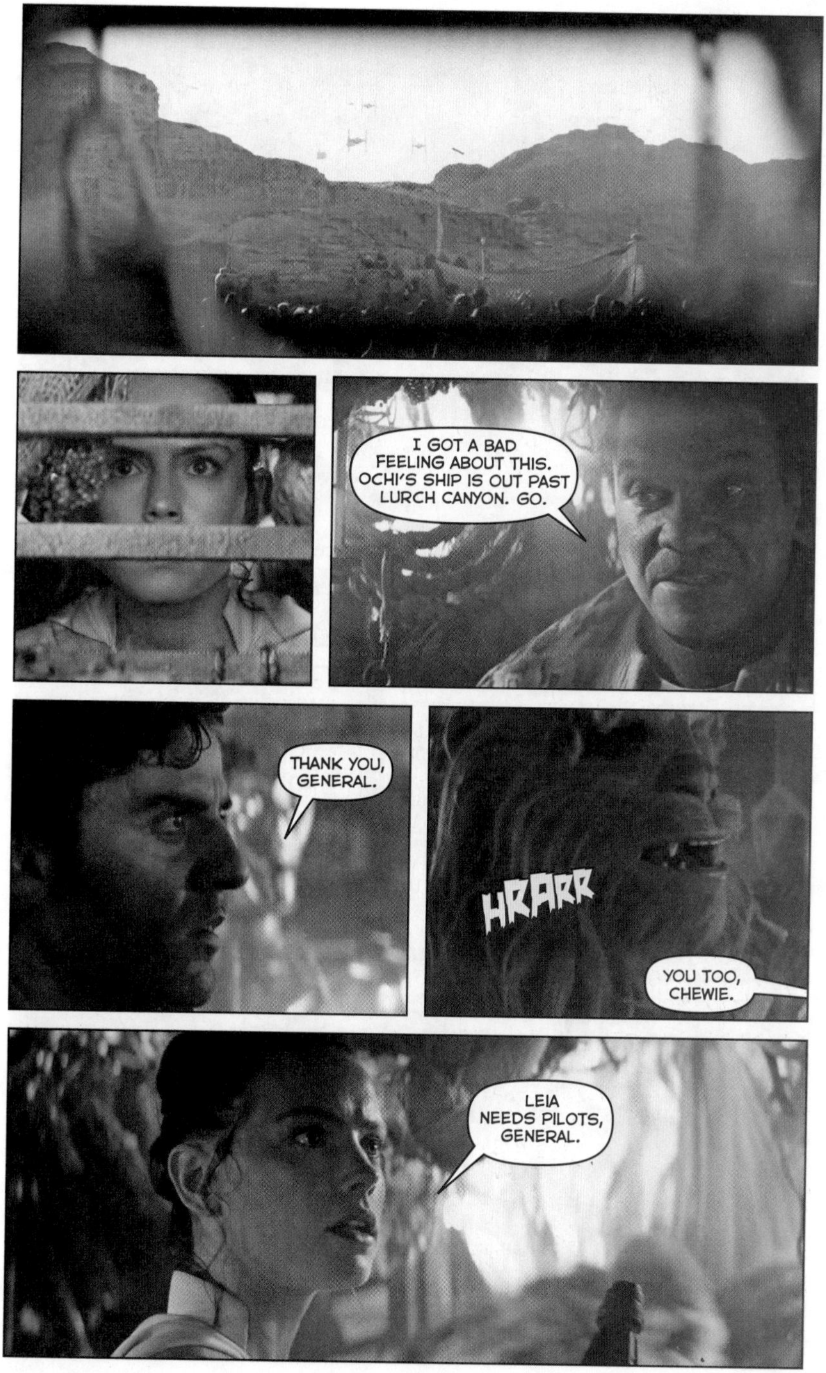
I GOT A BAD FEELING ABOUT THIS. OCHI'S SHIP IS OUT PAST LURCH CANYON. GO.
THANK YOU, GENERAL.
HRARR
YOU TOO, CHEWIE.
LEIA NEEDS PILOTS, GENERAL.

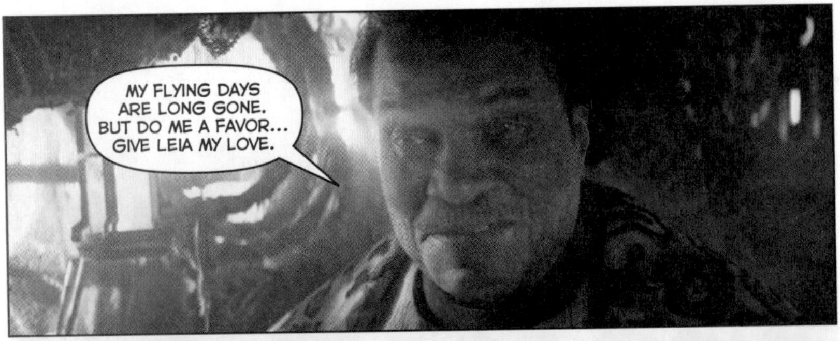
MY FLYING DAYS ARE LONG GONE. BUT DO ME A FAVOR... GIVE LEIA MY LOVE.

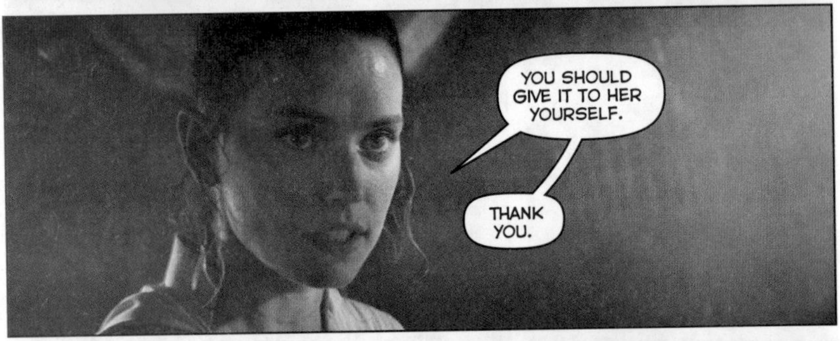
YOU SHOULD GIVE IT TO HER YOURSELF.
THANK YOU.

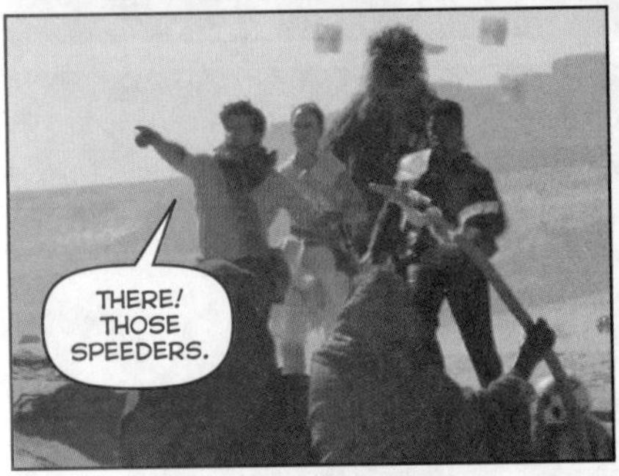
THERE! THOSE SPEEDERS.

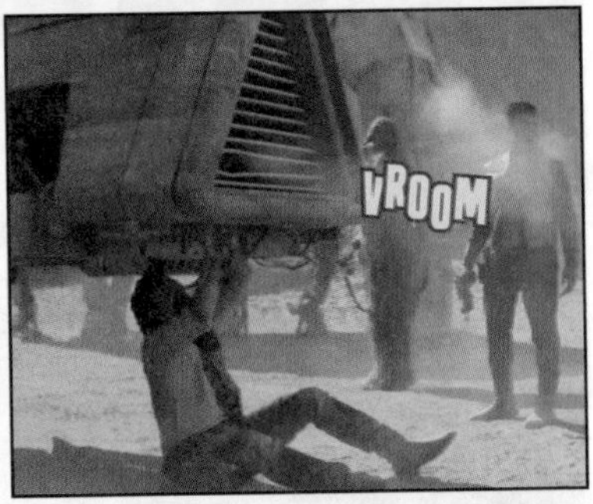
VROOM

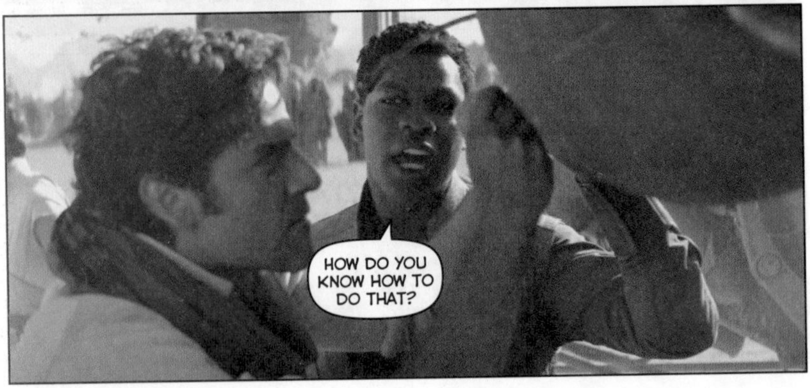
HOW DO YOU KNOW HOW TO DO THAT?

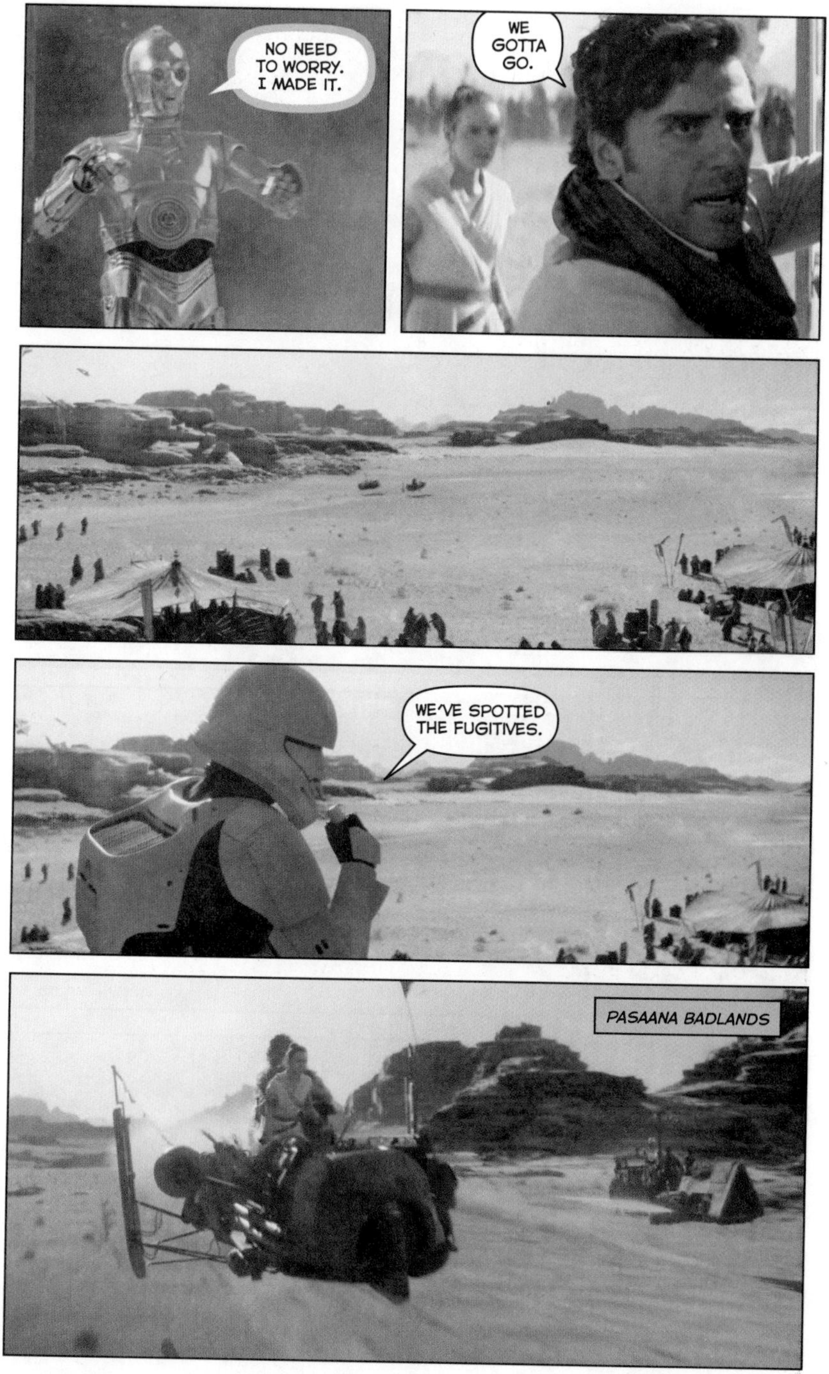
NO NEED TO WORRY. I MADE IT.
WE GOTTA GO.
WE'VE SPOTTED THE FUGITIVES.
PASAANA BADLANDS

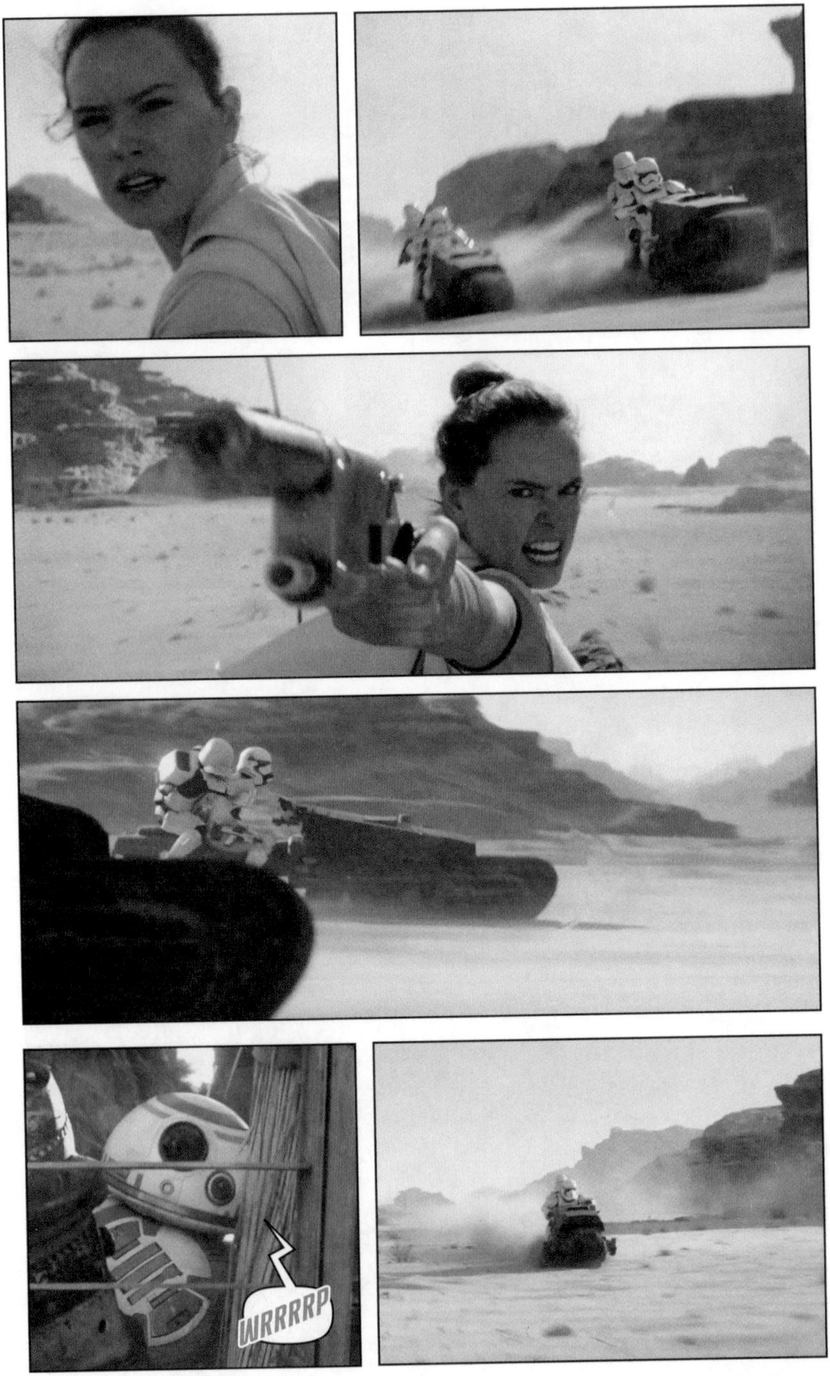
WRRRRP

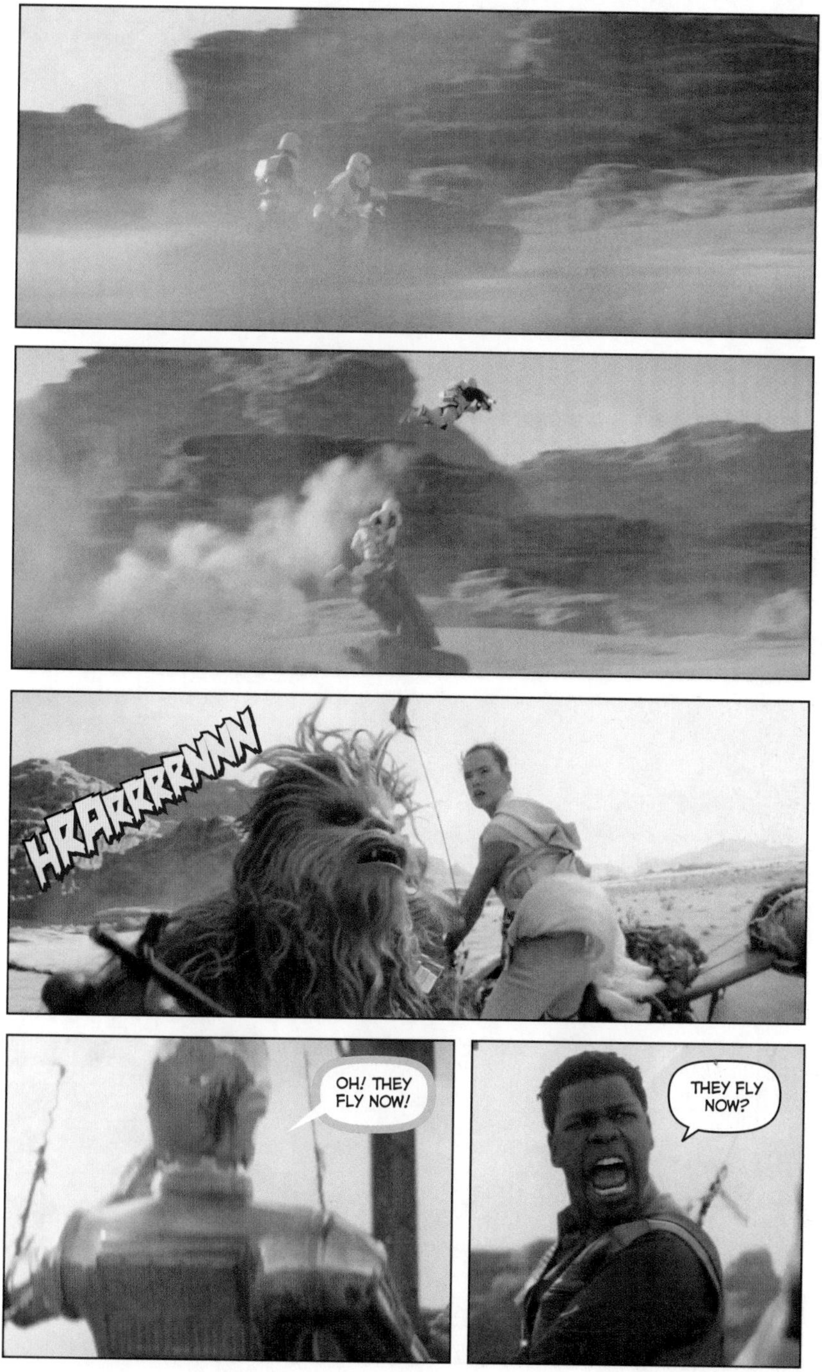
HRARRRRNNN
OH! THEY FLY NOW!
THEY FLY NOW?

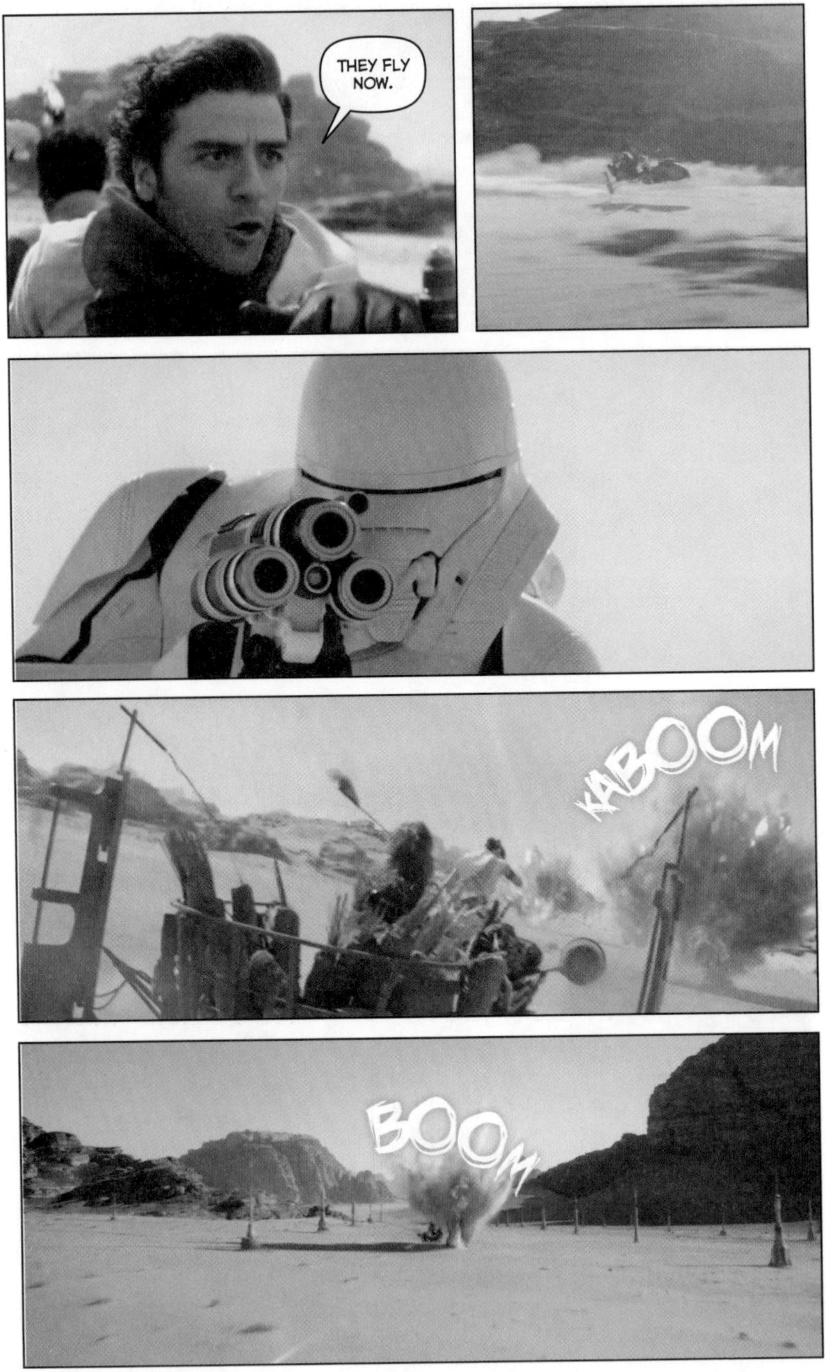
THEY FLY NOW.
KABOOM
BOOM

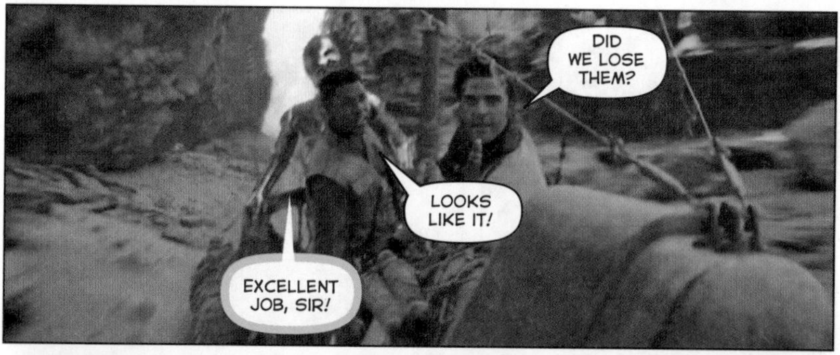
DID WE LOSE THEM?
LOOKS LIKE IT!
EXCELLENT JOB, SIR!

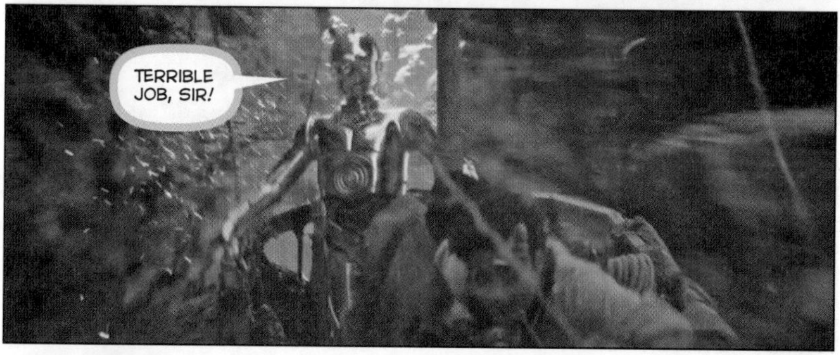
TERRIBLE JOB, SIR!

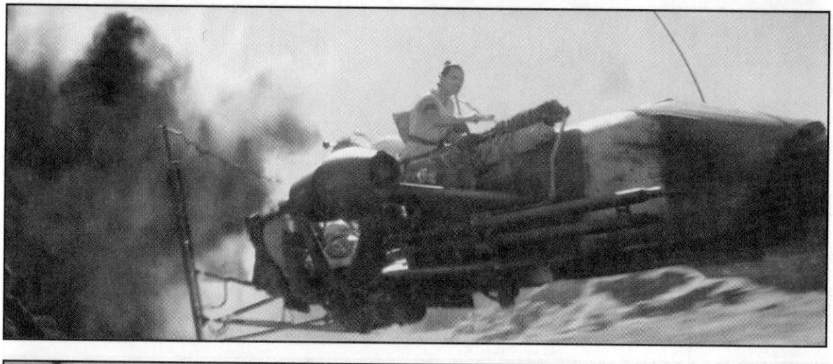

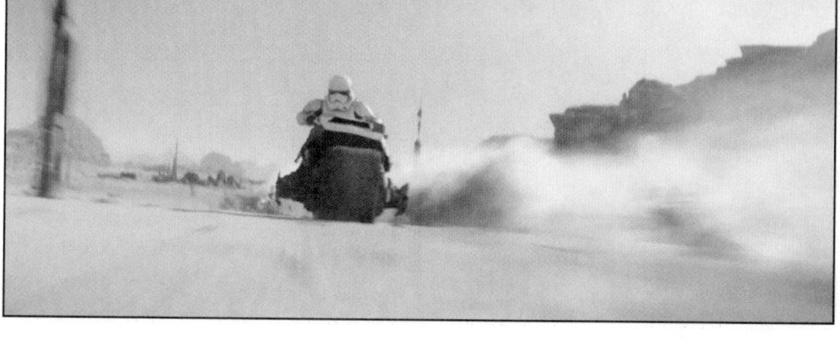

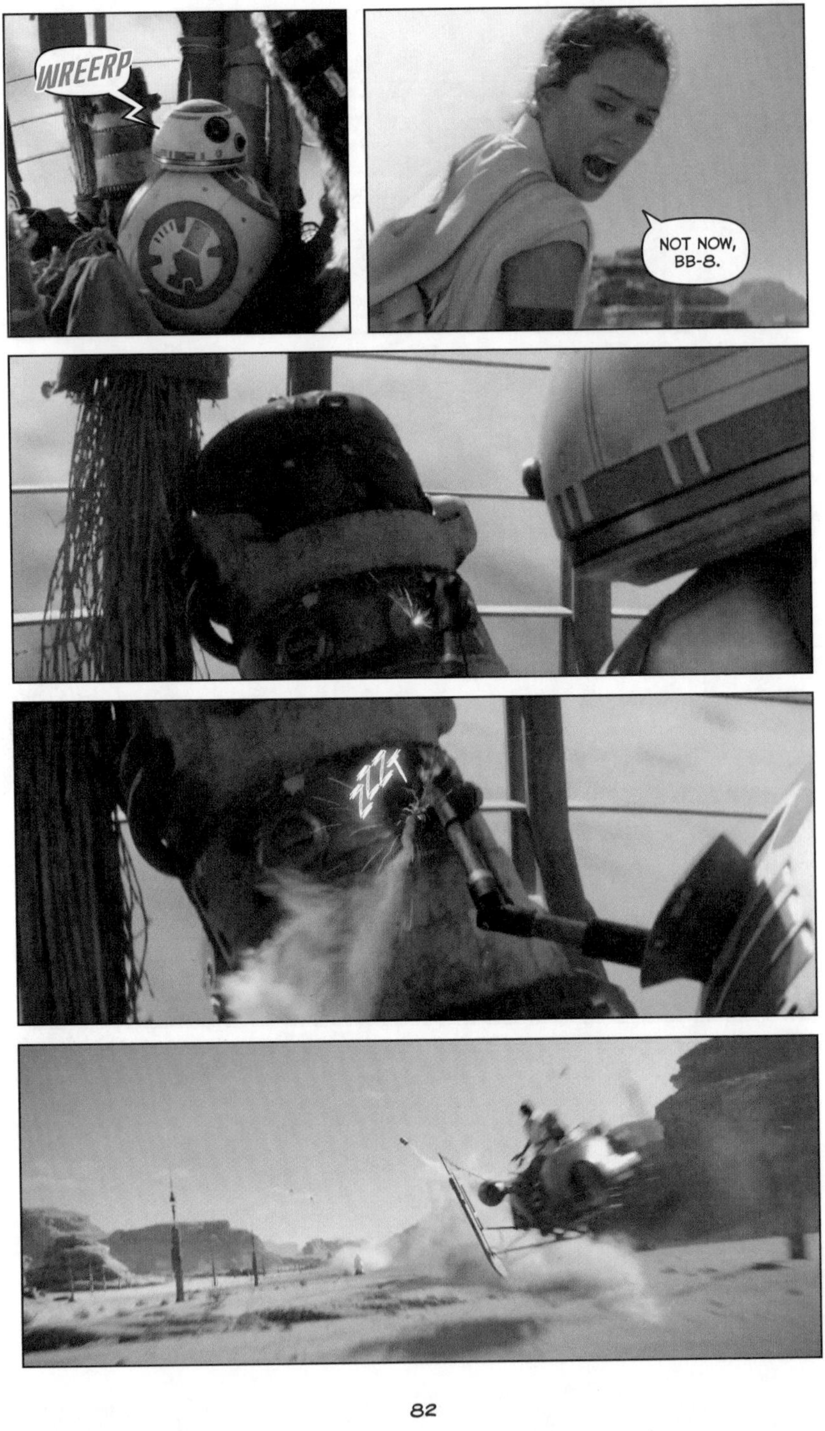
WREERP
NOT NOW, BB-8.
ZZZT

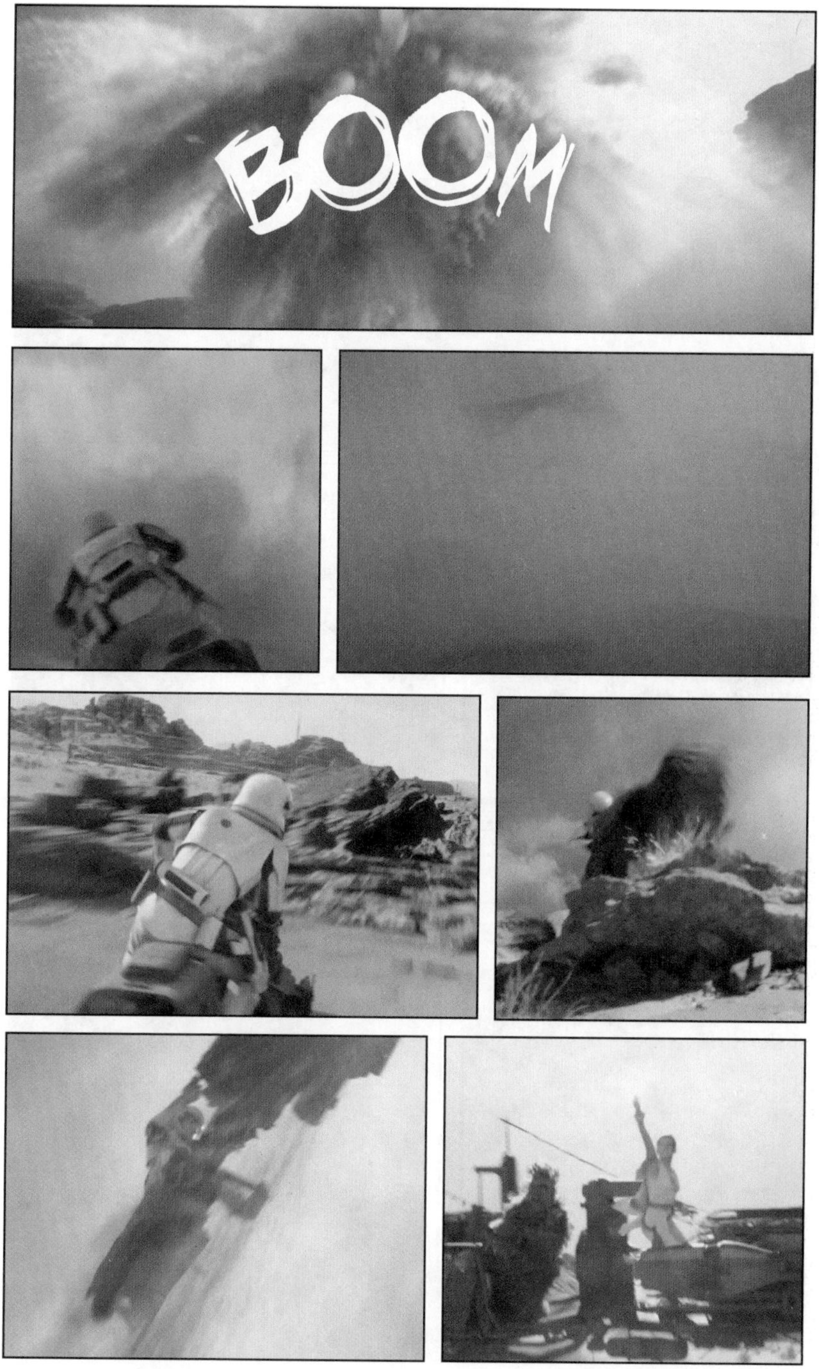
BOOM

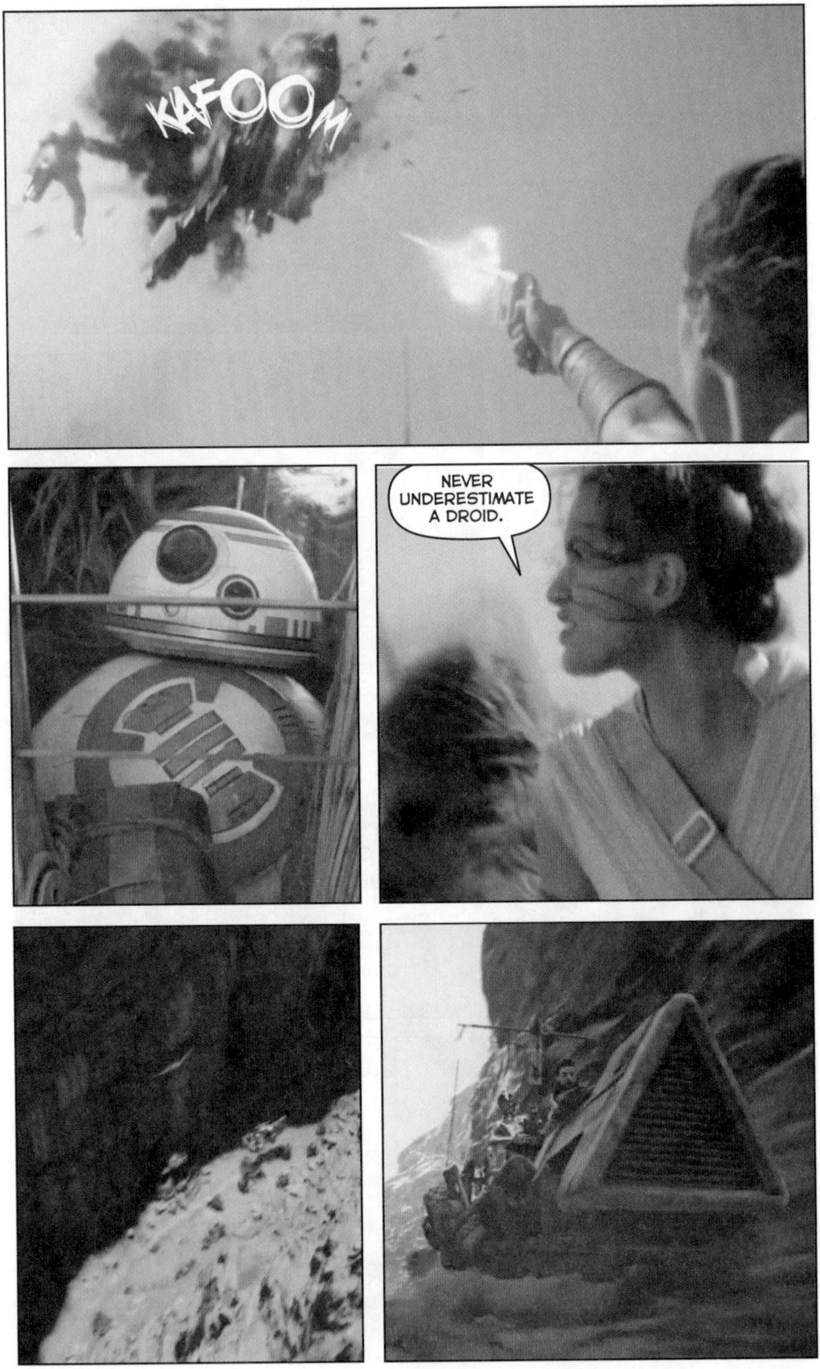
KAFOOM
NEVER UNDERESTIMATE A DROID.

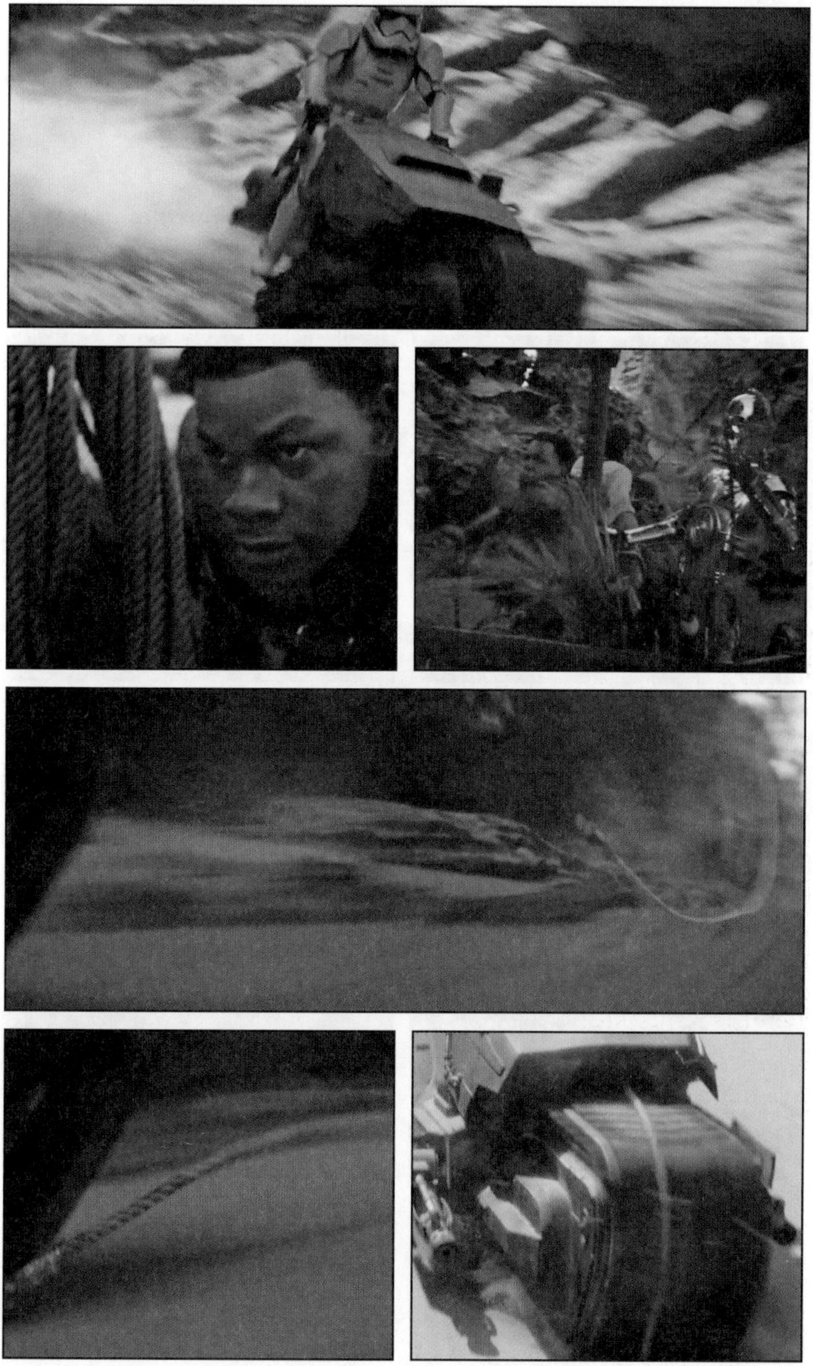

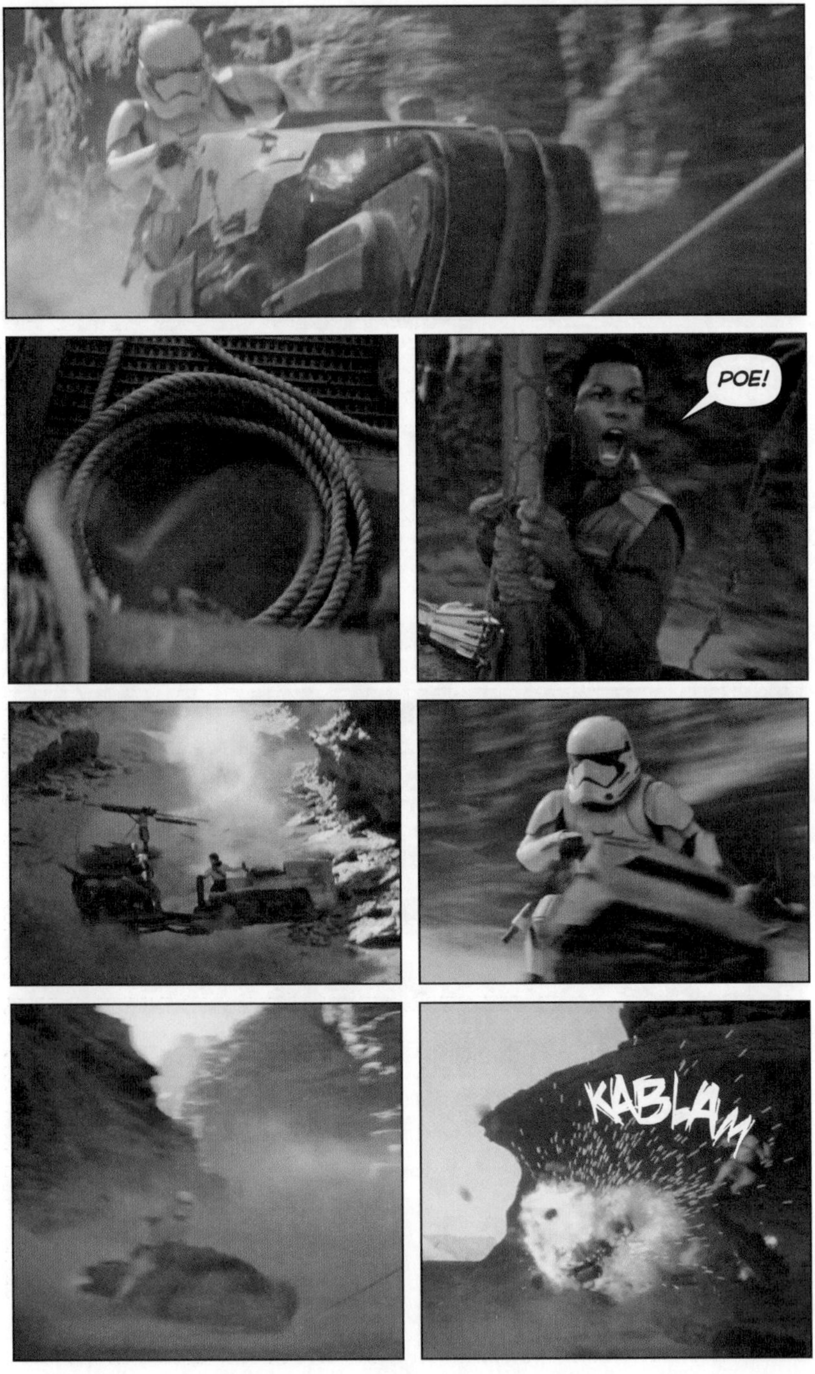
POE!
KABLAM

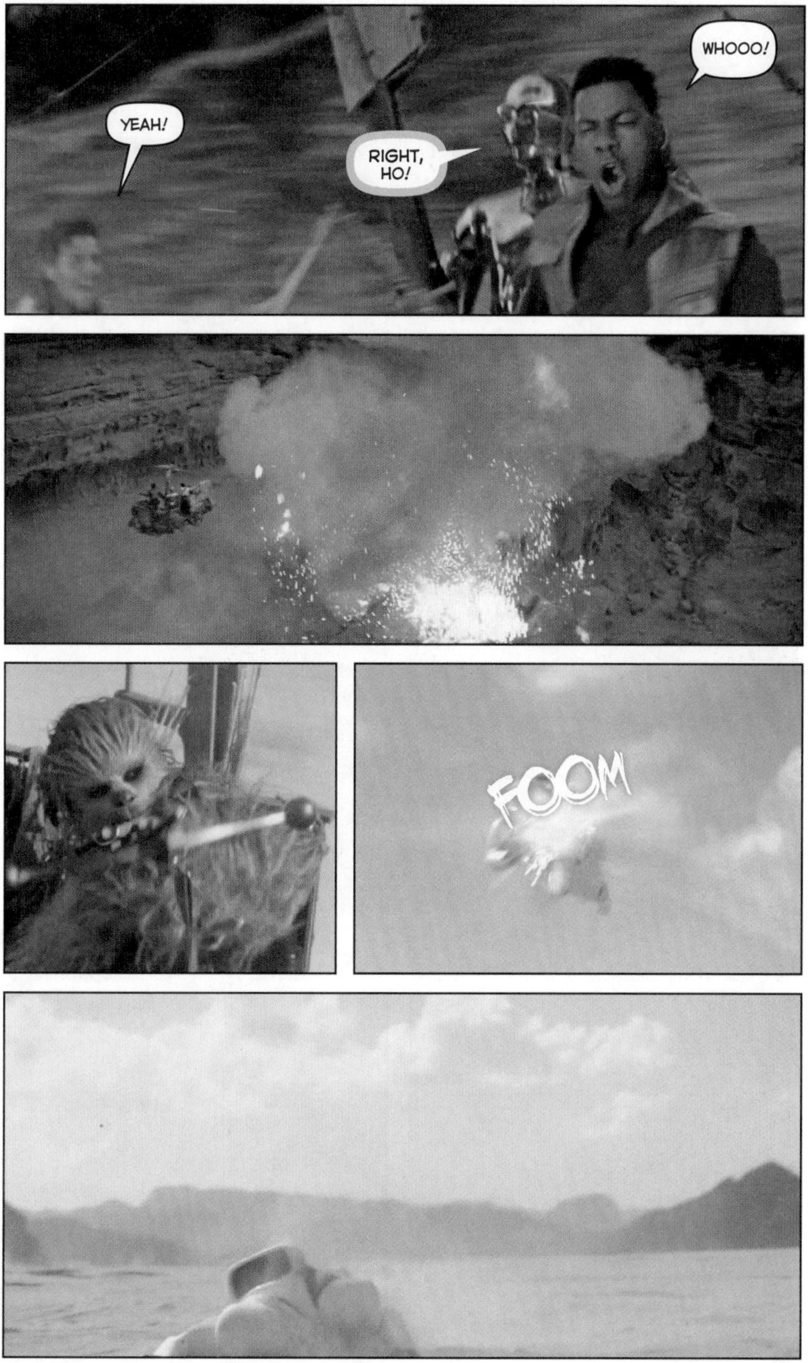
YEAH!
RIGHT, HO!
WHOOO!
FOOM

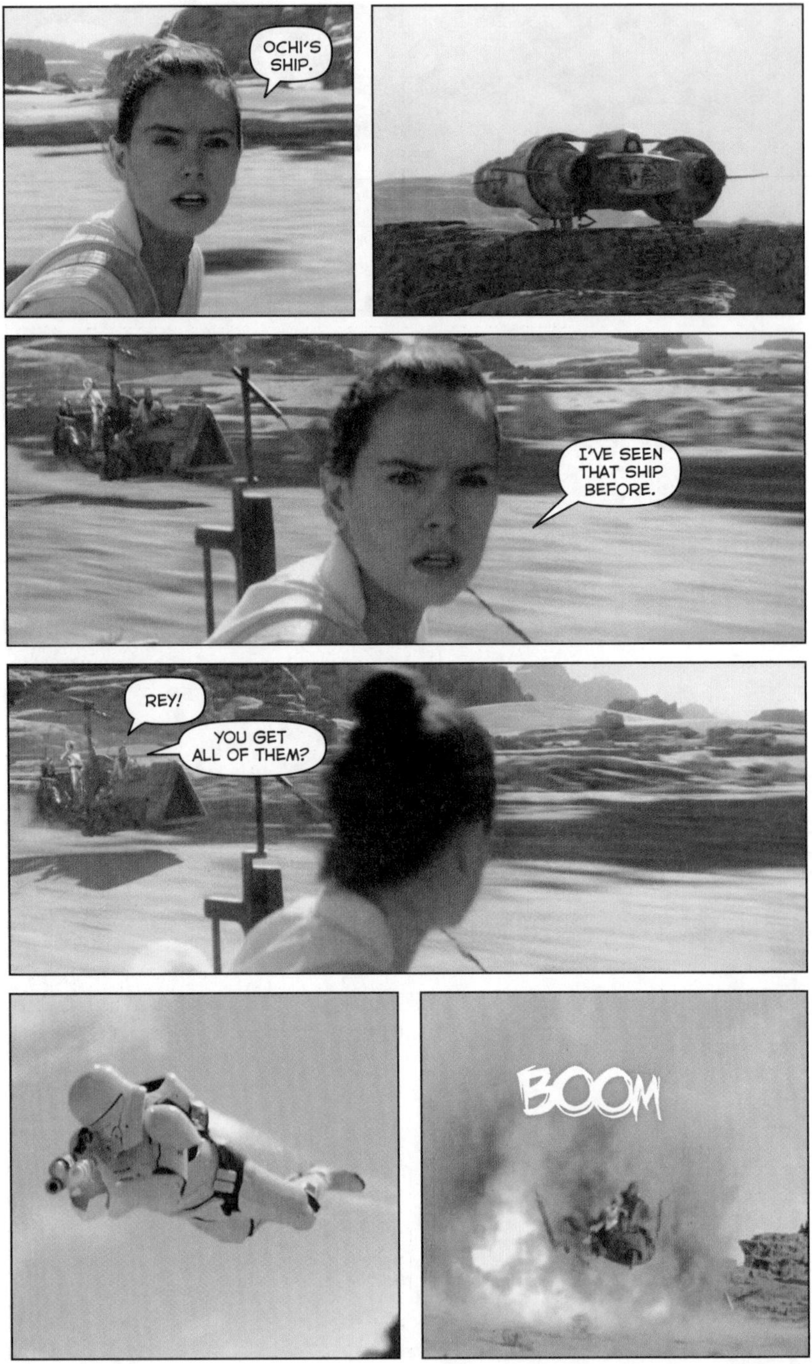
OCHI'S SHIP.
I'VE SEEN THAT SHIP BEFORE.
REY!
YOU GET ALL OF THEM?
BOOM

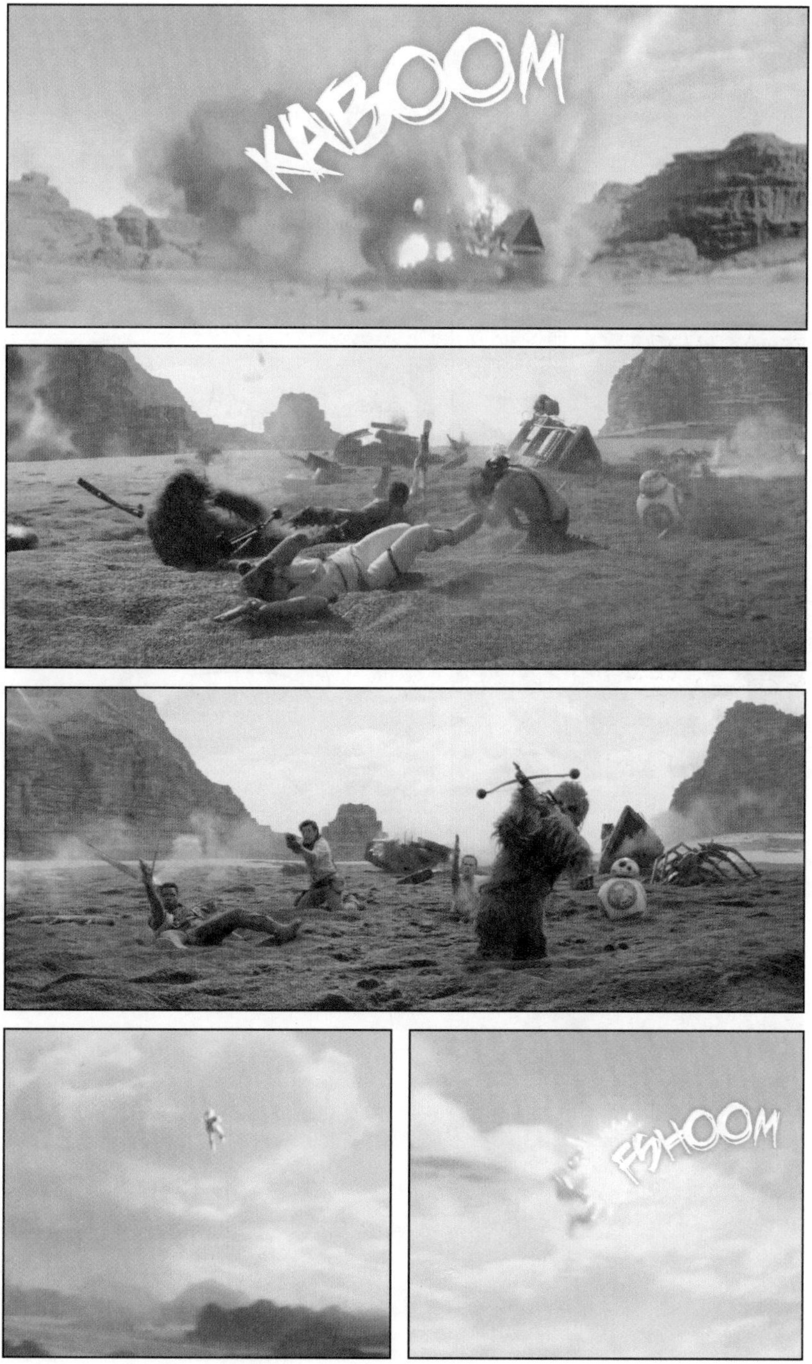
KABOOM
FSHOOM

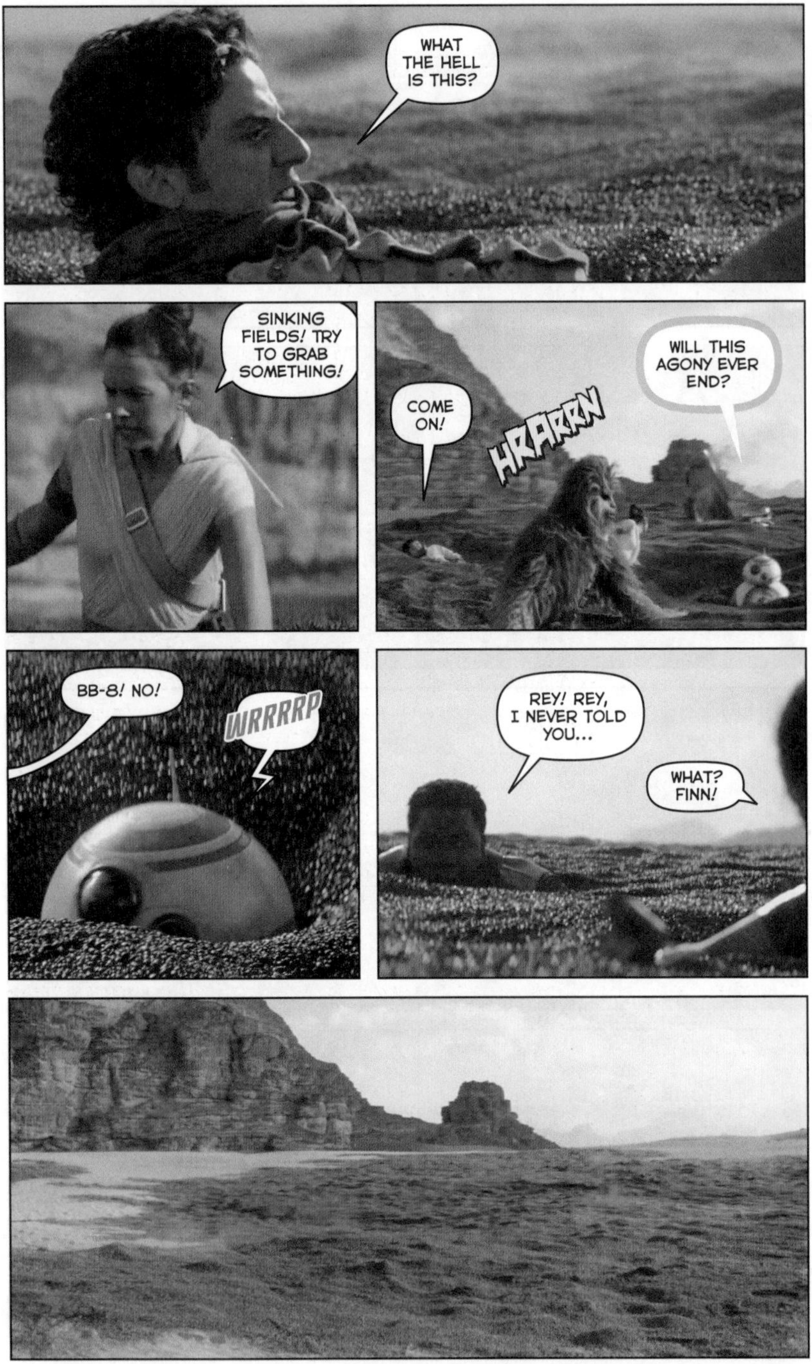
WHAT THE HELL IS THIS?
SINKING FIELDS! TRY TO GRAB SOMETHING!
COME ON!
HRARRN
WILL THIS AGONY EVER END?
BB-8! NO!
WRRRRP
REY! REY, I NEVER TOLD YOU...
WHAT? FINN!

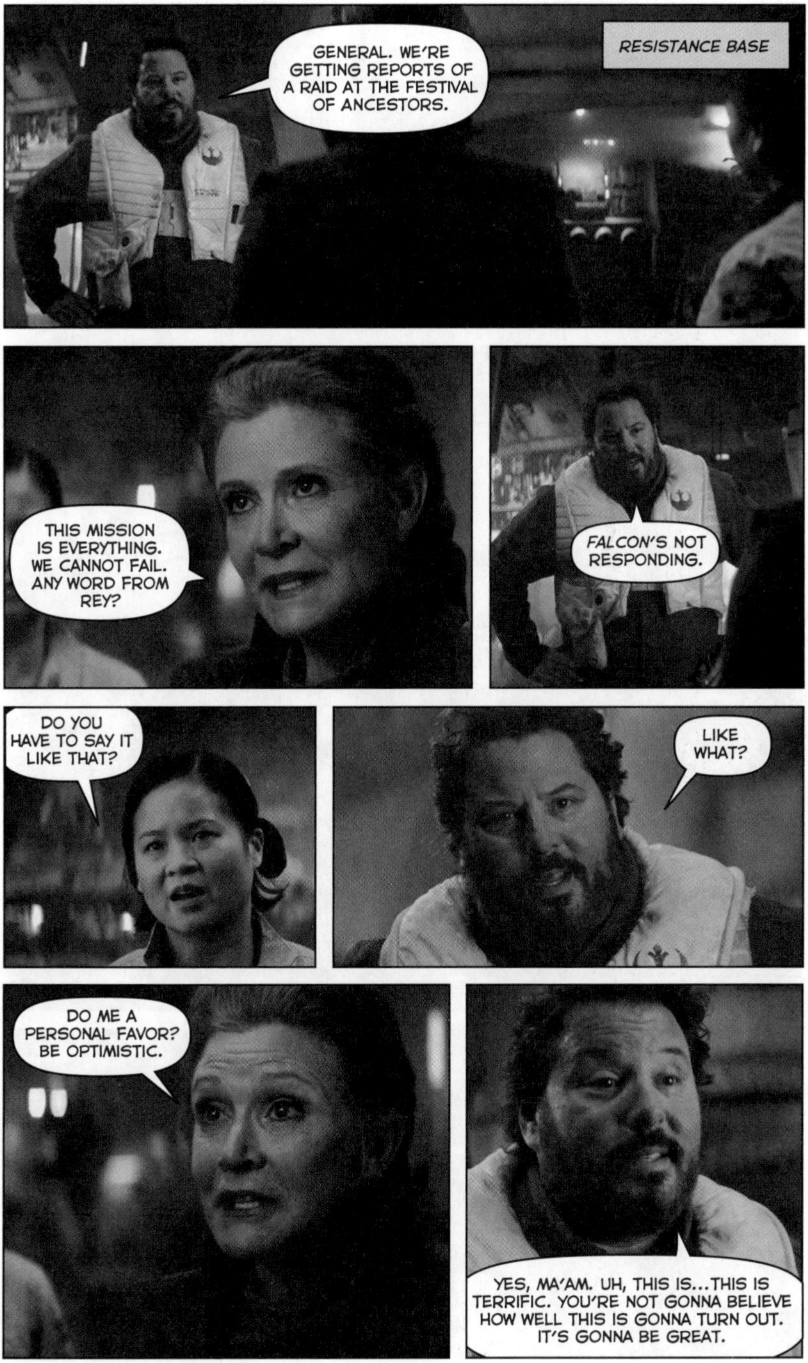
RESISTANCE BASE
GENERAL. WE'RE GETTING REPORTS OF A RAID AT THE FESTIVAL OF ANCESTORS.
THIS MISSION IS EVERYTHING. WE CANNOT FAIL. ANY WORD FROM REY?
FALCON'S NOT RESPONDING.
DO YOU HAVE TO SAY IT LIKE THAT?
LIKE WHAT?
DO ME A PERSONAL FAVOR? BE OPTIMISTIC.
YES, MA'AM. UH, THIS IS...THIS IS TERRIFIC. YOU'RE NOT GONNA BELIEVE HOW WELL THIS IS GONNA TURN OUT. IT'S GONNA BE GREAT.

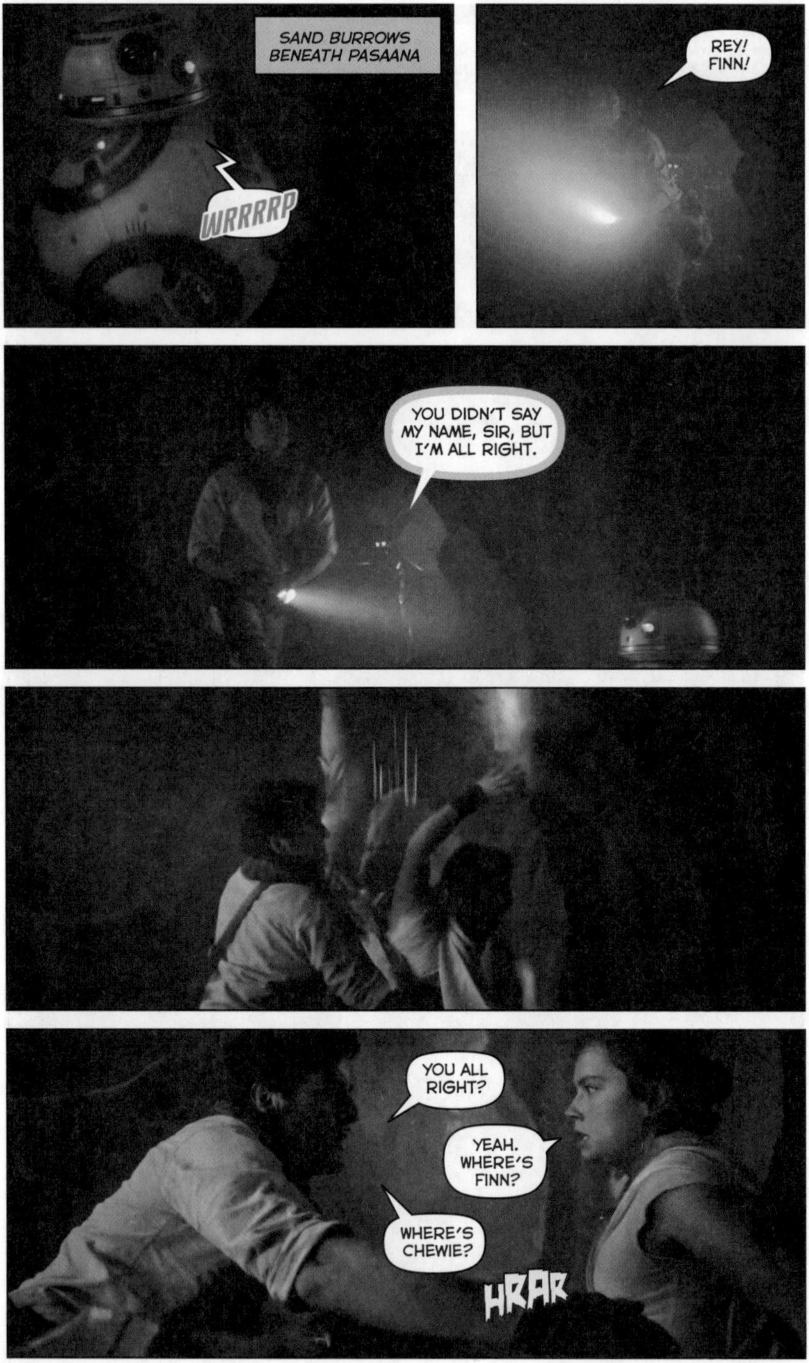
SAND BURROWS BENEATH PASAANA
WRRRRP
REY! FINN!
YOU DIDN'T SAY MY NAME, SIR, BUT I'M ALL RIGHT.
YOU ALL RIGHT?
YEAH. WHERE'S FINN?
WHERE'S CHEWIE?
HRAR

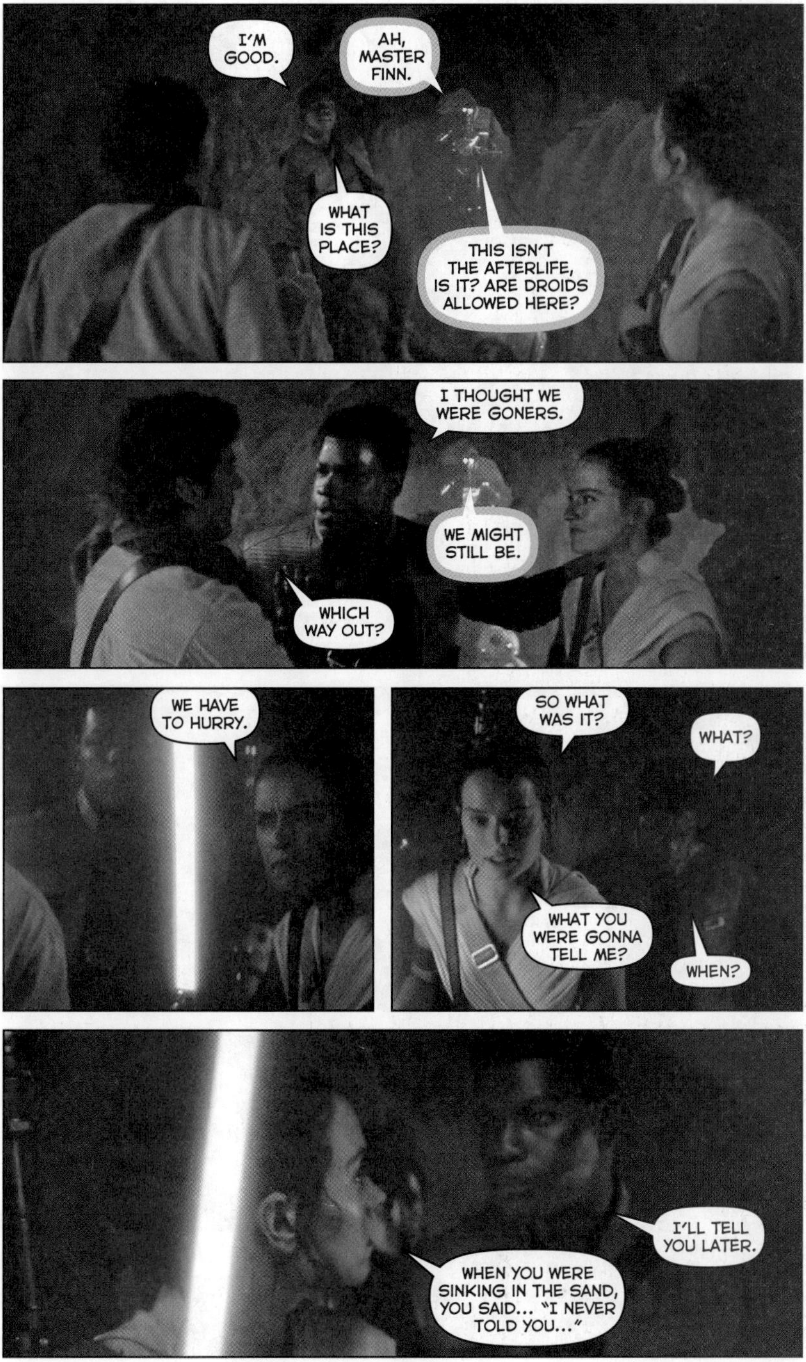
I'M GOOD.
AH, MASTER FINN.
WHAT IS THIS PLACE?
THIS ISN'T THE AFTERLIFE, IS IT? ARE DROIDS ALLOWED HERE?
I THOUGHT WE WERE GONERS.
WE MIGHT STILL BE.
WHICH WAY OUT?
WE HAVE TO HURRY.
SO WHAT WAS IT?
WHAT?
WHAT YOU WERE GONNA TELL ME?
WHEN?
WHEN YOU WERE SINKING IN THE SAND, YOU SAID... "I NEVER TOLD YOU..."
I'LL TELL YOU LATER.

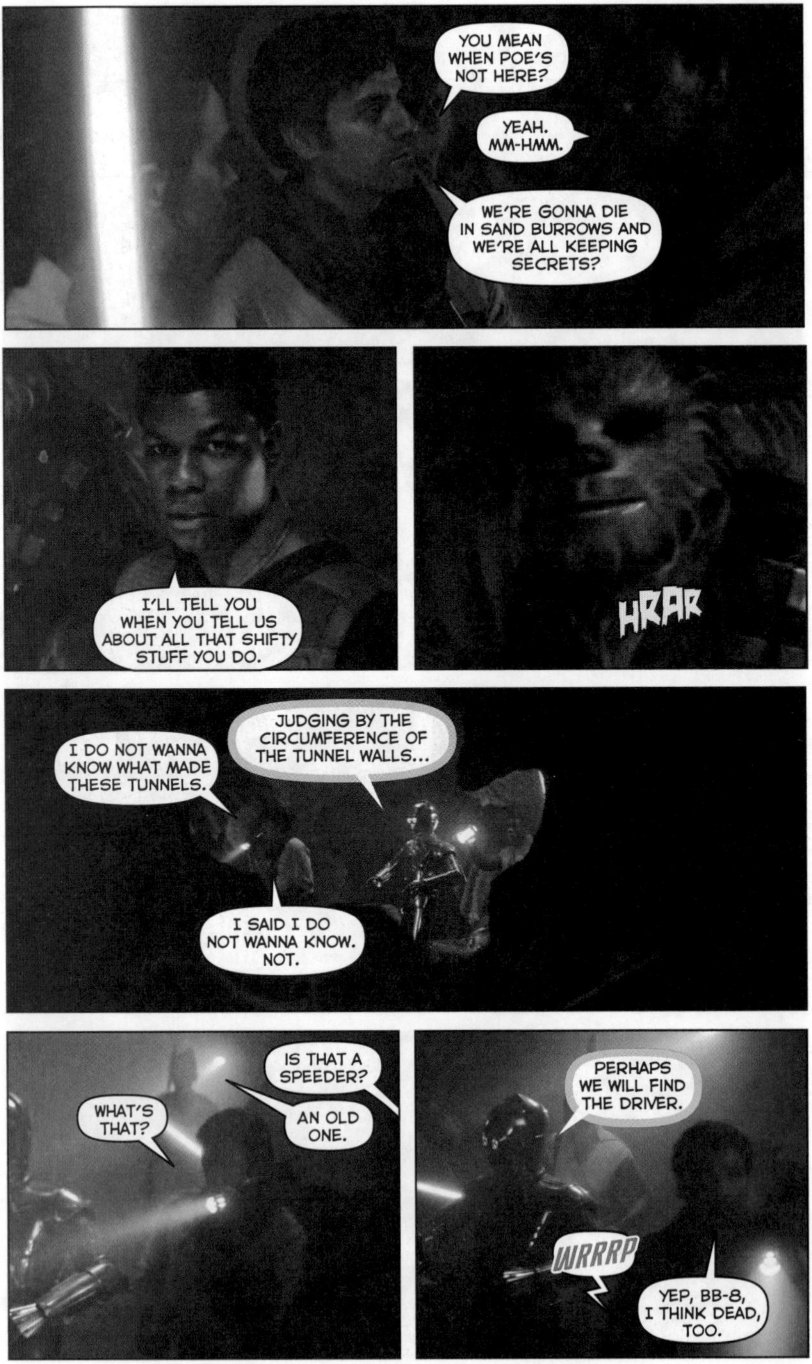
YOU MEAN WHEN POE'S NOT HERE?
YEAH. MM-HMM.
WE'RE GONNA DIE IN SAND BURROWS AND WE'RE ALL KEEPING SECRETS?
I'LL TELL YOU WHEN YOU TELL US ABOUT ALL THAT SHIFTY STUFF YOU DO.
HRAR
I DO NOT WANNA KNOW WHAT MADE THESE TUNNELS.
JUDGING BY THE CIRCUMFERENCE OF THE TUNNEL WALLS...
I SAID I DO NOT WANNA KNOW. NOT.
WHAT'S THAT?
IS THAT A SPEEDER?
AN OLD ONE.
PERHAPS WE WILL FIND THE DRIVER.
WRRRP
YEP, BB-8, I THINK DEAD, TOO.

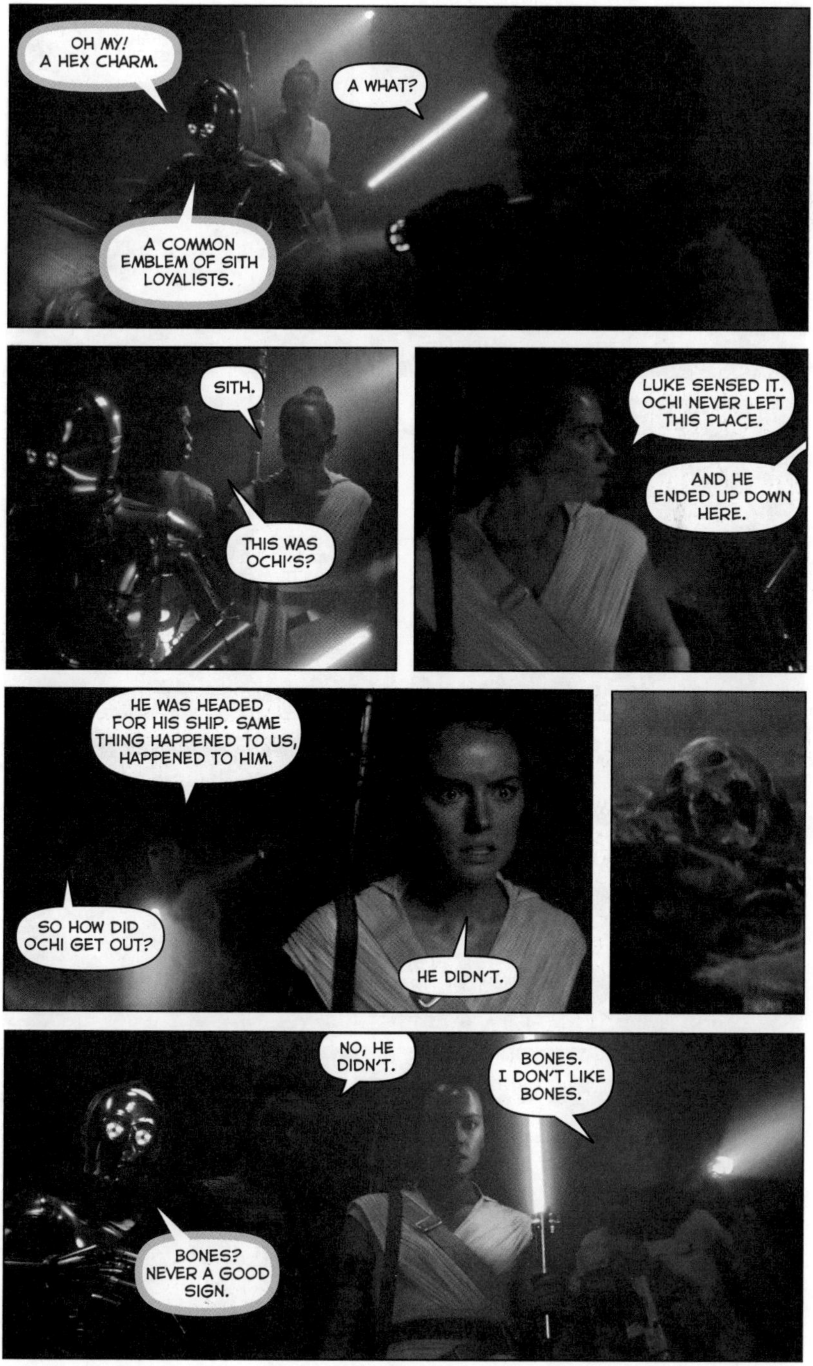
OH MY! A HEX CHARM.
A WHAT?
A COMMON EMBLEM OF SITH LOYALISTS.
SITH.
THIS WAS OCHI'S?
LUKE SENSED IT. OCHI NEVER LEFT THIS PLACE.
AND HE ENDED UP DOWN HERE.
HE WAS HEADED FOR HIS SHIP. SAME THING HAPPENED TO US, HAPPENED TO HIM.
SO HOW DID OCHI GET OUT?
HE DIDN'T.
NO, HE DIDN'T.
BONES. I DON'T LIKE BONES.
BONES? NEVER A GOOD SIGN.

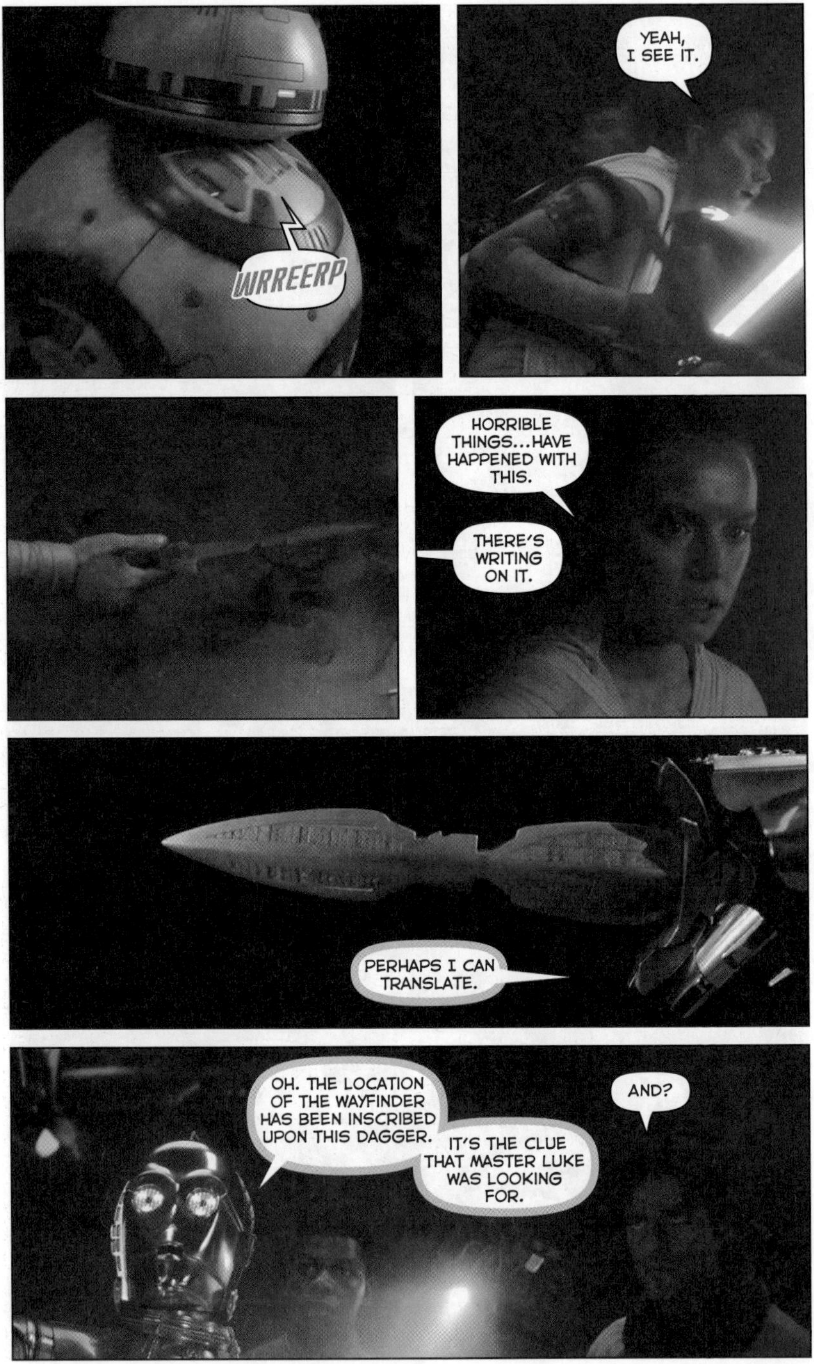
WRREERP
YEAH, I SEE IT.
HORRIBLE THINGS...HAVE HAPPENED WITH THIS.
THERE'S WRITING ON IT.
PERHAPS I CAN TRANSLATE.
OH. THE LOCATION OF THE WAYFINDER HAS BEEN INSCRIBED UPON THIS DAGGER.
IT'S THE CLUE THAT MASTER LUKE WAS LOOKING FOR.
AND?

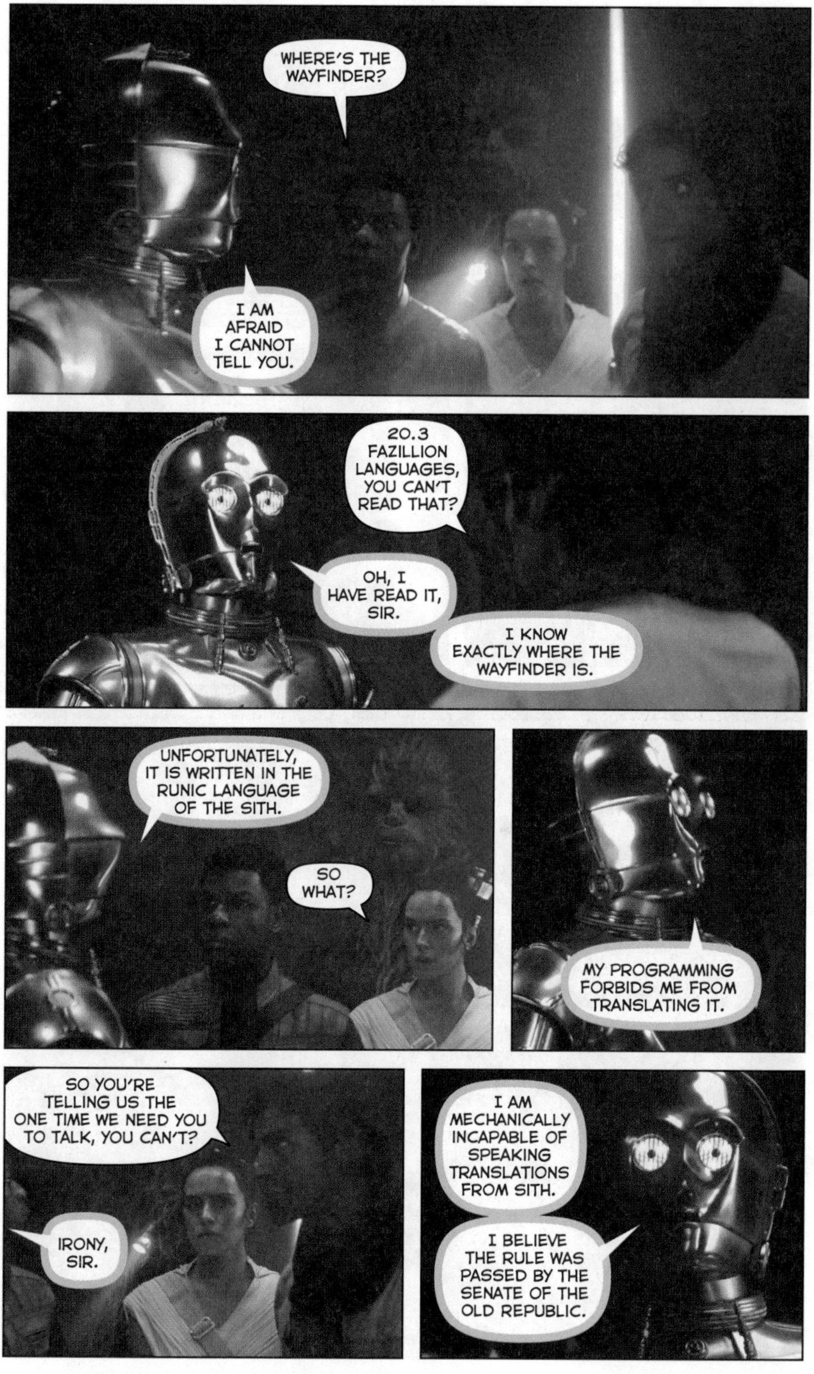
WHERE'S THE WAYFINDER?
I AM AFRAID I CANNOT TELL YOU.
20.3 FAZILLION LANGUAGES, YOU CAN'T READ THAT?
OH, I HAVE READ IT, SIR.
I KNOW EXACTLY WHERE THE WAYFINDER IS.
UNFORTUNATELY, IT IS WRITTEN IN THE RUNIC LANGUAGE OF THE SITH.
SO WHAT?
MY PROGRAMMING FORBIDS ME FROM TRANSLATING IT.
SO YOU'RE TELLING US THE ONE TIME WE NEED YOU TO TALK, YOU CAN'T?
IRONY, SIR.
I AM MECHANICALLY INCAPABLE OF SPEAKING TRANSLATIONS FROM SITH.
I BELIEVE THE RULE WAS PASSED BY THE SENATE OF THE OLD REPUBLIC.

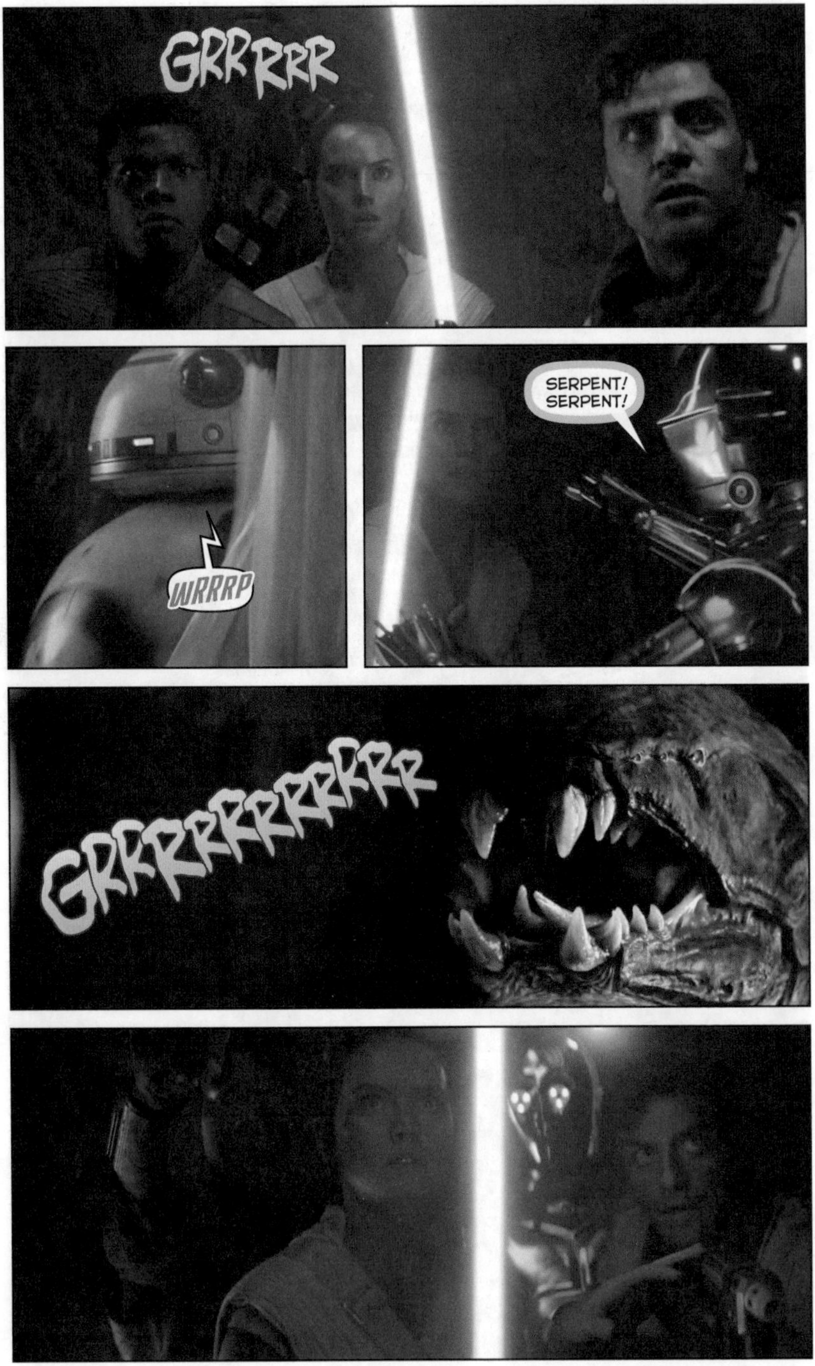
GRRRRR
WRRRP
SERPENT! SERPENT!
GRRRRRRRRRRR

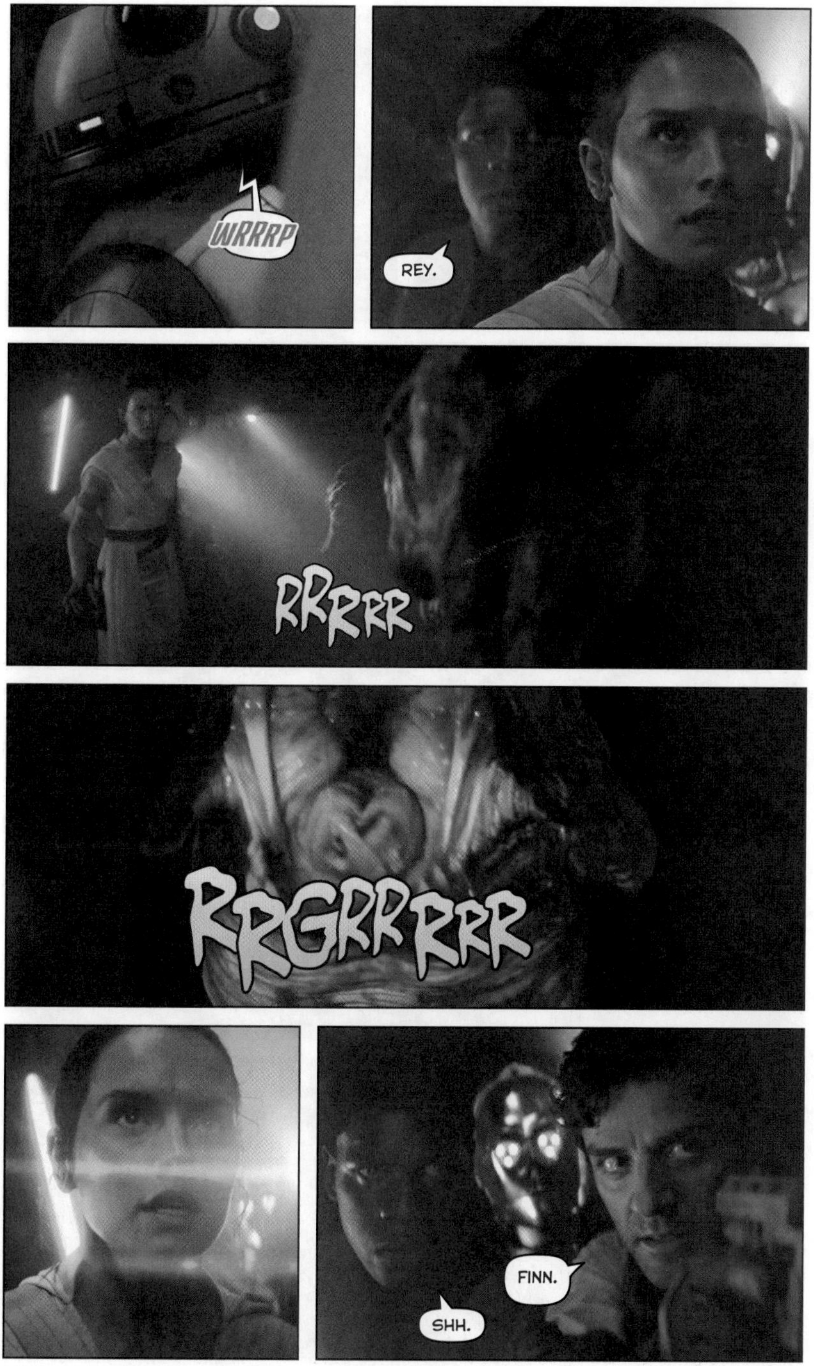
WRRRP
REY.
RRRRR
RRGRRRRR
FINN.
SHH.

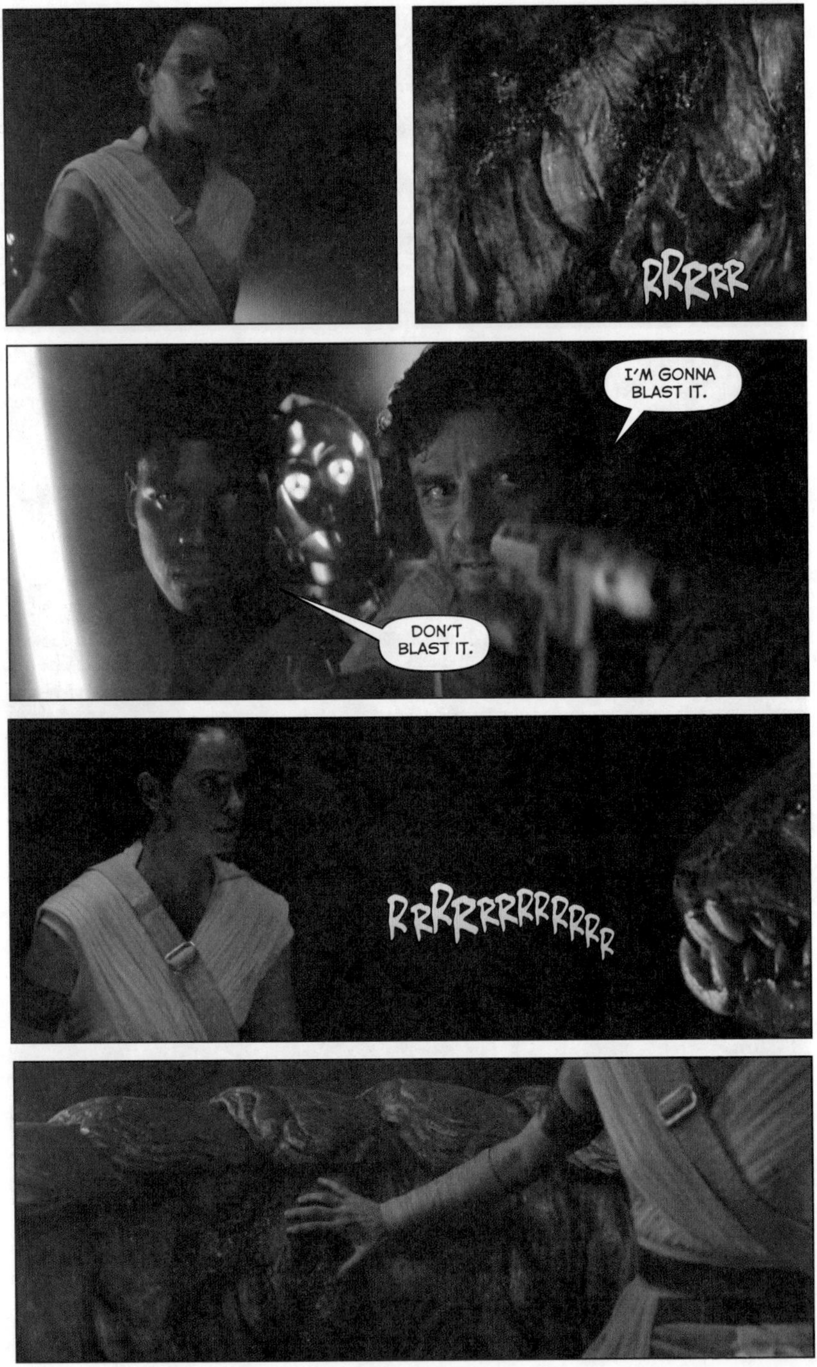
RRRRR
I'M GONNA BLAST IT.
DON'T BLAST IT.
RRRRRRRRRRRR

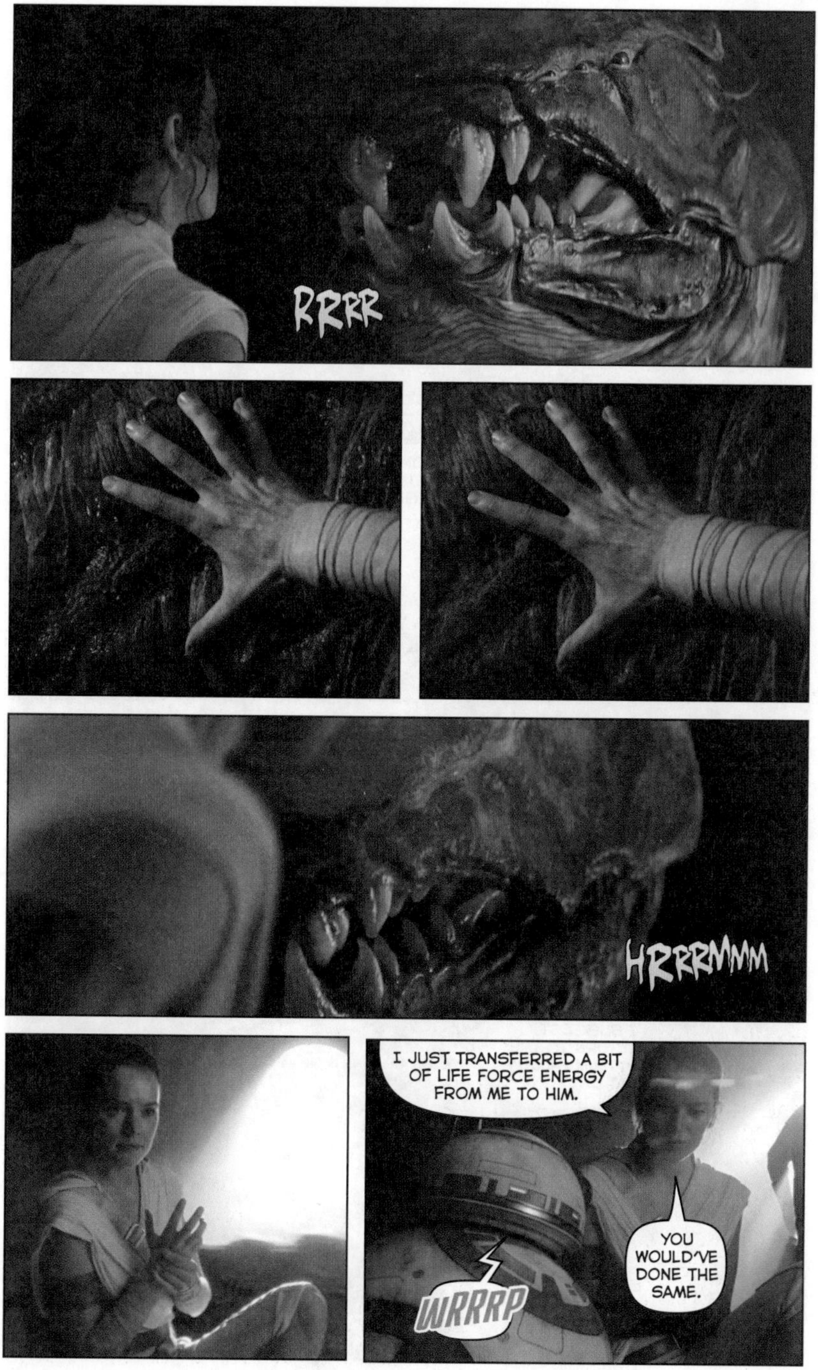
RRRR
HRRRMMM
I JUST TRANSFERRED A BIT OF LIFE FORCE ENERGY FROM ME TO HIM.
WRRRP
YOU WOULD'VE DONE THE SAME.

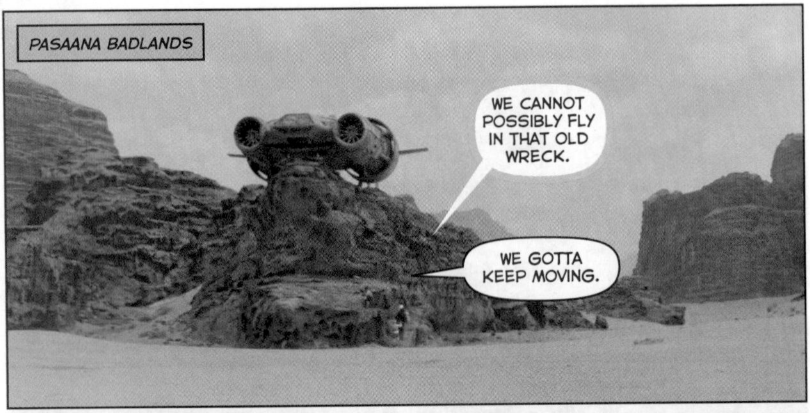
PASAANA BADLANDS
WE CANNOT POSSIBLY FLY IN THAT OLD WRECK.
WE GOTTA KEEP MOVING.

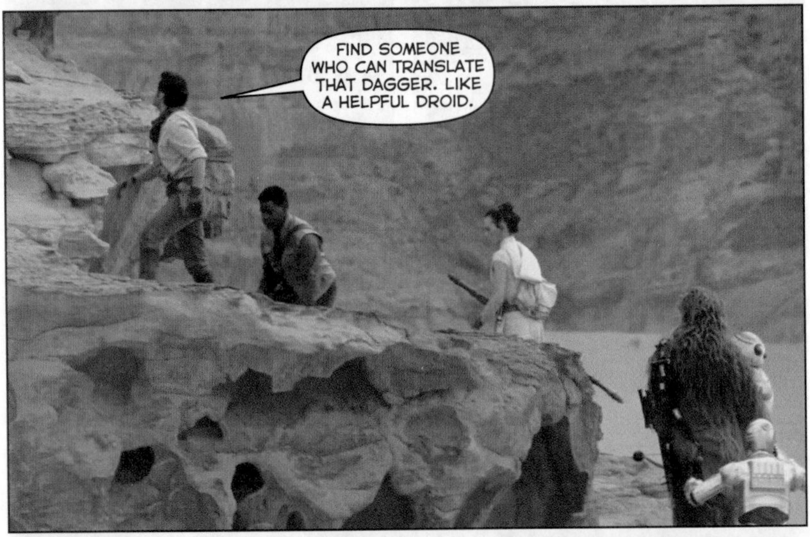
FIND SOMEONE WHO CAN TRANSLATE THAT DAGGER. LIKE A HELPFUL DROID.

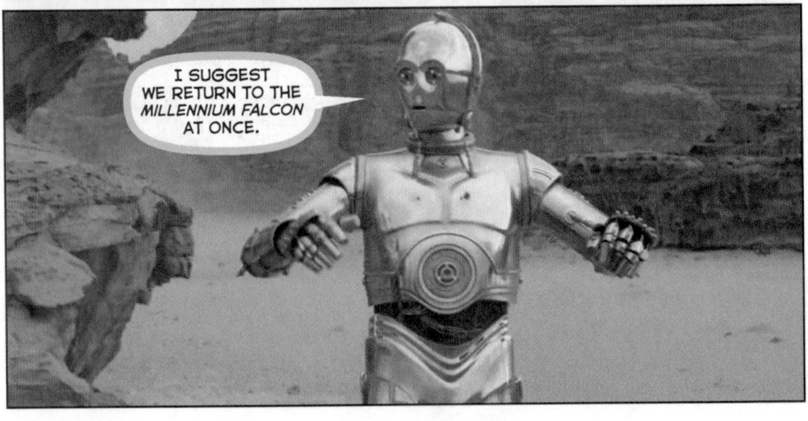
I SUGGEST WE RETURN TO THE *MILLENNIUM FALCON* AT ONCE.

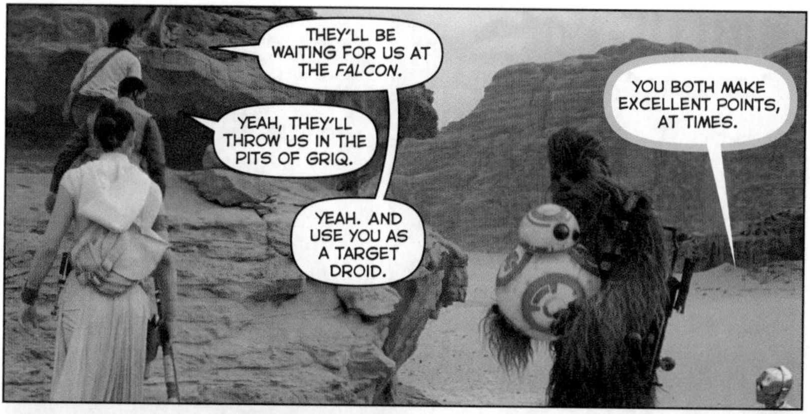
THEY'LL BE WAITING FOR US AT THE *FALCON*.
YEAH, THEY'LL THROW US IN THE PITS OF GRIQ.
YEAH. AND USE YOU AS A TARGET DROID.
YOU BOTH MAKE EXCELLENT POINTS, AT TIMES.

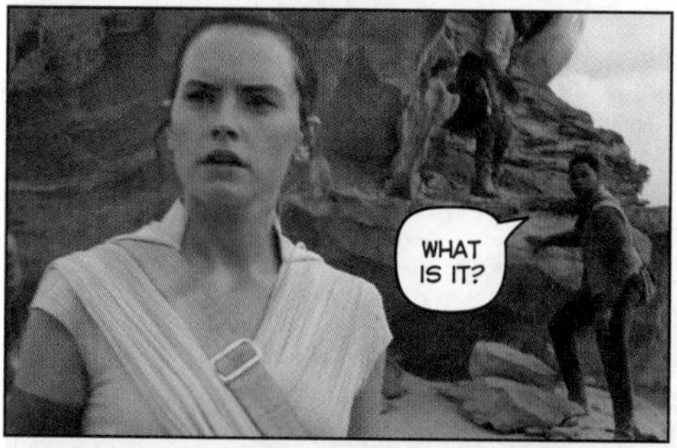
WHAT IS IT?

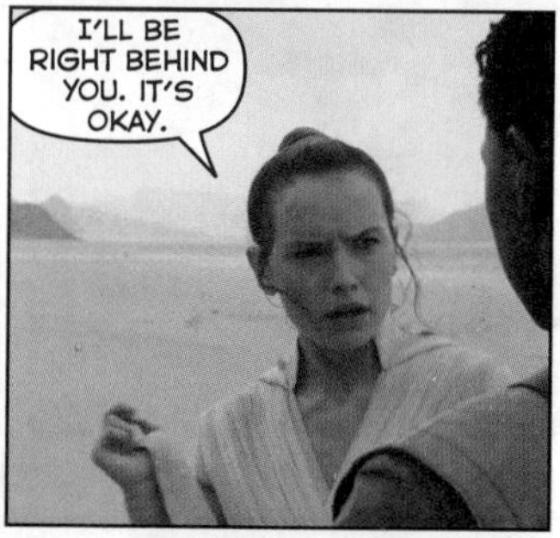
I'LL BE RIGHT BEHIND YOU. IT'S OKAY.

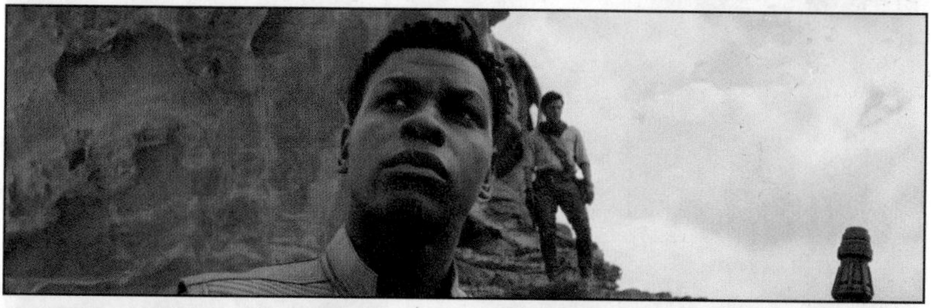

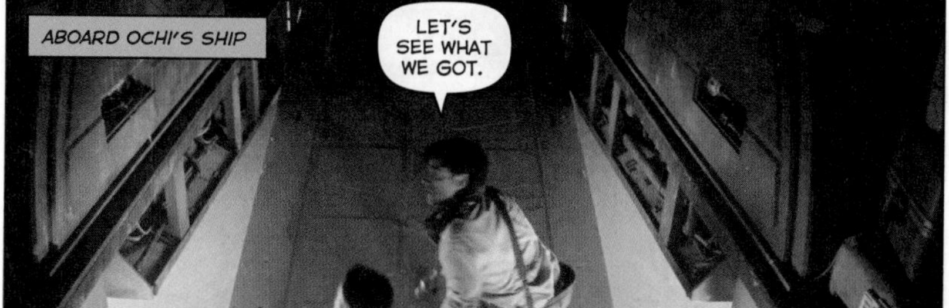
ABOARD OCHI'S SHIP
LET'S SEE WHAT WE GOT.

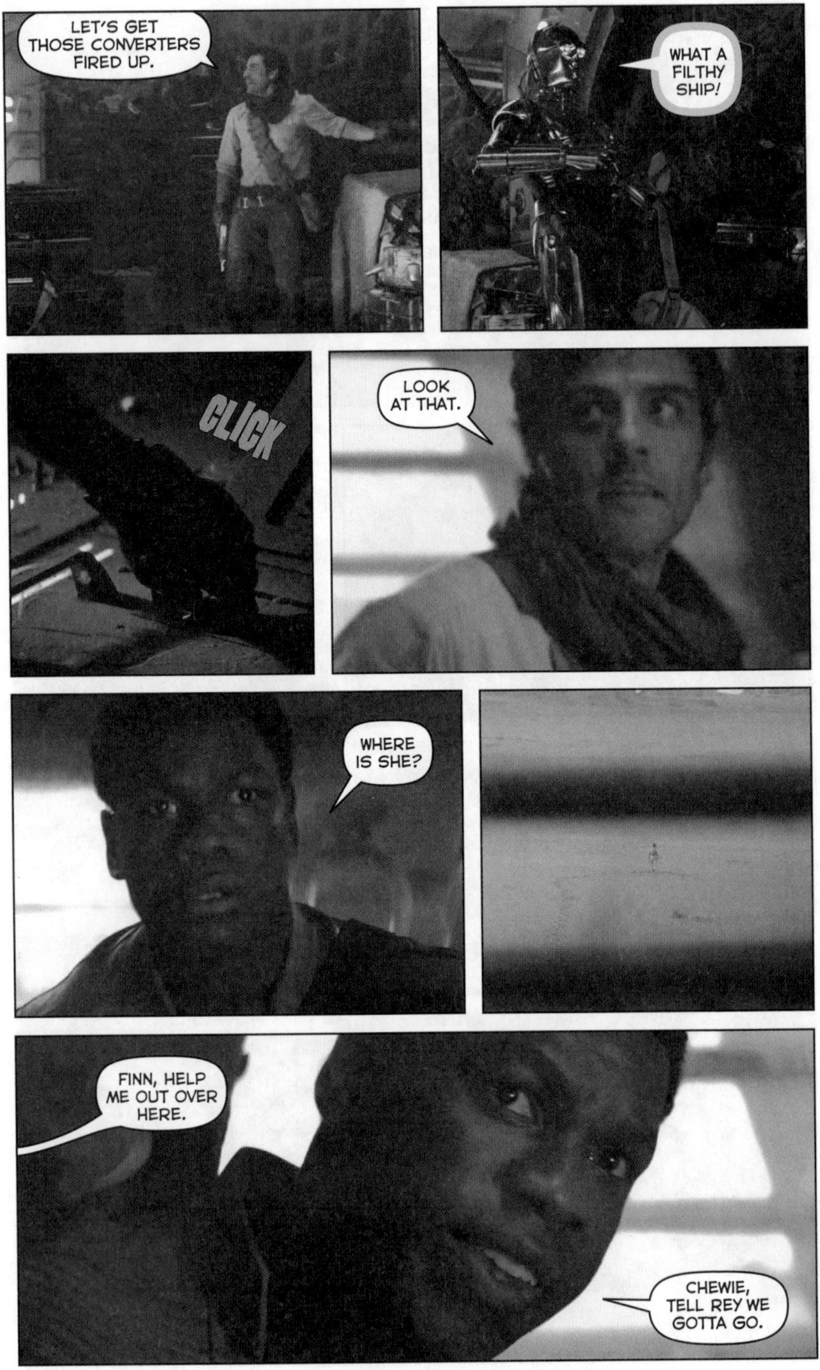
LET'S GET THOSE CONVERTERS FIRED UP.
WHAT A FILTHY SHIP!
CLICK
LOOK AT THAT.
WHERE IS SHE?
FINN, HELP ME OUT OVER HERE.
CHEWIE, TELL REY WE GOTTA GO.

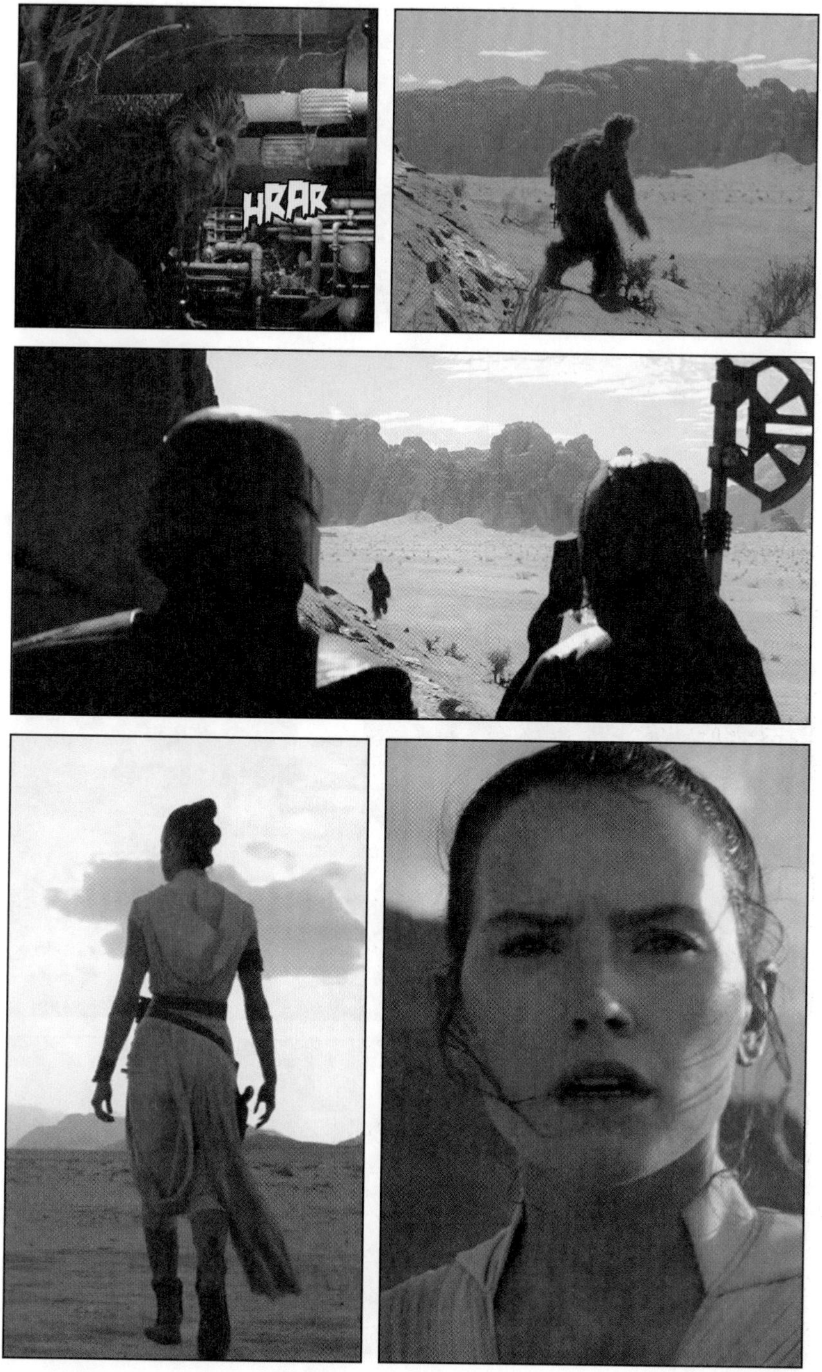
HRAR

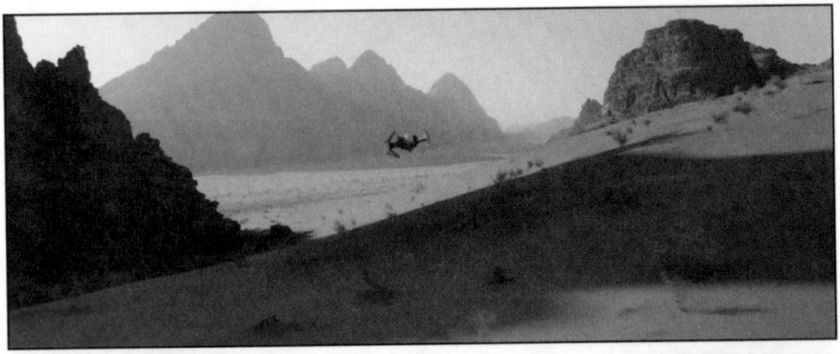

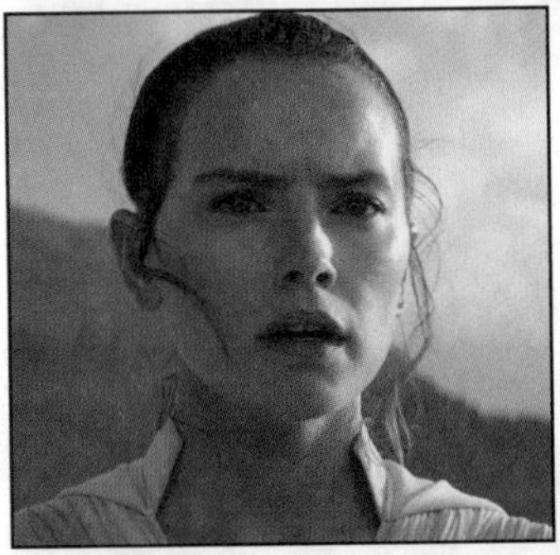

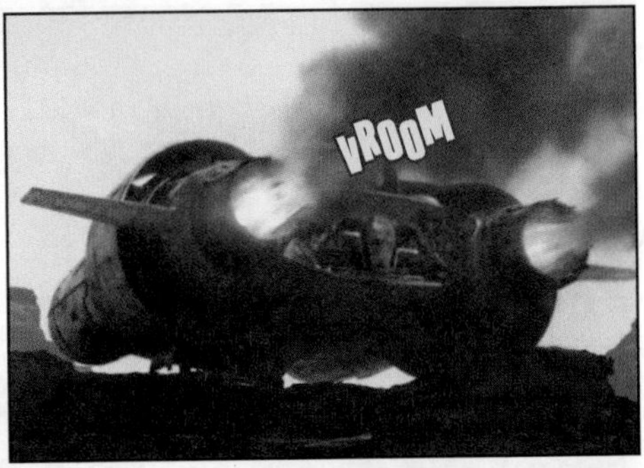
VROOM

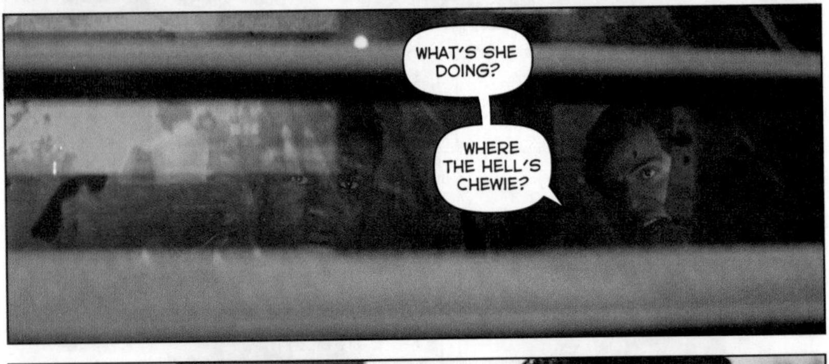
WHAT'S SHE DOING?
WHERE THE HELL'S CHEWIE?

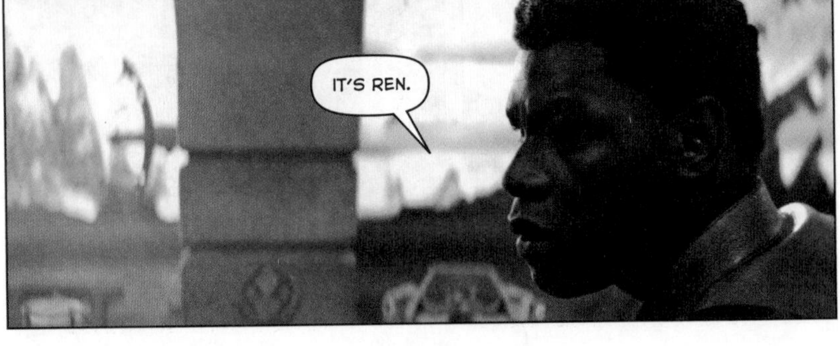
IT'S REN.

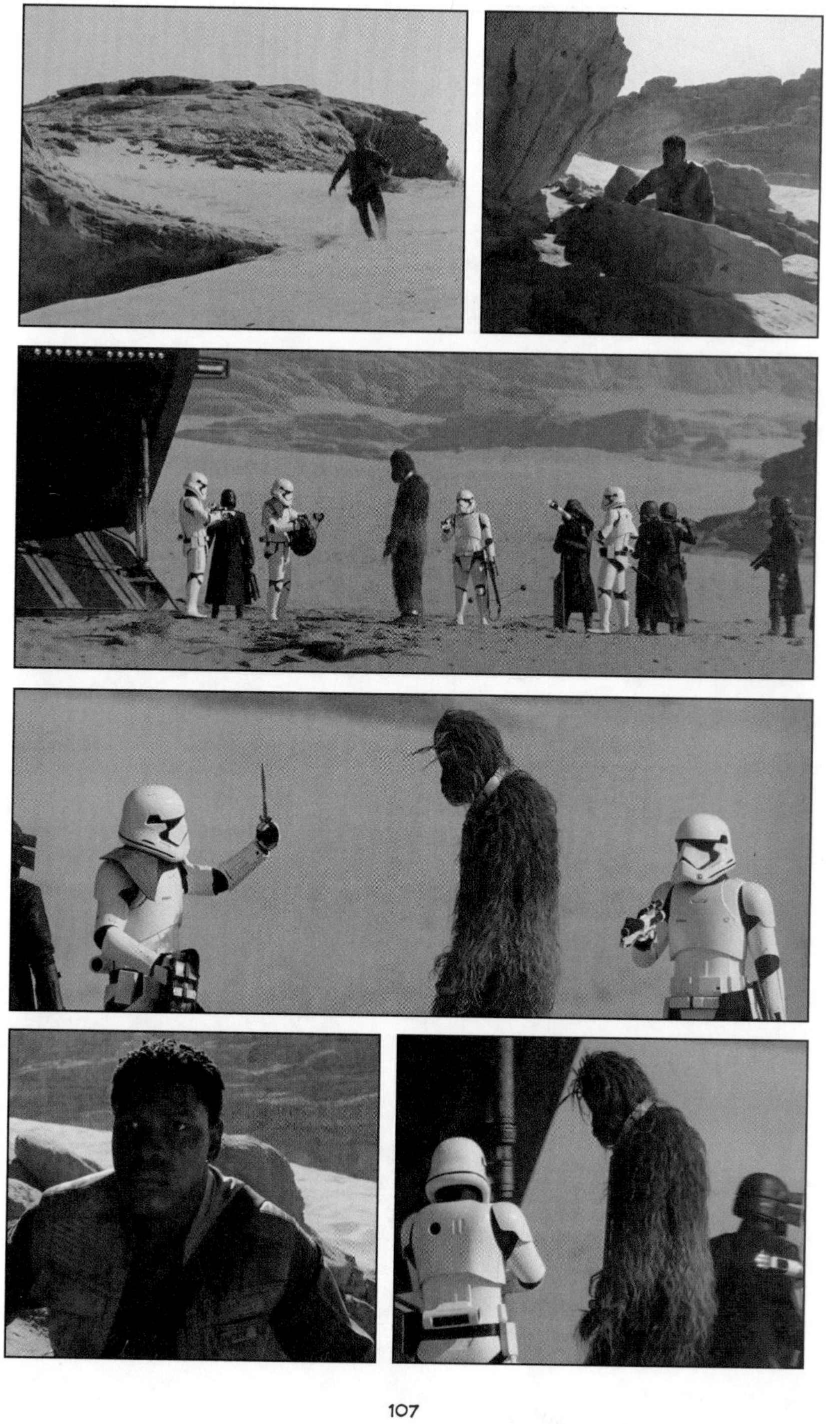

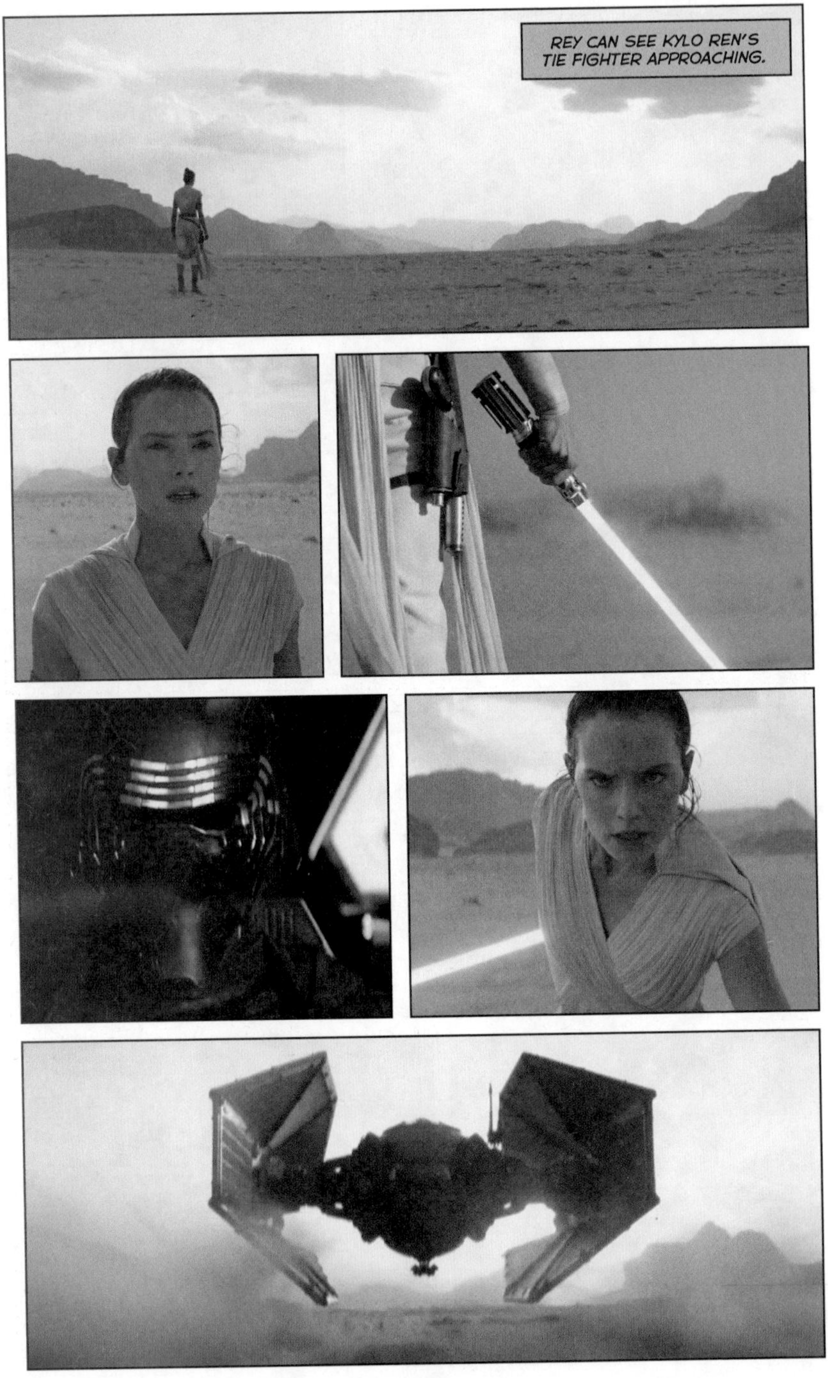
REY CAN SEE KYLO REN'S
TIE FIGHTER APPROACHING.

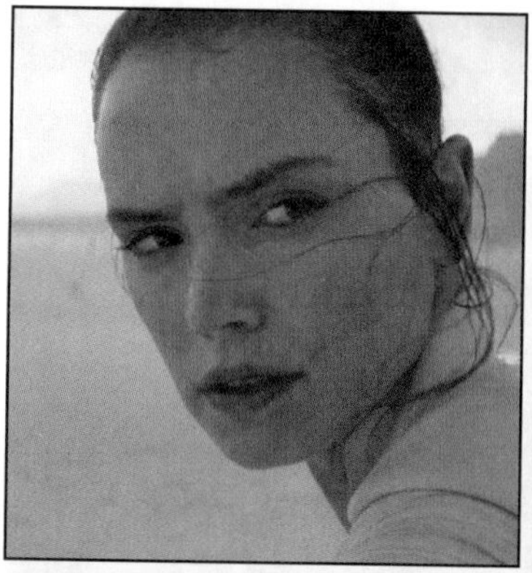
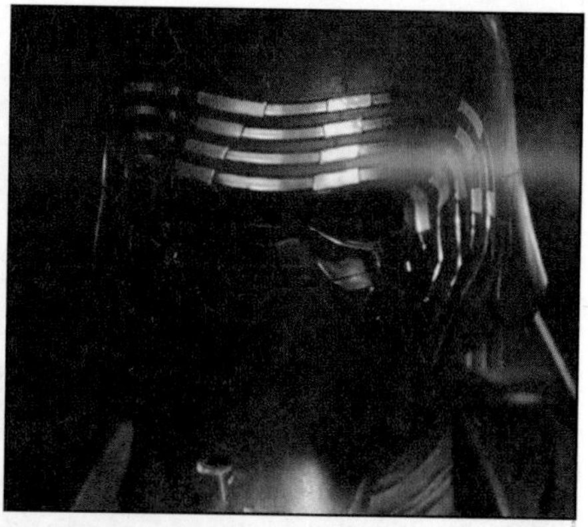
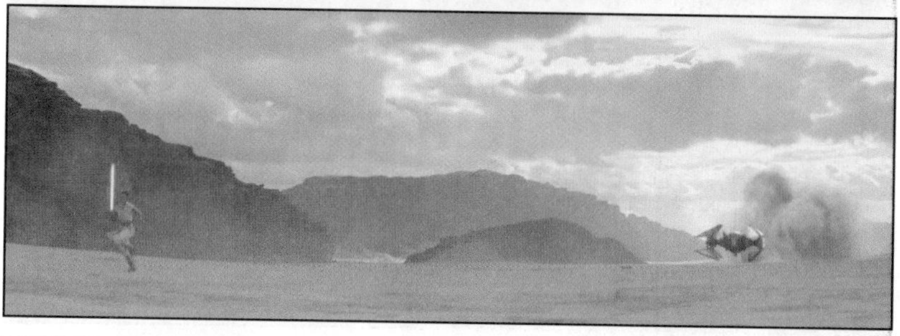
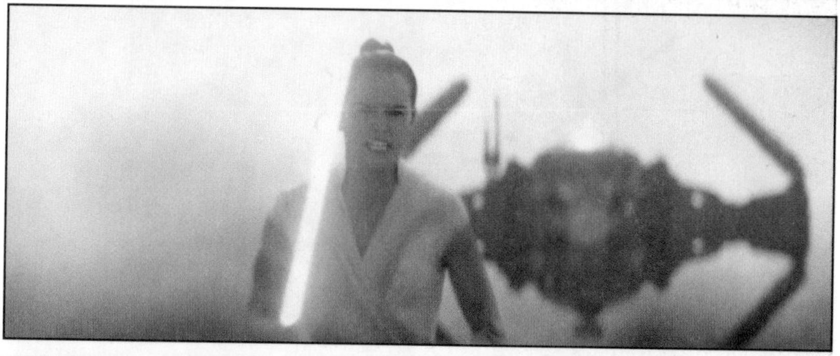
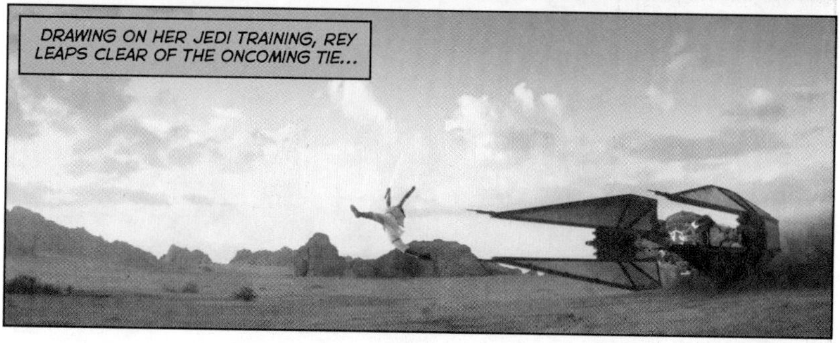
DRAWING ON HER JEDI TRAINING, REY
LEAPS CLEAR OF THE ONCOMING TIE...

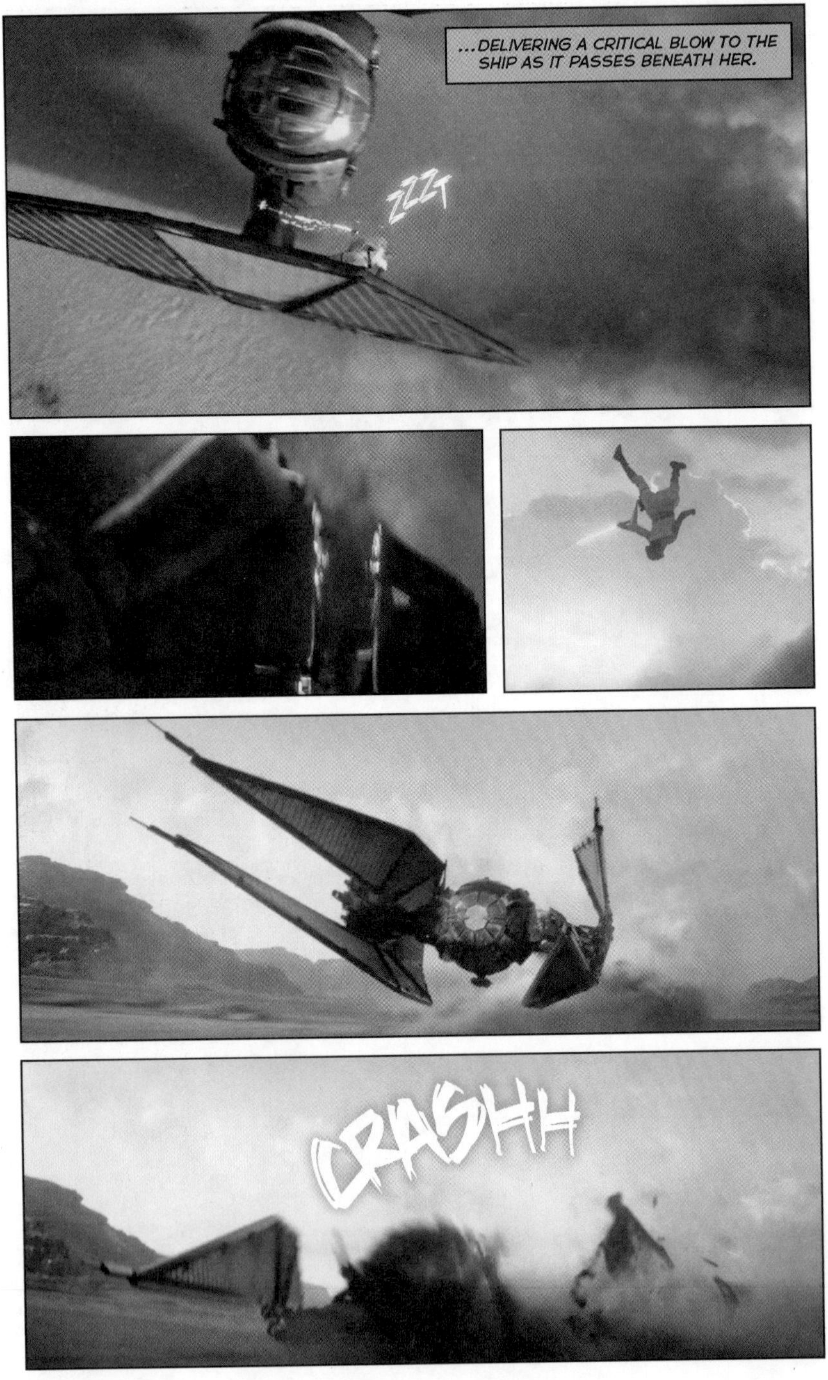
...DELIVERING A CRITICAL BLOW TO THE SHIP AS IT PASSES BENEATH HER.
ZZZT
CRASHH

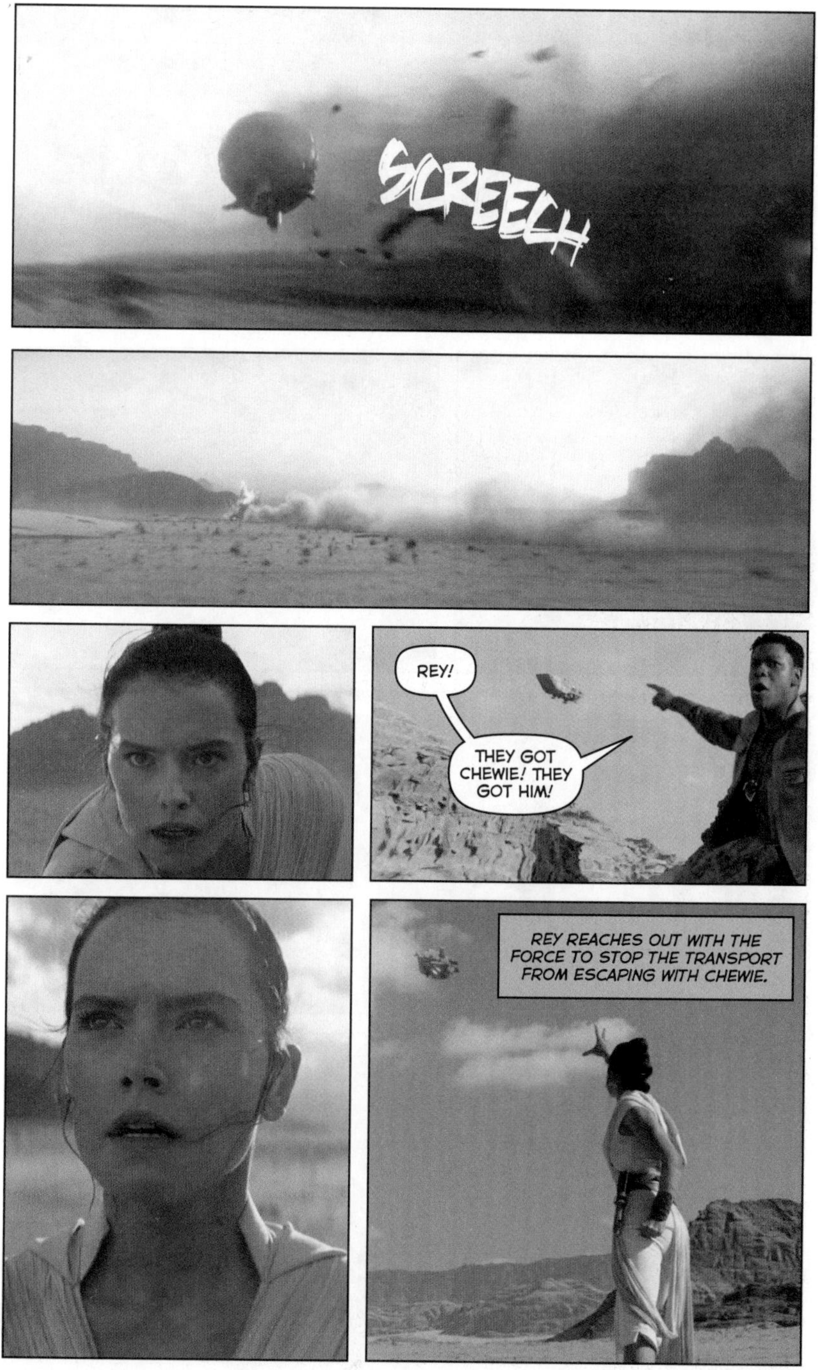
SCREECH
REY!
THEY GOT CHEWIE! THEY GOT HIM!
REY REACHES OUT WITH THE FORCE TO STOP THE TRANSPORT FROM ESCAPING WITH CHEWIE.

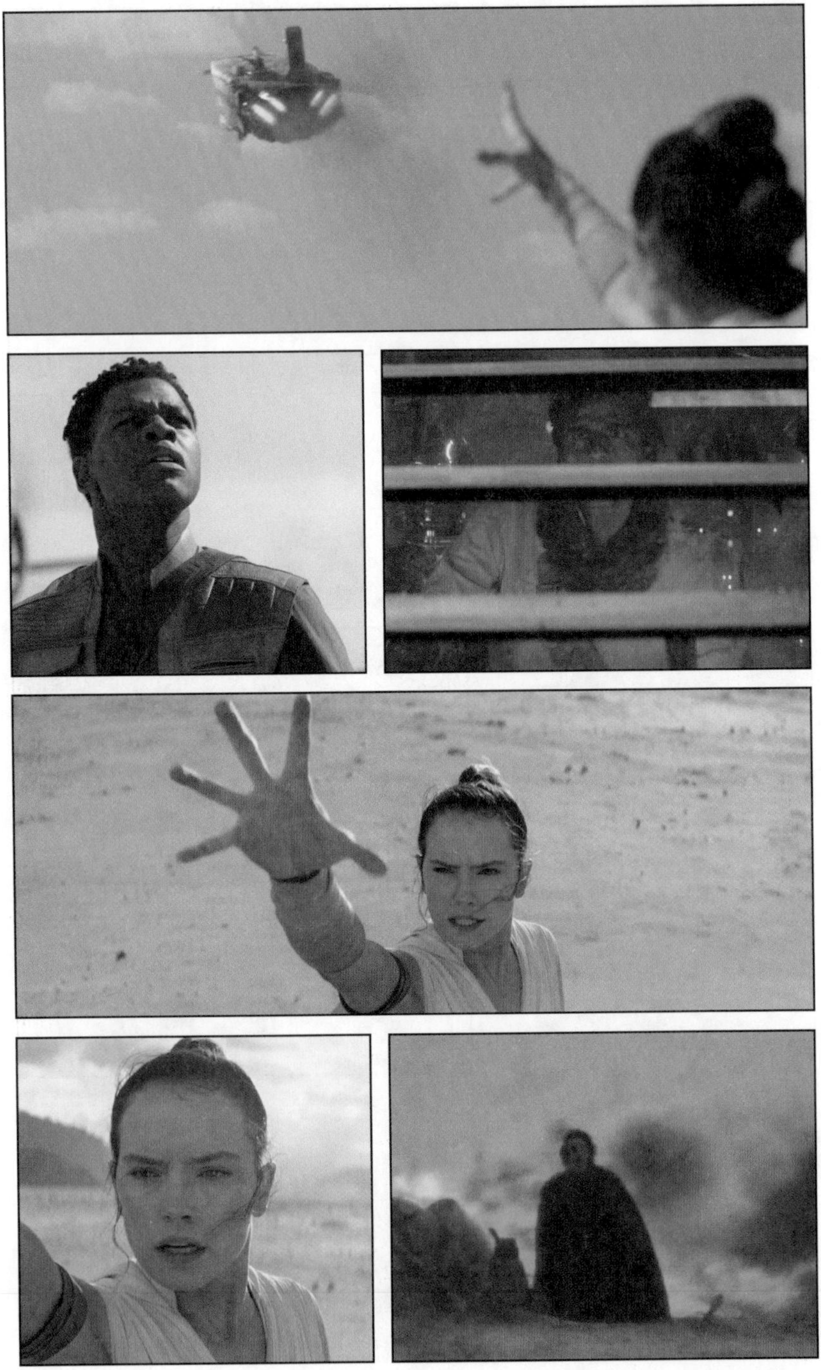

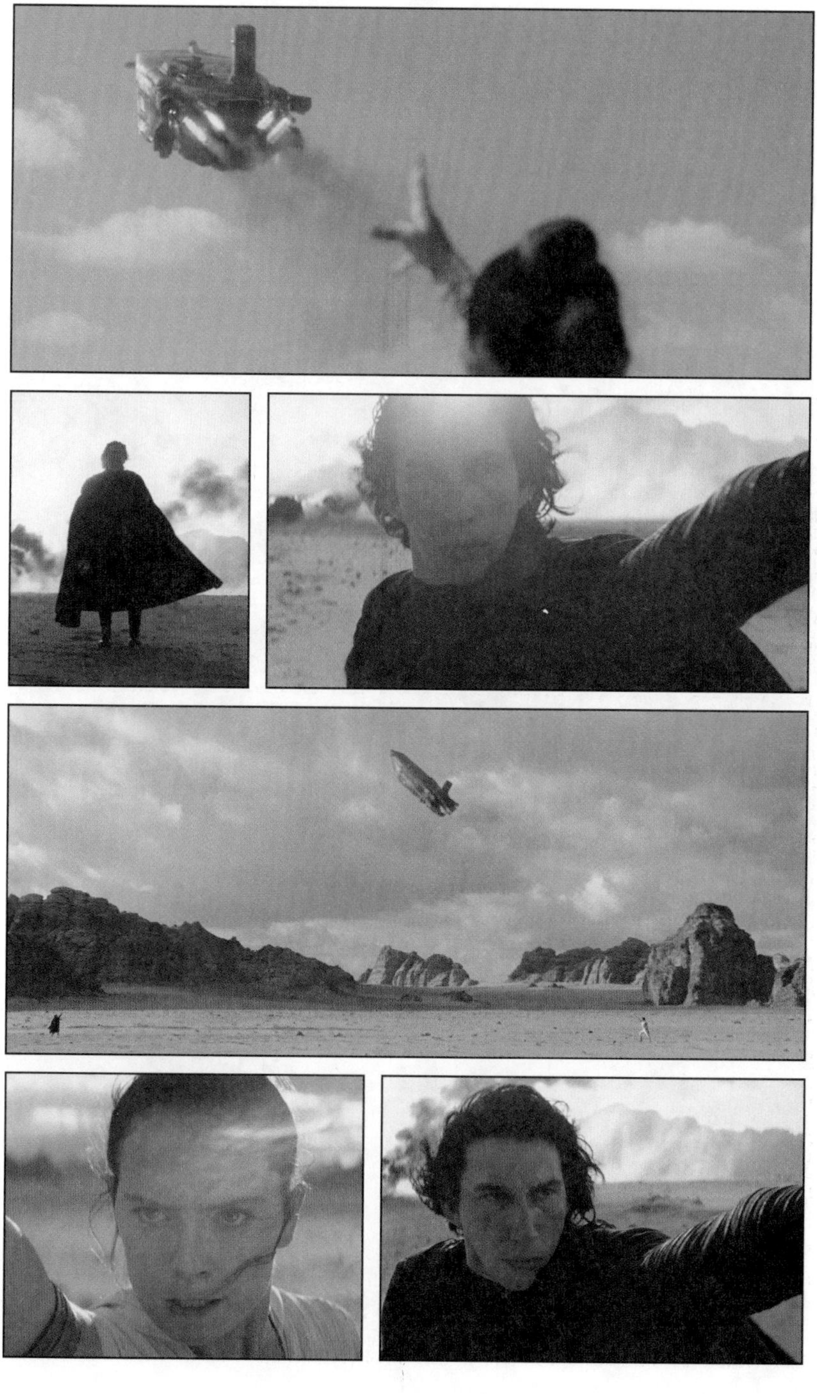

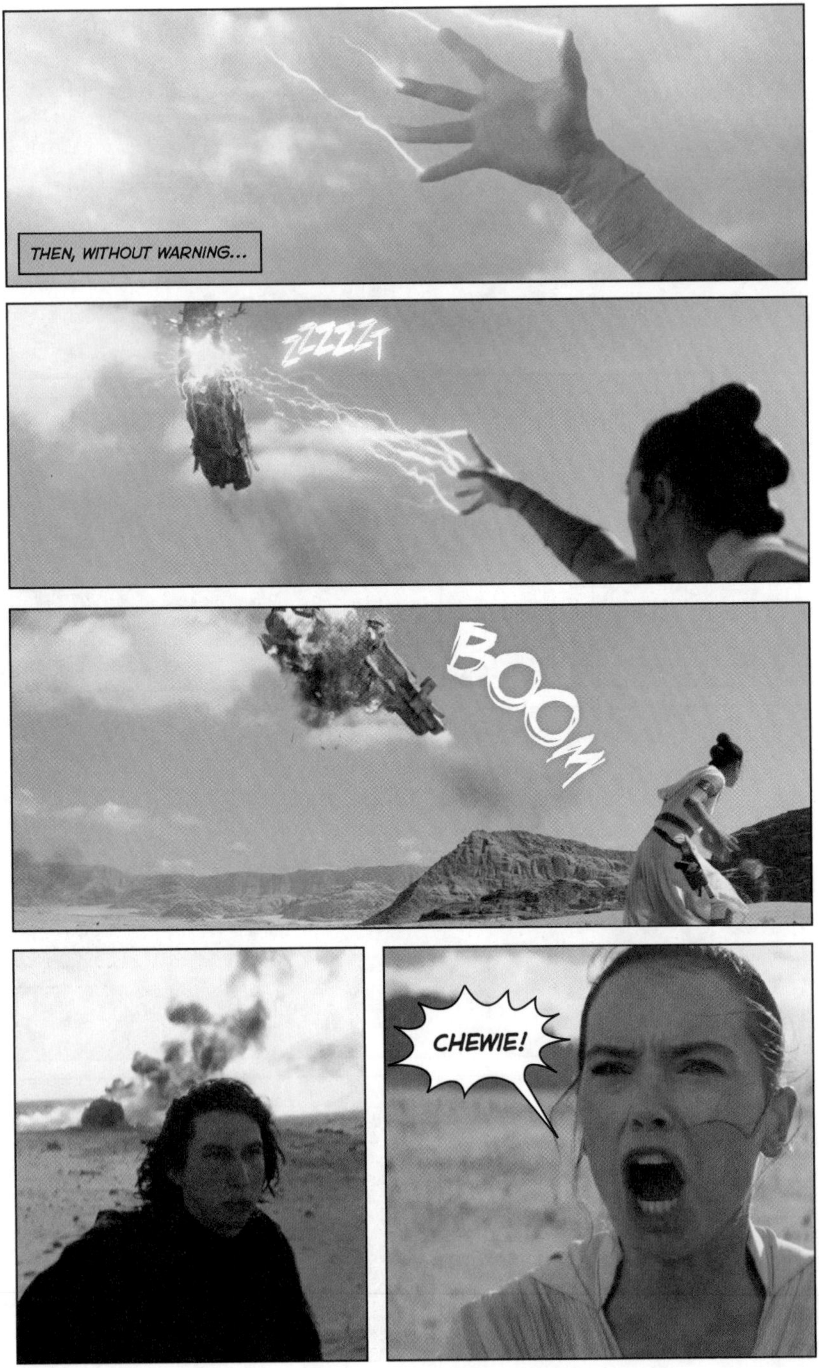
THEN, WITHOUT WARNING...
ZZZZZT
BOOM
CHEWIE!

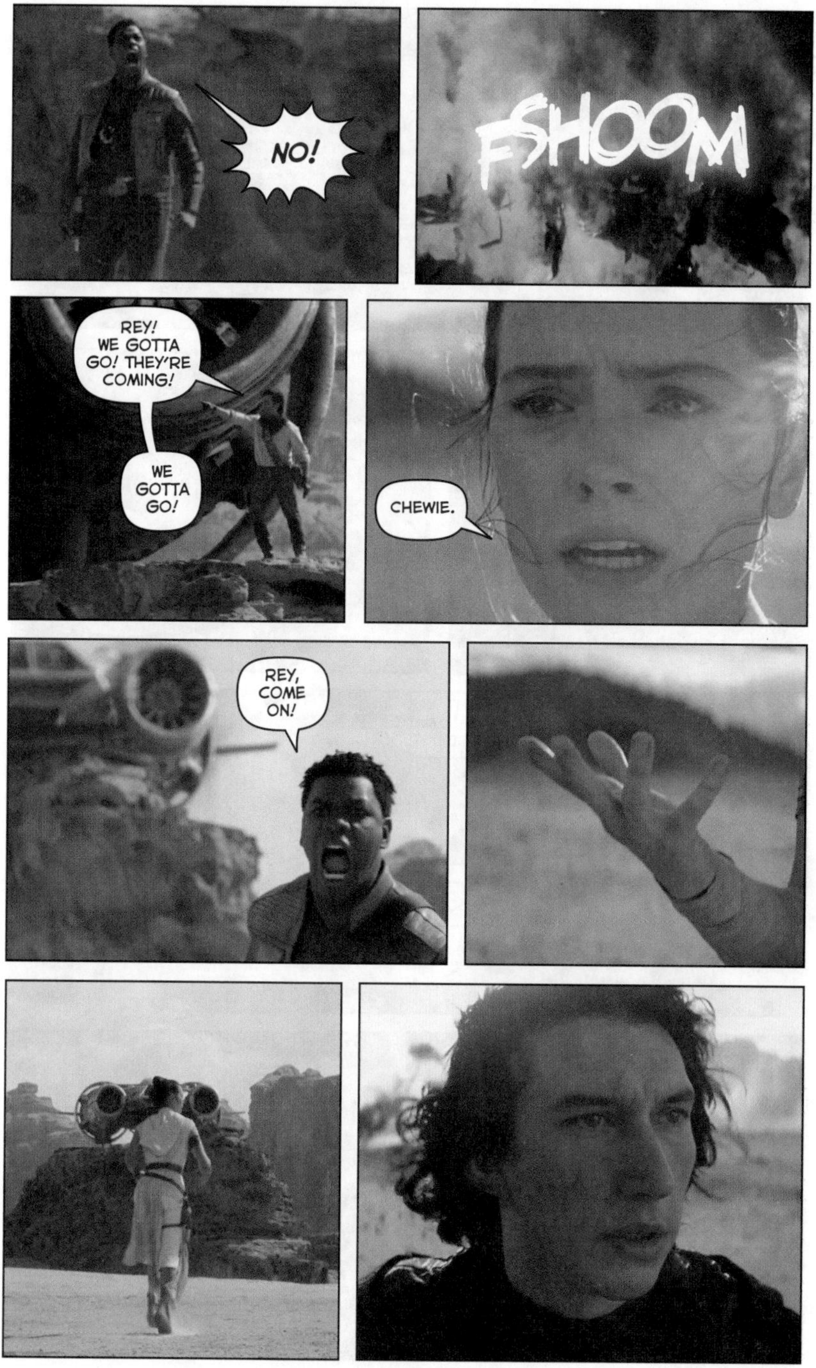
NO!
FSHOOM
REY! WE GOTTA GO! THEY'RE COMING!
WE GOTTA GO!
CHEWIE.
REY, COME ON!

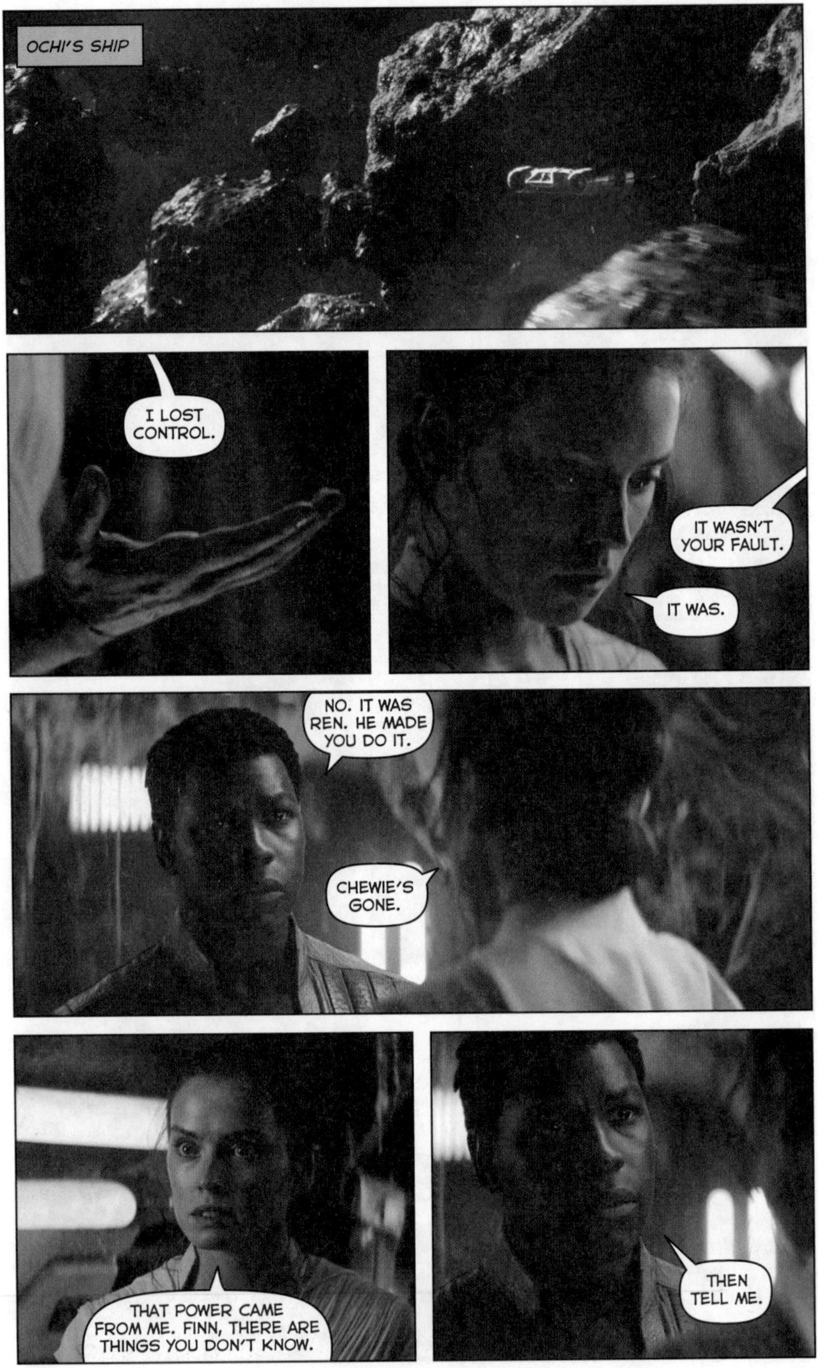
OCHI'S SHIP
I LOST CONTROL.
IT WASN'T YOUR FAULT.
IT WAS.
NO. IT WAS REN. HE MADE YOU DO IT.
CHEWIE'S GONE.
THAT POWER CAME FROM ME. FINN, THERE ARE THINGS YOU DON'T KNOW.
THEN TELL ME.

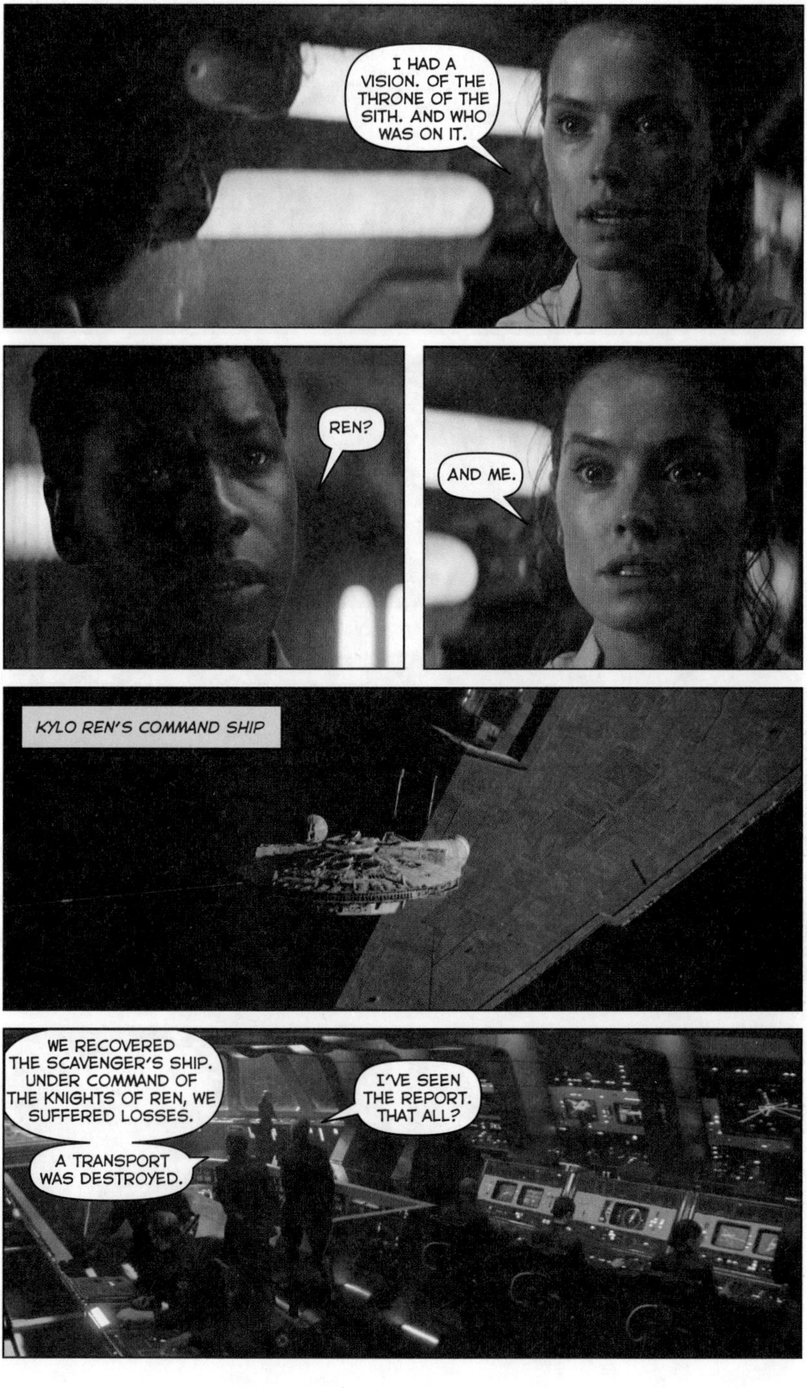
I HAD A VISION. OF THE THRONE OF THE SITH. AND WHO WAS ON IT.
REN?
AND ME.
KYLO REN'S COMMAND SHIP
WE RECOVERED THE SCAVENGER'S SHIP. UNDER COMMAND OF THE KNIGHTS OF REN, WE SUFFERED LOSSES.
A TRANSPORT WAS DESTROYED.
I'VE SEEN THE REPORT. THAT ALL?

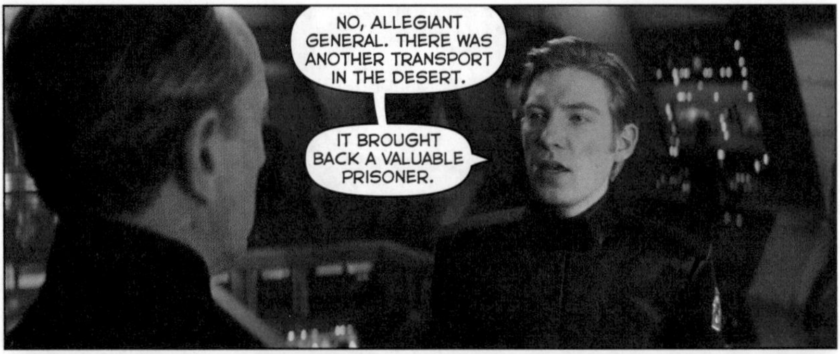
NO, ALLEGIANT GENERAL. THERE WAS ANOTHER TRANSPORT IN THE DESERT.
IT BROUGHT BACK A VALUABLE PRISONER.

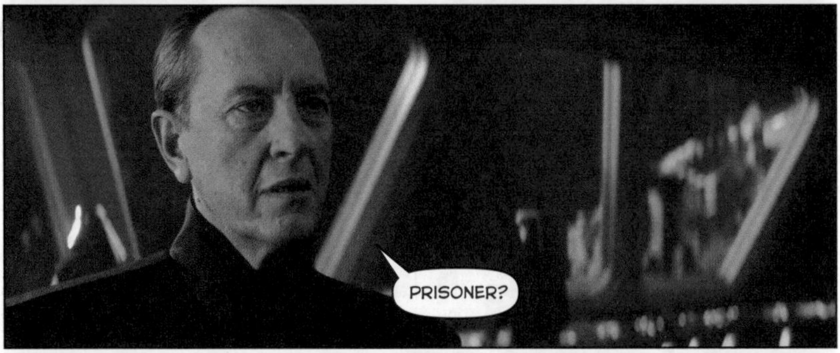
PRISONER?

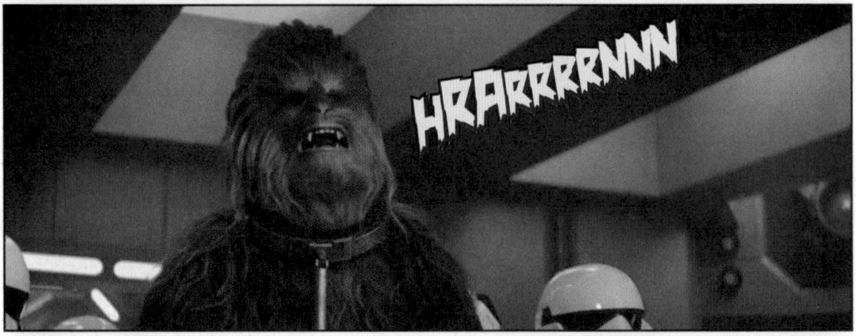
HRARRRRNNN

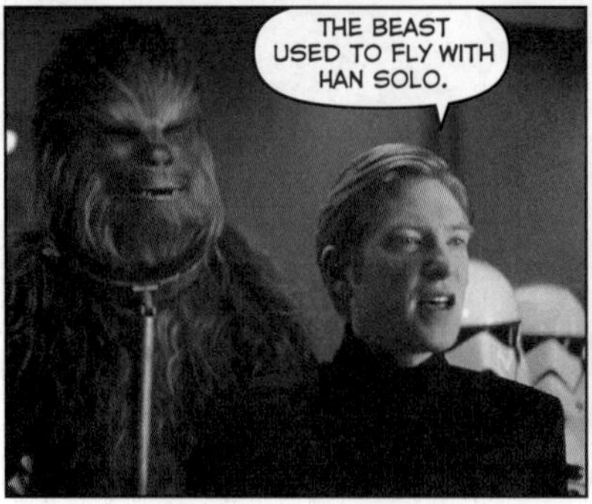
THE BEAST USED TO FLY WITH HAN SOLO.

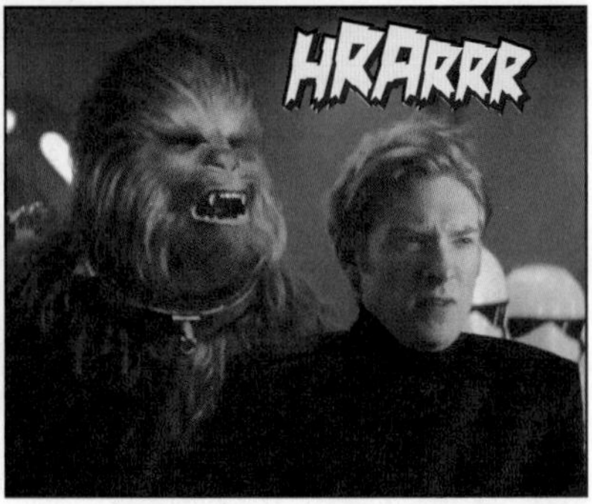
HRARRR

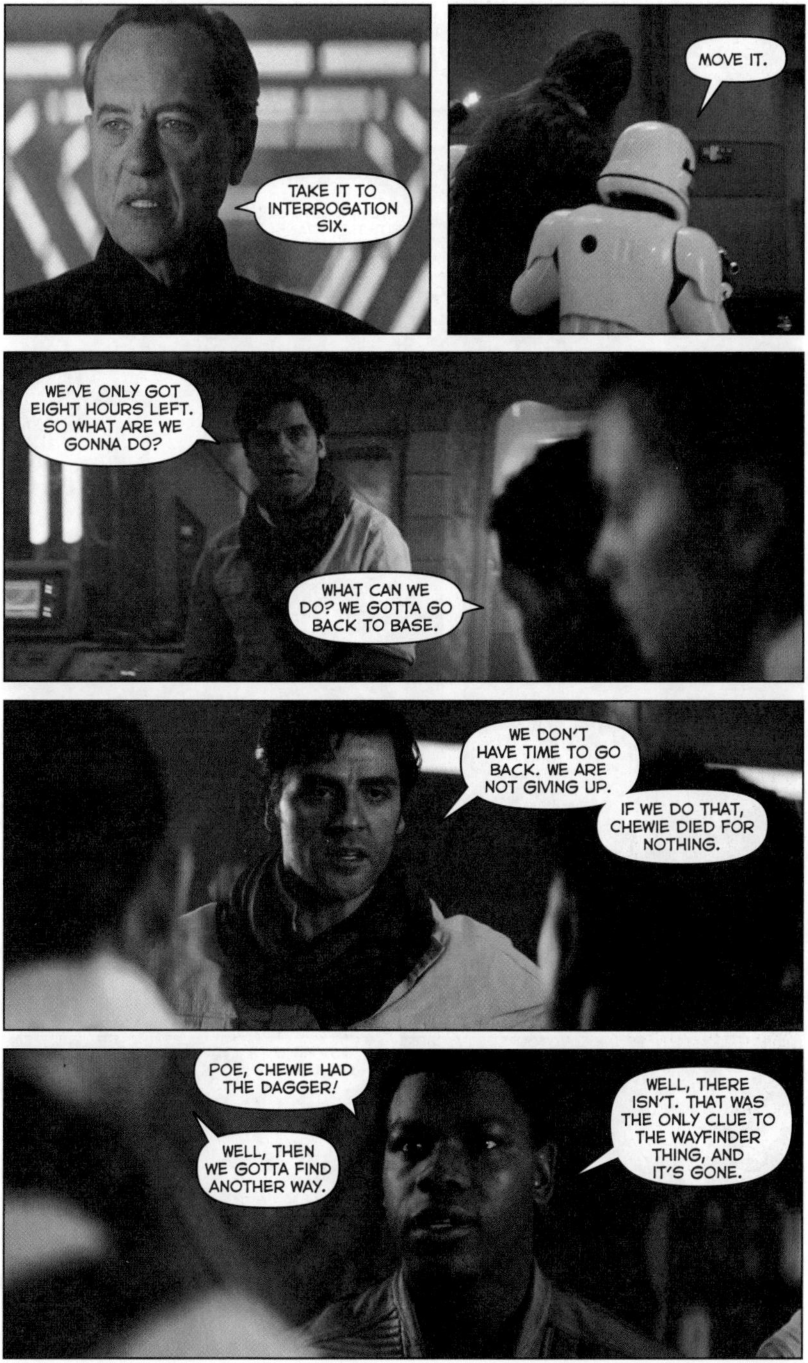
TAKE IT TO INTERROGATION SIX.
MOVE IT.
WE'VE ONLY GOT EIGHT HOURS LEFT. SO WHAT ARE WE GONNA DO?
WHAT CAN WE DO? WE GOTTA GO BACK TO BASE.
WE DON'T HAVE TIME TO GO BACK. WE ARE NOT GIVING UP.
IF WE DO THAT, CHEWIE DIED FOR NOTHING.
POE, CHEWIE HAD THE DAGGER!
WELL, THEN WE GOTTA FIND ANOTHER WAY.
WELL, THERE ISN'T. THAT WAS THE ONLY CLUE TO THE WAYFINDER THING, AND IT'S GONE.

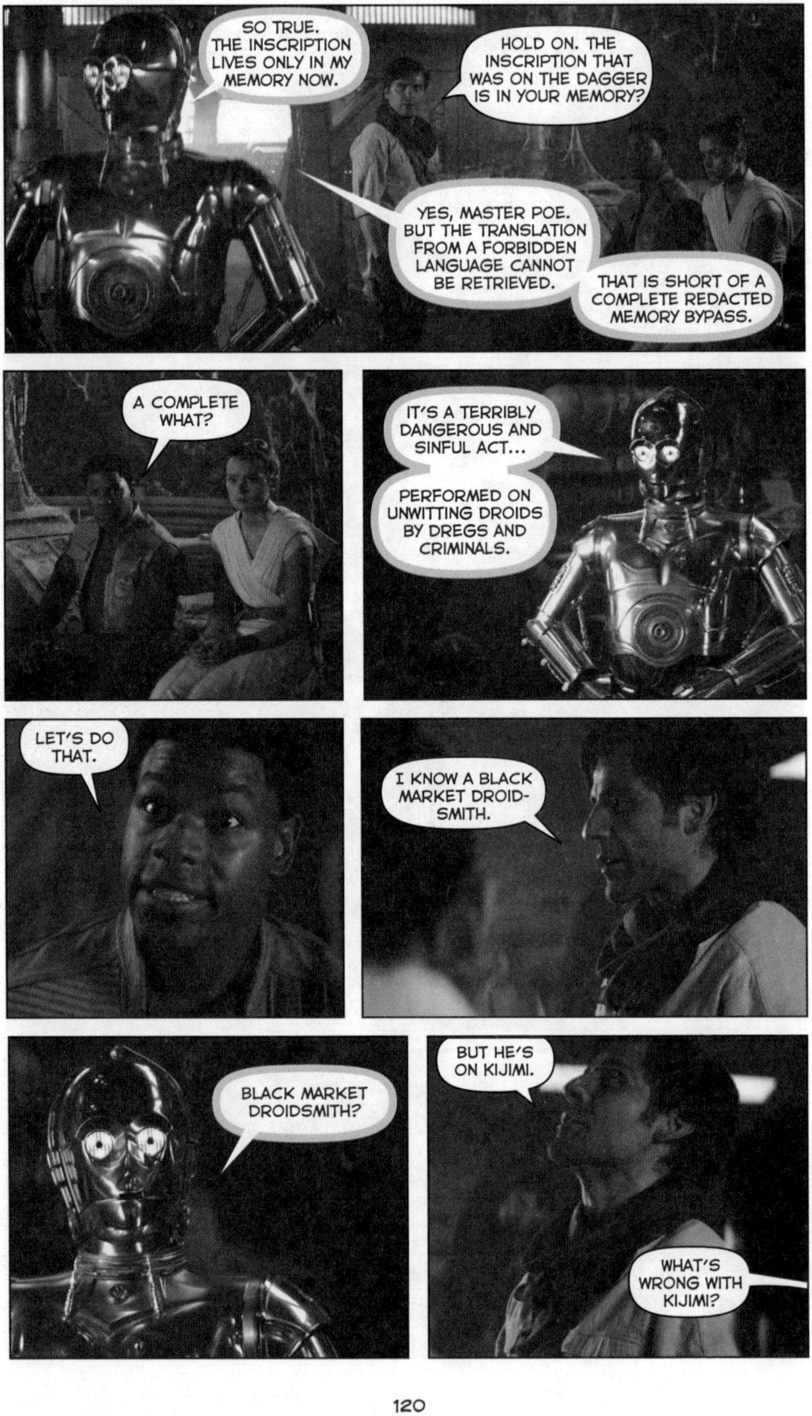
SO TRUE. THE INSCRIPTION LIVES ONLY IN MY MEMORY NOW.
HOLD ON. THE INSCRIPTION THAT WAS ON THE DAGGER IS IN YOUR MEMORY?
YES, MASTER POE. BUT THE TRANSLATION FROM A FORBIDDEN LANGUAGE CANNOT BE RETRIEVED.
THAT IS SHORT OF A COMPLETE REDACTED MEMORY BYPASS.
A COMPLETE WHAT?
IT'S A TERRIBLY DANGEROUS AND SINFUL ACT...
PERFORMED ON UNWITTING DROIDS BY DREGS AND CRIMINALS.
LET'S DO THAT.
I KNOW A BLACK MARKET DROID-SMITH.
BLACK MARKET DROIDSMITH?
BUT HE'S ON KIJIMI.
WHAT'S WRONG WITH KIJIMI?

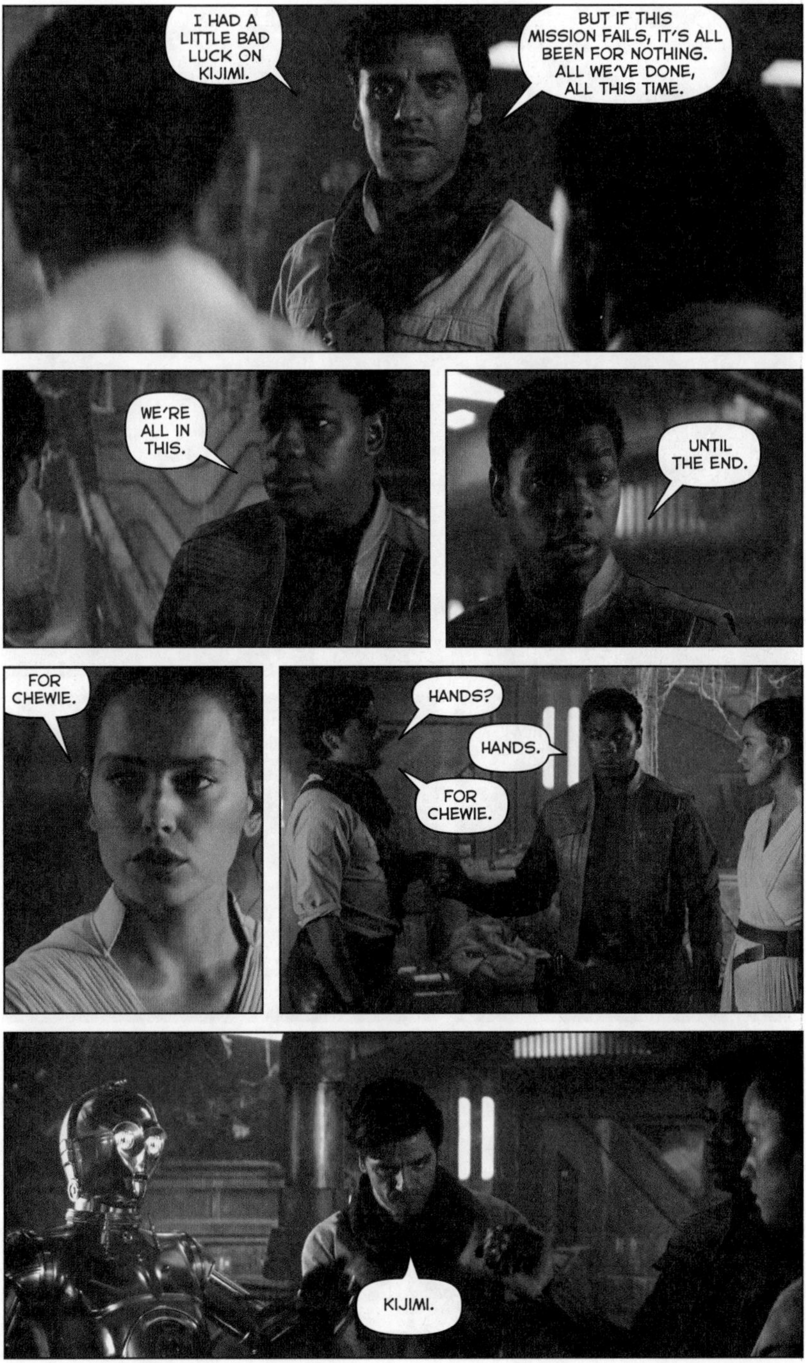
I HAD A LITTLE BAD LUCK ON KIJIMI.
BUT IF THIS MISSION FAILS, IT'S ALL BEEN FOR NOTHING. ALL WE'VE DONE, ALL THIS TIME.
WE'RE ALL IN THIS.
UNTIL THE END.
FOR CHEWIE.
HANDS?
HANDS.
FOR CHEWIE.
KIJIMI.

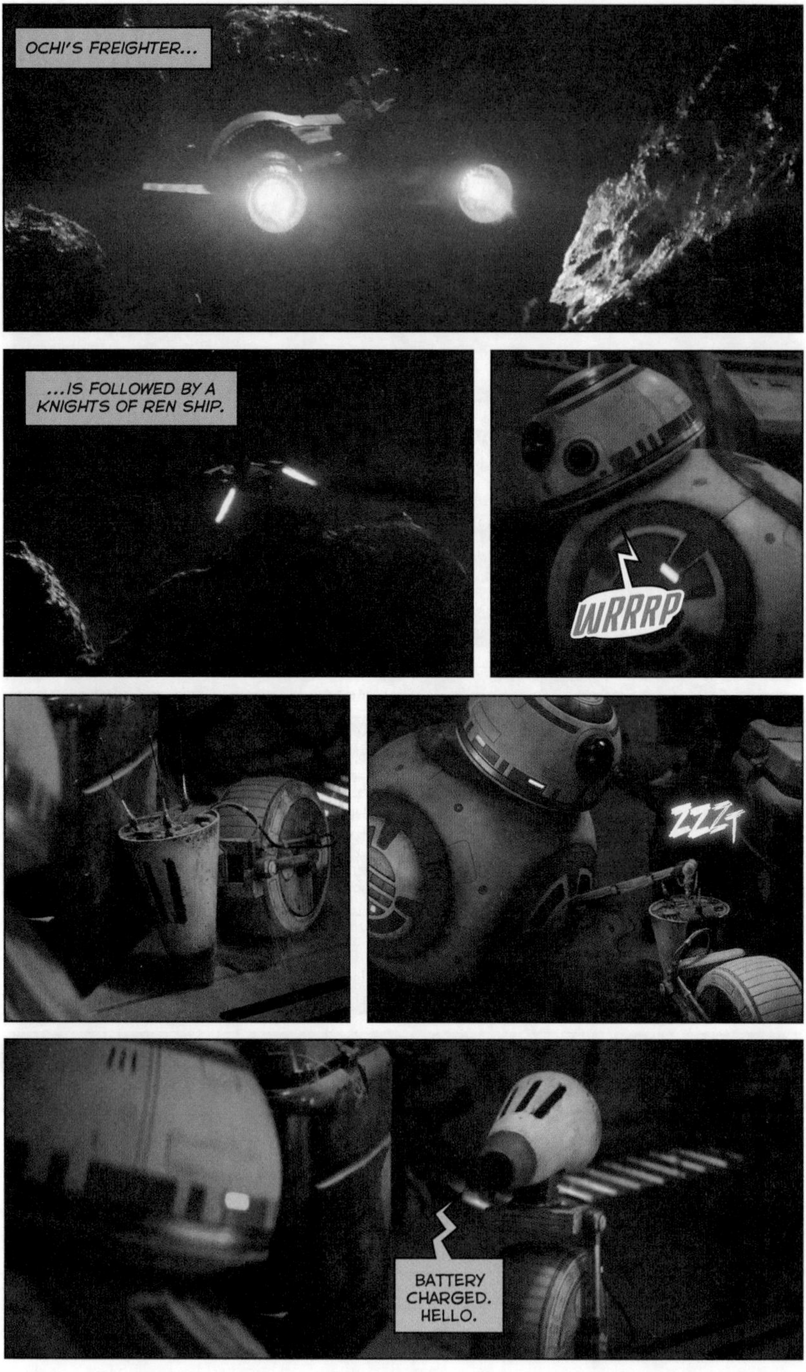
OCHI'S FREIGHTER...
...IS FOLLOWED BY A KNIGHTS OF REN SHIP.
WRRRP
ZZZT
BATTERY CHARGED. HELLO.

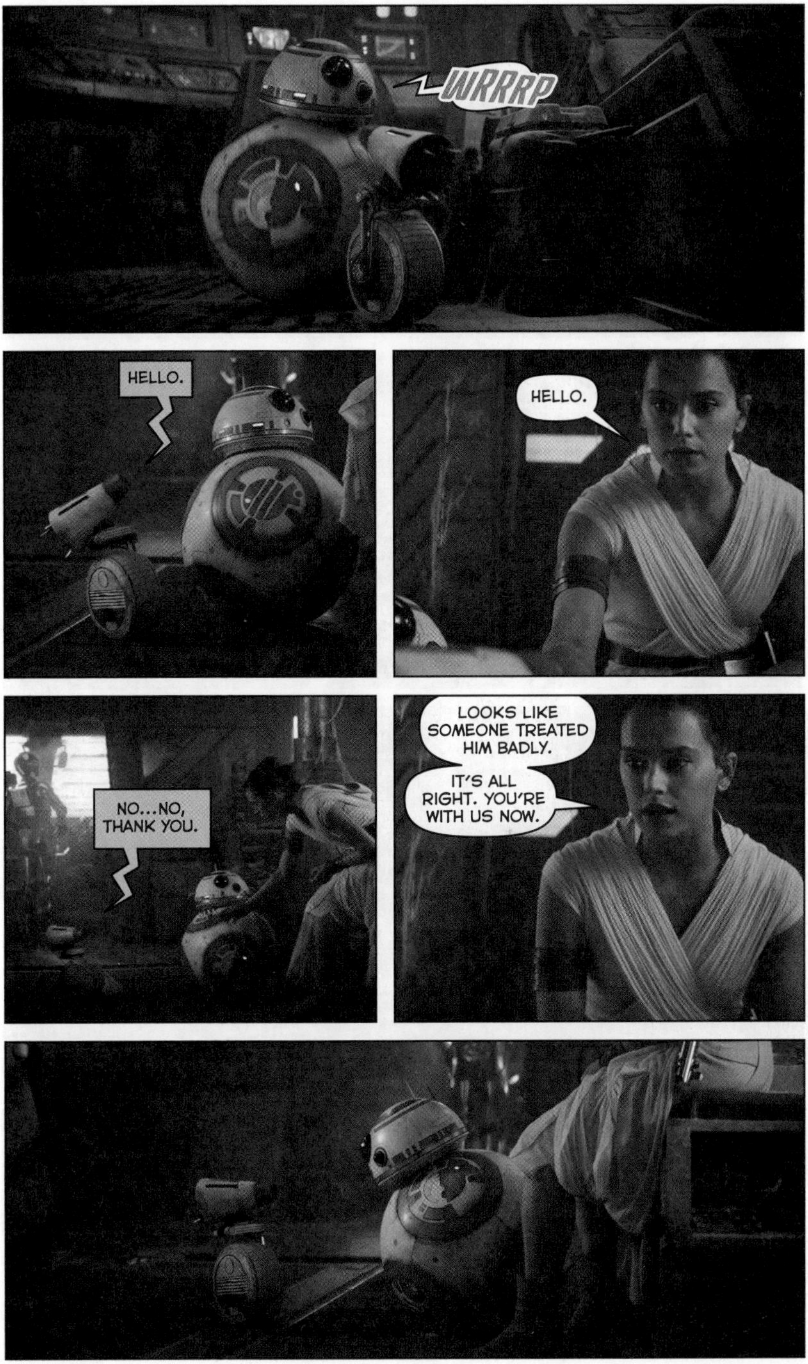

WRRRP
HELLO.
HELLO.
NO...NO, THANK YOU.
LOOKS LIKE SOMEONE TREATED HIM BADLY.
IT'S ALL RIGHT. YOU'RE WITH US NOW.

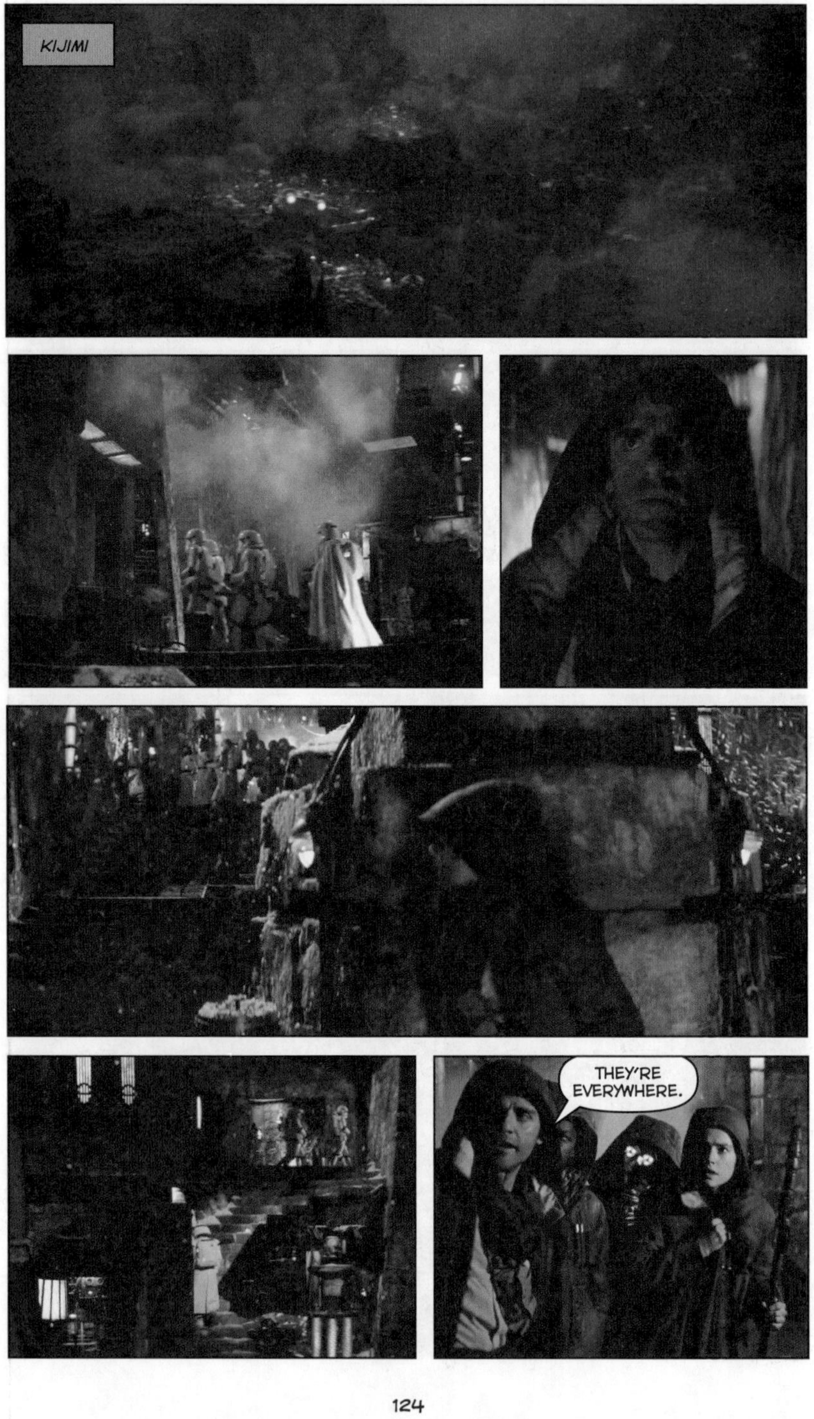
KIJIMI
THEY'RE EVERYWHERE.

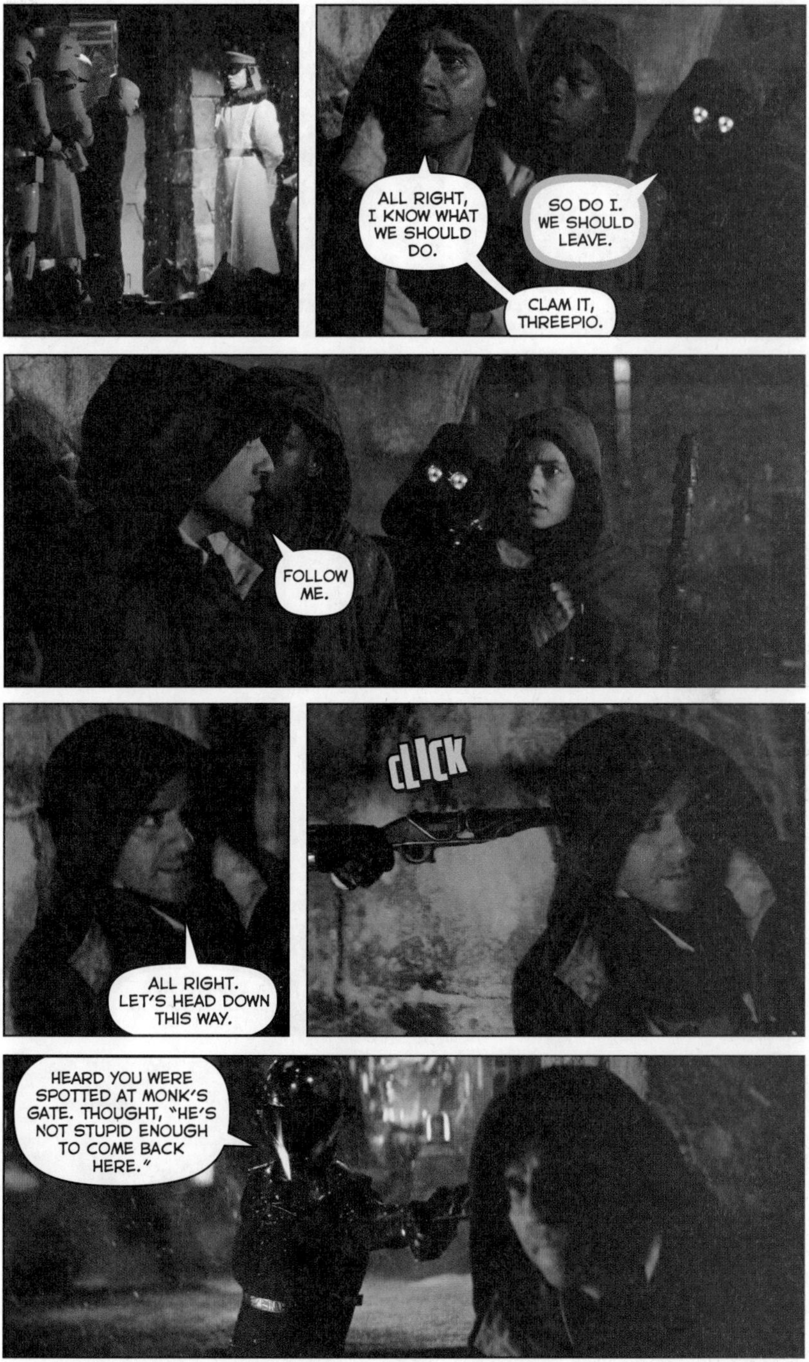
ALL RIGHT, I KNOW WHAT WE SHOULD DO.
SO DO I. WE SHOULD LEAVE.
CLAM IT, THREEPIO.
FOLLOW ME.
ALL RIGHT. LET'S HEAD DOWN THIS WAY.
CLICK
HEARD YOU WERE SPOTTED AT MONK'S GATE. THOUGHT, "HE'S NOT STUPID ENOUGH TO COME BACK HERE."

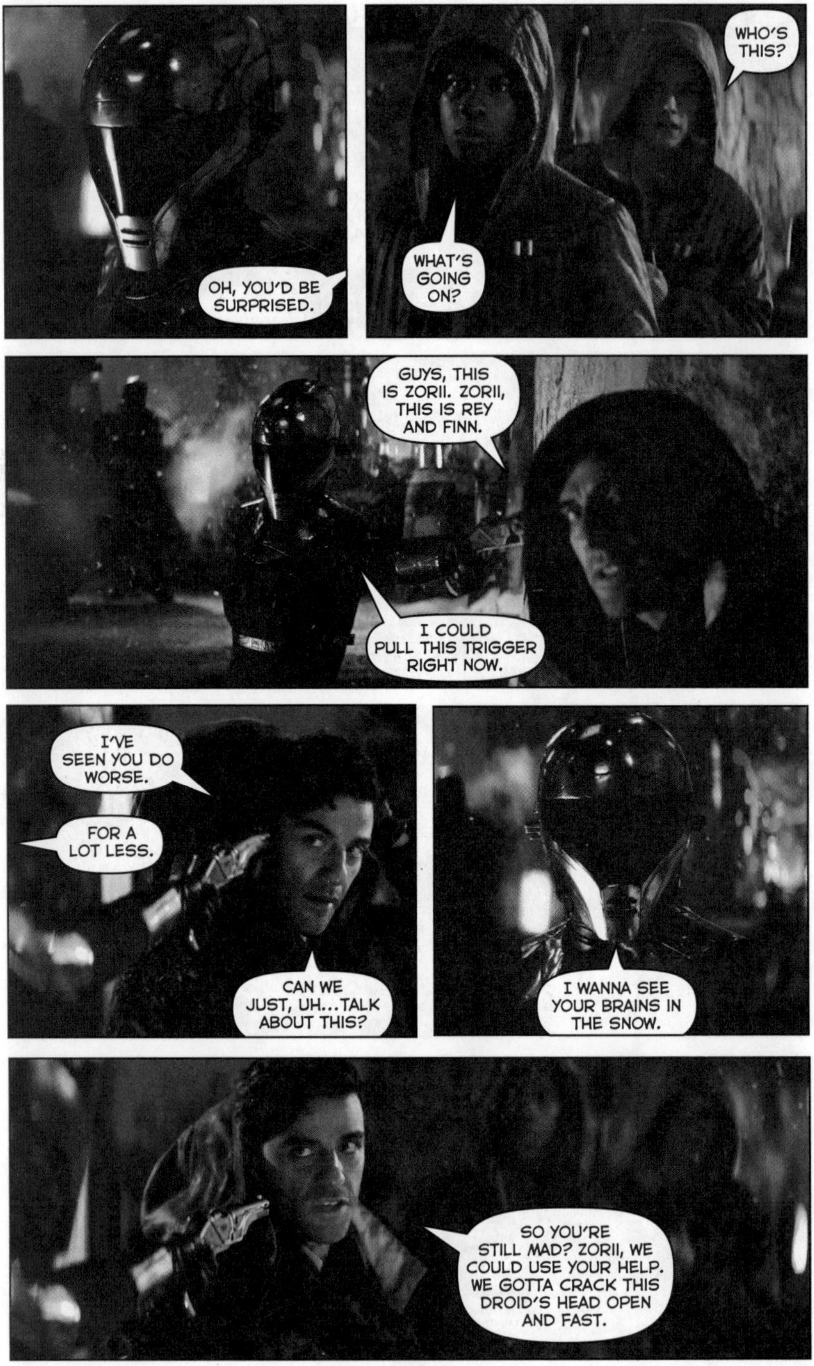
OH, YOU'D BE SURPRISED.
WHO'S THIS?
WHAT'S GOING ON?
GUYS, THIS IS ZORII. ZORII, THIS IS REY AND FINN.
I COULD PULL THIS TRIGGER RIGHT NOW.
I'VE SEEN YOU DO WORSE.
FOR A LOT LESS.
CAN WE JUST, UH...TALK ABOUT THIS?
I WANNA SEE YOUR BRAINS IN THE SNOW.
SO YOU'RE STILL MAD? ZORII, WE COULD USE YOUR HELP. WE GOTTA CRACK THIS DROID'S HEAD OPEN AND FAST.

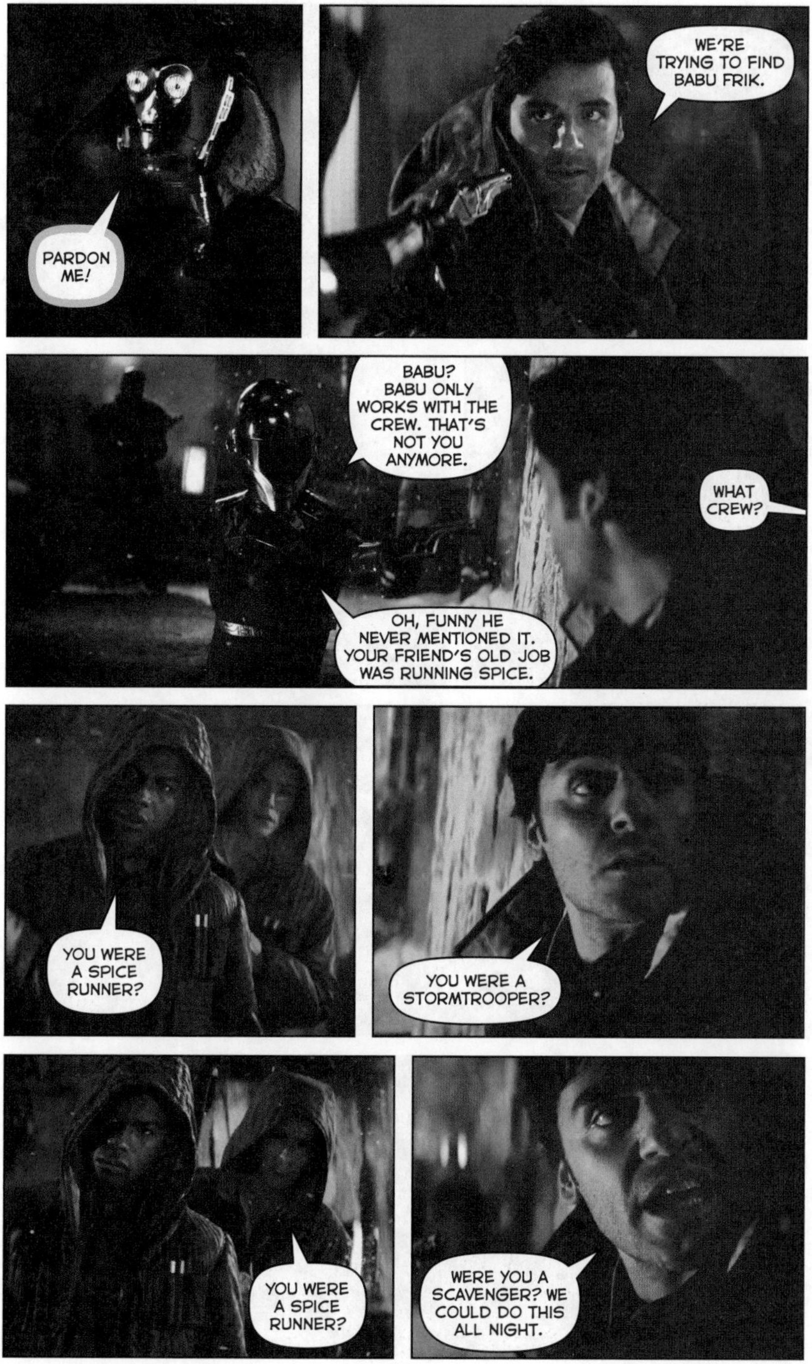
PARDON ME!
WE'RE TRYING TO FIND BABU FRIK.
BABU? BABU ONLY WORKS WITH THE CREW. THAT'S NOT YOU ANYMORE.
WHAT CREW?
OH, FUNNY HE NEVER MENTIONED IT. YOUR FRIEND'S OLD JOB WAS RUNNING SPICE.
YOU WERE A SPICE RUNNER?
YOU WERE A STORMTROOPER?
YOU WERE A SPICE RUNNER?
WERE YOU A SCAVENGER? WE COULD DO THIS ALL NIGHT.

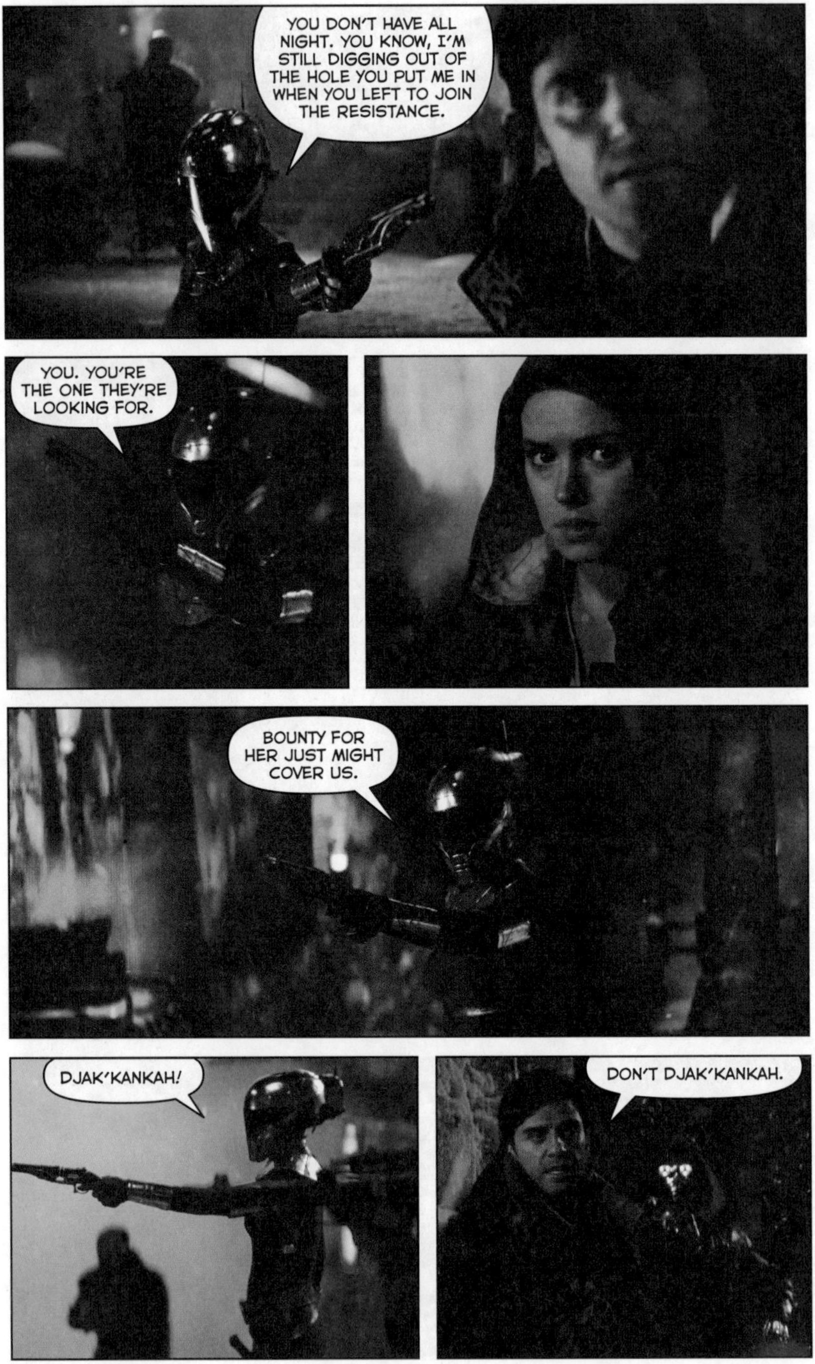
YOU DON'T HAVE ALL NIGHT. YOU KNOW, I'M STILL DIGGING OUT OF THE HOLE YOU PUT ME IN WHEN YOU LEFT TO JOIN THE RESISTANCE.
YOU. YOU'RE THE ONE THEY'RE LOOKING FOR.
BOUNTY FOR HER JUST MIGHT COVER US.
DJAK'KANKAH!
DON'T DJAK'KANKAH.

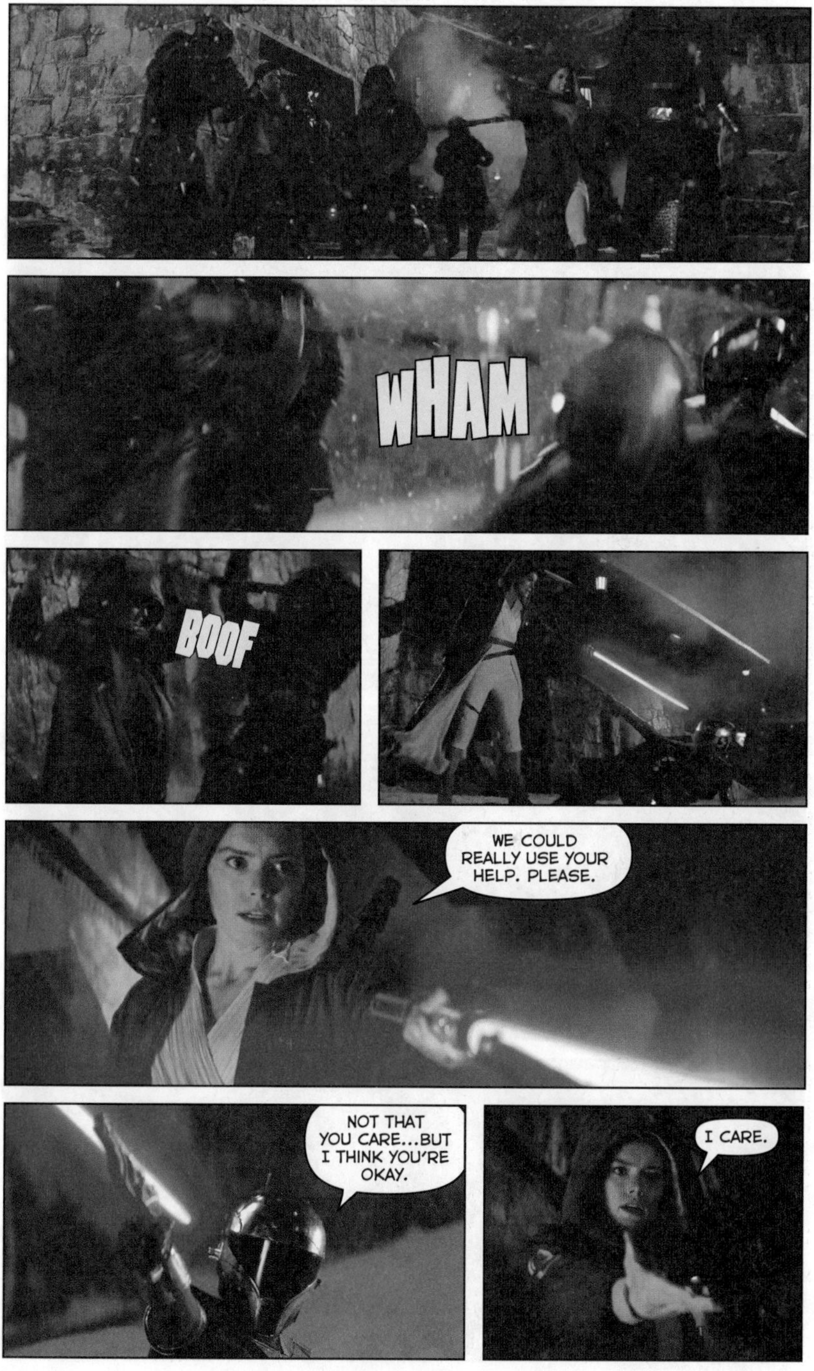
WHAM
BOOF
WE COULD REALLY USE YOUR HELP. PLEASE.
NOT THAT YOU CARE...BUT I THINK YOU'RE OKAY.
I CARE.

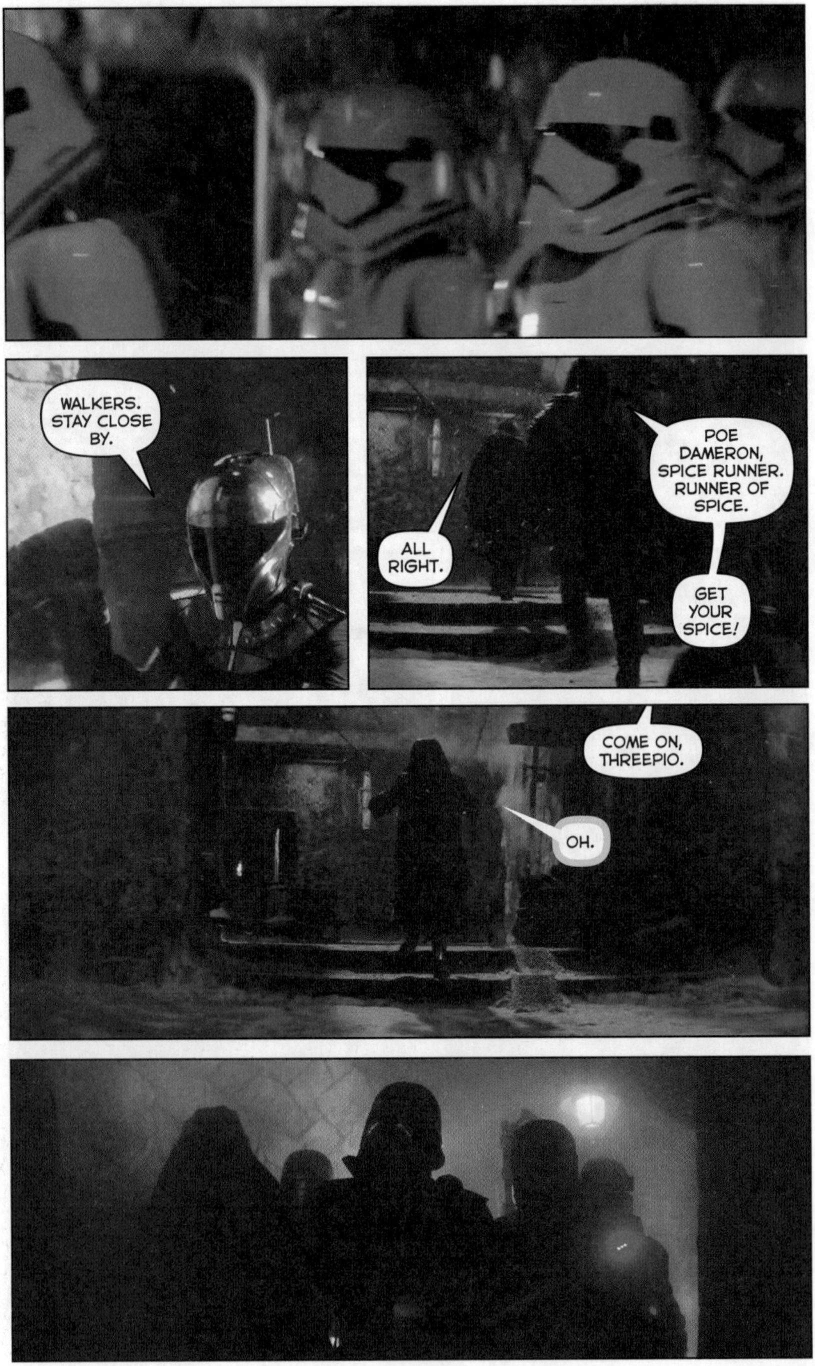
WALKERS. STAY CLOSE BY.
POE DAMERON, SPICE RUNNER. RUNNER OF SPICE.
GET YOUR SPICE!
ALL RIGHT.
COME ON, THREEPIO.
OH.

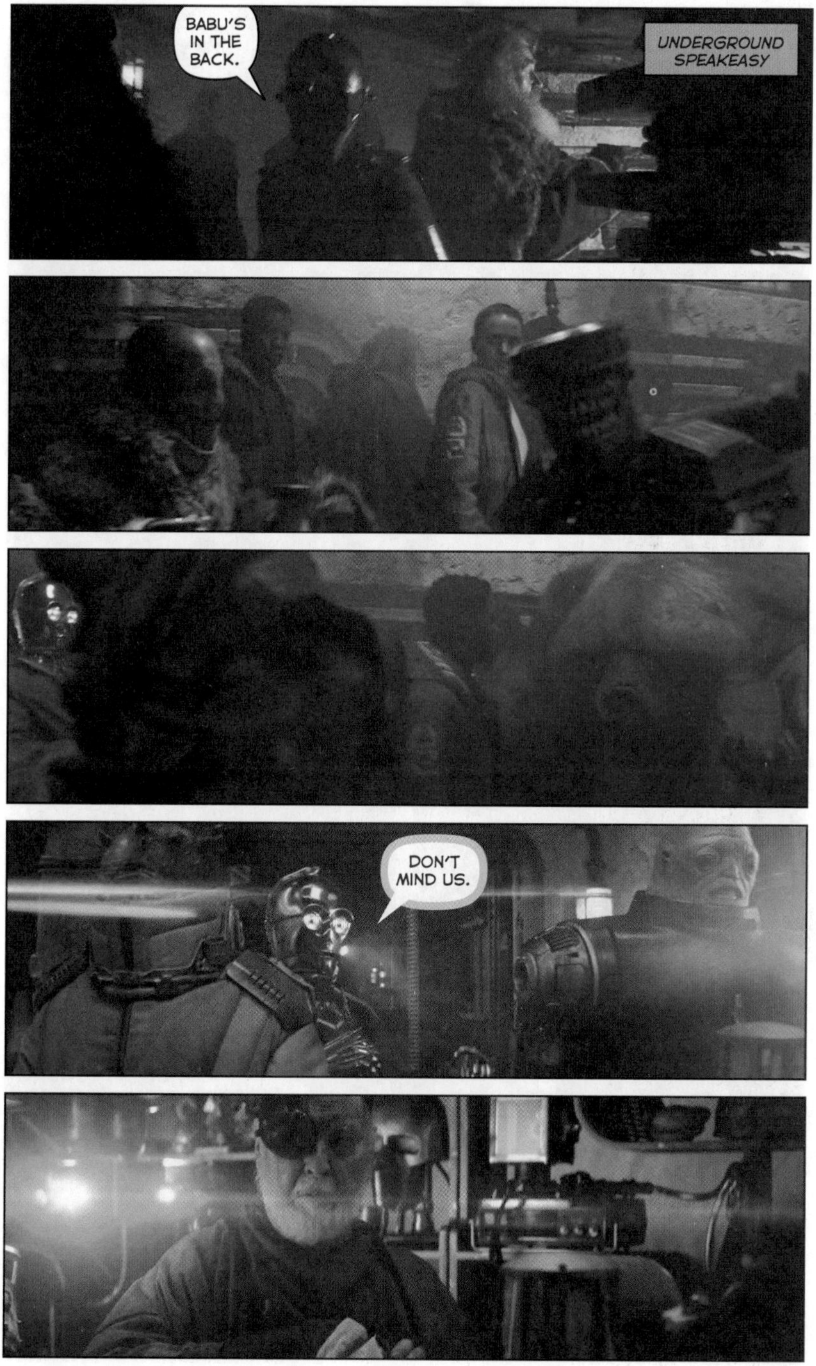
UNDERGROUND SPEAKEASY
BABU'S IN THE BACK.
DON'T MIND US.

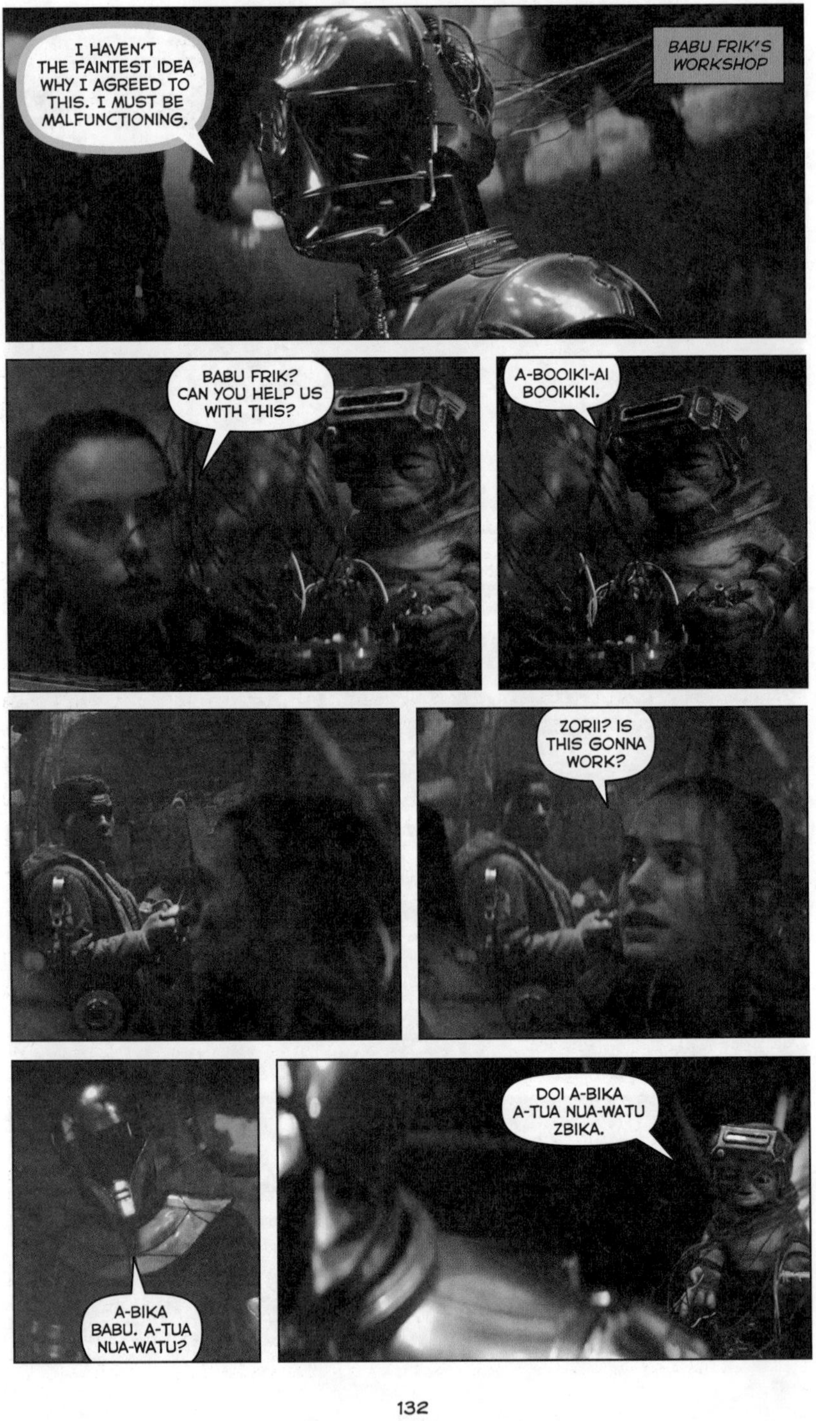
BABU FRIK'S WORKSHOP
I HAVEN'T THE FAINTEST IDEA WHY I AGREED TO THIS. I MUST BE MALFUNCTIONING.
BABU FRIK? CAN YOU HELP US WITH THIS?
A-BOOIKI-AI BOOIKIKI.
ZORII? IS THIS GONNA WORK?
A-BIKA BABU. A-TUA NUA-WATU?
DOI A-BIKA A-TUA NUA-WATU ZBIKA.

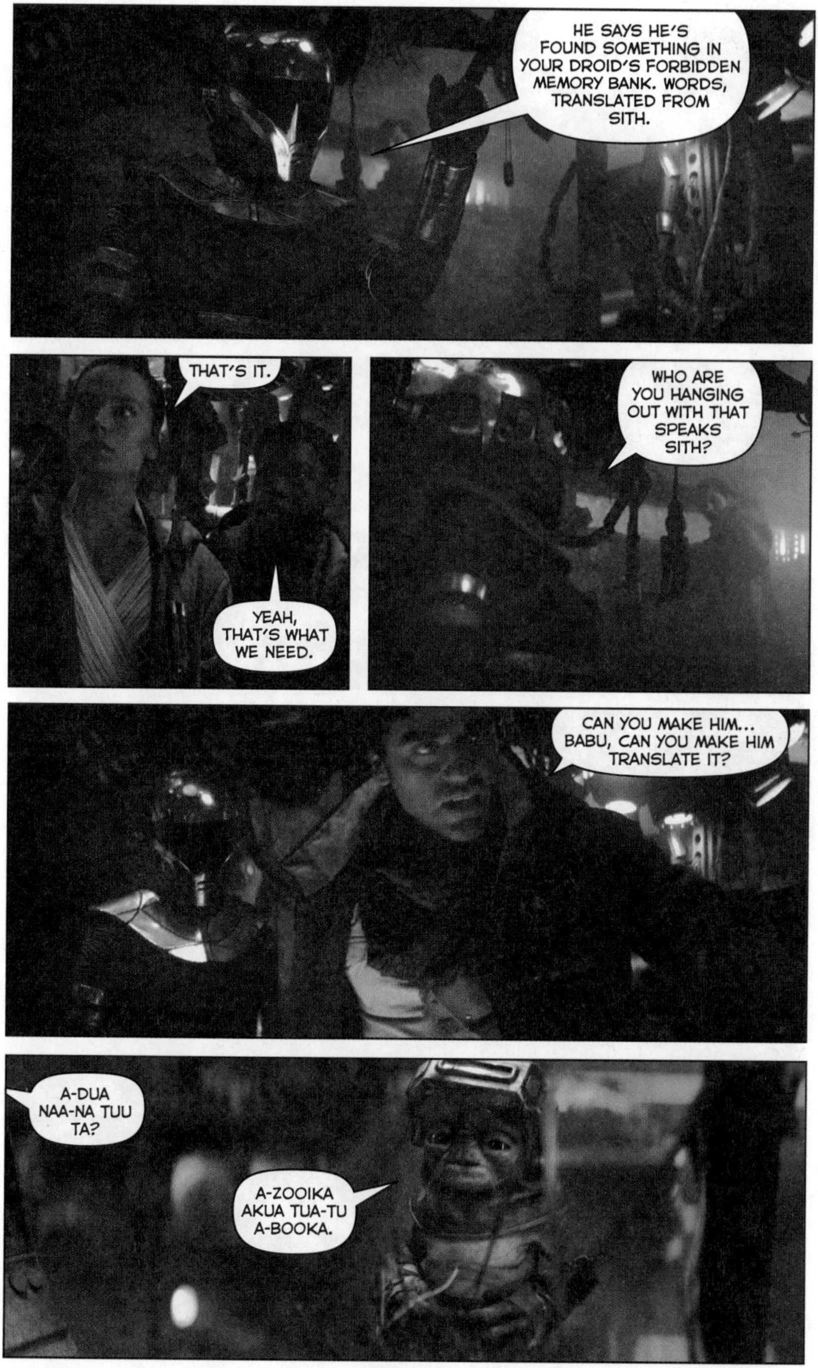
HE SAYS HE'S FOUND SOMETHING IN YOUR DROID'S FORBIDDEN MEMORY BANK. WORDS, TRANSLATED FROM SITH.
THAT'S IT.
YEAH, THAT'S WHAT WE NEED.
WHO ARE YOU HANGING OUT WITH THAT SPEAKS SITH?
CAN YOU MAKE HIM... BABU, CAN YOU MAKE HIM TRANSLATE IT?
A-DUA NAA-NA TUU TA?
A-ZOOIKA AKUA TUA-TU A-BOOKA.

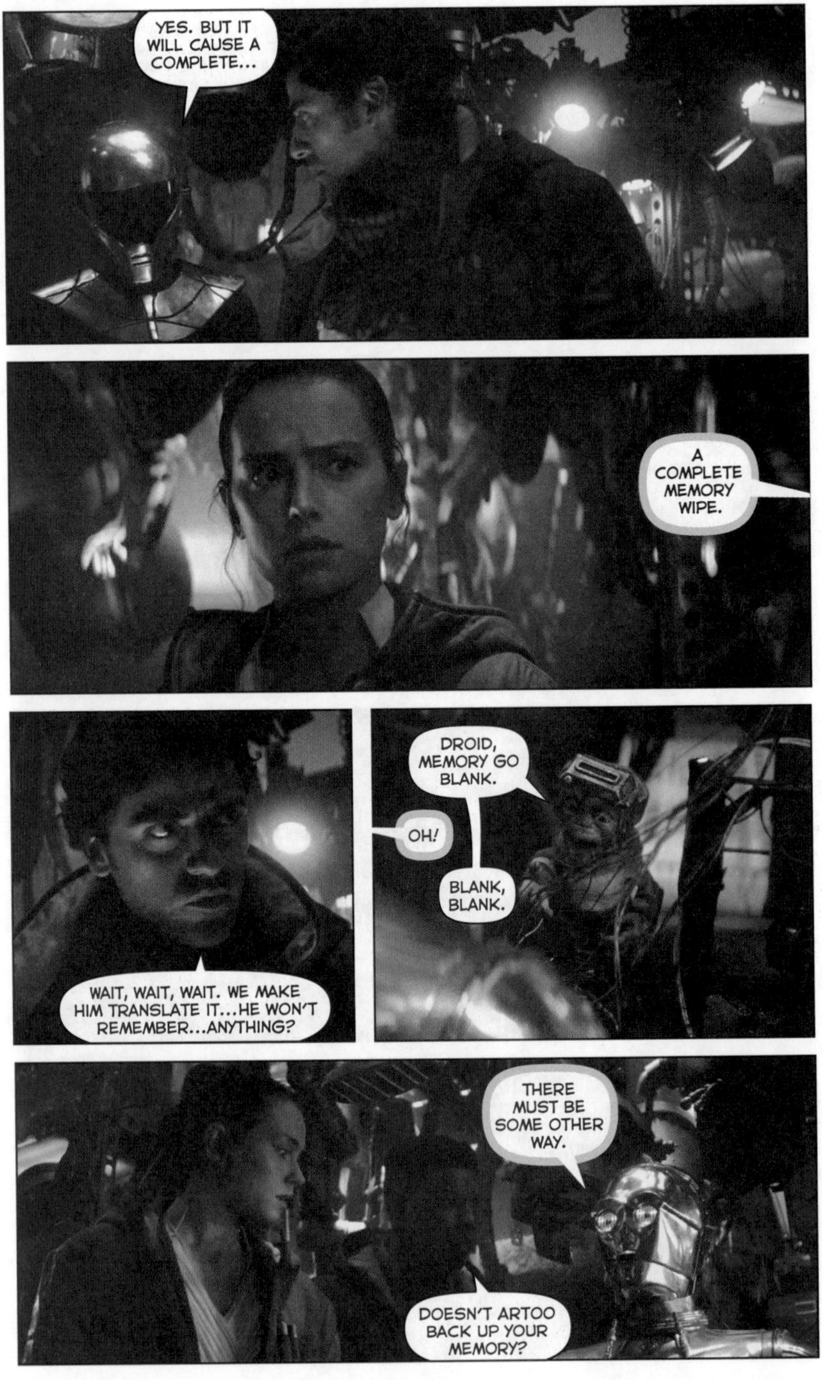
YES. BUT IT WILL CAUSE A COMPLETE...
A COMPLETE MEMORY WIPE.
WAIT, WAIT, WAIT. WE MAKE HIM TRANSLATE IT...HE WON'T REMEMBER...ANYTHING?
DROID, MEMORY GO BLANK.
OH!
BLANK, BLANK.
THERE MUST BE SOME OTHER WAY.
DOESN'T ARTOO BACK UP YOUR MEMORY?

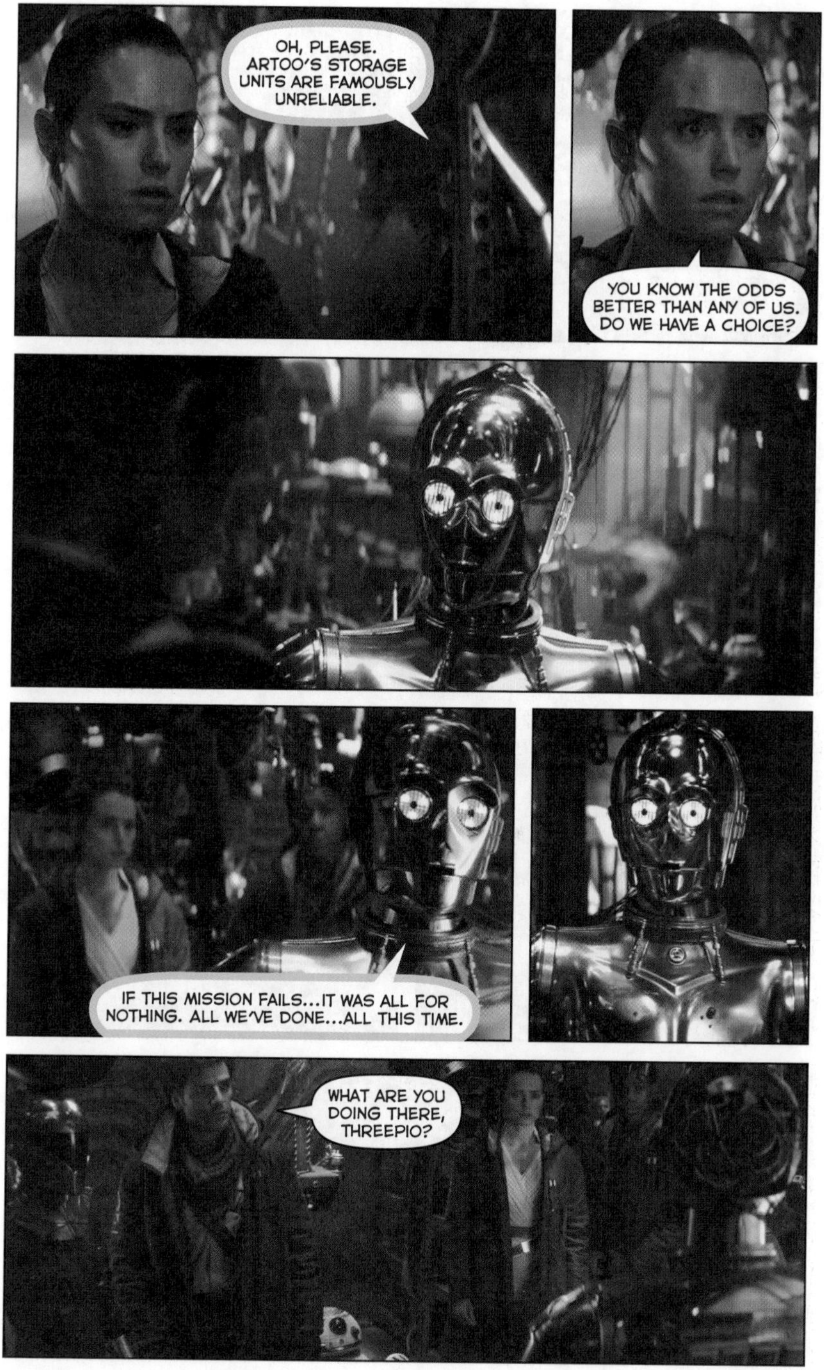
OH, PLEASE. ARTOO'S STORAGE UNITS ARE FAMOUSLY UNRELIABLE.
YOU KNOW THE ODDS BETTER THAN ANY OF US. DO WE HAVE A CHOICE?
IF THIS MISSION FAILS...IT WAS ALL FOR NOTHING. ALL WE'VE DONE...ALL THIS TIME.
WHAT ARE YOU DOING THERE, THREEPIO?

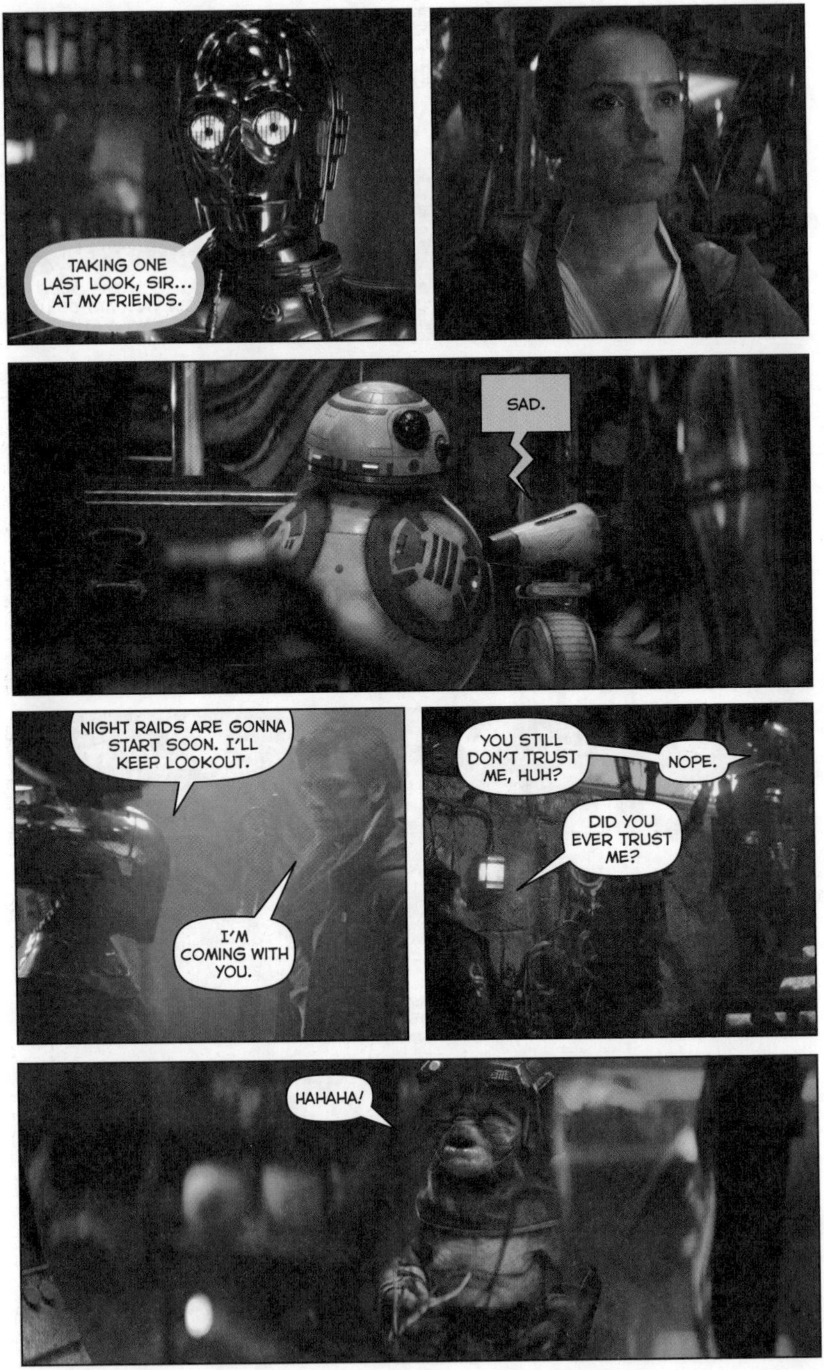
TAKING ONE LAST LOOK, SIR... AT MY FRIENDS.
SAD.
NIGHT RAIDS ARE GONNA START SOON. I'LL KEEP LOOKOUT.
I'M COMING WITH YOU.
YOU STILL DON'T TRUST ME, HUH?
NOPE.
DID YOU EVER TRUST ME?
HAHAHA!

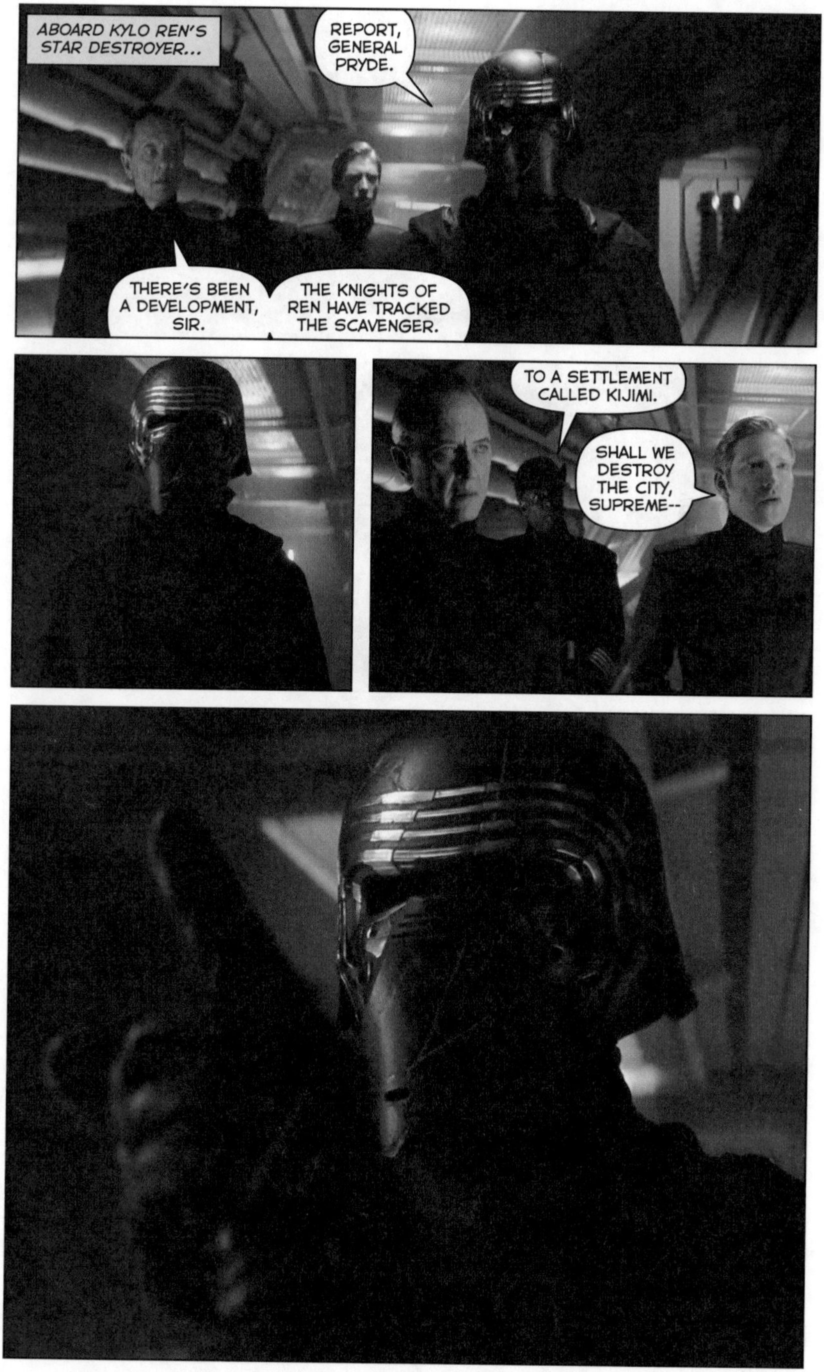
ABOARD KYLO REN'S STAR DESTROYER...
REPORT, GENERAL PRYDE.
THERE'S BEEN A DEVELOPMENT, SIR.
THE KNIGHTS OF REN HAVE TRACKED THE SCAVENGER.
TO A SETTLEMENT CALLED KIJIMI.
SHALL WE DESTROY THE CITY, SUPREME--

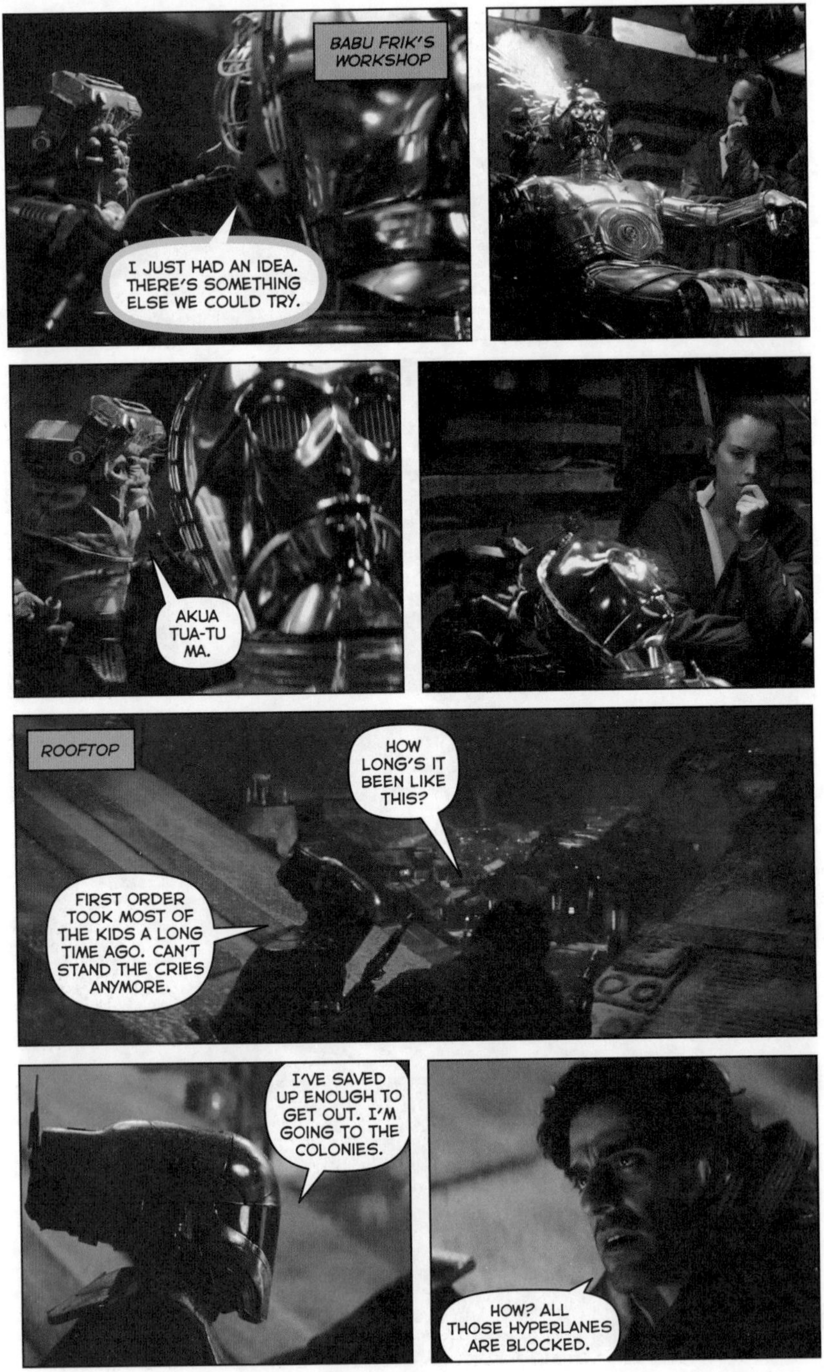
BABU FRIK'S WORKSHOP
I JUST HAD AN IDEA. THERE'S SOMETHING ELSE WE COULD TRY.
AKUA TUA-TU MA.
ROOFTOP
HOW LONG'S IT BEEN LIKE THIS?
FIRST ORDER TOOK MOST OF THE KIDS A LONG TIME AGO. CAN'T STAND THE CRIES ANYMORE.
I'VE SAVED UP ENOUGH TO GET OUT. I'M GOING TO THE COLONIES.
HOW? ALL THOSE HYPERLANES ARE BLOCKED.

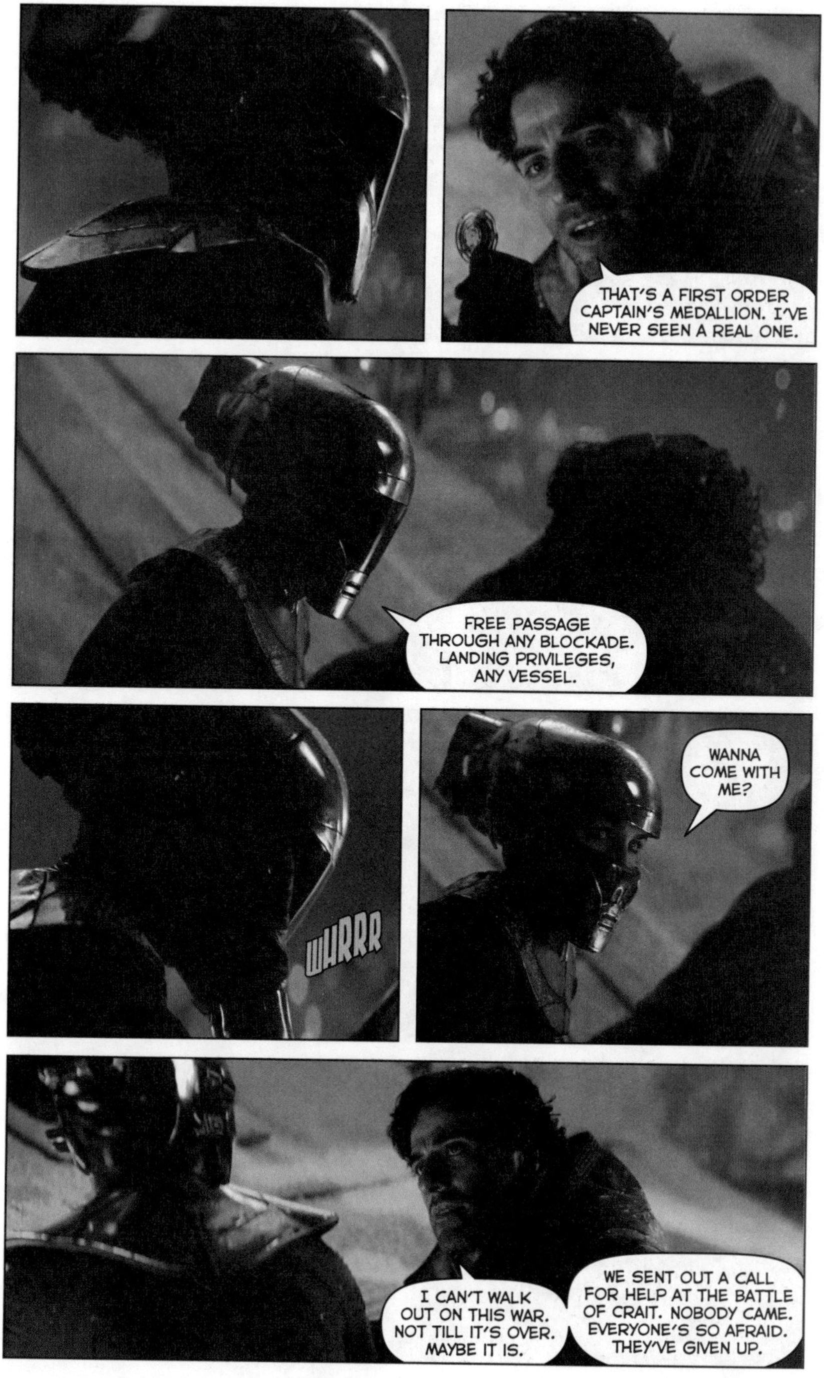
THAT'S A FIRST ORDER CAPTAIN'S MEDALLION. I'VE NEVER SEEN A REAL ONE.
FREE PASSAGE THROUGH ANY BLOCKADE. LANDING PRIVILEGES, ANY VESSEL.
WHRRR
WANNA COME WITH ME?
I CAN'T WALK OUT ON THIS WAR. NOT TILL IT'S OVER. MAYBE IT IS.
WE SENT OUT A CALL FOR HELP AT THE BATTLE OF CRAIT. NOBODY CAME. EVERYONE'S SO AFRAID. THEY'VE GIVEN UP.

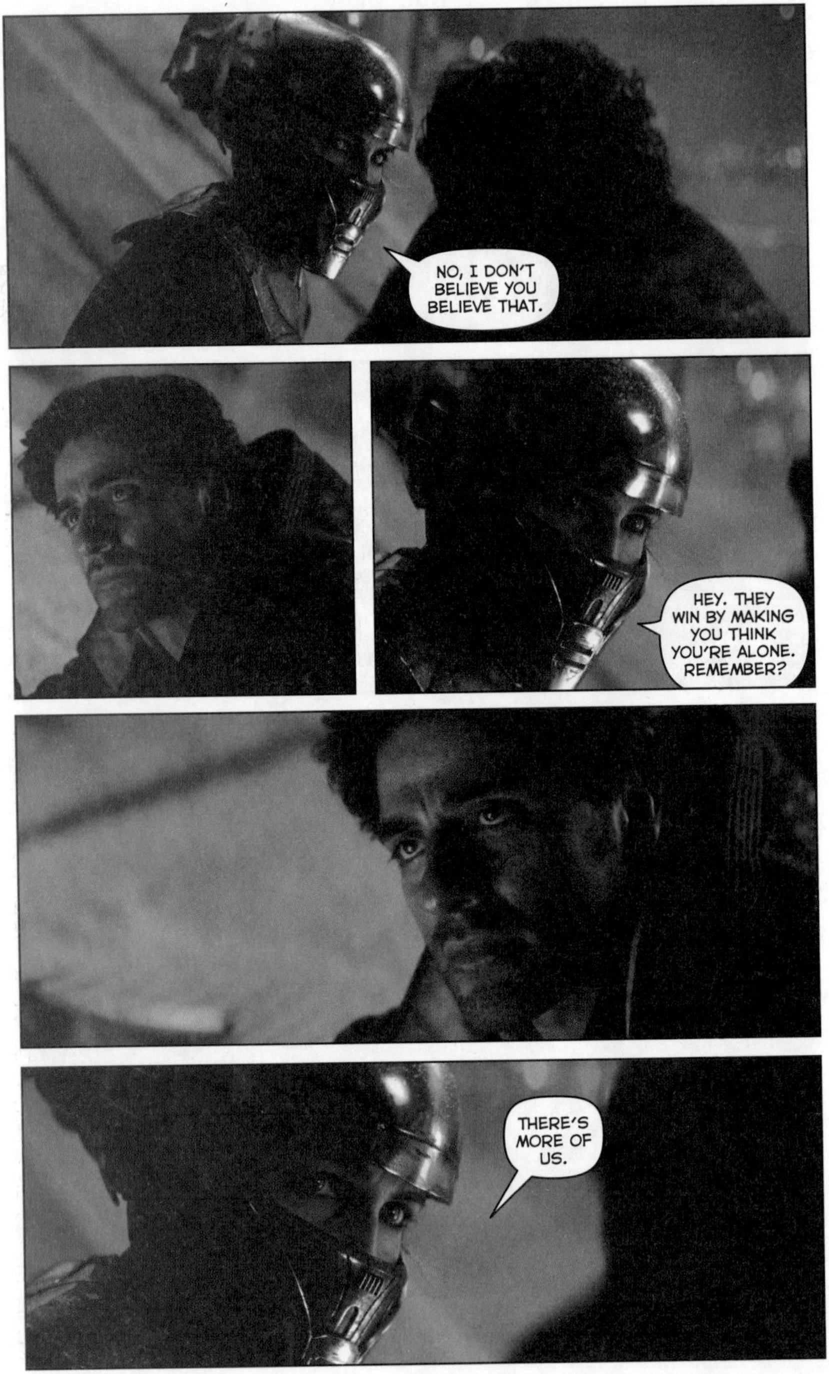
NO, I DON'T BELIEVE YOU BELIEVE THAT.
HEY. THEY WIN BY MAKING YOU THINK YOU'RE ALONE. REMEMBER?
THERE'S MORE OF US.

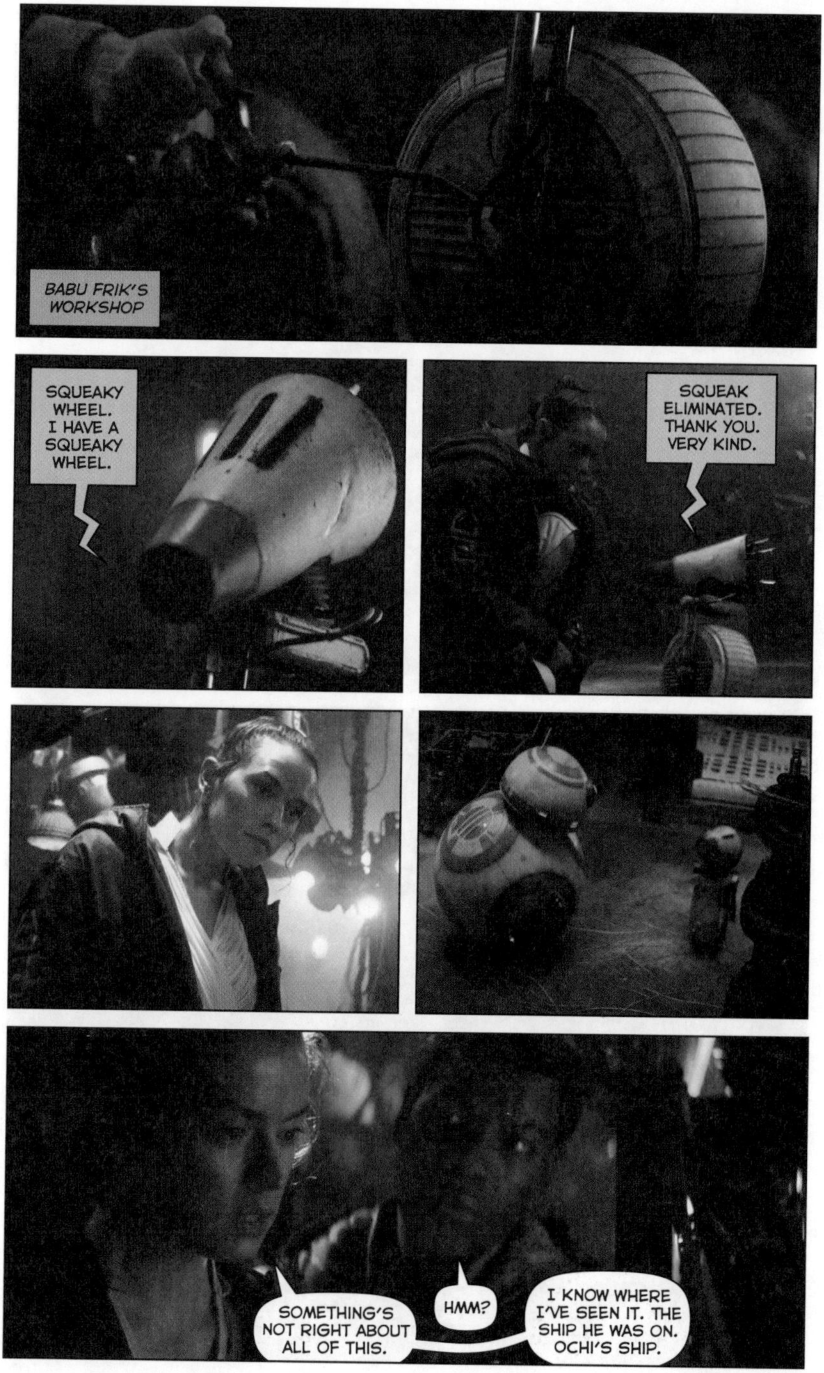

BABU FRIK'S WORKSHOP
SQUEAKY WHEEL. I HAVE A SQUEAKY WHEEL.
SQUEAK ELIMINATED. THANK YOU. VERY KIND.
SOMETHING'S NOT RIGHT ABOUT ALL OF THIS.
HMM?
I KNOW WHERE I'VE SEEN IT. THE SHIP HE WAS ON. OCHI'S SHIP.

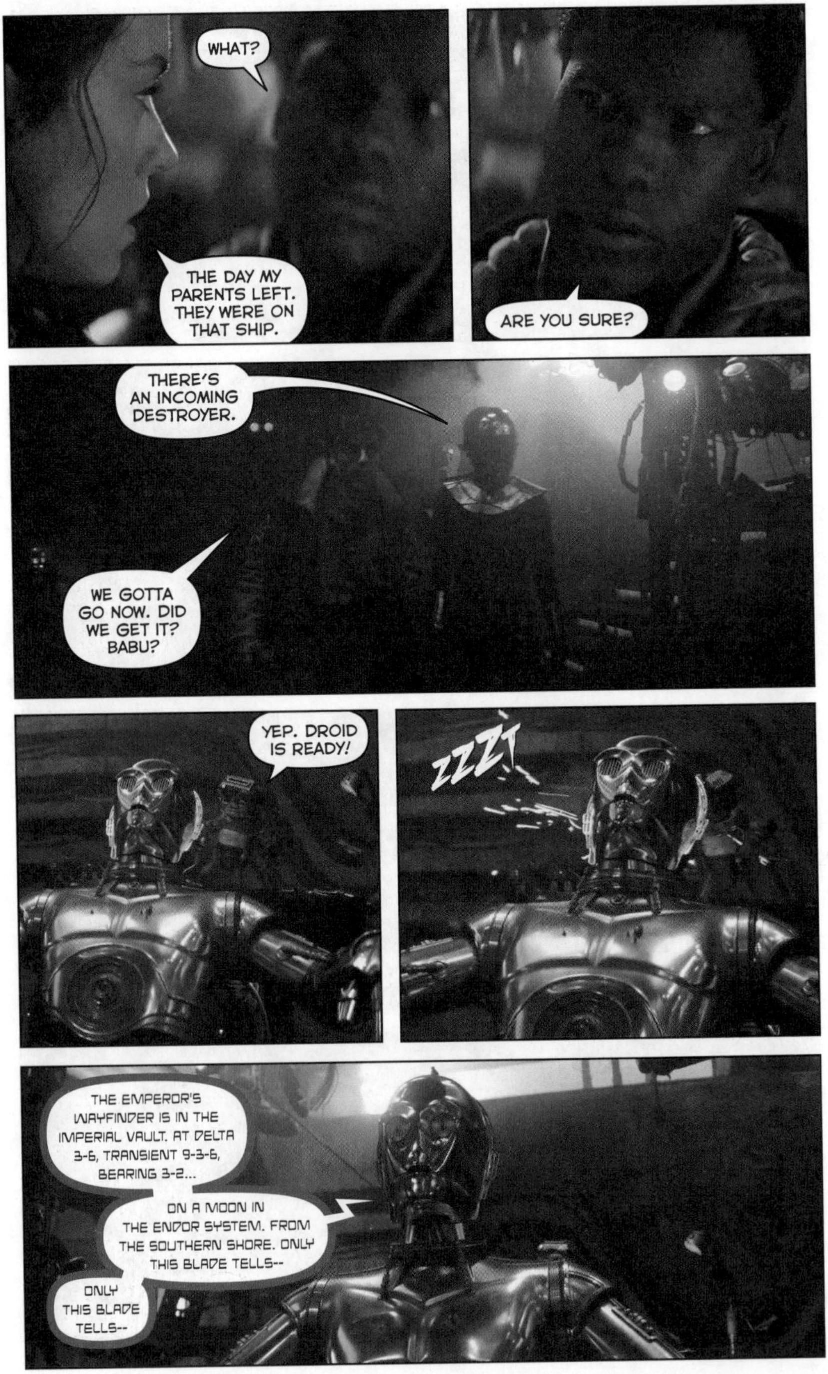
WHAT?
THE DAY MY PARENTS LEFT. THEY WERE ON THAT SHIP.
ARE YOU SURE?
THERE'S AN INCOMING DESTROYER.
WE GOTTA GO NOW. DID WE GET IT? BABU?
YEP. DROID IS READY!
ZZZT
THE EMPEROR'S WAYFINDER IS IN THE IMPERIAL VAULT. AT DELTA 3-6, TRANSIENT 9-3-6, BEARING 3-2...
ON A MOON IN THE ENDOR SYSTEM. FROM THE SOUTHERN SHORE. ONLY THIS BLADE TELLS--
ONLY THIS BLADE TELLS--

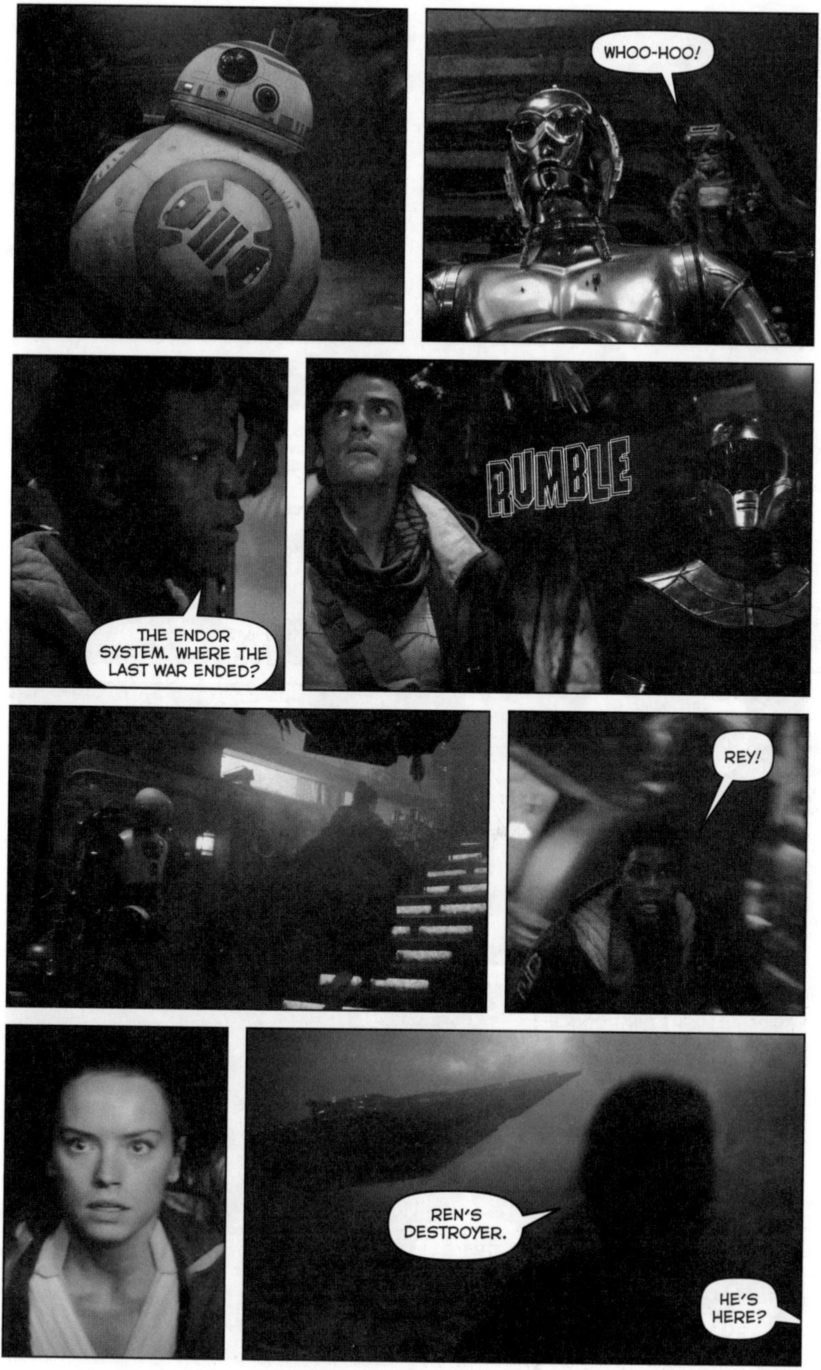
WHOO-HOO!
RUMBLE
THE ENDOR SYSTEM. WHERE THE LAST WAR ENDED?
REY!
REN'S DESTROYER.
HE'S HERE?

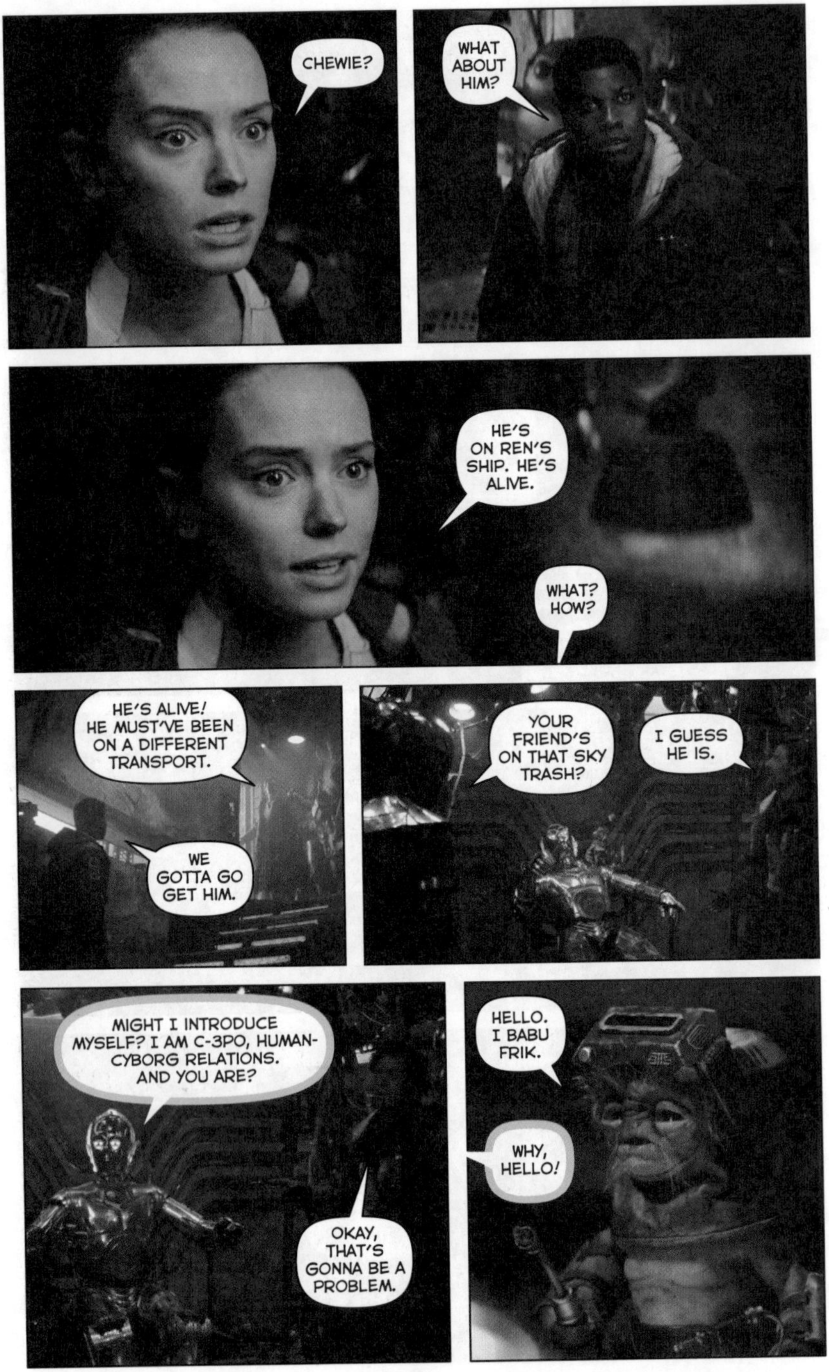
CHEWIE?
WHAT ABOUT HIM?
HE'S ON REN'S SHIP. HE'S ALIVE.
WHAT? HOW?
HE'S ALIVE! HE MUST'VE BEEN ON A DIFFERENT TRANSPORT.
WE GOTTA GO GET HIM.
YOUR FRIEND'S ON THAT SKY TRASH?
I GUESS HE IS.
MIGHT I INTRODUCE MYSELF? I AM C-3PO, HUMAN-CYBORG RELATIONS. AND YOU ARE?
OKAY, THAT'S GONNA BE A PROBLEM.
HELLO. I BABU FRIK.
WHY, HELLO!

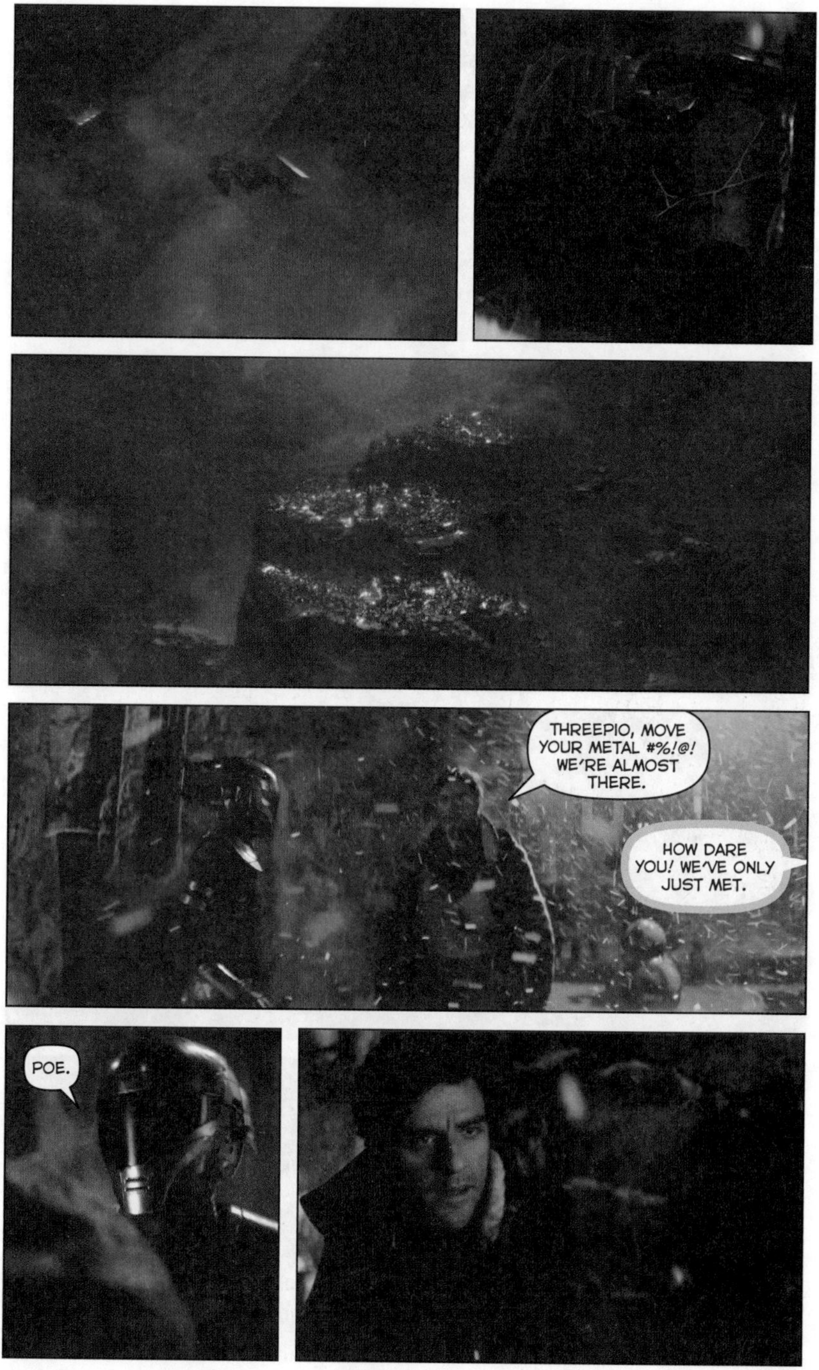
THREEPIO, MOVE YOUR METAL #%!@! WE'RE ALMOST THERE.
HOW DARE YOU! WE'VE ONLY JUST MET.
POE.

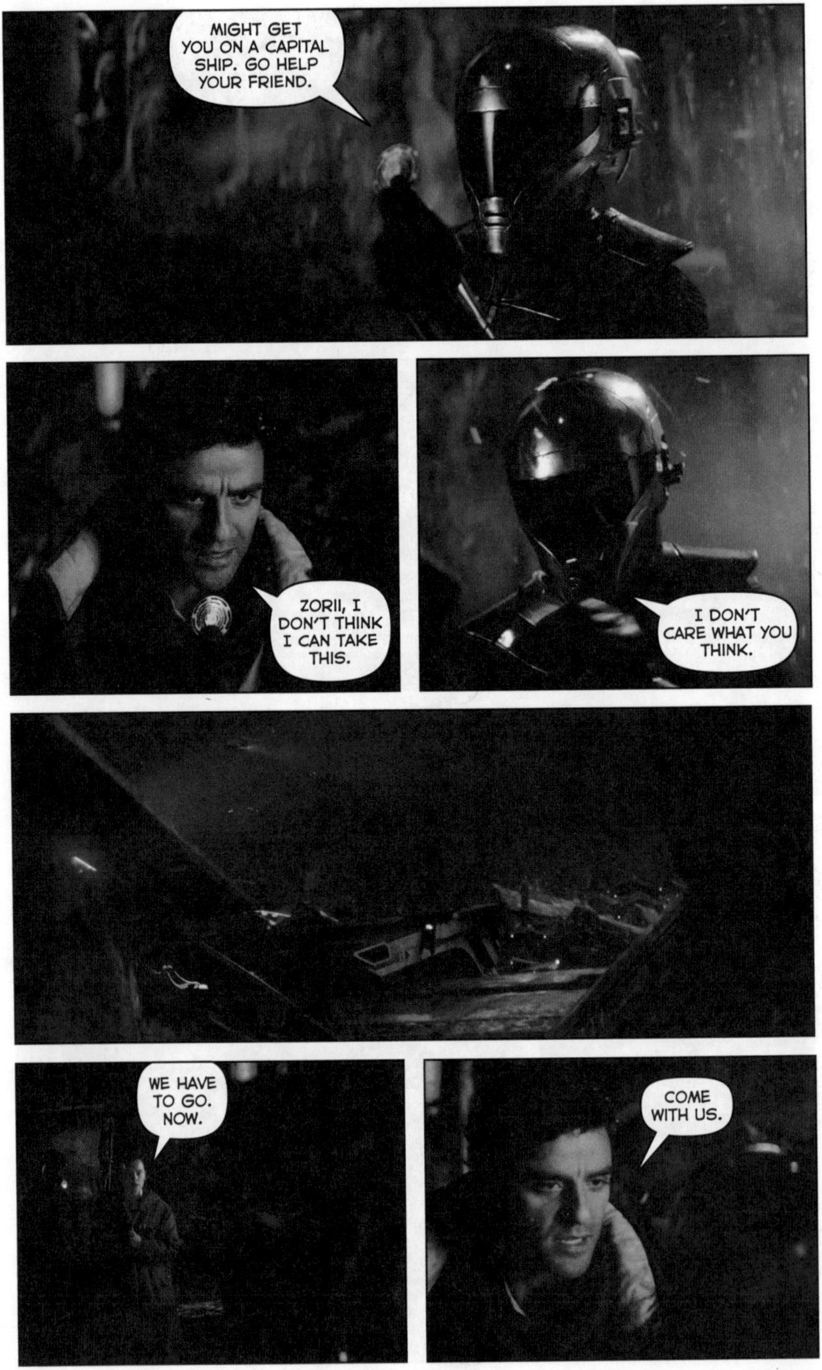
MIGHT GET YOU ON A CAPITAL SHIP. GO HELP YOUR FRIEND.
ZORII, I DON'T THINK I CAN TAKE THIS.
I DON'T CARE WHAT YOU THINK.
WE HAVE TO GO. NOW.
COME WITH US.

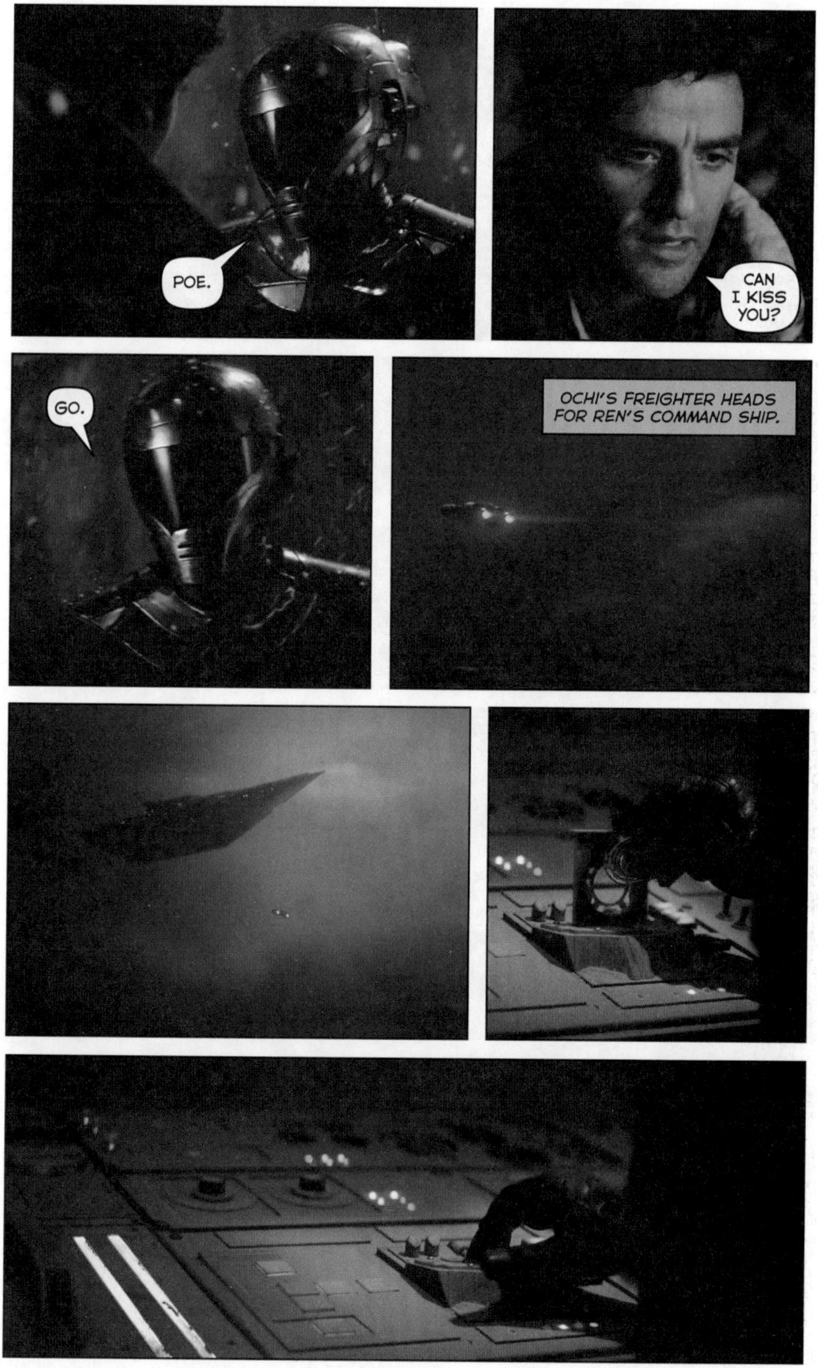
POE.
CAN I KISS YOU?
GO.
OCHI'S FREIGHTER HEADS FOR REN'S COMMAND SHIP.

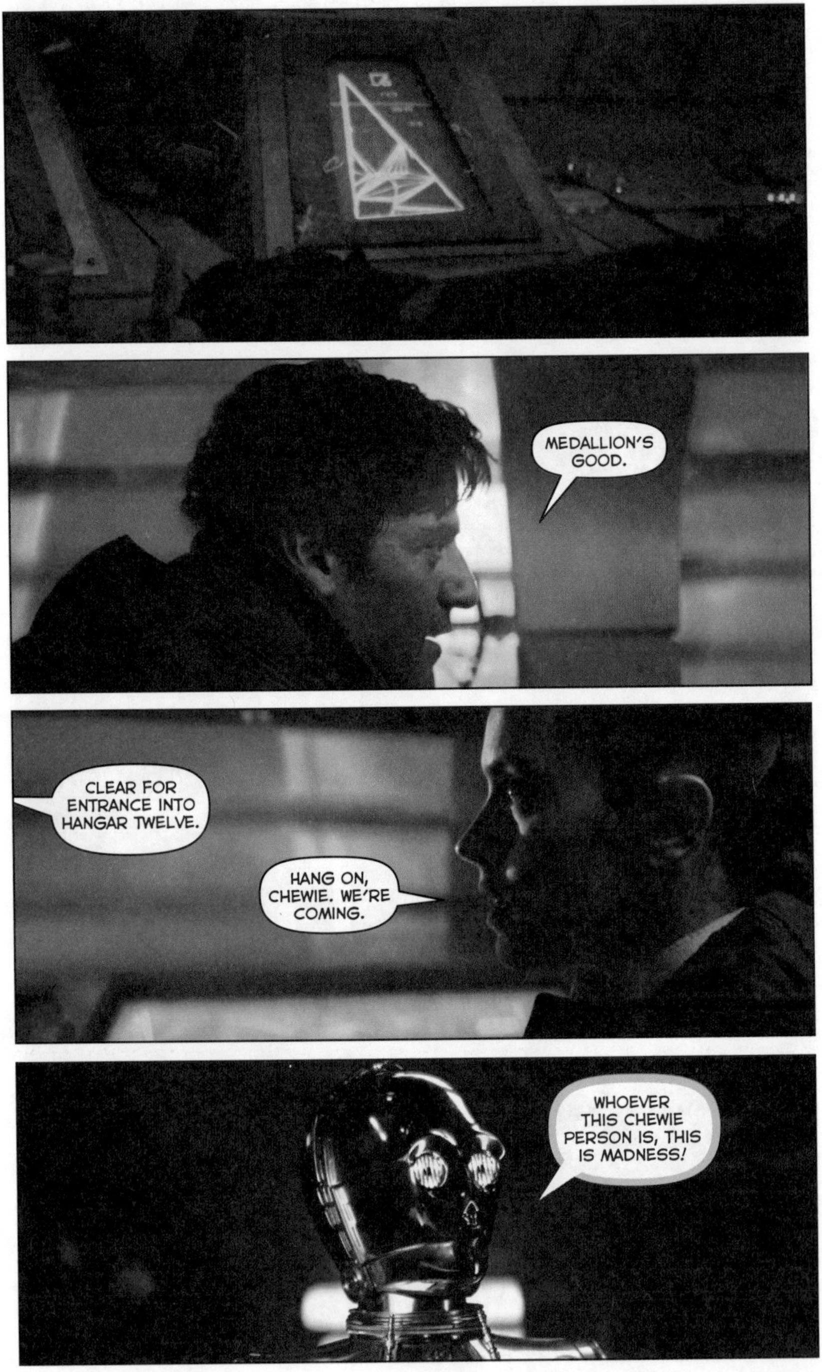

MEDALLION'S GOOD.
CLEAR FOR ENTRANCE INTO HANGAR TWELVE.
HANG ON, CHEWIE. WE'RE COMING.
WHOEVER THIS CHEWIE PERSON IS, THIS IS MADNESS!

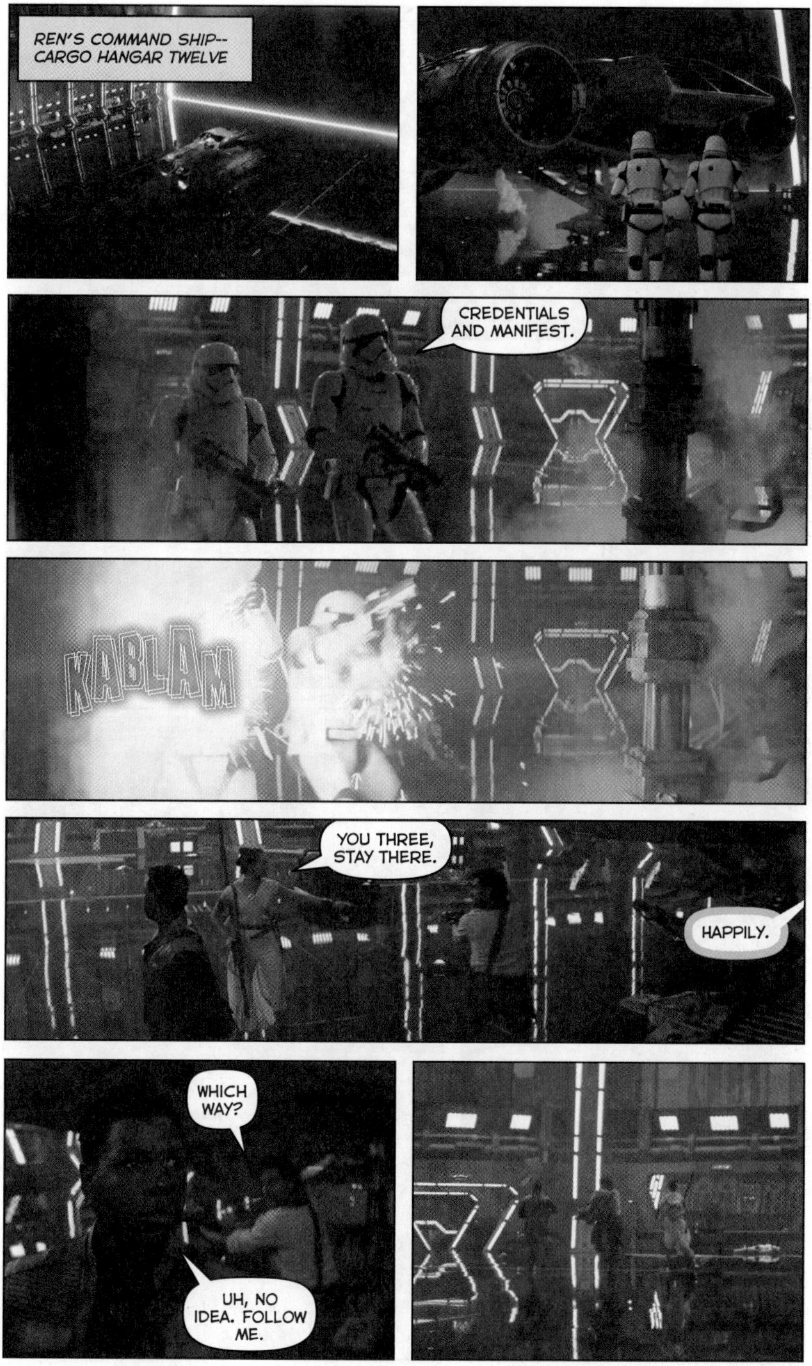
REN'S COMMAND SHIP--
CARGO HANGAR TWELVE
CREDENTIALS AND MANIFEST.
KABLAM
YOU THREE, STAY THERE.
HAPPILY.
WHICH WAY?
UH, NO IDEA. FOLLOW ME.

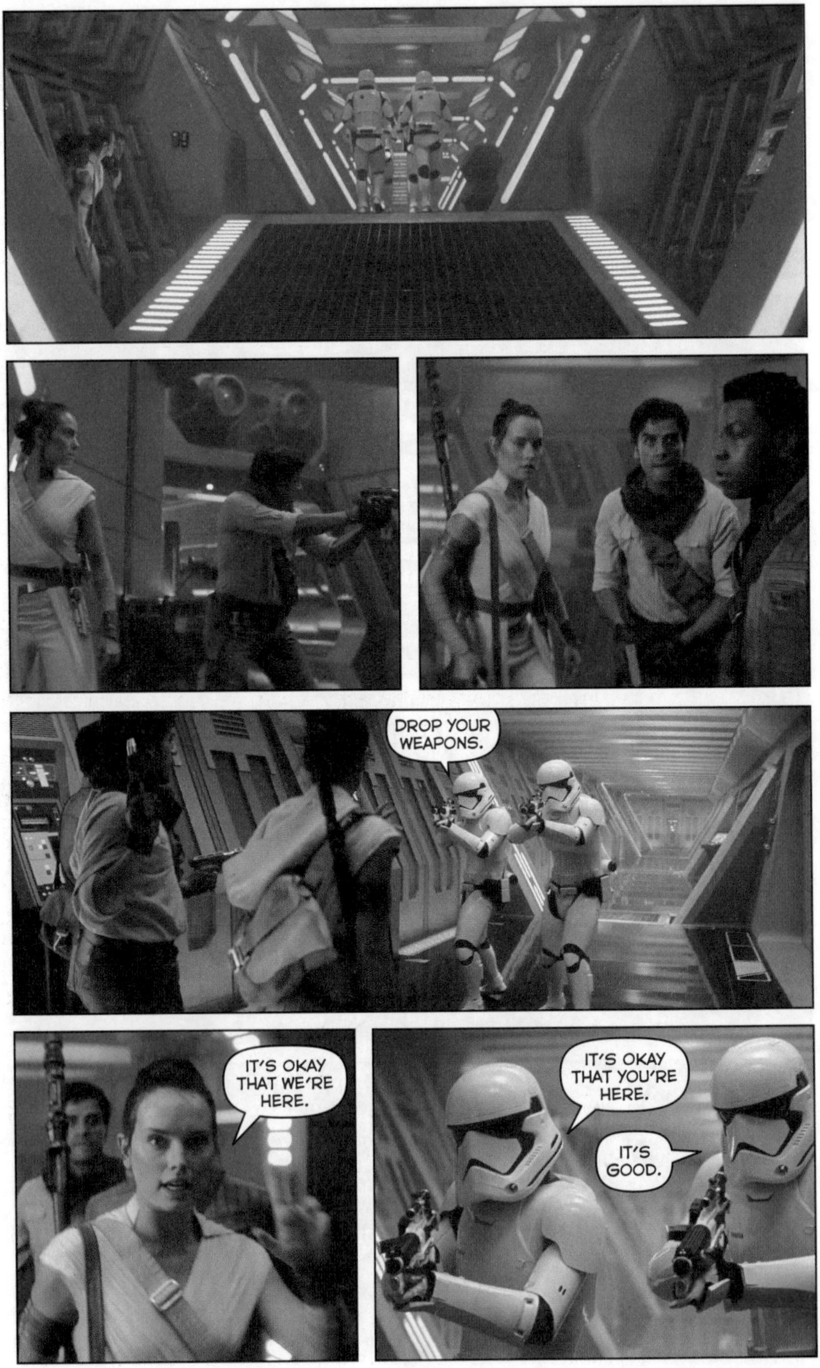
DROP YOUR WEAPONS.
IT'S OKAY THAT WE'RE HERE.
IT'S OKAY THAT YOU'RE HERE.
IT'S GOOD.

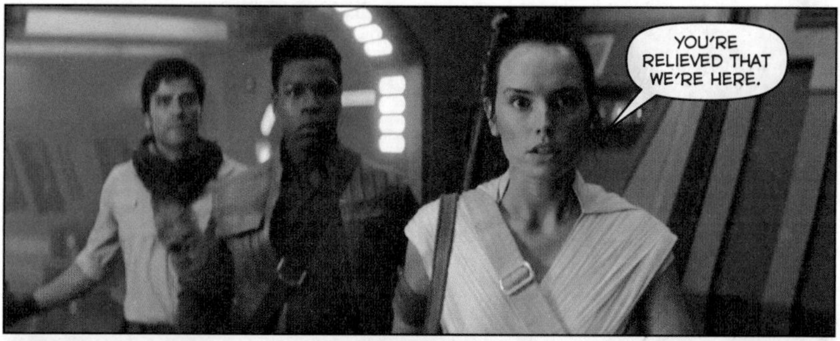
YOU'RE RELIEVED THAT WE'RE HERE.

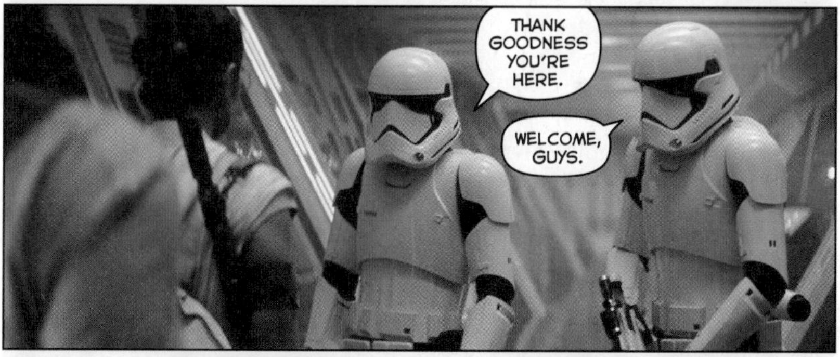
THANK GOODNESS YOU'RE HERE.
WELCOME, GUYS.

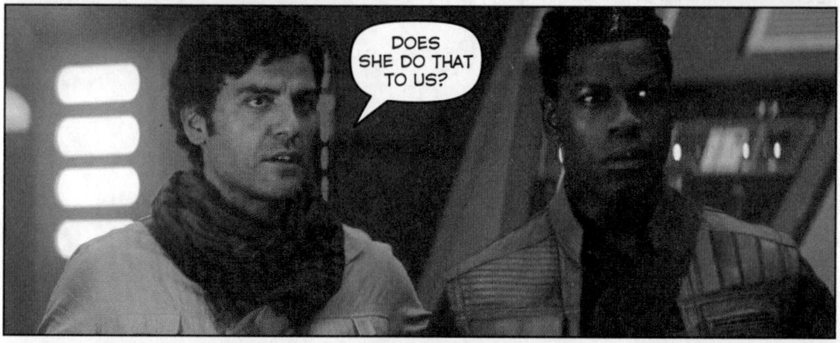
DOES SHE DO THAT TO US?

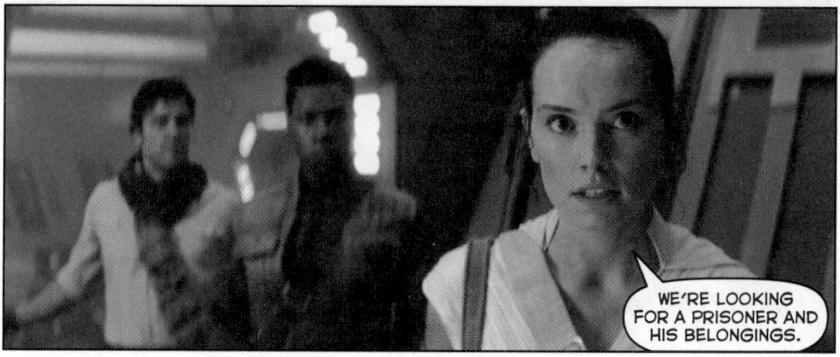
WE'RE LOOKING FOR A PRISONER AND HIS BELONGINGS.

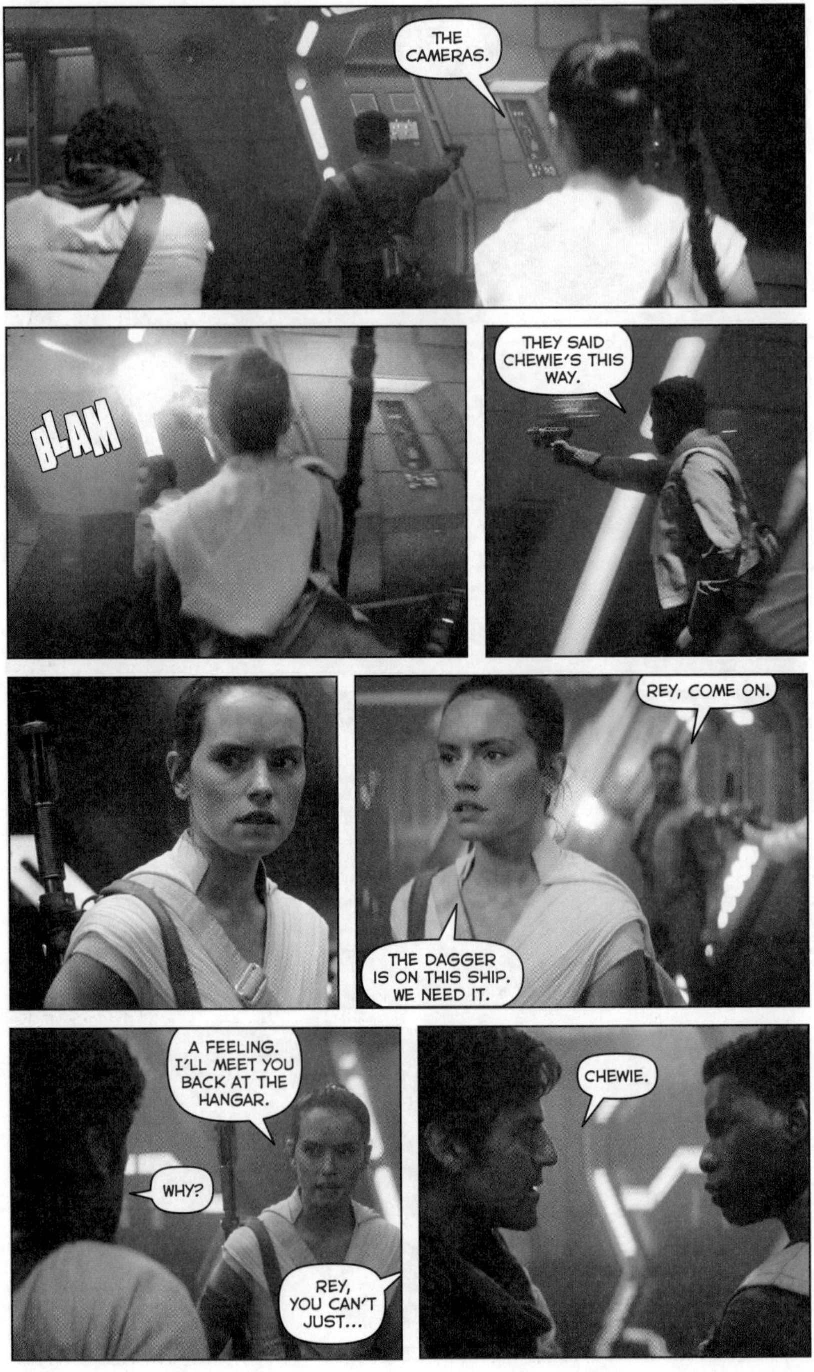
THE CAMERAS.
BLAM
THEY SAID CHEWIE'S THIS WAY.
REY, COME ON.
THE DAGGER IS ON THIS SHIP. WE NEED IT.
A FEELING. I'LL MEET YOU BACK AT THE HANGAR.
WHY?
REY, YOU CAN'T JUST...
CHEWIE.

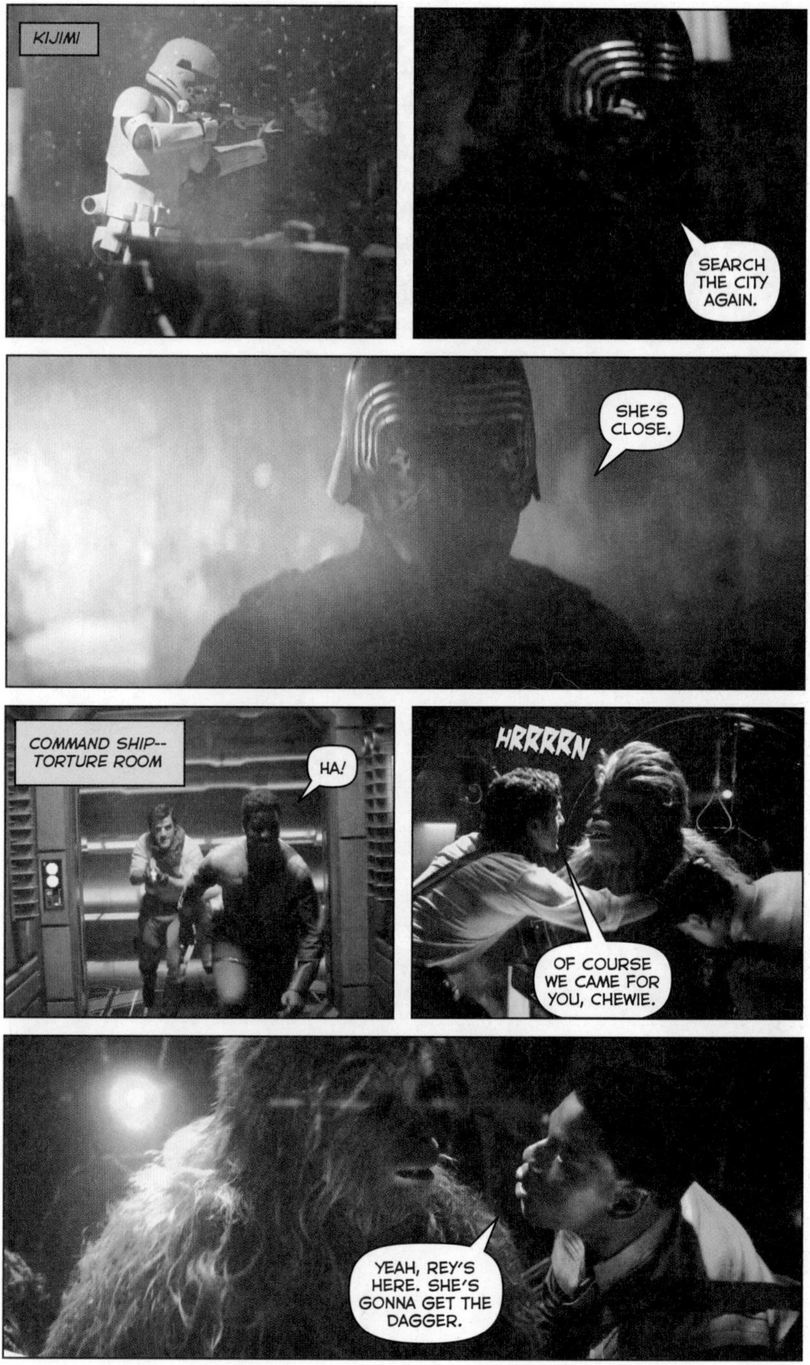
KIJIMI
SEARCH THE CITY AGAIN.
SHE'S CLOSE.
COMMAND SHIP-- TORTURE ROOM
HA!
HRRRRN
OF COURSE WE CAME FOR YOU, CHEWIE.
YEAH, REY'S HERE. SHE'S GONNA GET THE DAGGER.

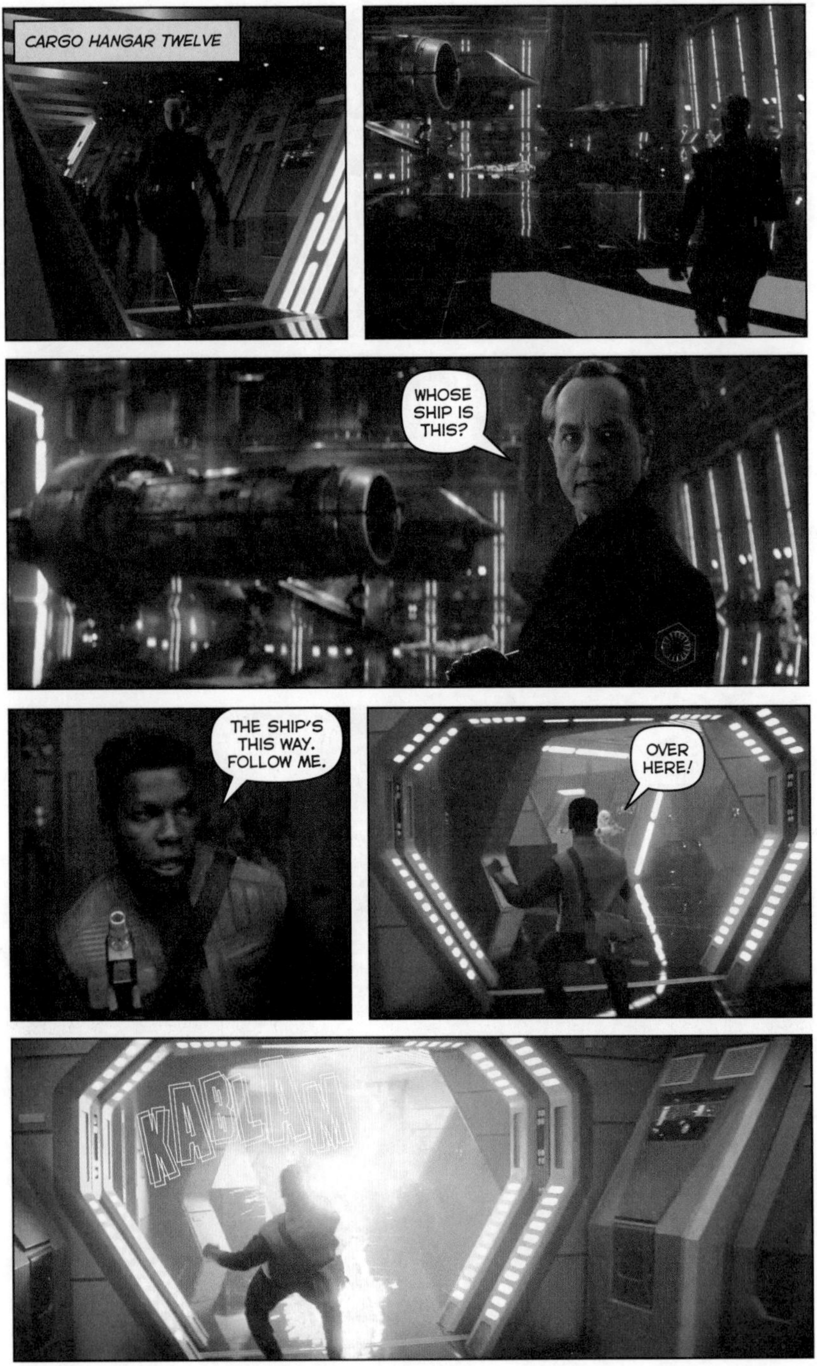
CARGO HANGAR TWELVE
WHOSE SHIP IS THIS?
THE SHIP'S THIS WAY. FOLLOW ME.
OVER HERE!
KABLAM

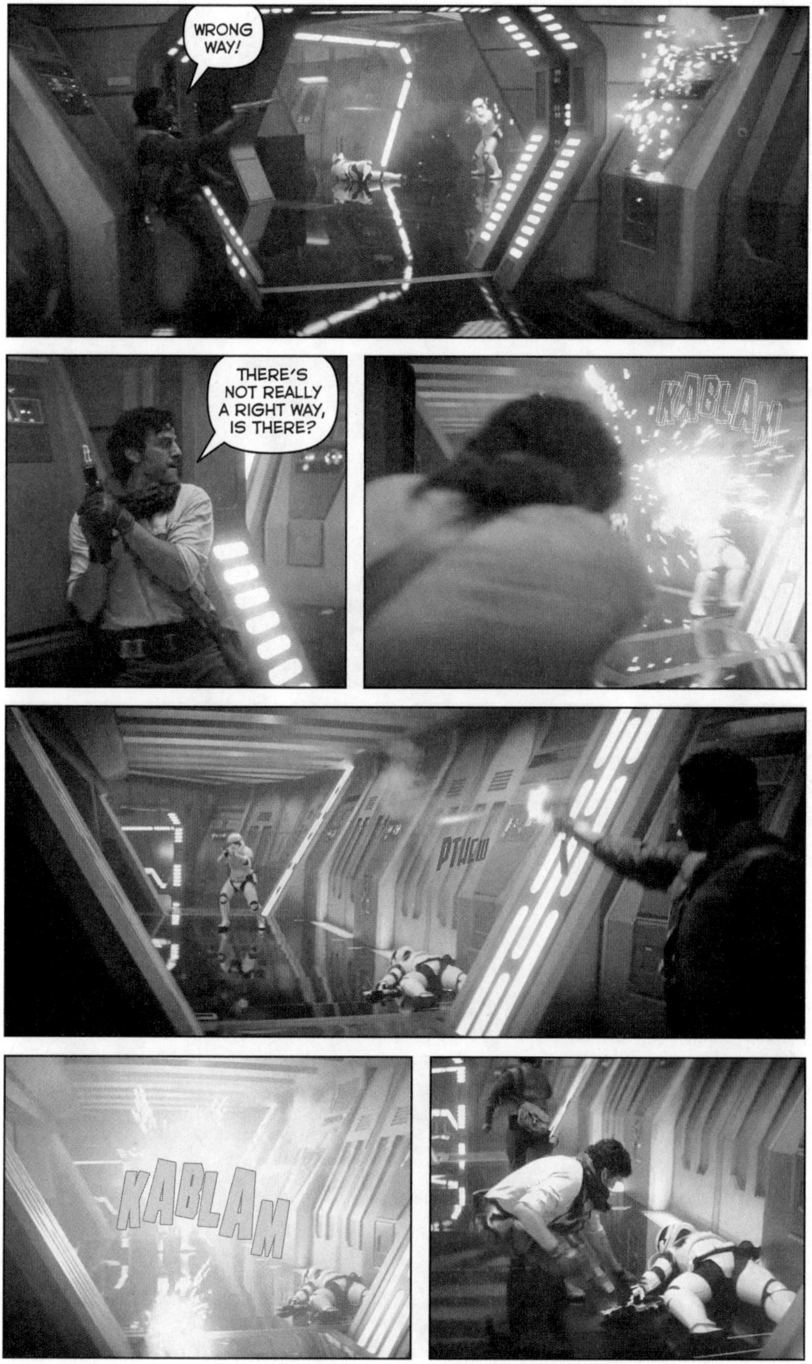
WRONG WAY!
THERE'S NOT REALLY A RIGHT WAY, IS THERE?
KABLAM
PTHEW
KABLAM

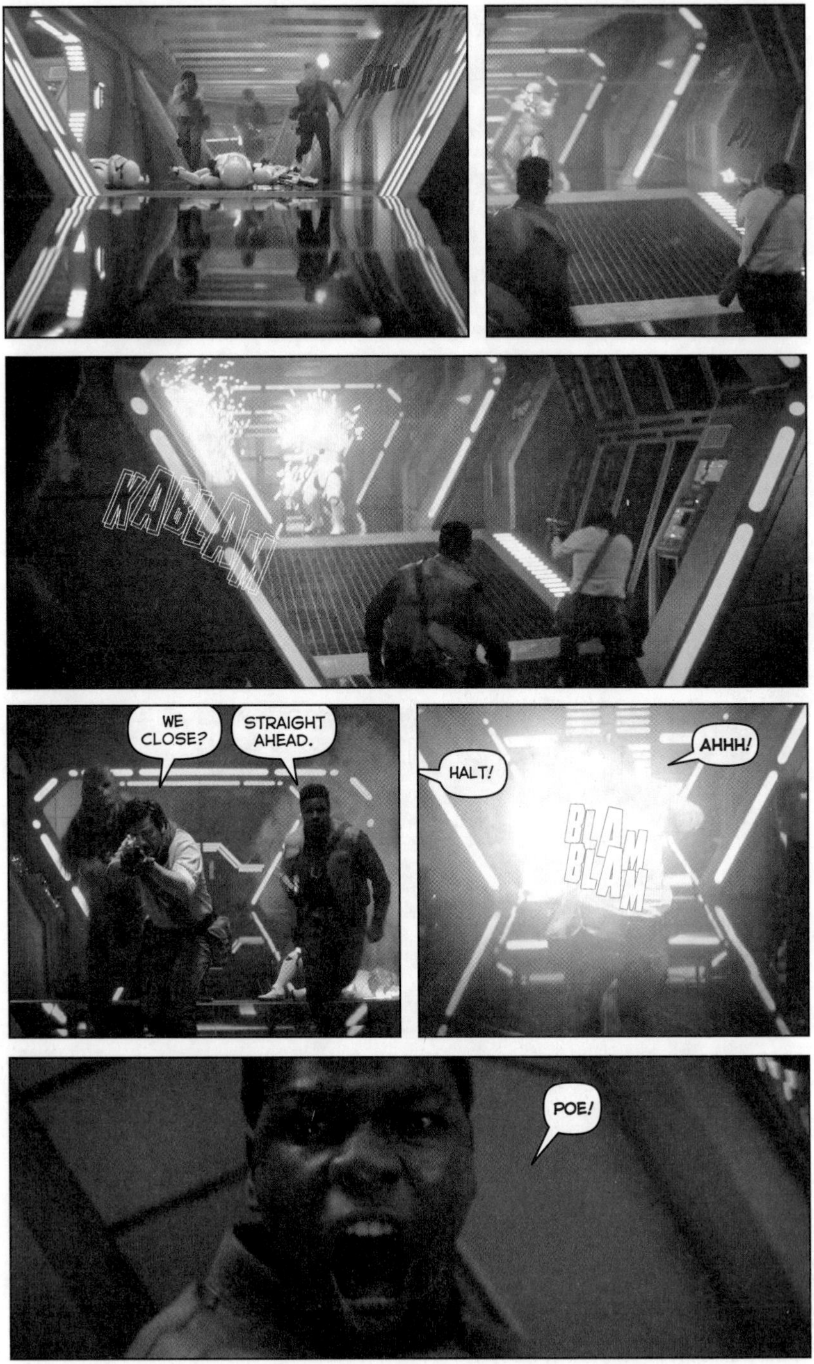
KABLAM
WE CLOSE?
STRAIGHT AHEAD.
HALT!
AHHH!
BLAM
BLAM
POE!

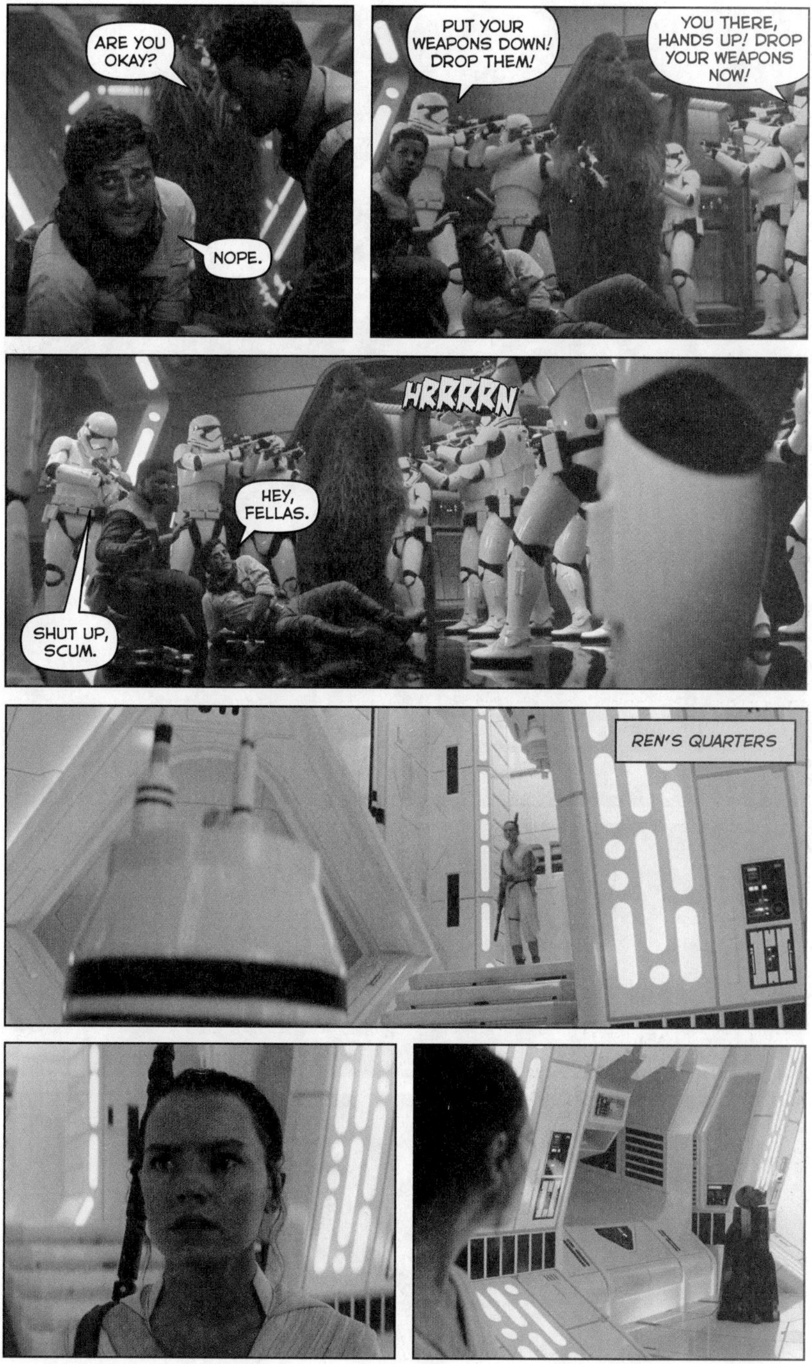
ARE YOU OKAY?
NOPE.
PUT YOUR WEAPONS DOWN! DROP THEM!
YOU THERE, HANDS UP! DROP YOUR WEAPONS NOW!
HRRRRN
HEY, FELLAS.
SHUT UP, SCUM.
REN'S QUARTERS

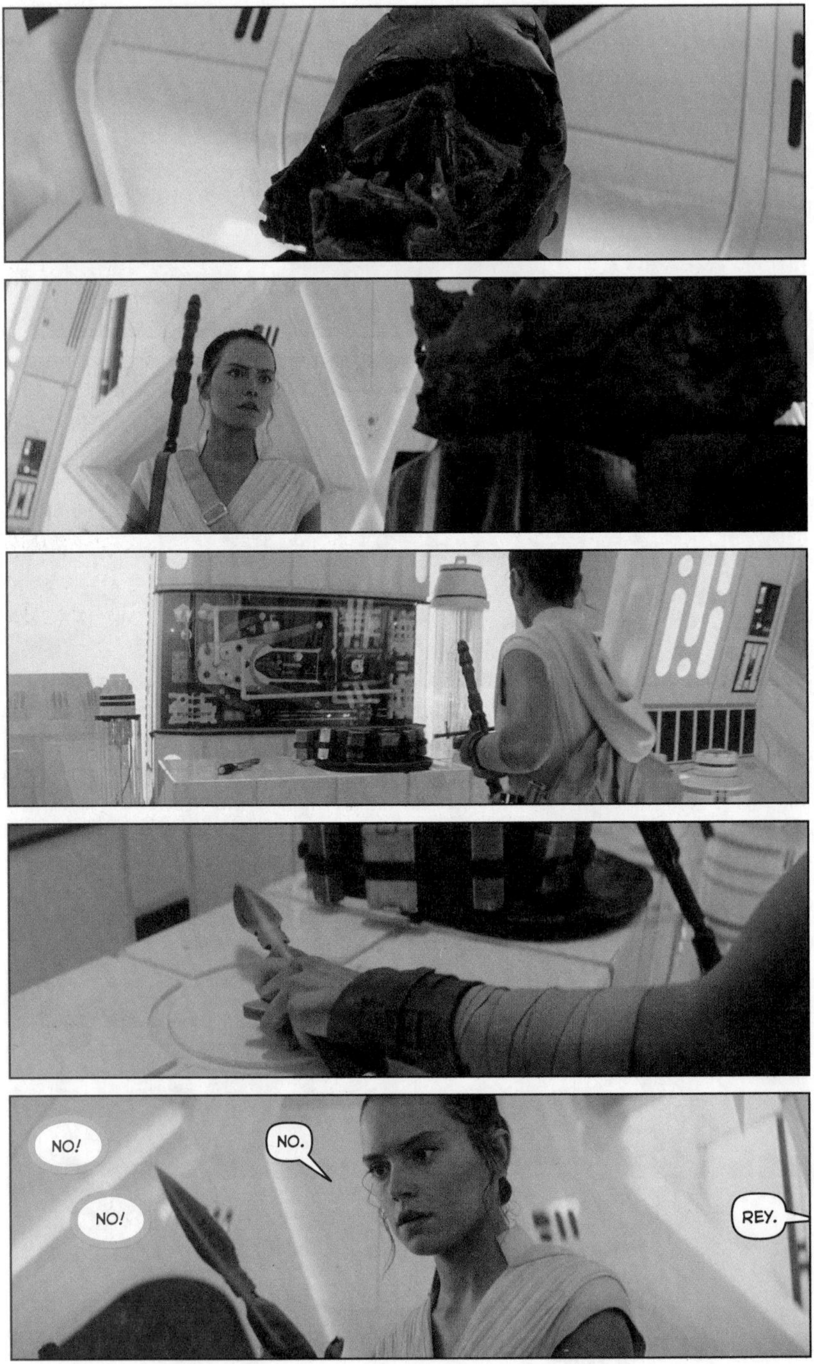
NO!
NO!
NO.
REY.

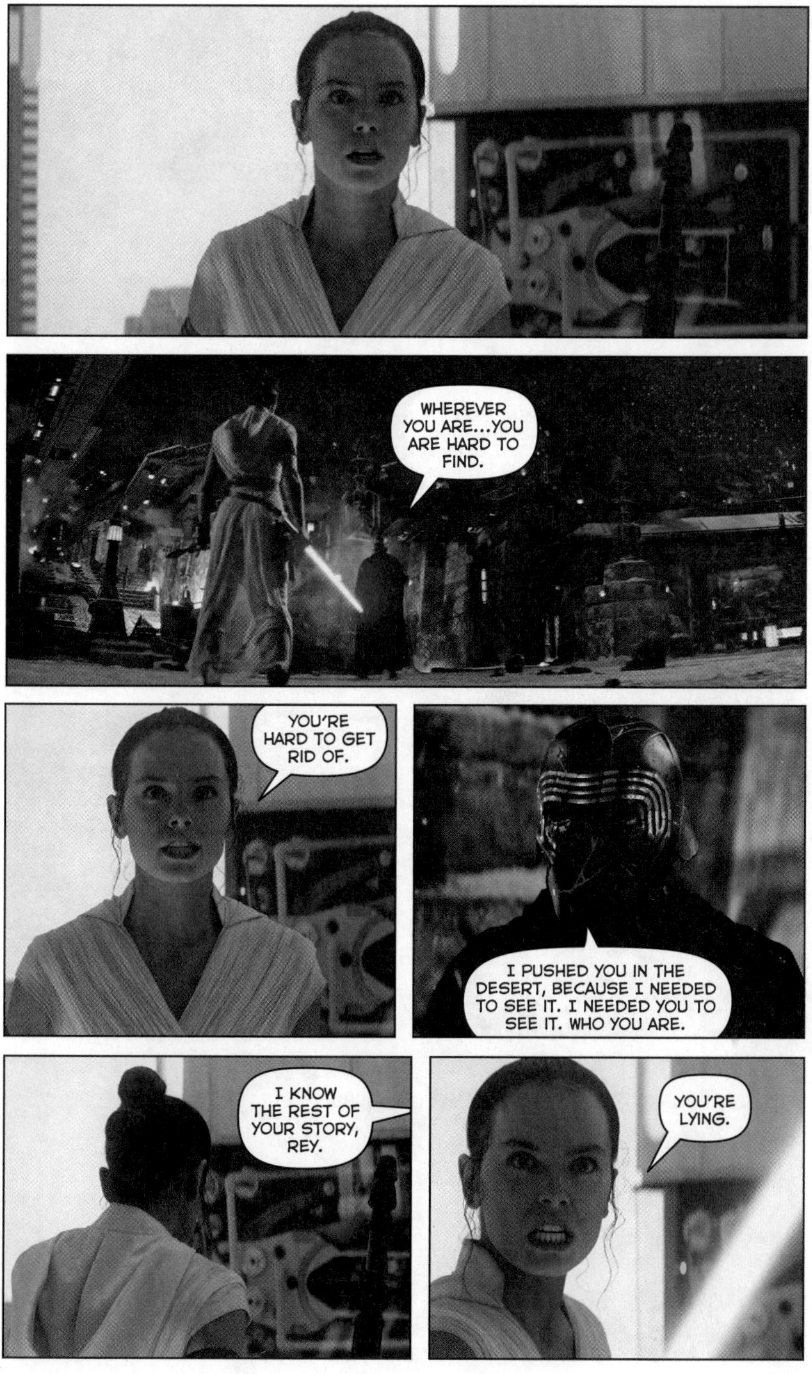
WHEREVER YOU ARE...YOU ARE HARD TO FIND.
YOU'RE HARD TO GET RID OF.
I PUSHED YOU IN THE DESERT, BECAUSE I NEEDED TO SEE IT. I NEEDED YOU TO SEE IT. WHO YOU ARE.
I KNOW THE REST OF YOUR STORY, REY.
YOU'RE LYING.

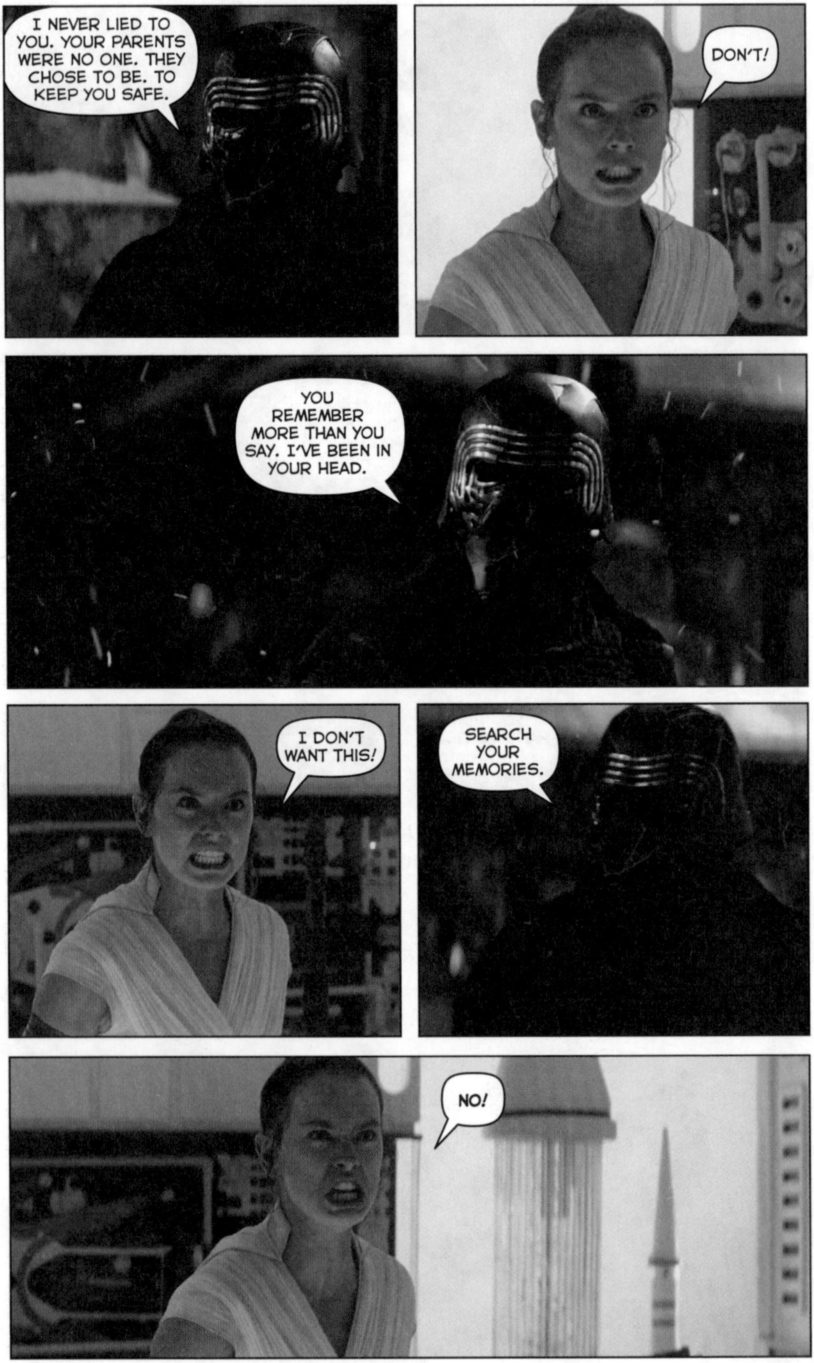
I NEVER LIED TO YOU. YOUR PARENTS WERE NO ONE. THEY CHOSE TO BE. TO KEEP YOU SAFE.
DON'T!
YOU REMEMBER MORE THAN YOU SAY. I'VE BEEN IN YOUR HEAD.
I DON'T WANT THIS!
SEARCH YOUR MEMORIES.
NO!

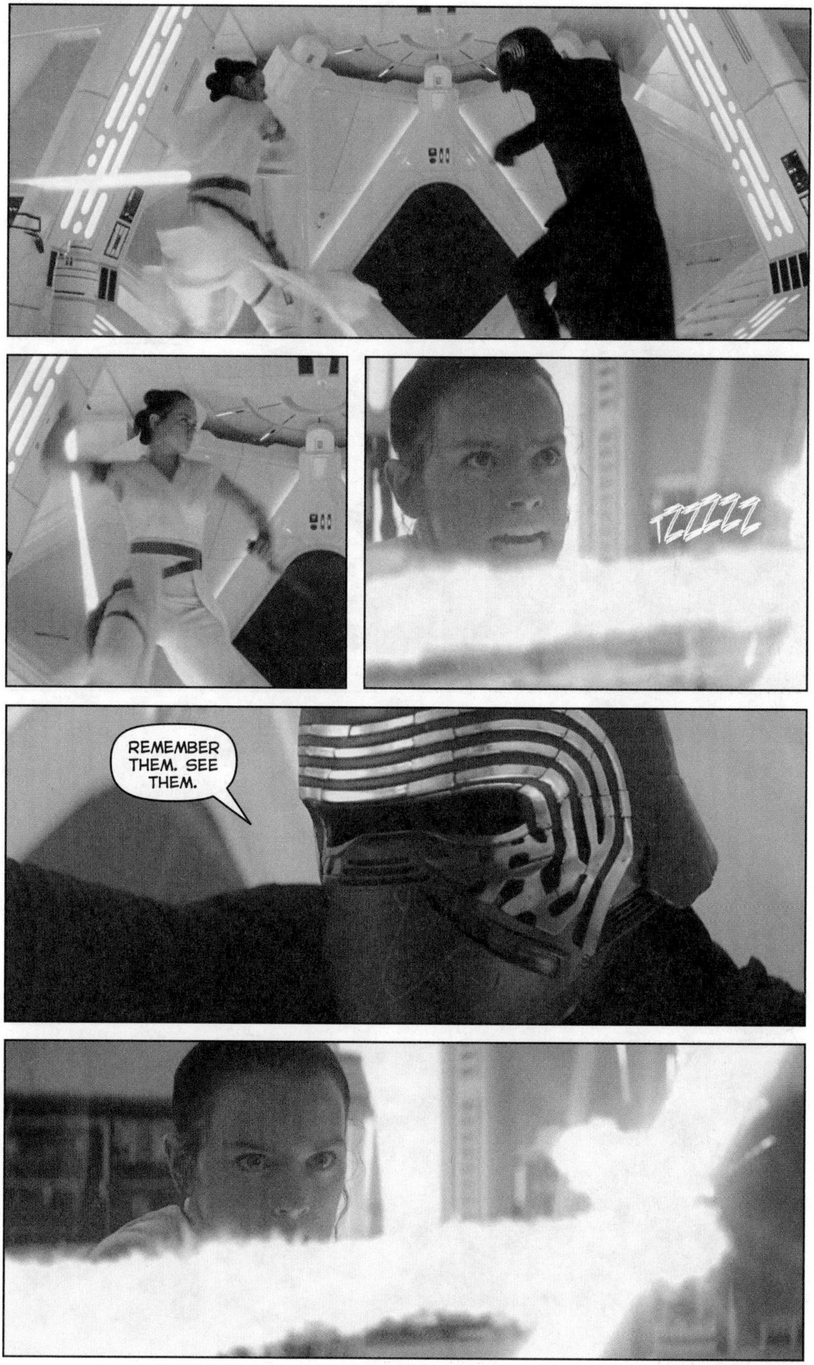
TZZZZZ
REMEMBER THEM. SEE THEM.

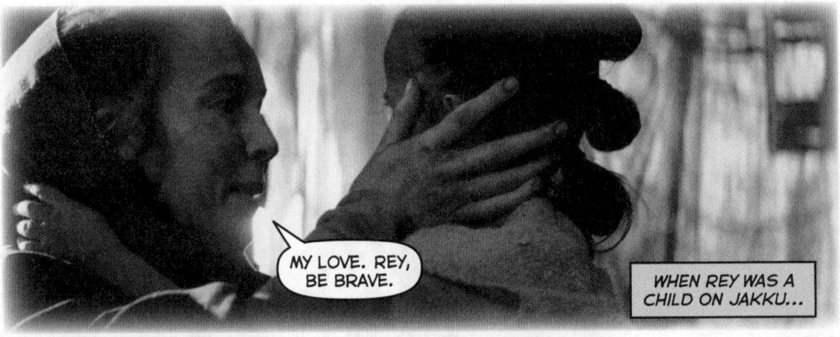
WHEN REY WAS A CHILD ON JAKKU...
MY LOVE. REY, BE BRAVE.

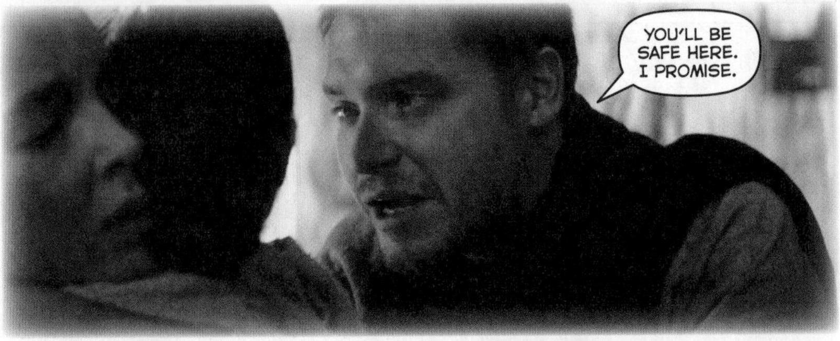
YOU'LL BE SAFE HERE. I PROMISE.

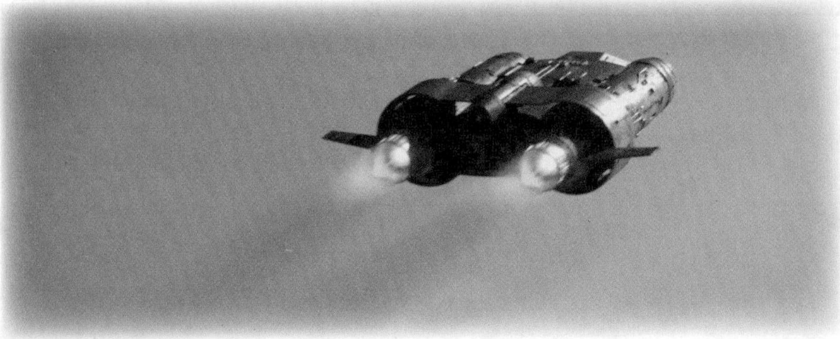

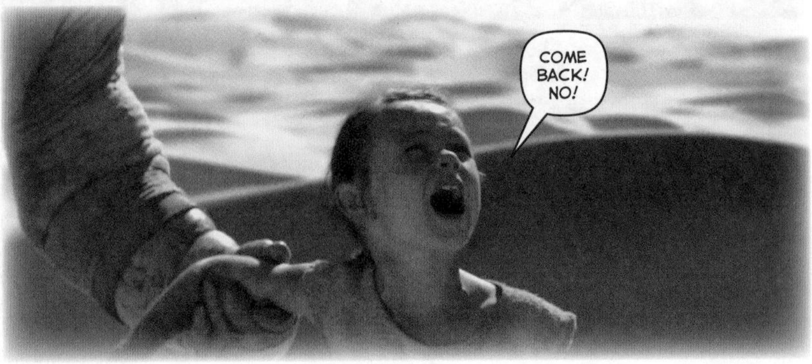
COME BACK! NO!

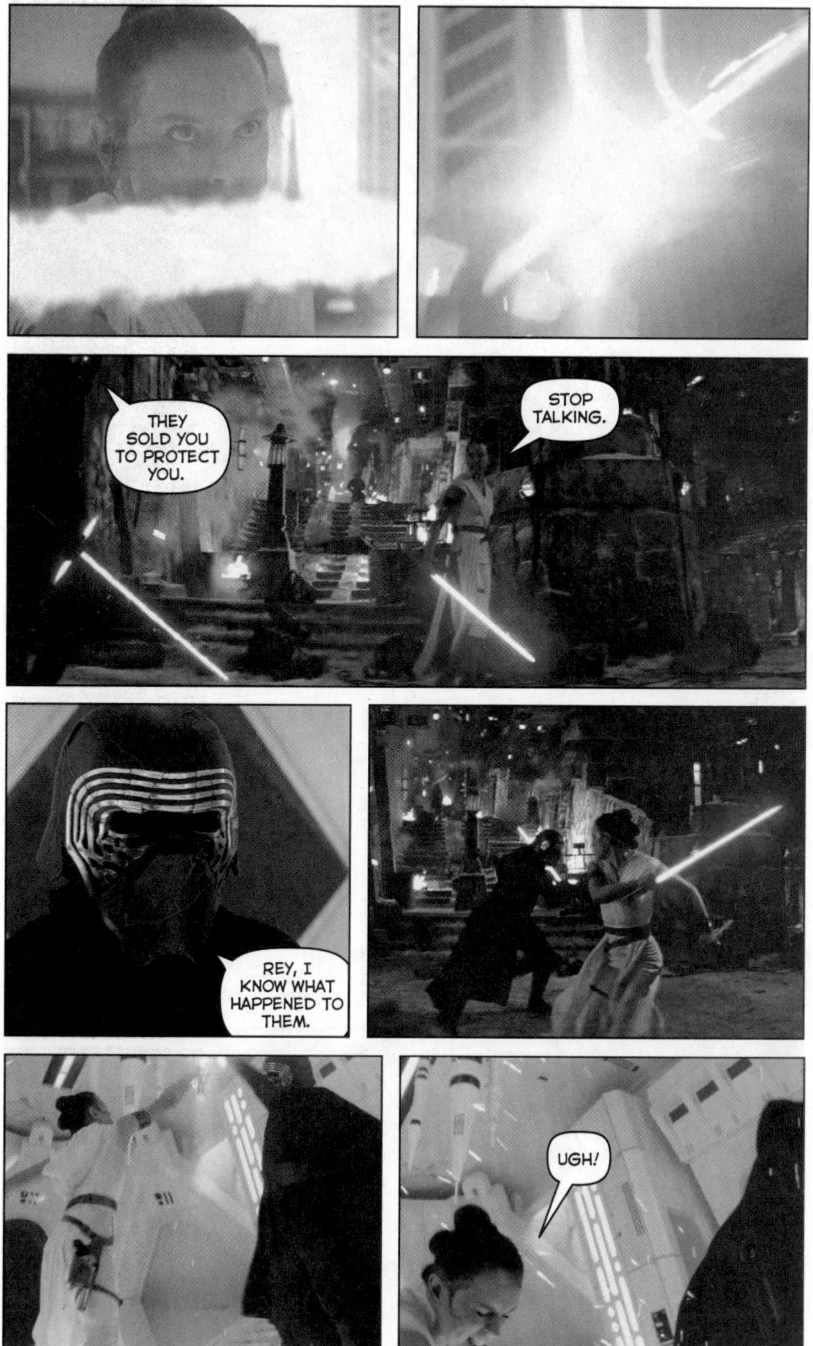
THEY SOLD YOU TO PROTECT YOU.
STOP TALKING.
REY, I KNOW WHAT HAPPENED TO THEM.
UGH!

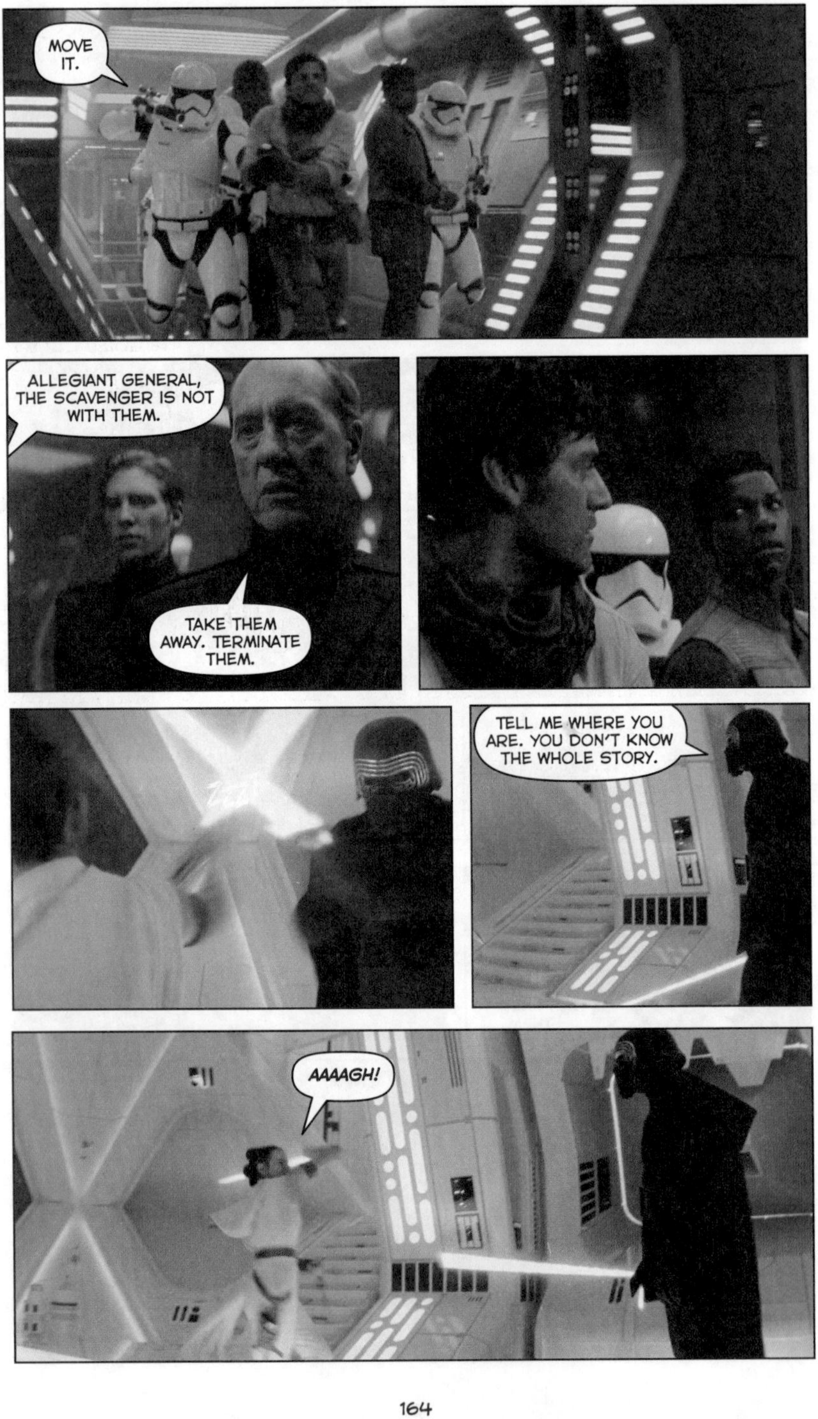
MOVE IT.
ALLEGIANT GENERAL, THE SCAVENGER IS NOT WITH THEM.
TAKE THEM AWAY. TERMINATE THEM.
TELL ME WHERE YOU ARE. YOU DON'T KNOW THE WHOLE STORY.
AAAAGH!

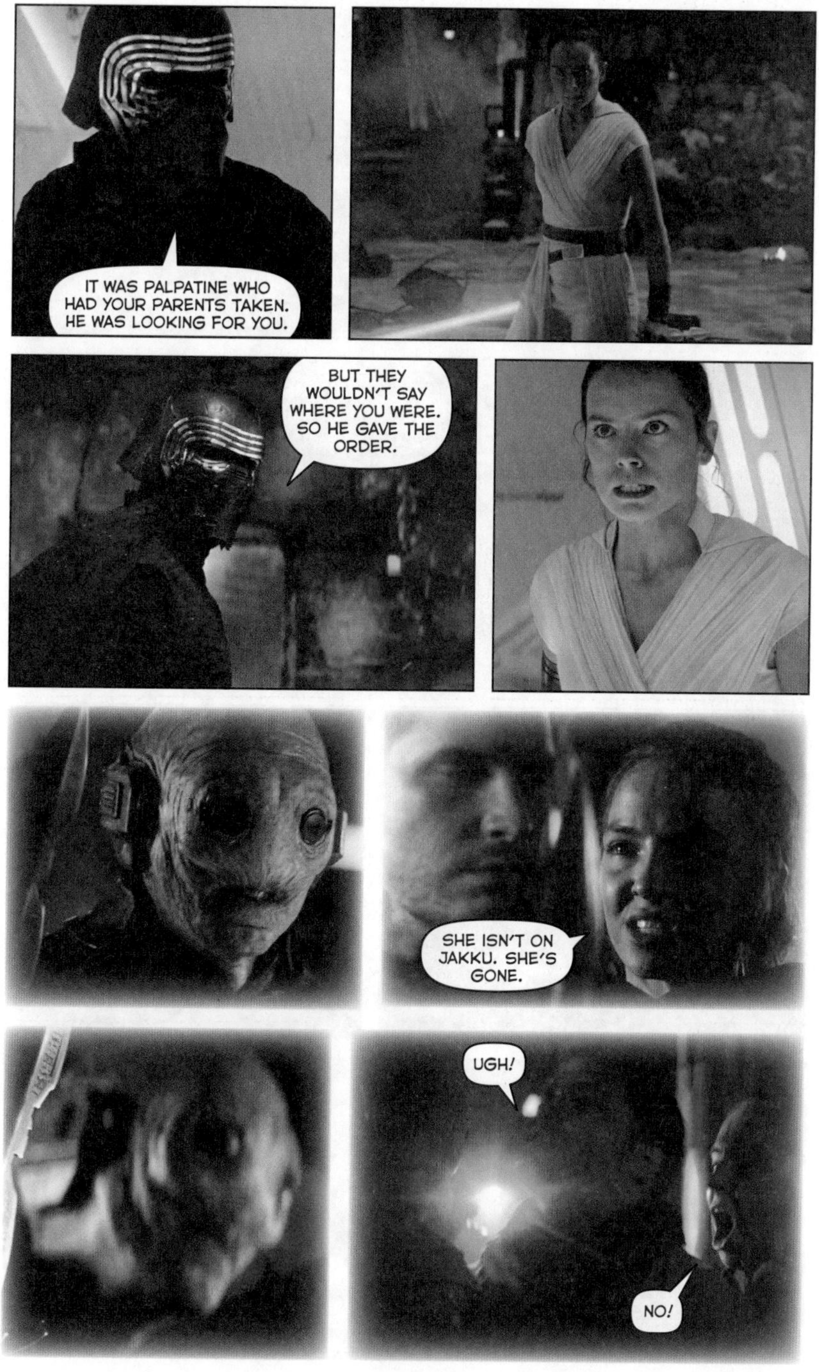
IT WAS PALPATINE WHO HAD YOUR PARENTS TAKEN. HE WAS LOOKING FOR YOU.
BUT THEY WOULDN'T SAY WHERE YOU WERE. SO HE GAVE THE ORDER.
SHE ISN'T ON JAKKU. SHE'S GONE.
UGH!
NO!

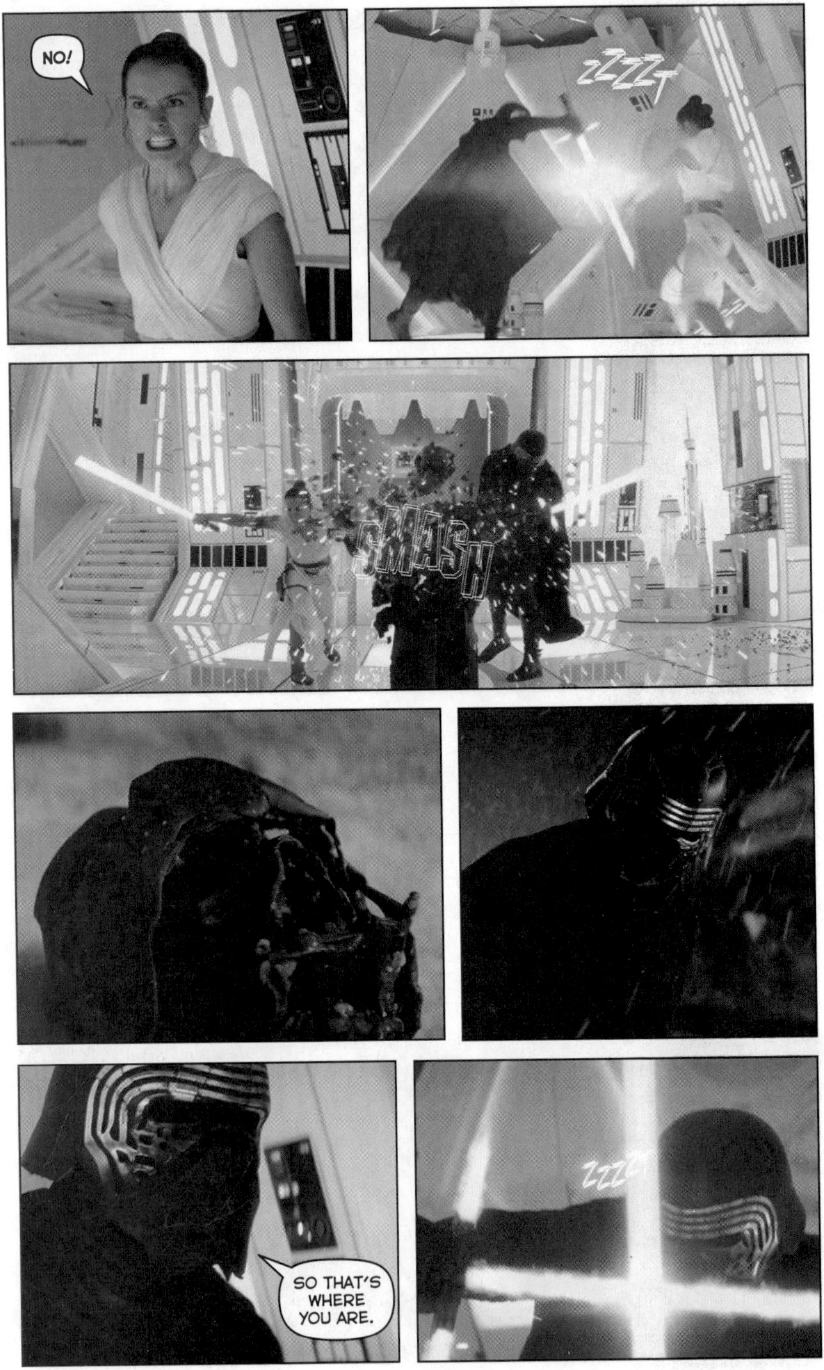
NO!
ZZZZT
SMASH
ZZZT
SO THAT'S WHERE YOU ARE.

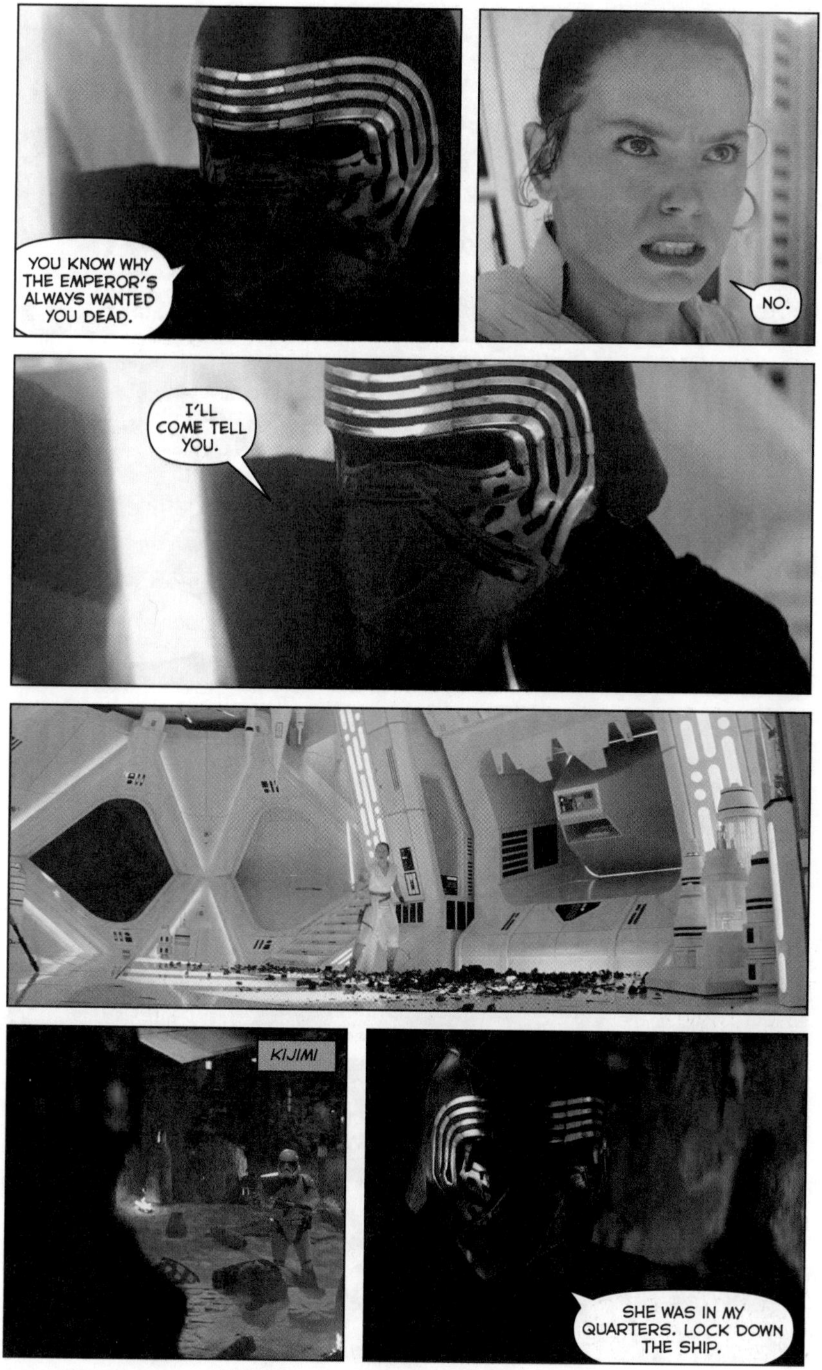
YOU KNOW WHY THE EMPEROR'S ALWAYS WANTED YOU DEAD.
NO.
I'LL COME TELL YOU.
KIJIMI
SHE WAS IN MY QUARTERS. LOCK DOWN THE SHIP.

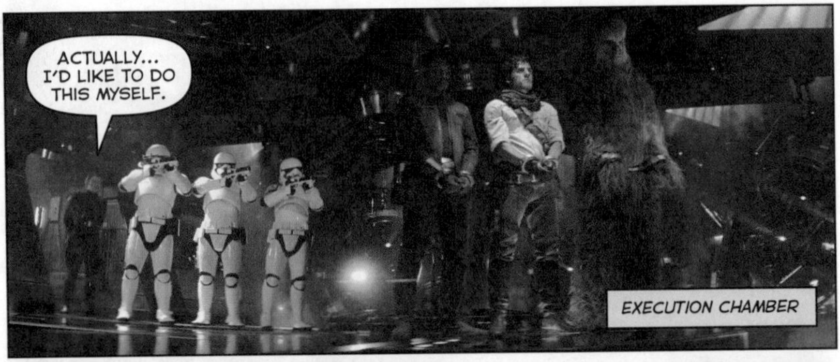
ACTUALLY... I'D LIKE TO DO THIS MYSELF.
EXECUTION CHAMBER

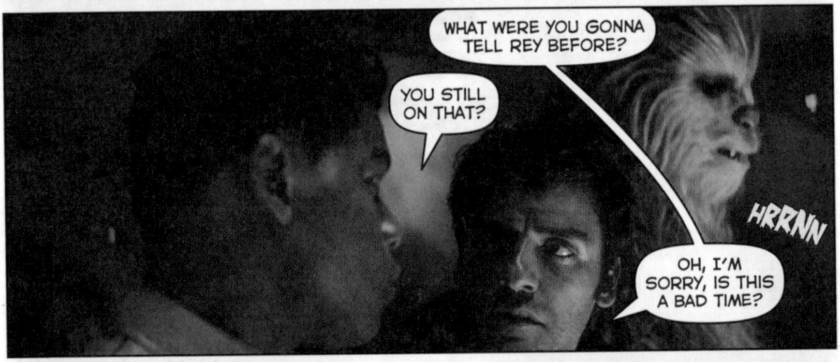
WHAT WERE YOU GONNA TELL REY BEFORE?
YOU STILL ON THAT?
HRRNN
OH, I'M SORRY, IS THIS A BAD TIME?

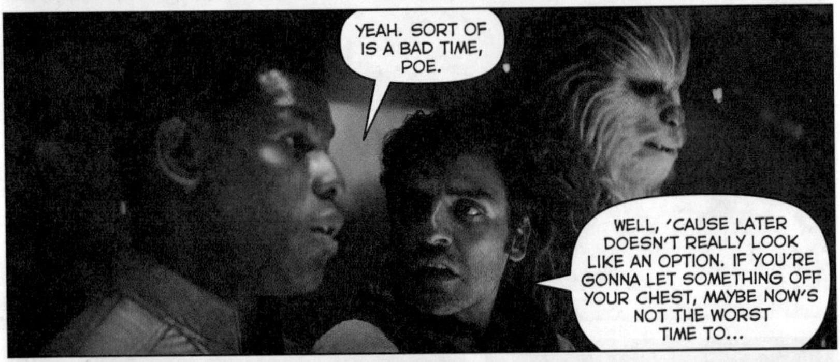
YEAH. SORT OF IS A BAD TIME, POE.
WELL, 'CAUSE LATER DOESN'T REALLY LOOK LIKE AN OPTION. IF YOU'RE GONNA LET SOMETHING OFF YOUR CHEST, MAYBE NOW'S NOT THE WORST TIME TO...

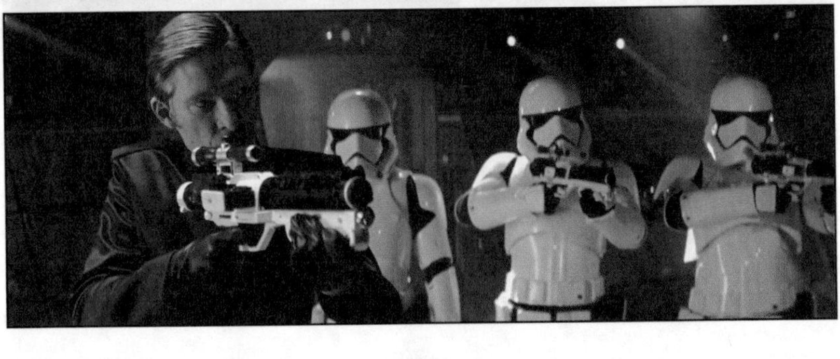

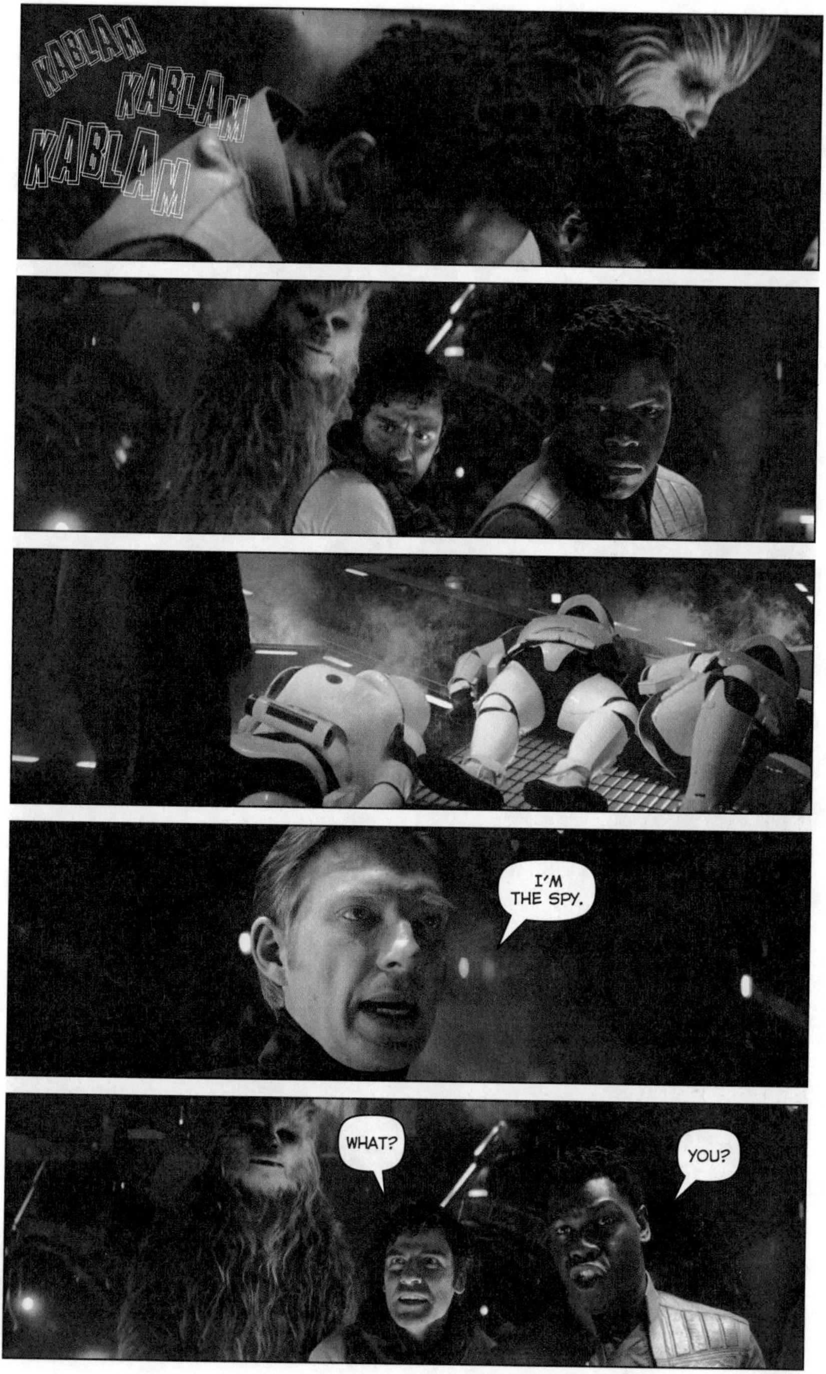
KABLAM
KABLAM
KABLAM
I'M THE SPY.
WHAT?
YOU?

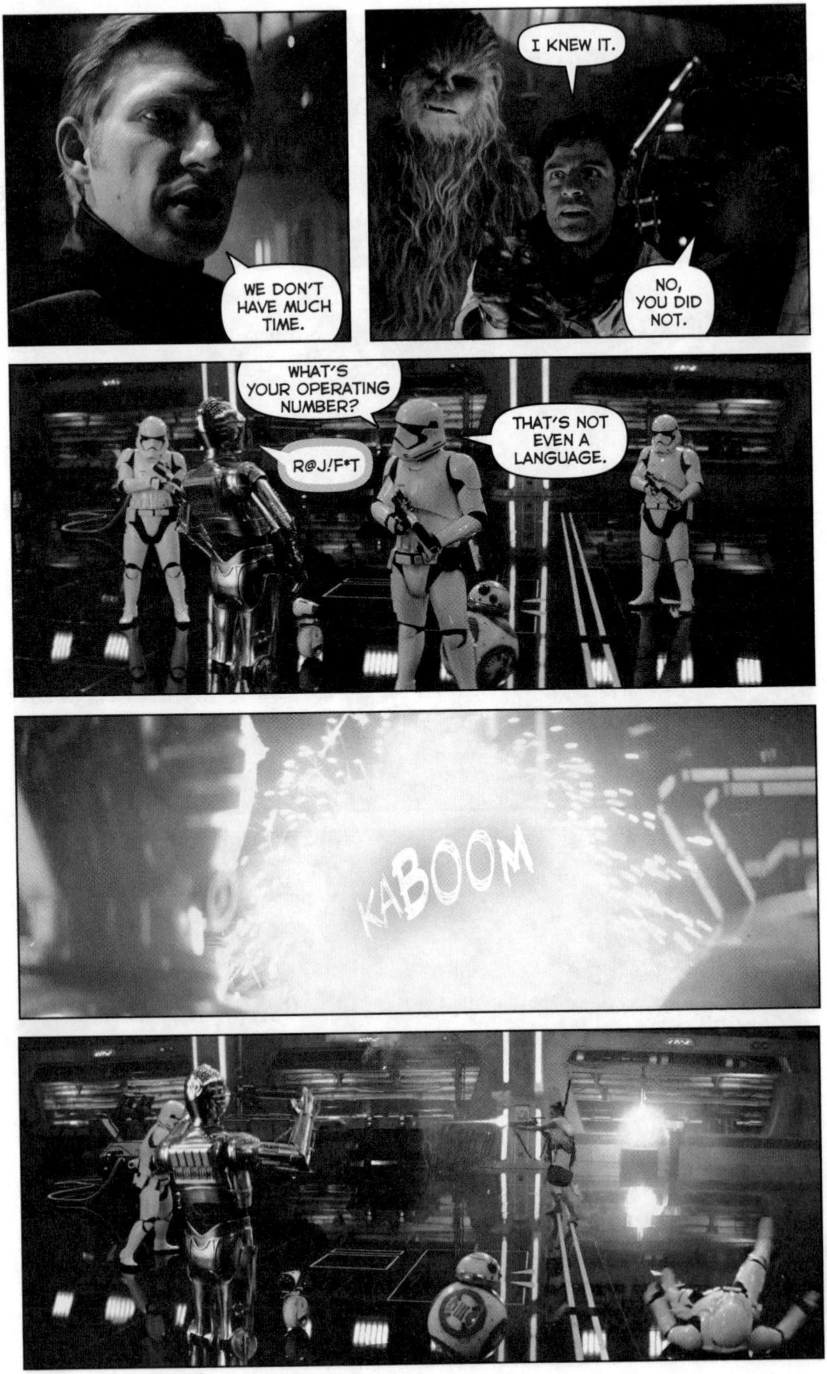
WE DON'T HAVE MUCH TIME.
I KNEW IT.
NO, YOU DID NOT.
WHAT'S YOUR OPERATING NUMBER?
R@J!F*T
THAT'S NOT EVEN A LANGUAGE.
KABOOM

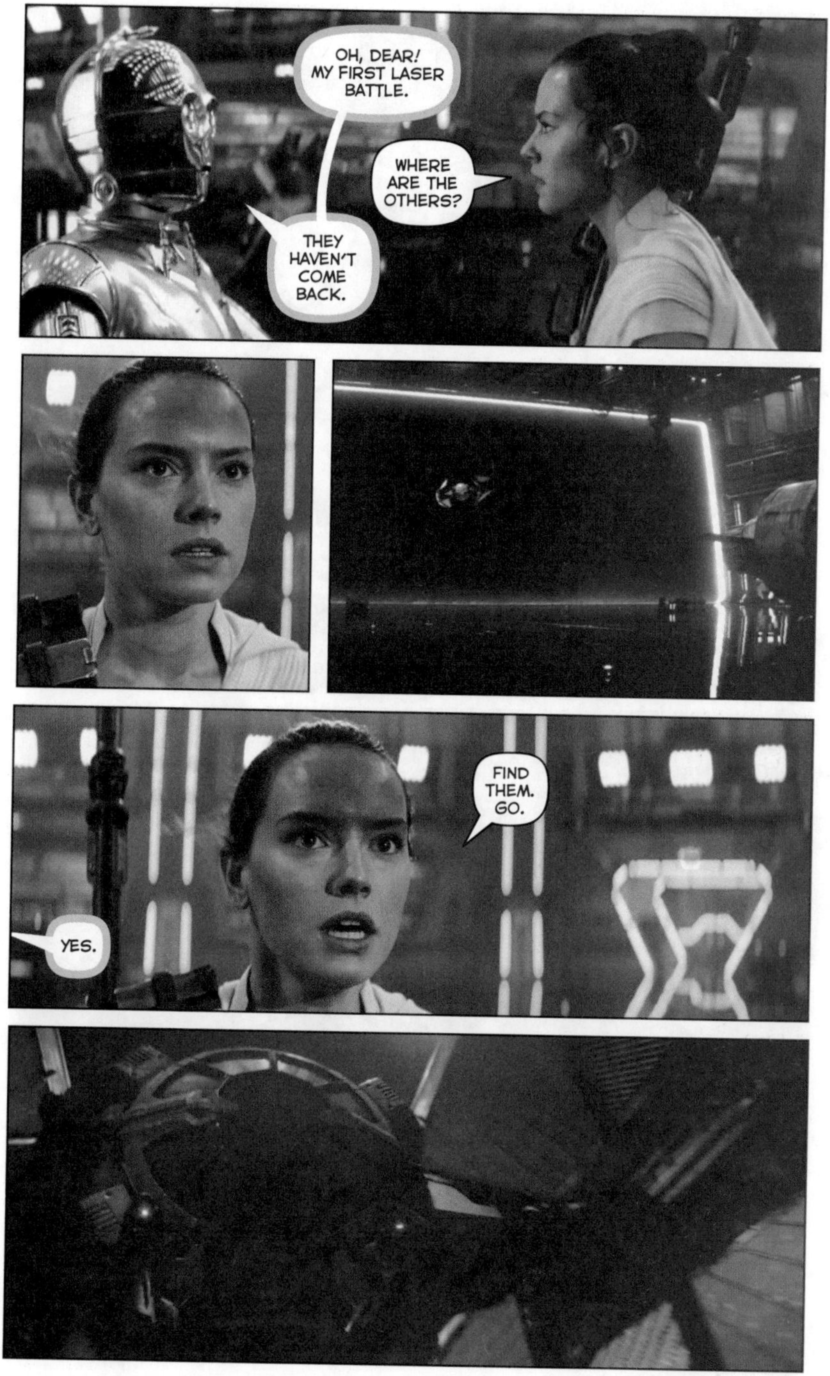
OH, DEAR! MY FIRST LASER BATTLE.
WHERE ARE THE OTHERS?
THEY HAVEN'T COME BACK.
FIND THEM. GO.
YES.

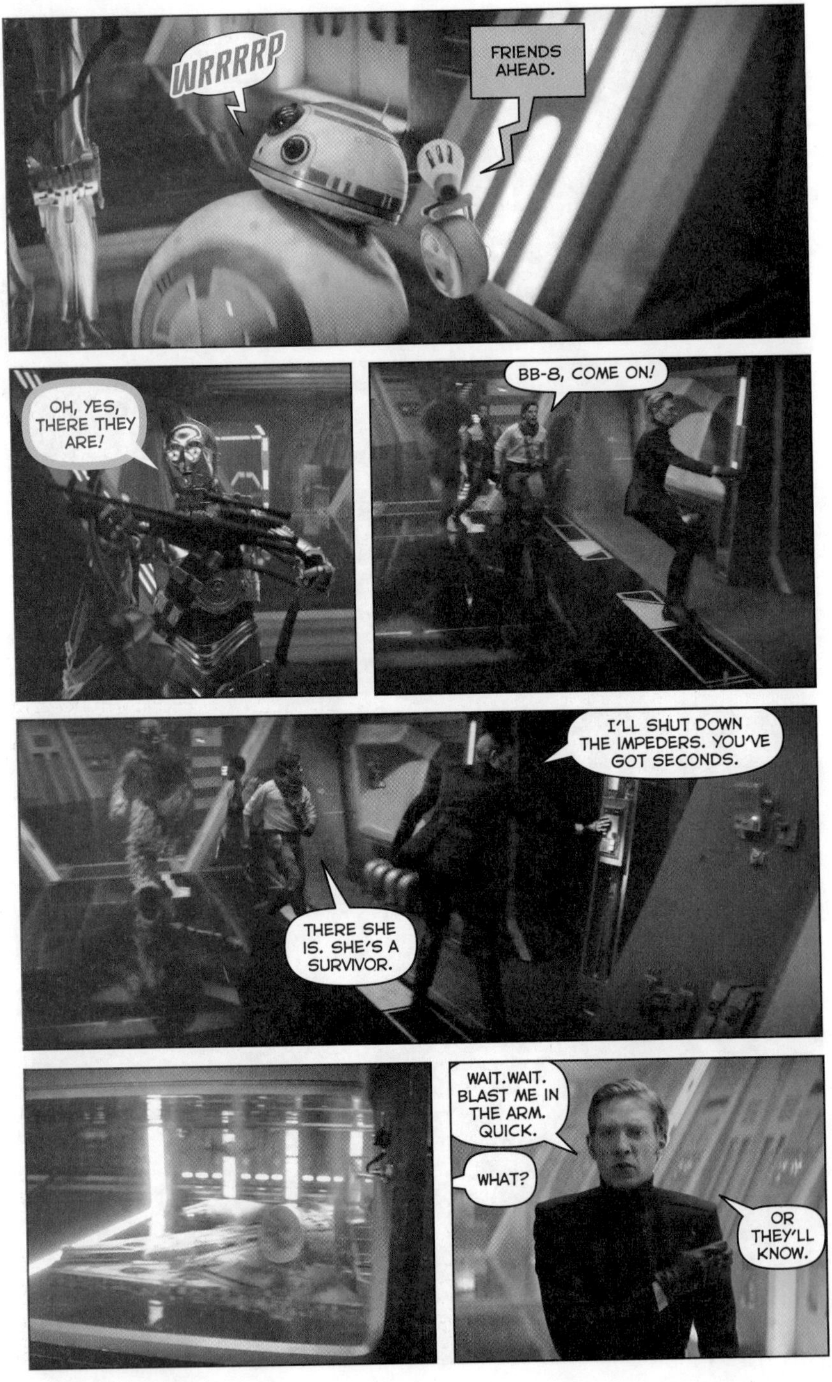
WRRRRP
FRIENDS AHEAD.
OH, YES, THERE THEY ARE!
BB-8, COME ON!
I'LL SHUT DOWN THE IMPEDERS. YOU'VE GOT SECONDS.
THERE SHE IS. SHE'S A SURVIVOR.
WAIT.WAIT. BLAST ME IN THE ARM. QUICK.
WHAT?
OR THEY'LL KNOW.

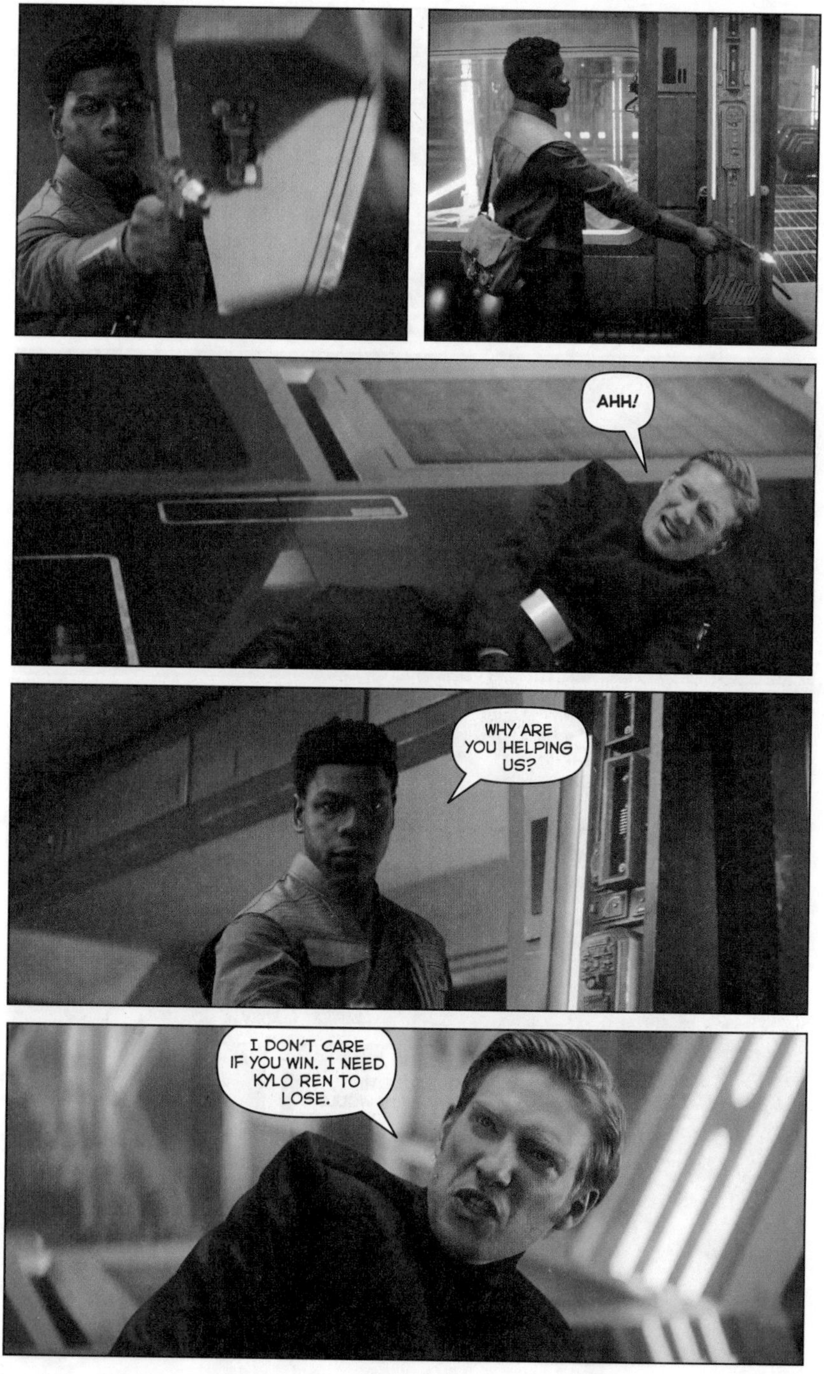
AHH!
WHY ARE YOU HELPING US?
I DON'T CARE IF YOU WIN. I NEED KYLO REN TO LOSE.

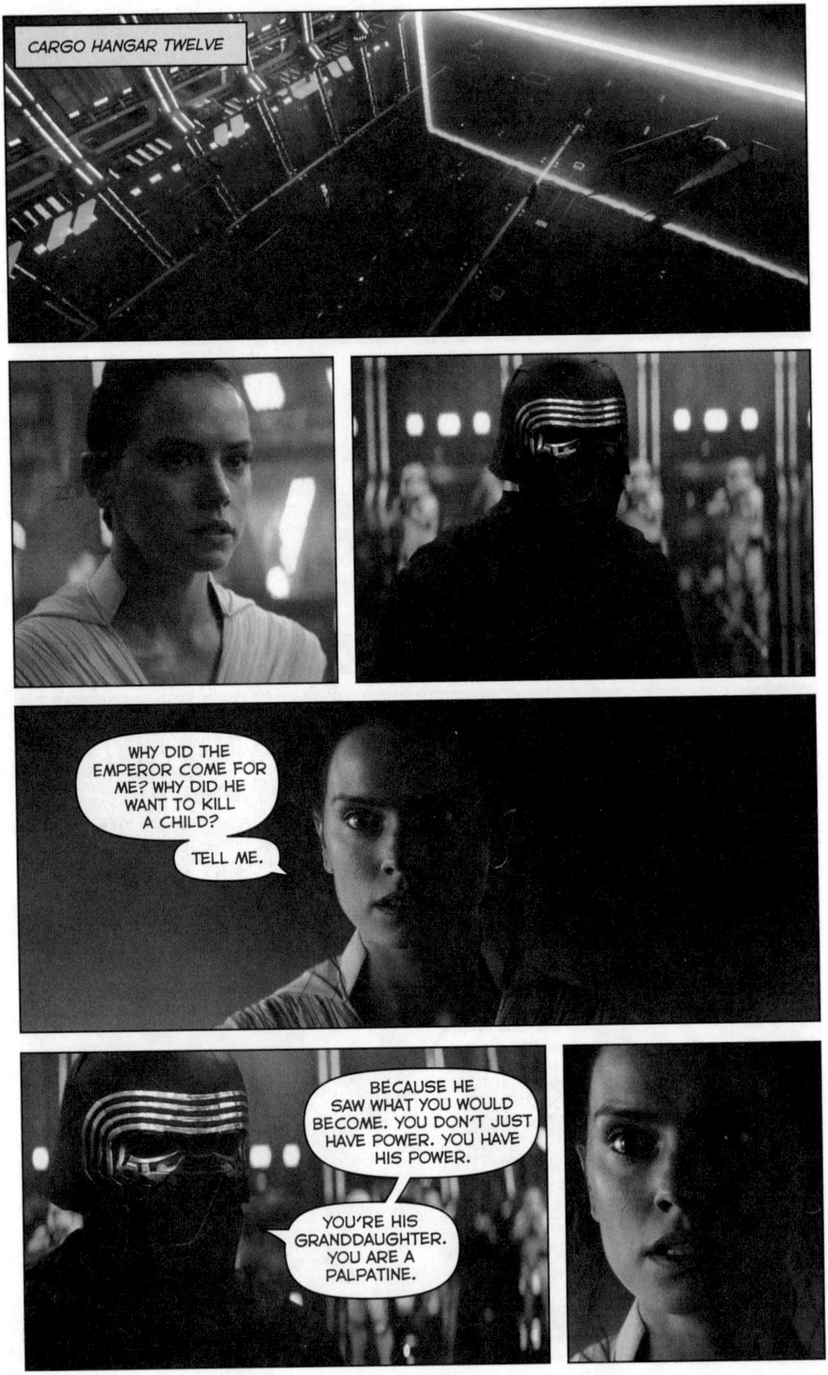
CARGO HANGAR TWELVE
WHY DID THE EMPEROR COME FOR ME? WHY DID HE WANT TO KILL A CHILD?
TELL ME.
BECAUSE HE SAW WHAT YOU WOULD BECOME. YOU DON'T JUST HAVE POWER. YOU HAVE HIS POWER.
YOU'RE HIS GRANDDAUGHTER. YOU ARE A PALPATINE.

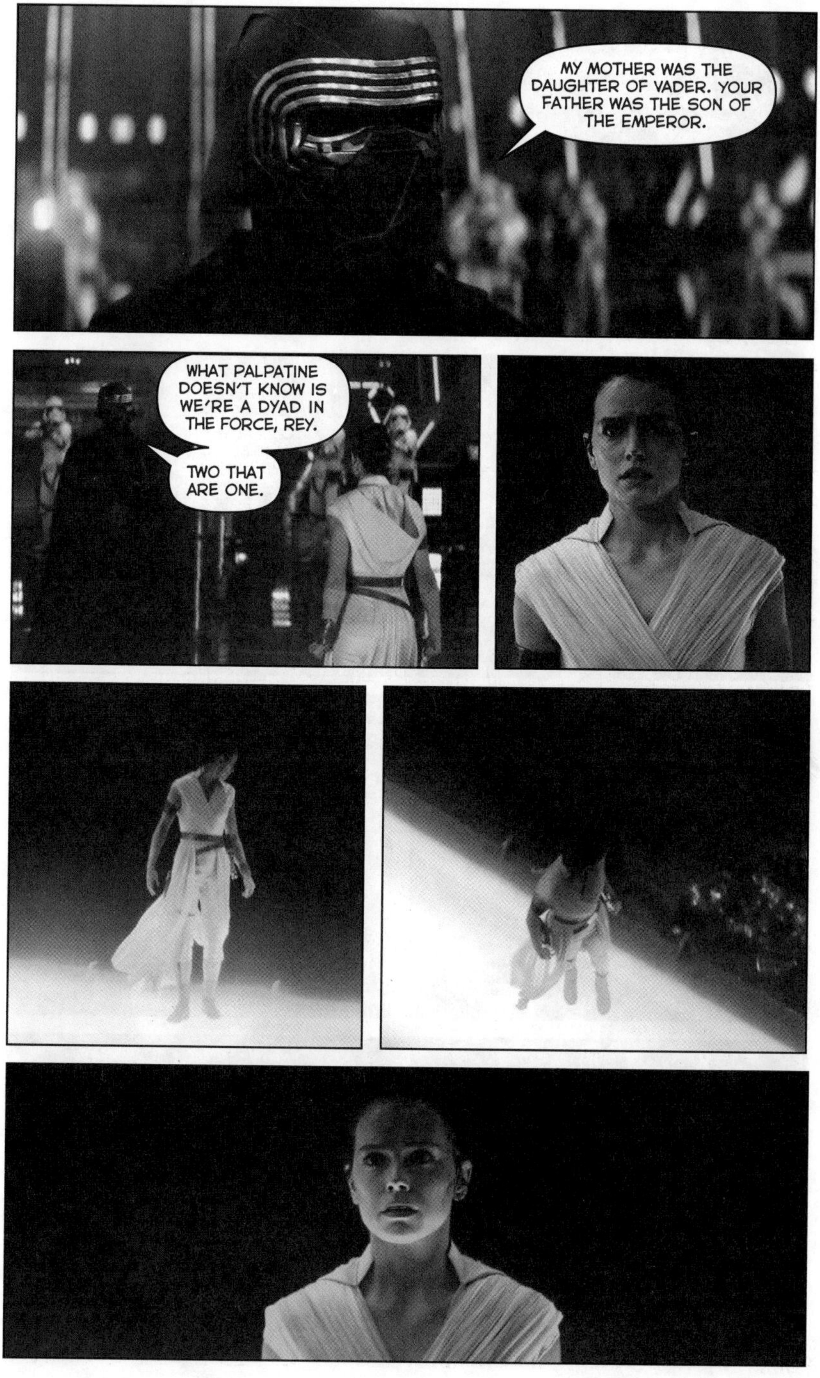
MY MOTHER WAS THE DAUGHTER OF VADER. YOUR FATHER WAS THE SON OF THE EMPEROR.
WHAT PALPATINE DOESN'T KNOW IS WE'RE A DYAD IN THE FORCE, REY.
TWO THAT ARE ONE.

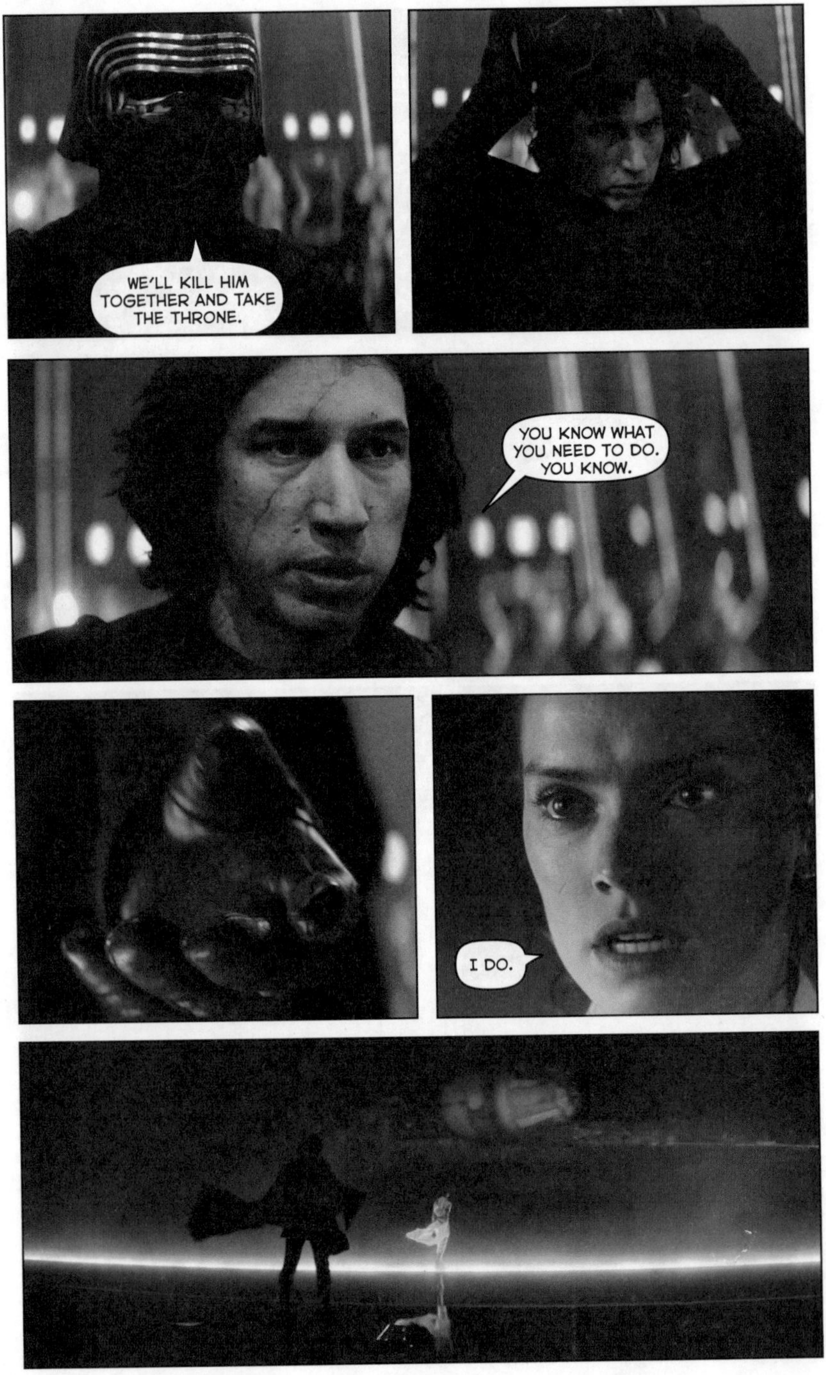
WE'LL KILL HIM TOGETHER AND TAKE THE THRONE.
YOU KNOW WHAT YOU NEED TO DO. YOU KNOW.
I DO.

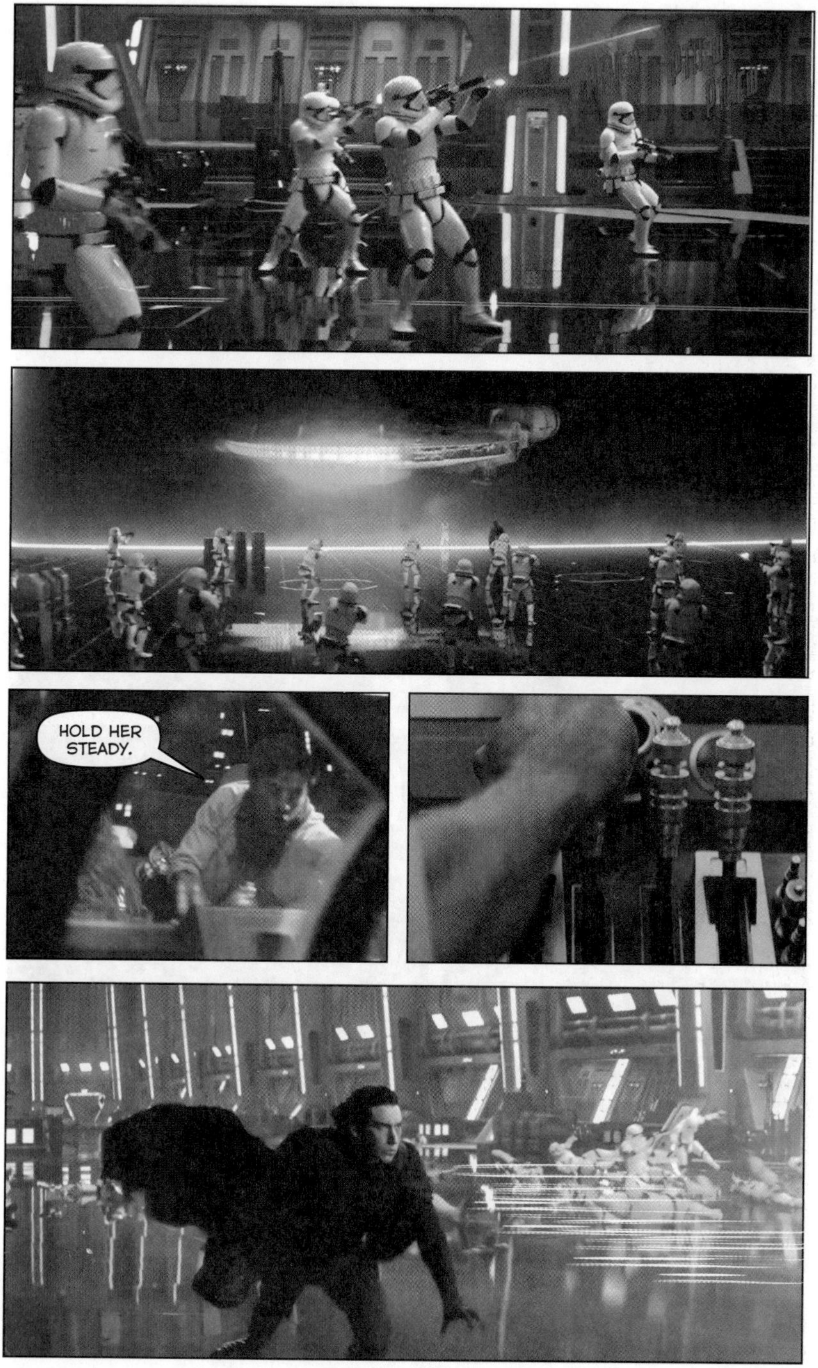
HOLD HER
STEADY.

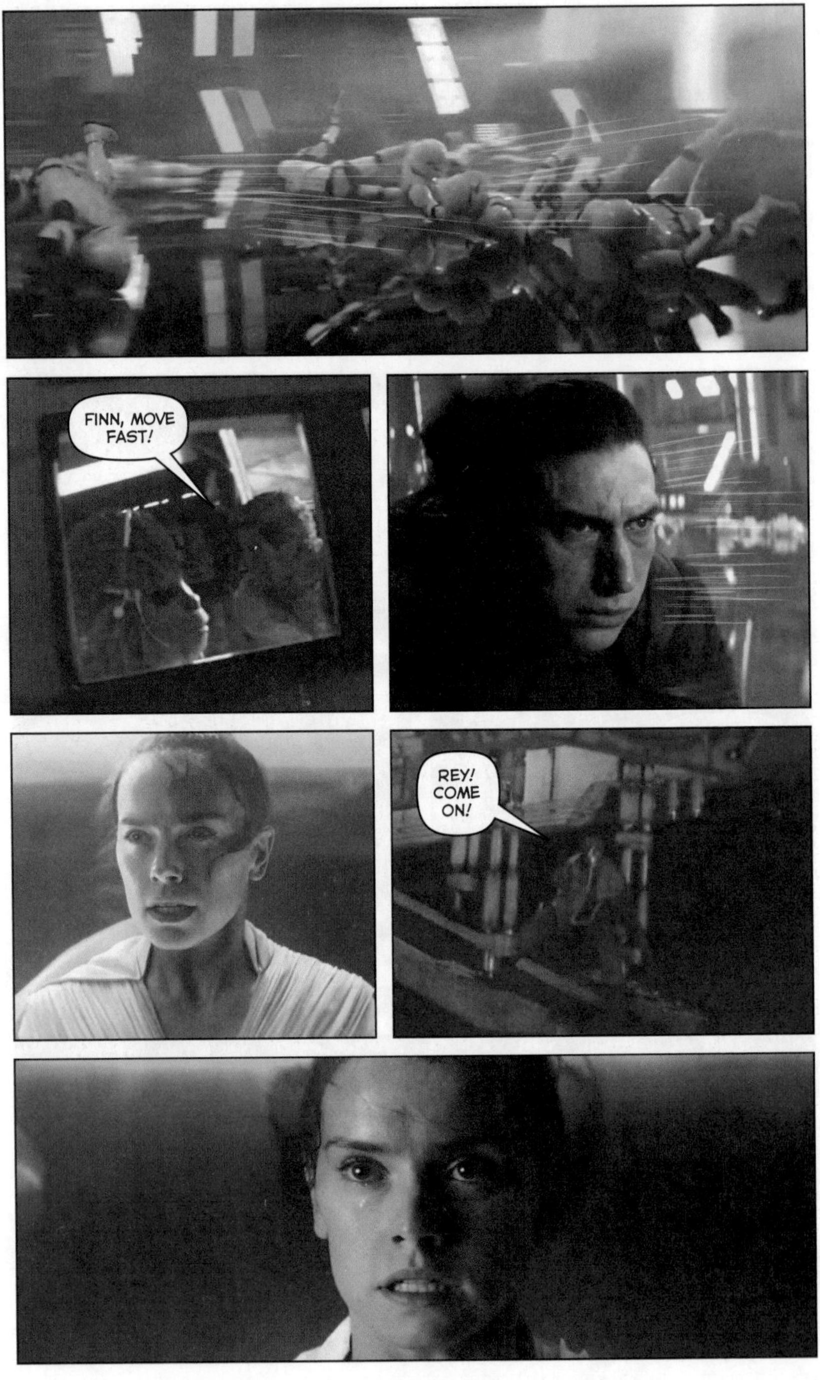
FINN, MOVE FAST!
REY! COME ON!

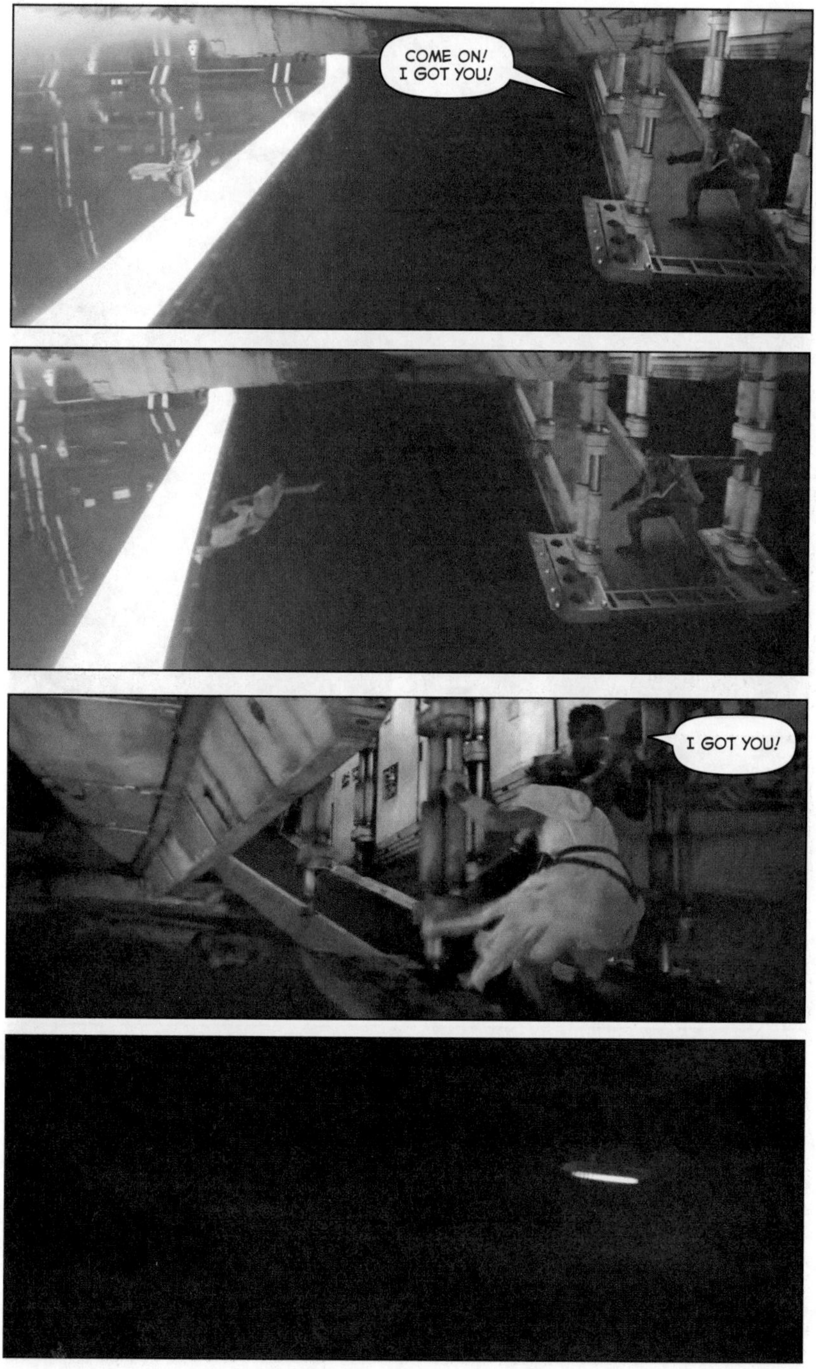
COME ON!
I GOT YOU!
I GOT YOU!

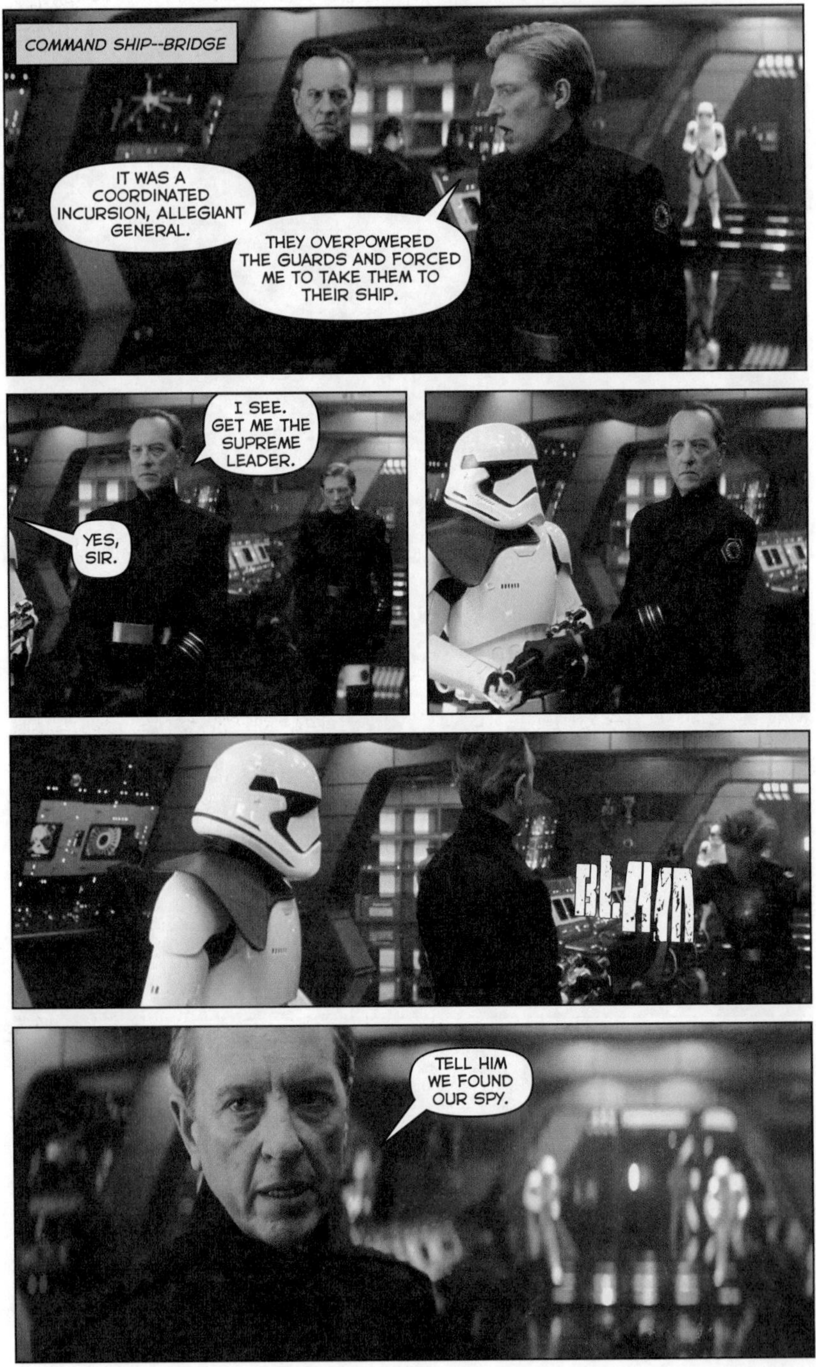
COMMAND SHIP--BRIDGE
IT WAS A COORDINATED INCURSION, ALLEGIANT GENERAL.
THEY OVERPOWERED THE GUARDS AND FORCED ME TO TAKE THEM TO THEIR SHIP.
I SEE. GET ME THE SUPREME LEADER.
YES, SIR.
BLAM
TELL HIM WE FOUND OUR SPY.

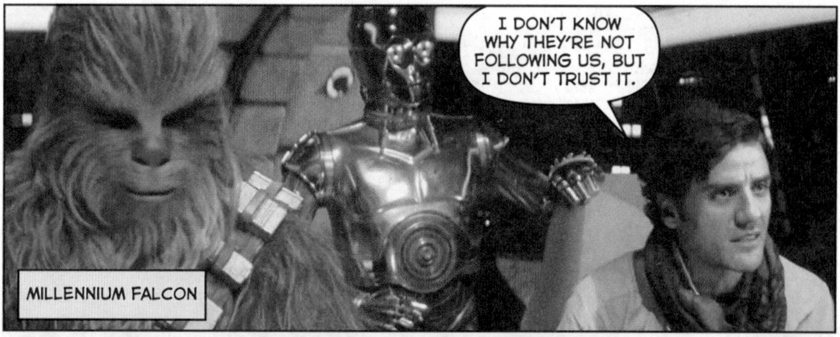
MILLENNIUM FALCON
I DON'T KNOW WHY THEY'RE NOT FOLLOWING US, BUT I DON'T TRUST IT.

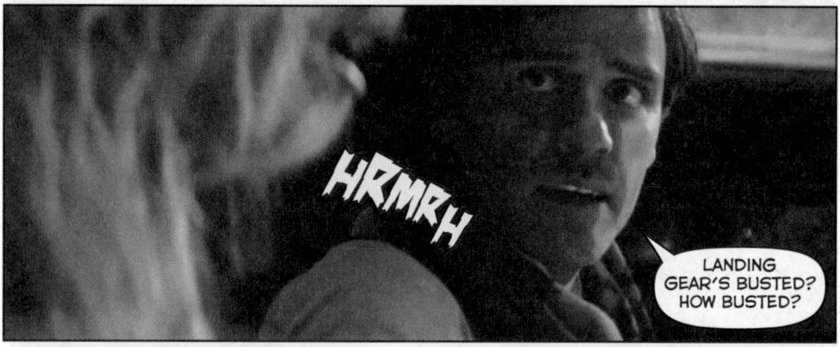
HRMRH
LANDING GEAR'S BUSTED? HOW BUSTED?

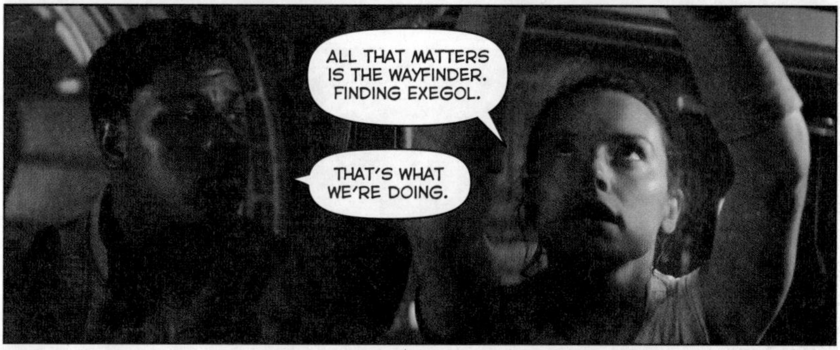
ALL THAT MATTERS IS THE WAYFINDER. FINDING EXEGOL.
THAT'S WHAT WE'RE DOING.

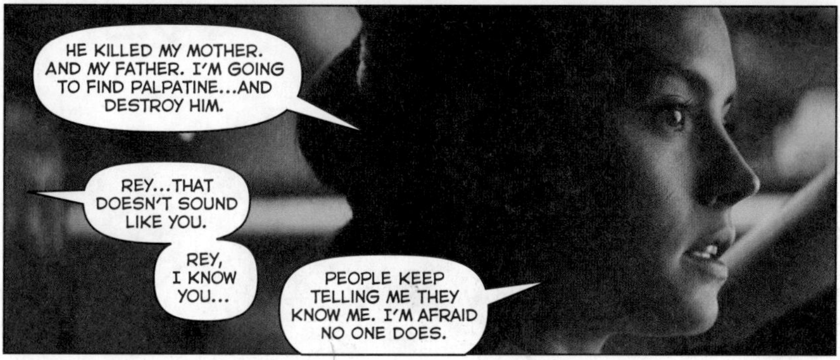
HE KILLED MY MOTHER. AND MY FATHER. I'M GOING TO FIND PALPATINE...AND DESTROY HIM.
REY...THAT DOESN'T SOUND LIKE YOU.
REY, I KNOW YOU...
PEOPLE KEEP TELLING ME THEY KNOW ME. I'M AFRAID NO ONE DOES.

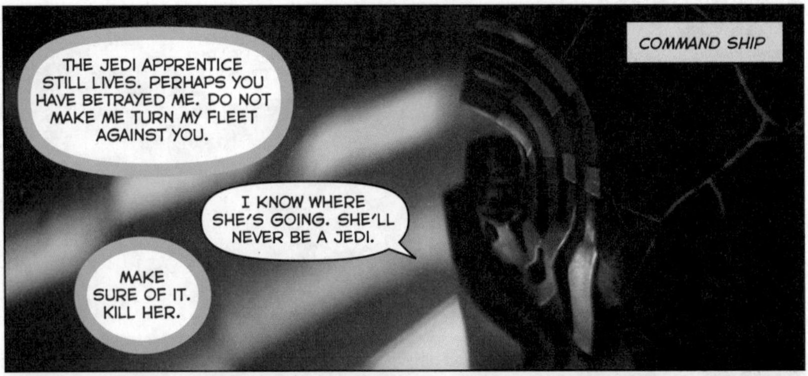
COMMAND SHIP
THE JEDI APPRENTICE STILL LIVES. PERHAPS YOU HAVE BETRAYED ME. DO NOT MAKE ME TURN MY FLEET AGAINST YOU.
I KNOW WHERE SHE'S GOING. SHE'LL NEVER BE A JEDI.
MAKE SURE OF IT. KILL HER.

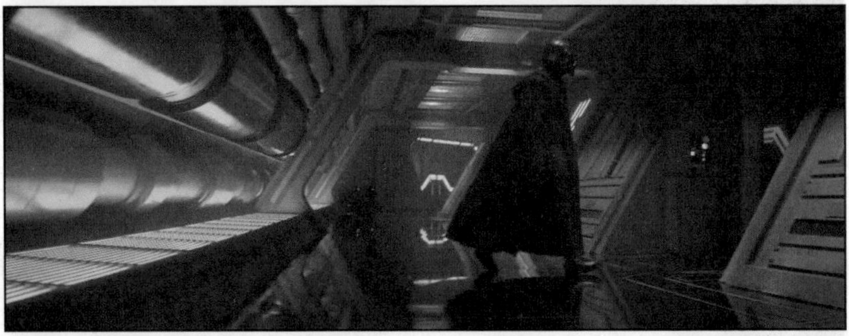

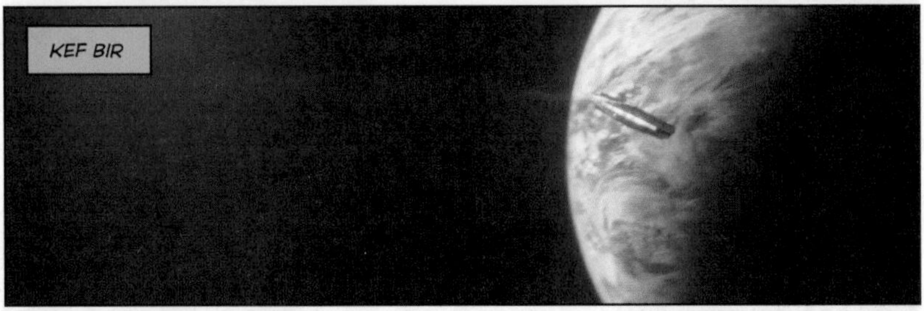
KEF BIR

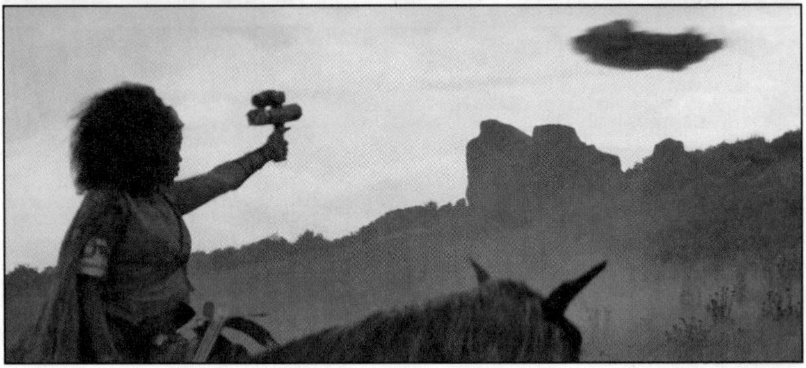

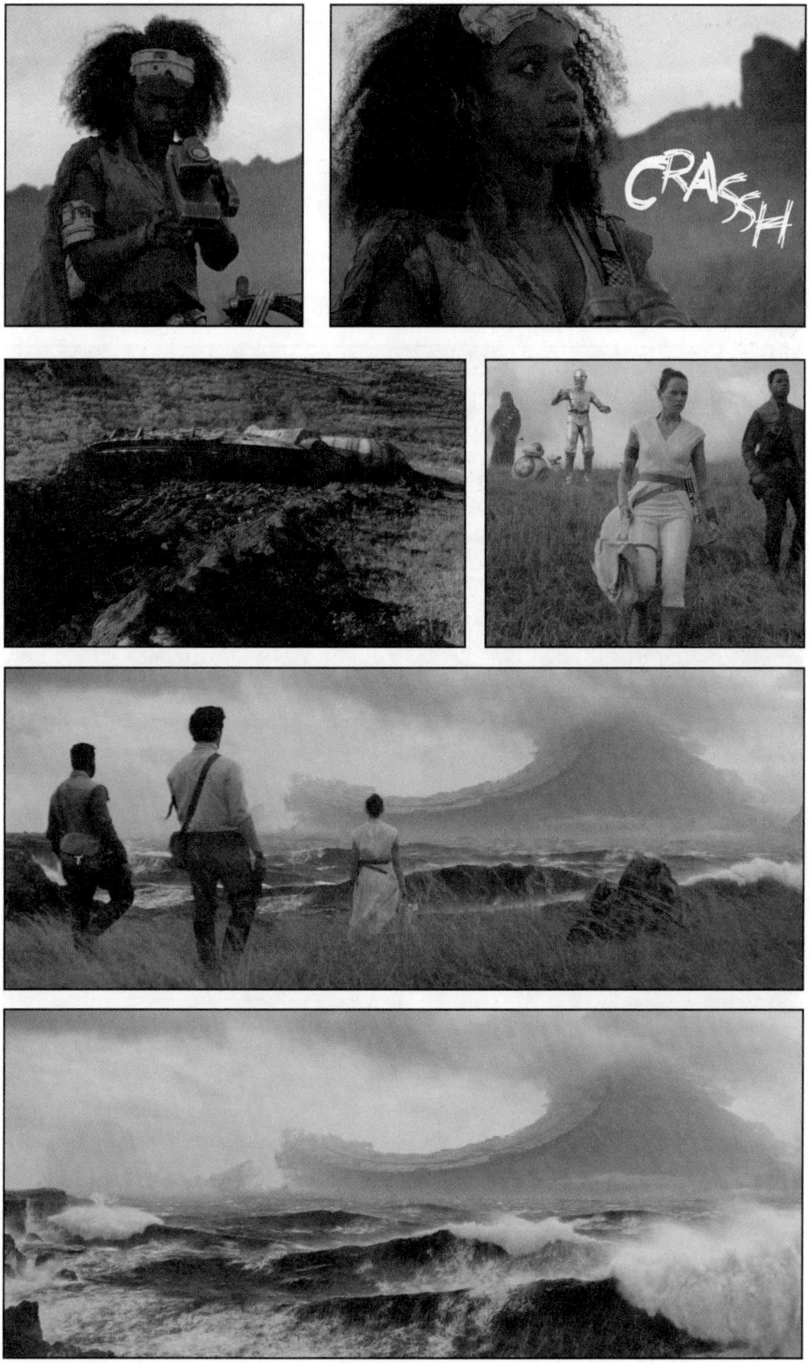
CRASSH

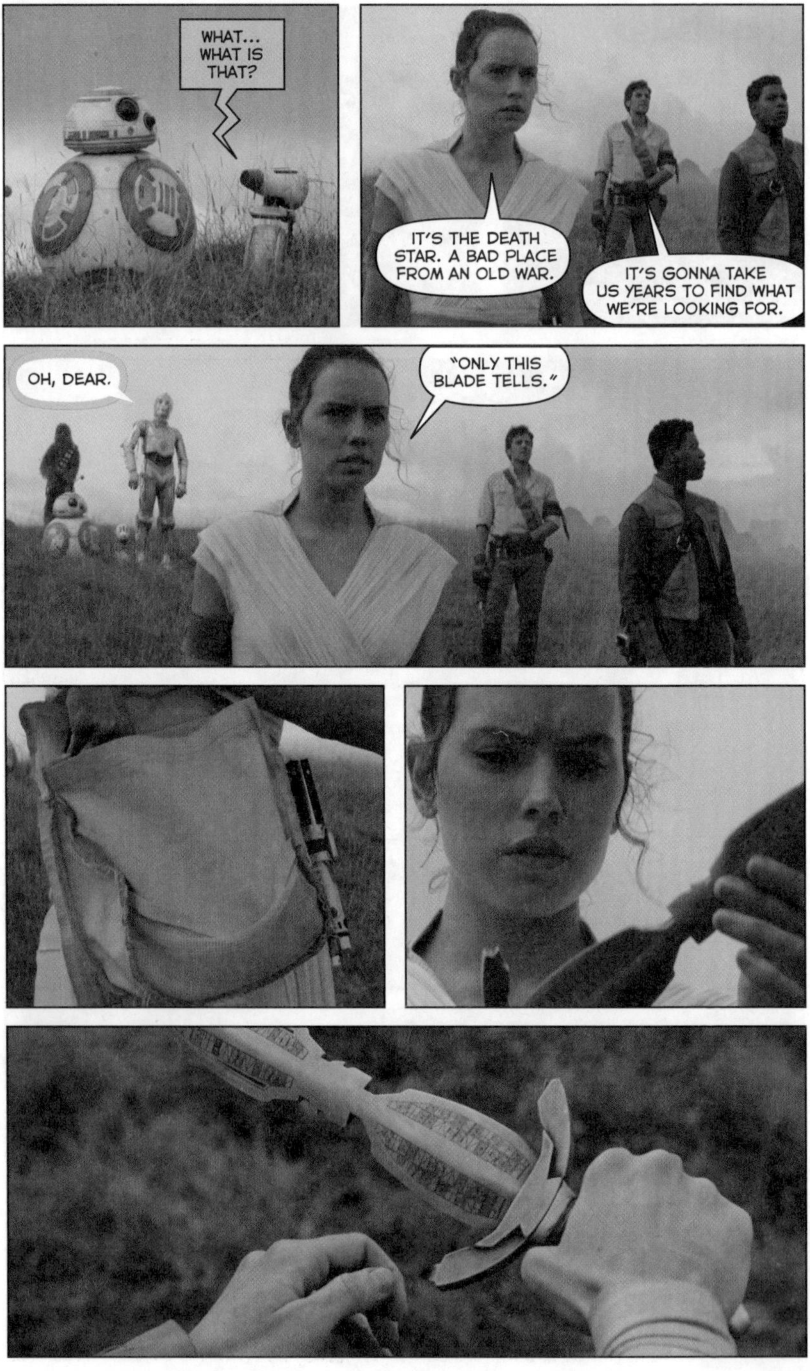
WHAT... WHAT IS THAT?
IT'S THE DEATH STAR. A BAD PLACE FROM AN OLD WAR.
IT'S GONNA TAKE US YEARS TO FIND WHAT WE'RE LOOKING FOR.
OH, DEAR.
"ONLY THIS BLADE TELLS."

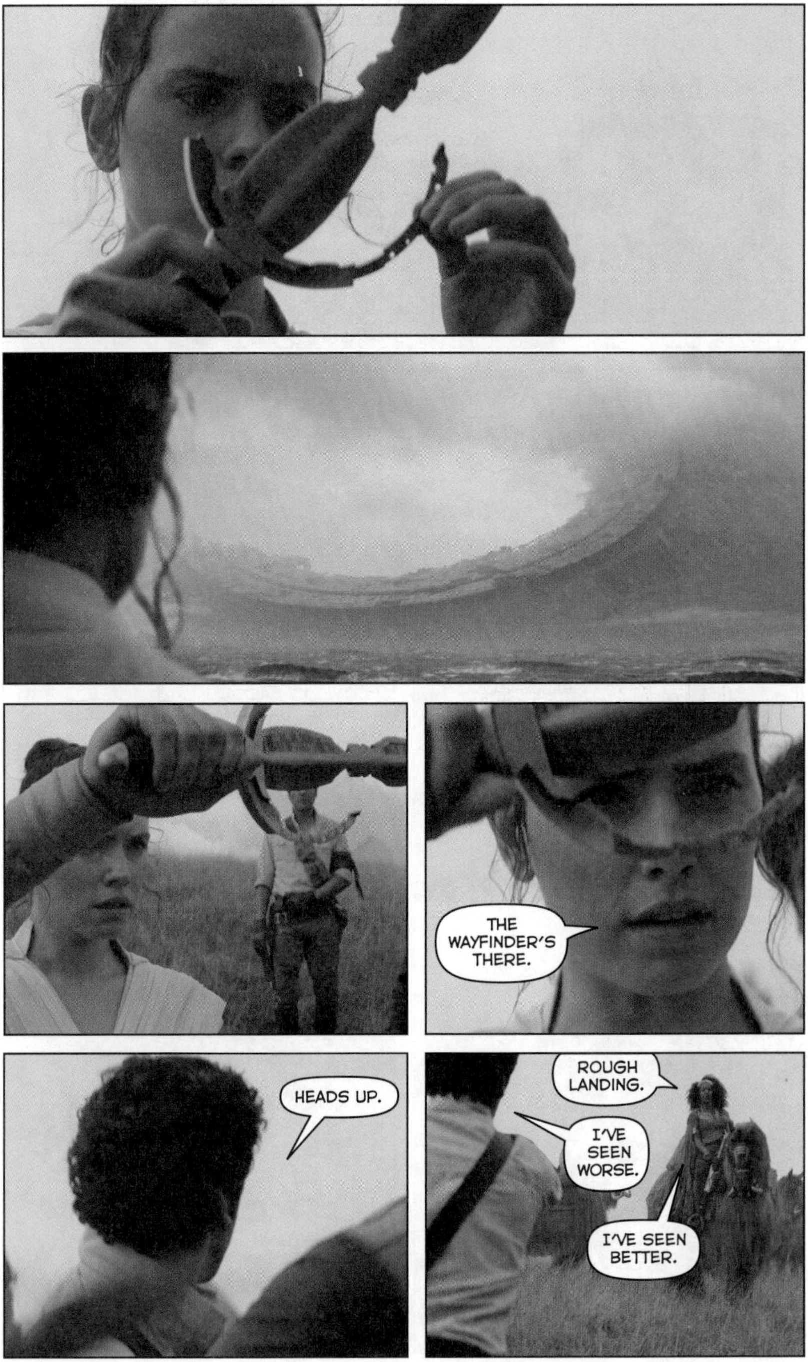
THE WAYFINDER'S THERE.
HEADS UP.
ROUGH LANDING.
I'VE SEEN WORSE.
I'VE SEEN BETTER.

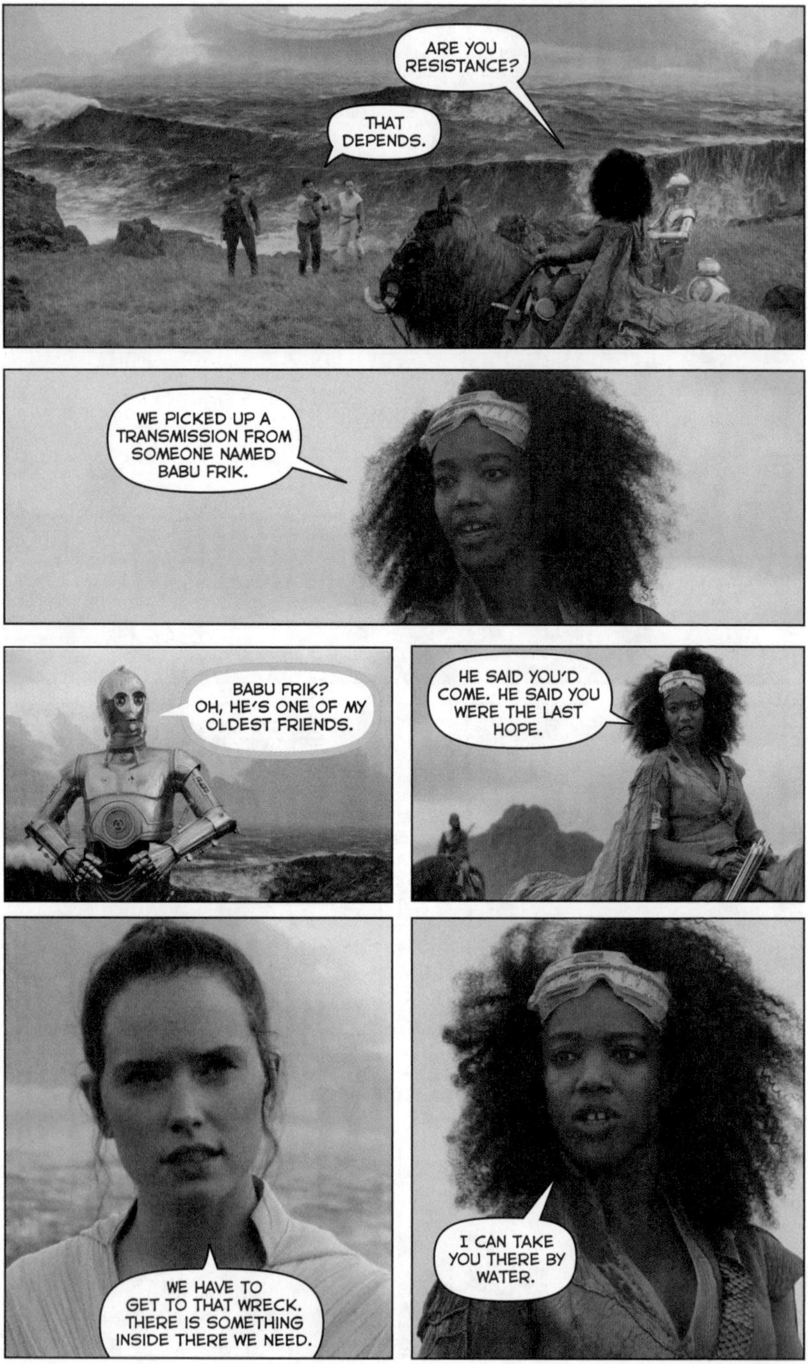
ARE YOU RESISTANCE?
THAT DEPENDS.
WE PICKED UP A TRANSMISSION FROM SOMEONE NAMED BABU FRIK.
BABU FRIK? OH, HE'S ONE OF MY OLDEST FRIENDS.
HE SAID YOU'D COME. HE SAID YOU WERE THE LAST HOPE.
WE HAVE TO GET TO THAT WRECK. THERE IS SOMETHING INSIDE THERE WE NEED.
I CAN TAKE YOU THERE BY WATER.

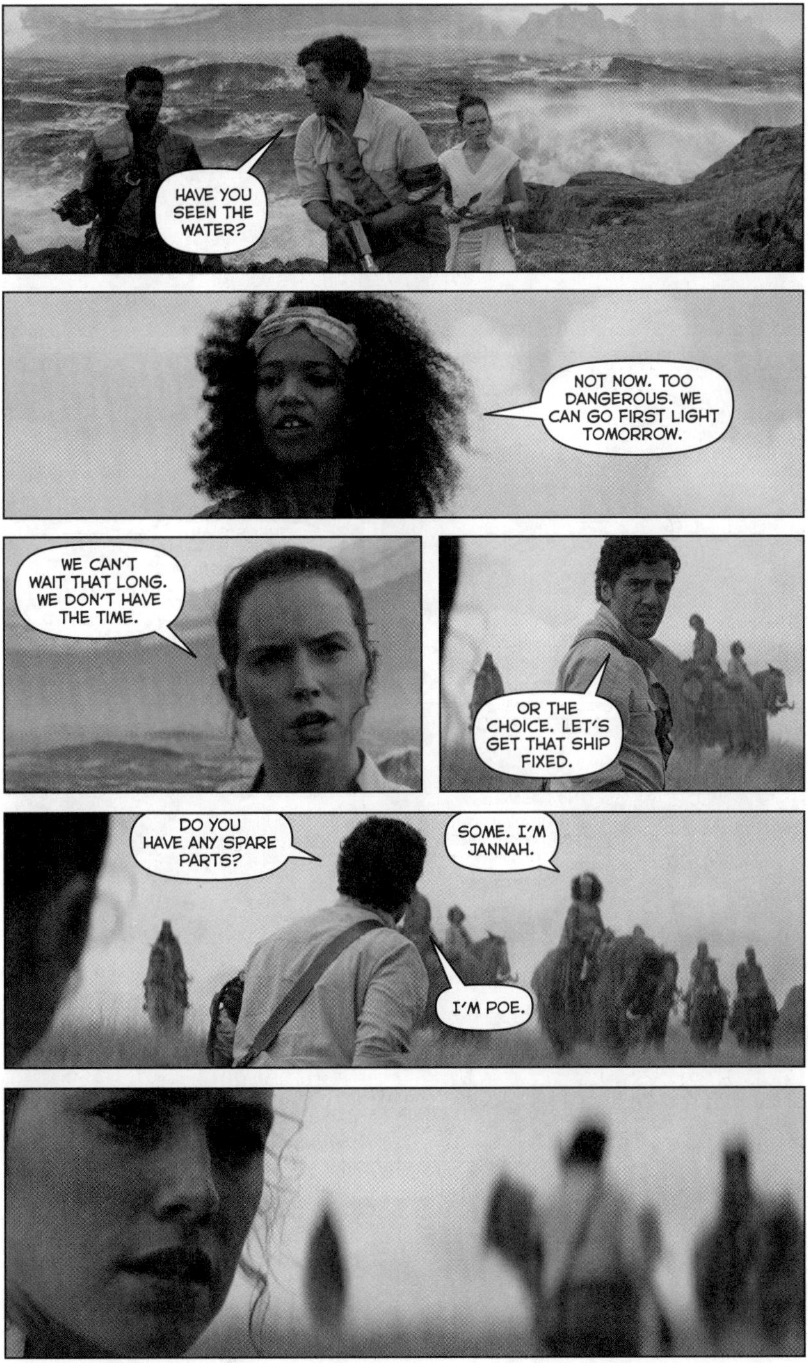
HAVE YOU SEEN THE WATER?
NOT NOW. TOO DANGEROUS. WE CAN GO FIRST LIGHT TOMORROW.
WE CAN'T WAIT THAT LONG. WE DON'T HAVE THE TIME.
OR THE CHOICE. LET'S GET THAT SHIP FIXED.
DO YOU HAVE ANY SPARE PARTS?
SOME. I'M JANNAH.
I'M POE.

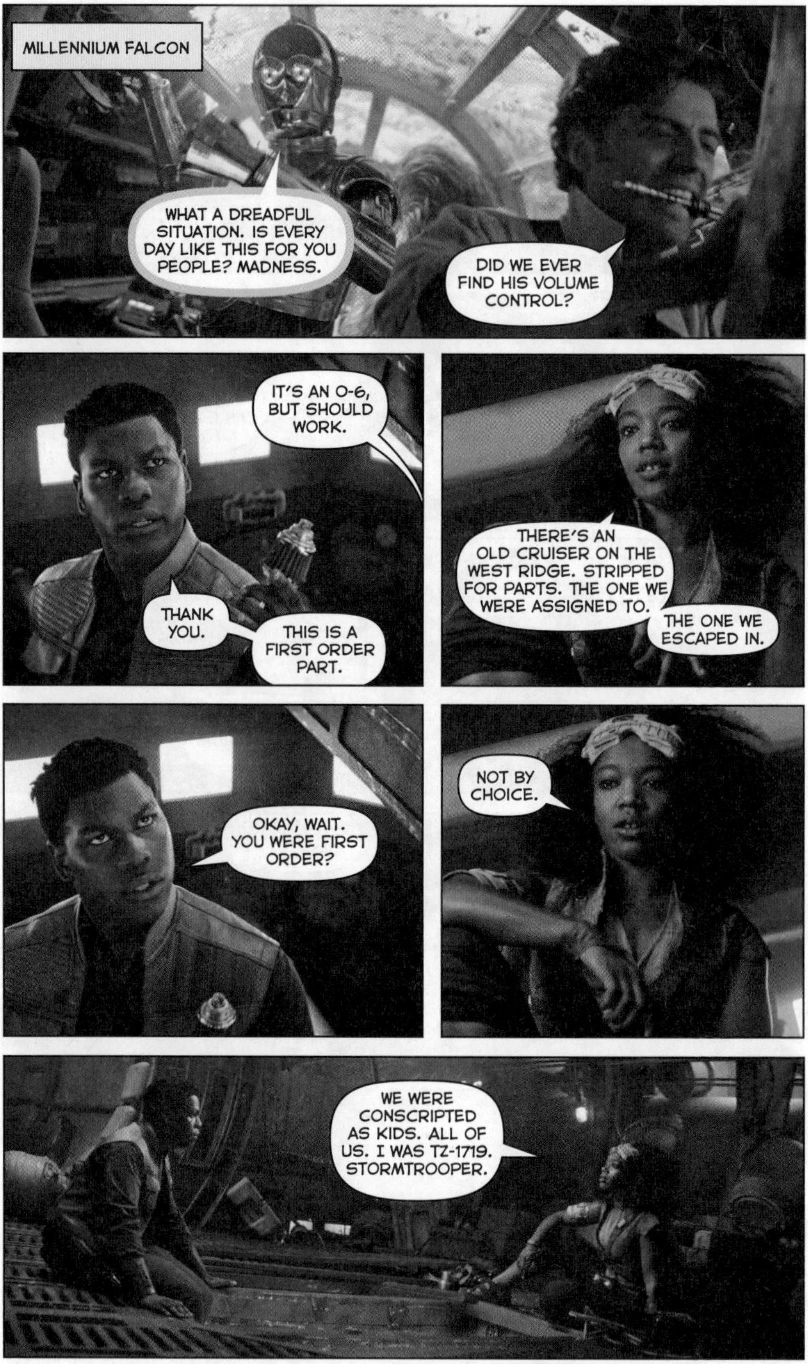
MILLENNIUM FALCON
WHAT A DREADFUL SITUATION. IS EVERY DAY LIKE THIS FOR YOU PEOPLE? MADNESS.
DID WE EVER FIND HIS VOLUME CONTROL?
IT'S AN O-6, BUT SHOULD WORK.
THANK YOU.
THIS IS A FIRST ORDER PART.
THERE'S AN OLD CRUISER ON THE WEST RIDGE. STRIPPED FOR PARTS. THE ONE WE WERE ASSIGNED TO.
THE ONE WE ESCAPED IN.
OKAY, WAIT. YOU WERE FIRST ORDER?
NOT BY CHOICE.
WE WERE CONSCRIPTED AS KIDS. ALL OF US. I WAS TZ-1719. STORMTROOPER.

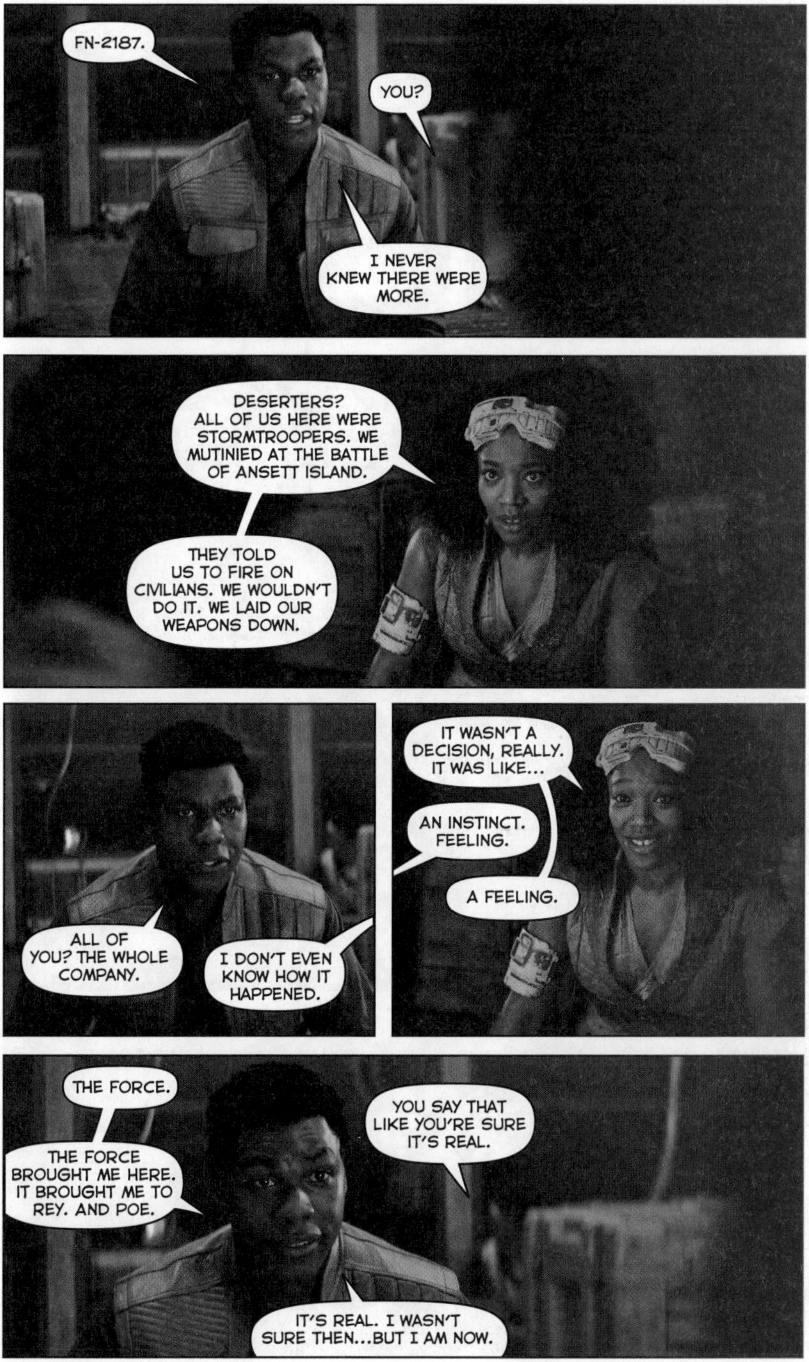
FN-2187.
YOU?
I NEVER KNEW THERE WERE MORE.
DESERTERS? ALL OF US HERE WERE STORMTROOPERS. WE MUTINIED AT THE BATTLE OF ANSETT ISLAND.
THEY TOLD US TO FIRE ON CIVILIANS. WE WOULDN'T DO IT. WE LAID OUR WEAPONS DOWN.
ALL OF YOU? THE WHOLE COMPANY.
I DON'T EVEN KNOW HOW IT HAPPENED.
IT WASN'T A DECISION, REALLY. IT WAS LIKE...
AN INSTINCT. FEELING.
A FEELING.
THE FORCE.
THE FORCE BROUGHT ME HERE. IT BROUGHT ME TO REY. AND POE.
YOU SAY THAT LIKE YOU'RE SURE IT'S REAL.
IT'S REAL. I WASN'T SURE THEN...BUT I AM NOW.

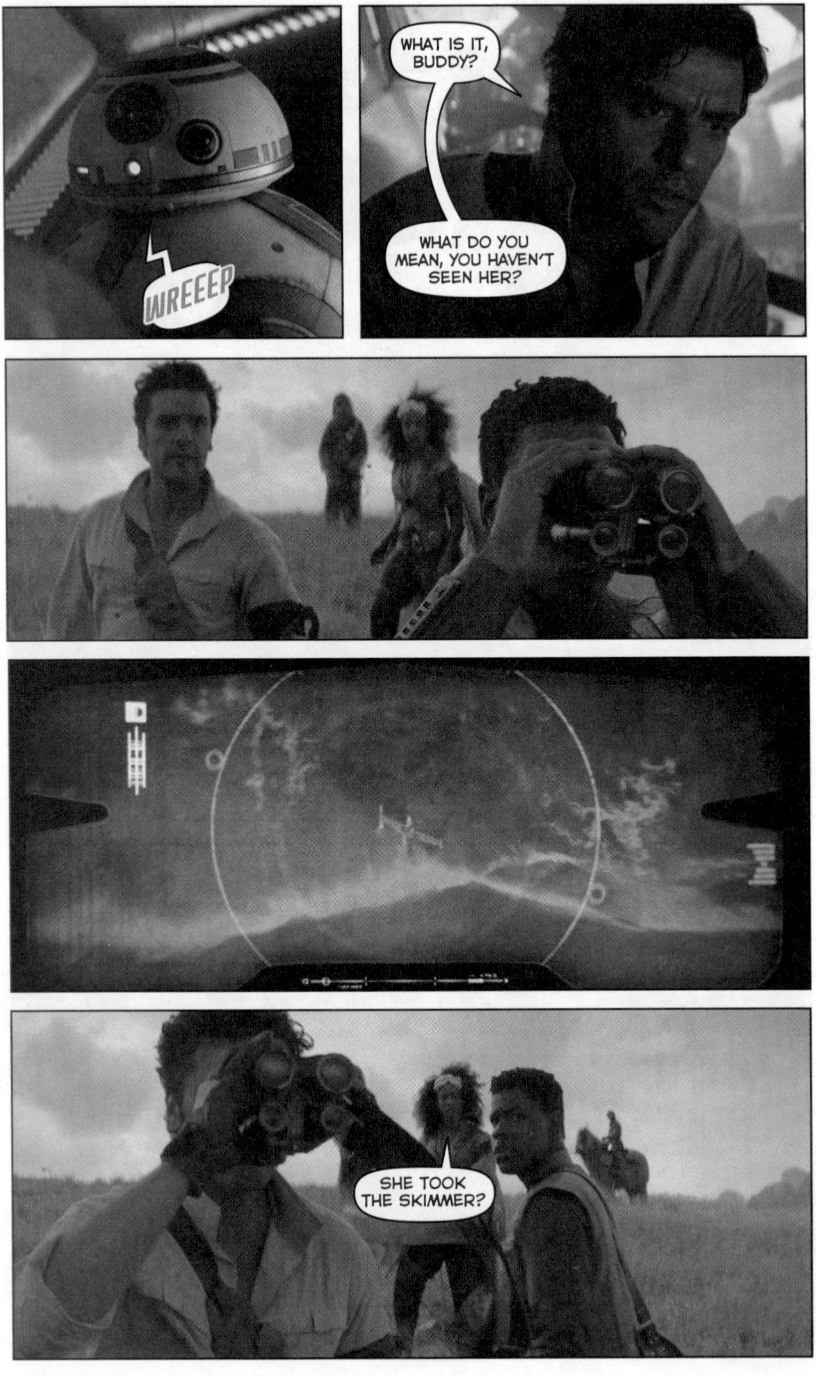
WREEEP
WHAT IS IT, BUDDY?
WHAT DO YOU MEAN, YOU HAVEN'T SEEN HER?
SHE TOOK THE SKIMMER?

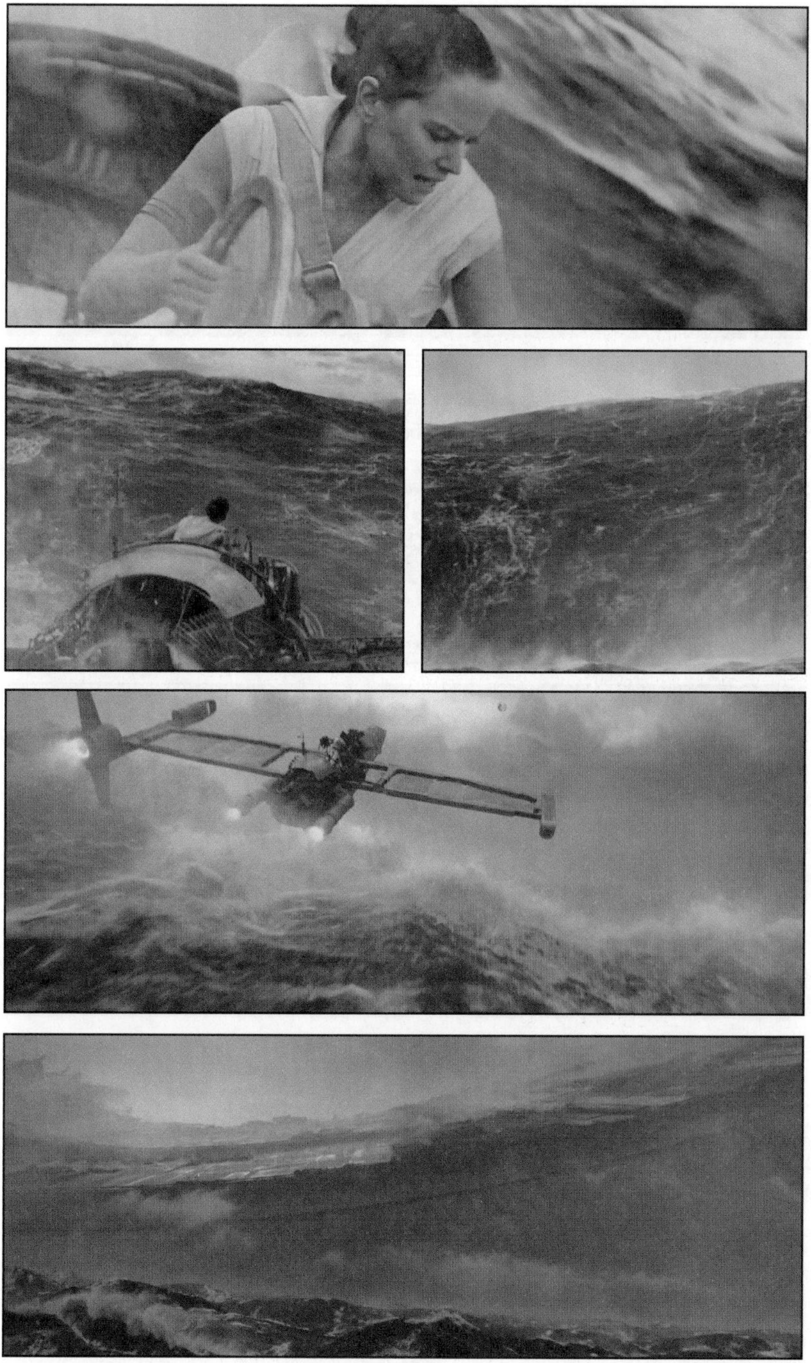

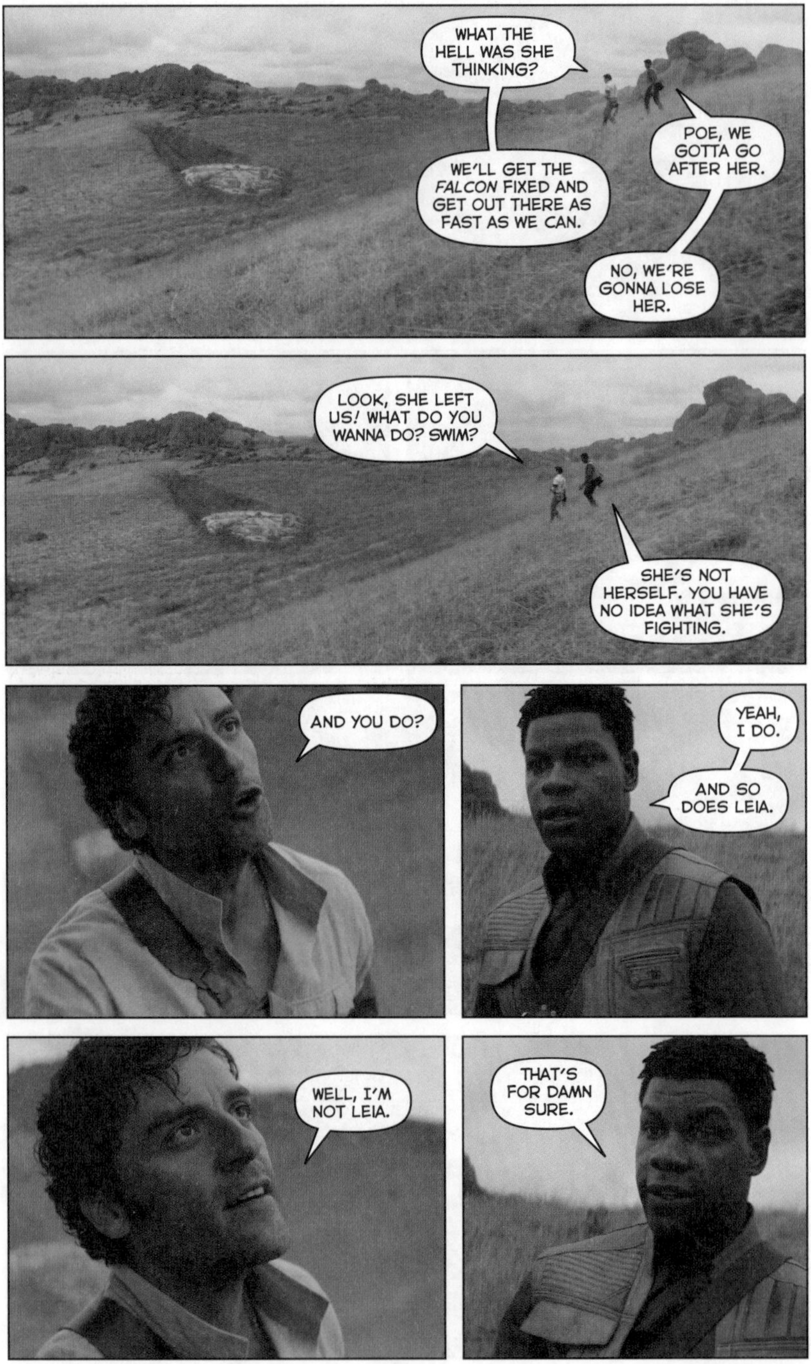

WHAT THE HELL WAS SHE THINKING?
POE, WE GOTTA GO AFTER HER.
WE'LL GET THE *FALCON* FIXED AND GET OUT THERE AS FAST AS WE CAN.
NO, WE'RE GONNA LOSE HER.
LOOK, SHE LEFT US! WHAT DO YOU WANNA DO? SWIM?
SHE'S NOT HERSELF. YOU HAVE NO IDEA WHAT SHE'S FIGHTING.
AND YOU DO?
YEAH, I DO.
AND SO DOES LEIA.
WELL, I'M NOT LEIA.
THAT'S FOR DAMN SURE.

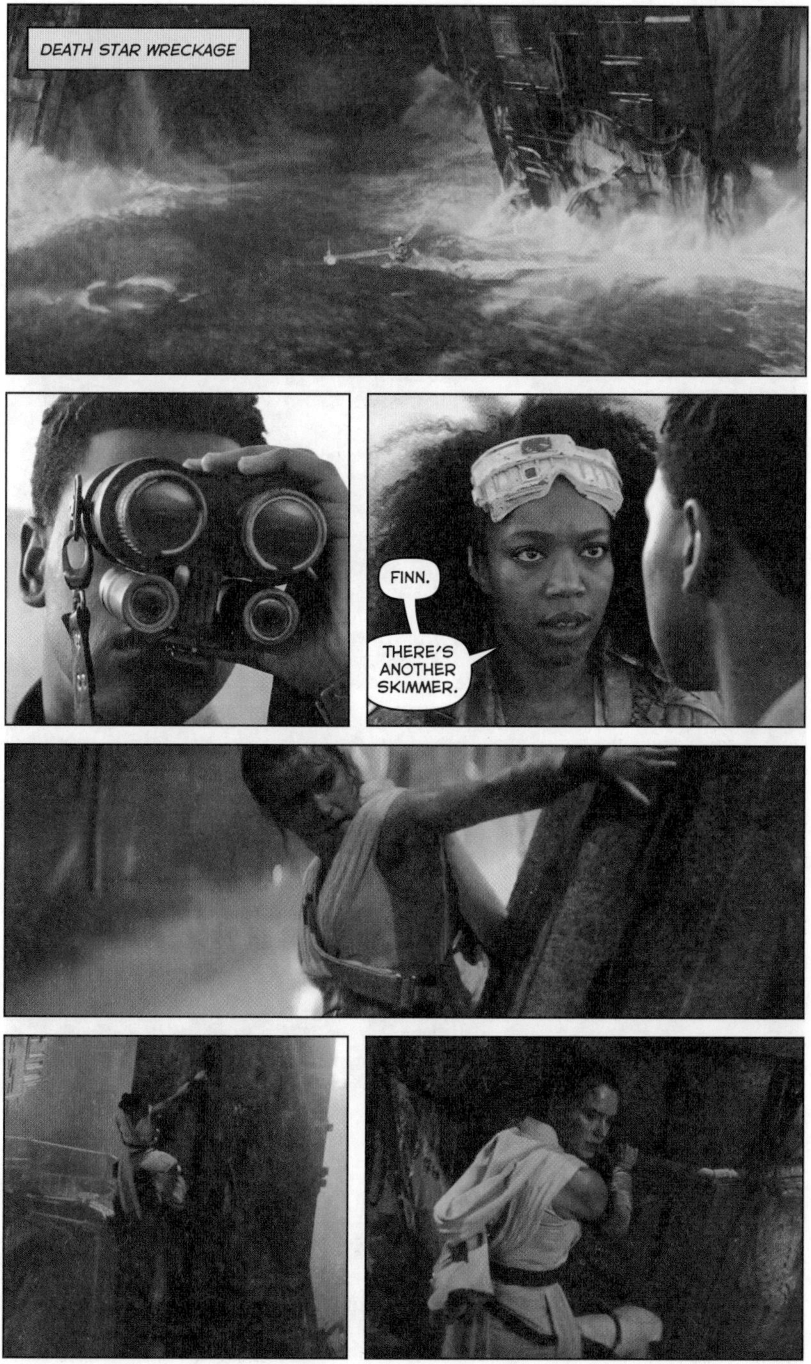
DEATH STAR WRECKAGE
FINN.
THERE'S ANOTHER SKIMMER.

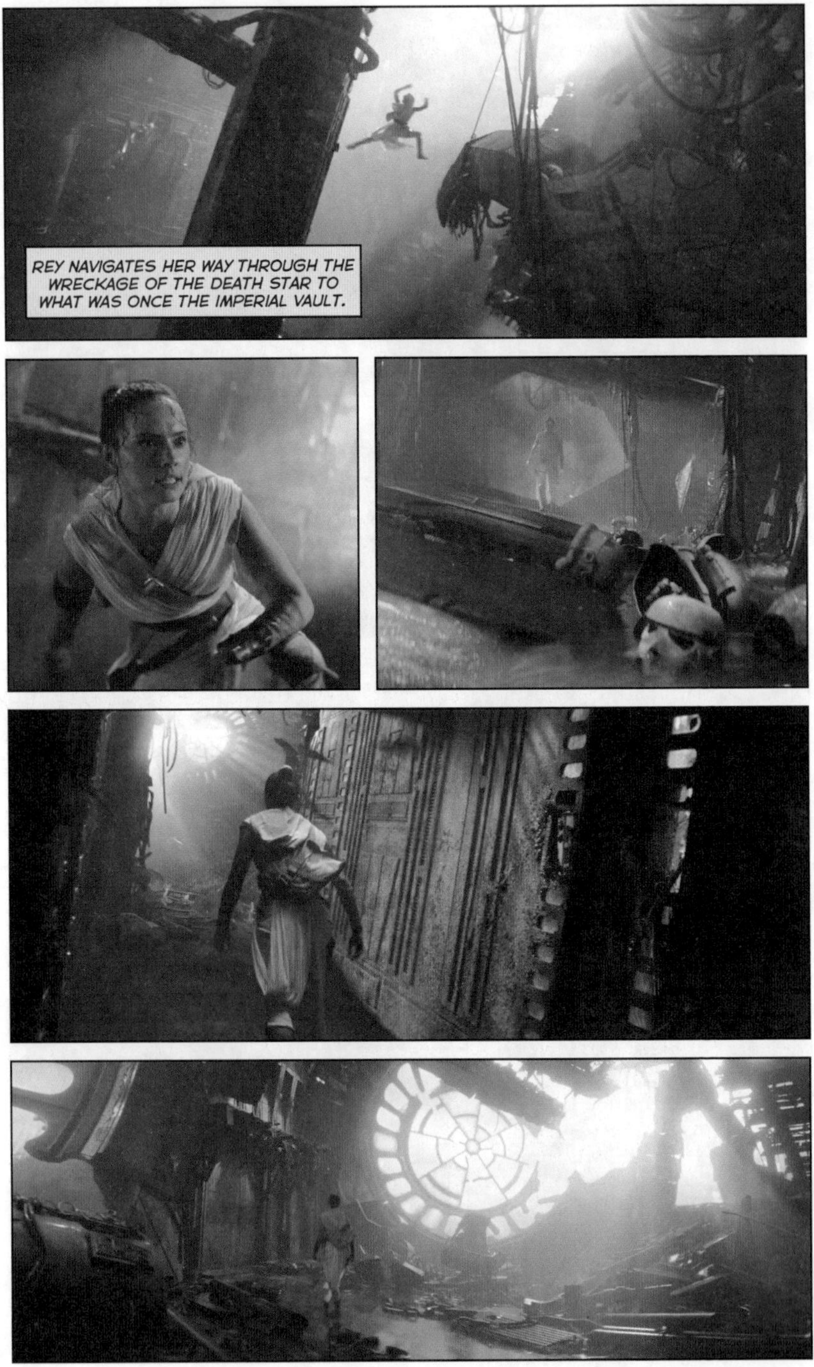
REY NAVIGATES HER WAY THROUGH THE WRECKAGE OF THE DEATH STAR TO WHAT WAS ONCE THE IMPERIAL VAULT.

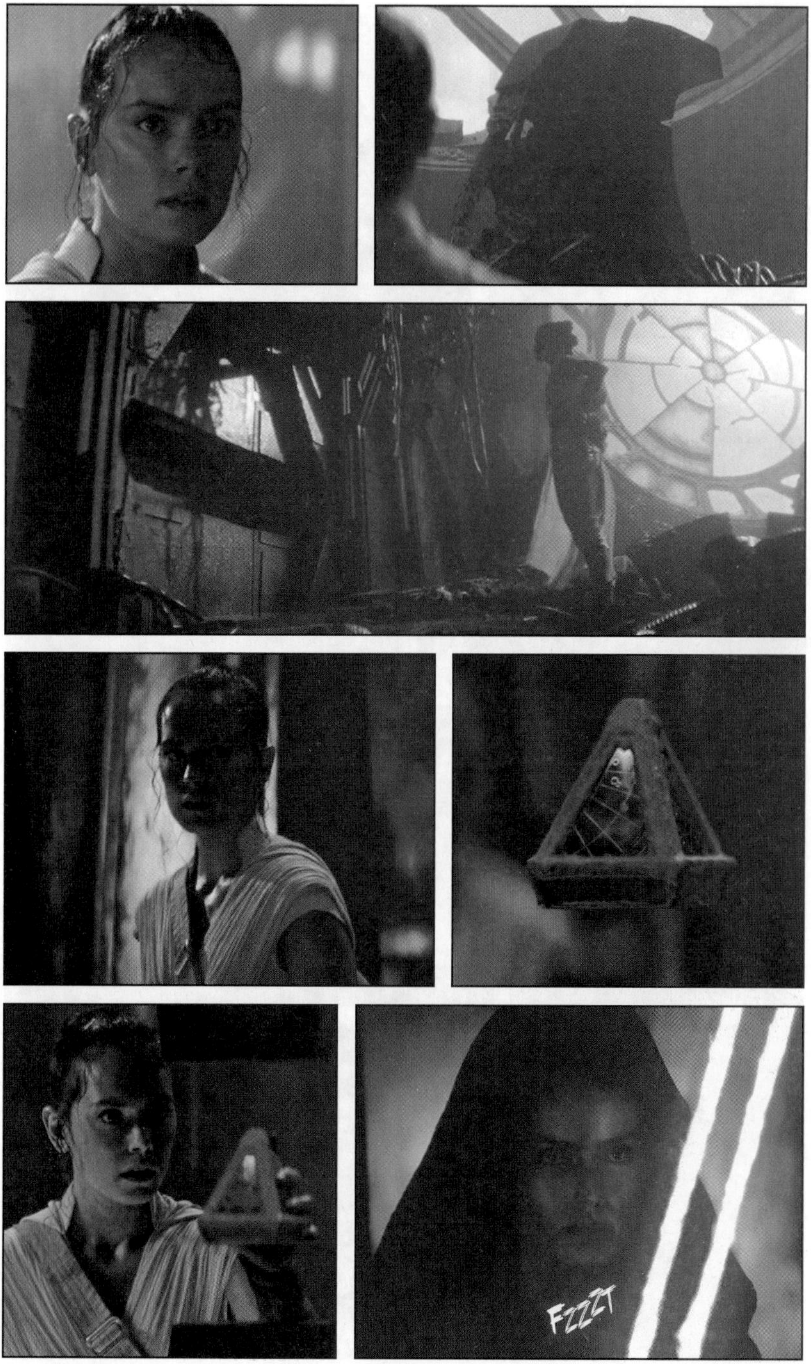
FZZZT

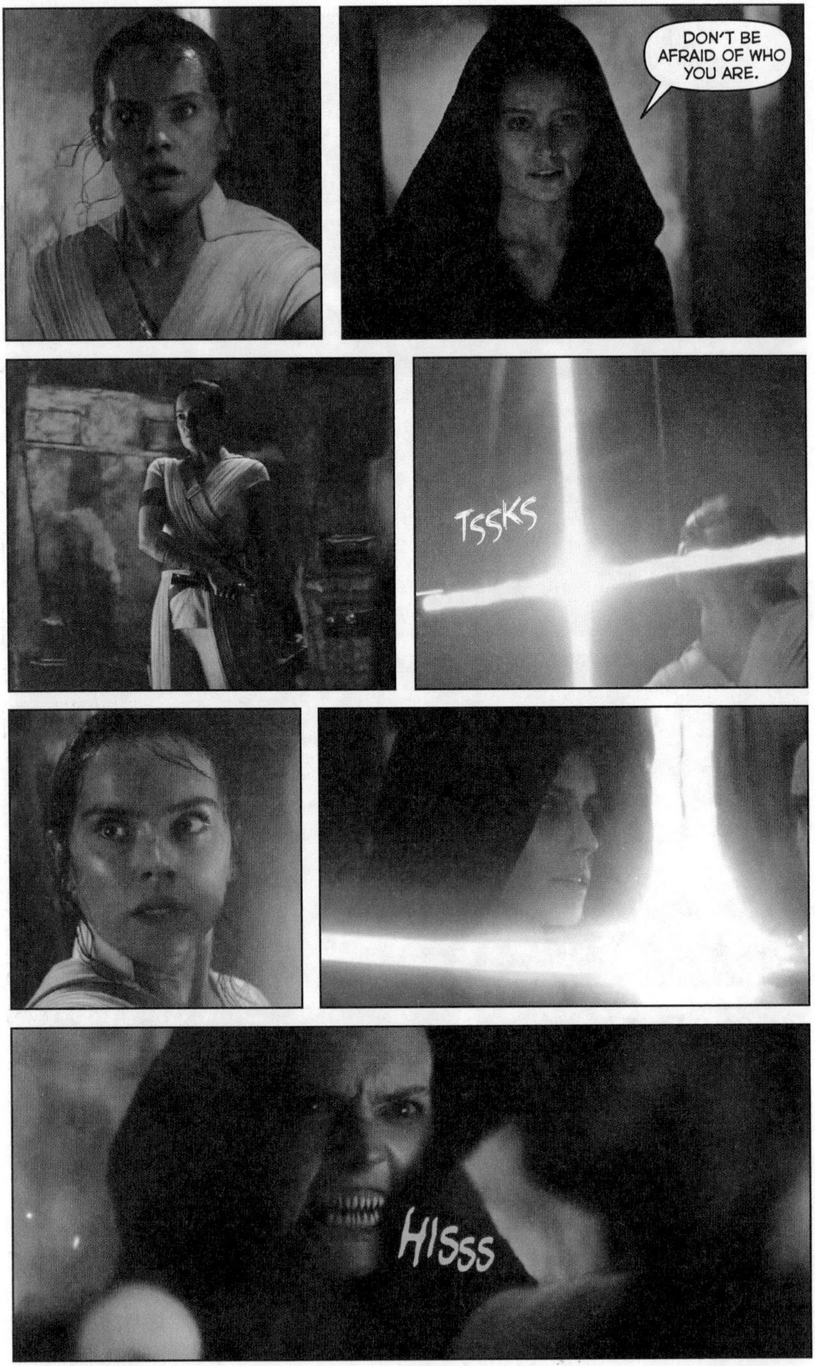
DON'T BE AFRAID OF WHO YOU ARE.
TSSKS
HISSS

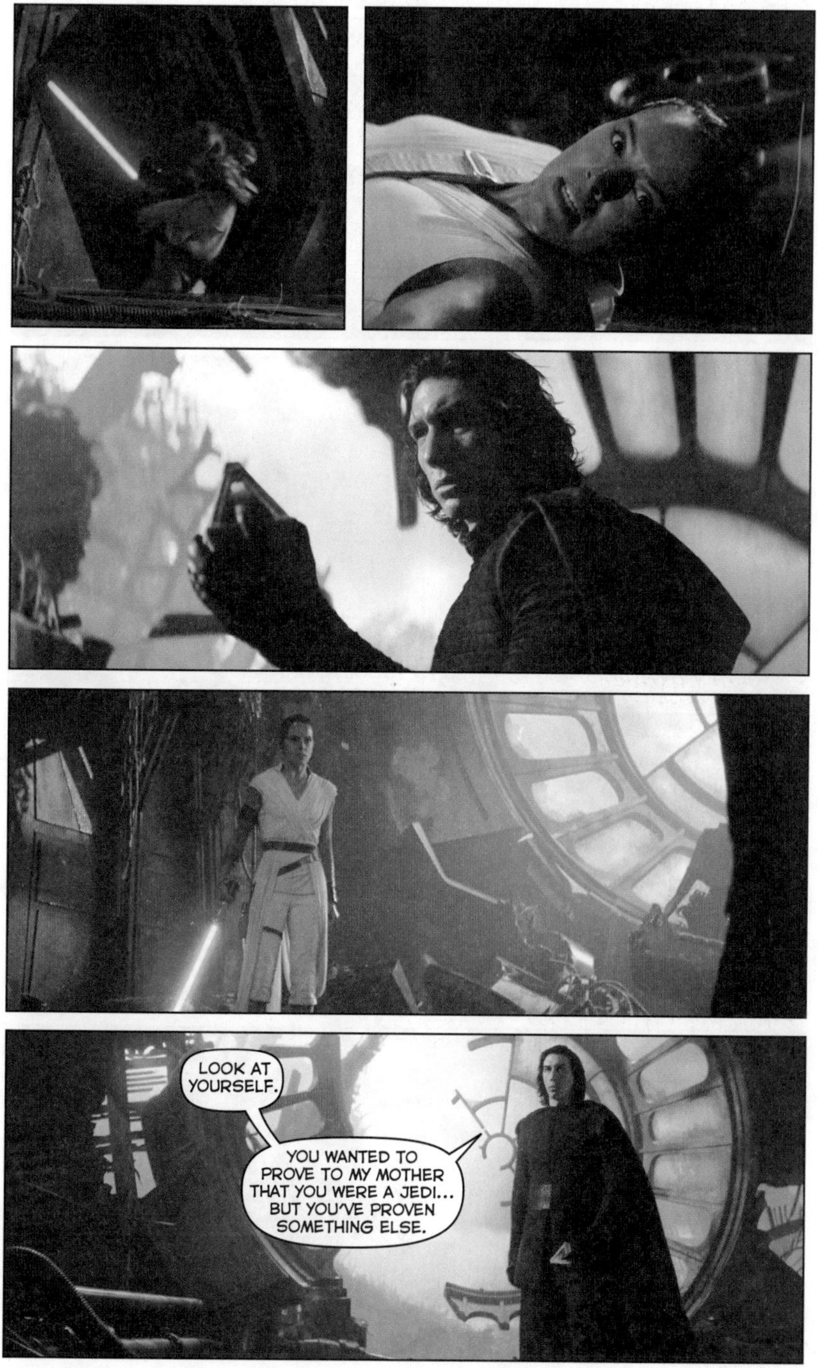
LOOK AT YOURSELF.
YOU WANTED TO PROVE TO MY MOTHER THAT YOU WERE A JEDI... BUT YOU'VE PROVEN SOMETHING ELSE.

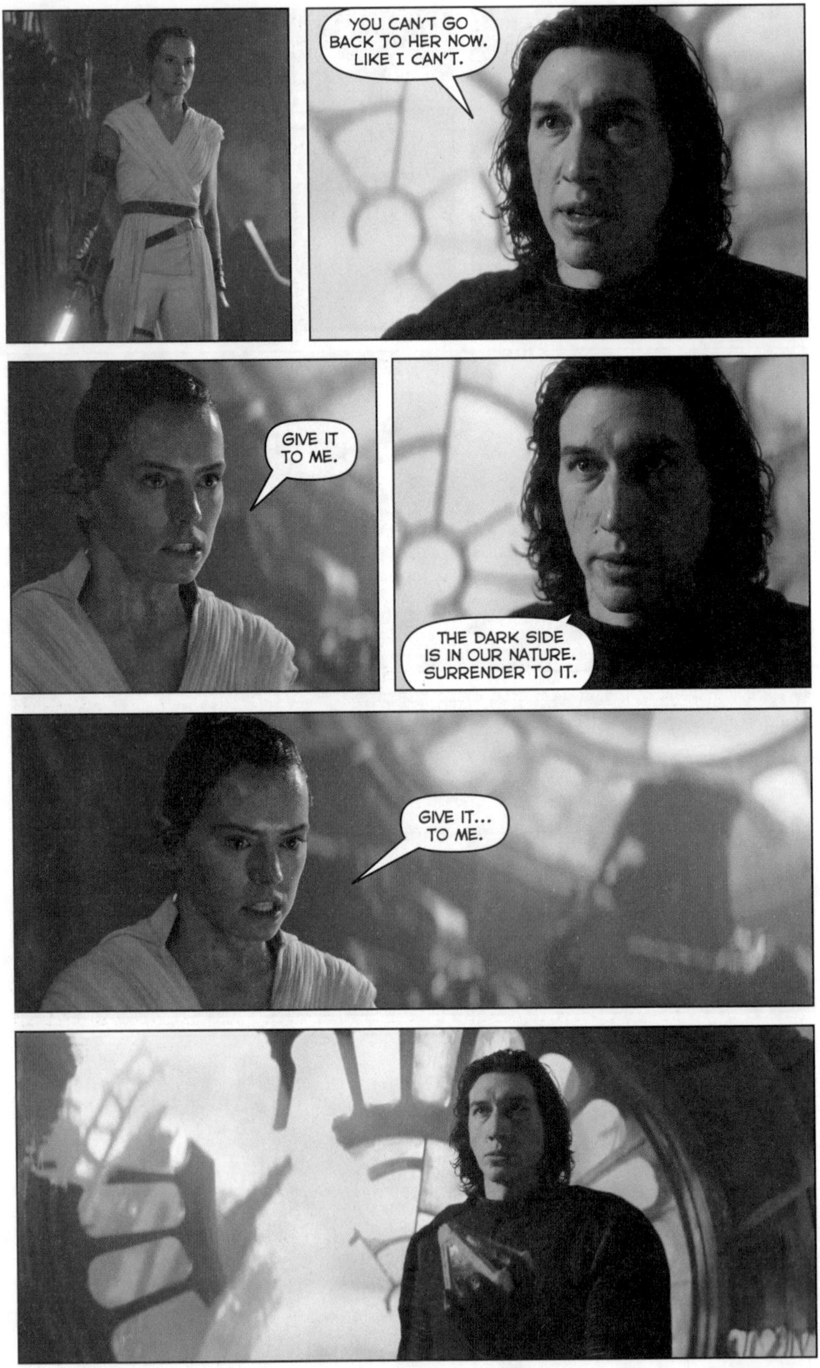
YOU CAN'T GO BACK TO HER NOW. LIKE I CAN'T.
GIVE IT TO ME.
THE DARK SIDE IS IN OUR NATURE. SURRENDER TO IT.
GIVE IT... TO ME.

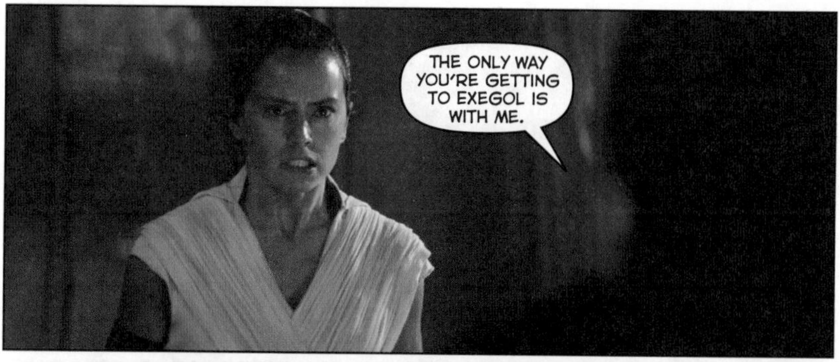
THE ONLY WAY YOU'RE GETTING TO EXEGOL IS WITH ME.

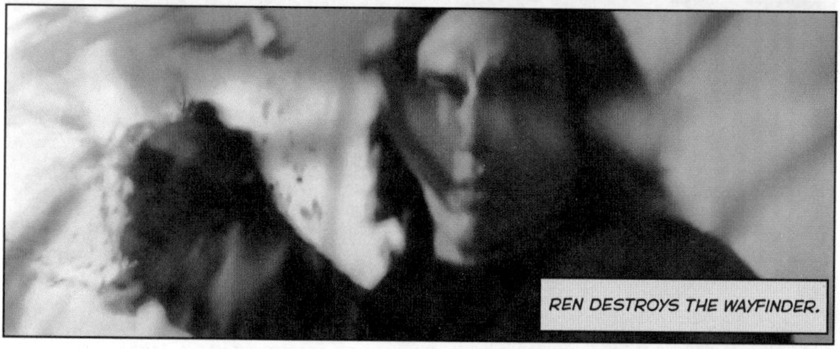
REN DESTROYS THE WAYFINDER.

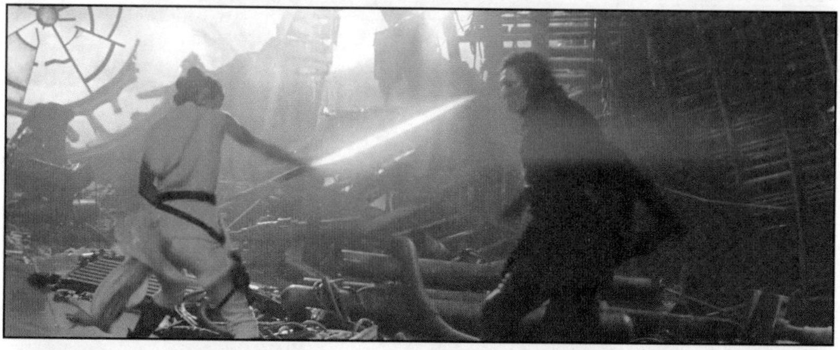

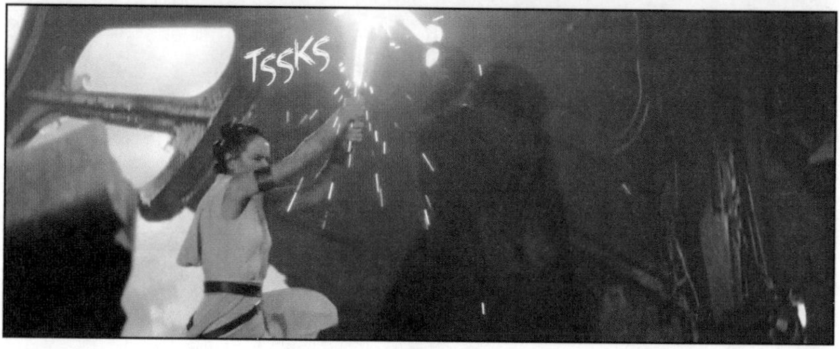
TSSKS

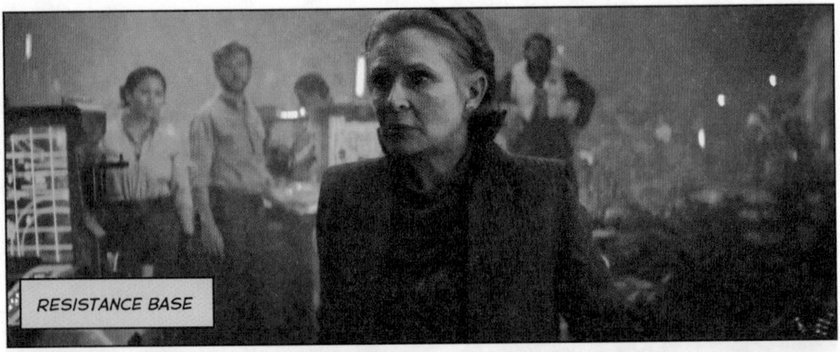
RESISTANCE BASE

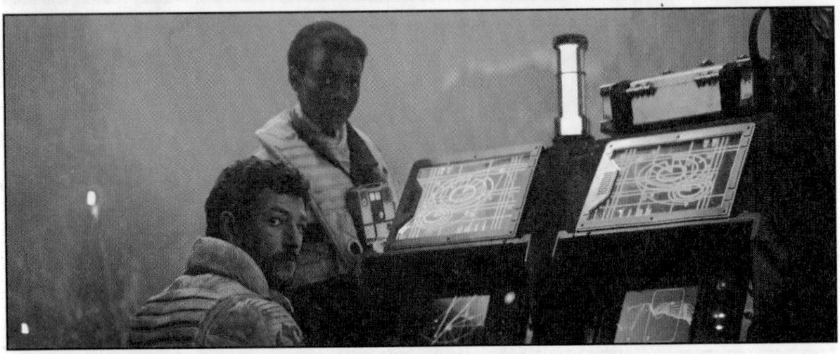

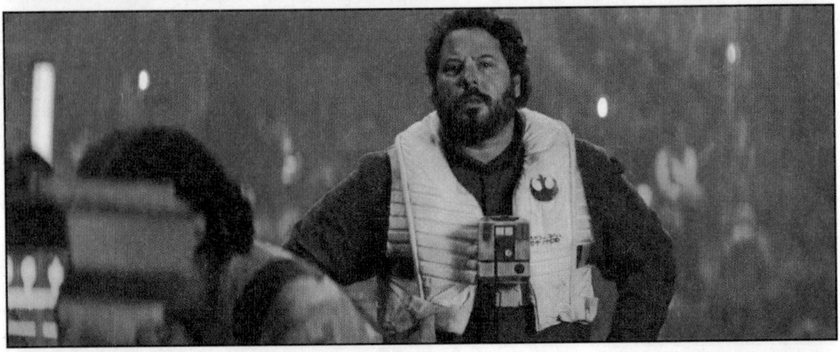

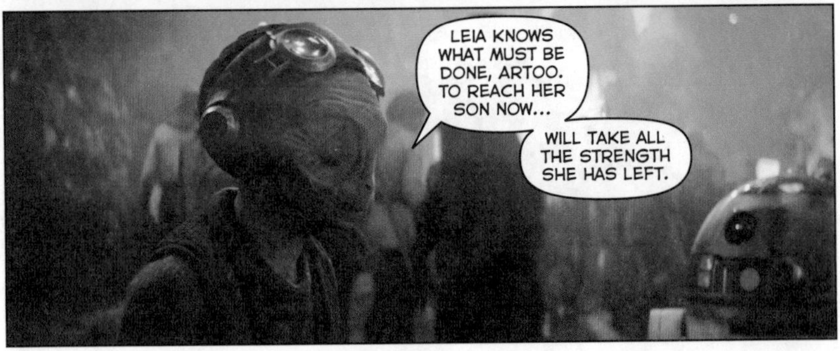
LEIA KNOWS WHAT MUST BE DONE, ARTOO. TO REACH HER SON NOW...
WILL TAKE ALL THE STRENGTH SHE HAS LEFT.

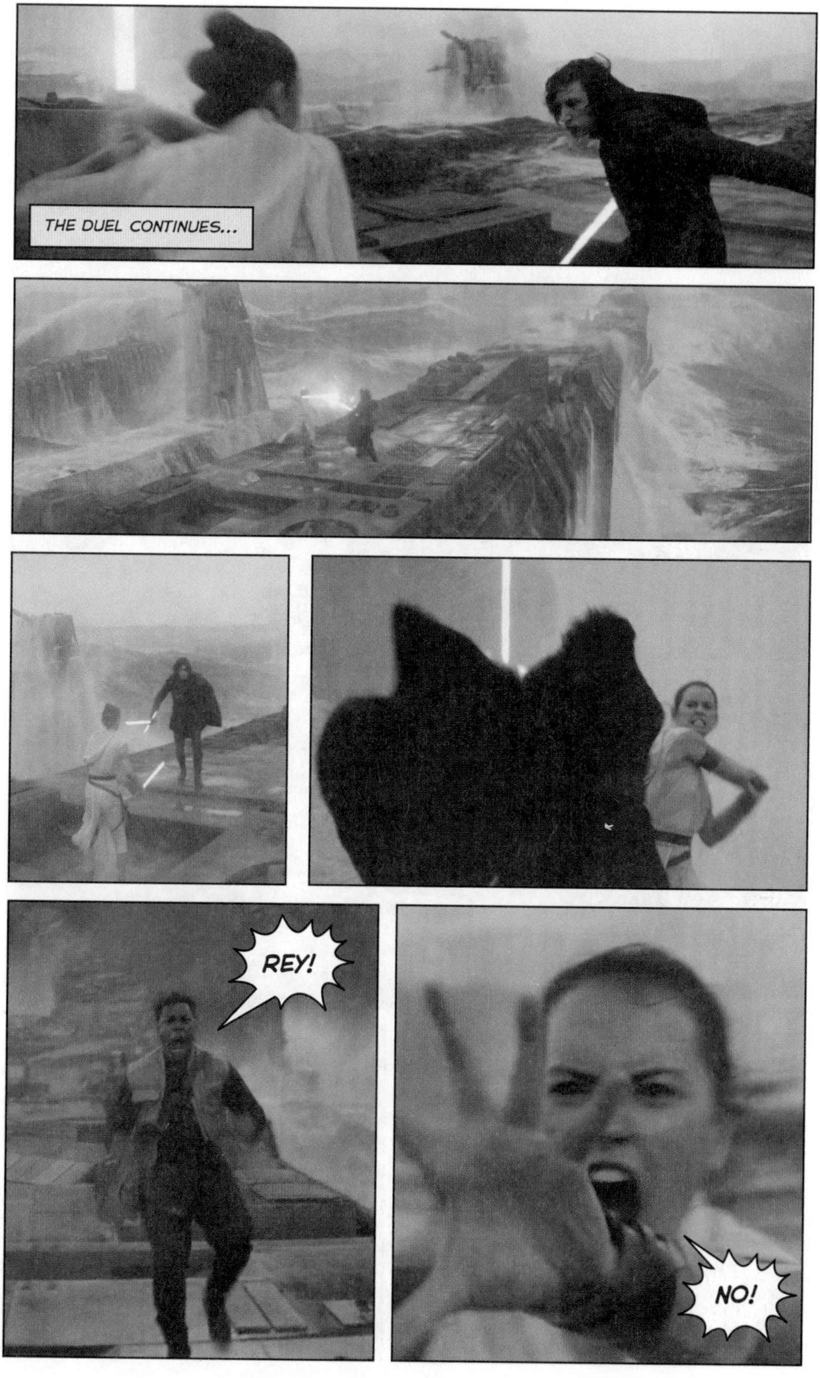
THE DUEL CONTINUES...
REY!
NO!

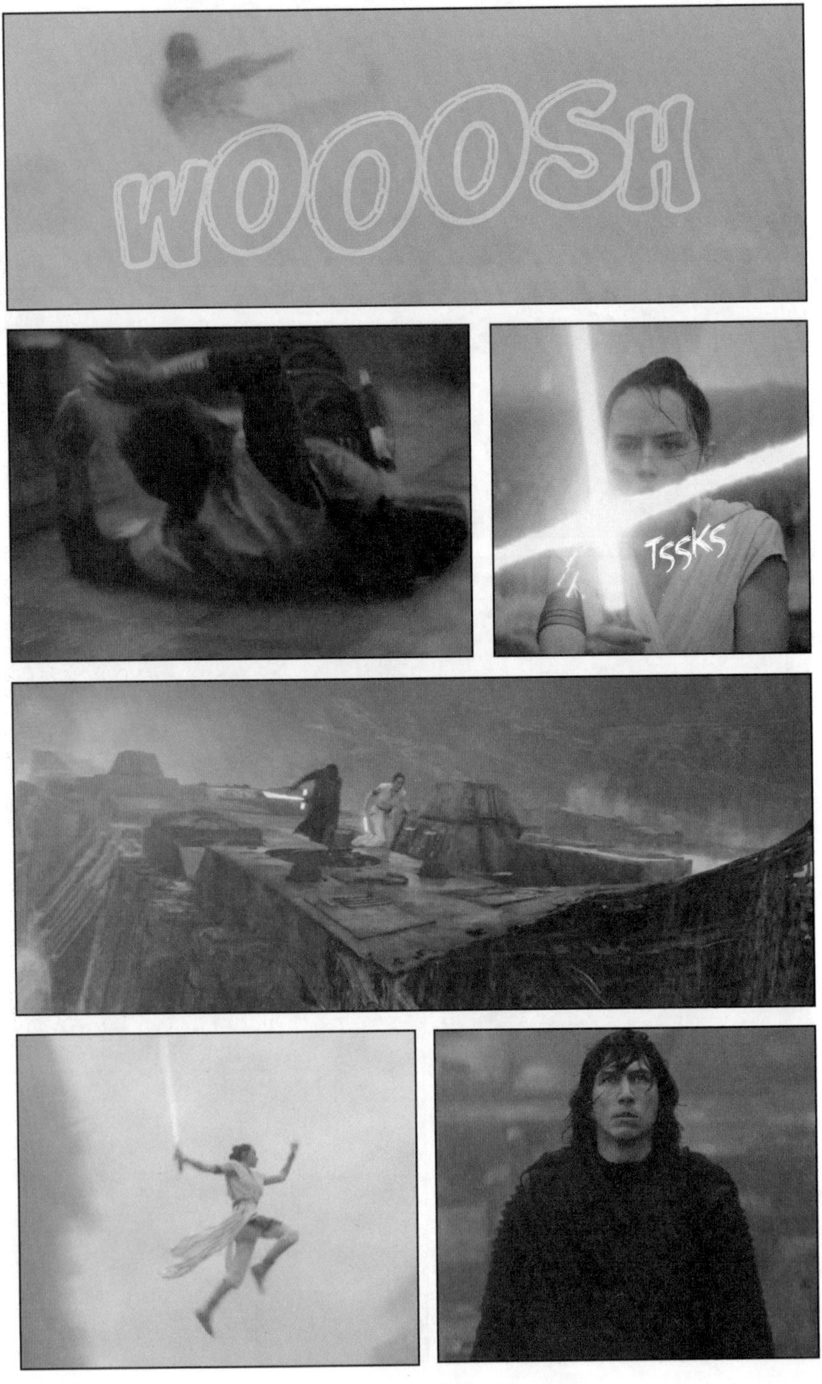
WOOOSH
TSSKS

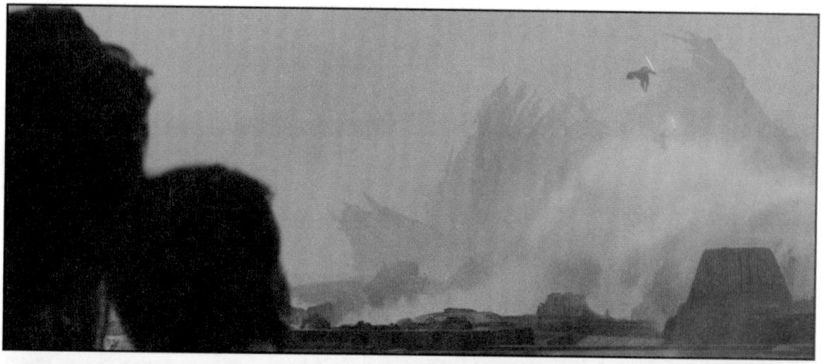

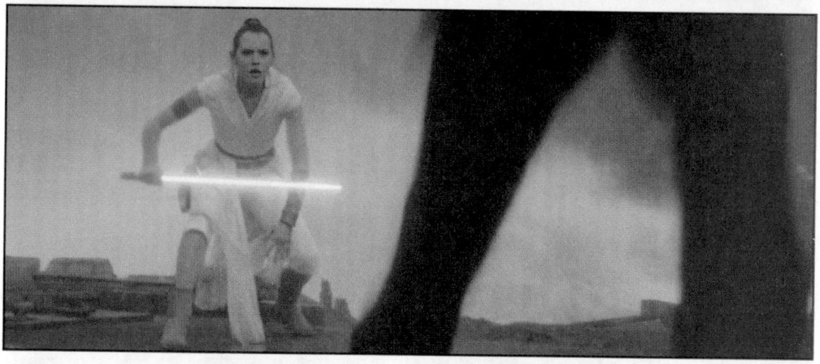

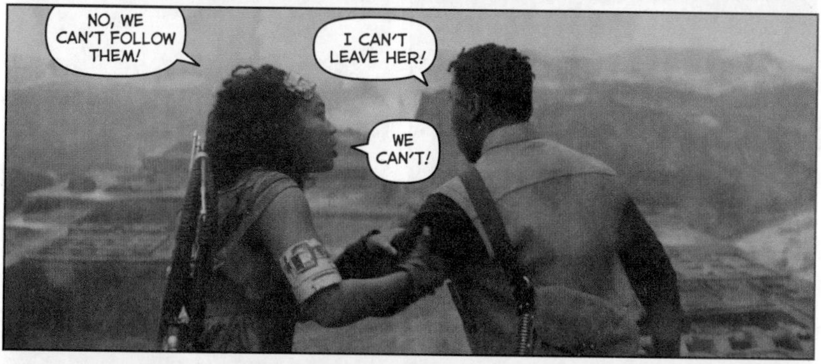
NO, WE CAN'T FOLLOW THEM!
I CAN'T LEAVE HER!
WE CAN'T!

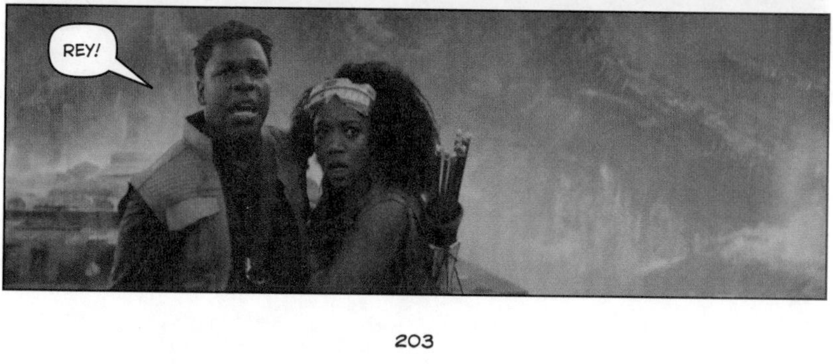
REY!

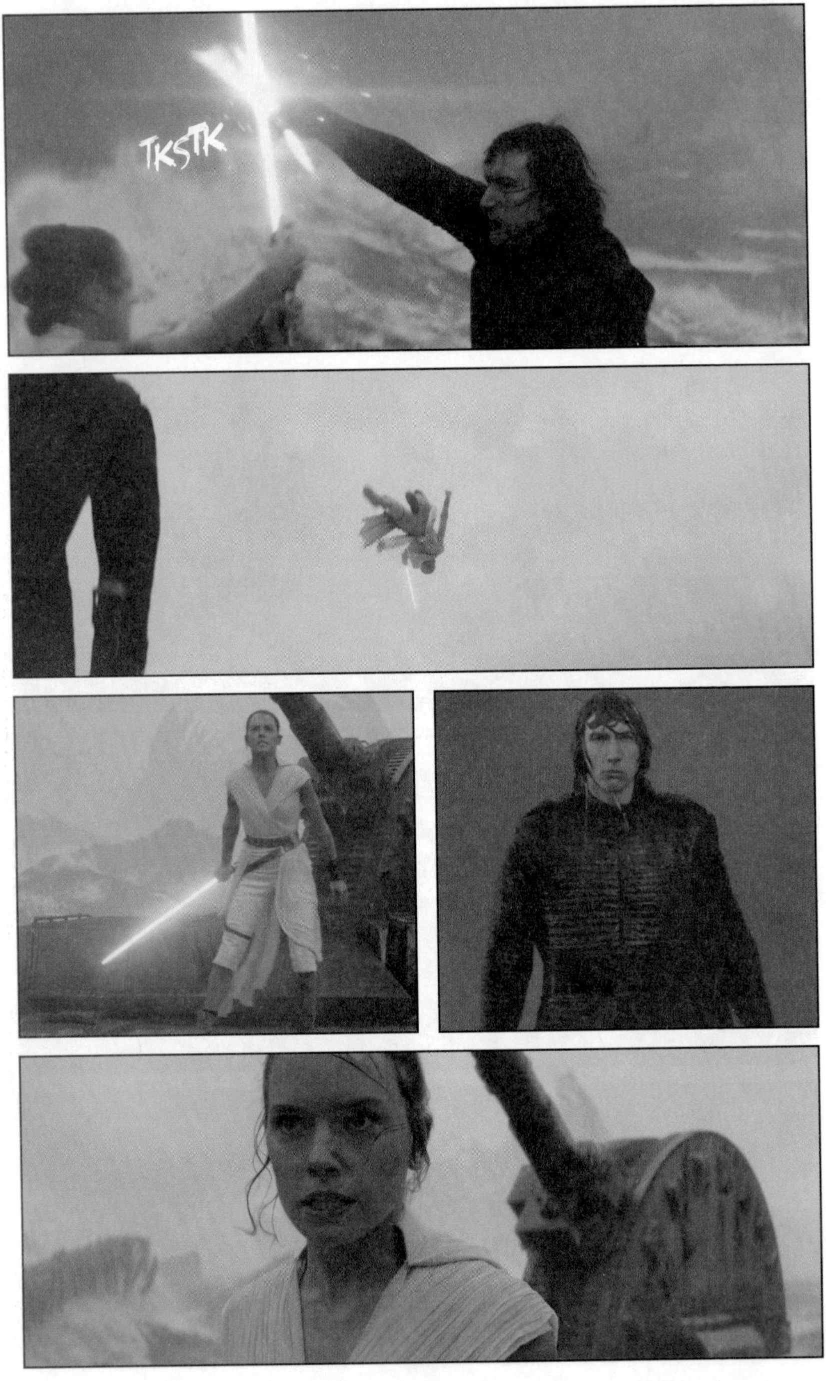
TKSTK

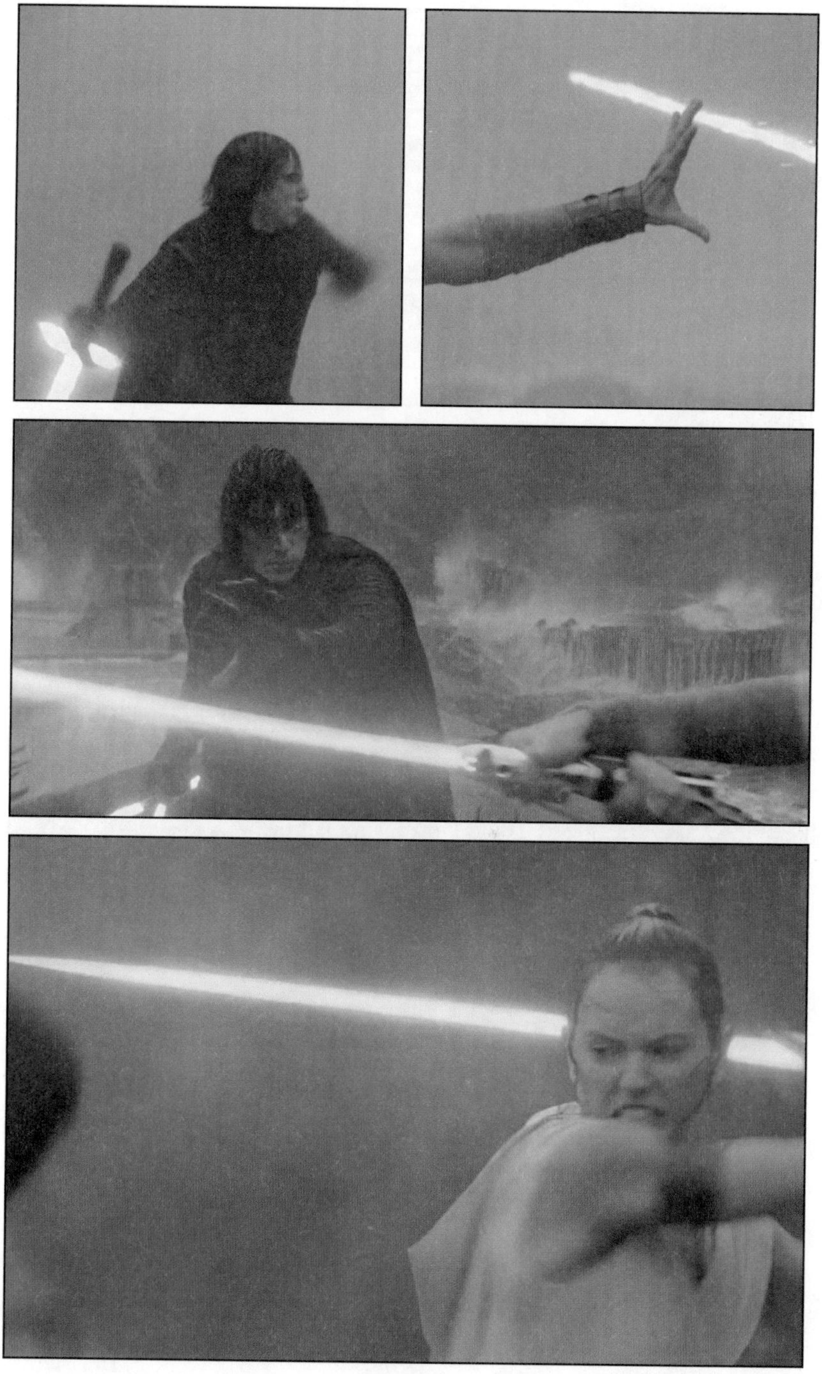

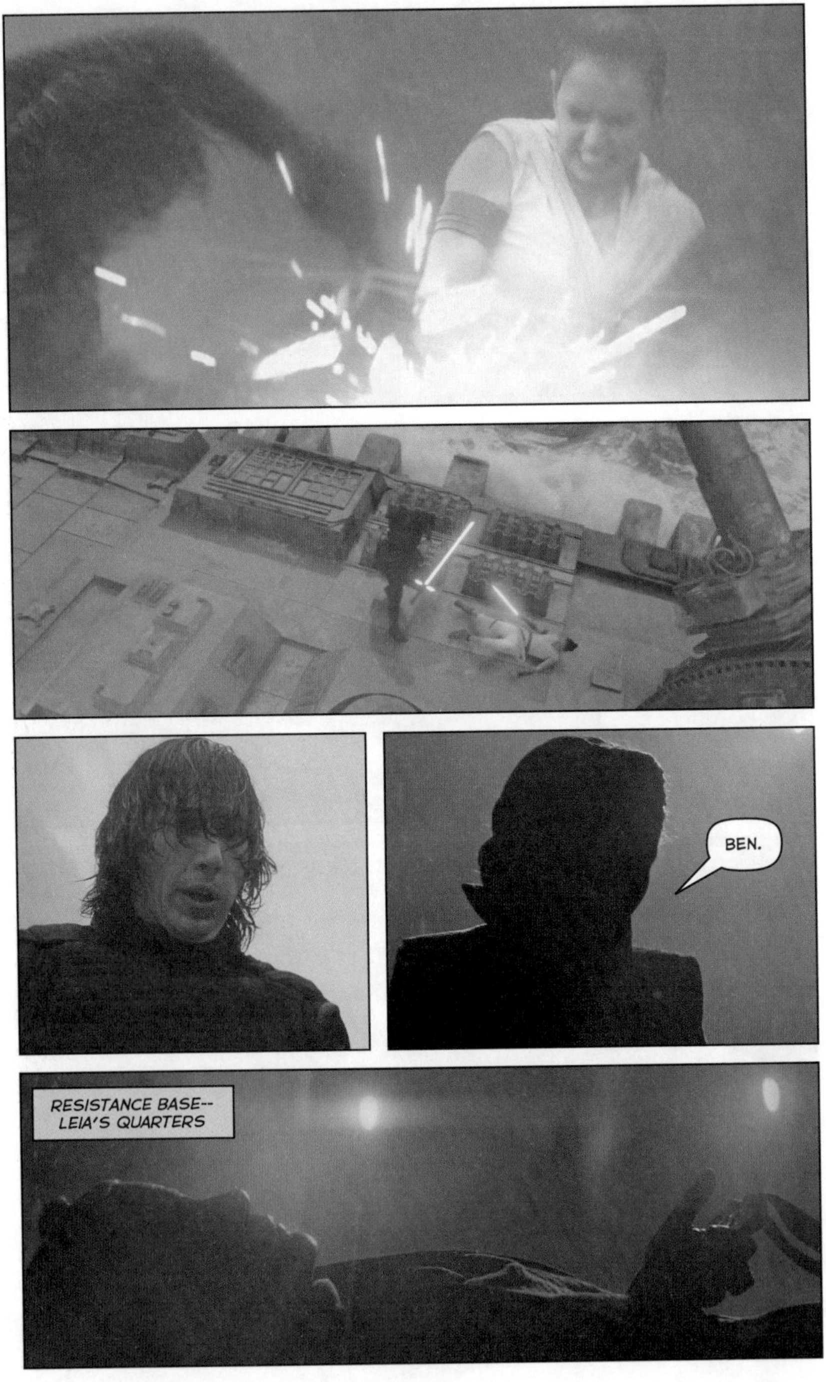
BEN.
RESISTANCE BASE--
LEIA'S QUARTERS

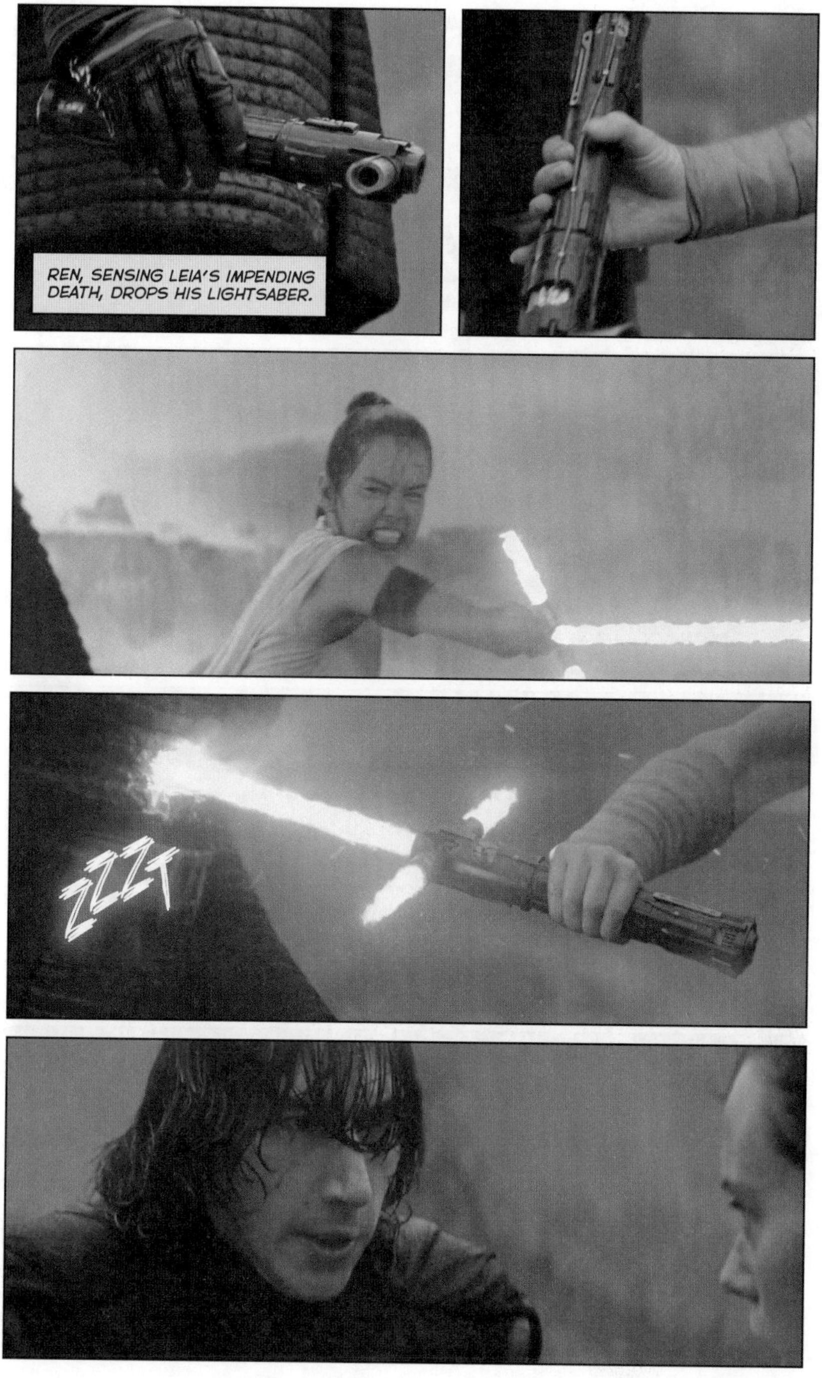
REN, SENSING LEIA'S IMPENDING DEATH, DROPS HIS LIGHTSABER.
ZZZT

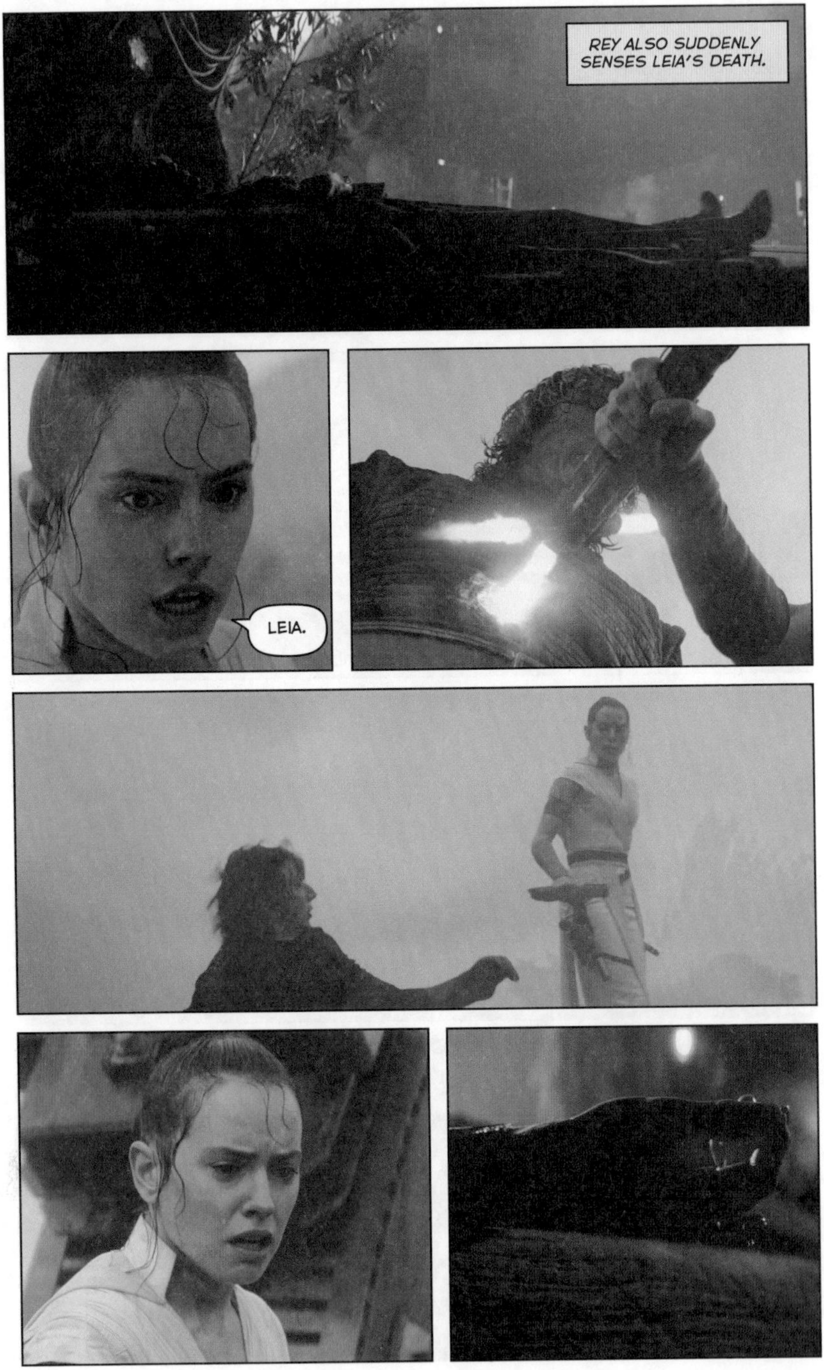
REY ALSO SUDDENLY SENSES LEIA'S DEATH.
LEIA.

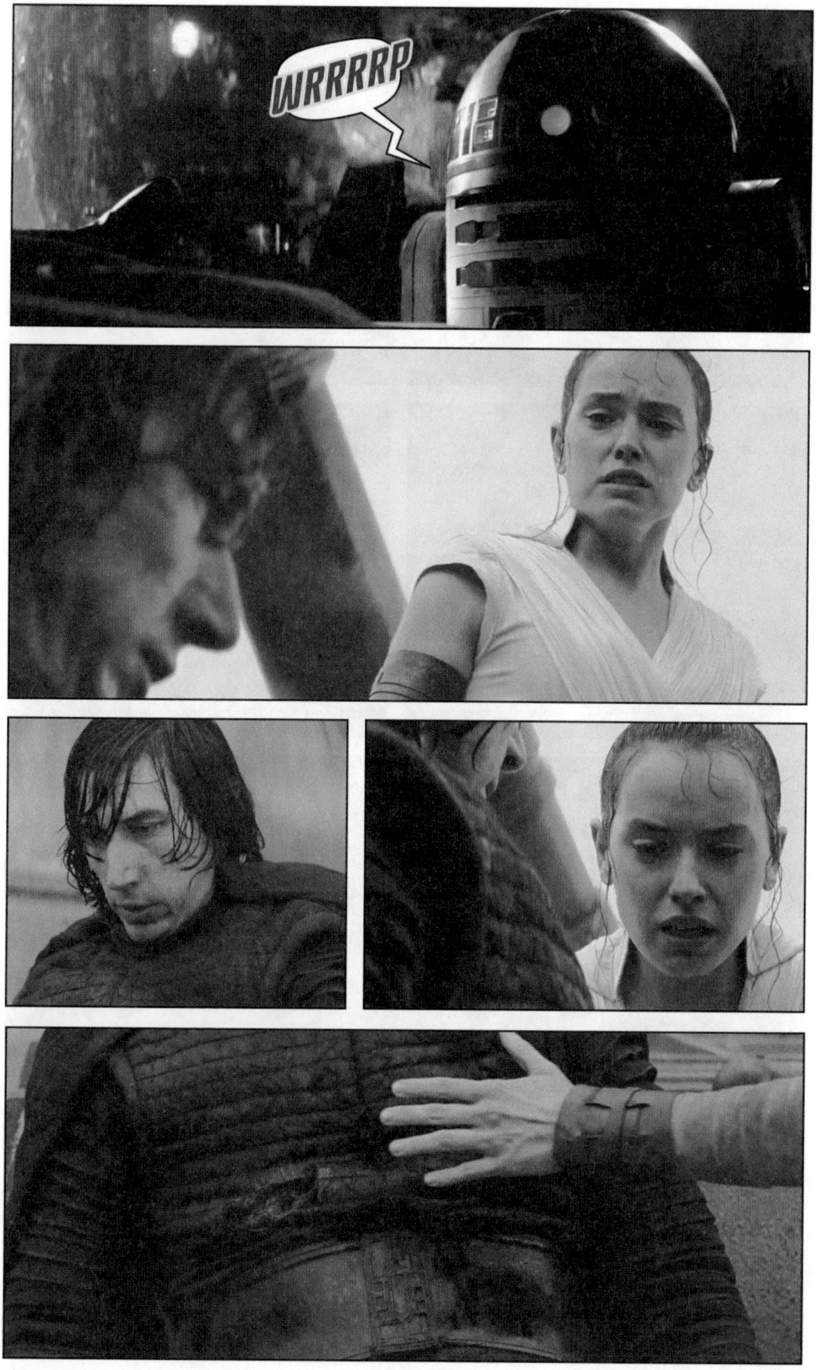
WRRRRP

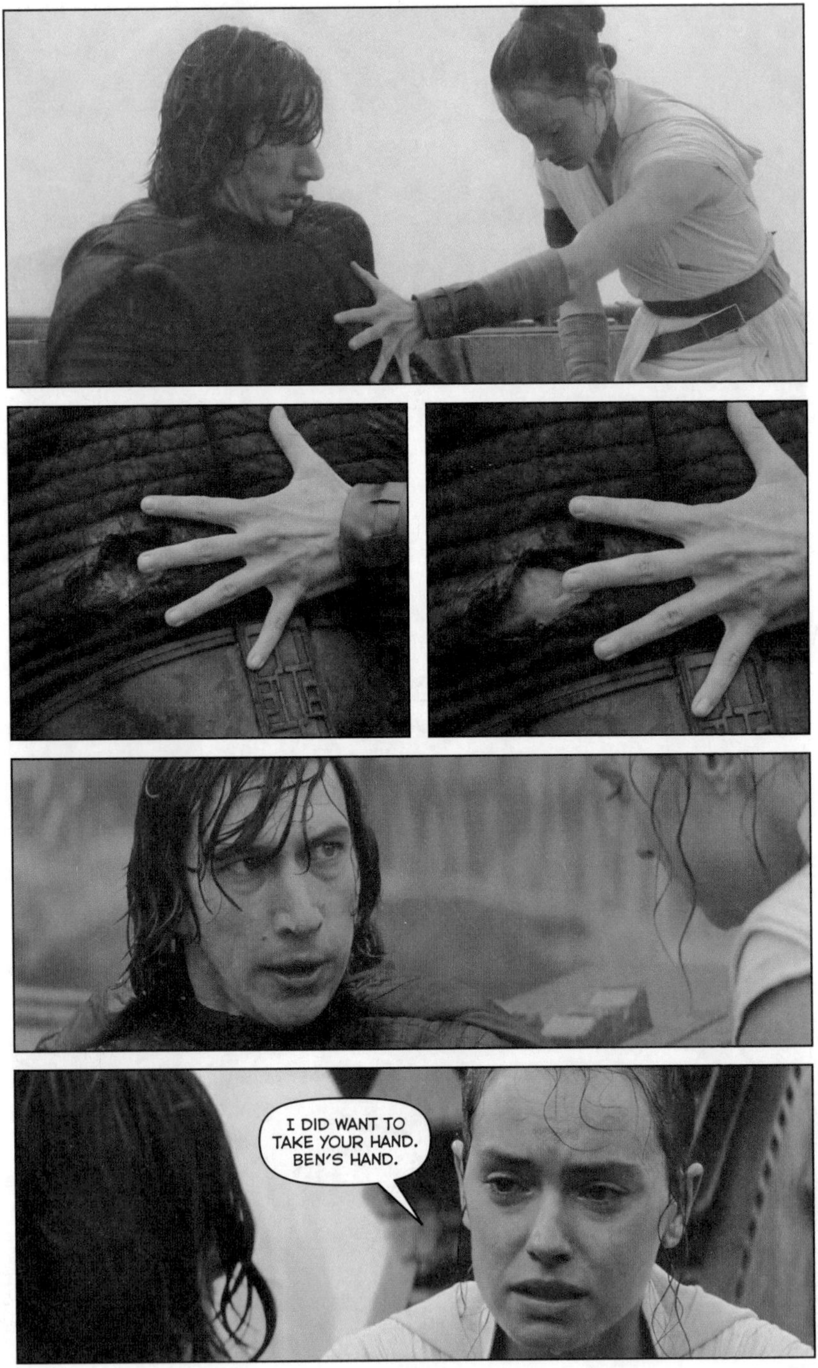
I DID WANT TO TAKE YOUR HAND. BEN'S HAND.

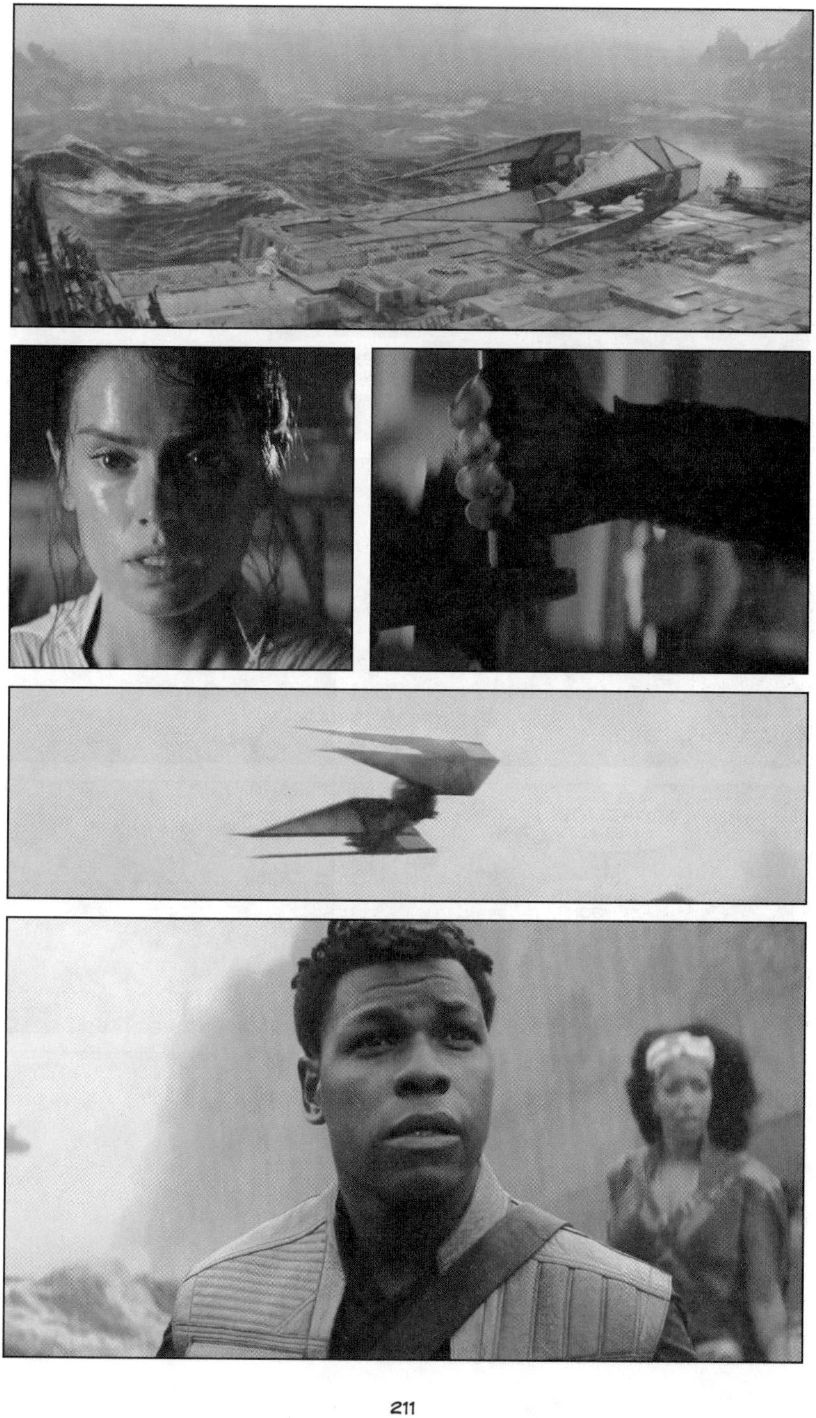

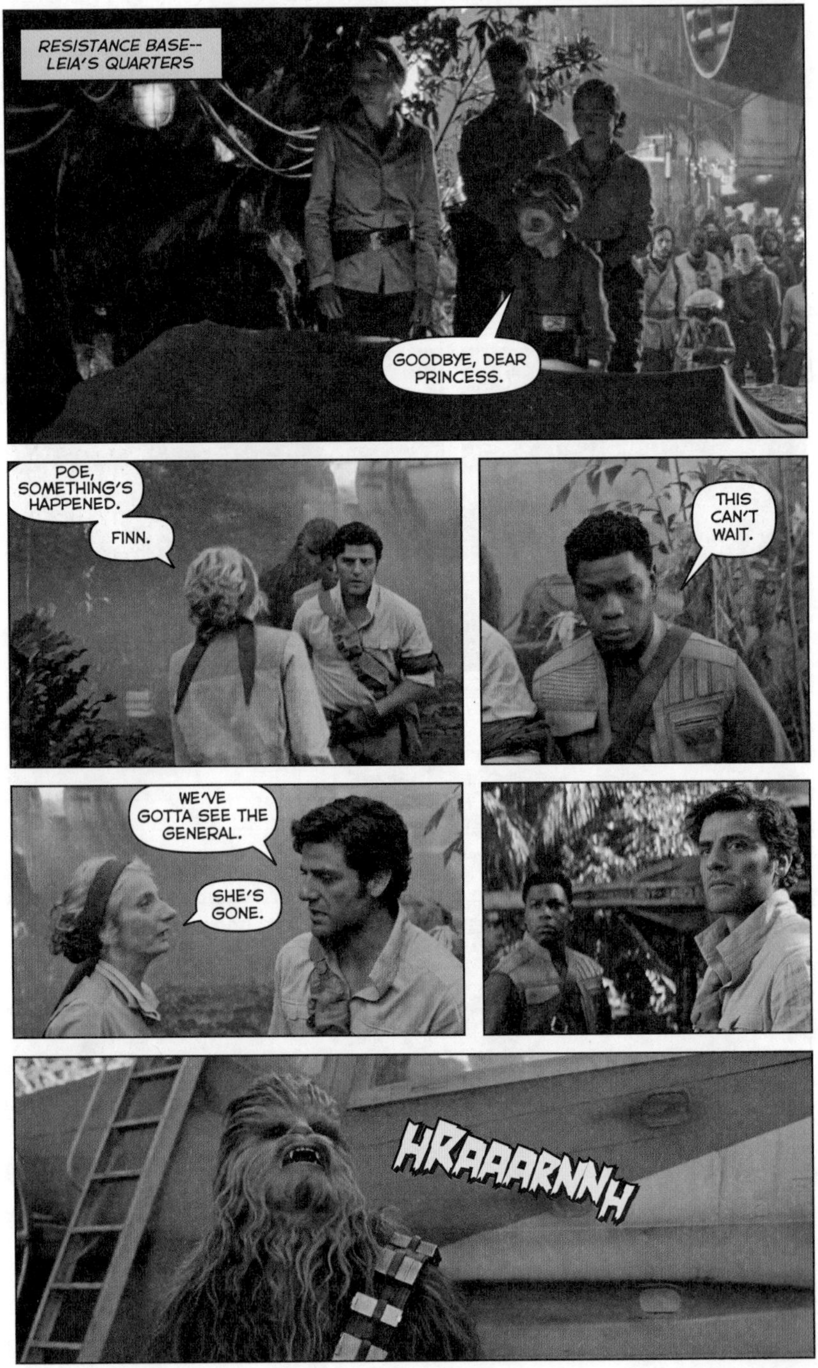
RESISTANCE BASE--
LEIA'S QUARTERS
GOODBYE, DEAR PRINCESS.
POE, SOMETHING'S HAPPENED.
FINN.
THIS CAN'T WAIT.
WE'VE GOTTA SEE THE GENERAL.
SHE'S GONE.
HRAAARNNH

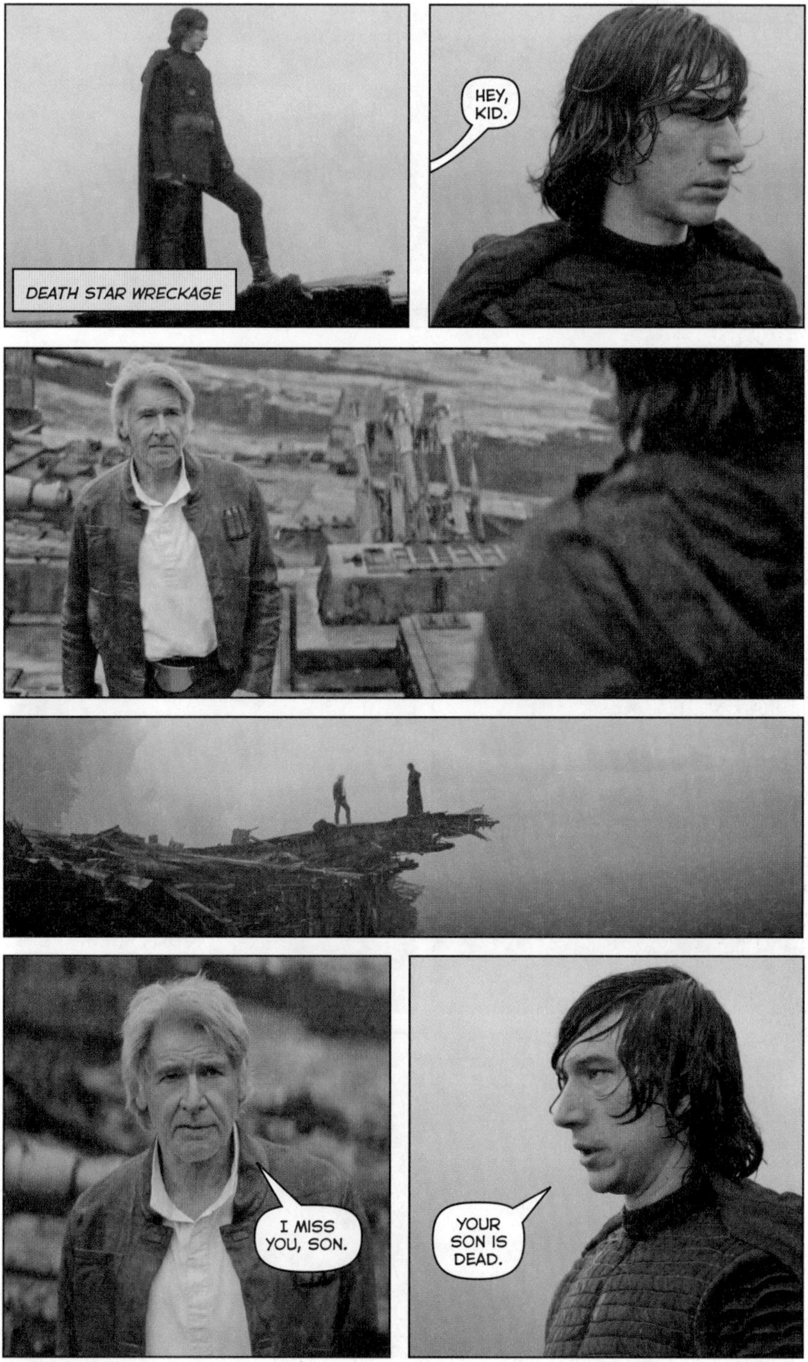
DEATH STAR WRECKAGE
HEY, KID.
I MISS YOU, SON.
YOUR SON IS DEAD.

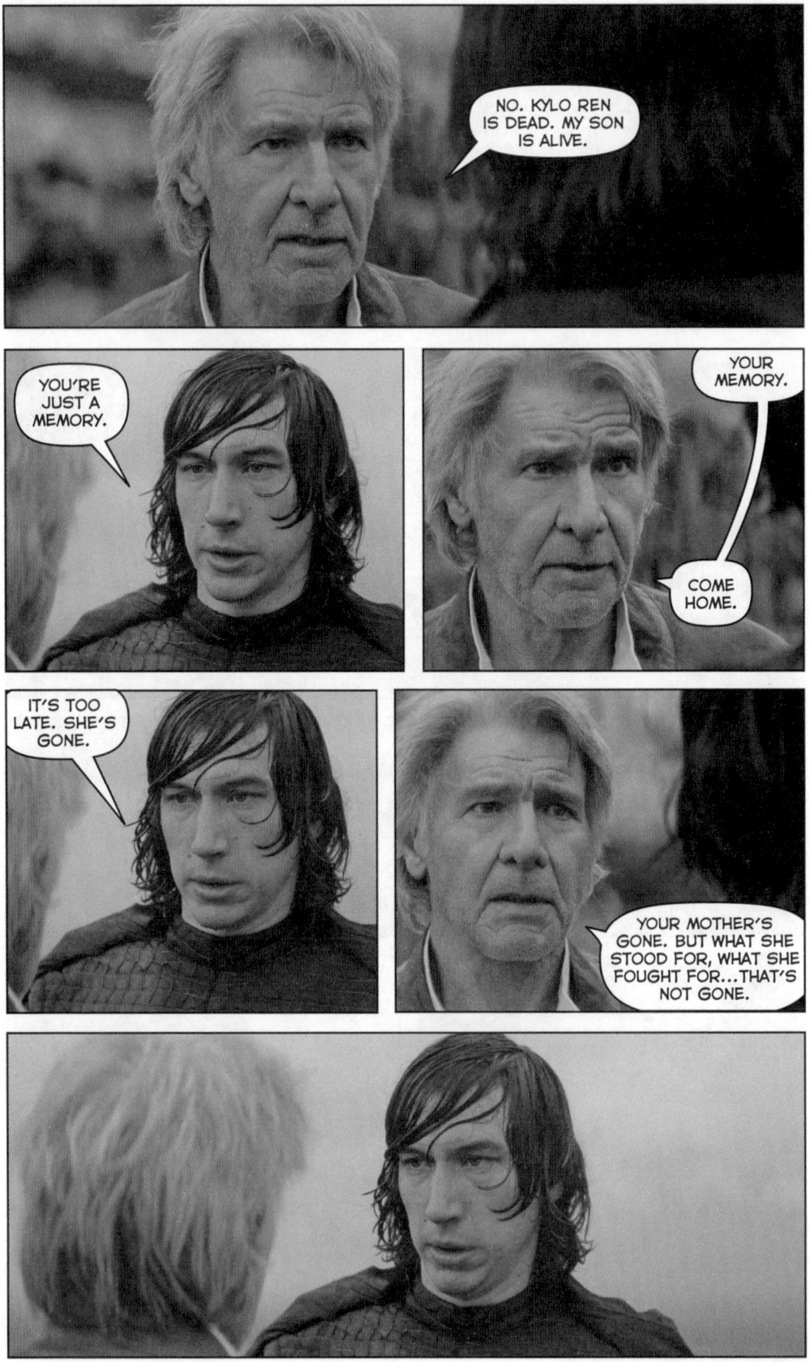
NO. KYLO REN IS DEAD. MY SON IS ALIVE.
YOU'RE JUST A MEMORY.
YOUR MEMORY.
COME HOME.
IT'S TOO LATE. SHE'S GONE.
YOUR MOTHER'S GONE. BUT WHAT SHE STOOD FOR, WHAT SHE FOUGHT FOR...THAT'S NOT GONE.

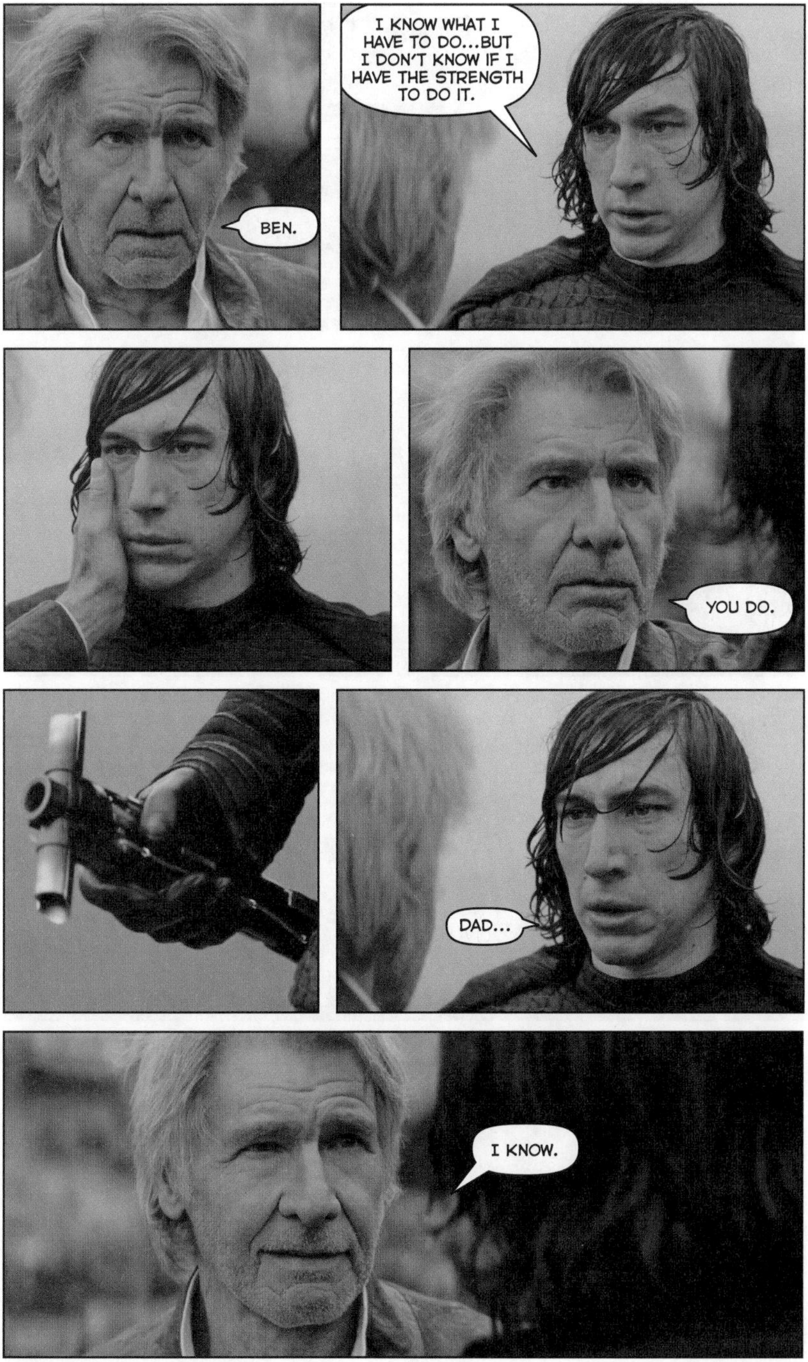
BEN.
I KNOW WHAT I HAVE TO DO...BUT I DON'T KNOW IF I HAVE THE STRENGTH TO DO IT.
YOU DO.
DAD...
I KNOW.

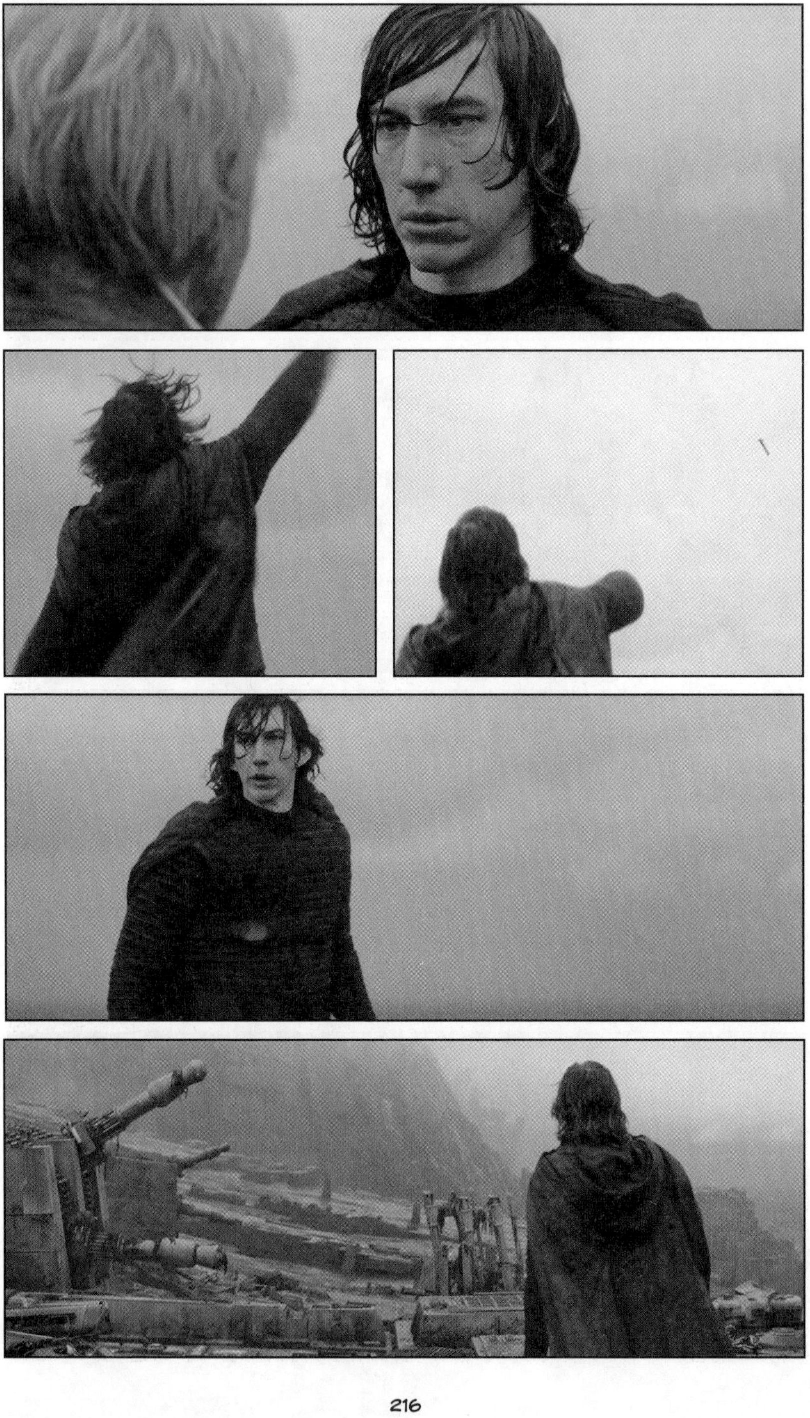

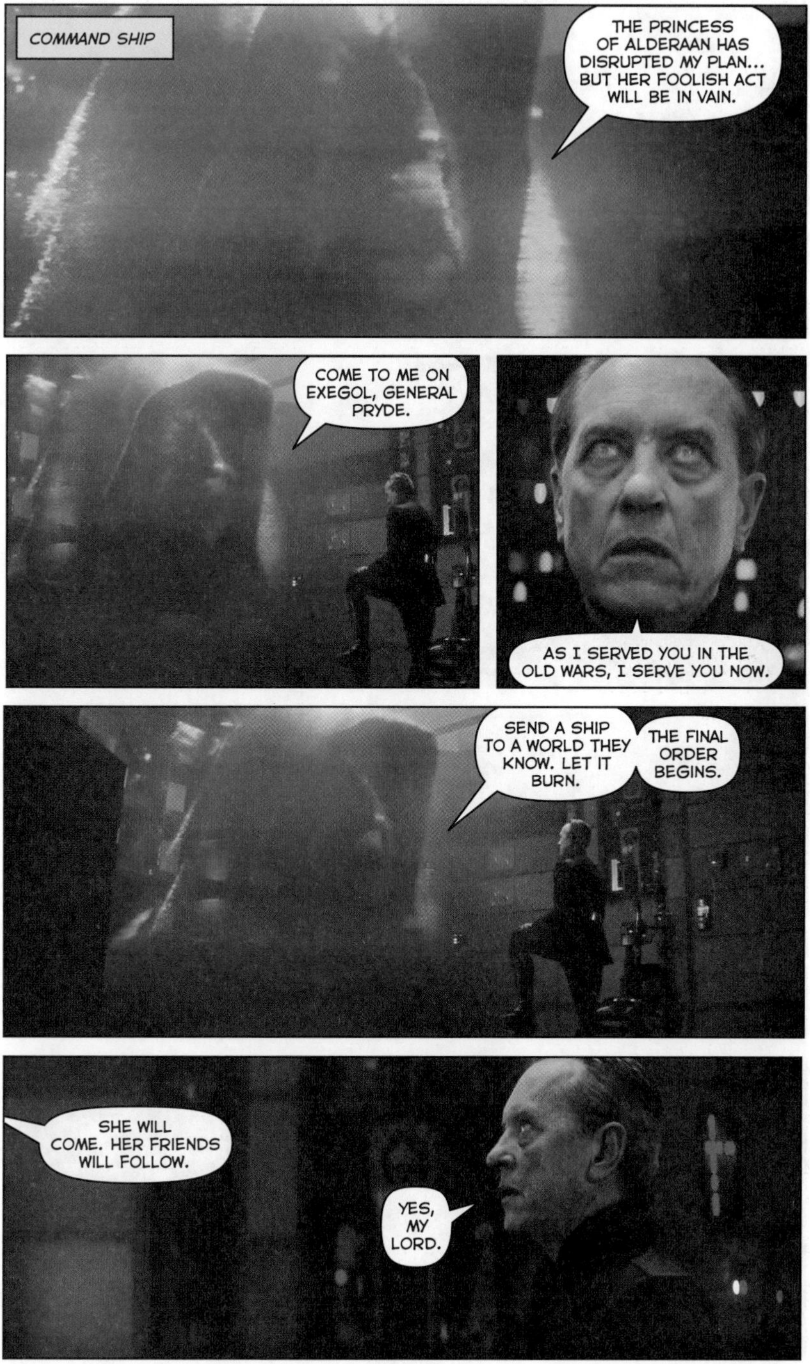
COMMAND SHIP
THE PRINCESS OF ALDERAAN HAS DISRUPTED MY PLAN... BUT HER FOOLISH ACT WILL BE IN VAIN.
COME TO ME ON EXEGOL, GENERAL PRYDE.
AS I SERVED YOU IN THE OLD WARS, I SERVE YOU NOW.
SEND A SHIP TO A WORLD THEY KNOW. LET IT BURN.
THE FINAL ORDER BEGINS.
SHE WILL COME. HER FRIENDS WILL FOLLOW.
YES, MY LORD.

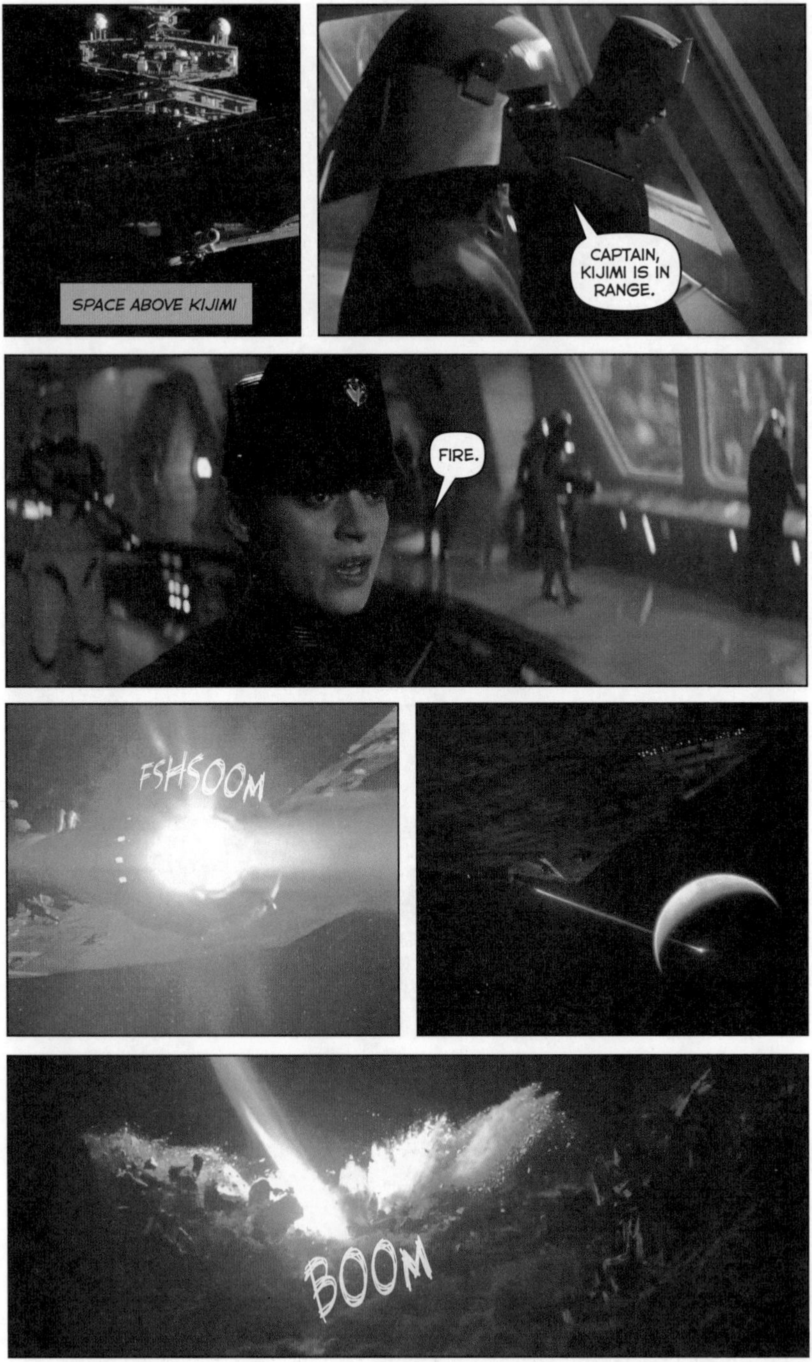
SPACE ABOVE KIJIMI
CAPTAIN, KIJIMI IS IN RANGE.
FIRE.
FSHSOOM
BOOM

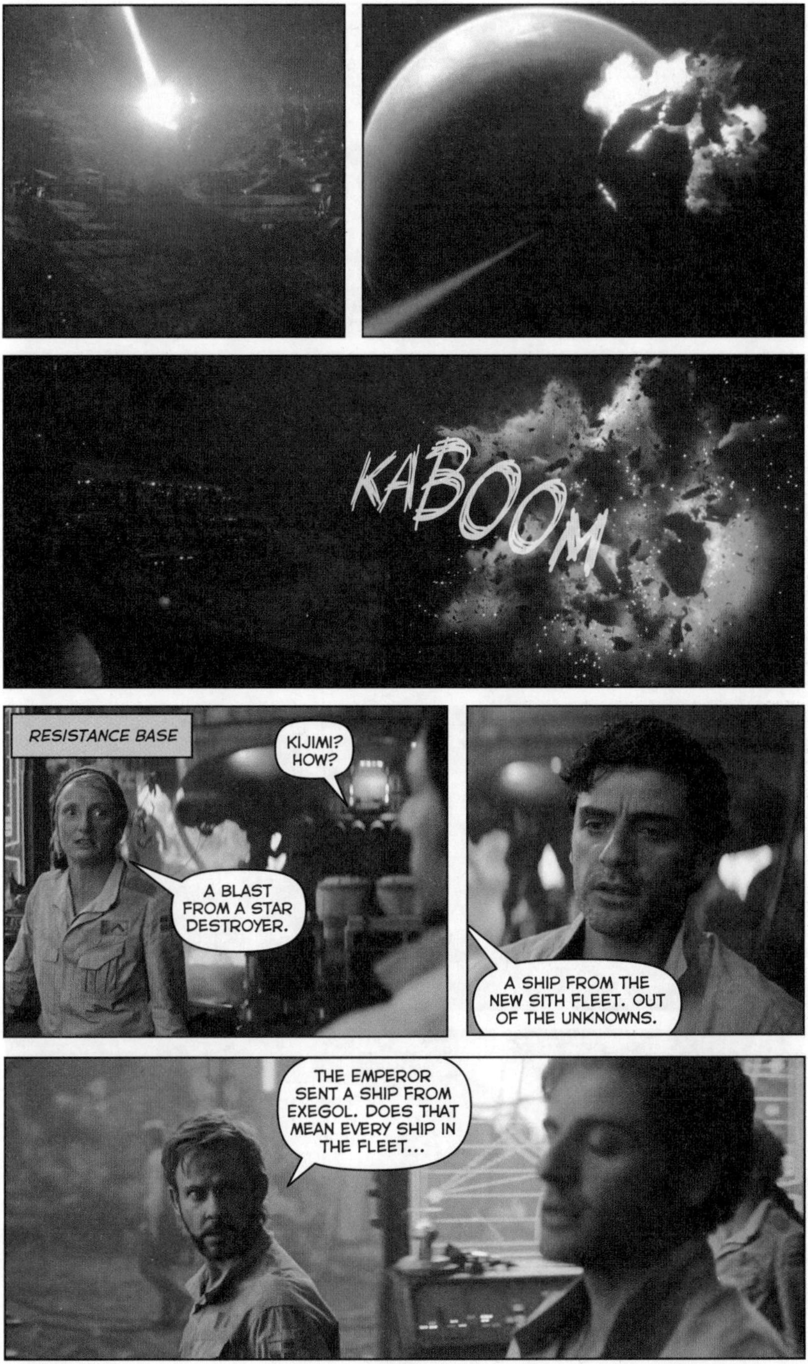
KABOOM
RESISTANCE BASE
KIJIMI? HOW?
A BLAST FROM A STAR DESTROYER.
A SHIP FROM THE NEW SITH FLEET. OUT OF THE UNKNOWNS.
THE EMPEROR SENT A SHIP FROM EXEGOL. DOES THAT MEAN EVERY SHIP IN THE FLEET...

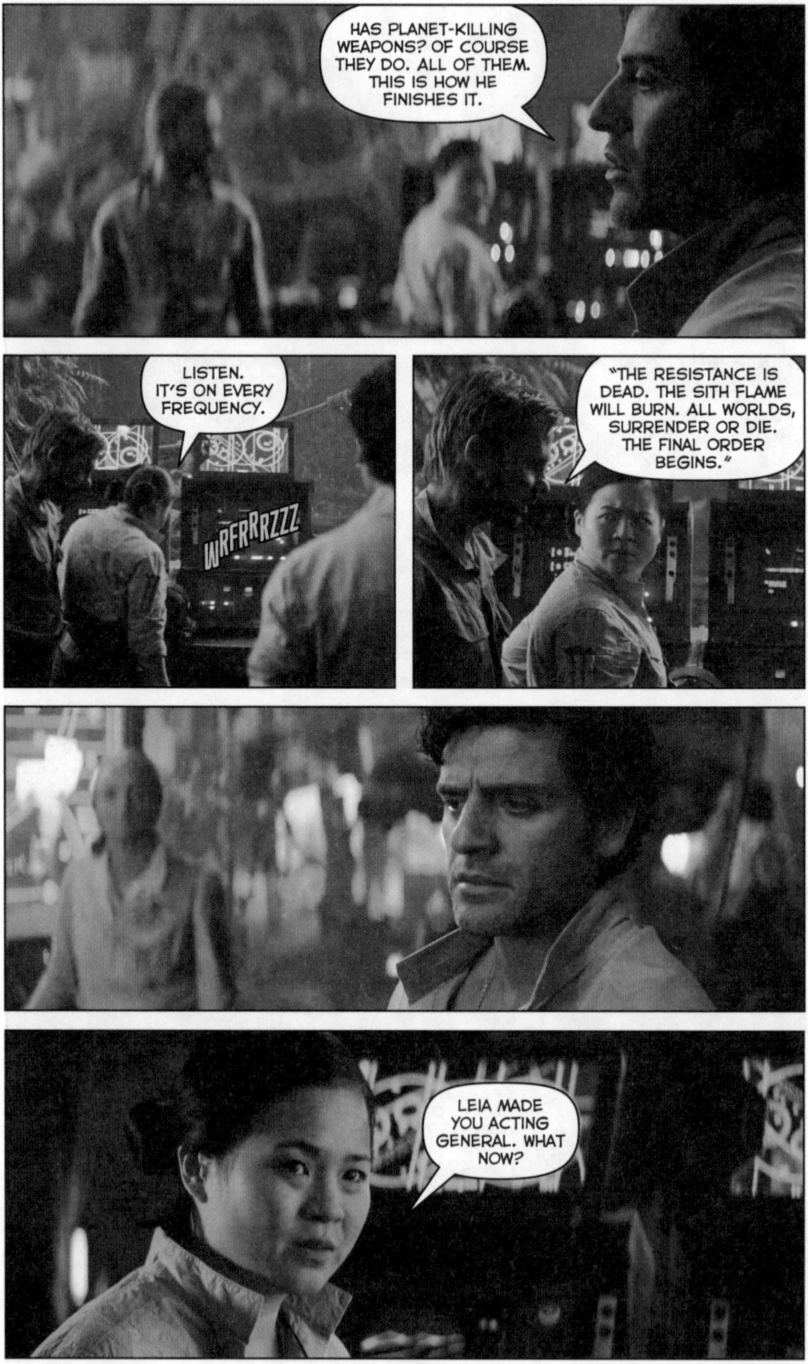
HAS PLANET-KILLING WEAPONS? OF COURSE THEY DO. ALL OF THEM. THIS IS HOW HE FINISHES IT.
LISTEN. IT'S ON EVERY FREQUENCY.
WRFRRRZZZ
"THE RESISTANCE IS DEAD. THE SITH FLAME WILL BURN. ALL WORLDS, SURRENDER OR DIE. THE FINAL ORDER BEGINS."
LEIA MADE YOU ACTING GENERAL. WHAT NOW?

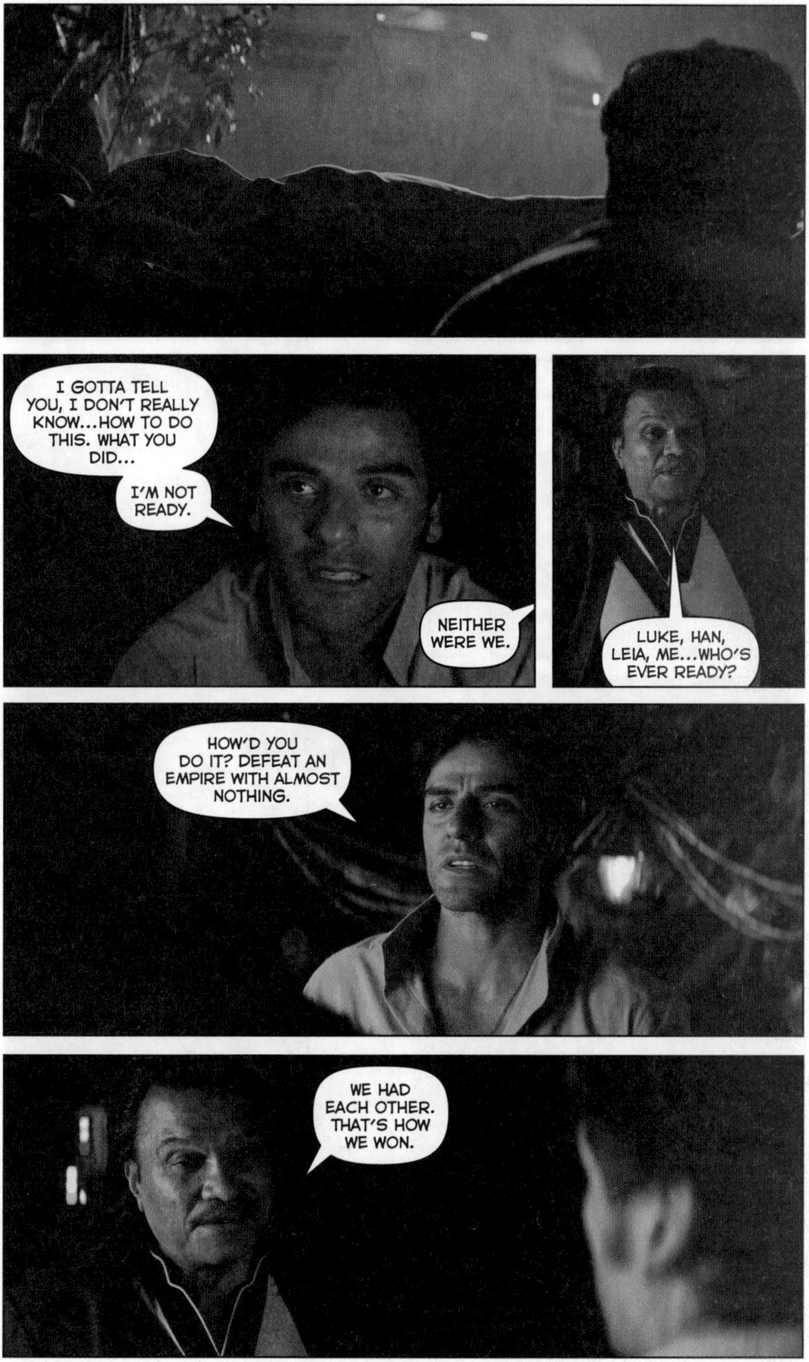
I GOTTA TELL YOU, I DON'T REALLY KNOW...HOW TO DO THIS. WHAT YOU DID...
I'M NOT READY.
NEITHER WERE WE.
LUKE, HAN, LEIA, ME...WHO'S EVER READY?
HOW'D YOU DO IT? DEFEAT AN EMPIRE WITH ALMOST NOTHING.
WE HAD EACH OTHER. THAT'S HOW WE WON.

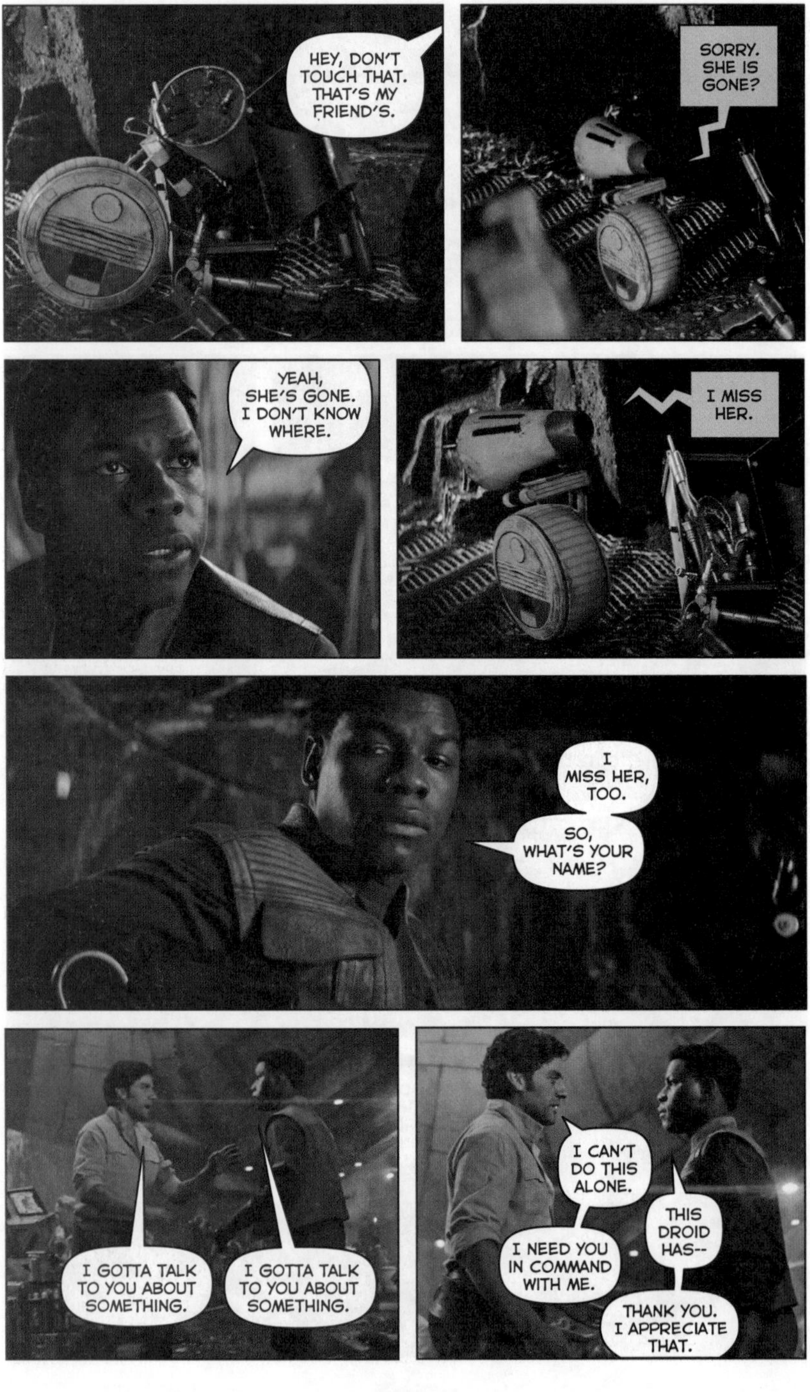
HEY, DON'T TOUCH THAT. THAT'S MY FRIEND'S.
SORRY. SHE IS GONE?
YEAH, SHE'S GONE. I DON'T KNOW WHERE.
I MISS HER.
I MISS HER, TOO.
SO, WHAT'S YOUR NAME?
I GOTTA TALK TO YOU ABOUT SOMETHING.
I GOTTA TALK TO YOU ABOUT SOMETHING.
I CAN'T DO THIS ALONE.
I NEED YOU IN COMMAND WITH ME.
THIS DROID HAS--
THANK YOU. I APPRECIATE THAT.

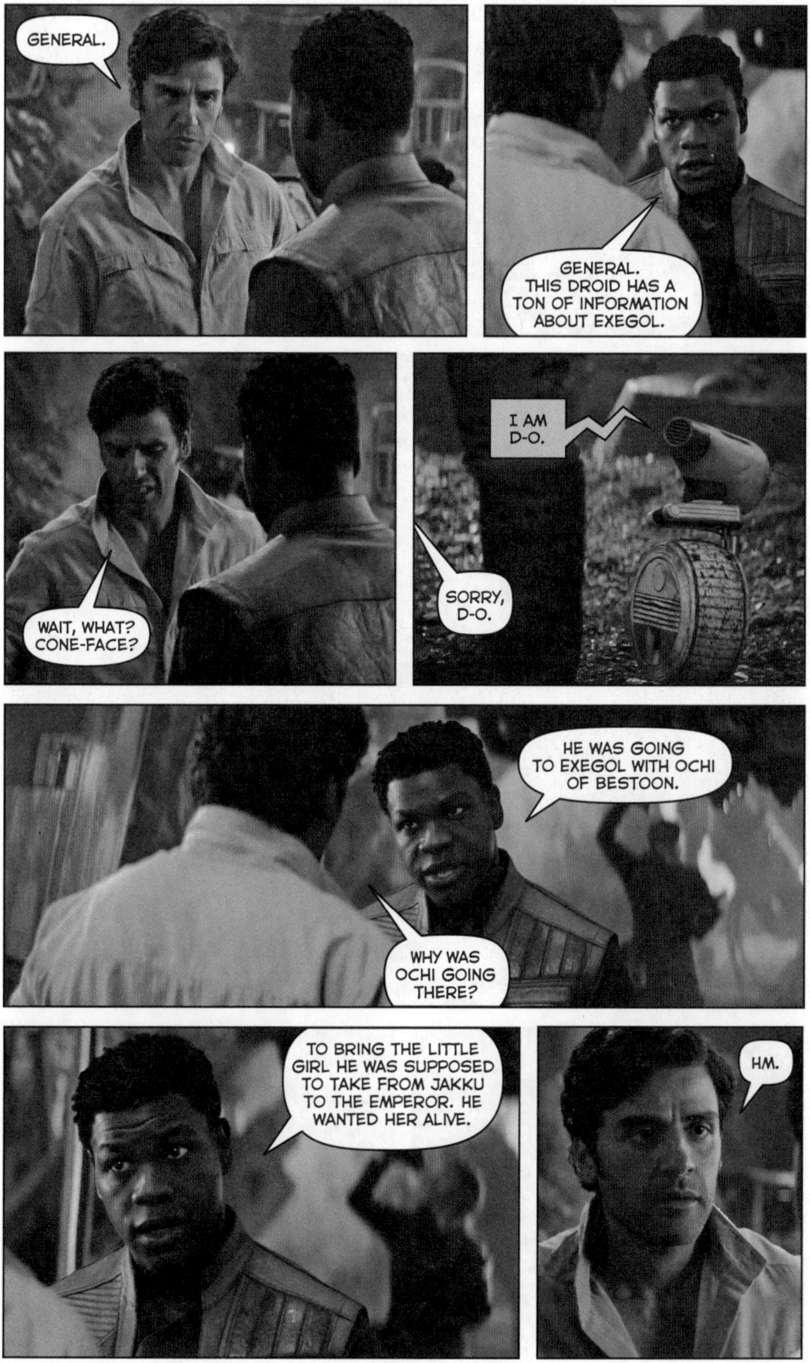
GENERAL.
GENERAL. THIS DROID HAS A TON OF INFORMATION ABOUT EXEGOL.
WAIT, WHAT? CONE-FACE?
I AM D-O.
SORRY, D-O.
HE WAS GOING TO EXEGOL WITH OCHI OF BESTOON.
WHY WAS OCHI GOING THERE?
TO BRING THE LITTLE GIRL HE WAS SUPPOSED TO TAKE FROM JAKKU TO THE EMPEROR. HE WANTED HER ALIVE.
HM.

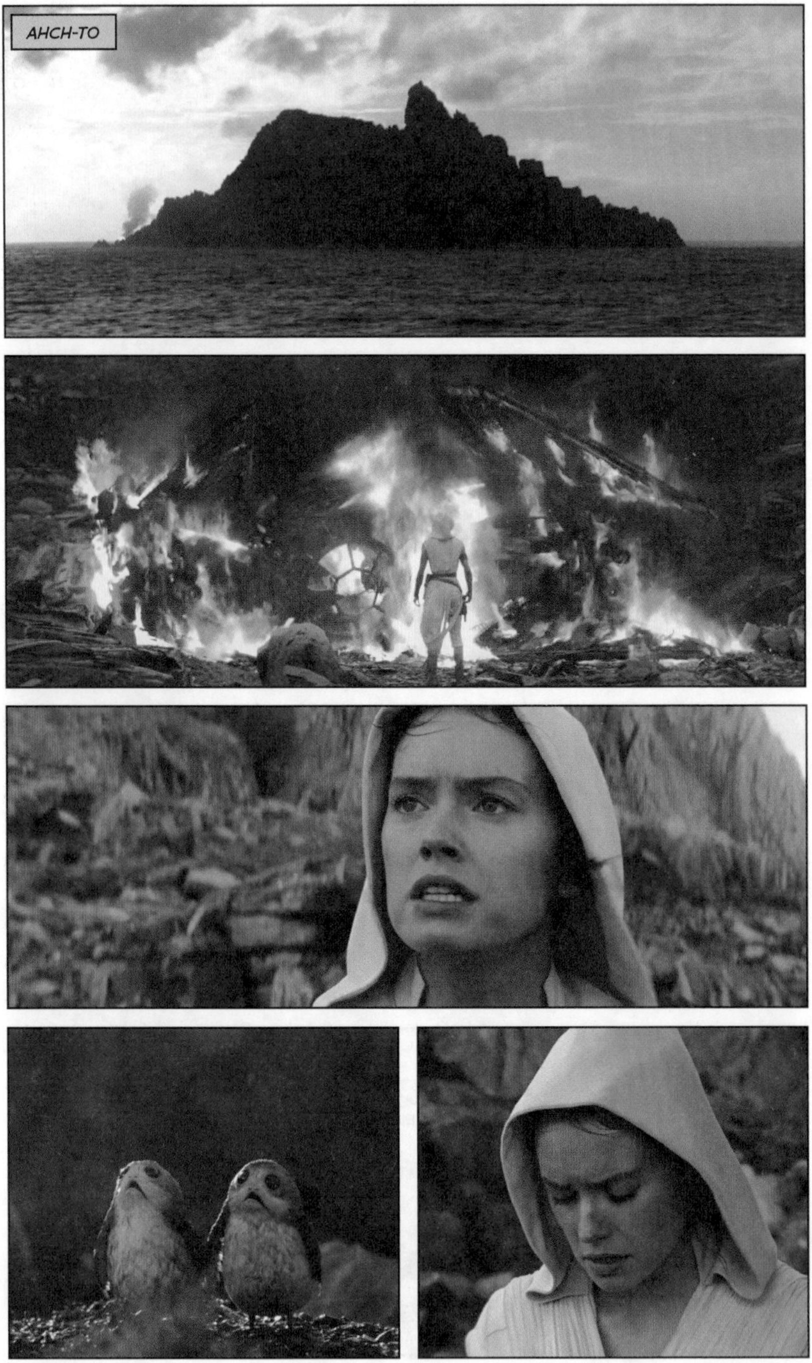
AHCH-TO

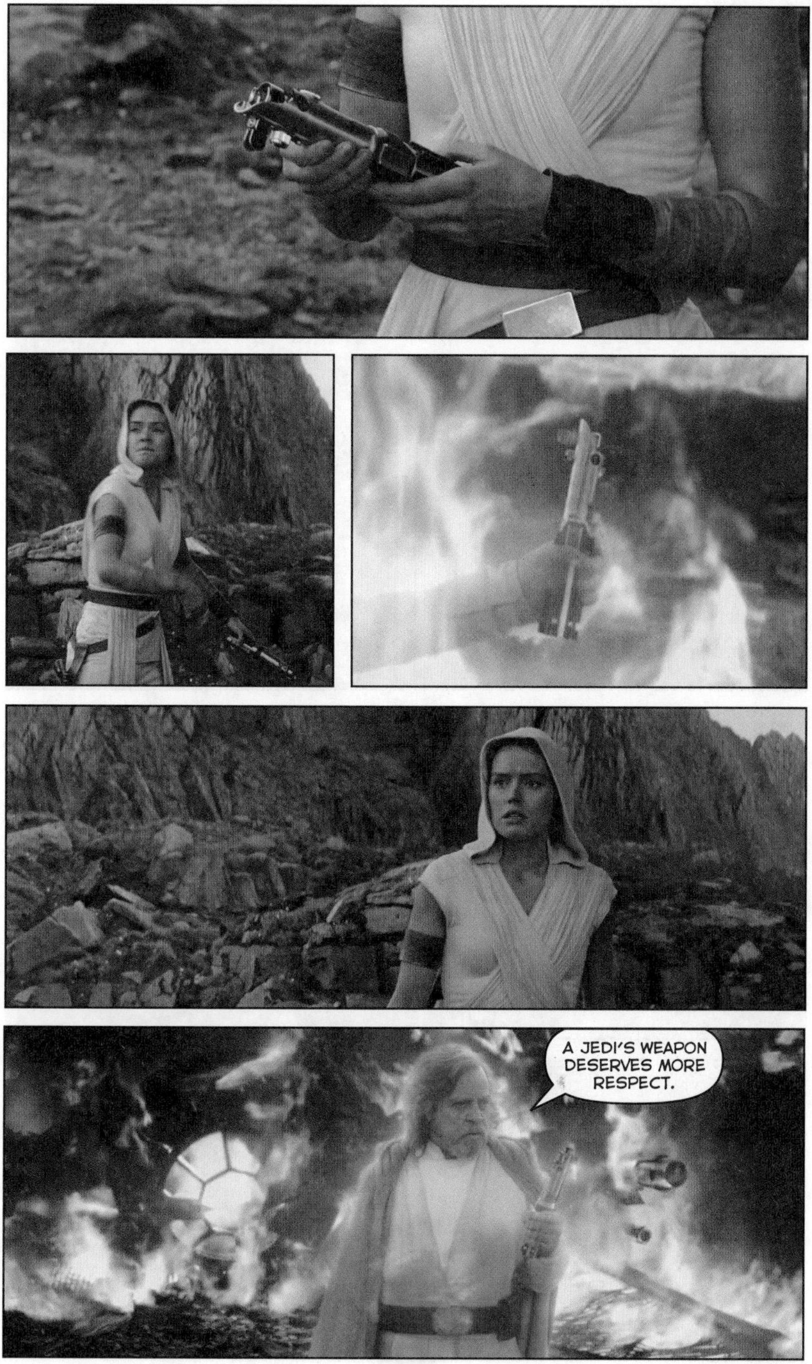
A JEDI'S WEAPON
DESERVES MORE
RESPECT.

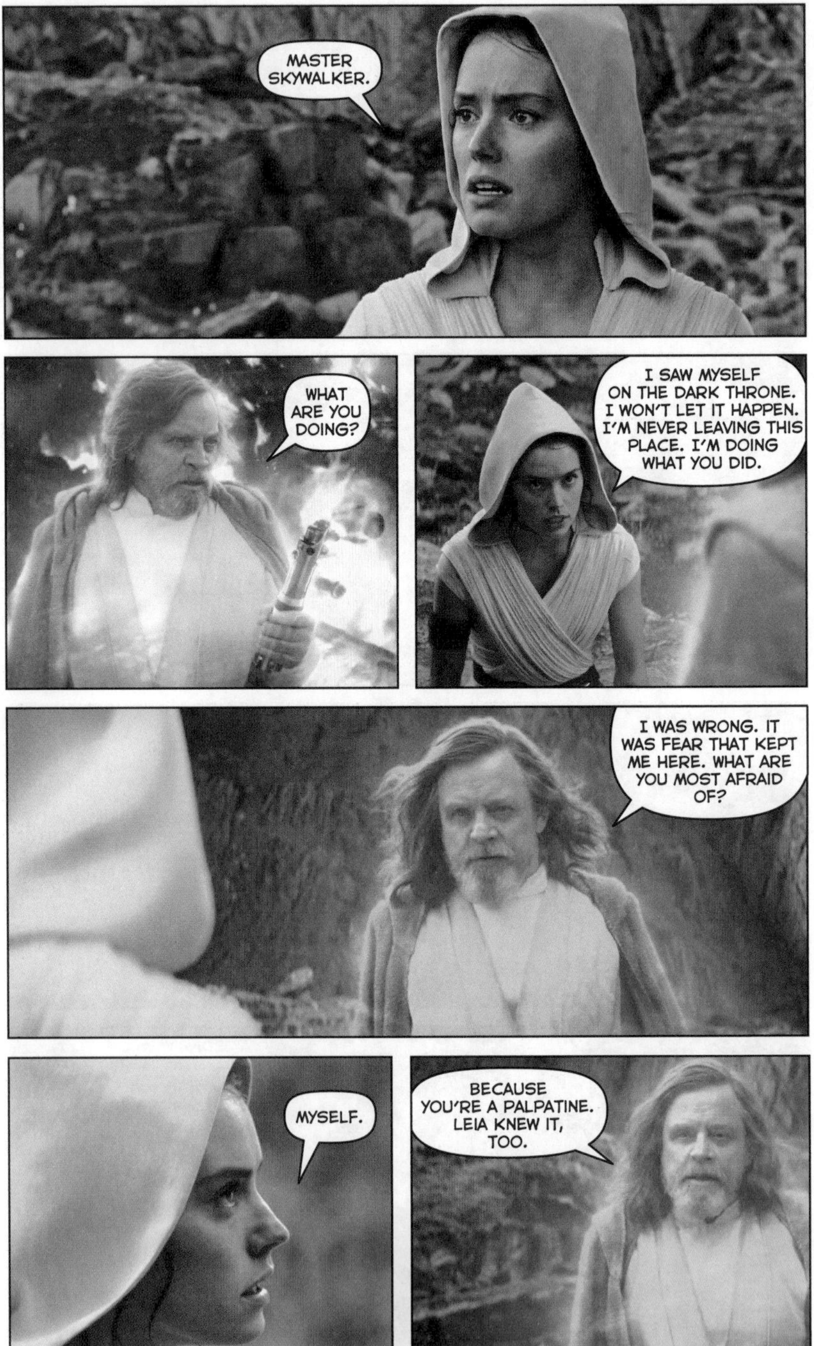
MASTER SKYWALKER.
WHAT ARE YOU DOING?
I SAW MYSELF ON THE DARK THRONE. I WON'T LET IT HAPPEN. I'M NEVER LEAVING THIS PLACE. I'M DOING WHAT YOU DID.
I WAS WRONG. IT WAS FEAR THAT KEPT ME HERE. WHAT ARE YOU MOST AFRAID OF?
MYSELF.
BECAUSE YOU'RE A PALPATINE. LEIA KNEW IT, TOO.

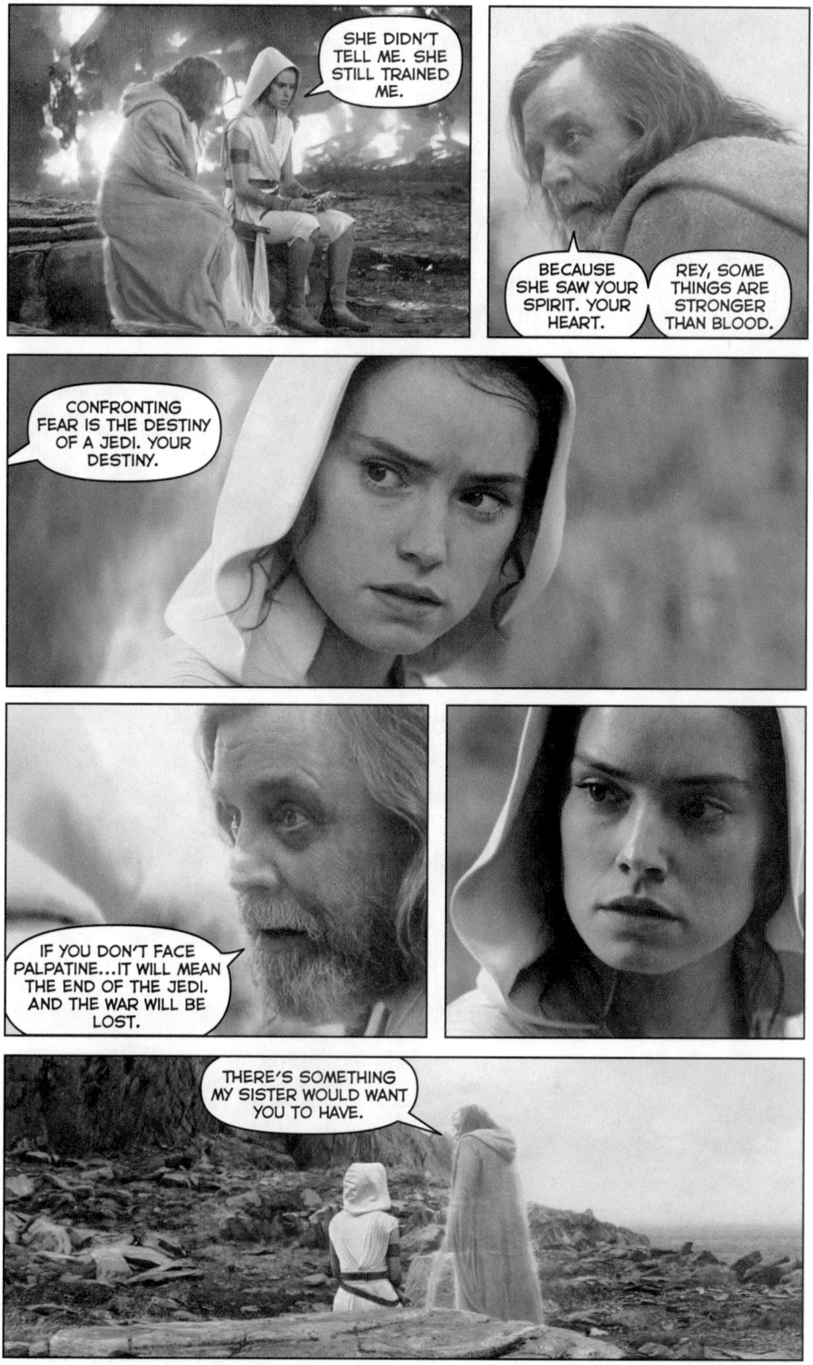
SHE DIDN'T TELL ME. SHE STILL TRAINED ME.
BECAUSE SHE SAW YOUR SPIRIT. YOUR HEART.
REY, SOME THINGS ARE STRONGER THAN BLOOD.
CONFRONTING FEAR IS THE DESTINY OF A JEDI. YOUR DESTINY.
IF YOU DON'T FACE PALPATINE...IT WILL MEAN THE END OF THE JEDI. AND THE WAR WILL BE LOST.
THERE'S SOMETHING MY SISTER WOULD WANT YOU TO HAVE.

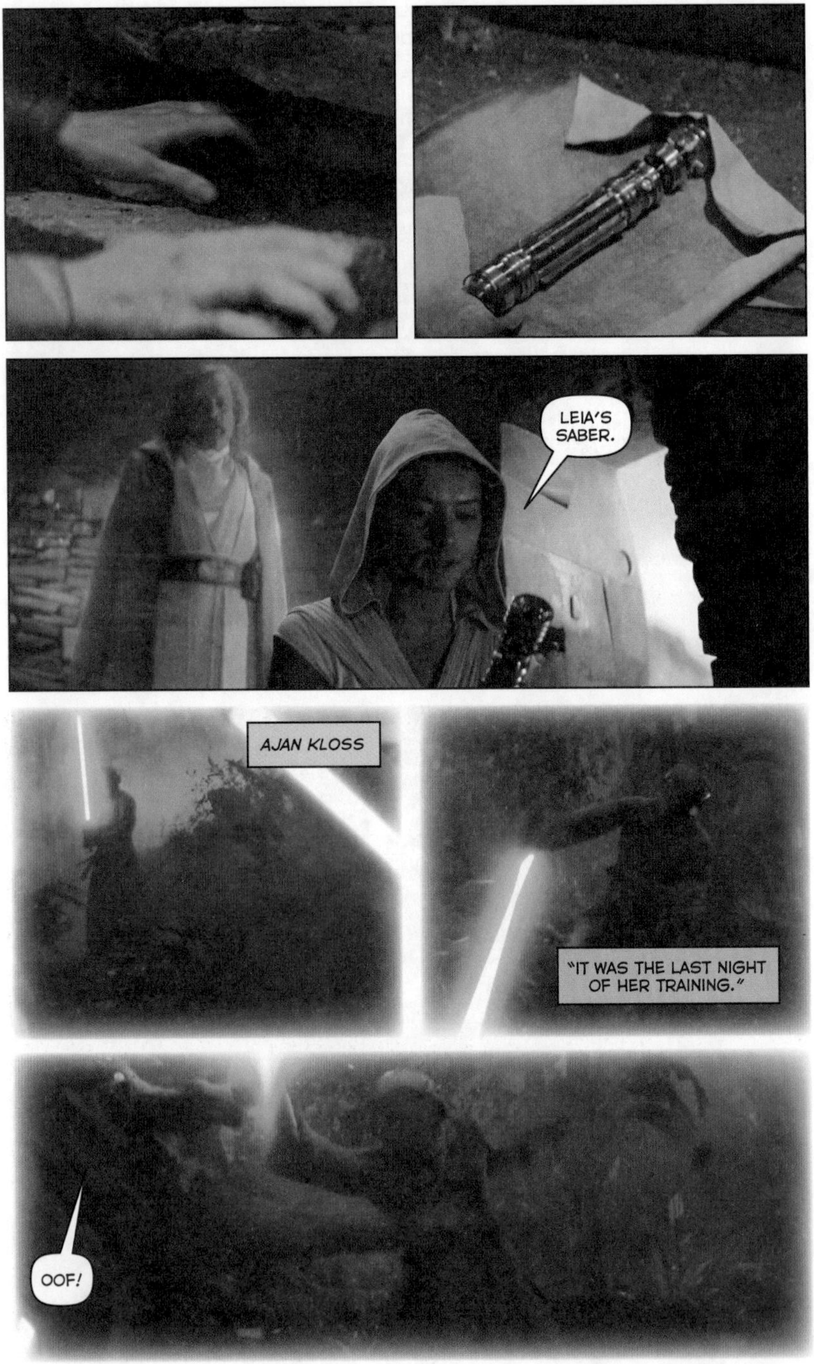
LEIA'S SABER.
AJAN KLOSS
"IT WAS THE LAST NIGHT OF HER TRAINING."
OOF!

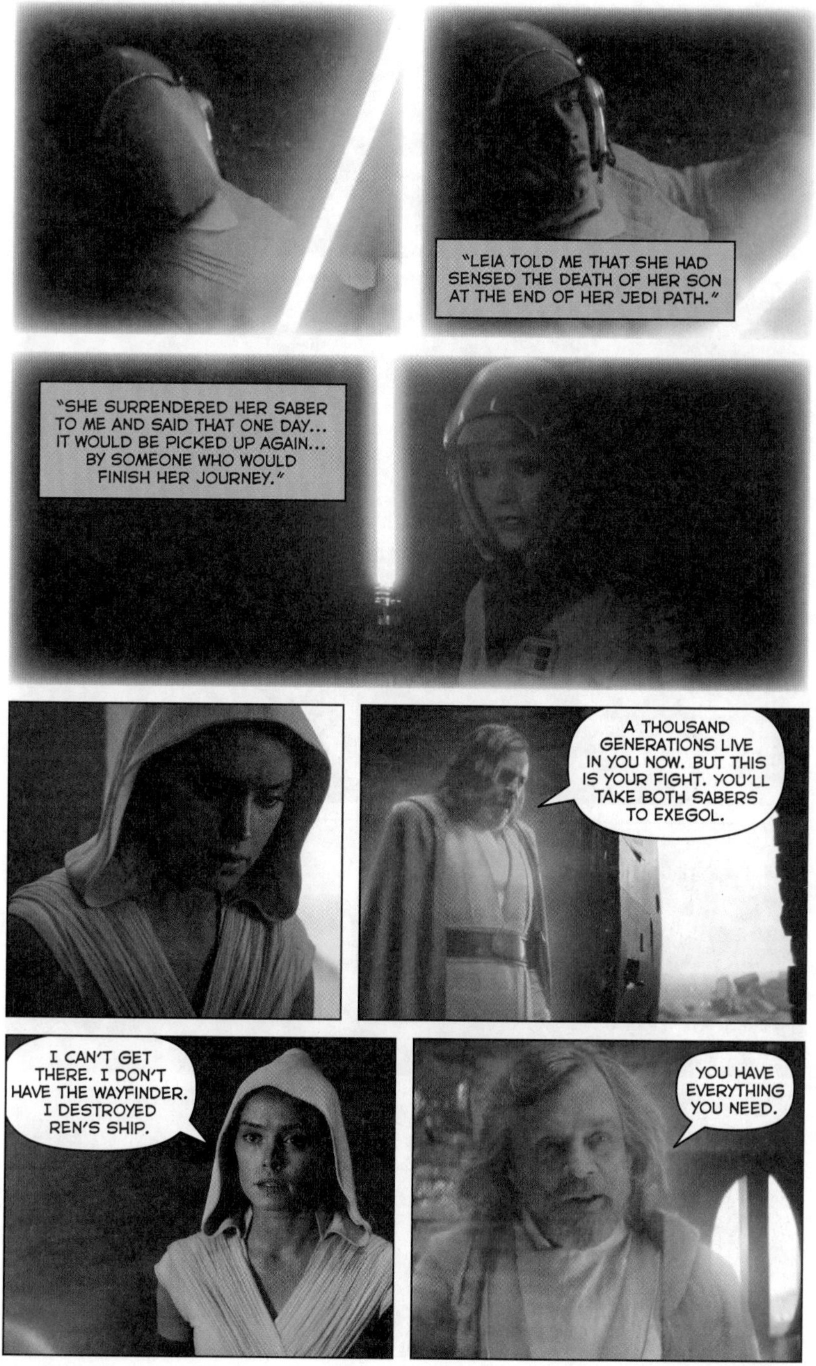
"LEIA TOLD ME THAT SHE HAD SENSED THE DEATH OF HER SON AT THE END OF HER JEDI PATH."
"SHE SURRENDERED HER SABER TO ME AND SAID THAT ONE DAY... IT WOULD BE PICKED UP AGAIN... BY SOMEONE WHO WOULD FINISH HER JOURNEY."
A THOUSAND GENERATIONS LIVE IN YOU NOW. BUT THIS IS YOUR FIGHT. YOU'LL TAKE BOTH SABERS TO EXEGOL.
I CAN'T GET THERE. I DON'T HAVE THE WAYFINDER. I DESTROYED REN'S SHIP.
YOU HAVE EVERYTHING YOU NEED.

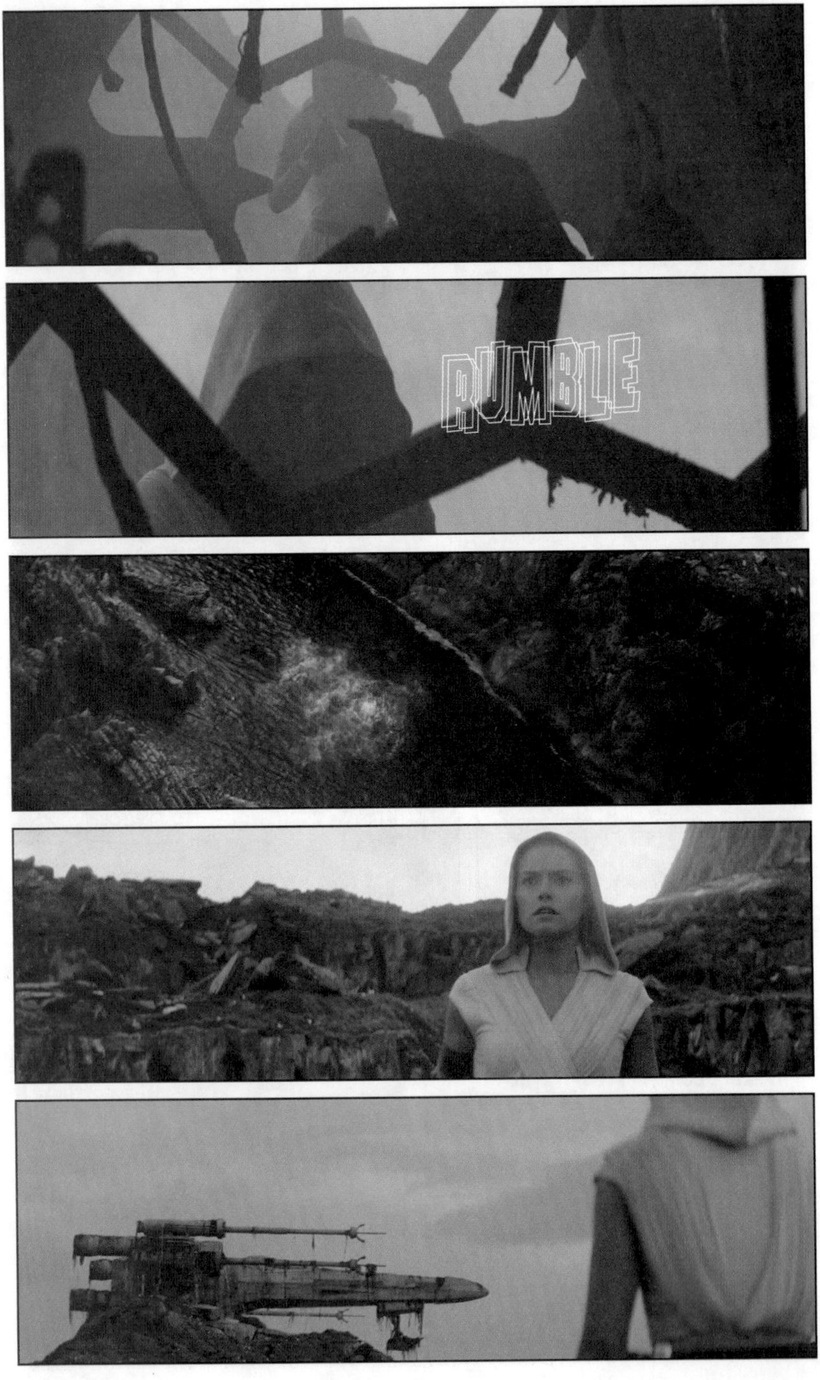
RUMBLE

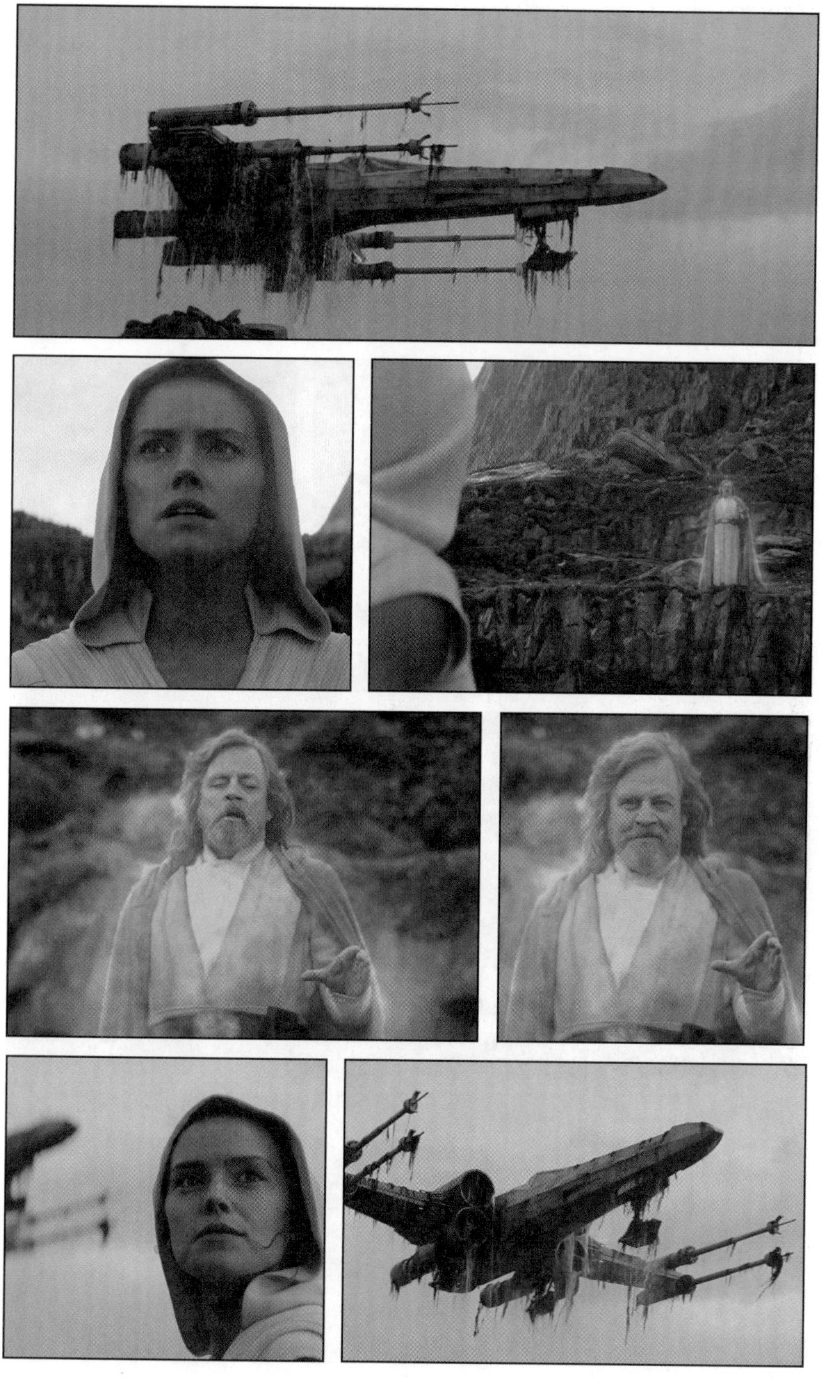

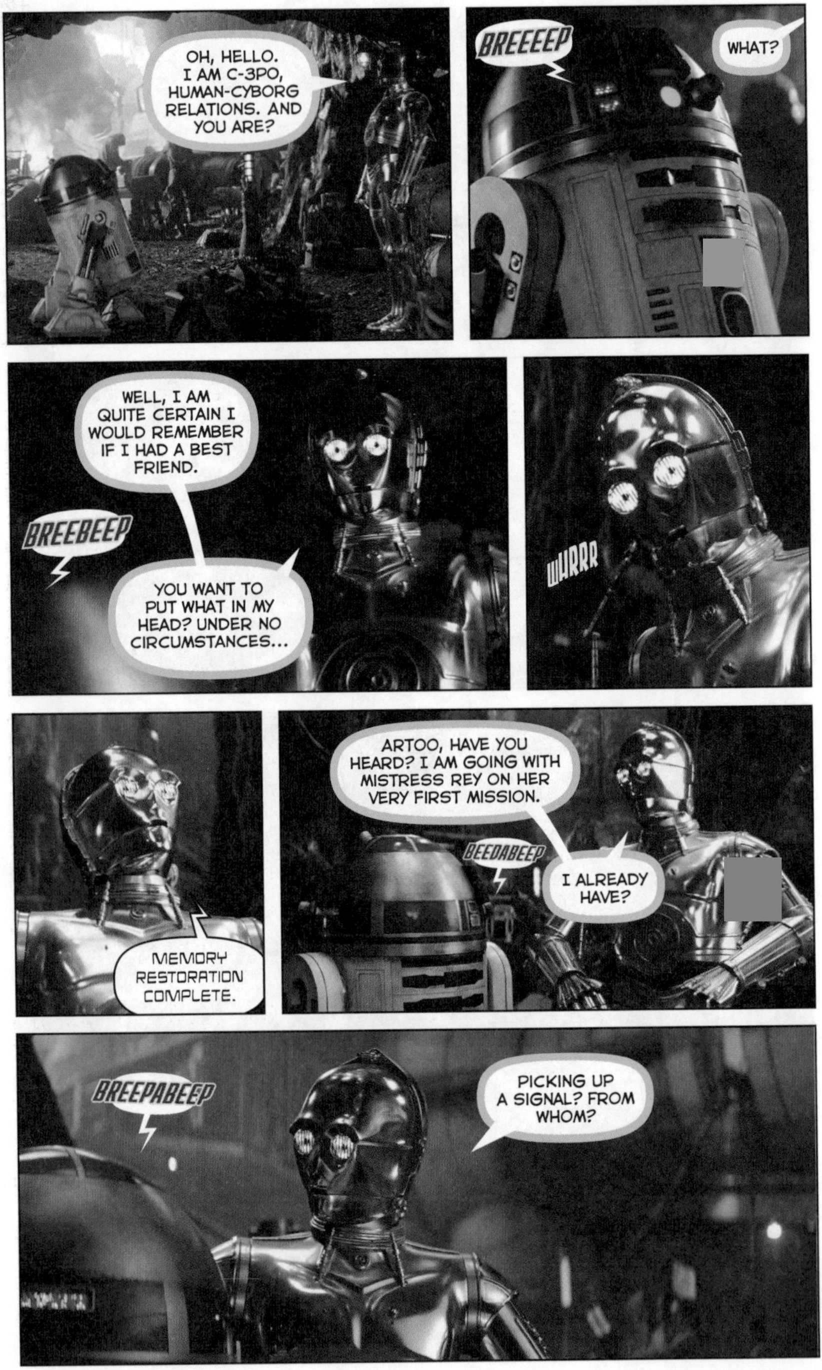
OH, HELLO. I AM C-3PO, HUMAN-CYBORG RELATIONS. AND YOU ARE?
BREEEEP
WHAT?
WELL, I AM QUITE CERTAIN I WOULD REMEMBER IF I HAD A BEST FRIEND.
BREEBEEP
YOU WANT TO PUT WHAT IN MY HEAD? UNDER NO CIRCUMSTANCES...
WHRRR
MEMORY RESTORATION COMPLETE.
ARTOO, HAVE YOU HEARD? I AM GOING WITH MISTRESS REY ON HER VERY FIRST MISSION.
BEEDABEEP
I ALREADY HAVE?
BREEPABEEP
PICKING UP A SIGNAL? FROM WHOM?

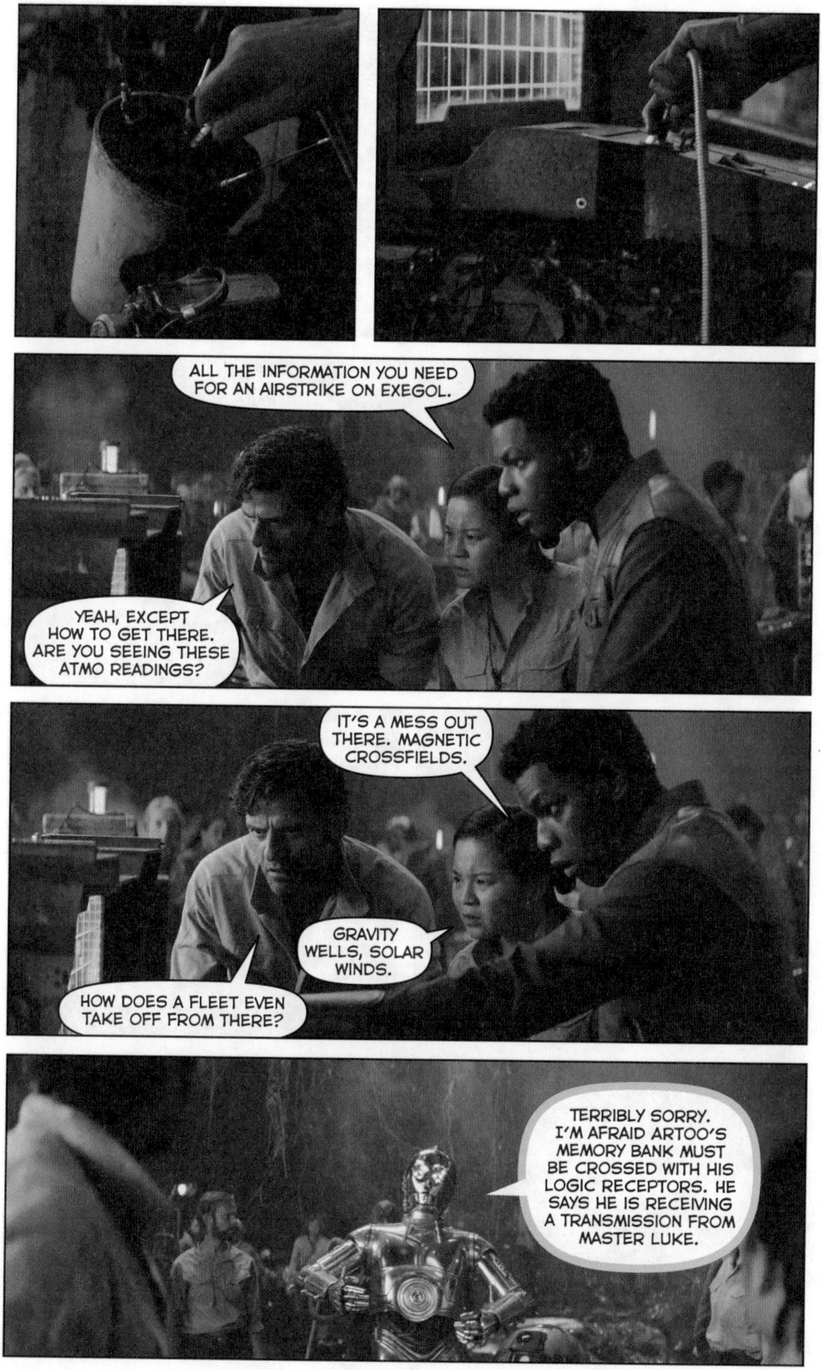
ALL THE INFORMATION YOU NEED FOR AN AIRSTRIKE ON EXEGOL.
YEAH, EXCEPT HOW TO GET THERE. ARE YOU SEEING THESE ATMO READINGS?
IT'S A MESS OUT THERE. MAGNETIC CROSSFIELDS.
GRAVITY WELLS, SOLAR WINDS.
HOW DOES A FLEET EVEN TAKE OFF FROM THERE?
TERRIBLY SORRY. I'M AFRAID ARTOO'S MEMORY BANK MUST BE CROSSED WITH HIS LOGIC RECEPTORS. HE SAYS HE IS RECEIVING A TRANSMISSION FROM MASTER LUKE.

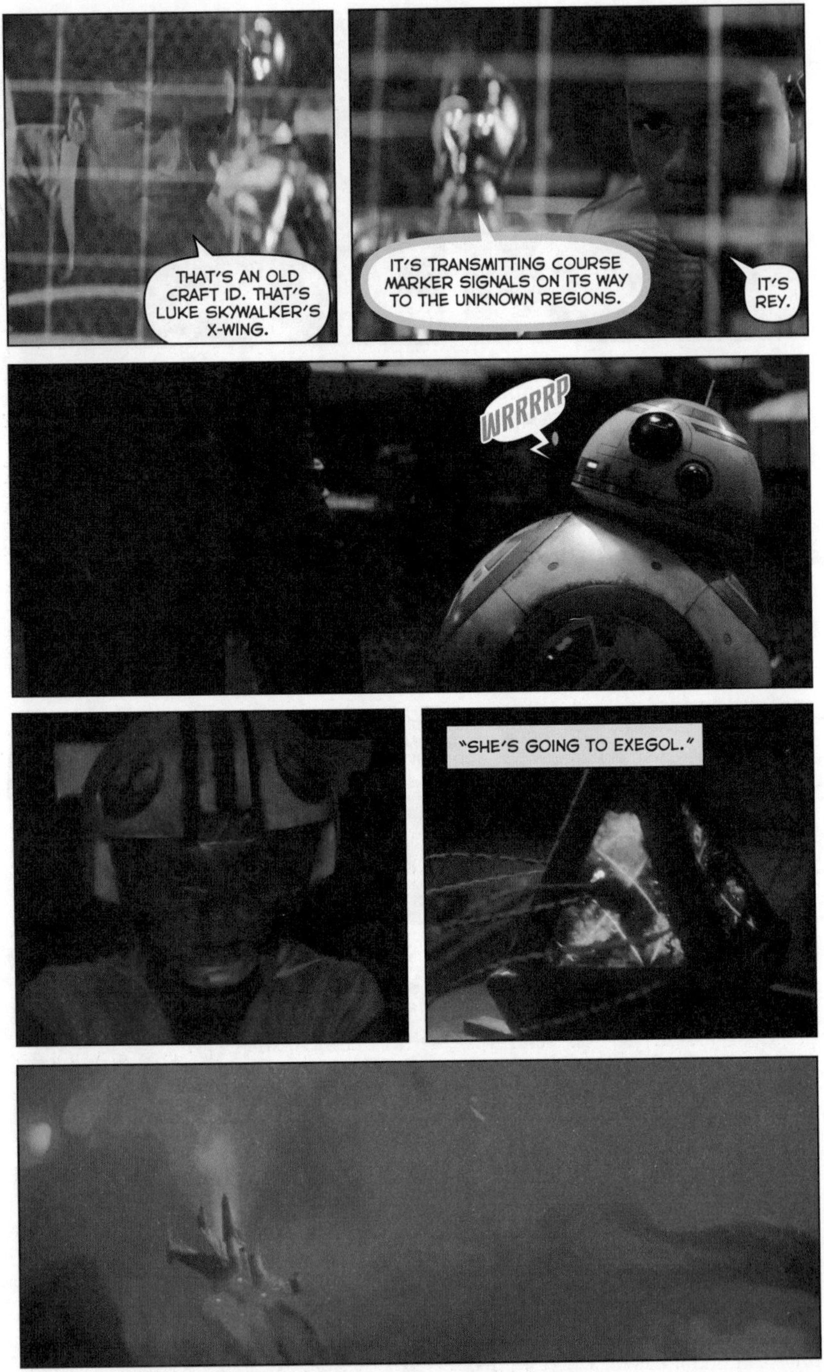
THAT'S AN OLD CRAFT ID. THAT'S LUKE SKYWALKER'S X-WING.
IT'S TRANSMITTING COURSE MARKER SIGNALS ON ITS WAY TO THE UNKNOWN REGIONS.
IT'S REY.
WRRRRP
"SHE'S GOING TO EXEGOL."

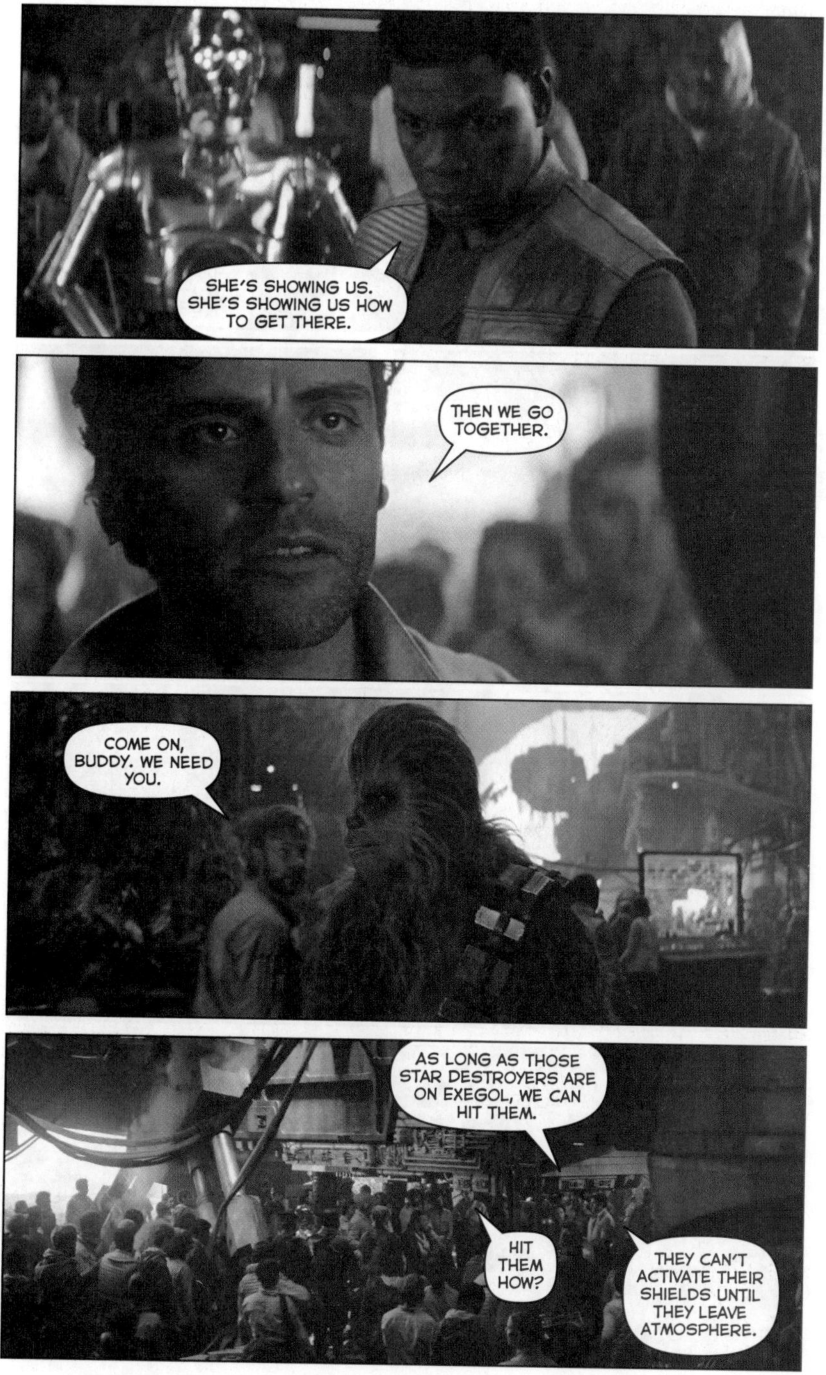
SHE'S SHOWING US. SHE'S SHOWING US HOW TO GET THERE.
THEN WE GO TOGETHER.
COME ON, BUDDY. WE NEED YOU.
AS LONG AS THOSE STAR DESTROYERS ARE ON EXEGOL, WE CAN HIT THEM.
HIT THEM HOW?
THEY CAN'T ACTIVATE THEIR SHIELDS UNTIL THEY LEAVE ATMOSPHERE.

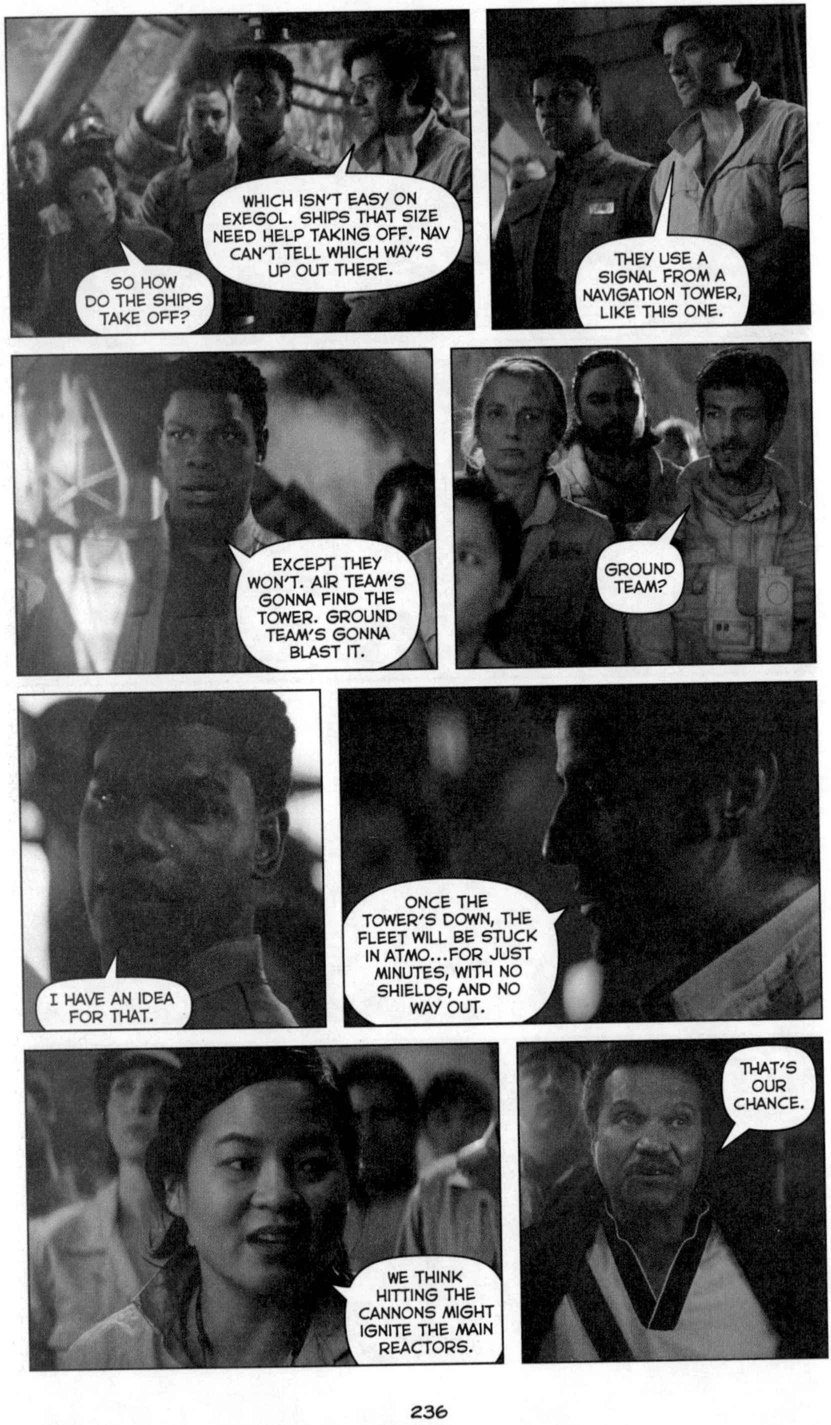
SO HOW DO THE SHIPS TAKE OFF?
WHICH ISN'T EASY ON EXEGOL. SHIPS THAT SIZE NEED HELP TAKING OFF. NAV CAN'T TELL WHICH WAY'S UP OUT THERE.
THEY USE A SIGNAL FROM A NAVIGATION TOWER, LIKE THIS ONE.
EXCEPT THEY WON'T. AIR TEAM'S GONNA FIND THE TOWER. GROUND TEAM'S GONNA BLAST IT.
GROUND TEAM?
I HAVE AN IDEA FOR THAT.
ONCE THE TOWER'S DOWN, THE FLEET WILL BE STUCK IN ATMO...FOR JUST MINUTES, WITH NO SHIELDS, AND NO WAY OUT.
WE THINK HITTING THE CANNONS MIGHT IGNITE THE MAIN REACTORS.
THAT'S OUR CHANCE.

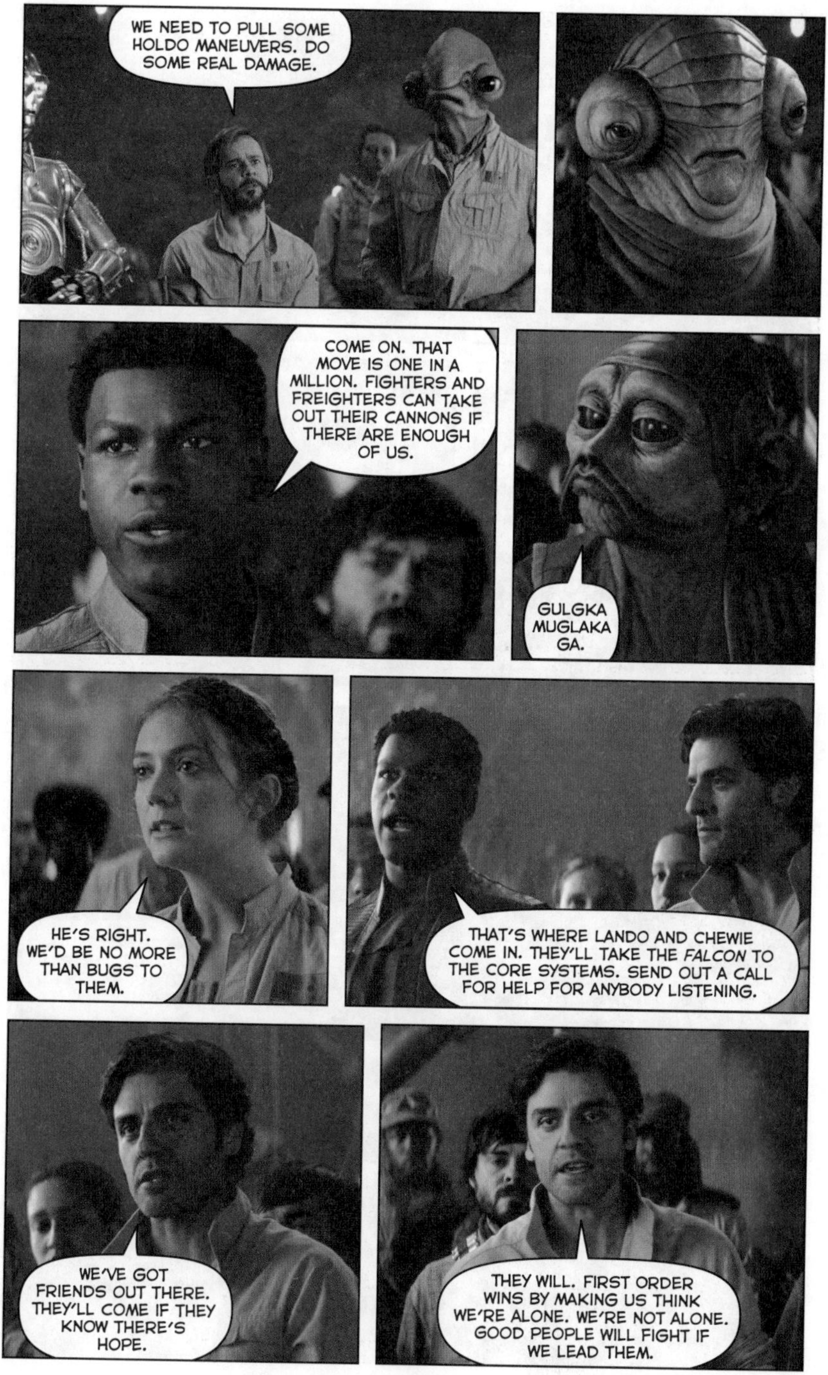
WE NEED TO PULL SOME HOLDO MANEUVERS. DO SOME REAL DAMAGE.
COME ON. THAT MOVE IS ONE IN A MILLION. FIGHTERS AND FREIGHTERS CAN TAKE OUT THEIR CANNONS IF THERE ARE ENOUGH OF US.
GULGKA MUGLAKA GA.
HE'S RIGHT. WE'D BE NO MORE THAN BUGS TO THEM.
THAT'S WHERE LANDO AND CHEWIE COME IN. THEY'LL TAKE THE *FALCON* TO THE CORE SYSTEMS. SEND OUT A CALL FOR HELP FOR ANYBODY LISTENING.
WE'VE GOT FRIENDS OUT THERE. THEY'LL COME IF THEY KNOW THERE'S HOPE.
THEY WILL. FIRST ORDER WINS BY MAKING US THINK WE'RE ALONE. WE'RE NOT ALONE. GOOD PEOPLE WILL FIGHT IF WE LEAD THEM.

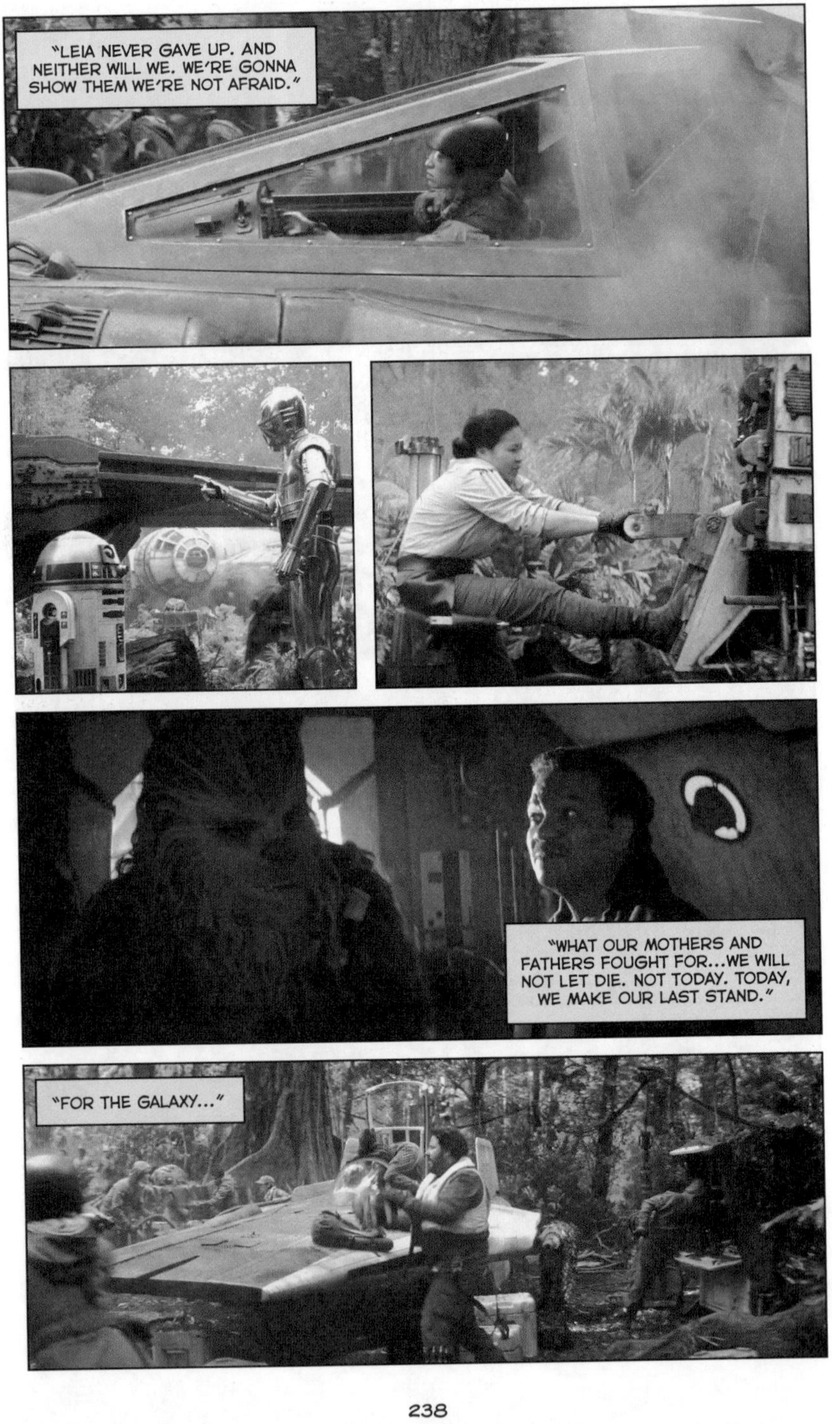
"LEIA NEVER GAVE UP. AND NEITHER WILL WE. WE'RE GONNA SHOW THEM WE'RE NOT AFRAID."
"WHAT OUR MOTHERS AND FATHERS FOUGHT FOR...WE WILL NOT LET DIE. NOT TODAY. TODAY, WE MAKE OUR LAST STAND."
"FOR THE GALAXY..."

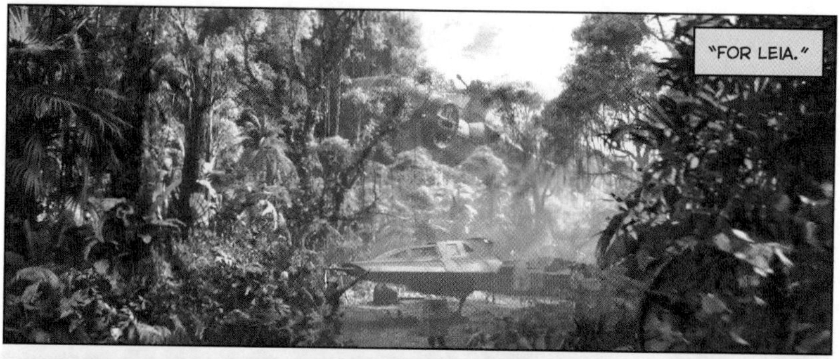
"FOR LEIA."

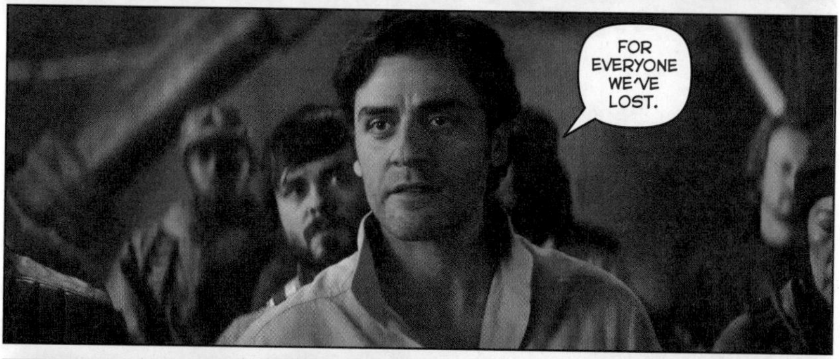
FOR EVERYONE WE'VE LOST.

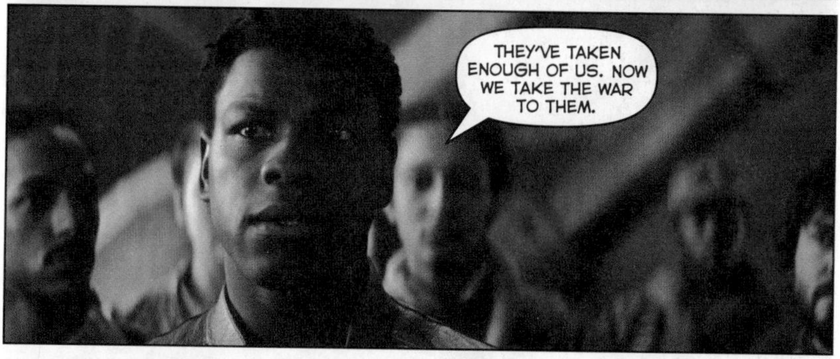
THEY'VE TAKEN ENOUGH OF US. NOW WE TAKE THE WAR TO THEM.

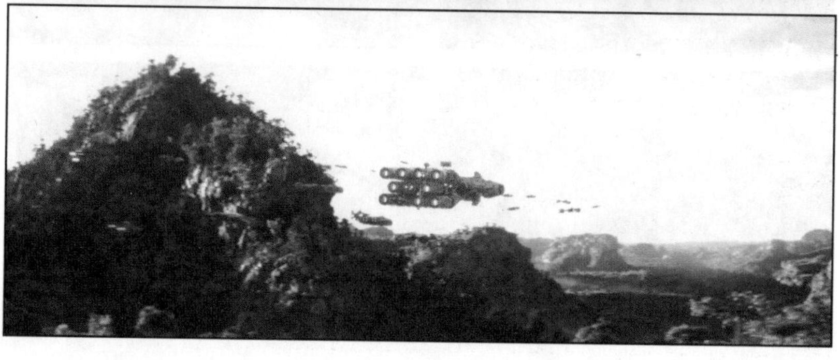

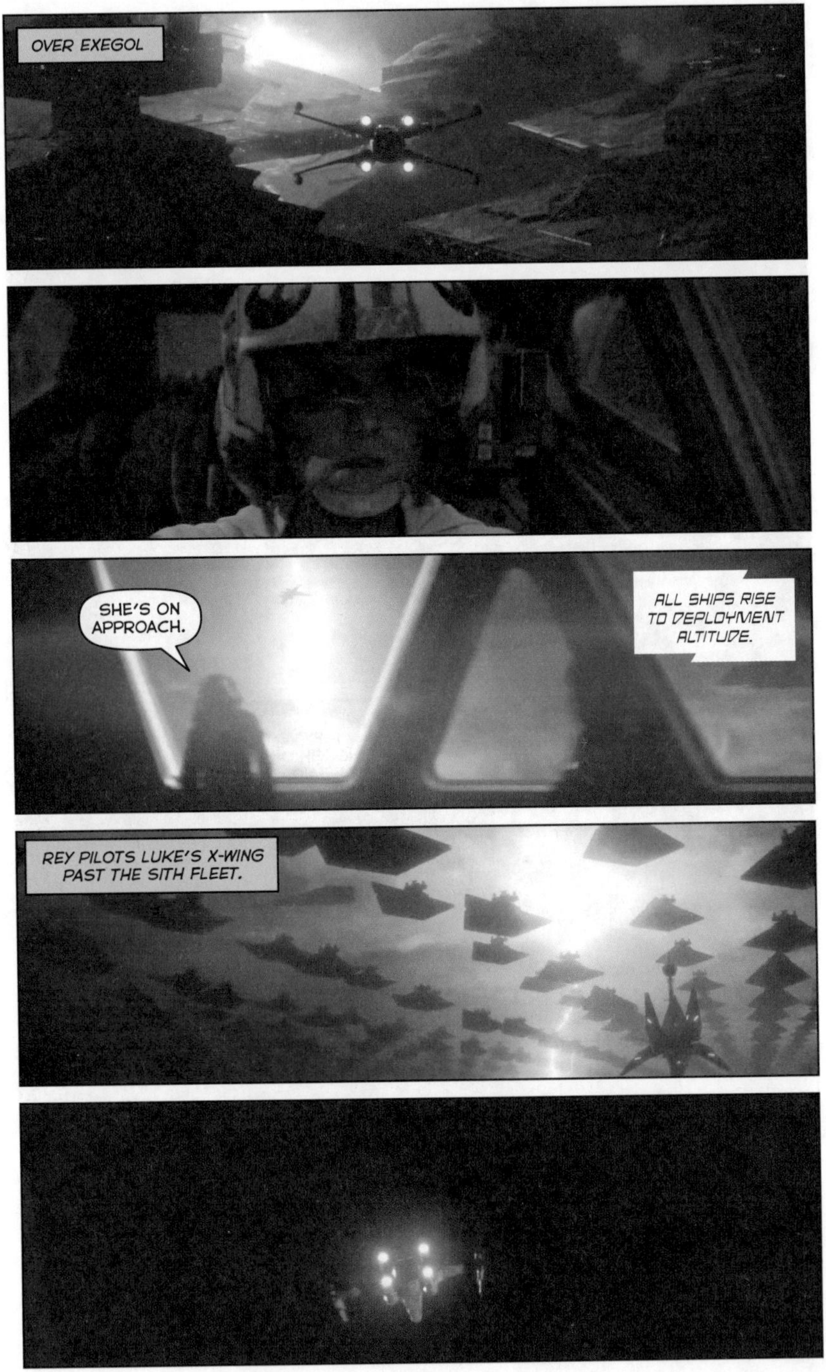

OVER EXEGOL
SHE'S ON APPROACH.
ALL SHIPS RISE TO DEPLOYMENT ALTITUDE.
REY PILOTS LUKE'S X-WING PAST THE SITH FLEET.

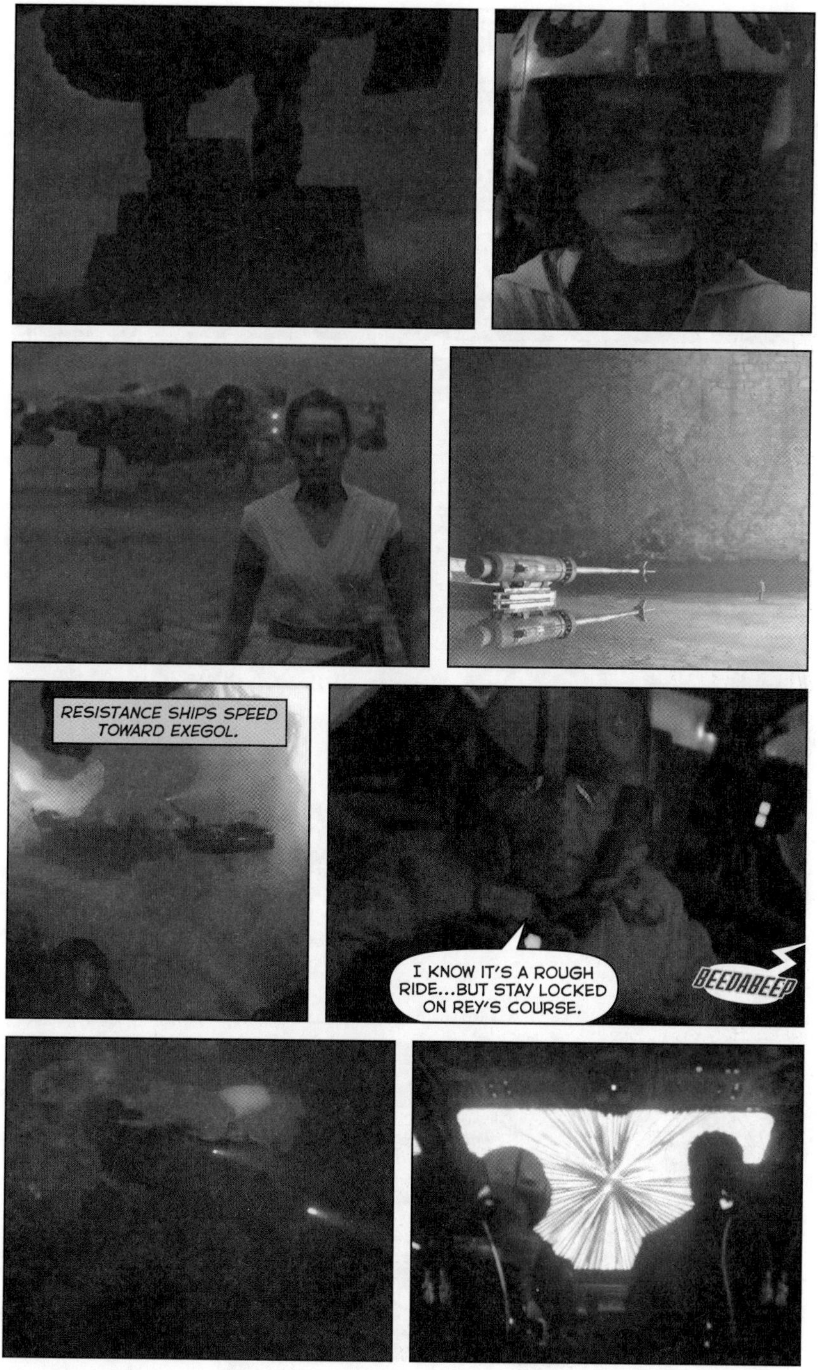
RESISTANCE SHIPS SPEED TOWARD EXEGOL.
I KNOW IT'S A ROUGH RIDE...BUT STAY LOCKED ON REY'S COURSE.
BEEDABEEP

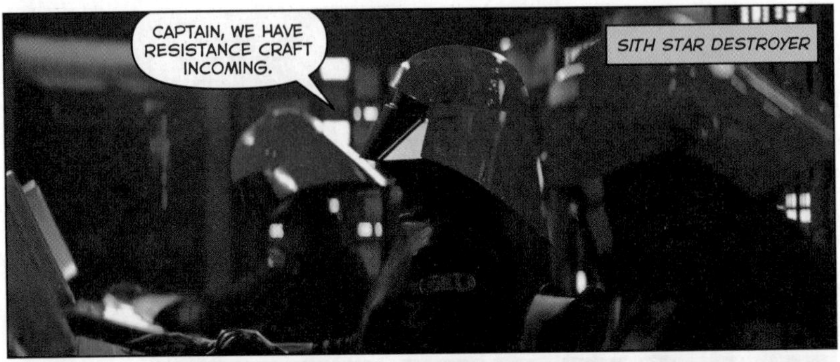
SITH STAR DESTROYER
CAPTAIN, WE HAVE RESISTANCE CRAFT INCOMING.

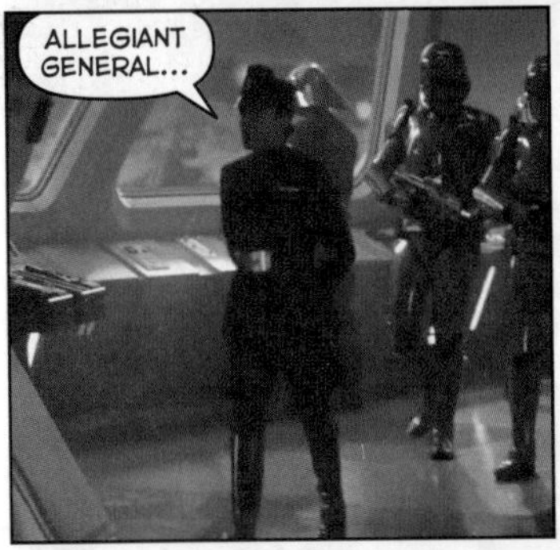
ALLEGIANT GENERAL...

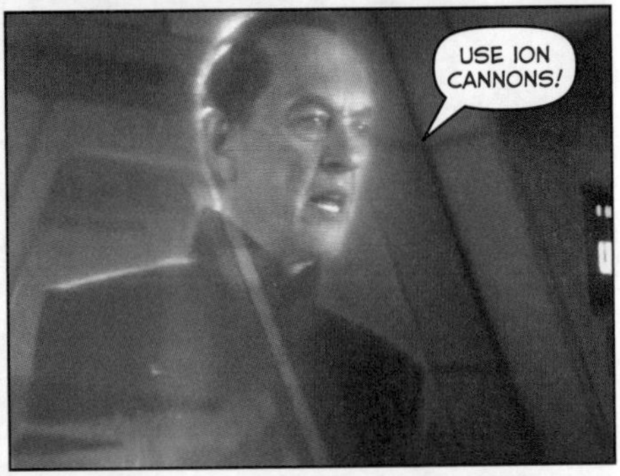
USE ION CANNONS!

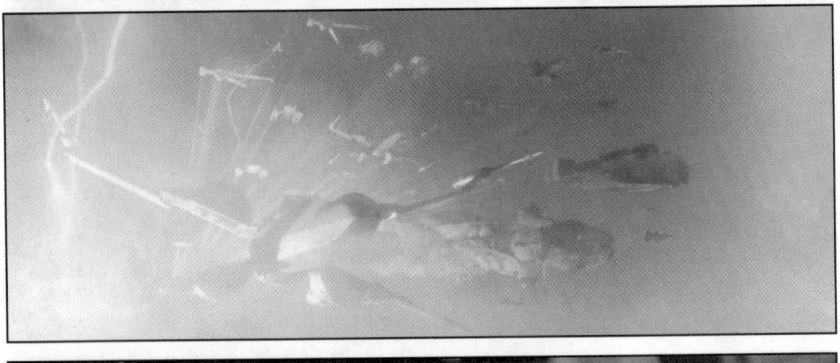

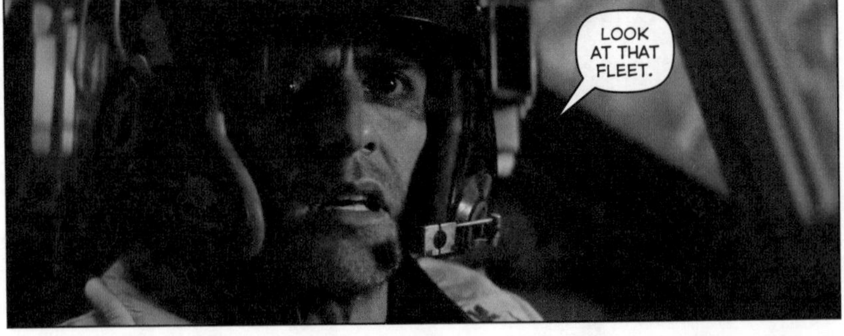
LOOK AT THAT FLEET.

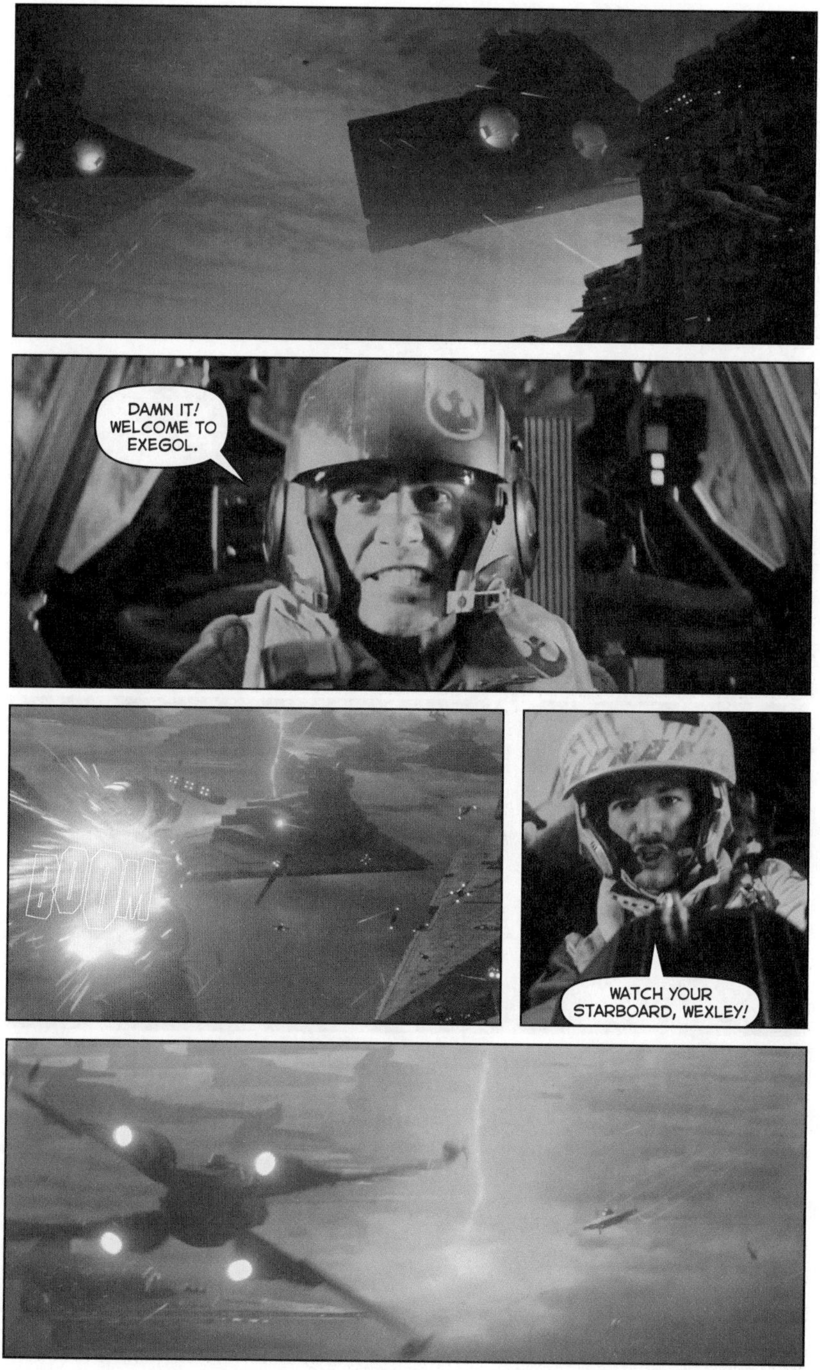
DAMN IT! WELCOME TO EXEGOL.
BOOM
WATCH YOUR STARBOARD, WEXLEY!

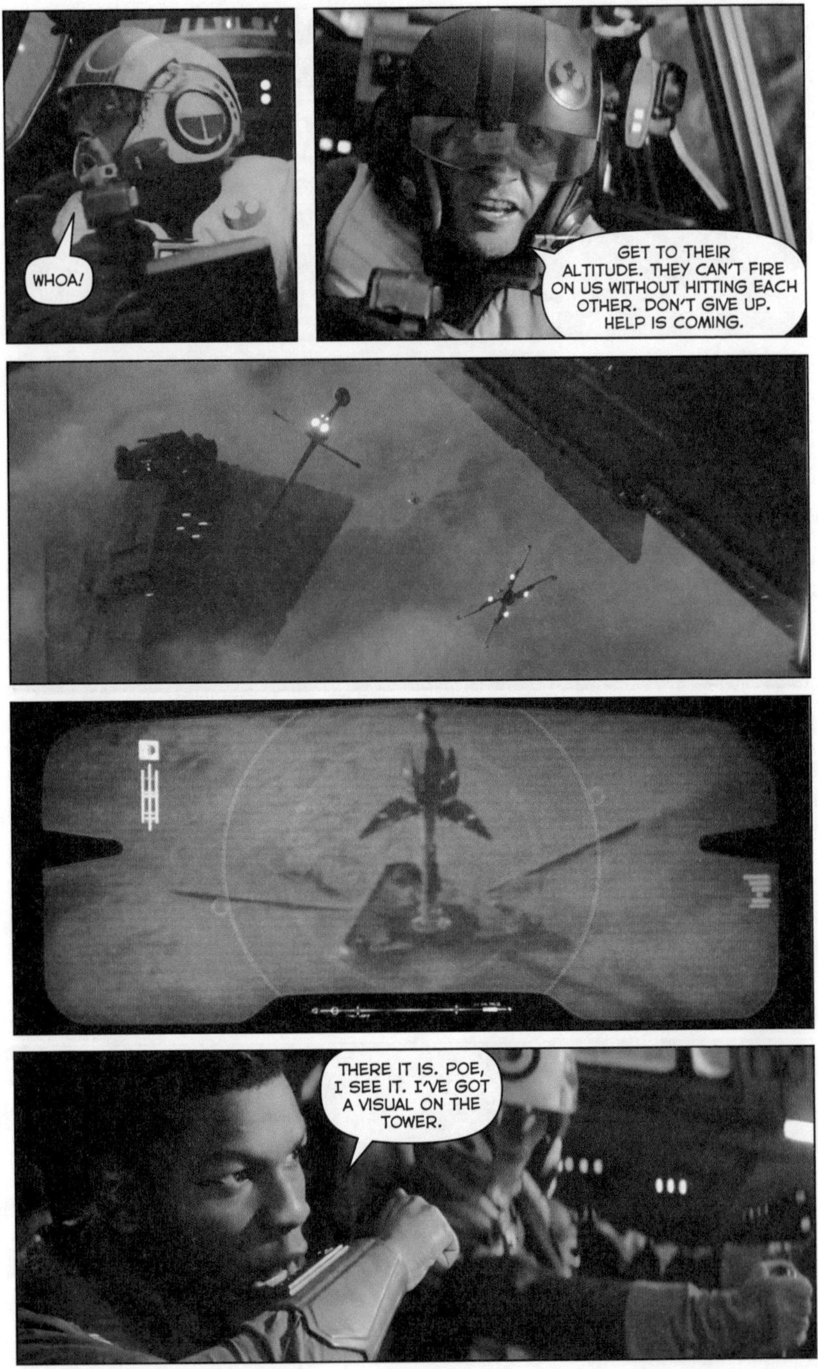
WHOA!
GET TO THEIR ALTITUDE. THEY CAN'T FIRE ON US WITHOUT HITTING EACH OTHER. DON'T GIVE UP. HELP IS COMING.
THERE IT IS. POE, I SEE IT. I'VE GOT A VISUAL ON THE TOWER.

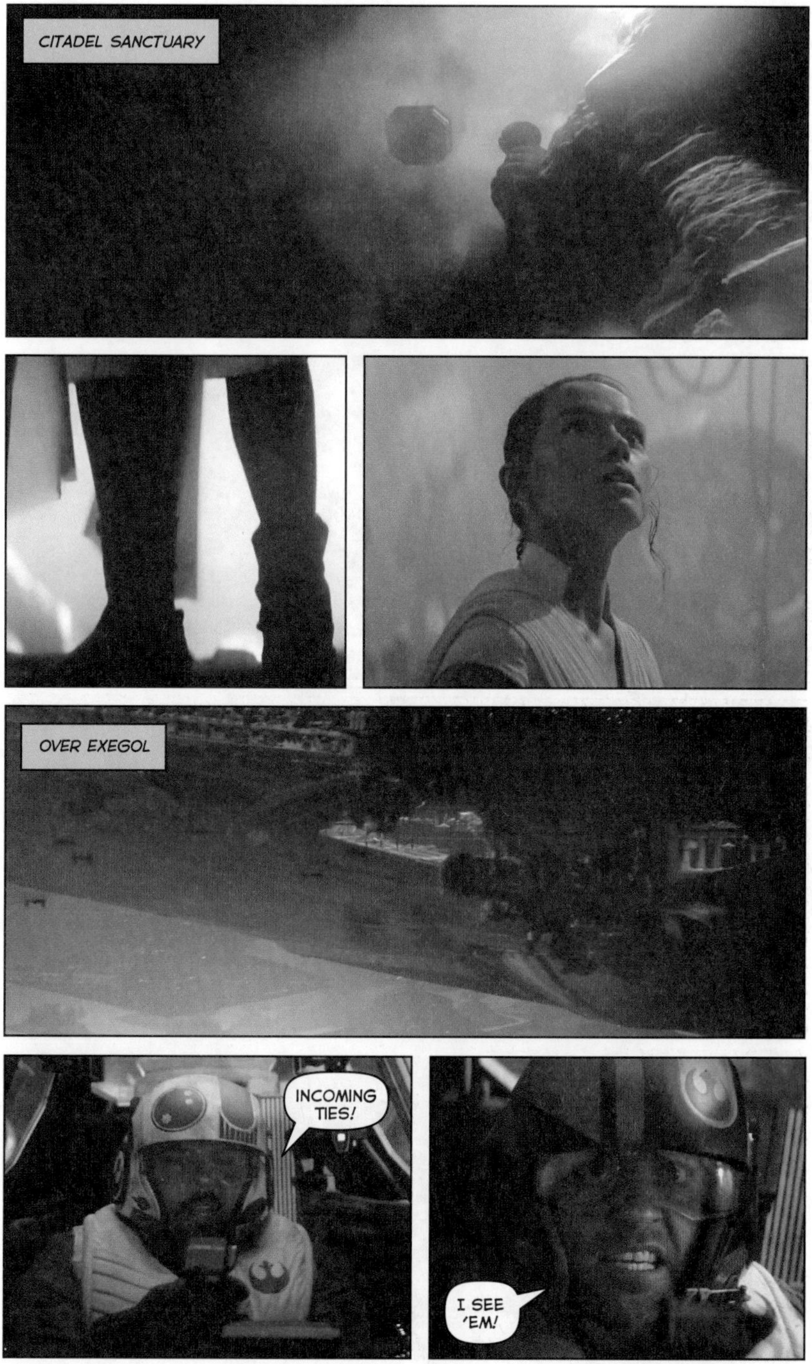
CITADEL SANCTUARY
OVER EXEGOL
INCOMING TIES!
I SEE 'EM!

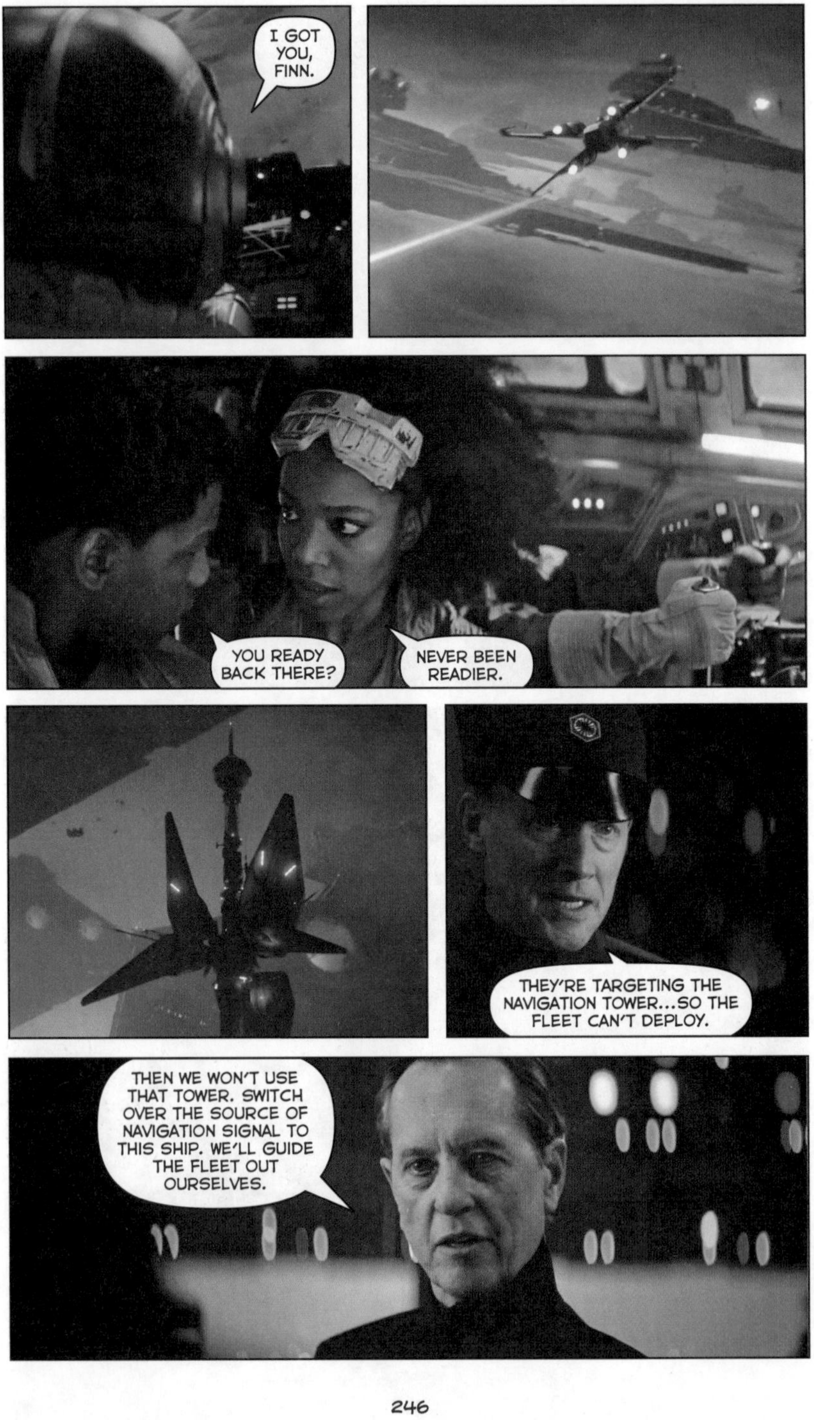
I GOT YOU, FINN.
YOU READY BACK THERE?
NEVER BEEN READIER.
THEY'RE TARGETING THE NAVIGATION TOWER...SO THE FLEET CAN'T DEPLOY.
THEN WE WON'T USE THAT TOWER. SWITCH OVER THE SOURCE OF NAVIGATION SIGNAL TO THIS SHIP. WE'LL GUIDE THE FLEET OUT OURSELVES.

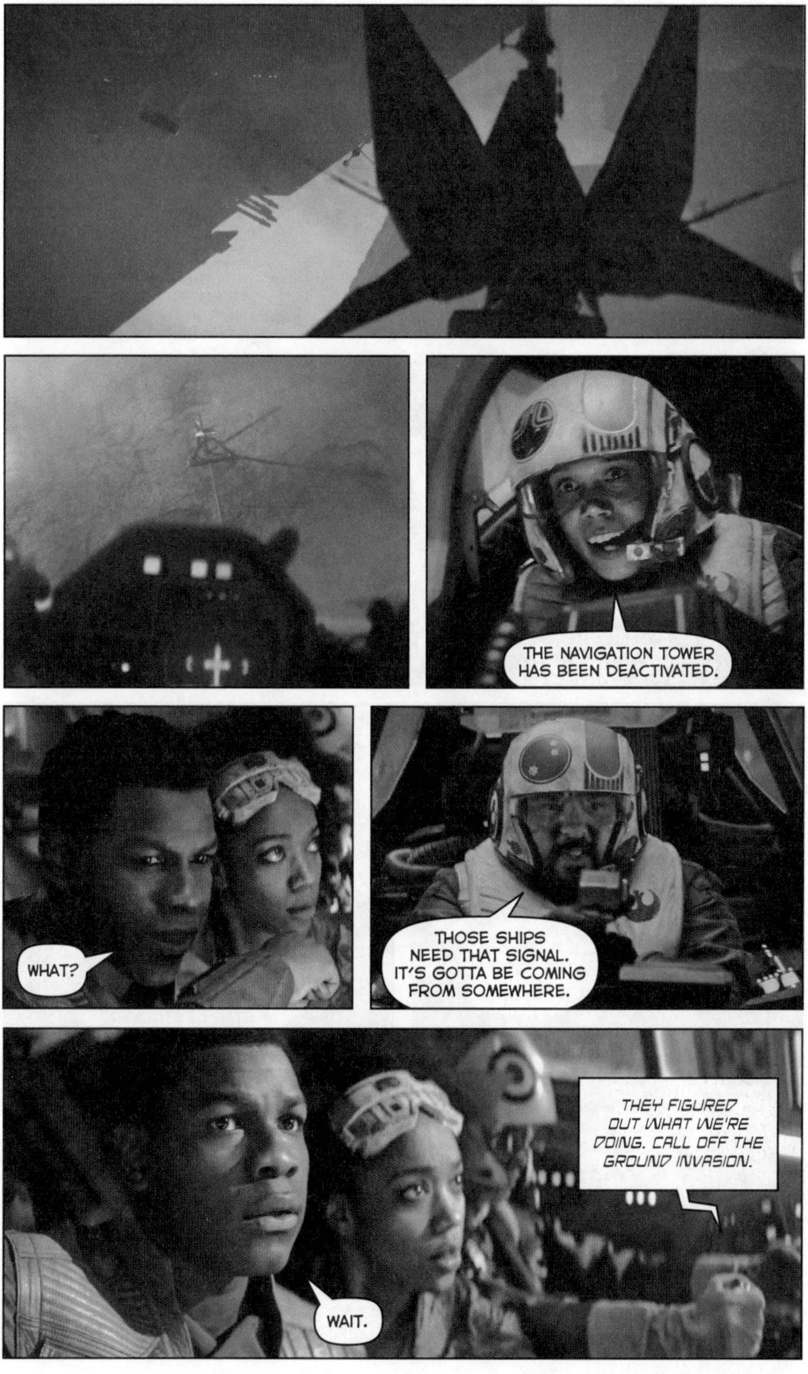
THE NAVIGATION TOWER HAS BEEN DEACTIVATED.
WHAT?
THOSE SHIPS NEED THAT SIGNAL. IT'S GOTTA BE COMING FROM SOMEWHERE.
THEY FIGURED OUT WHAT WE'RE DOING. CALL OFF THE GROUND INVASION.
WAIT.

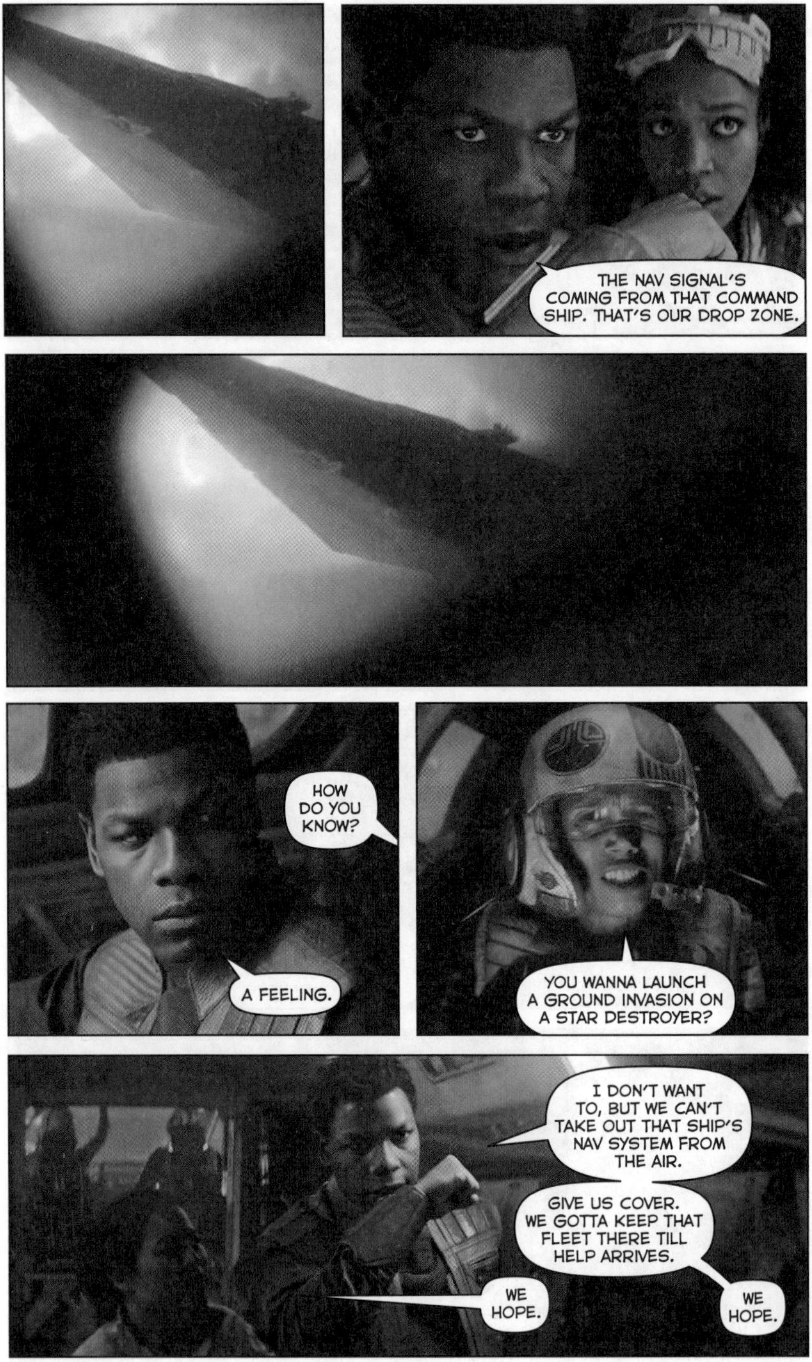
THE NAV SIGNAL'S COMING FROM THAT COMMAND SHIP. THAT'S OUR DROP ZONE.
HOW DO YOU KNOW?
A FEELING.
YOU WANNA LAUNCH A GROUND INVASION ON A STAR DESTROYER?
I DON'T WANT TO, BUT WE CAN'T TAKE OUT THAT SHIP'S NAV SYSTEM FROM THE AIR.
GIVE US COVER. WE GOTTA KEEP THAT FLEET THERE TILL HELP ARRIVES.
WE HOPE.
WE HOPE.

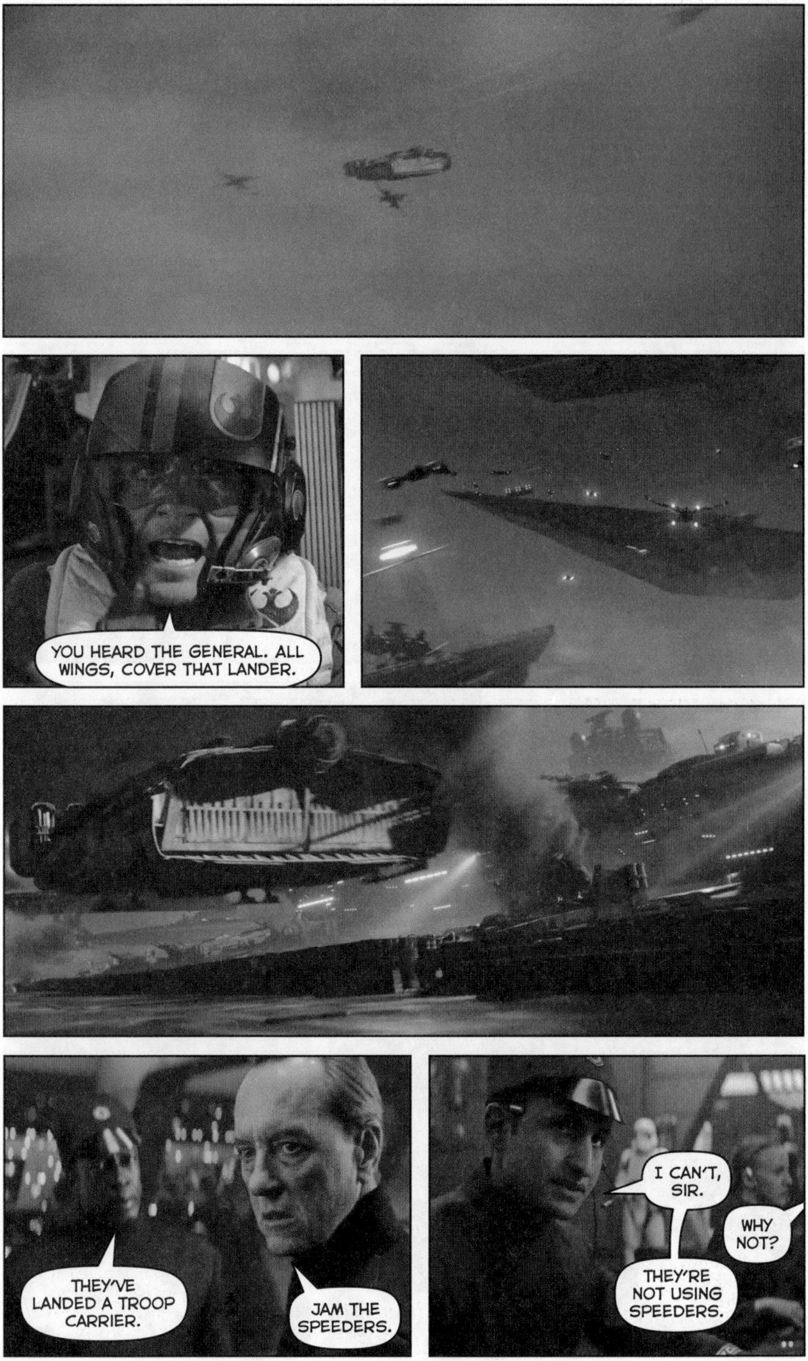
YOU HEARD THE GENERAL. ALL WINGS, COVER THAT LANDER.
THEY'VE LANDED A TROOP CARRIER.
JAM THE SPEEDERS.
I CAN'T, SIR.
WHY NOT?
THEY'RE NOT USING SPEEDERS.

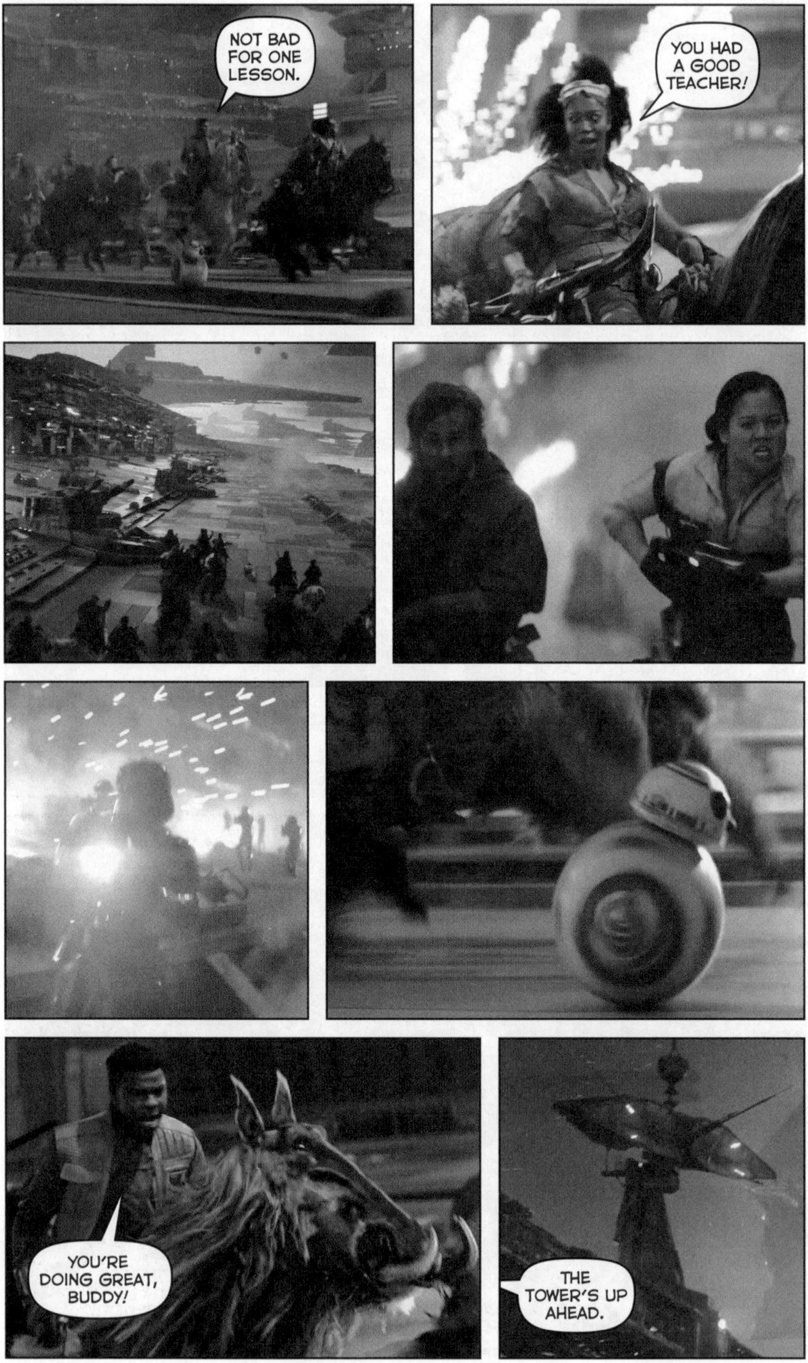
NOT BAD FOR ONE LESSON.
YOU HAD A GOOD TEACHER!
YOU'RE DOING GREAT, BUDDY!
THE TOWER'S UP AHEAD.

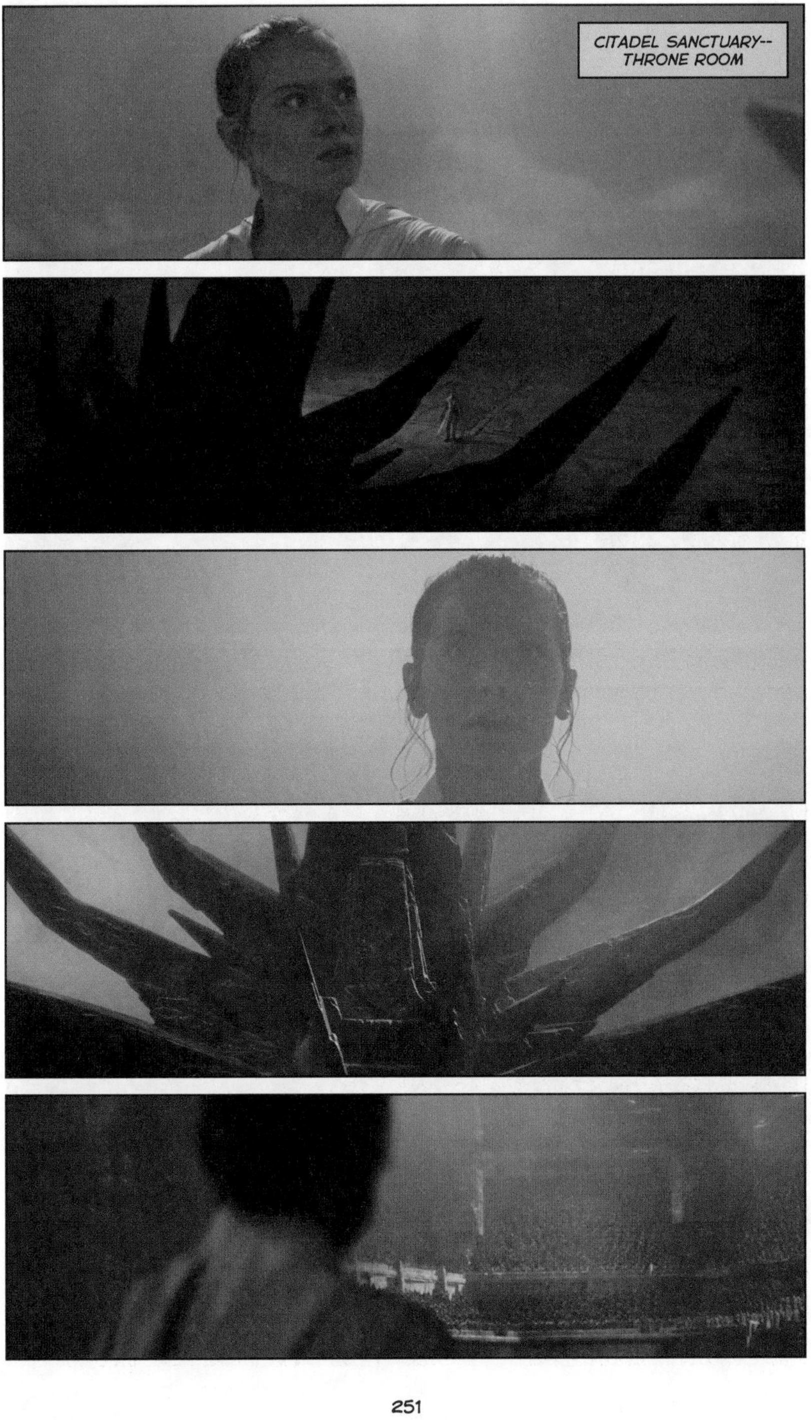
CITADEL SANCTUARY--
THRONE ROOM

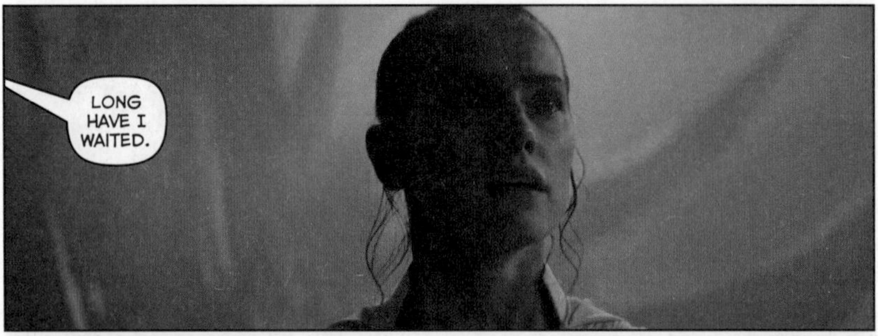
LONG HAVE I WAITED.

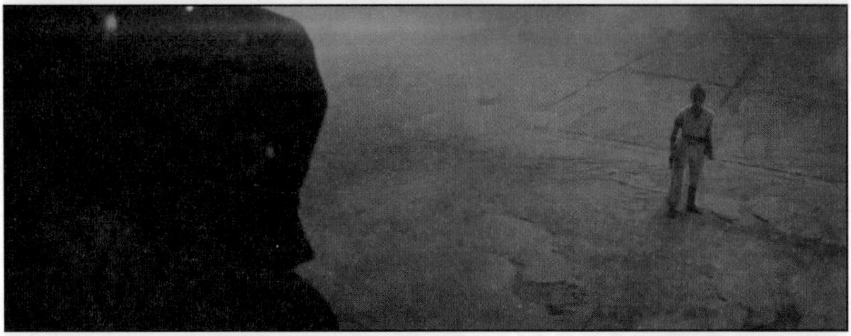

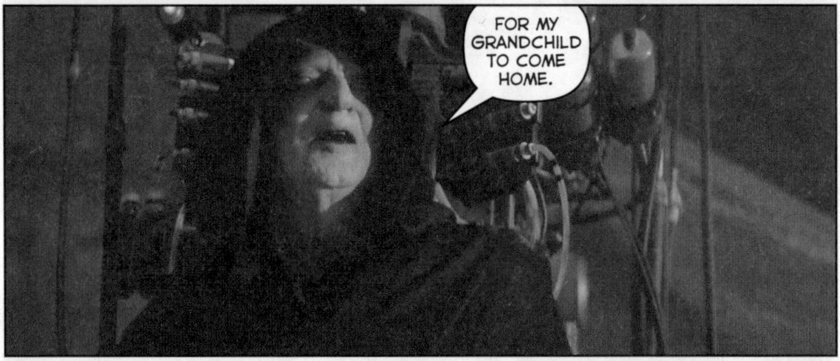
FOR MY GRANDCHILD TO COME HOME.

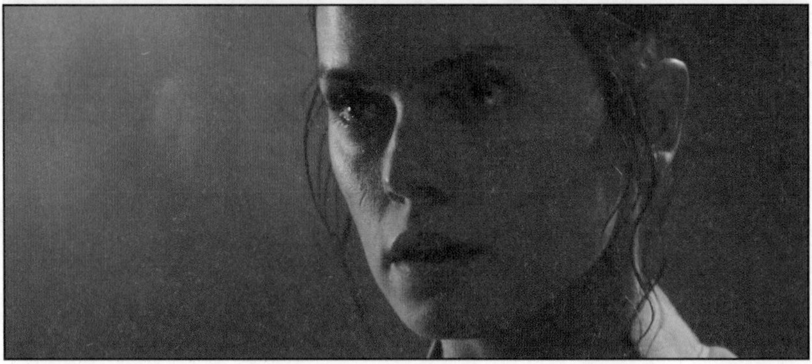

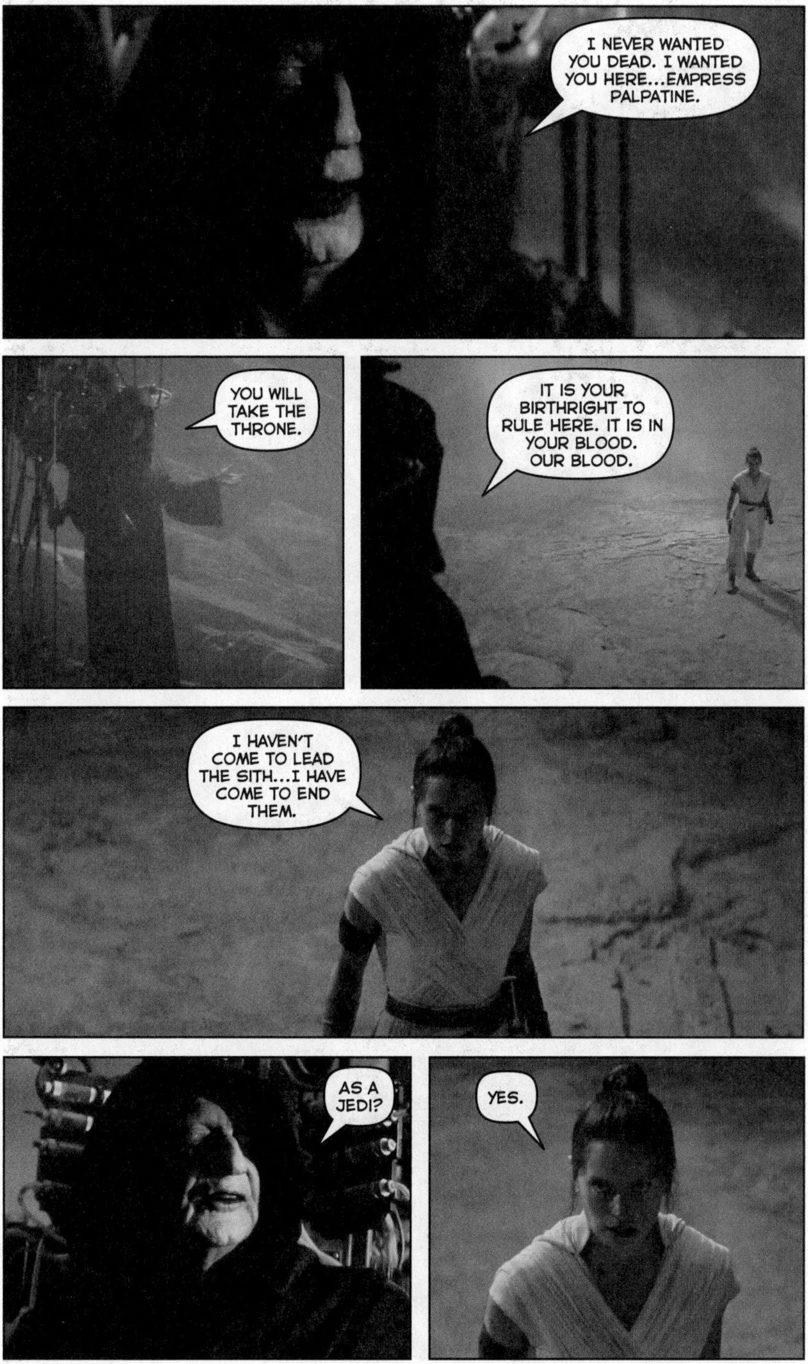
I NEVER WANTED YOU DEAD. I WANTED YOU HERE...EMPRESS PALPATINE.
YOU WILL TAKE THE THRONE.
IT IS YOUR BIRTHRIGHT TO RULE HERE. IT IS IN YOUR BLOOD. OUR BLOOD.
I HAVEN'T COME TO LEAD THE SITH...I HAVE COME TO END THEM.
AS A JEDI?
YES.

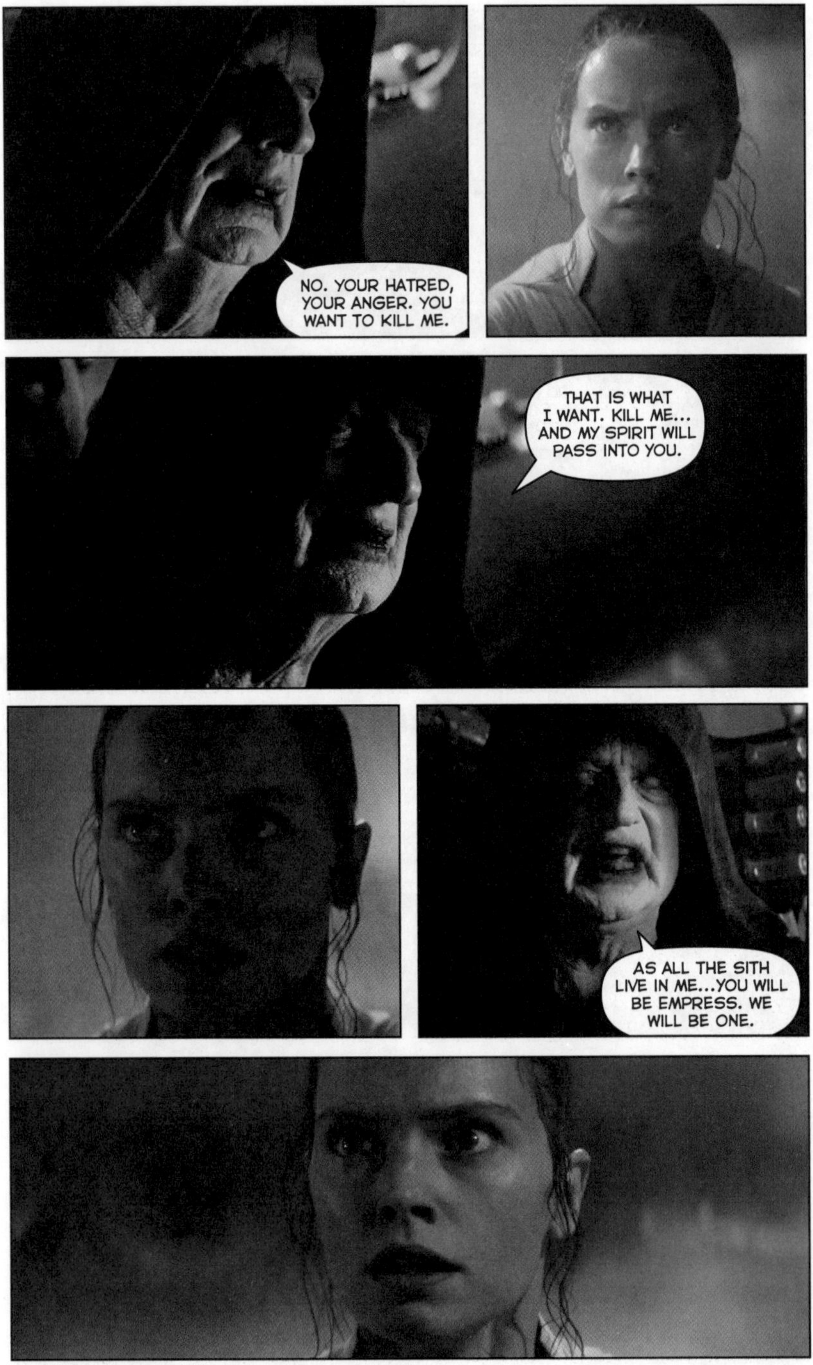
NO. YOUR HATRED, YOUR ANGER. YOU WANT TO KILL ME.
THAT IS WHAT I WANT. KILL ME... AND MY SPIRIT WILL PASS INTO YOU.
AS ALL THE SITH LIVE IN ME...YOU WILL BE EMPRESS. WE WILL BE ONE.

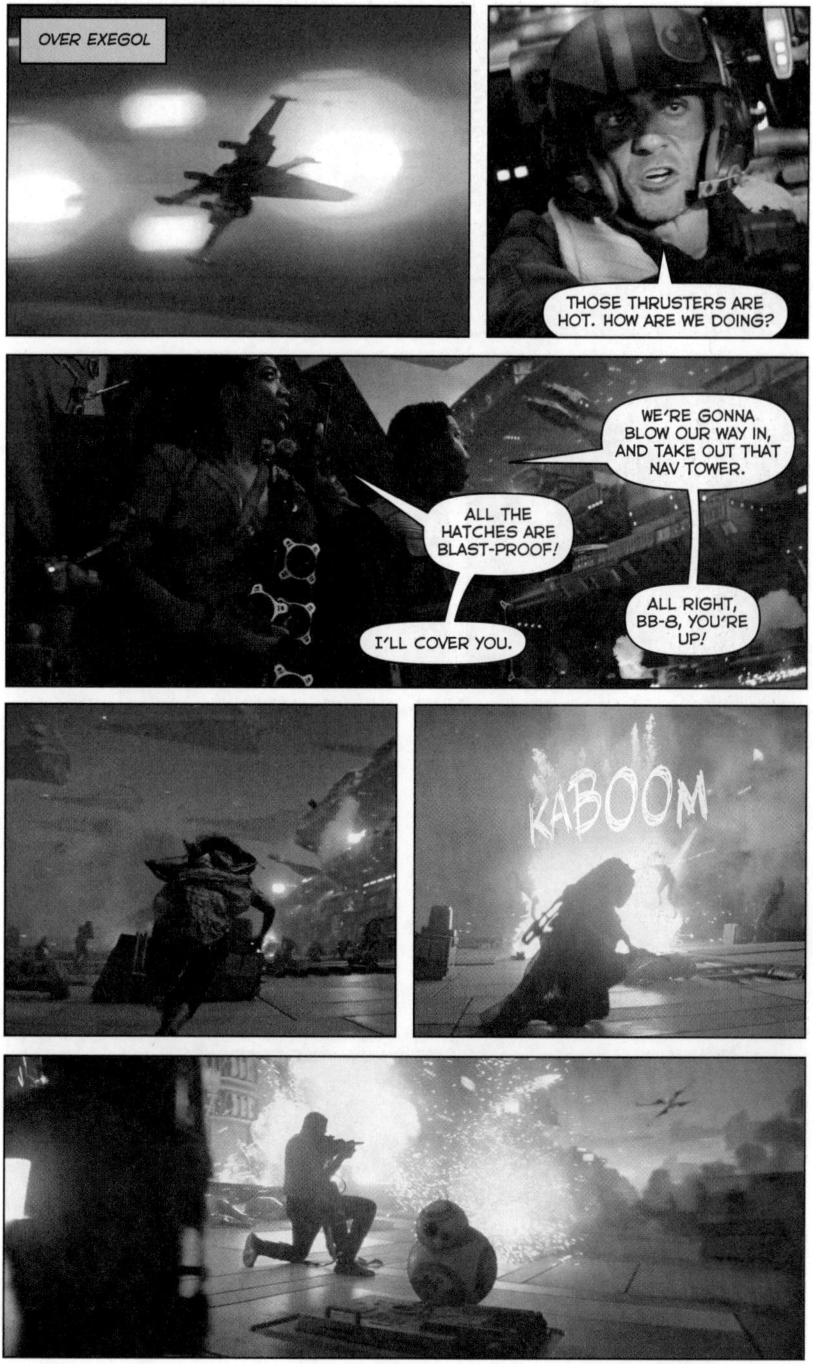
OVER EXEGOL
THOSE THRUSTERS ARE HOT. HOW ARE WE DOING?
WE'RE GONNA BLOW OUR WAY IN, AND TAKE OUT THAT NAV TOWER.
ALL THE HATCHES ARE BLAST-PROOF!
I'LL COVER YOU.
ALL RIGHT, BB-8, YOU'RE UP!
KABOOM

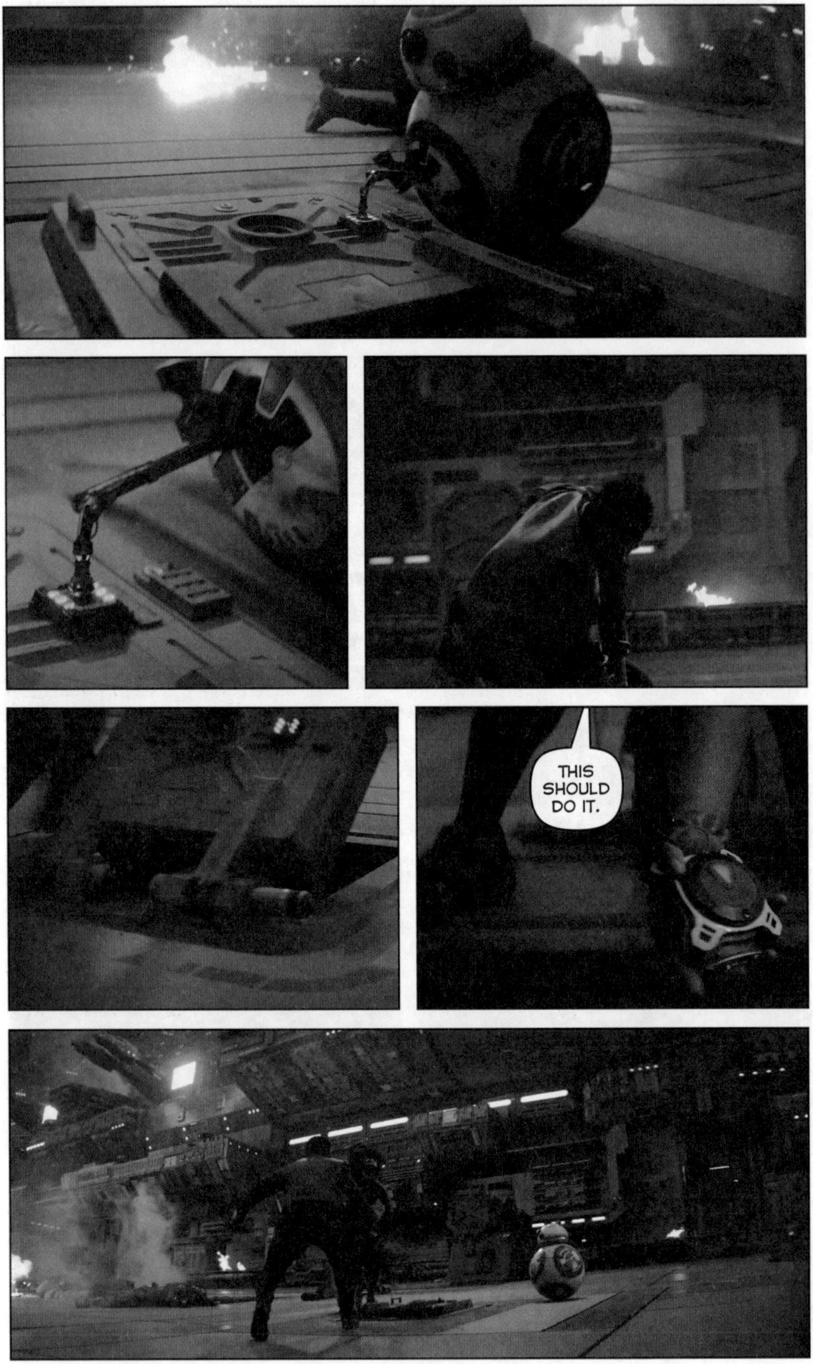
THIS SHOULD DO IT.

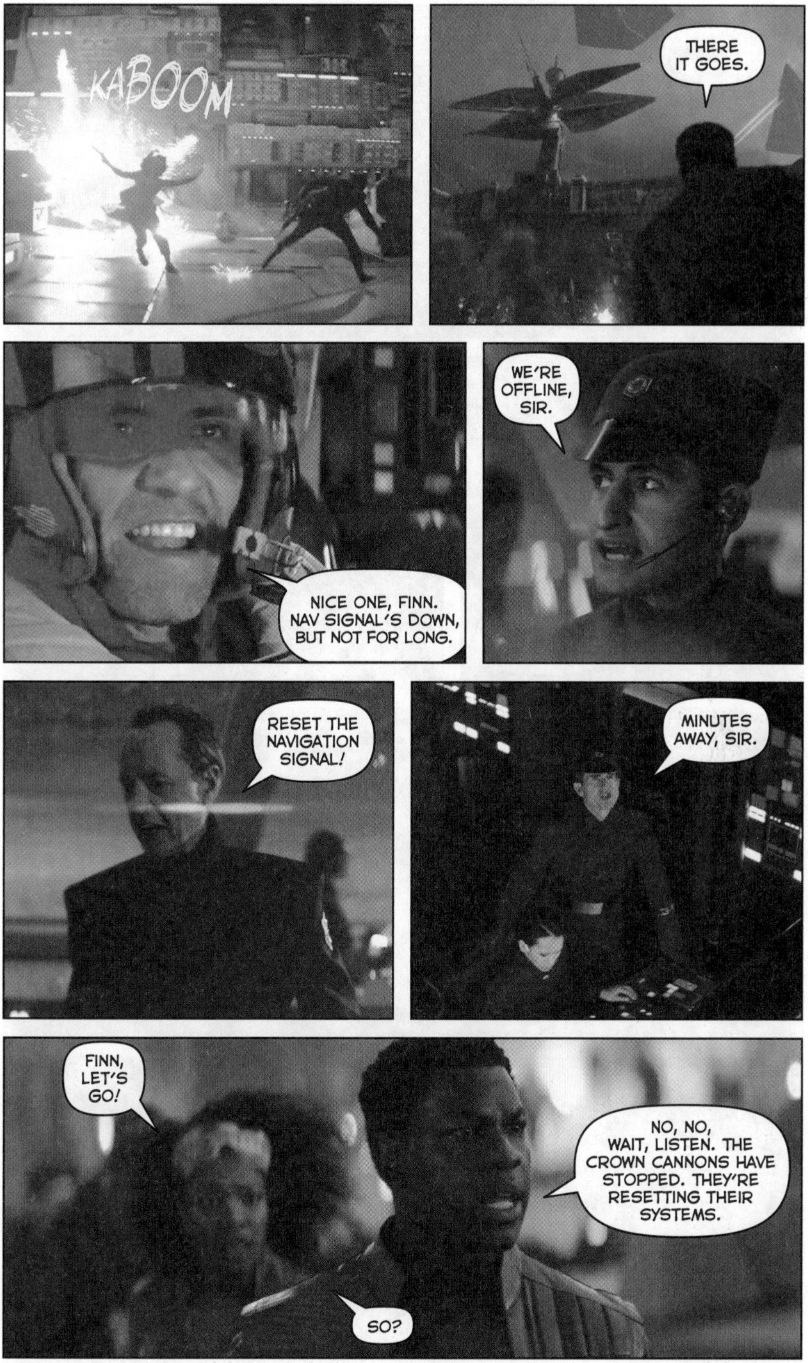
KABOOM
THERE IT GOES.
NICE ONE, FINN. NAV SIGNAL'S DOWN, BUT NOT FOR LONG.
WE'RE OFFLINE, SIR.
RESET THE NAVIGATION SIGNAL!
MINUTES AWAY, SIR.
FINN, LET'S GO!
NO, NO, WAIT, LISTEN. THE CROWN CANNONS HAVE STOPPED. THEY'RE RESETTING THEIR SYSTEMS.
SO?

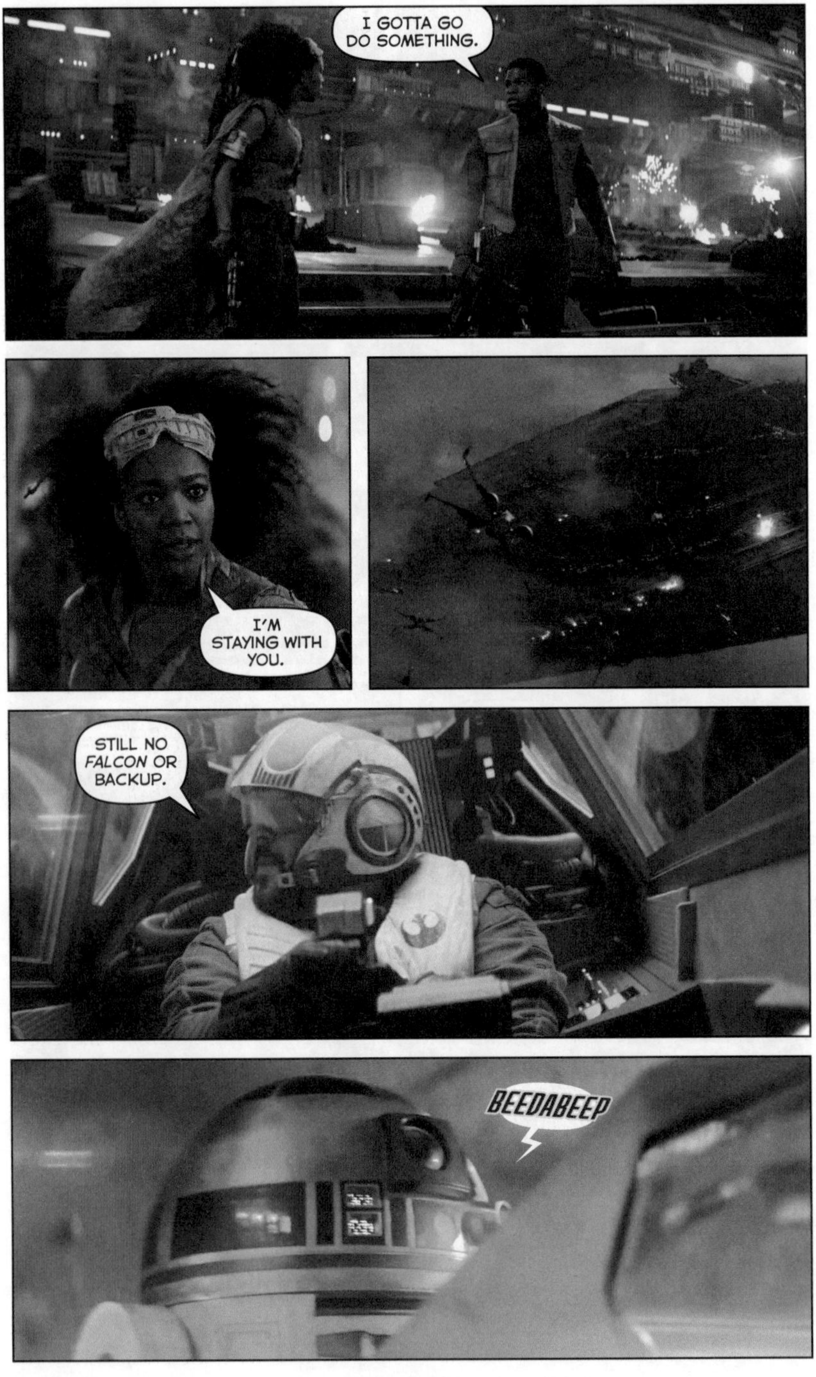

I GOTTA GO DO SOMETHING.
I'M STAYING WITH YOU.
STILL NO *FALCON* OR BACKUP.
BEEDABEEP

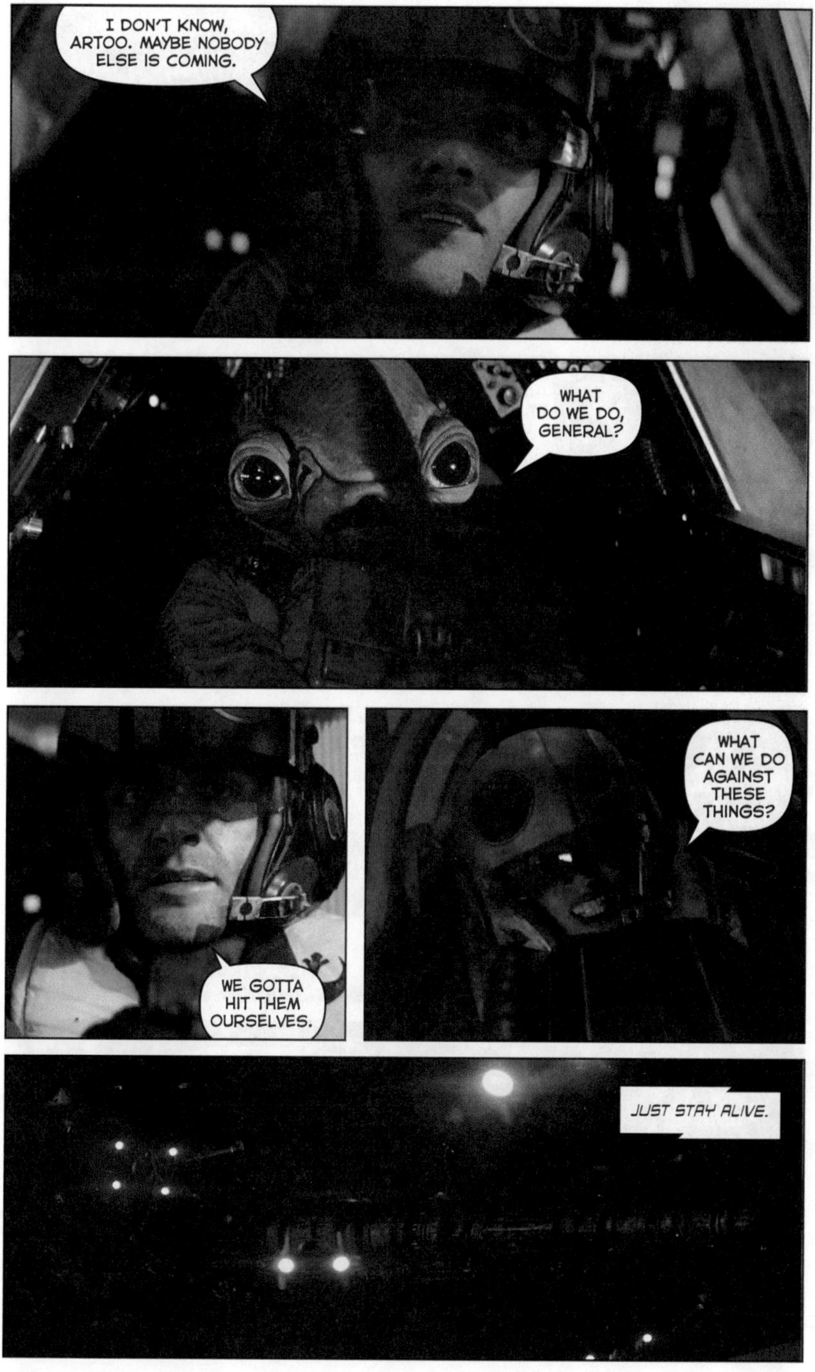
I DON'T KNOW, ARTOO. MAYBE NOBODY ELSE IS COMING.
WHAT DO WE DO, GENERAL?
WE GOTTA HIT THEM OURSELVES.
WHAT CAN WE DO AGAINST THESE THINGS?
JUST STAY ALIVE.

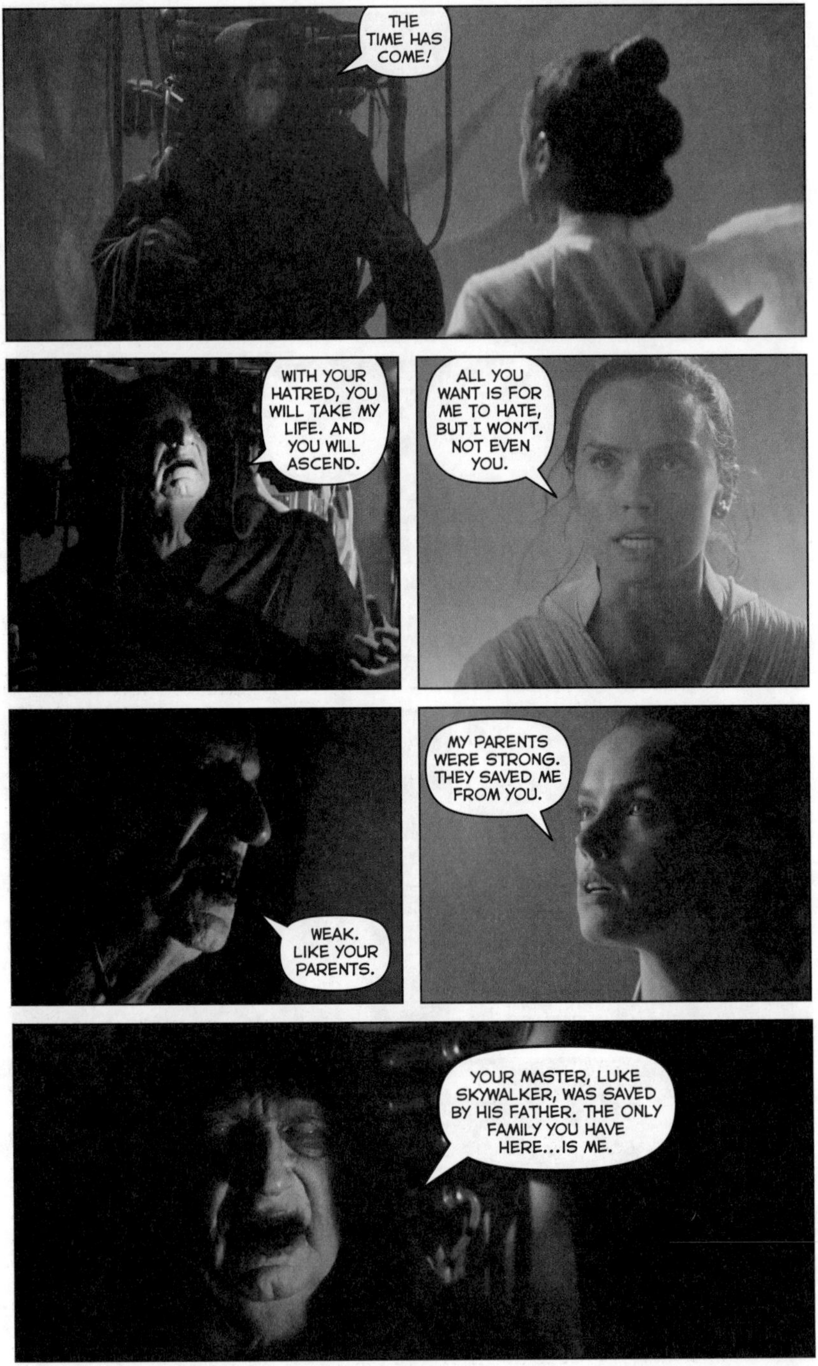
THE TIME HAS COME!
WITH YOUR HATRED, YOU WILL TAKE MY LIFE. AND YOU WILL ASCEND.
ALL YOU WANT IS FOR ME TO HATE, BUT I WON'T. NOT EVEN YOU.
WEAK. LIKE YOUR PARENTS.
MY PARENTS WERE STRONG. THEY SAVED ME FROM YOU.
YOUR MASTER, LUKE SKYWALKER, WAS SAVED BY HIS FATHER. THE ONLY FAMILY YOU HAVE HERE...IS ME.

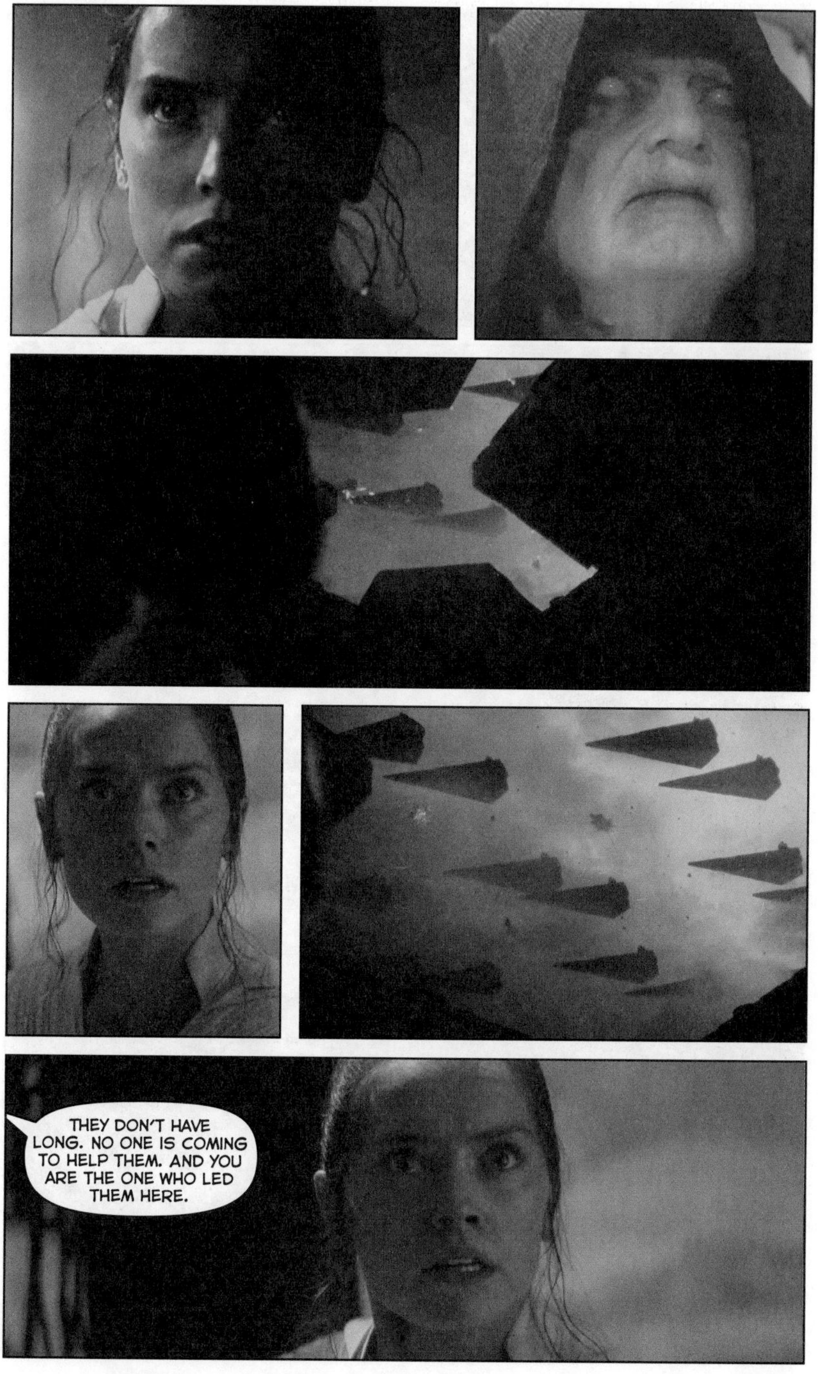
THEY DON'T HAVE LONG. NO ONE IS COMING TO HELP THEM. AND YOU ARE THE ONE WHO LED THEM HERE.

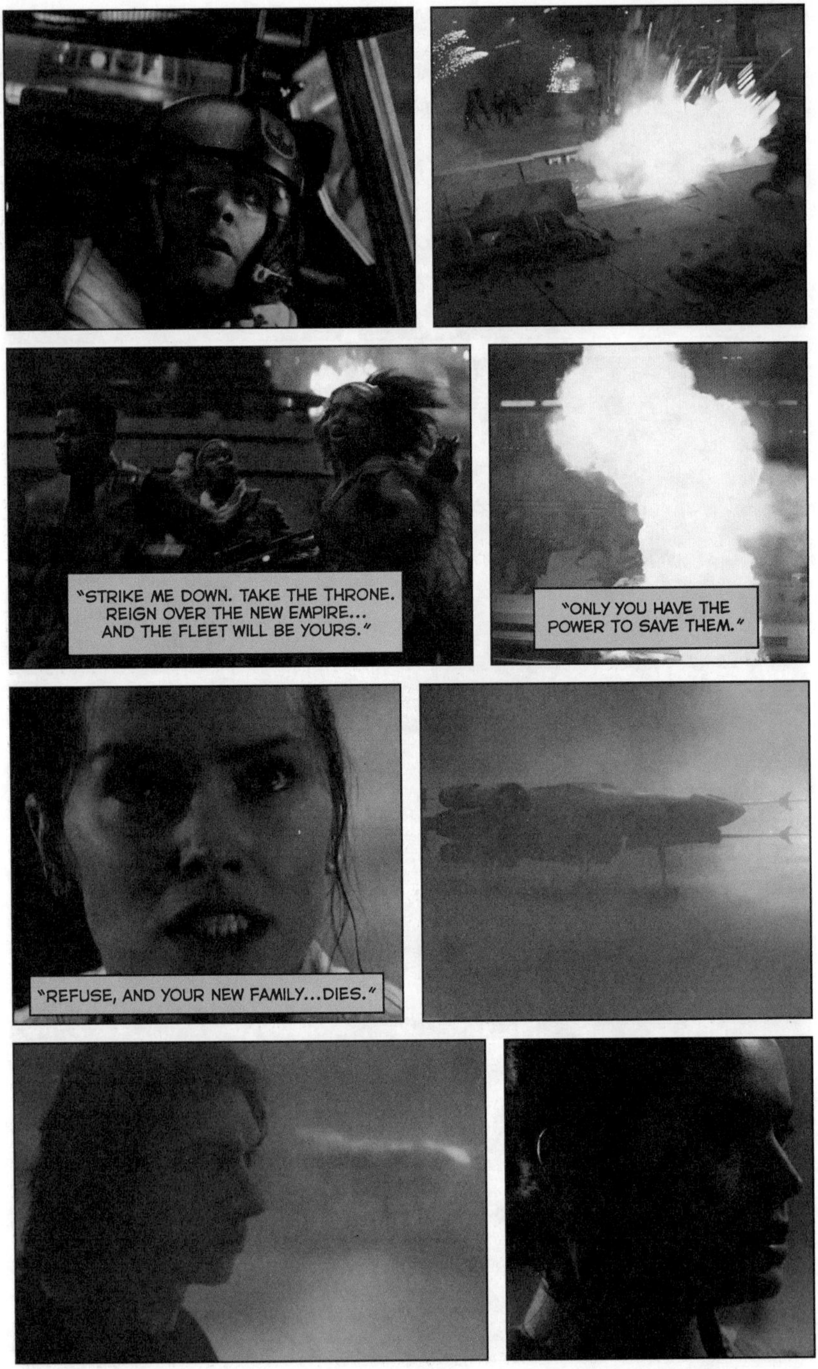
"STRIKE ME DOWN. TAKE THE THRONE. REIGN OVER THE NEW EMPIRE... AND THE FLEET WILL BE YOURS."
"ONLY YOU HAVE THE POWER TO SAVE THEM."
"REFUSE, AND YOUR NEW FAMILY...DIES."

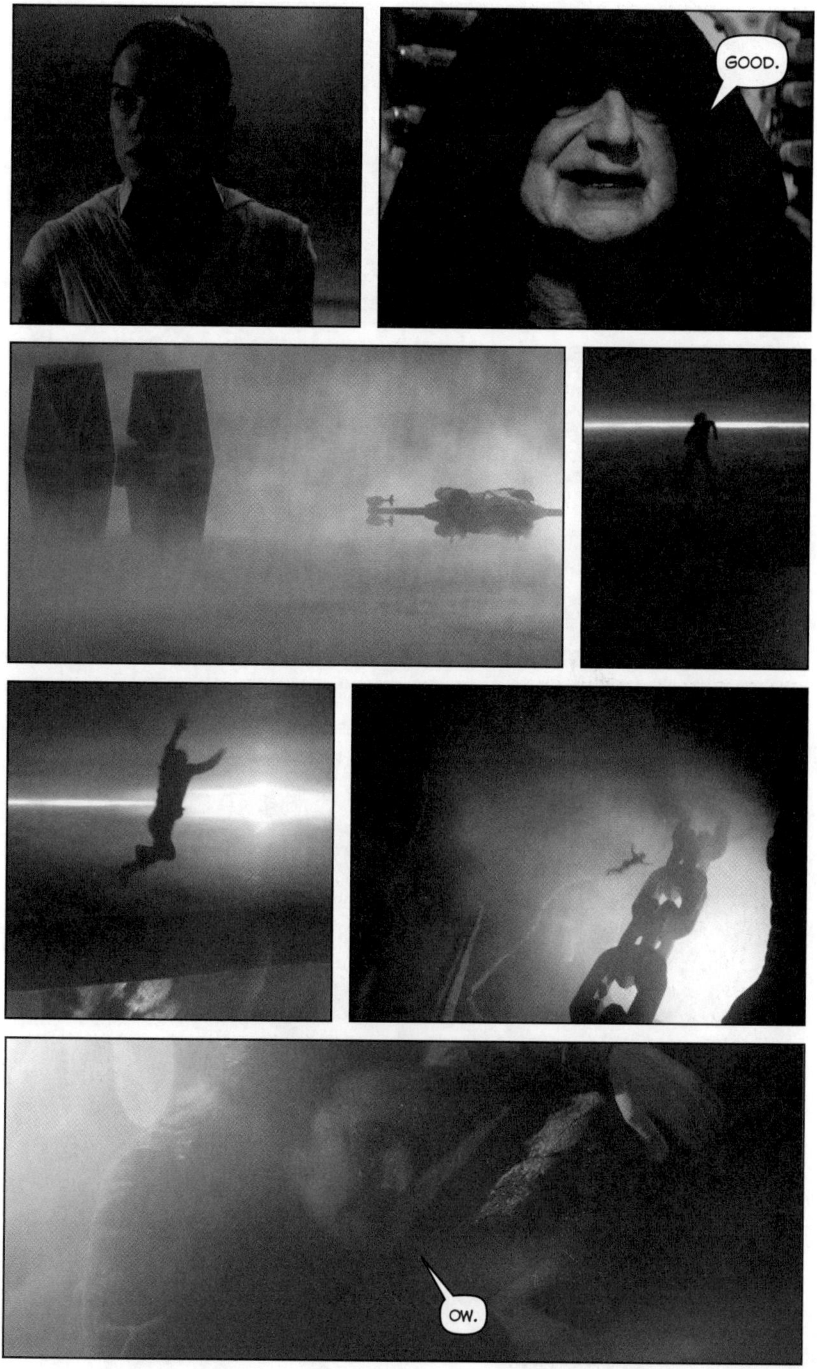
GOOD.
OW.

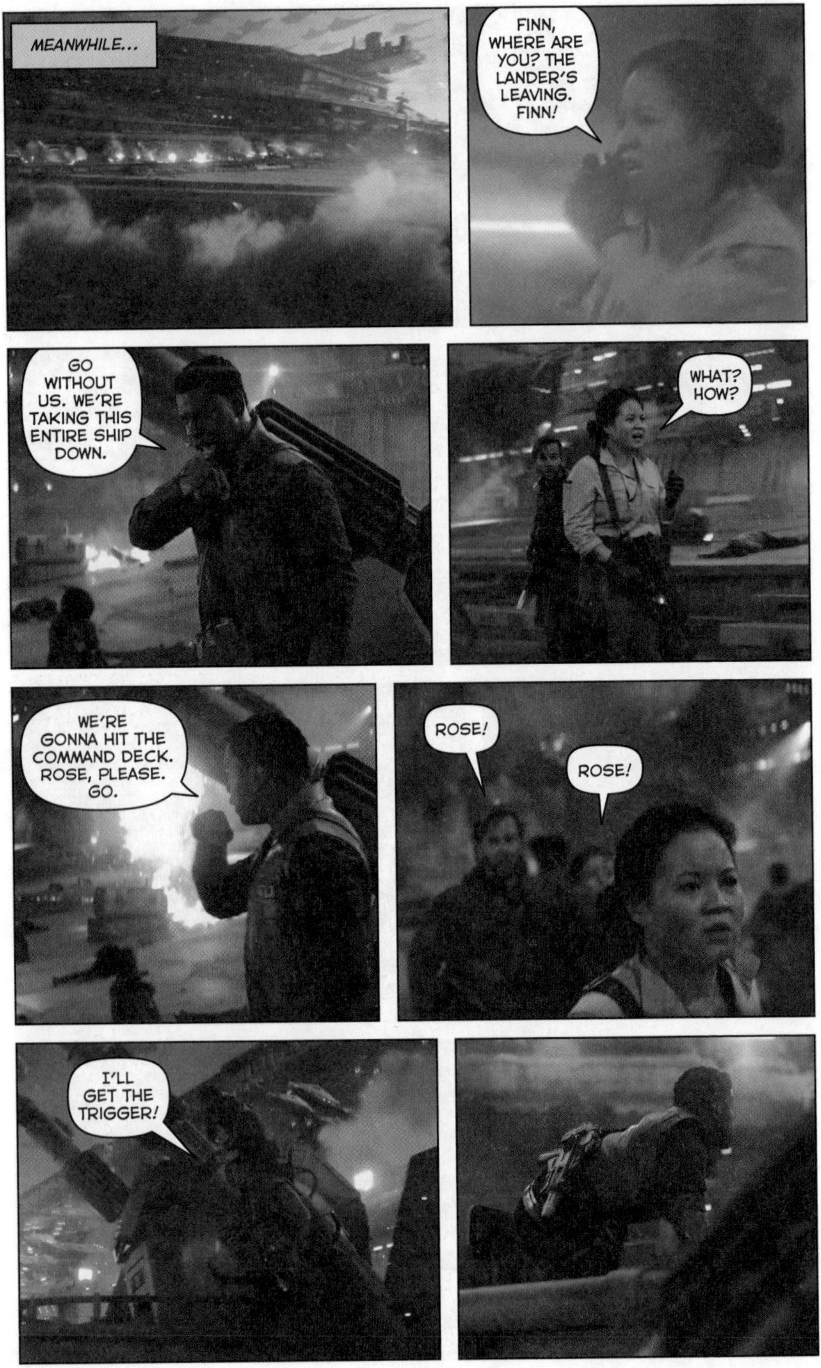
MEANWHILE...
FINN, WHERE ARE YOU? THE LANDER'S LEAVING. FINN!
GO WITHOUT US. WE'RE TAKING THIS ENTIRE SHIP DOWN.
WHAT? HOW?
WE'RE GONNA HIT THE COMMAND DECK. ROSE, PLEASE. GO.
ROSE!
ROSE!
I'LL GET THE TRIGGER!

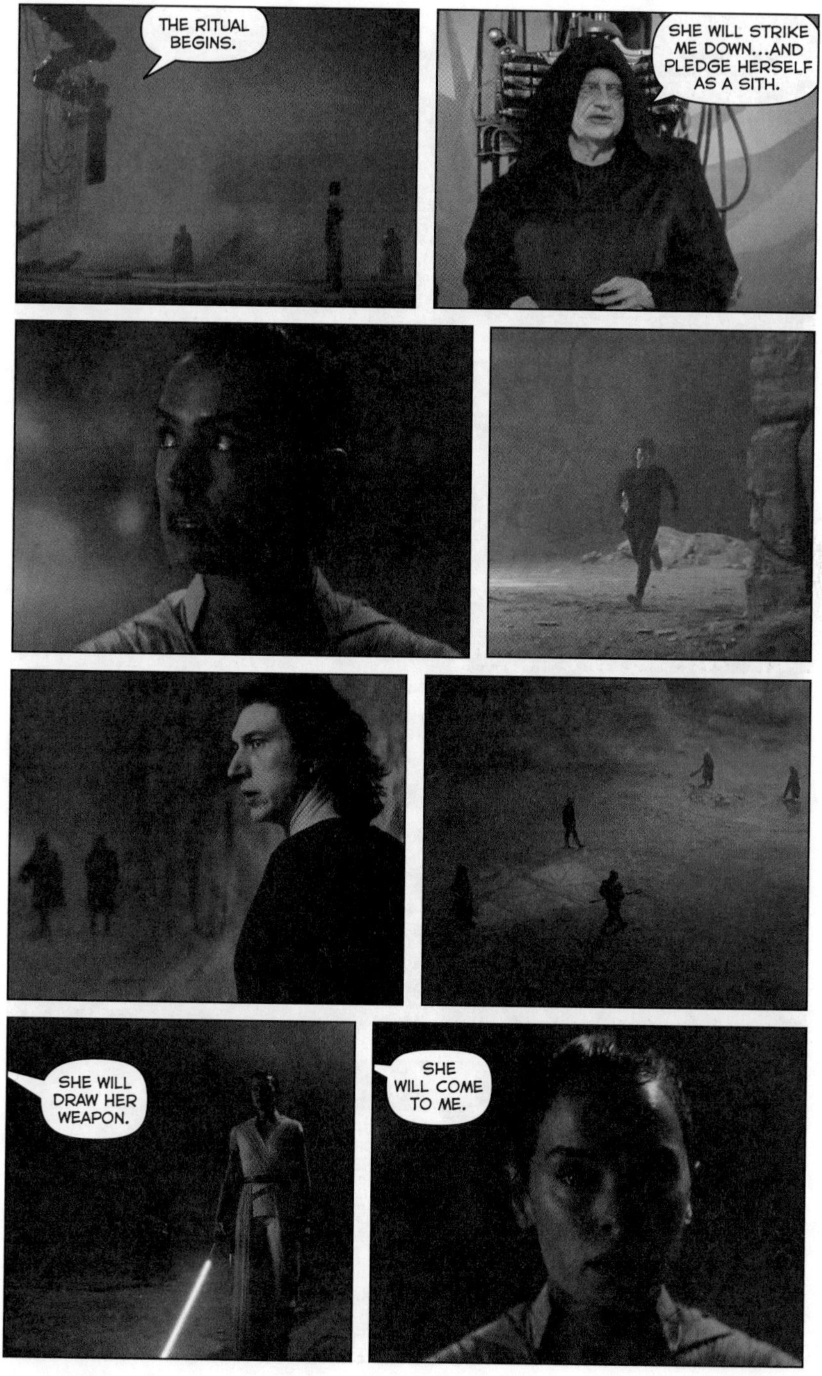
THE RITUAL BEGINS.
SHE WILL STRIKE ME DOWN...AND PLEDGE HERSELF AS A SITH.
SHE WILL DRAW HER WEAPON.
SHE WILL COME TO ME.

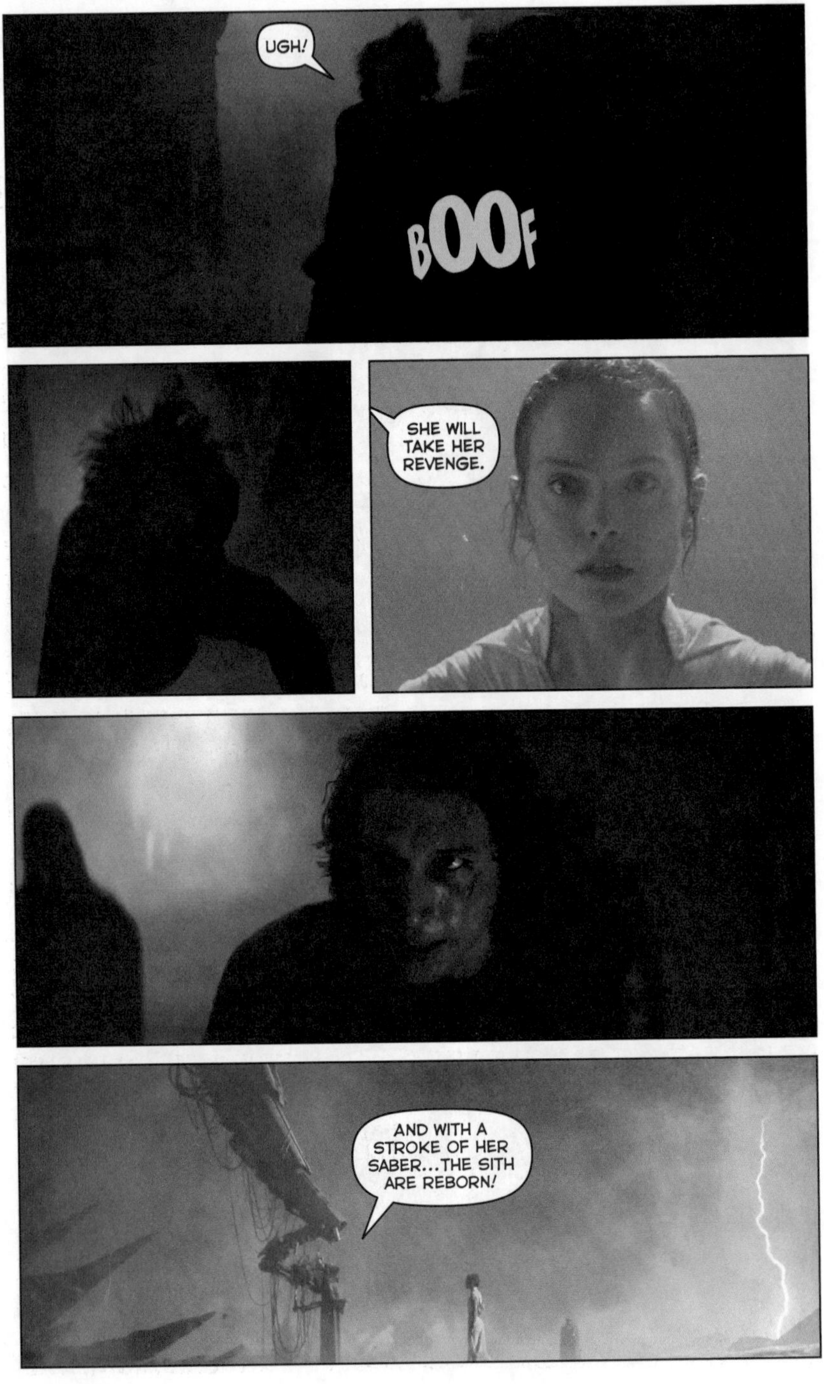
UGH!
BOOF
SHE WILL TAKE HER REVENGE.
AND WITH A STROKE OF HER SABER...THE SITH ARE REBORN!

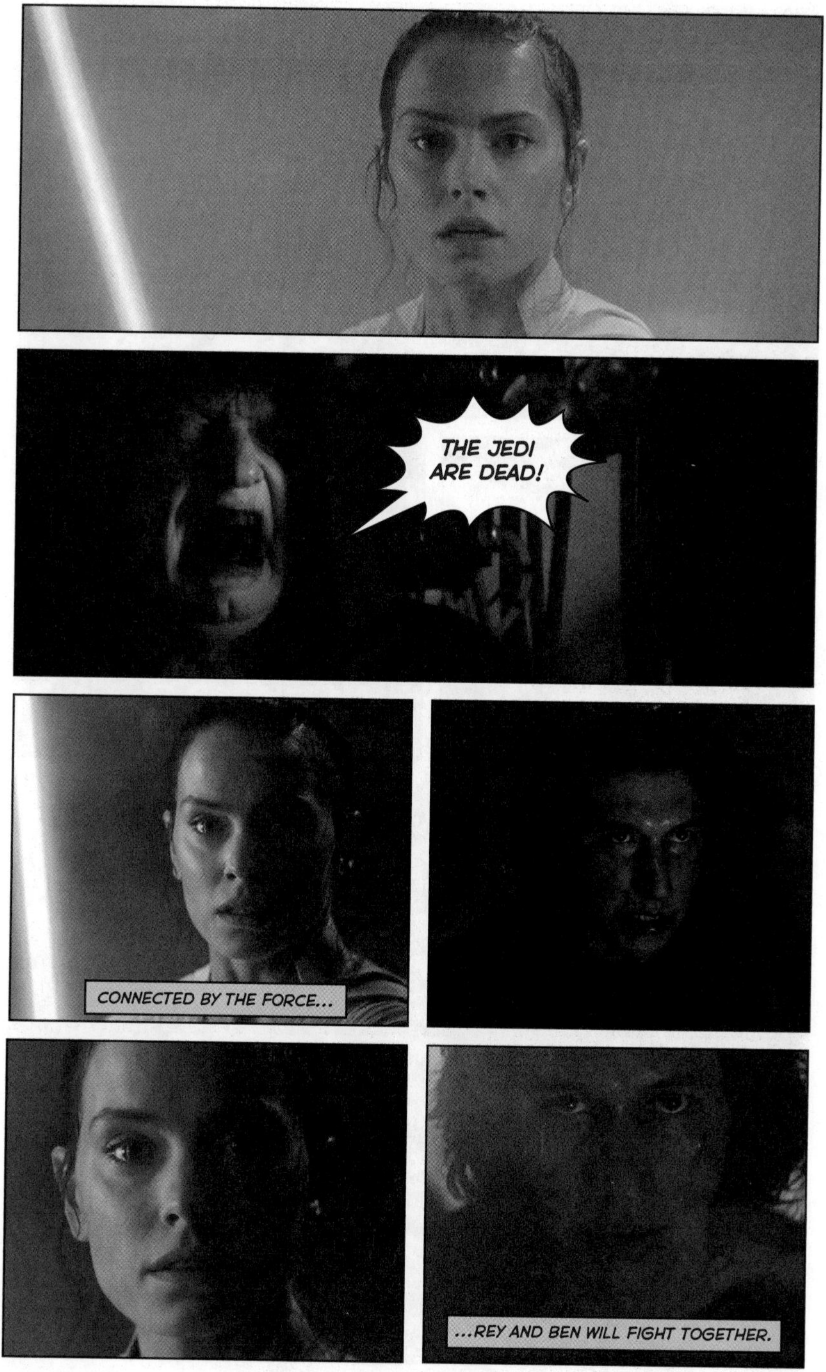
THE JEDI ARE DEAD!
CONNECTED BY THE FORCE...
...REY AND BEN WILL FIGHT TOGETHER.

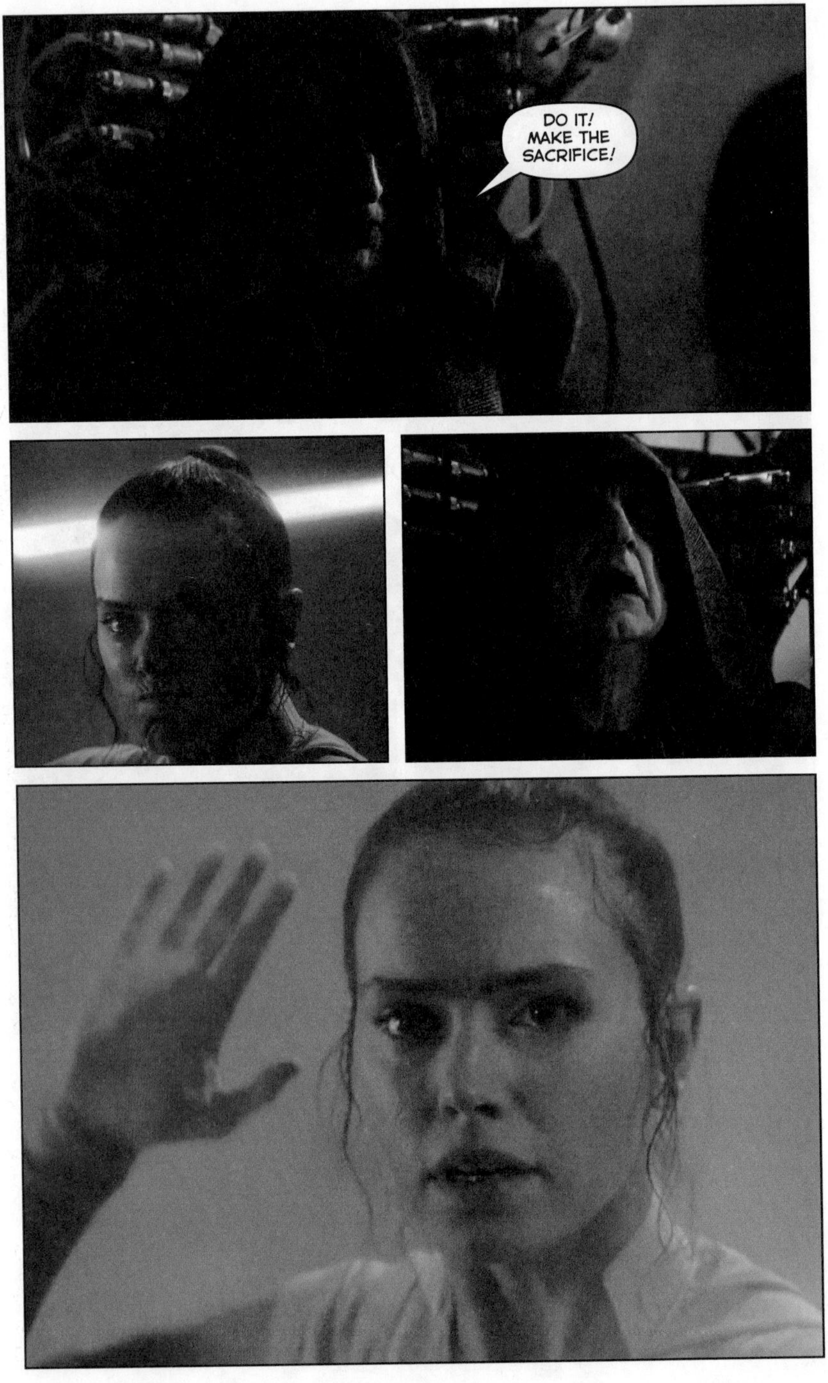
DO IT! MAKE THE SACRIFICE!

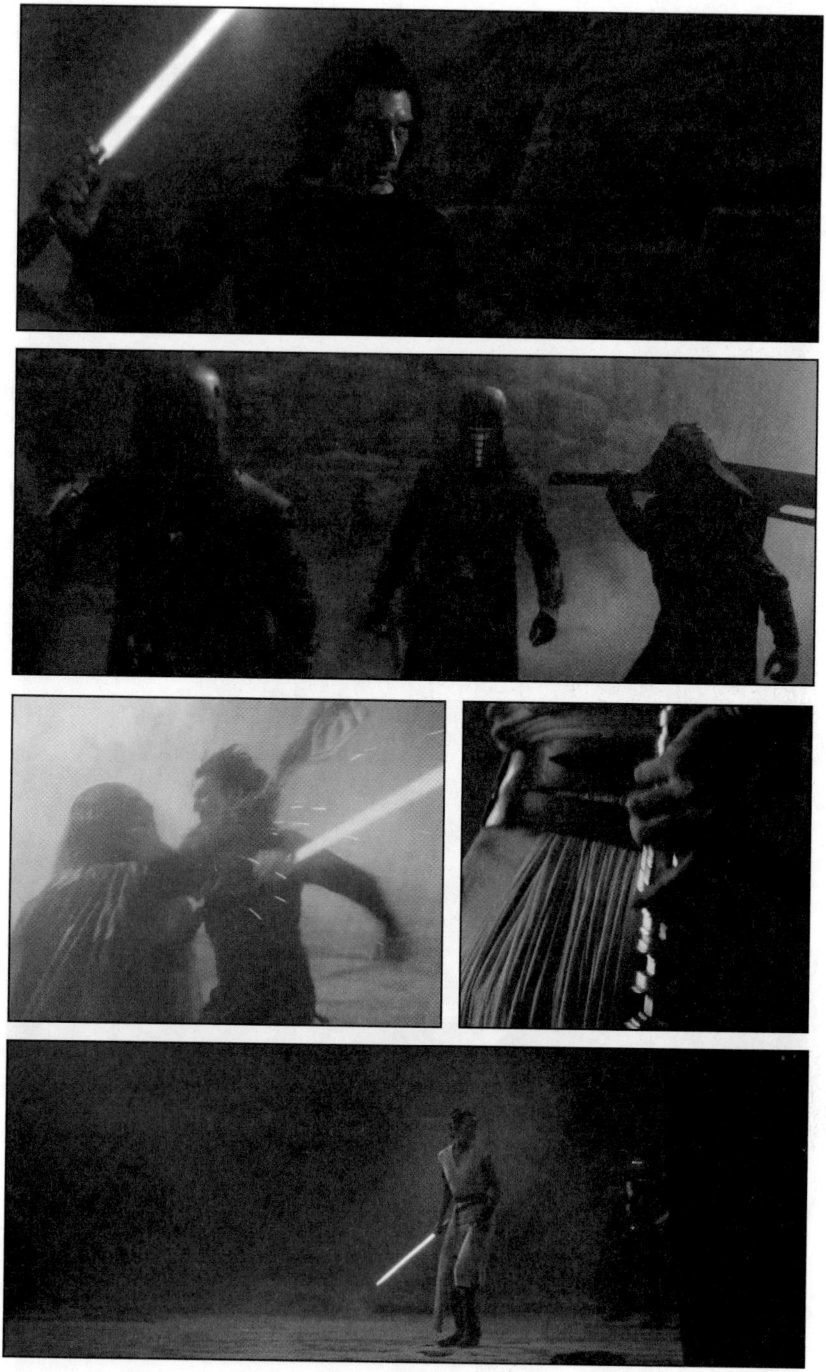

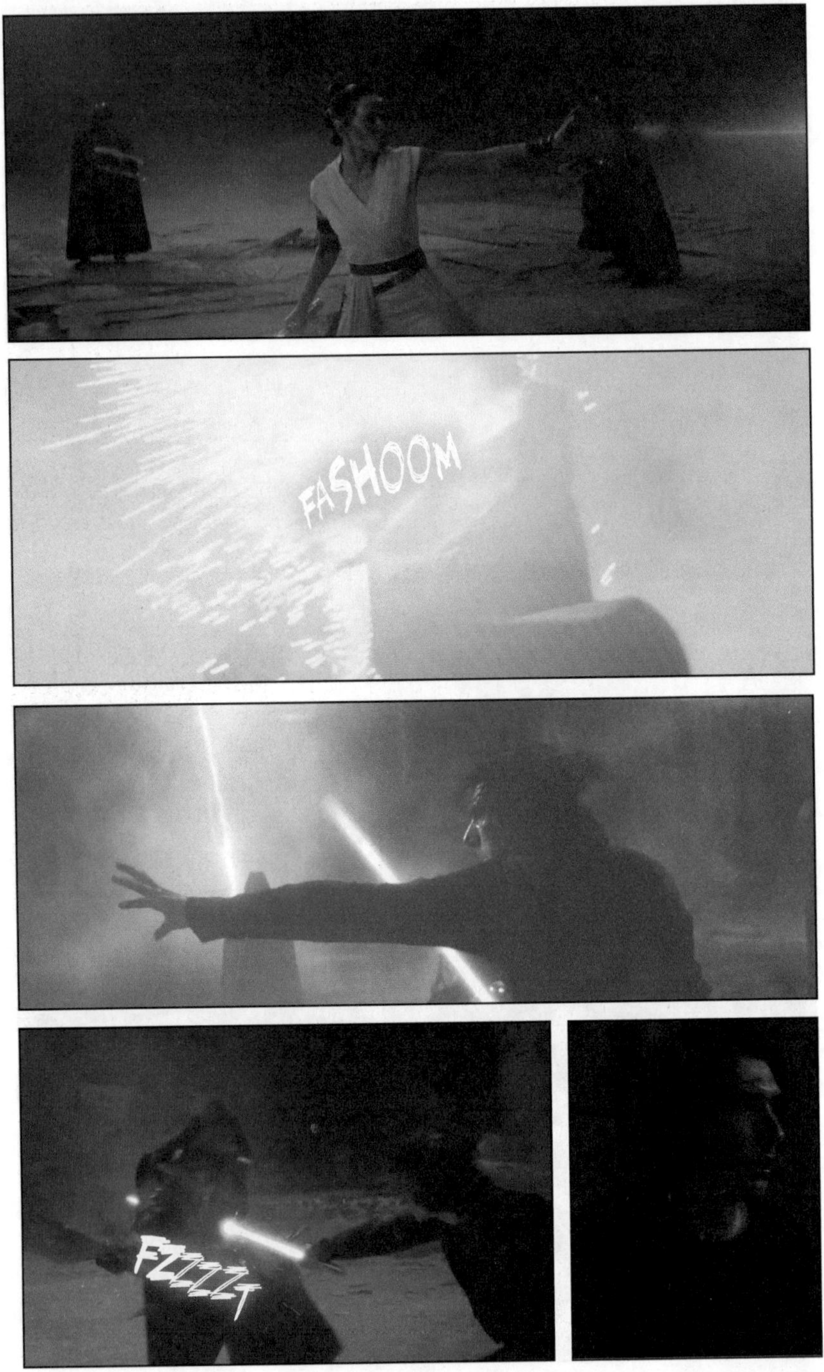
FASHOOM
FZZZZT

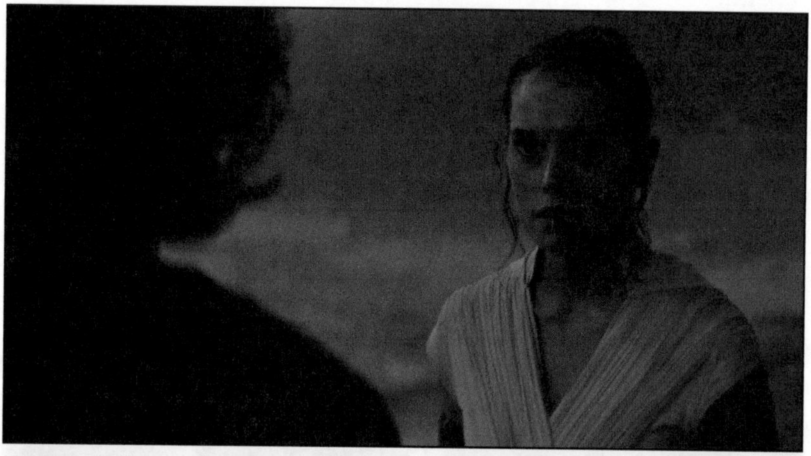

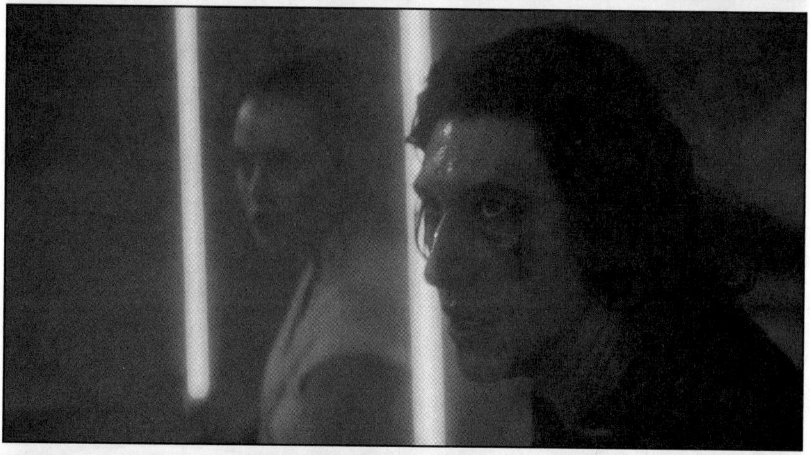

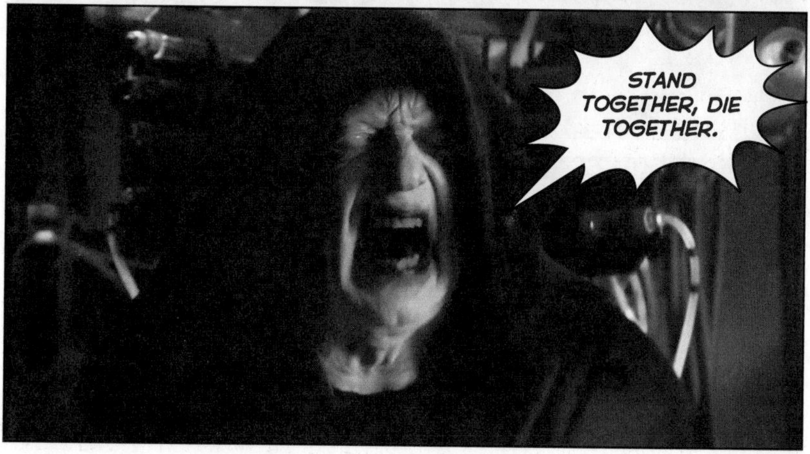
STAND TOGETHER, DIE TOGETHER.

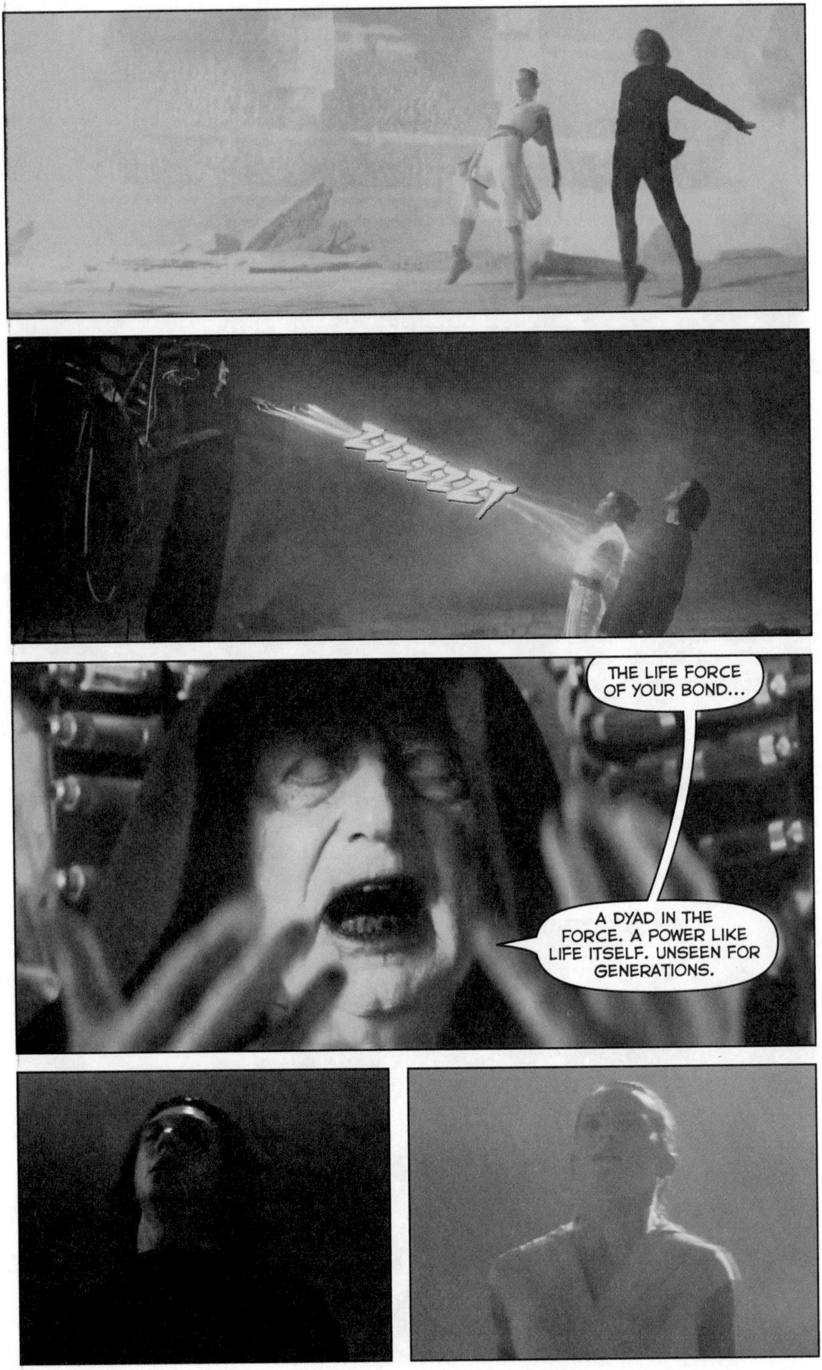
THE LIFE FORCE OF YOUR BOND...
A DYAD IN THE FORCE. A POWER LIKE LIFE ITSELF. UNSEEN FOR GENERATIONS.

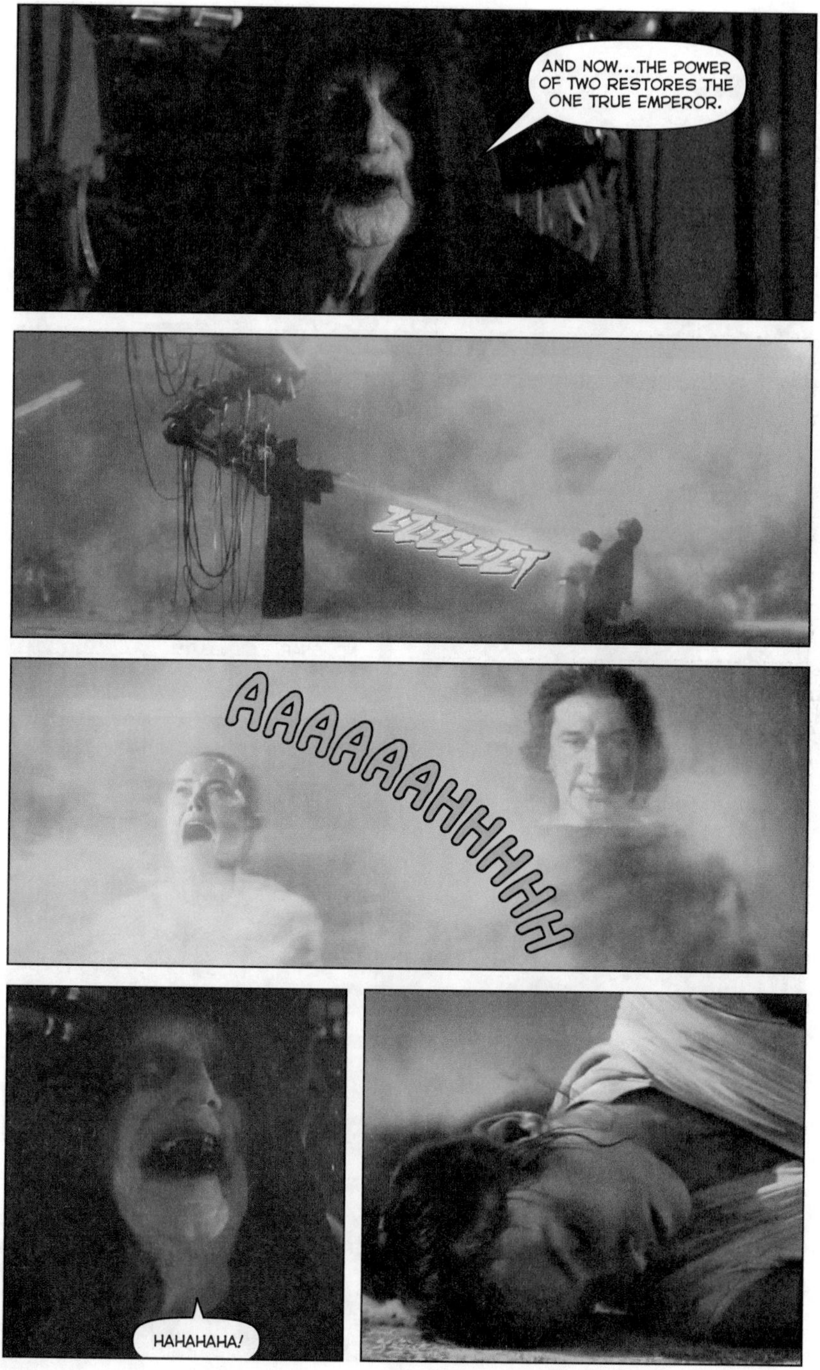
AND NOW...THE POWER OF TWO RESTORES THE ONE TRUE EMPEROR.
ZZZZZZZT
AAAAAAAHHHHHH
HAHAHAHA!

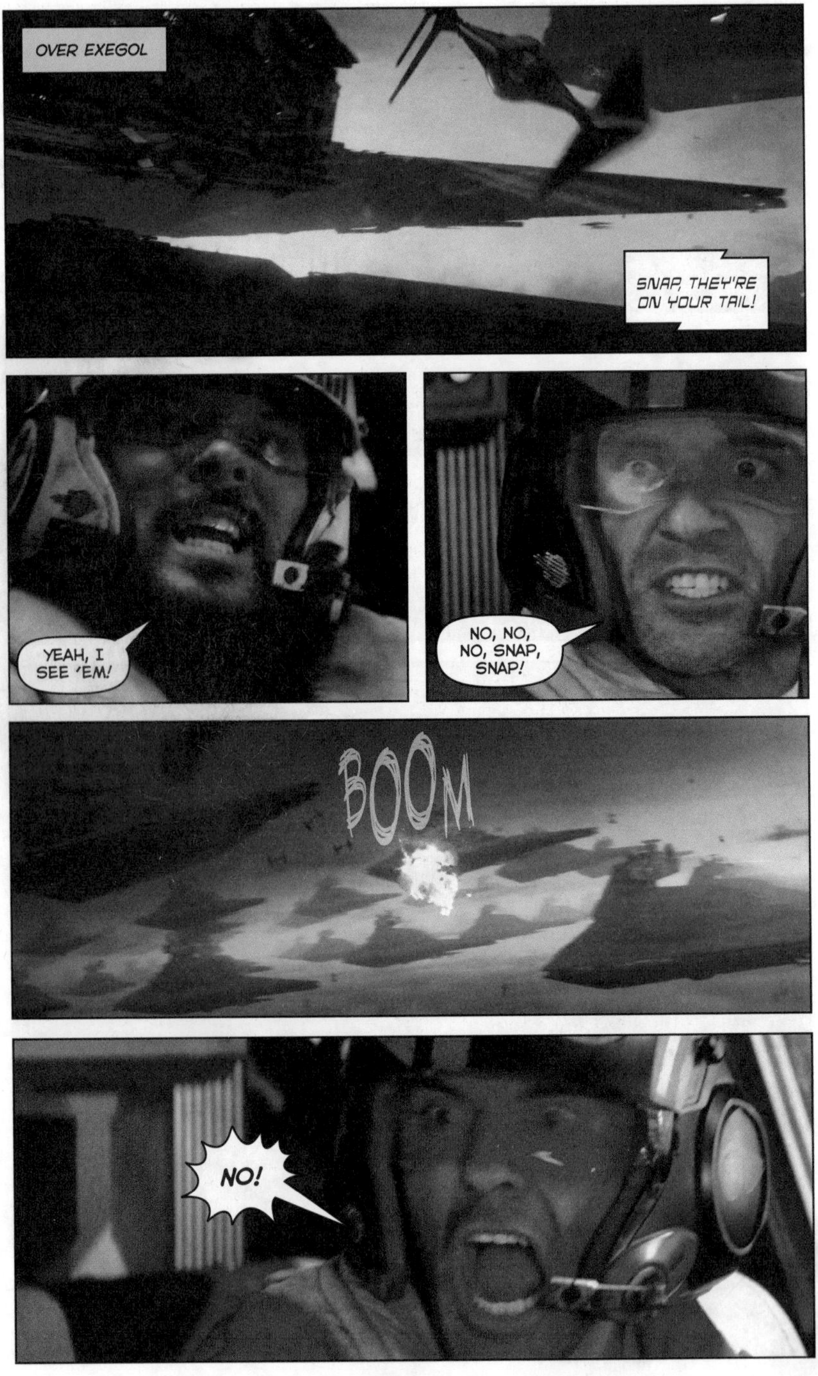
OVER EXEGOL
SNAP, THEY'RE ON YOUR TAIL!
YEAH, I SEE 'EM!
NO, NO, NO, SNAP, SNAP!
BOOM
NO!

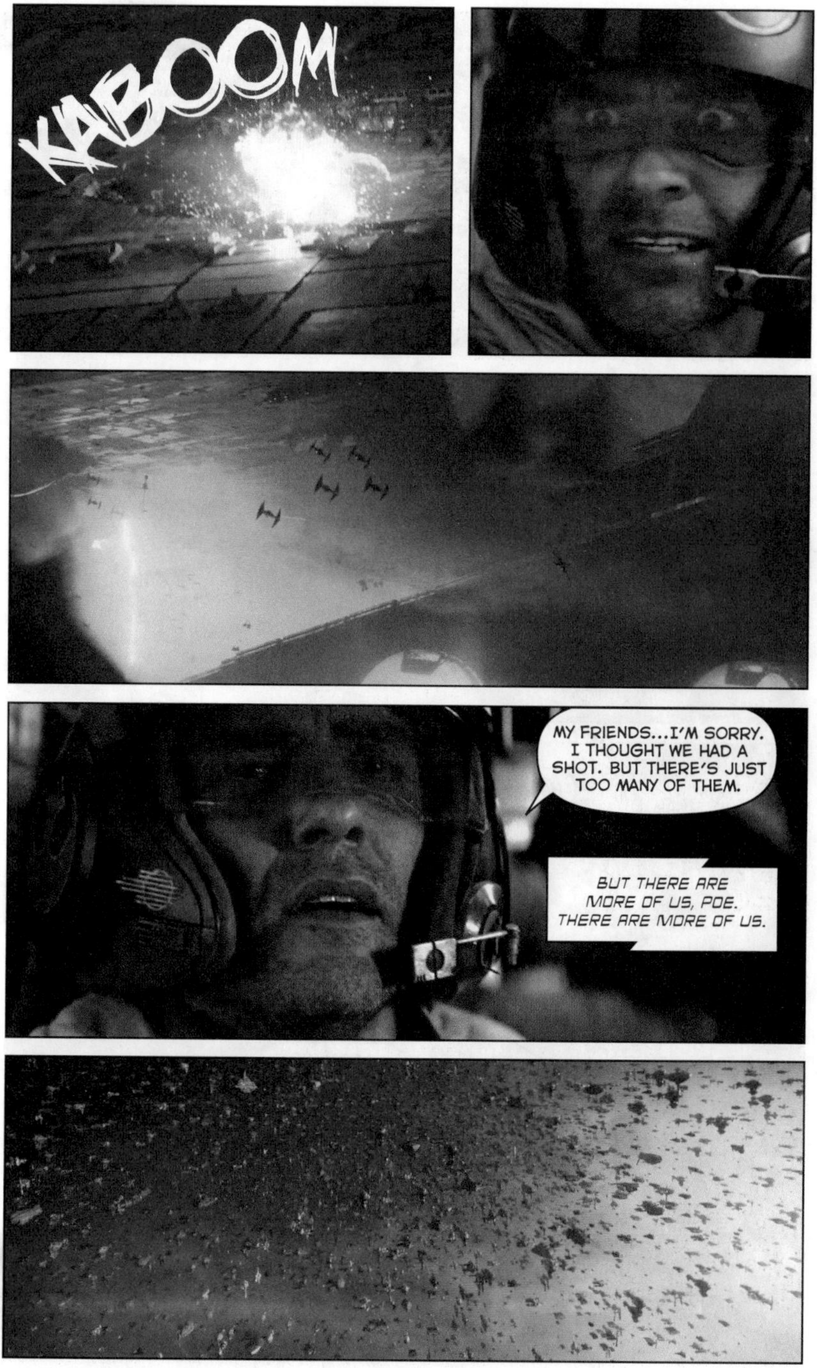
KABOOM
MY FRIENDS...I'M SORRY. I THOUGHT WE HAD A SHOT. BUT THERE'S JUST TOO MANY OF THEM.
BUT THERE ARE MORE OF US, POE. THERE ARE MORE OF US.

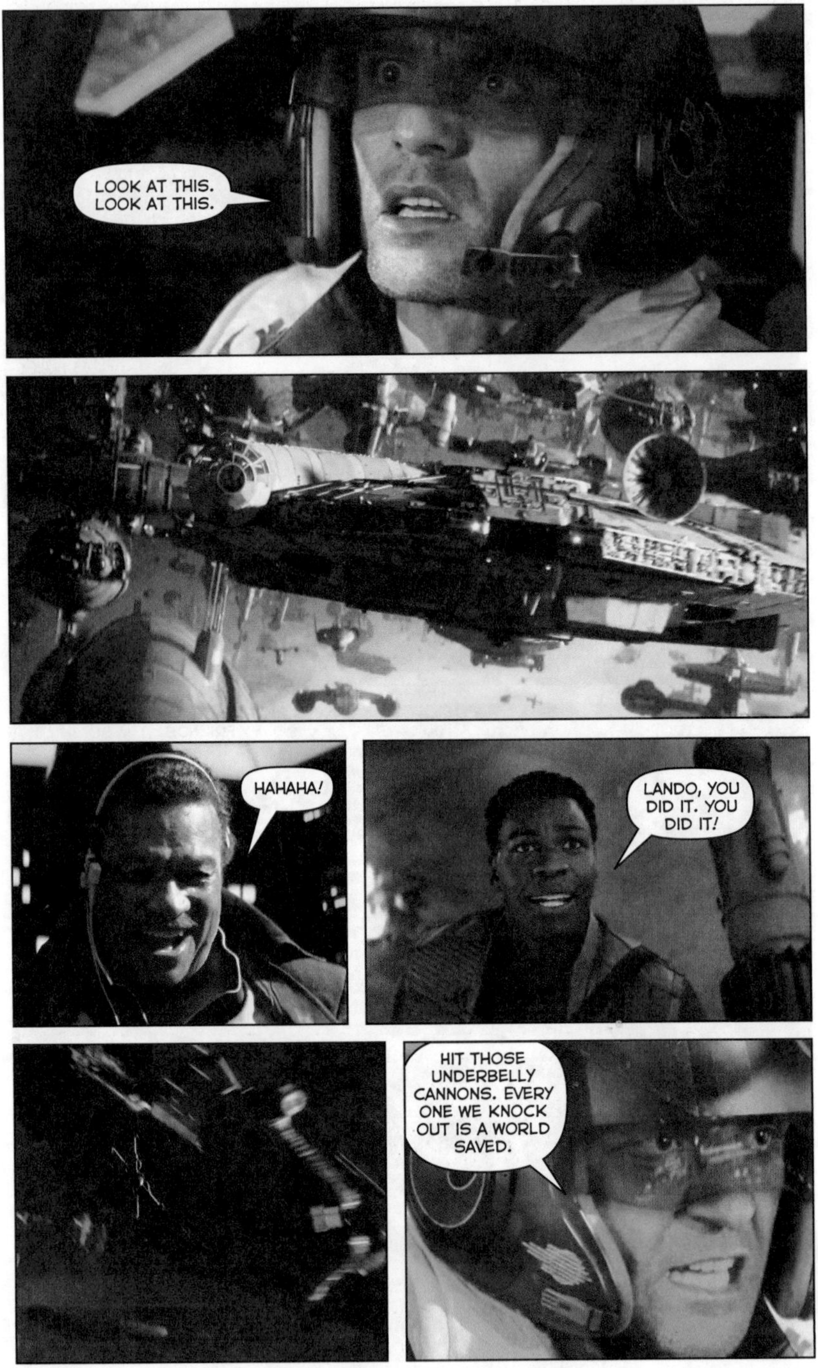
LOOK AT THIS. LOOK AT THIS.
HAHAHA!
LANDO, YOU DID IT. YOU DID IT!
HIT THOSE UNDERBELLY CANNONS. EVERY ONE WE KNOCK OUT IS A WORLD SAVED.

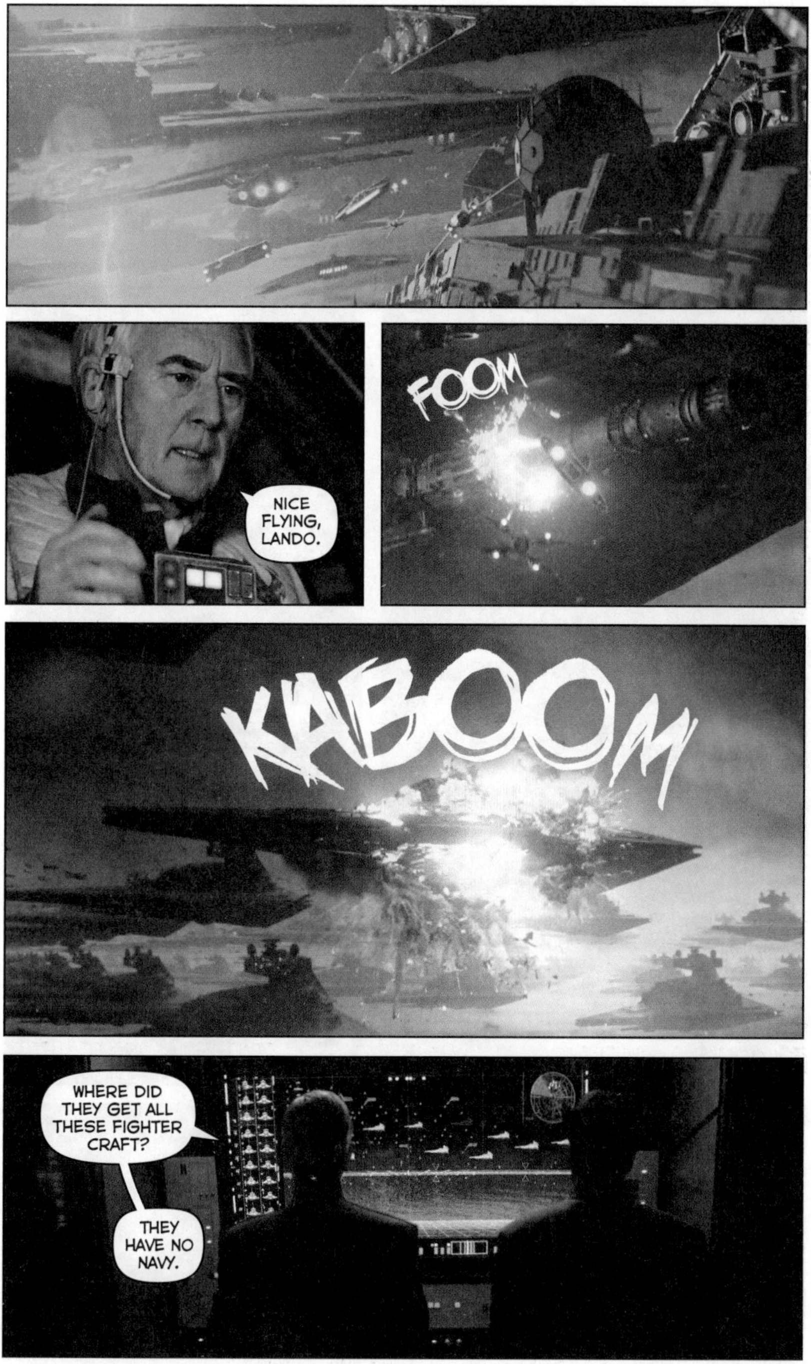
NICE FLYING, LANDO.
FOOM
KABOOM
WHERE DID THEY GET ALL THESE FIGHTER CRAFT?
THEY HAVE NO NAVY.

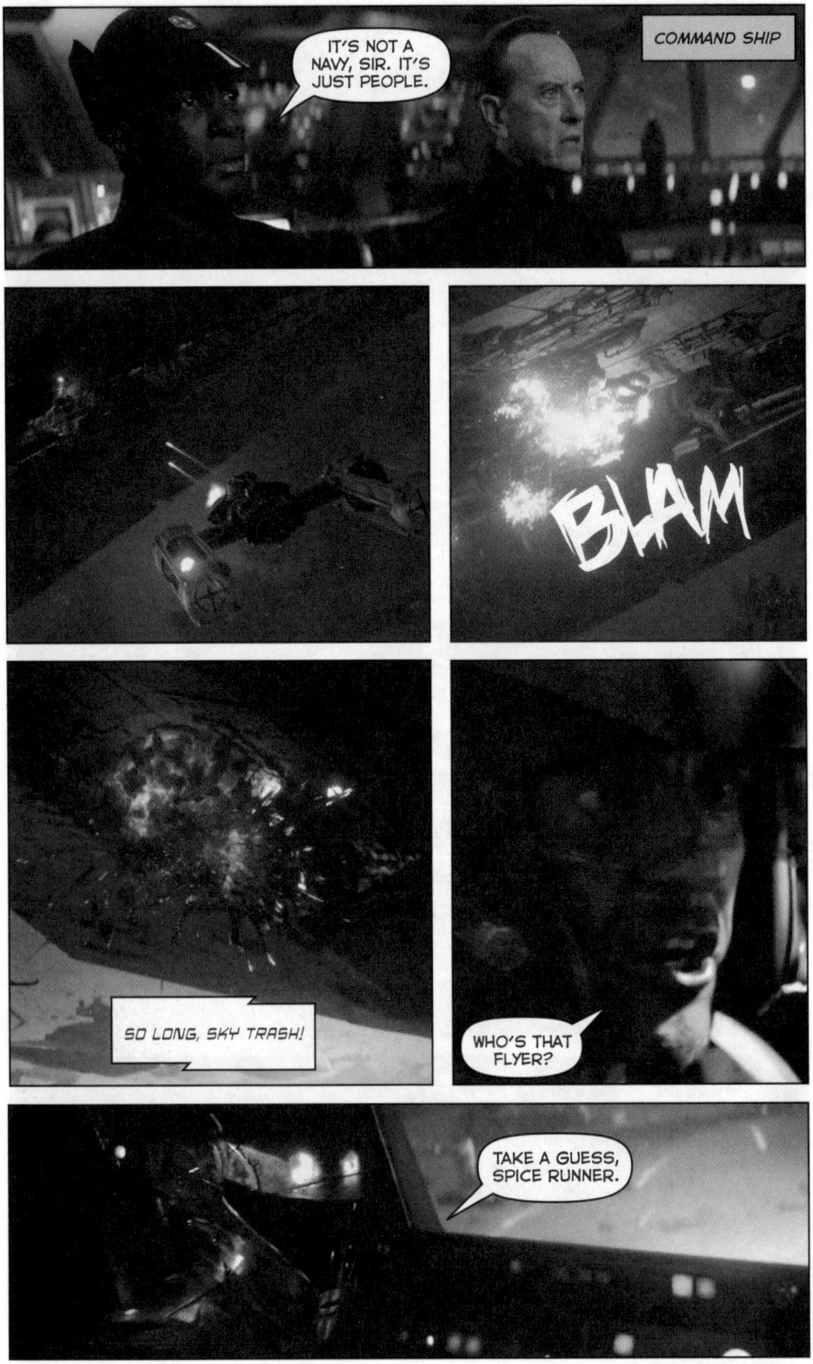
COMMAND SHIP
IT'S NOT A NAVY, SIR. IT'S JUST PEOPLE.
BLAM
SO LONG, SKY TRASH!
WHO'S THAT FLYER?
TAKE A GUESS, SPICE RUNNER.

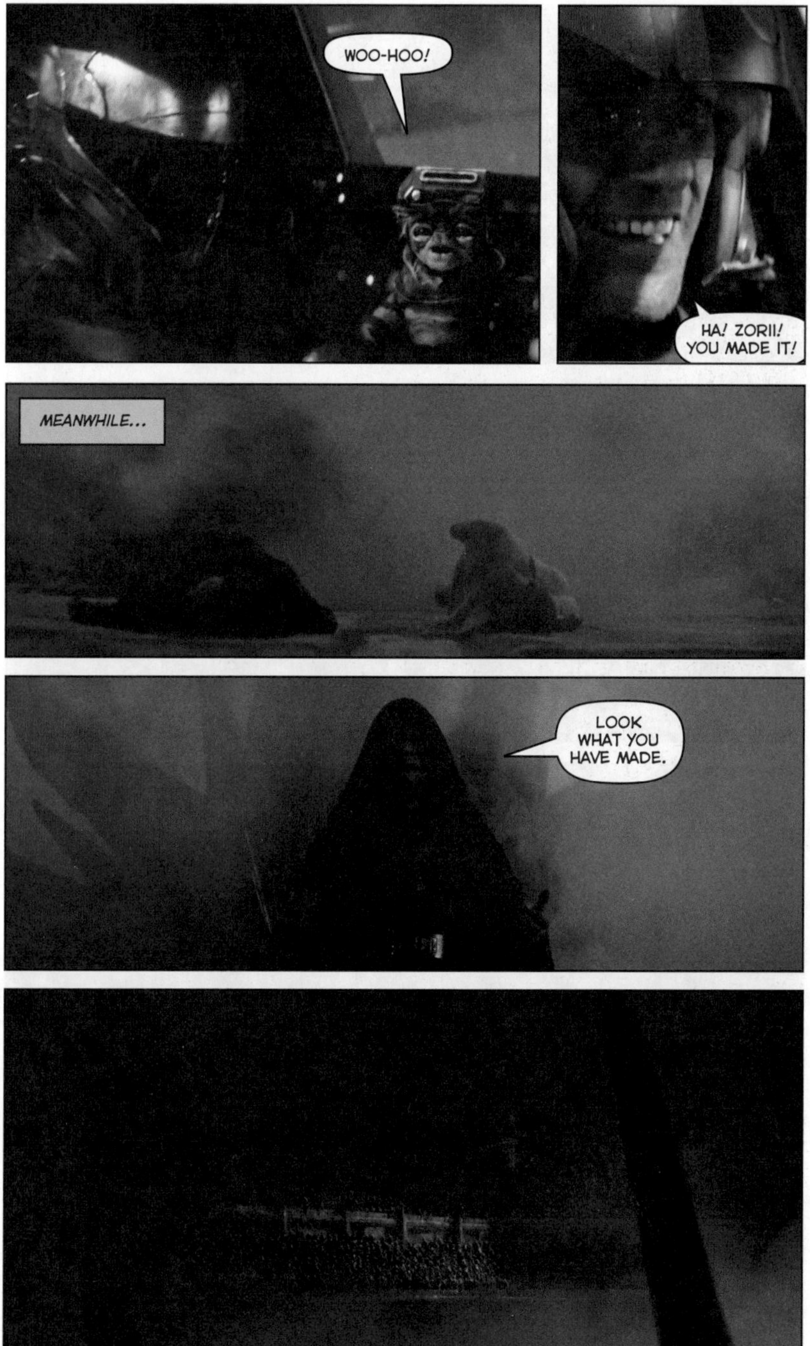
WOO-HOO!
HA! ZORII! YOU MADE IT!
MEANWHILE...
LOOK WHAT YOU HAVE MADE.

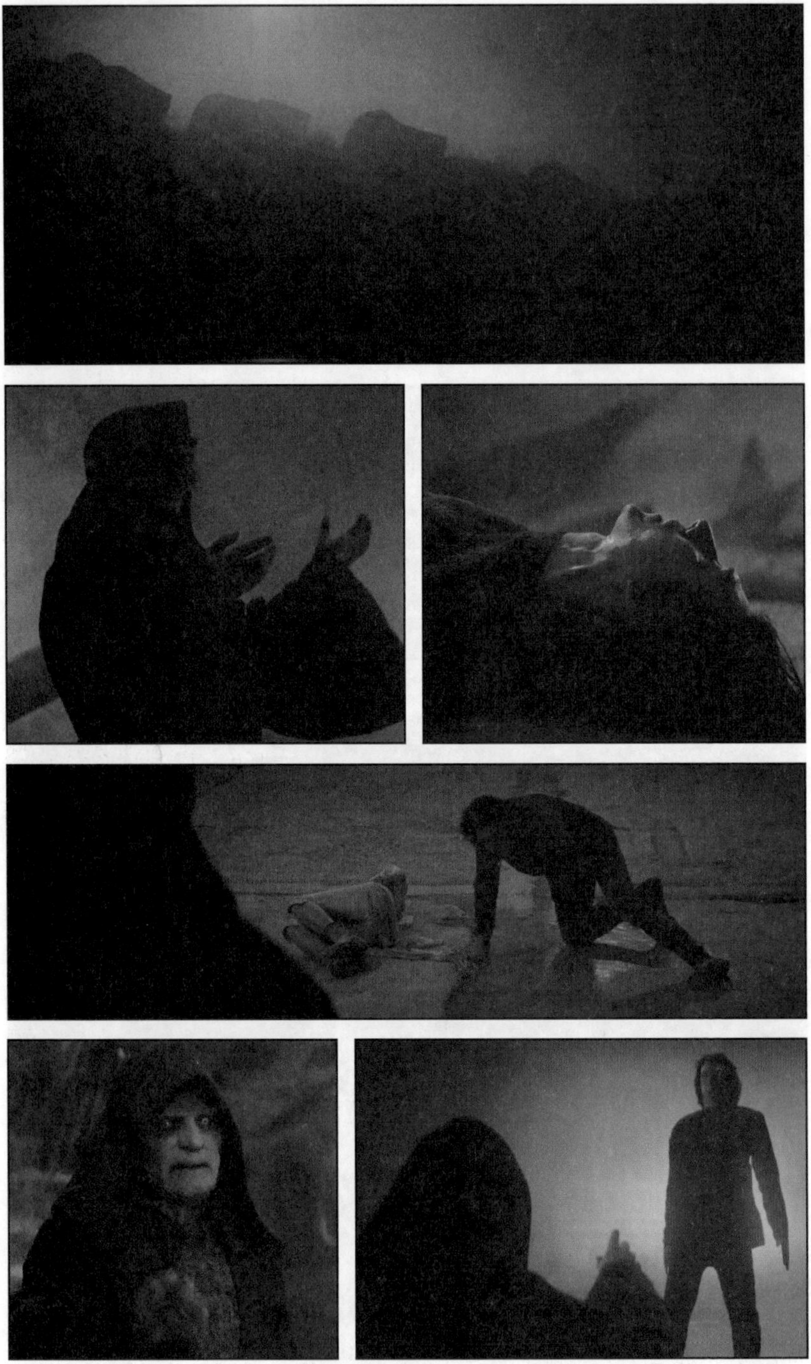

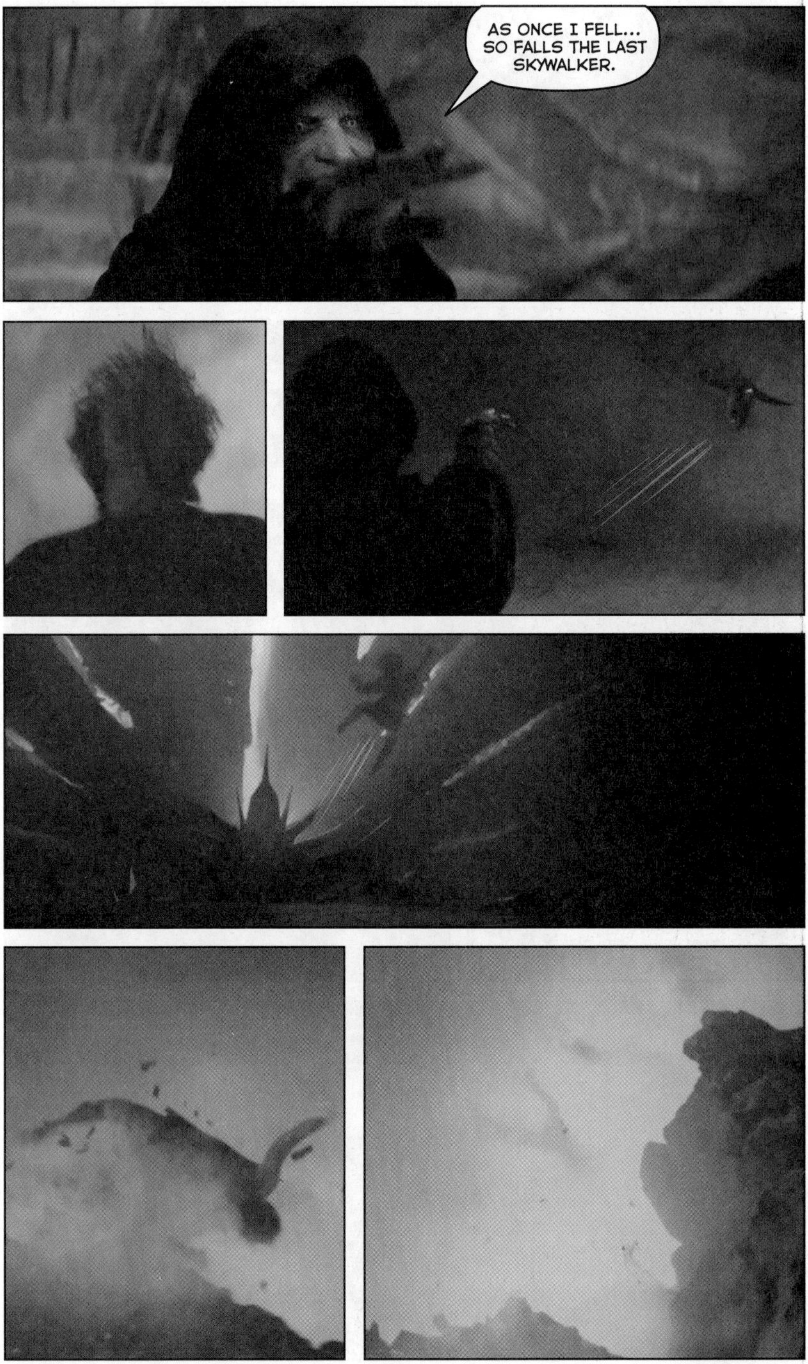
AS ONCE I FELL... SO FALLS THE LAST SKYWALKER.

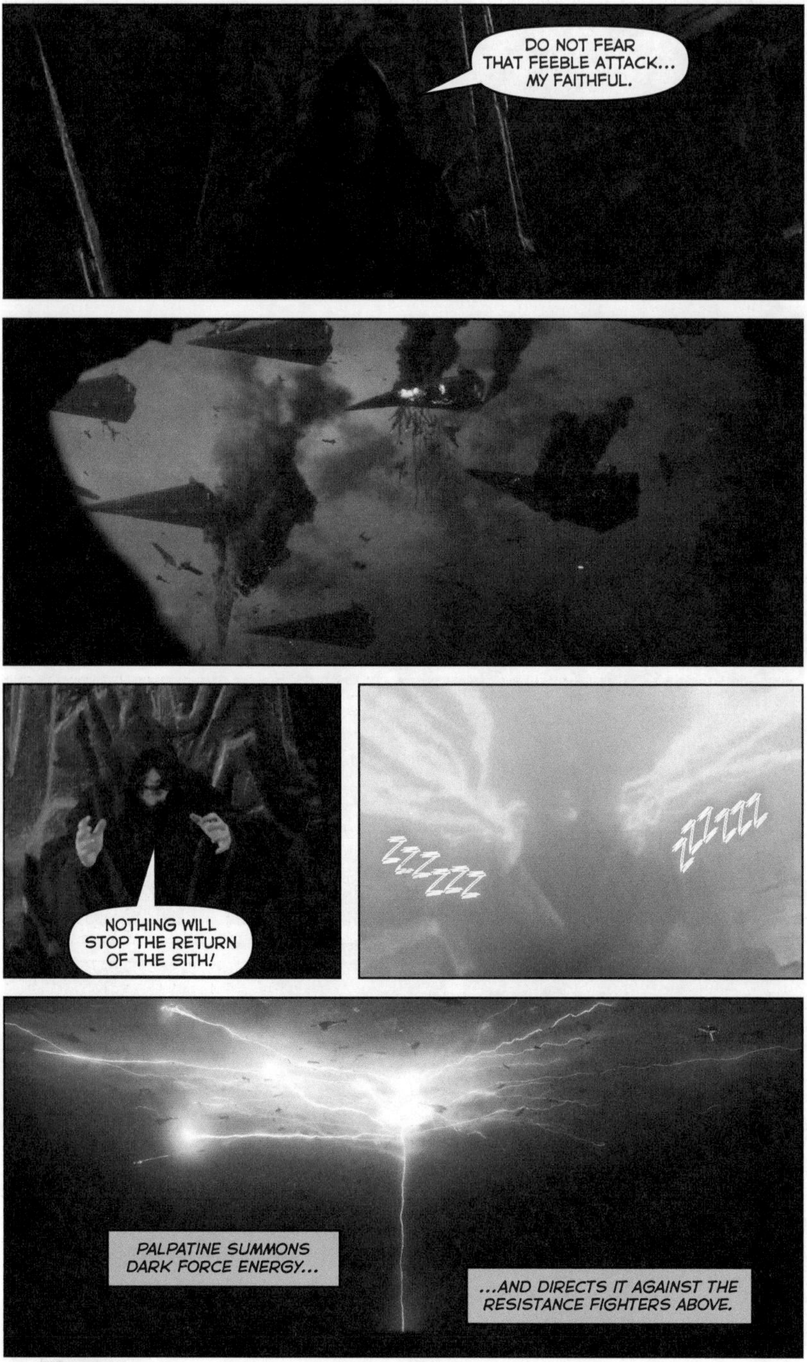
DO NOT FEAR THAT FEEBLE ATTACK... MY FAITHFUL.
NOTHING WILL STOP THE RETURN OF THE SITH!
ZZZZZZZ
ZZZZZZ
PALPATINE SUMMONS DARK FORCE ENERGY...
...AND DIRECTS IT AGAINST THE RESISTANCE FIGHTERS ABOVE.

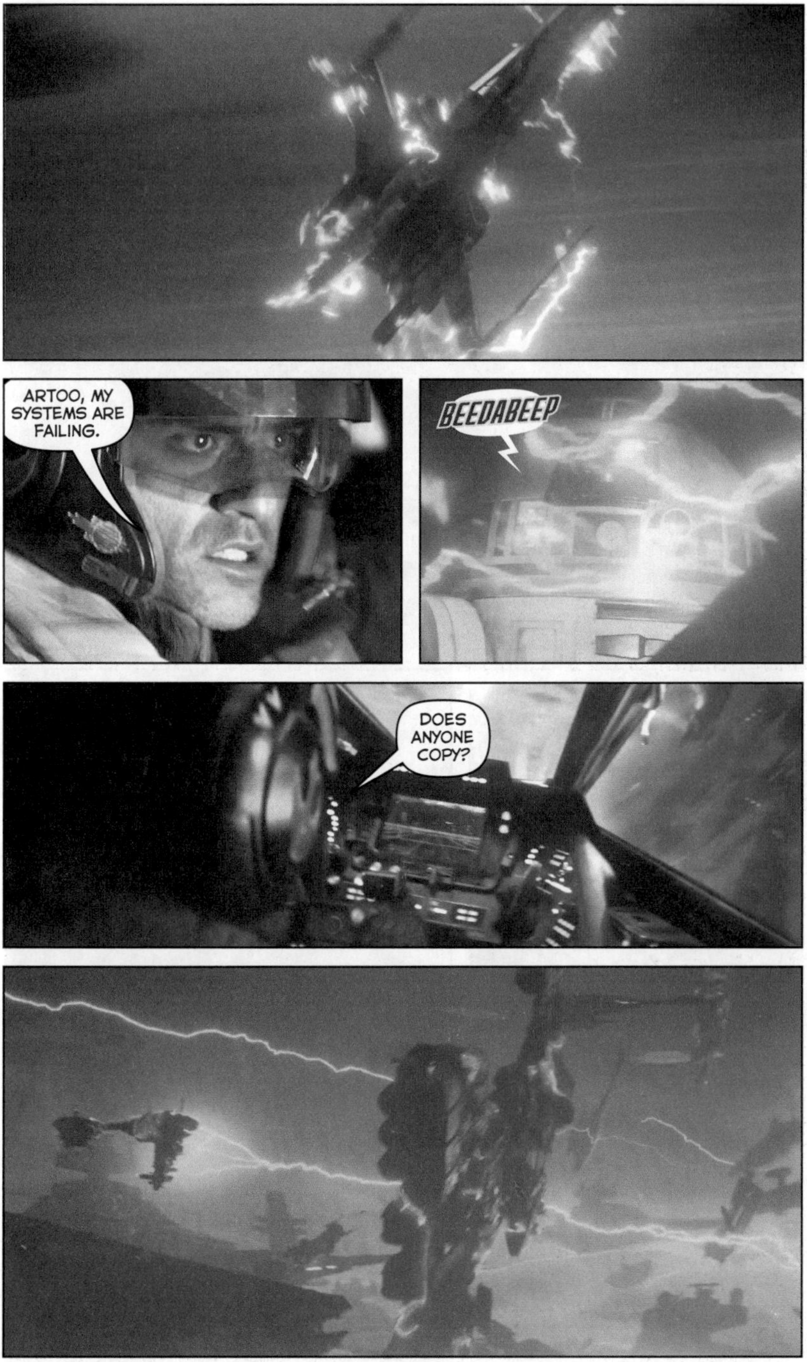
ARTOO, MY SYSTEMS ARE FAILING.
BEEDABEEP
DOES ANYONE COPY?

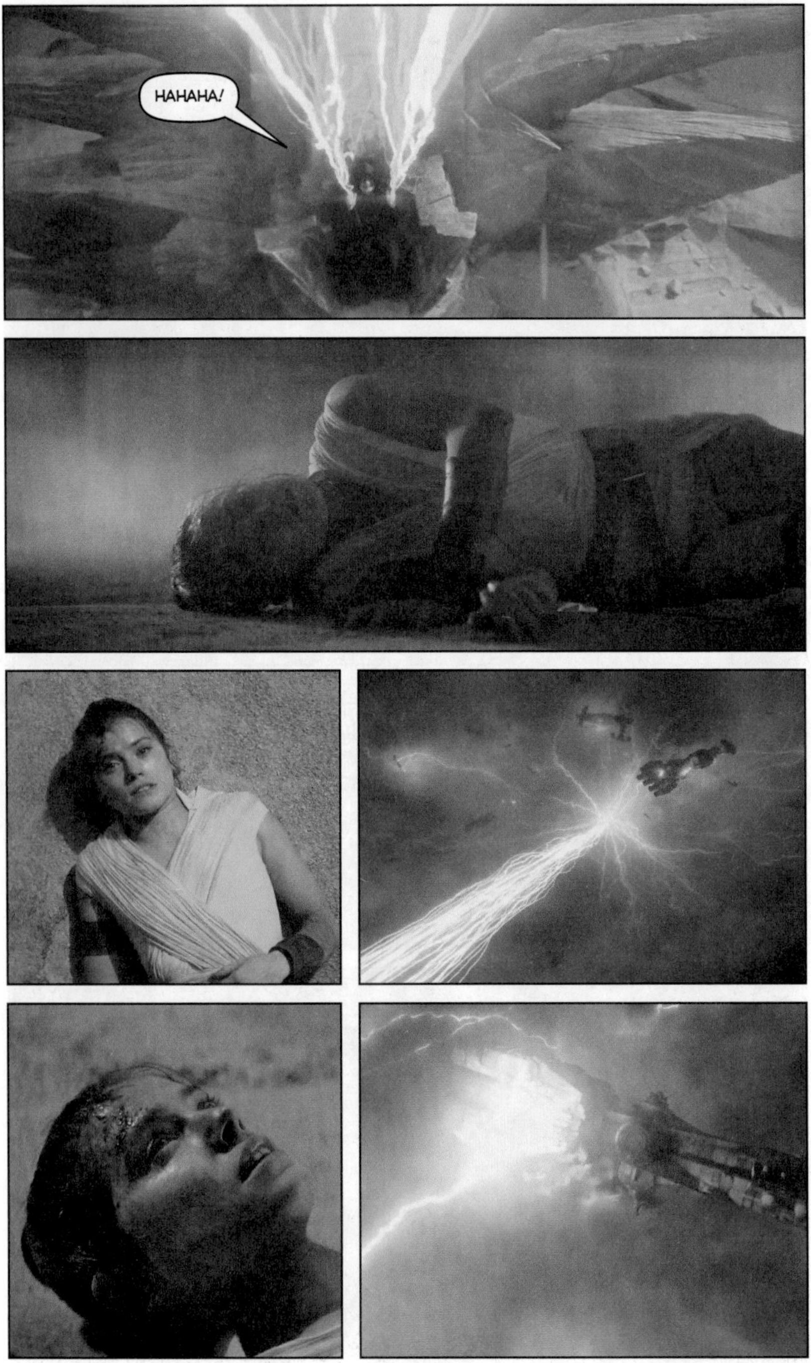
HAHAHA!

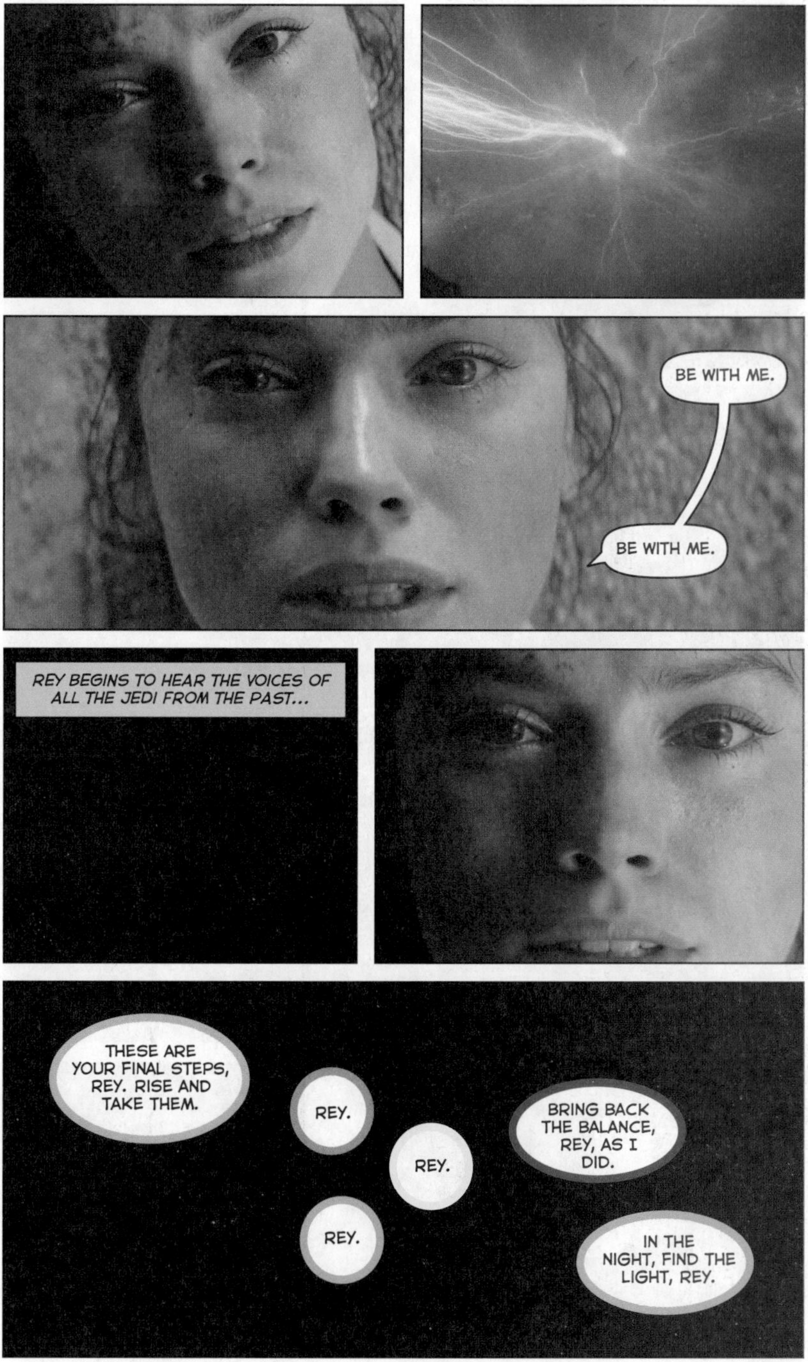
BE WITH ME.
BE WITH ME.
REY BEGINS TO HEAR THE VOICES OF ALL THE JEDI FROM THE PAST...
THESE ARE YOUR FINAL STEPS, REY. RISE AND TAKE THEM.
REY.
REY.
REY.
BRING BACK THE BALANCE, REY, AS I DID.
IN THE NIGHT, FIND THE LIGHT, REY.

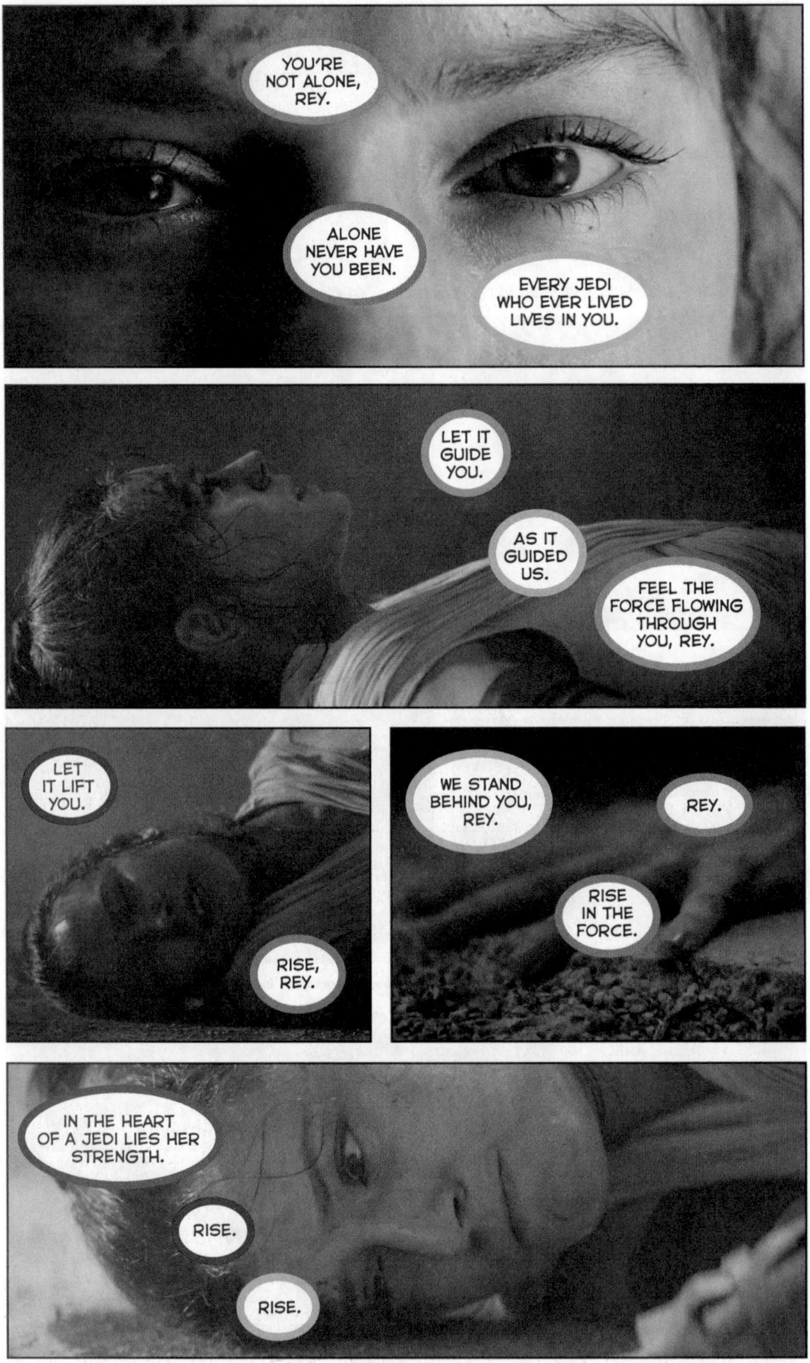
YOU'RE NOT ALONE, REY.
ALONE NEVER HAVE YOU BEEN.
EVERY JEDI WHO EVER LIVED LIVES IN YOU.
LET IT GUIDE YOU.
AS IT GUIDED US.
FEEL THE FORCE FLOWING THROUGH YOU, REY.
LET IT LIFT YOU.
RISE, REY.
WE STAND BEHIND YOU, REY.
REY.
RISE IN THE FORCE.
IN THE HEART OF A JEDI LIES HER STRENGTH.
RISE.
RISE.

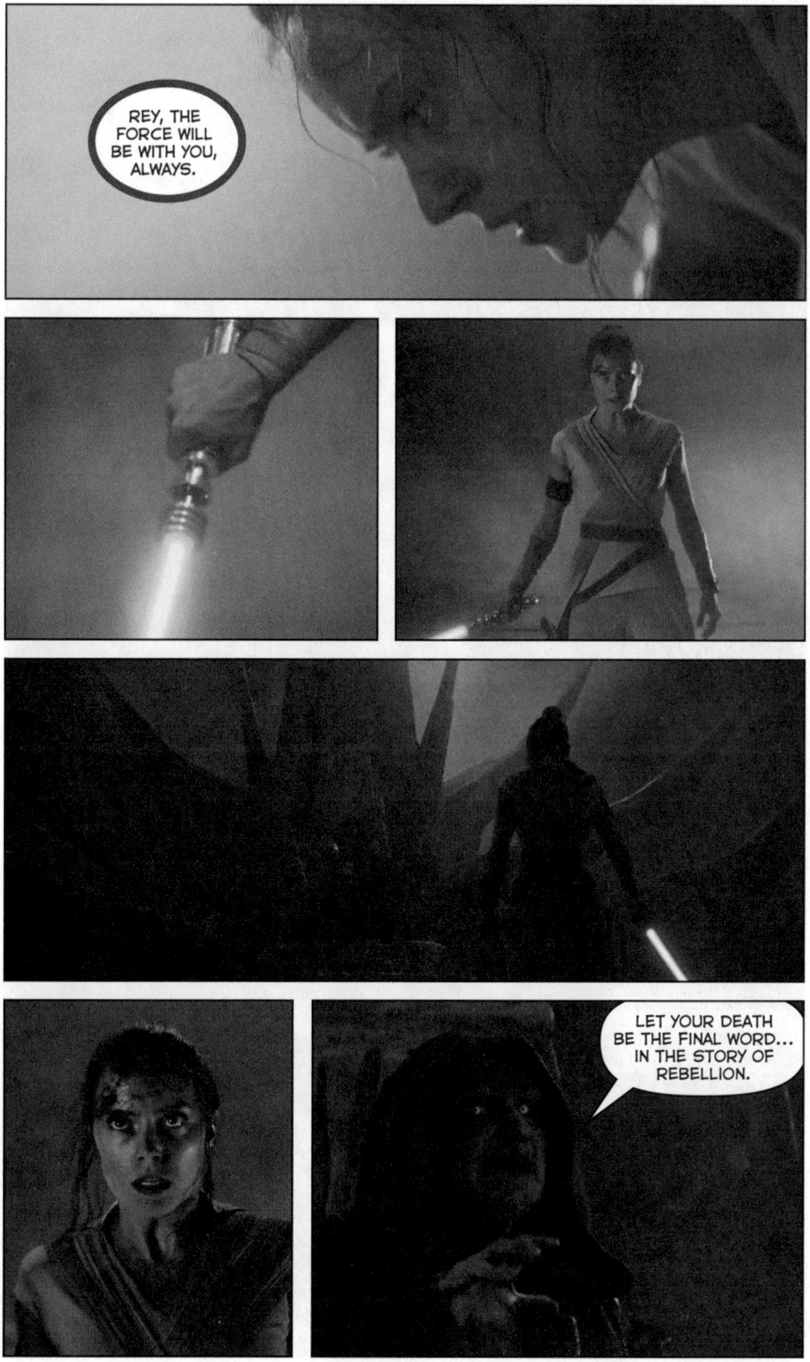
REY, THE FORCE WILL BE WITH YOU, ALWAYS.
LET YOUR DEATH BE THE FINAL WORD... IN THE STORY OF REBELLION.

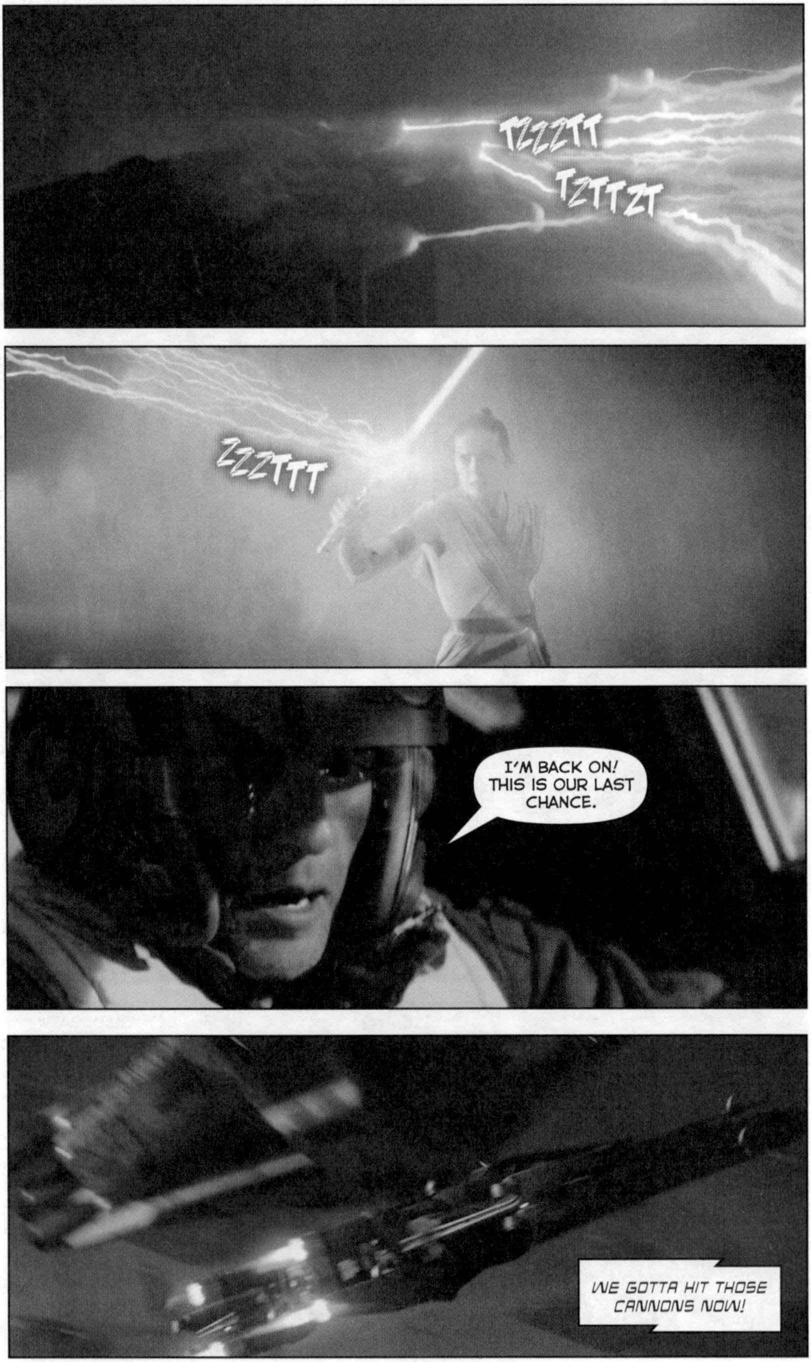
TZZZTT
TZTTZT
ZZZTTT
I'M BACK ON! THIS IS OUR LAST CHANCE.
WE GOTTA HIT THOSE CANNONS NOW!

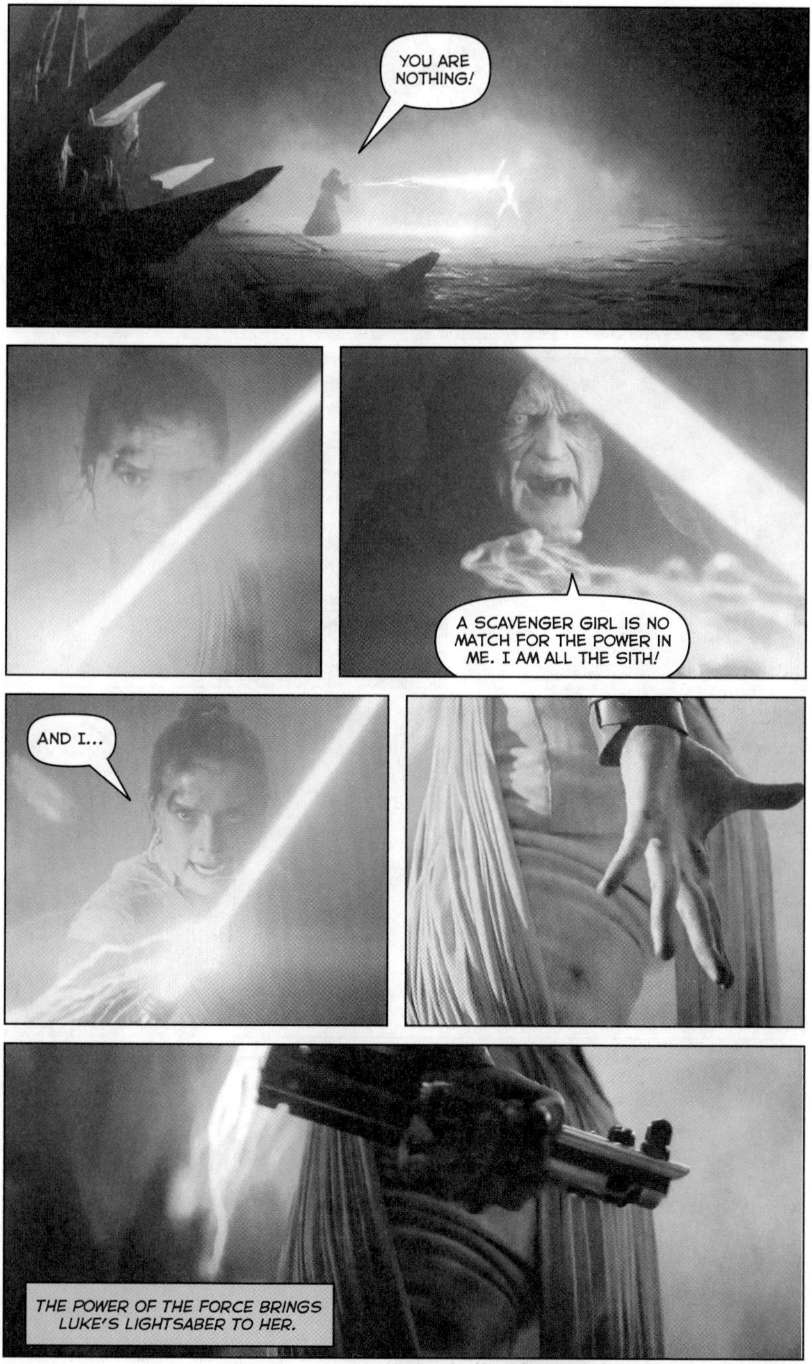

YOU ARE NOTHING!
A SCAVENGER GIRL IS NO MATCH FOR THE POWER IN ME. I AM ALL THE SITH!
AND I...
THE POWER OF THE FORCE BRINGS LUKE'S LIGHTSABER TO HER.

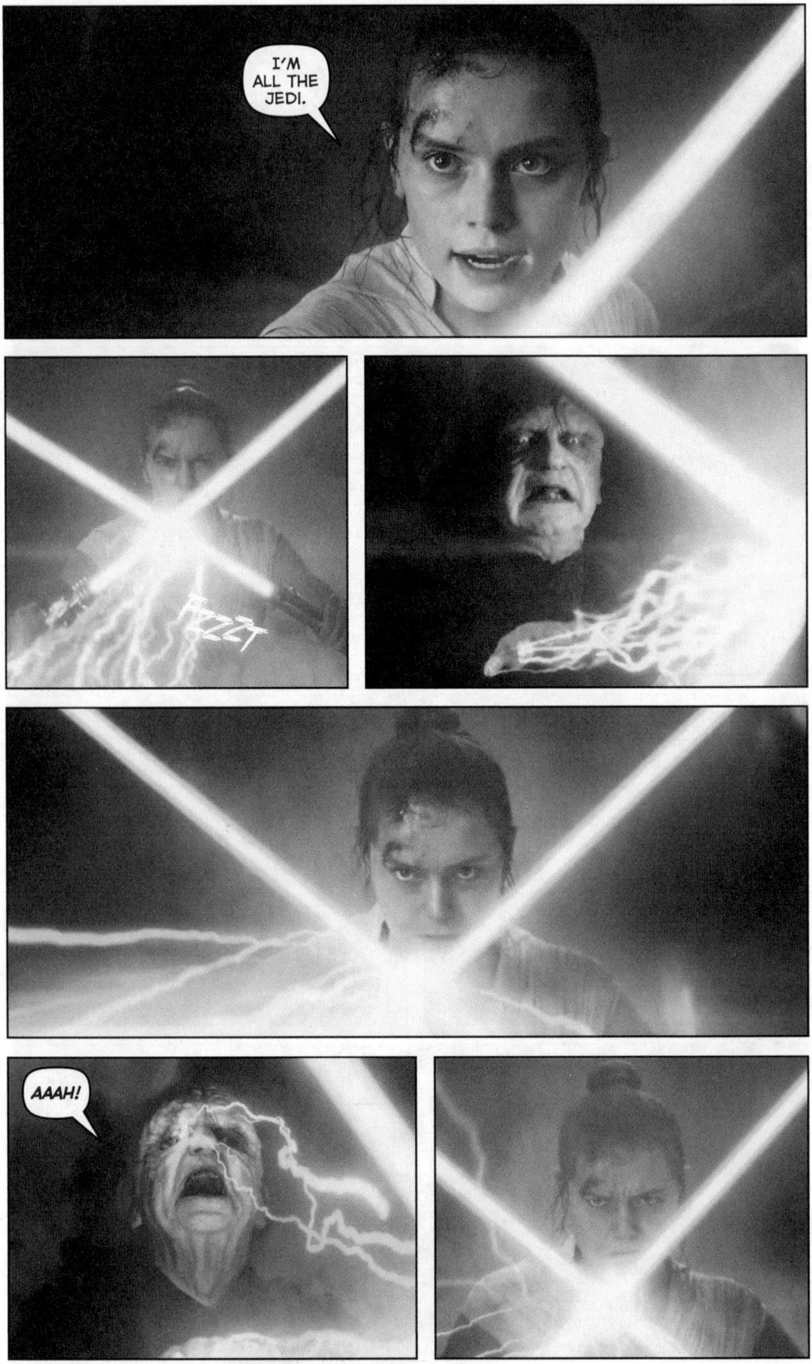
I'M ALL THE JEDI.
FZZZT
AAAH!

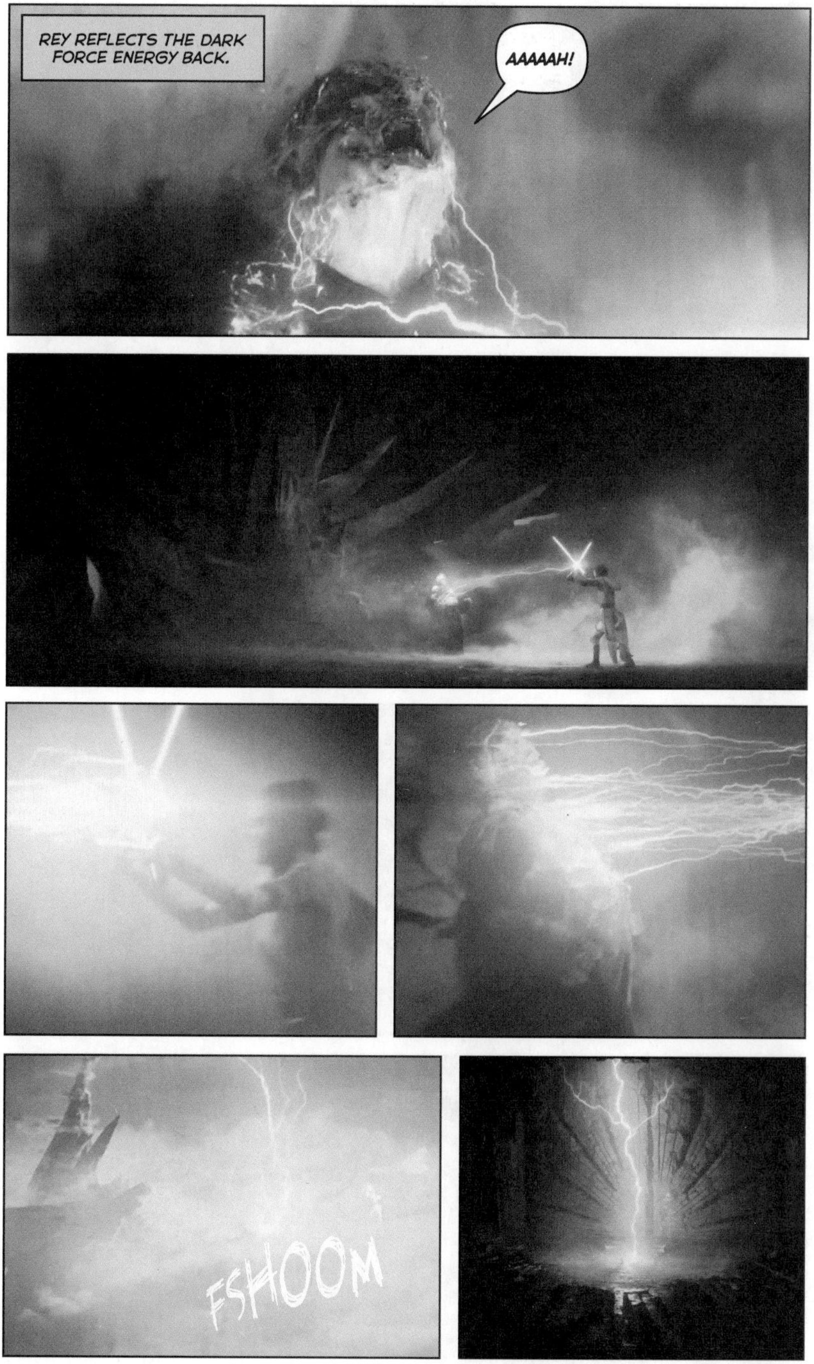
REY REFLECTS THE DARK FORCE ENERGY BACK.
AAAAAH!
FSHOOM

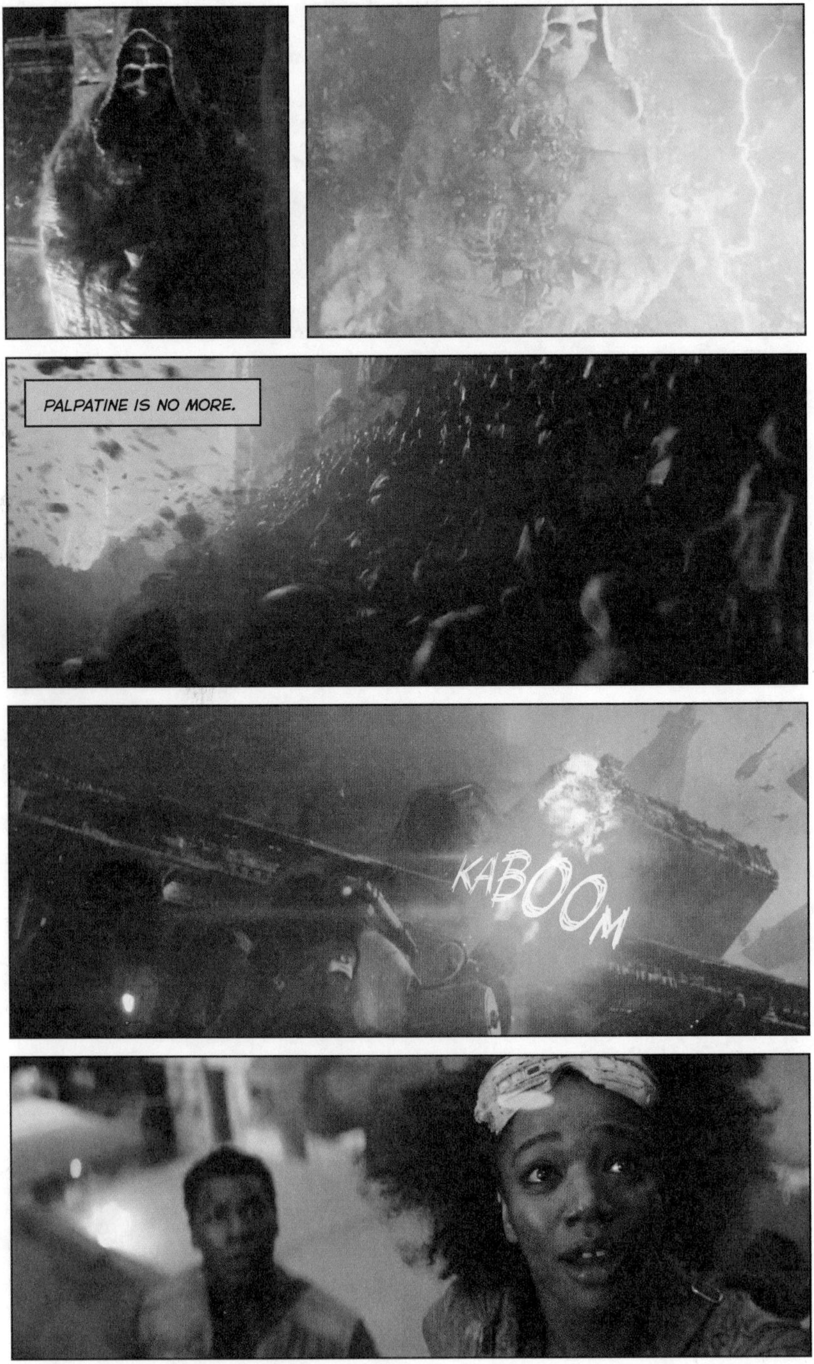
PALPATINE IS NO MORE.
KABOOM

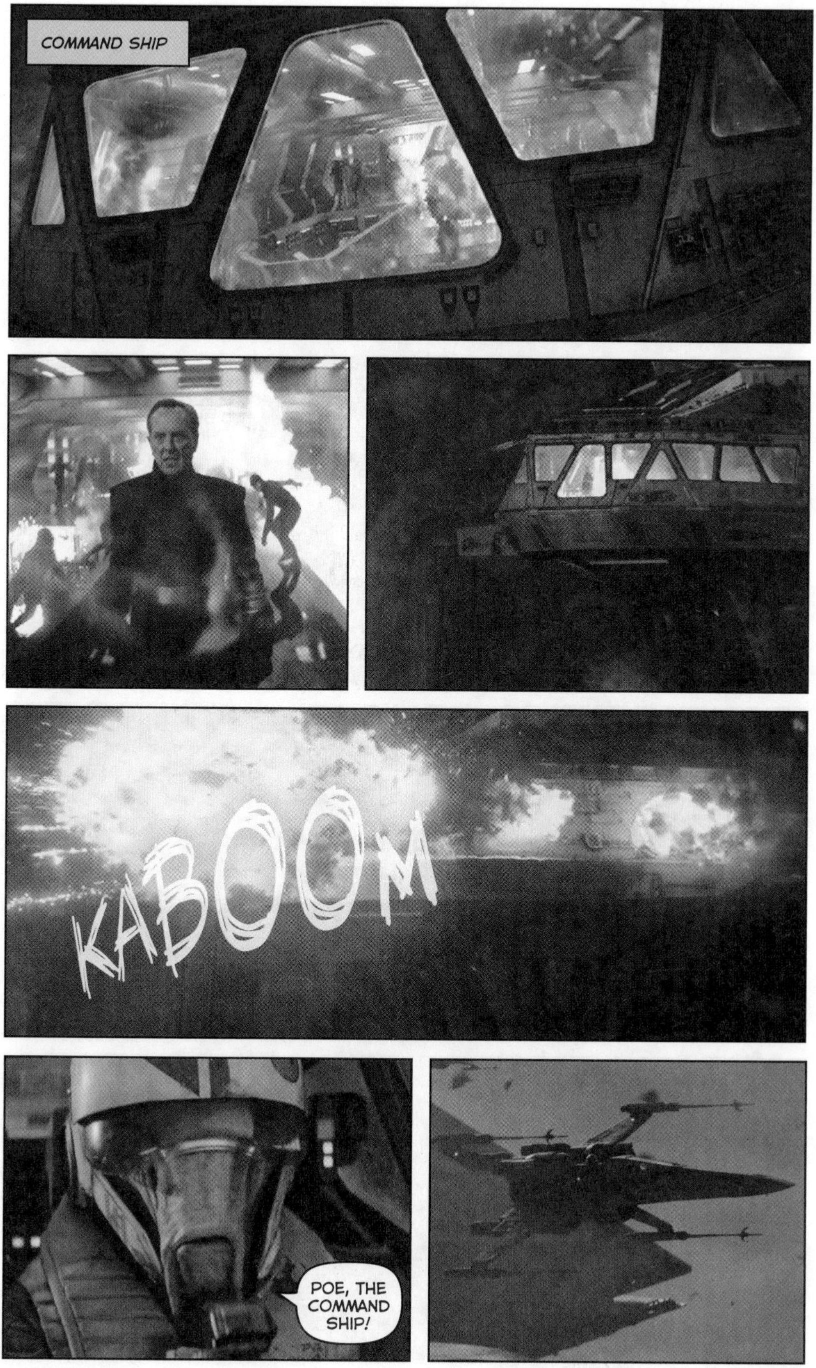
COMMAND SHIP
KABOOM
POE, THE COMMAND SHIP!

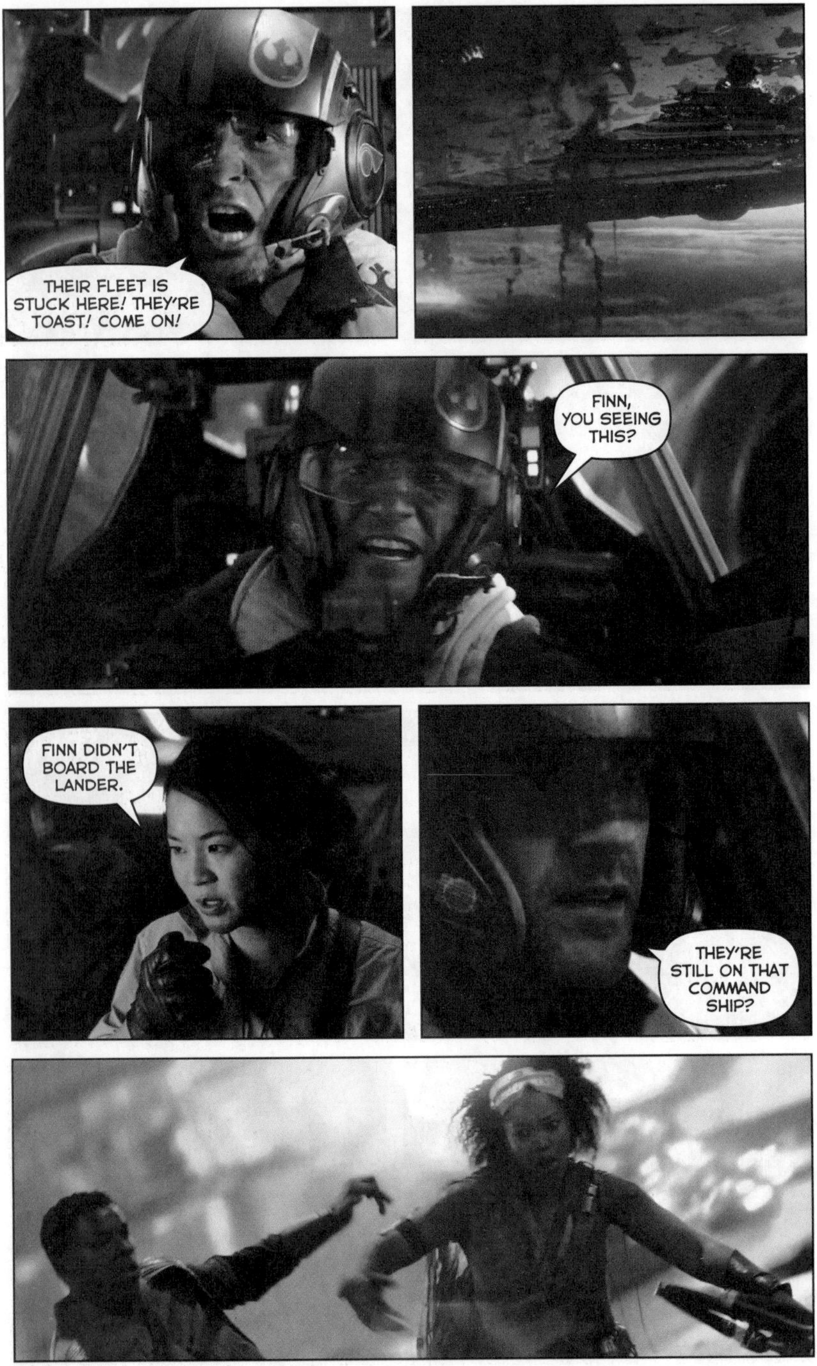
THEIR FLEET IS STUCK HERE! THEY'RE TOAST! COME ON!
FINN, YOU SEEING THIS?
FINN DIDN'T BOARD THE LANDER.
THEY'RE STILL ON THAT COMMAND SHIP?

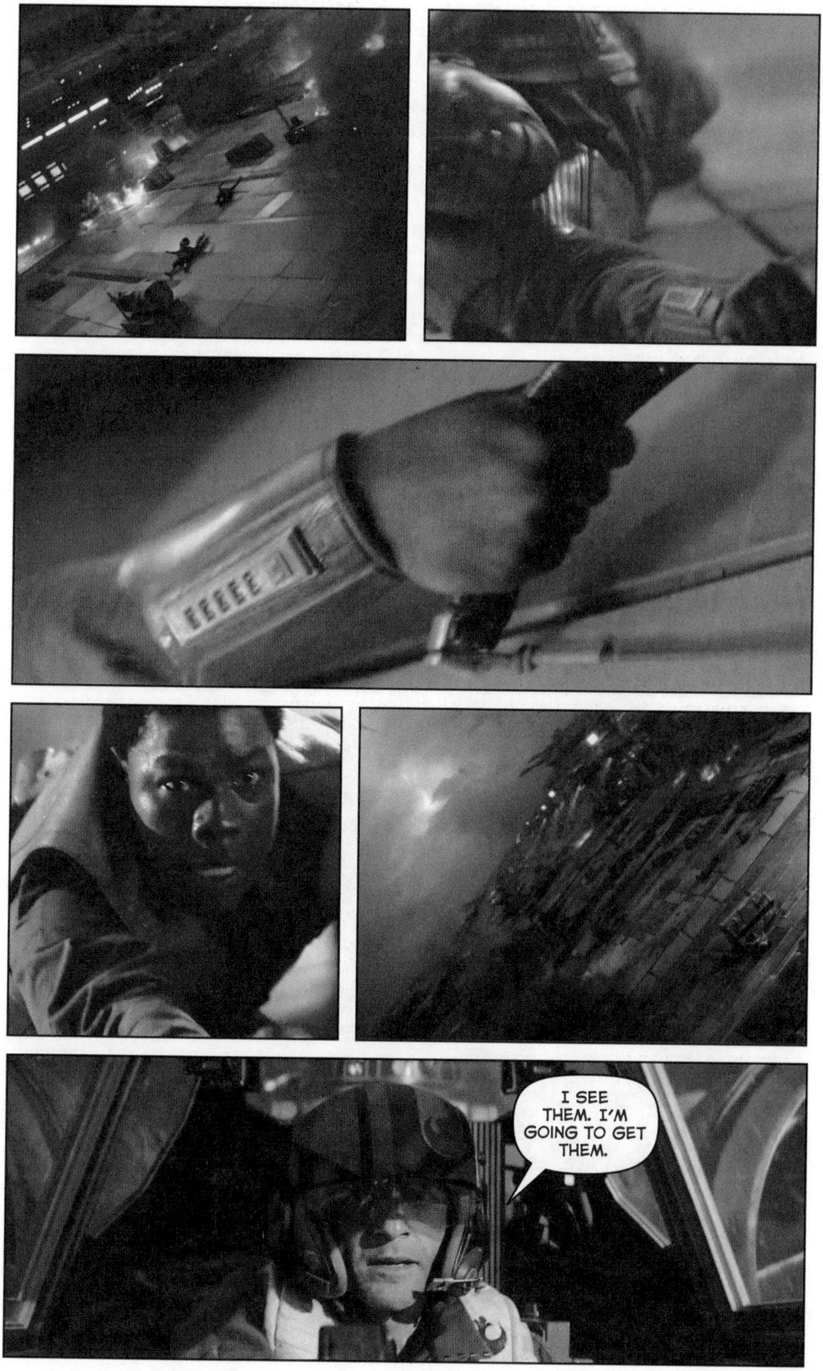
I SEE THEM. I'M GOING TO GET THEM.

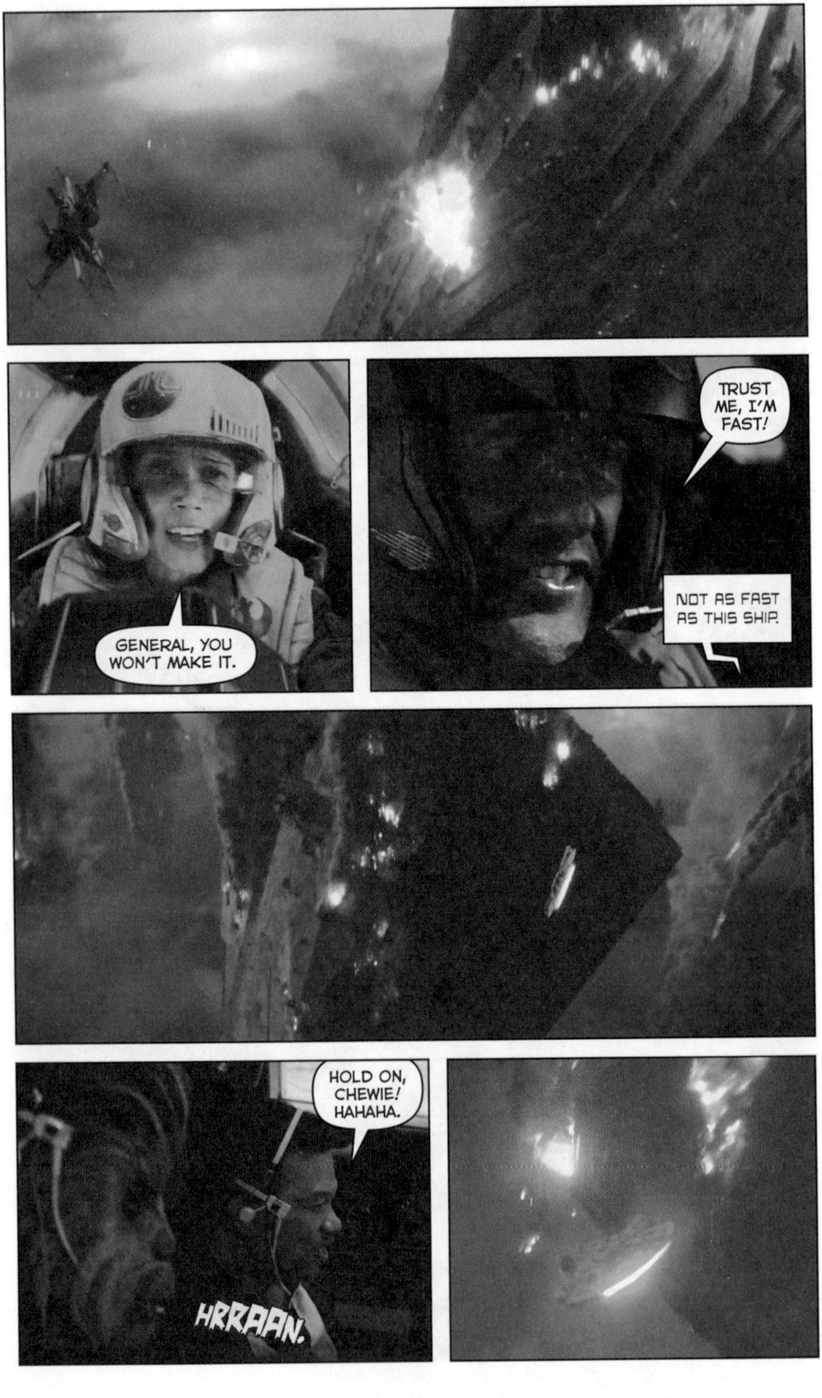

GENERAL, YOU WON'T MAKE IT.
TRUST ME, I'M FAST!
NOT AS FAST AS THIS SHIP.
HOLD ON, CHEWIE! HAHAHA.
HRRAAN.

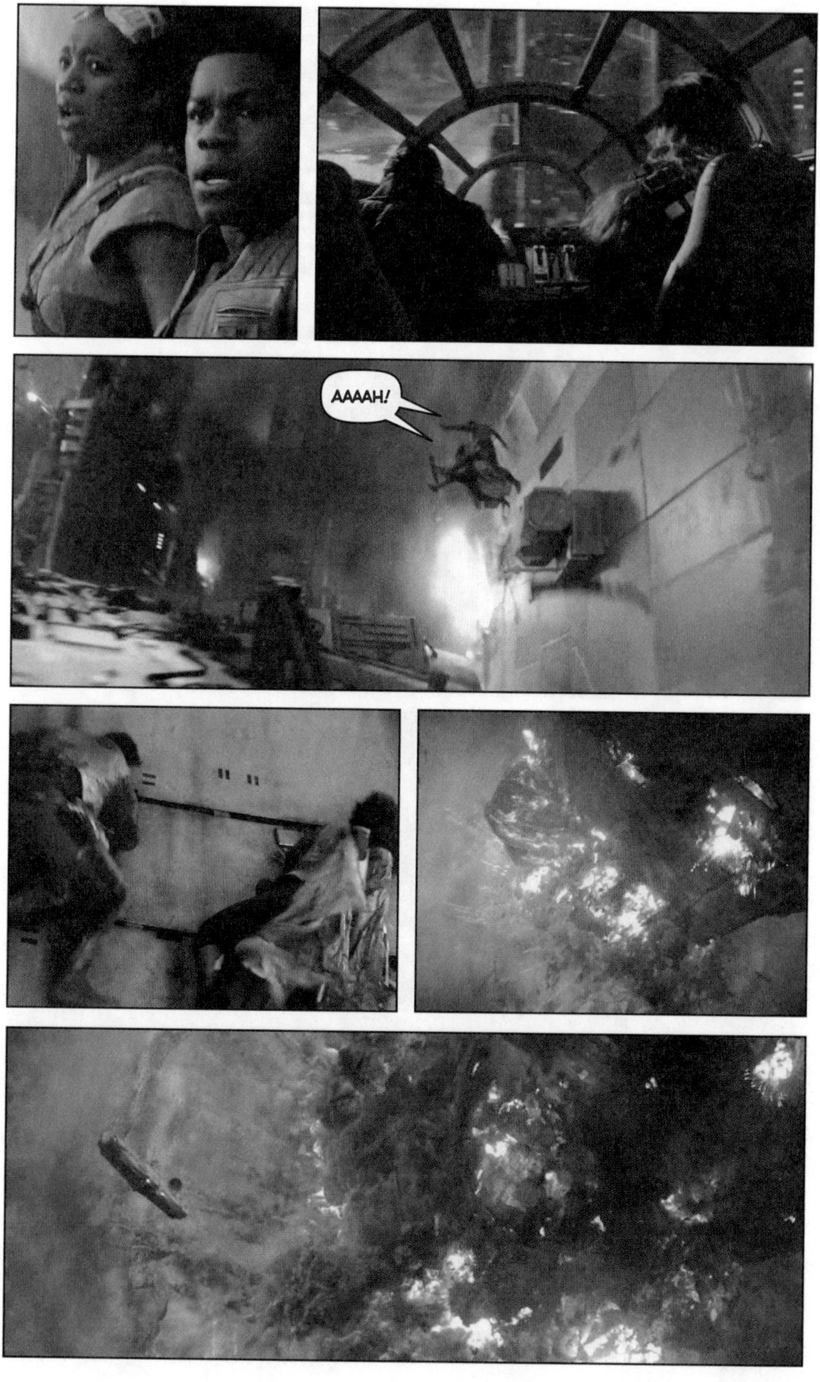
AAAAH!

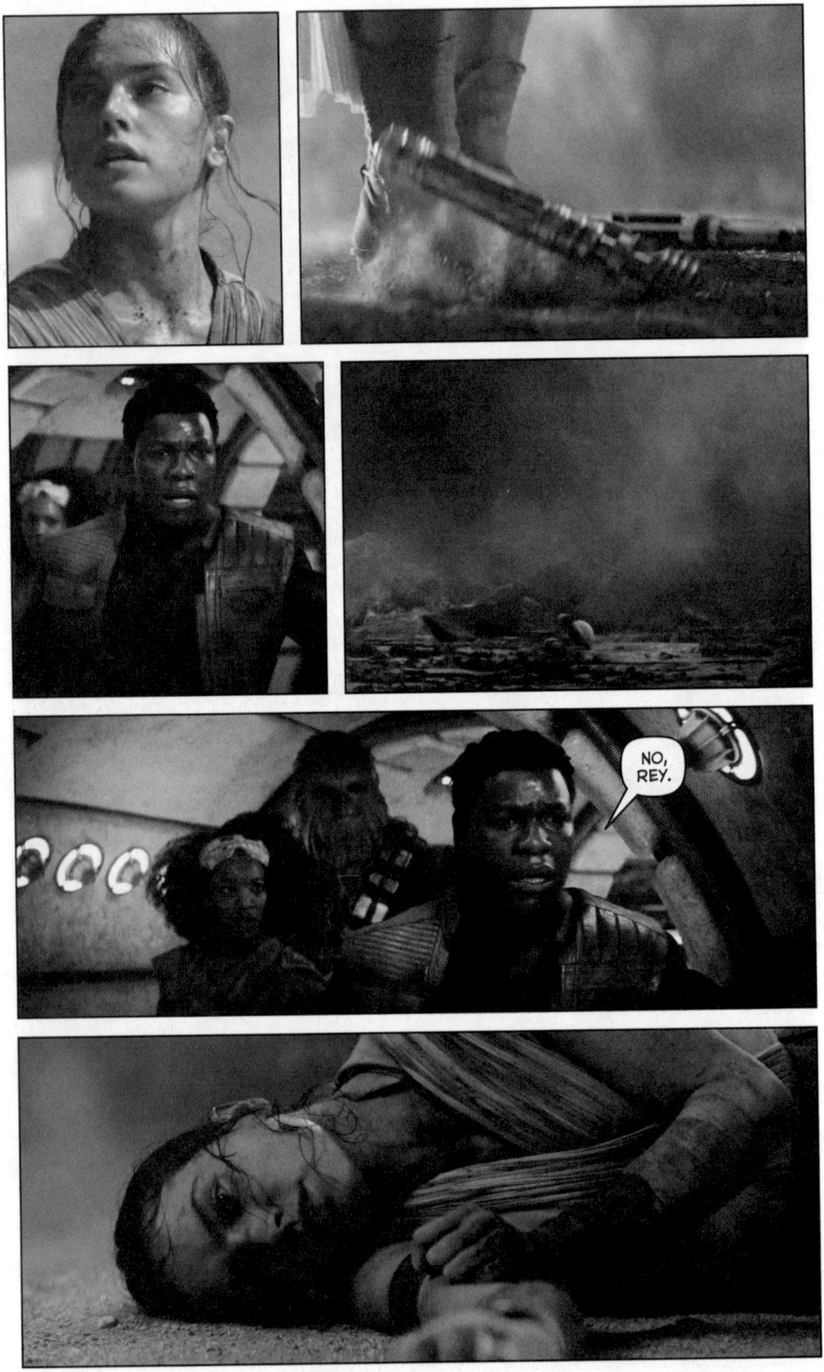
NO,
REY.

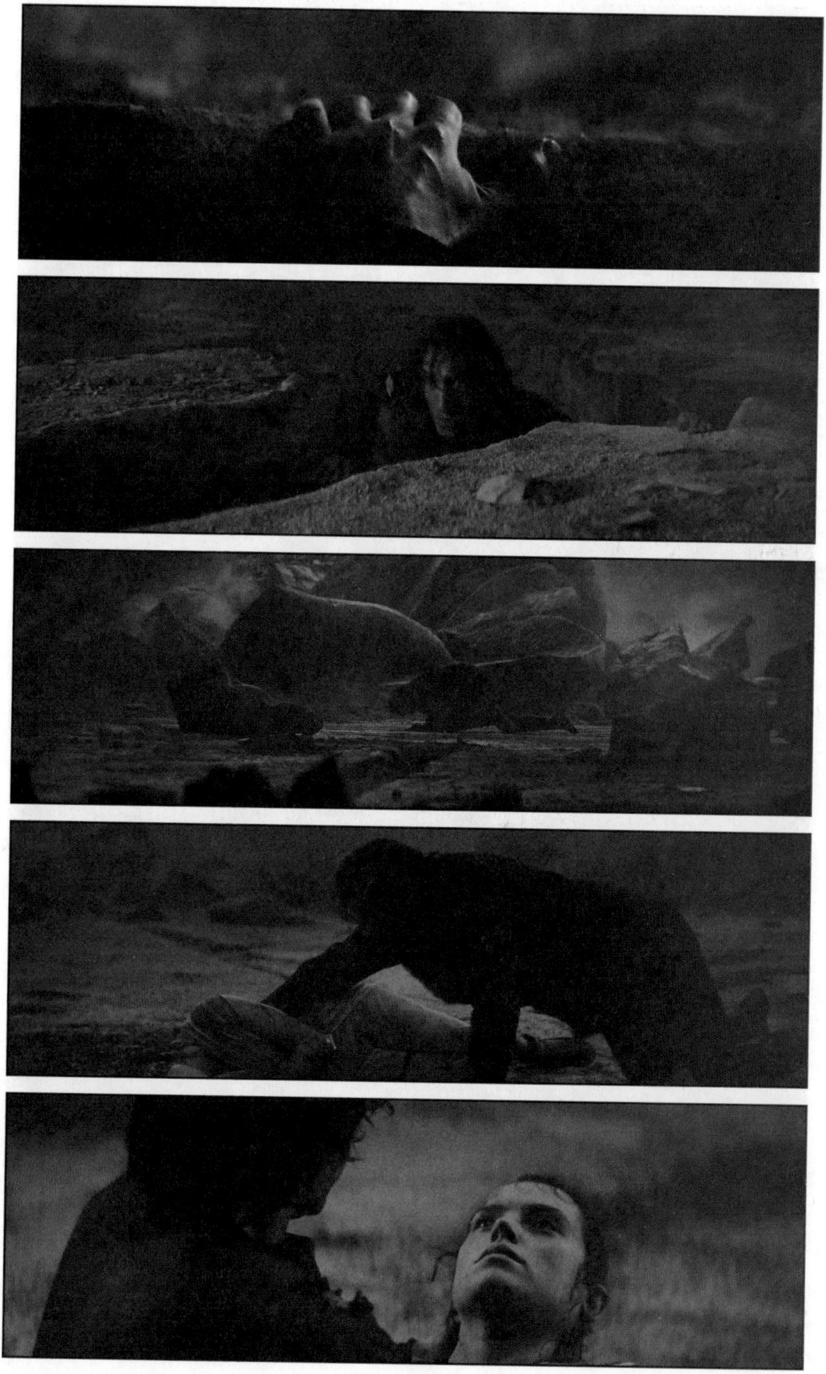

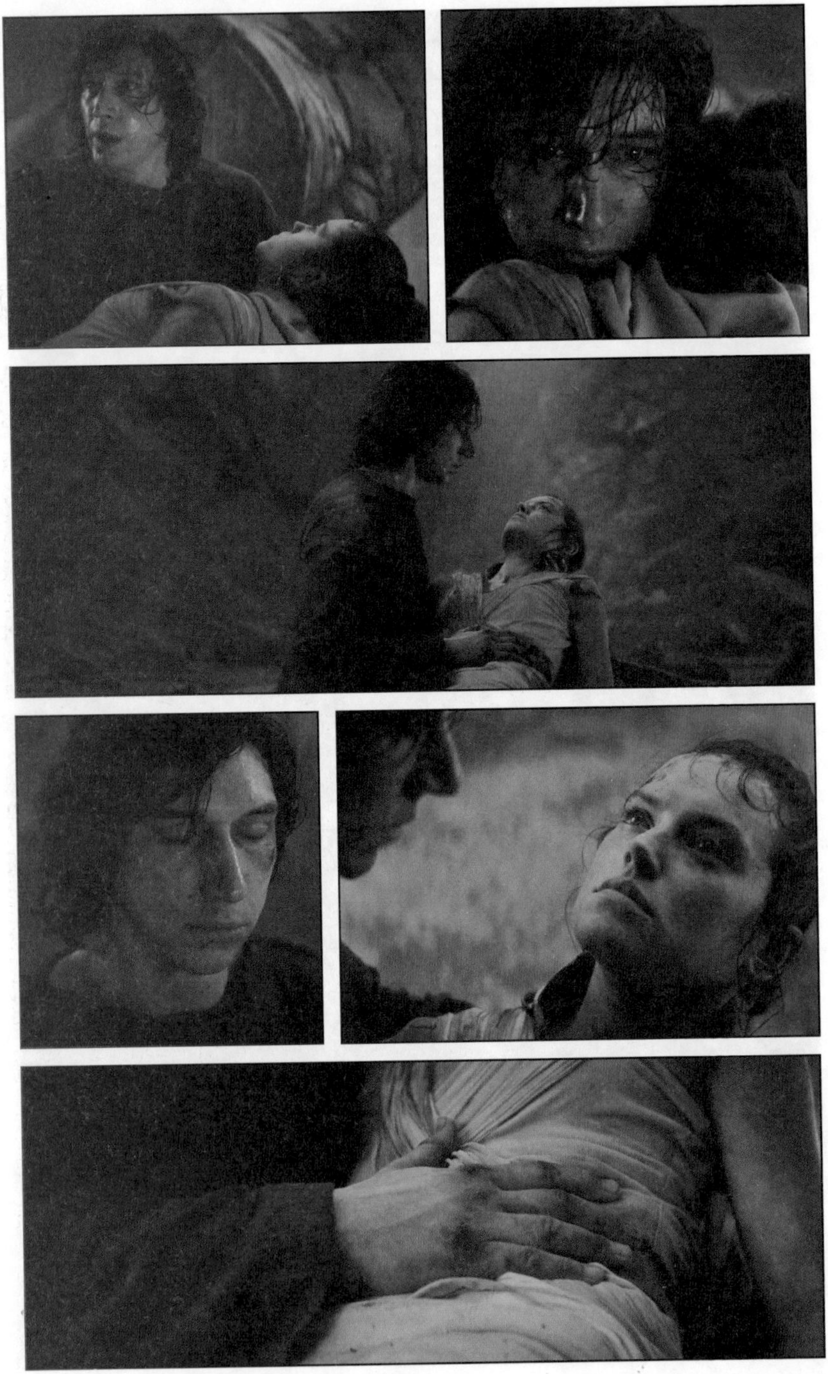

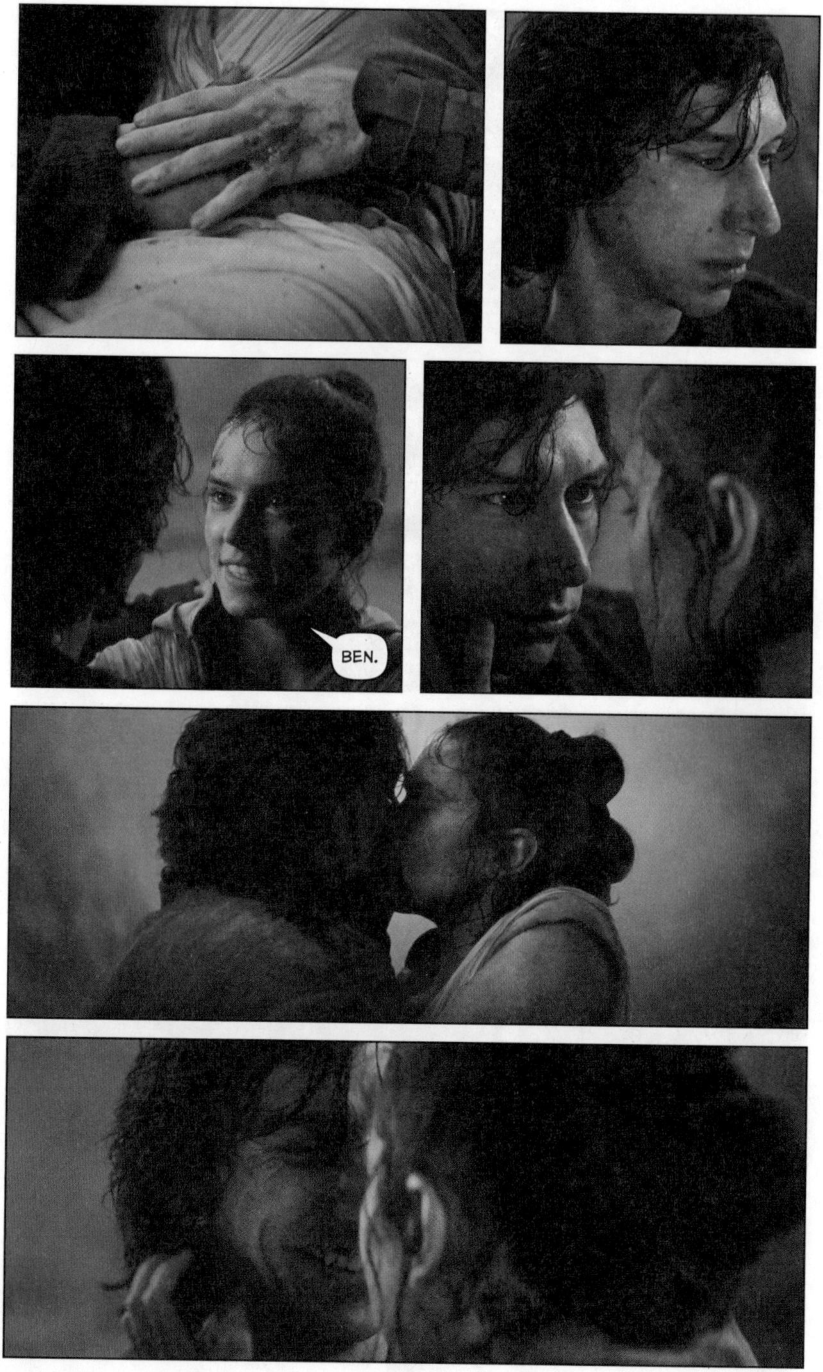
BEN.

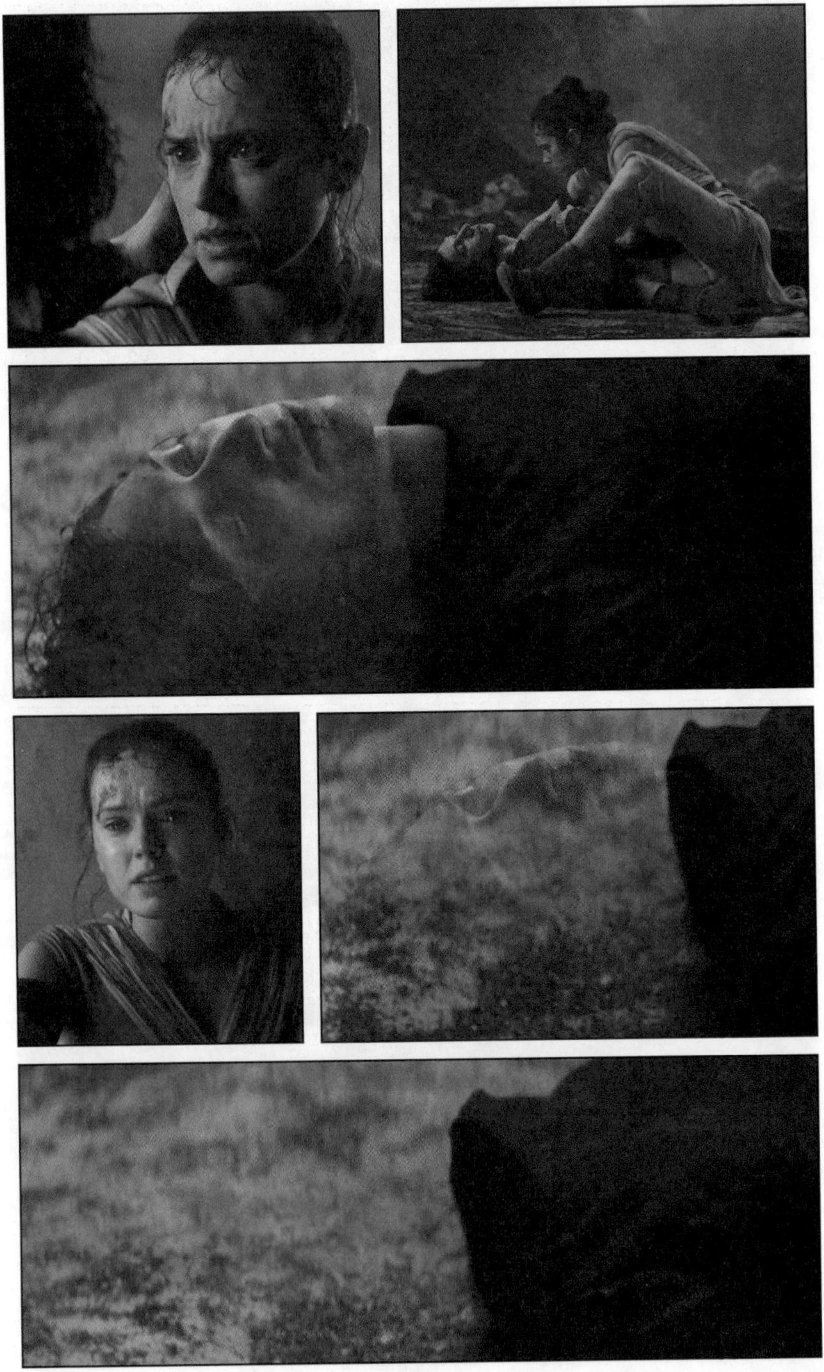

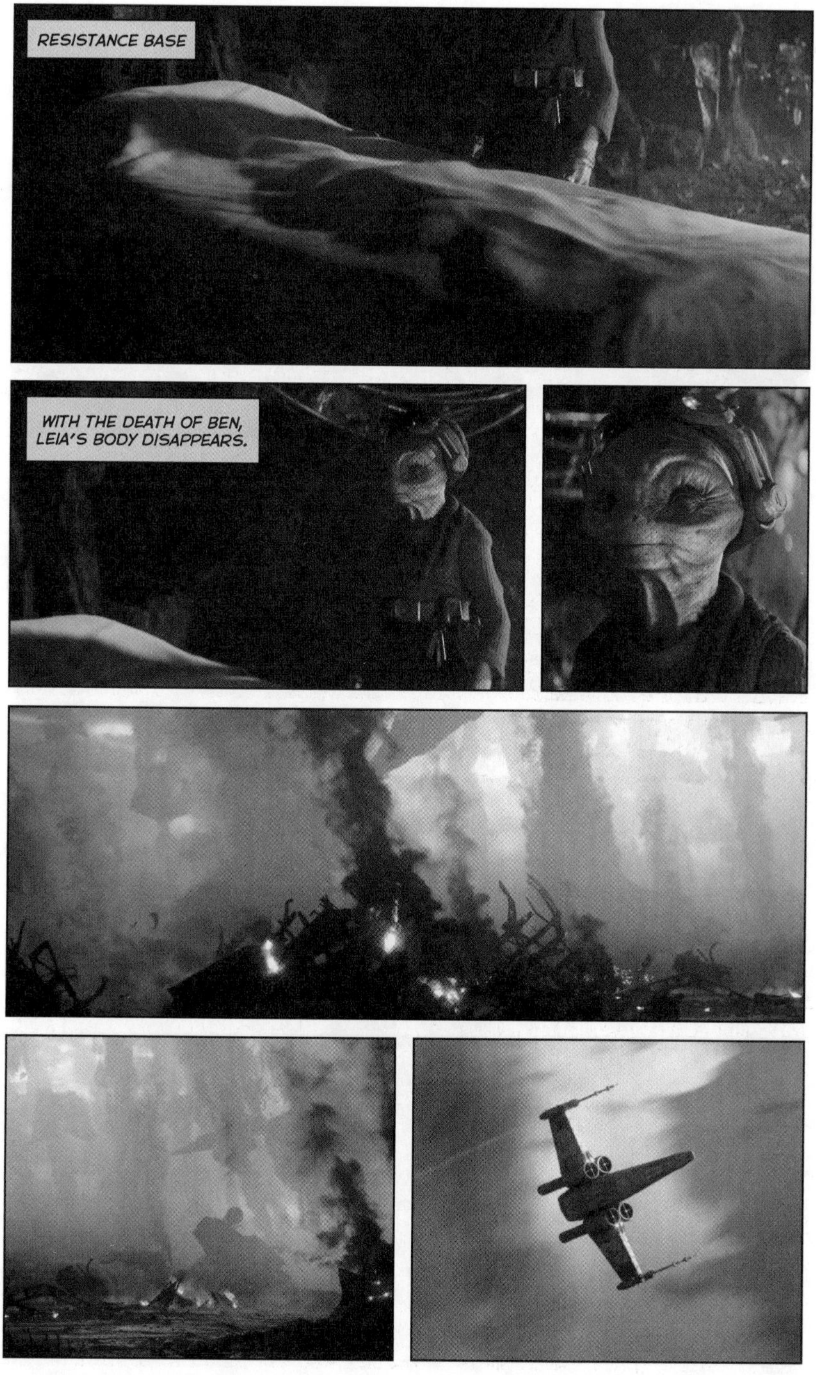
RESISTANCE BASE
WITH THE DEATH OF BEN, LEIA'S BODY DISAPPEARS.

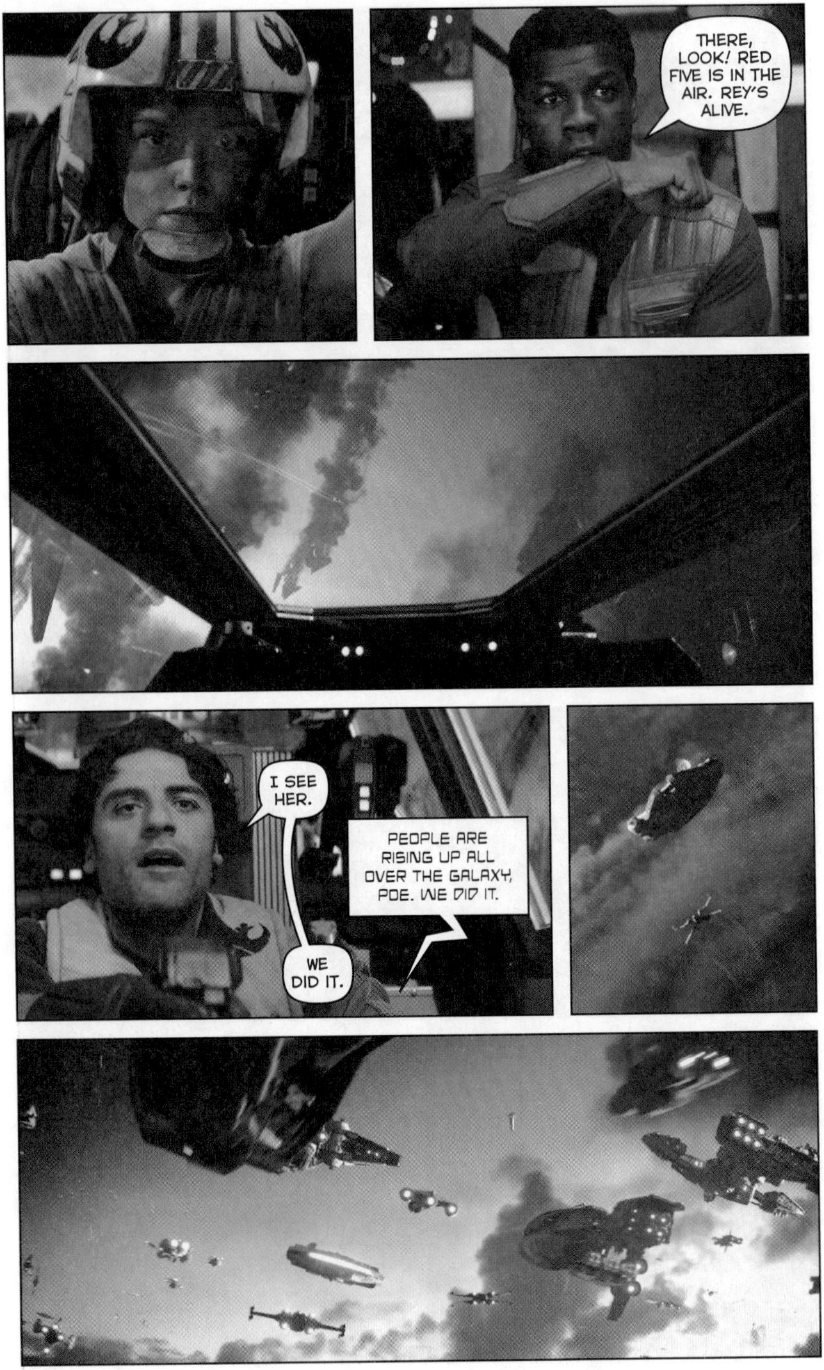
THERE, LOOK! RED FIVE IS IN THE AIR. REY'S ALIVE.
I SEE HER.
WE DID IT.
PEOPLE ARE RISING UP ALL OVER THE GALAXY, POE. WE DID IT.

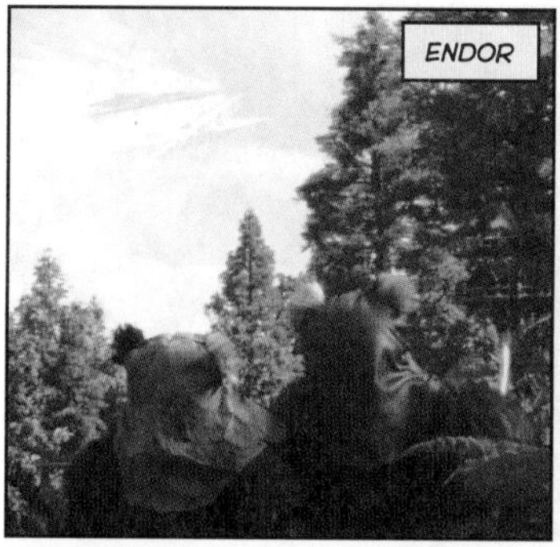
ENDOR

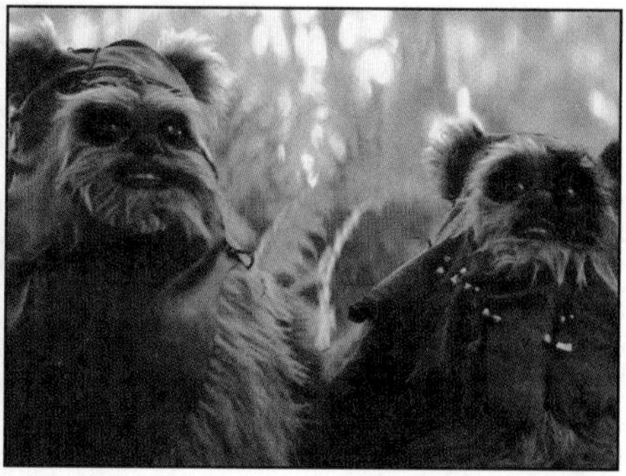

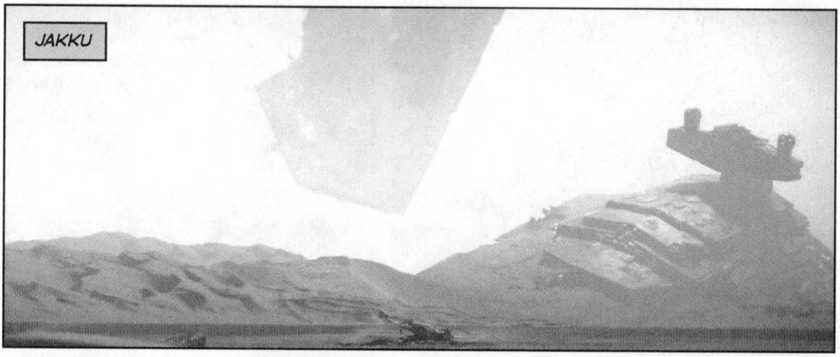
JAKKU

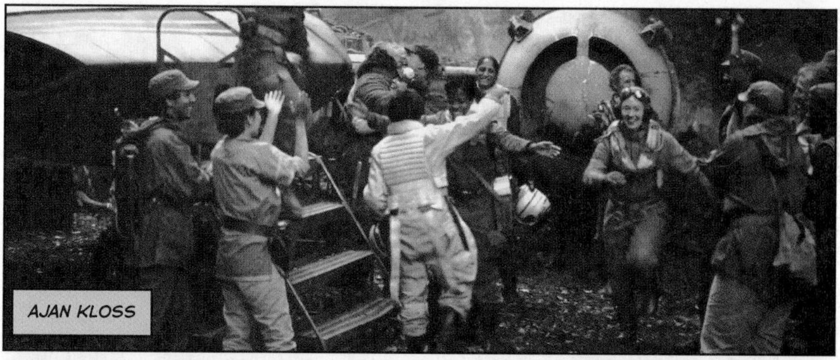
AJAN KLOSS

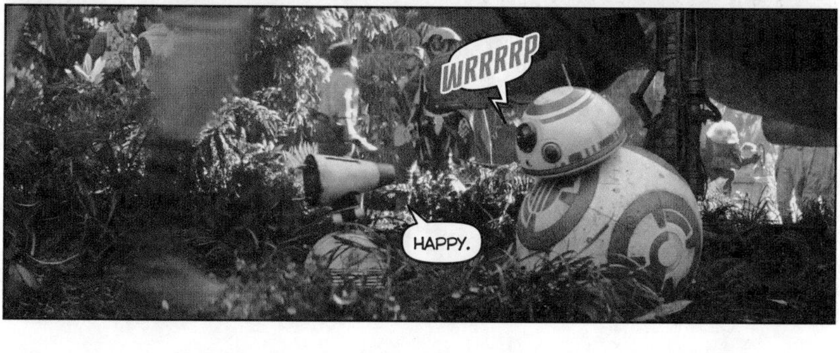
WRRRRP
HAPPY.

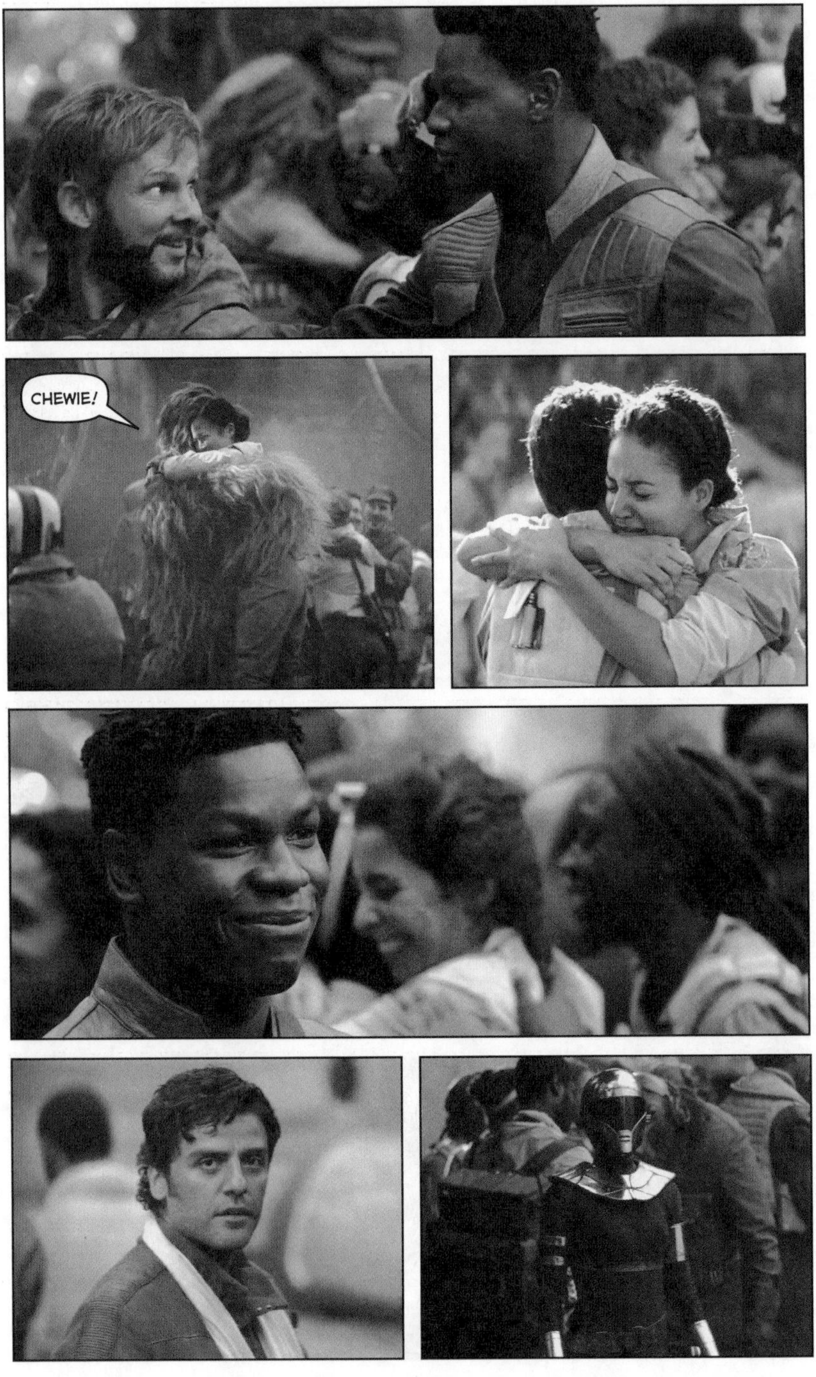
CHEWIE!

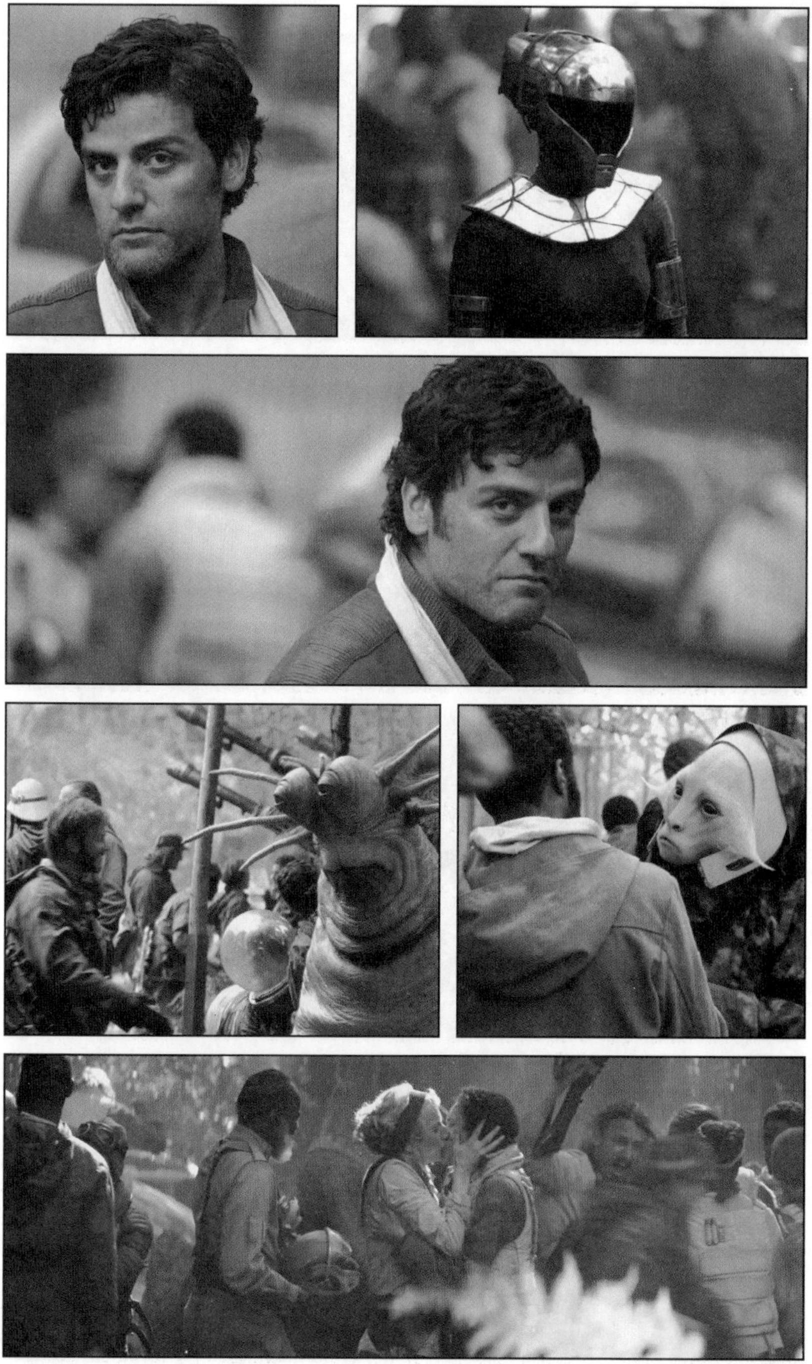

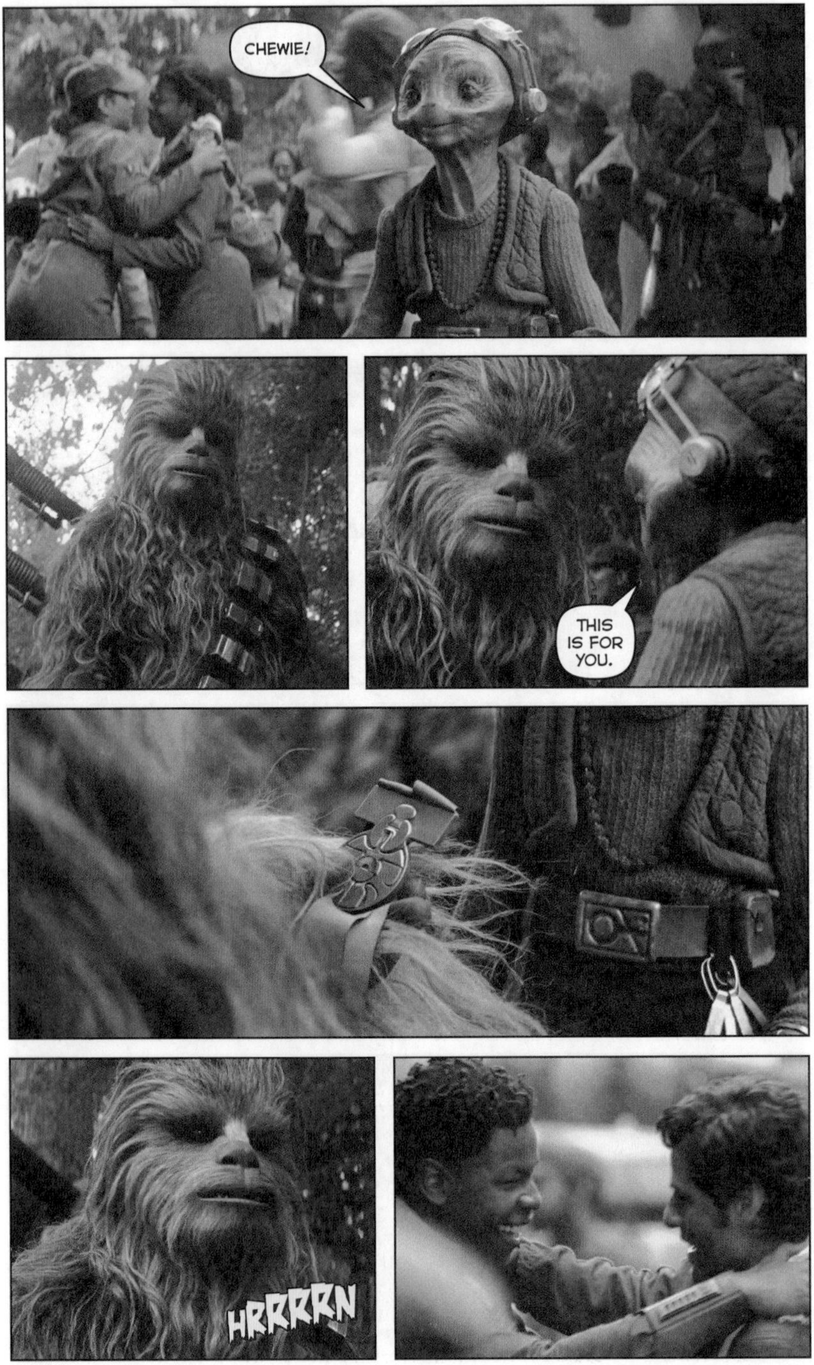
CHEWIE!
THIS IS FOR YOU.
HRRRRN

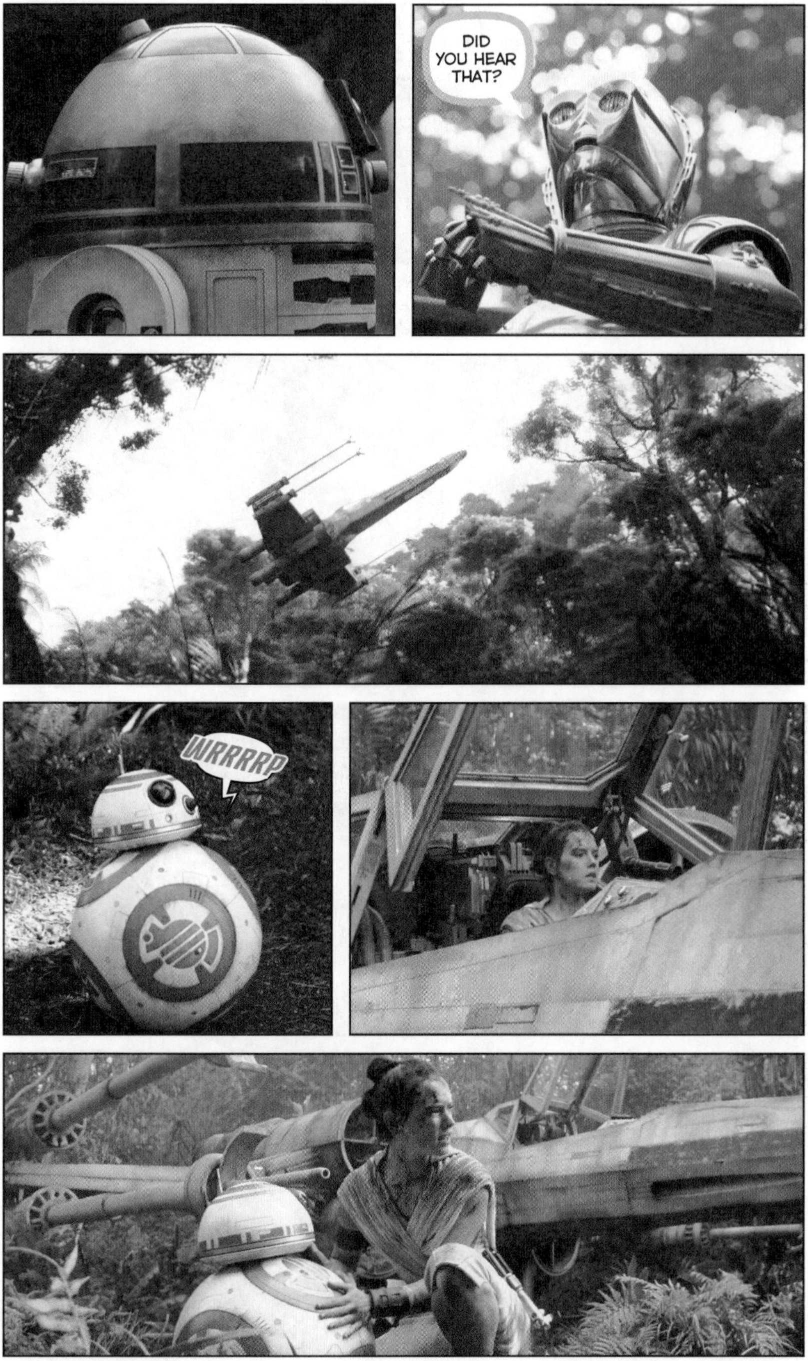
DID YOU HEAR THAT?
WRRRRP

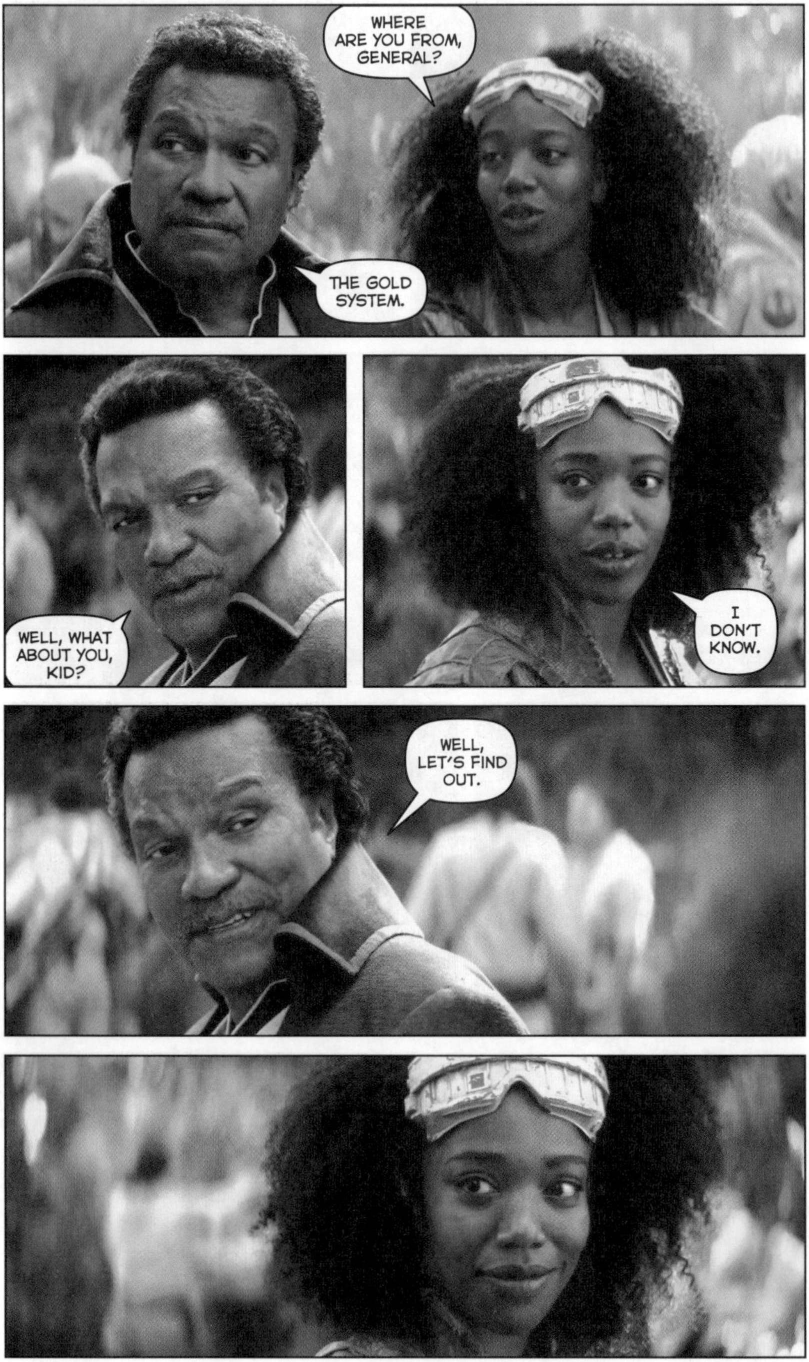
WHERE ARE YOU FROM, GENERAL?
THE GOLD SYSTEM.
WELL, WHAT ABOUT YOU, KID?
I DON'T KNOW.
WELL, LET'S FIND OUT.

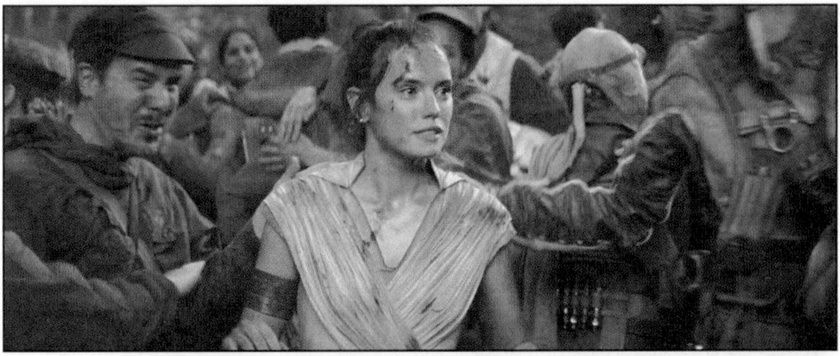
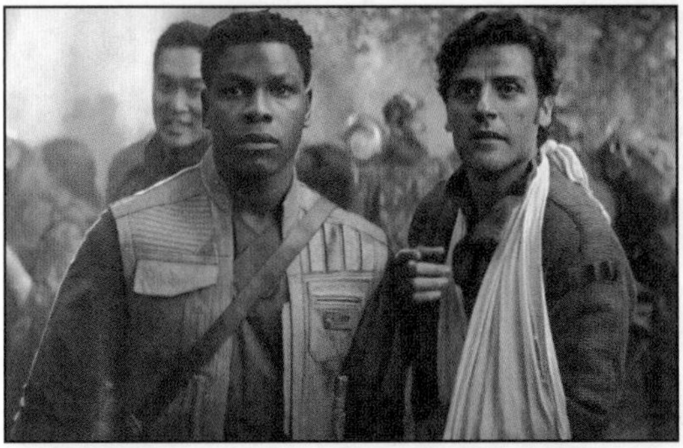
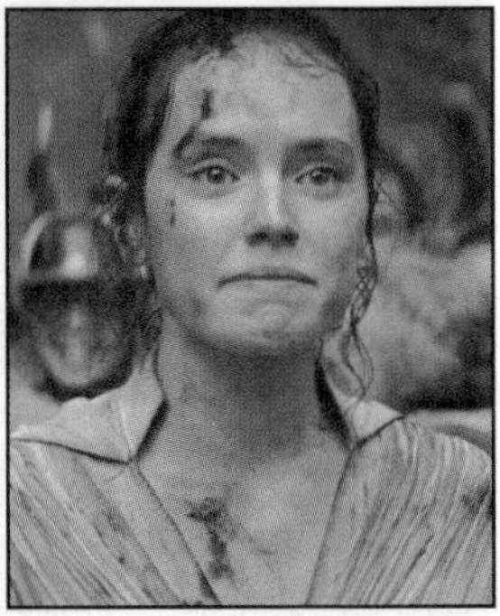
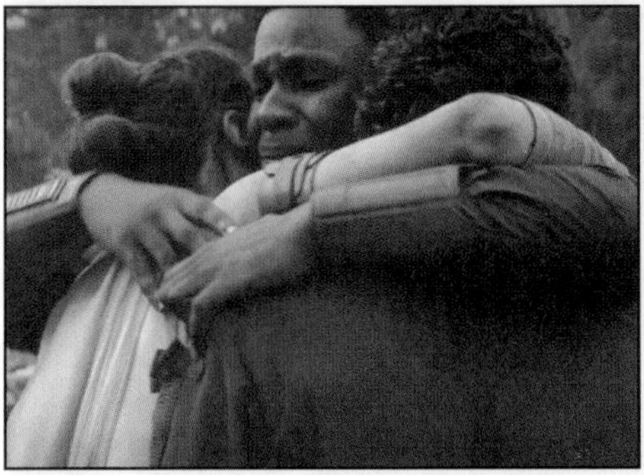
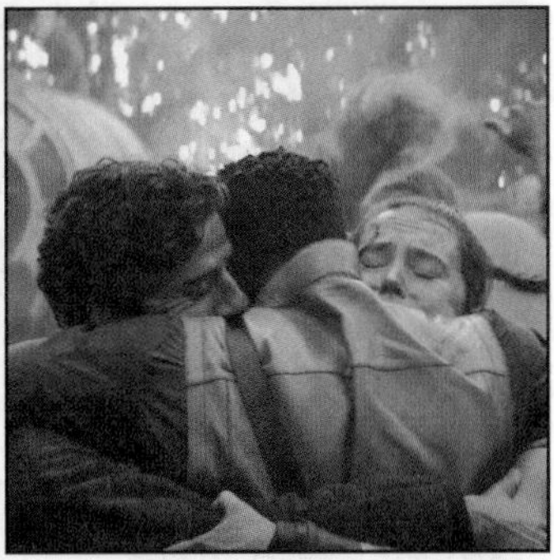
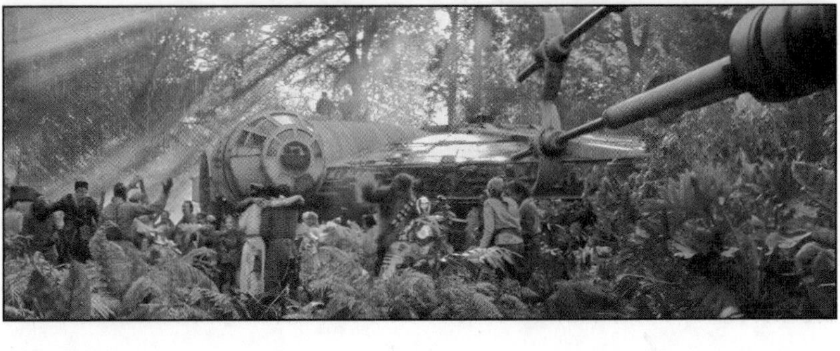

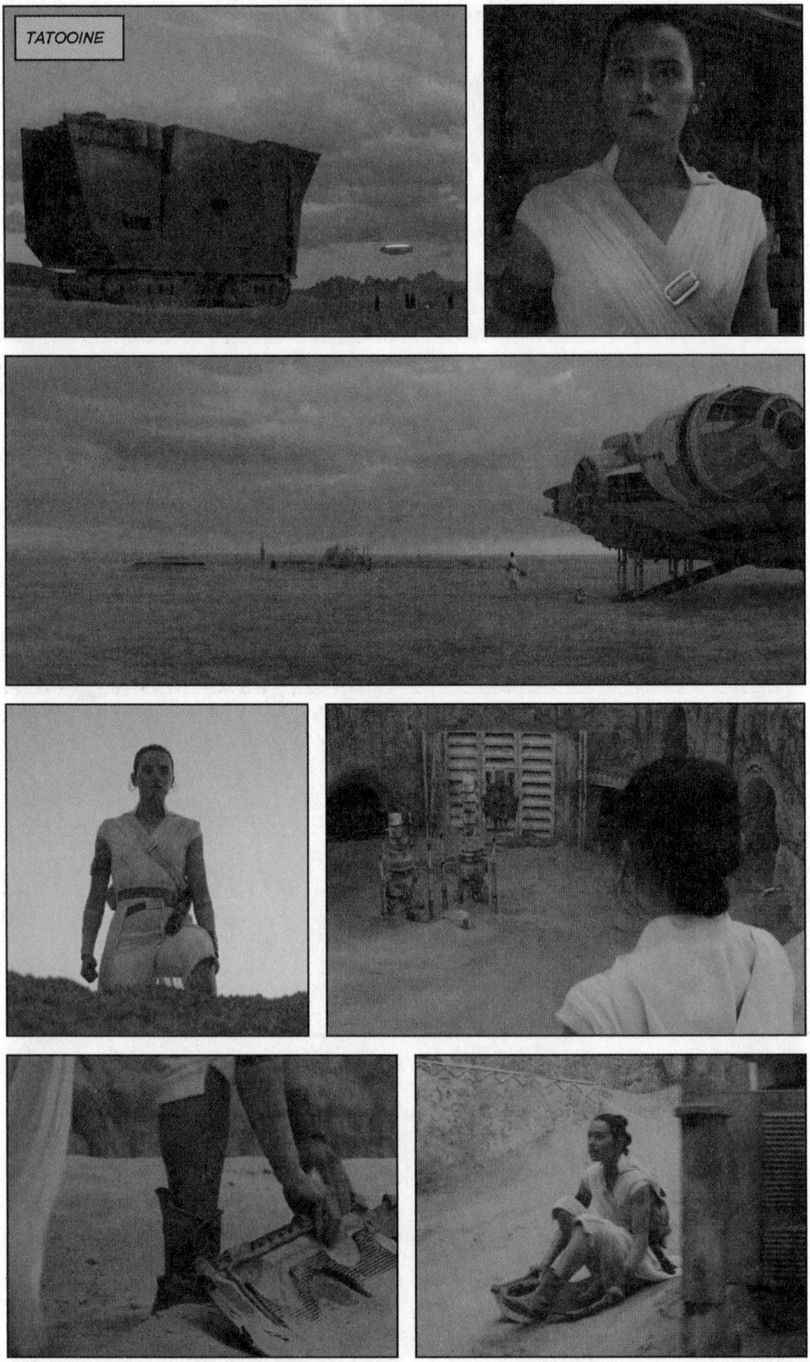
TATOOINE

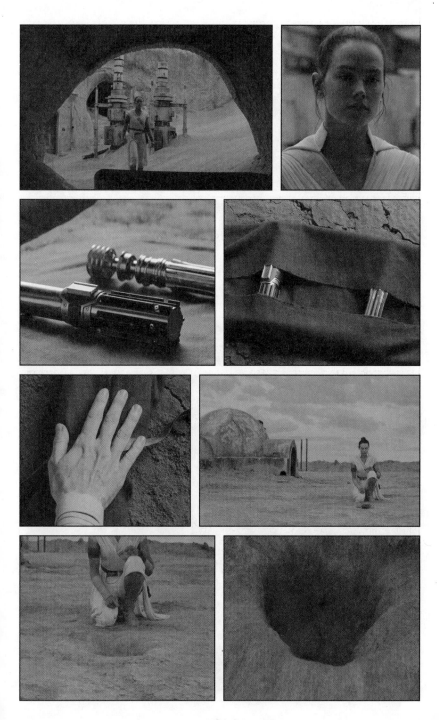

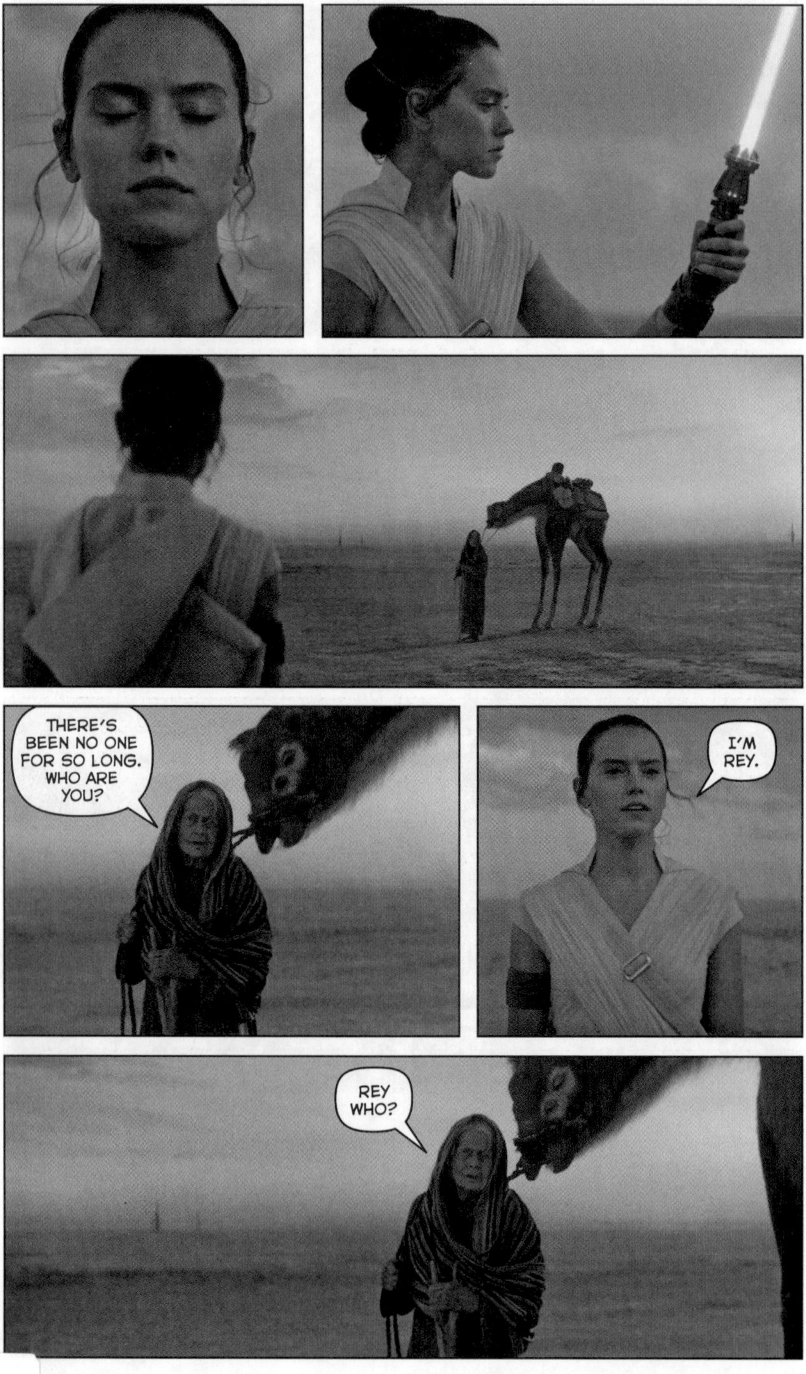
THERE'S BEEN NO ONE FOR SO LONG. WHO ARE YOU?
I'M REY.
REY WHO?

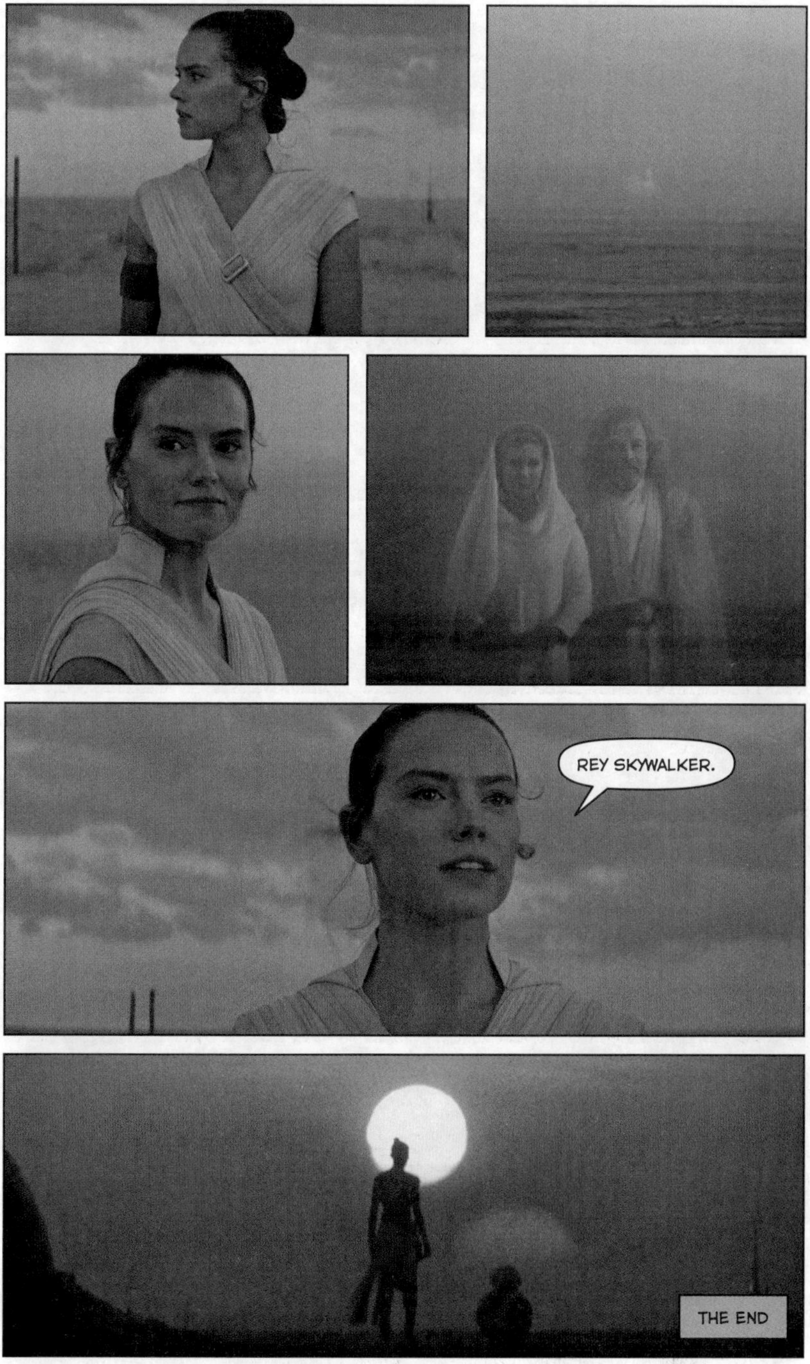

REY SKYWALKER.
THE END

STAR WARS

THE RISE OF SKYWALKER

Directed by
J.J. Abrams

Produced by
Kathleen Kennedy, p.g.a.
J.J. Abrams, p.g.a.
Michelle Rejwan, p.g.a.

Screenplay by
Chris Terrio
J.J. Abrams

Executive Producers
Callum Greene
Tommy Gormley
Jason McGatlin